PRAISE FOR NANCY McKENZIE

Queen of Camelot

"A rich and powerful tapestry of words layered in legend and myth . . . Surely Merlin's magic reached out to touch Nancy McKenzie's pen."

—ELAINE COFFMAN

"Guinevere comes alive—a strong, resourceful, and compassionate woman, accessible to modern folk . . . McKenzie makes a quantum leap in defining the character of Guinevere as a real, flesh-and-blood woman. The Arthur-Guinevere-Lancelot triangle comes alive as well—believable, poignant, and bearing the seeds of tragedy."

—KATHERINE KURTZ

Grail Prince

"Stunning . . . McKenzie continues to put her own unique spin on the Arthurian legend. . . . Brimming with romance, myth, and magic, this intriguing retelling of an ever-appealing fable will appease fans eager for twists and turns in the lives and times of King Arthur and the knights of the Round Table."

—Booklist

"Fans of Marion Zimmer Bradley's Mists of Avalon series and Persia Woolley's Guinevere trilogy will be delighted with this addition to the modern interpretation of Arthurian legend. . . . This tale of abiding love and enduring hope is highly recommended."

—Library Journal

Also by Nancy McKenzie
Published by Ballantine Books

QUEEN OF CAMELOT

GRAIL PRINCE

PRINCE
OF
DREAMS

NANCY McKENZIE

BALLANTINE BOOKS

NEW YORK

A Del Rey® Book
Published by The Random House Publishing Group

Prince of Dreams is a work of fiction. Names, places, and incidents either are
products of the author's imagination or are used fictitiously.

www.delreydigital.com

Library of Congress Control Number: 2003097809

ISBN 0-345-45650-5

Cover photograph by George Kerrigan
Cover design by David Stevenson

Manufactured in the United States of America

First Edition: January 2004

2   4   6   8   10   9   7   5   3   1

For James Gelston Affleck, my father

ACKNOWLEDGMENTS

Readers familiar with traditional versions of the legend of Tristan/Tristram and Iseult/Isolde will recognize in this retelling all the essential elements of the original story, plus a twist or two. The twists enable this tale to serve as a sequel to *Queen of Camelot* and *Grail Prince*, my previous novels of the Arthurian legend. This version of Tristan's story is based principally on the works of Beroul, Gottfried von Strassburg, and Sir Thomas Malory, men who lived between six hundred and nine hundred years ago. Like them, I have reshaped the story to suit a contemporary readership. Without them, I could not have written it.

I owe much to Jean Naggar, my agent, for her tireless efforts on my behalf. It has been a pleasure to rely on such professionalism and expertise. I owe even more to all those at Del Rey who have taken such good care of my work: to Shelly Shapiro, Editorial Director at Del Rey Books, for taking Tristan on; to David Stevenson for his stunning cover designs, not only for this book but for *Queen of Camelot* and *Grail Prince* as well; to Patricia Nicolescu for her untiring attention to detail and her care in seeing these books through the production process; and most of all to Kathleen O'Shea David, my editor, for her excellent advice, her clear head, and her ability to see the forest when I was lost among the trees.

It might not be difficult for some women writers of a torrid romance to show their work to their fathers, but it was difficult for me. I dedicate this book to my dad in heartfelt thanks for his strong and unswerving support over an entire lifetime, and, more particularly, for his liking *Prince of Dreams* the first time he read it.

—Nancy McKenzie
Father's Day, June 15, 2003

CONTENTS

Tristan's Britain

PICTS

Dunpeldyr

LOTHIAN

STRATHCLYDE

North Sea

RHEGED

Irish Sea

ELMET

Isle of Mona

York

Percival's Castle GWYNEDD

BRITAIN

ANGLES

IRELAND

NORHGALLIS

ANGLES

POWYS

DYFED GUENT

Caer Myrddin
Maridunum

Caerleon

Severn River LOGRIS

EAST SAXONS

Rook Point DUMNONIA

Amesbury

Thames R. Rutupiai

Camelot

SOUTH SAXONS

Tintagel

Morois Wood

CORNWALL

WEST SAXONS

Castle Dorr
DORRIA

LYONESSE

Pernam's Sanctuary

Narrow Sea

FRANKS

Lyon's Head

NEUSTRIA

Ryol's Lair

Benoic

BRITTANY LANASCOL

LESS BRITAIN

MAP BY DAVID LINDROTH INC.

PART I

1 ⛨ BORN BETWEEN THE STARS

Rain fell in sheets. The swollen river tore through its narrow valley, bearing sodden bodies like old logs, dashing them against rocks, spinning them heavily in swirling cataracts, heaving them up along the drowned shore, pale and bloated, a midnight feast for eager kites. Upstream where the forest thinned under the cliff face, a lone company of soldiers slogged wearily through the mud, heads down, shoulders hunched against the heavens' fury. Their captain sat on his horse, his face raised to the sky. He stretched out his arms as if to embrace the storm, the black night, the soaking wet, and gather them to himself. Through the din of the downpour they heard his cry.

"Gods of the high hills, gods of the moving deep, gods of the living forest, the birthless sky and the deathless night, accept our thanks! Praise be to Lord Mithra, the Bull-Slayer, the Light who conquers darkness! We honor your name. Great Goddess of Nemet, arbiter of fate, stay your bright sword and smile on us! We bend our knee to Yahweh, Lawgiver, whose vengeful eye can turn a man to stone! Hear our plea, sweet Jesu Christ, who died for all our sins—grant us the grace to forgive our enemies. Ai-ya! We have beaten back the Saxons and exult in victory!"

The captain turned in his saddle and grinned at his men. His face, under the dark mop of streaming hair, was the beardless face of a boy. "How's that, Bryn? Conwyl? Haeric? Did I leave anyone out?"

The soldiers laughed with affection, called him a Druid's spawn, and named forty gods he had forgotten. One man, a veteran, turned to his younger companion.

"Never saw a lad delight so in bad weather. Can't bear to be indoors when there's a storm outside. Begotten of the sea witch, he must have been."

"Aye," growled his companion, wiping blood from a cut in his cheek. "Sings like an angel and wields a sword like the very devil. Born between the stars, as we say in Lyonesse."

"Born under the Twins, you told me, Kerro, born too late. Don't they say in Lyonesse his fate's unlucky?"

Kerro squirmed. "His mother the queen died at his birthing, but that doesn't always bring bad luck."

The veteran hawked, turned his head and spat. "I'll tell you what's bad luck. His father's dying before the lad reached manhood. Ill-fated prince! Old enough to see his future just beyond his grasp. That'll bring black shadows down around anyone's ears."

"Black shadows, indeed! You and your superstitions. *I* don't think our prince is unlucky. He's a likely youth, strong and well favored, an excellent swordsman, a sensible fighter, a good head on his shoulders. You'll see, Haeric, someday he'll make us a fine king."

The veteran laughed, water streaming from his beard. "If he ever gets the chance."

"What do you mean?"

"His father Meliodas was King of Lyonesse and King of Cornwall, too, being firstborn of the High King Constantine. Young Tristan's sixteen and, as you say, a sensible fighter. He's the heir. Yet what's he king of?"

"Oh, come, Haeric, that's an old story. He was twelve when Meliodas died, too young for kingship. It's only right that Cornwall passed to his uncle Markion, Constantine's second son. Would you want to be led by a boy?"

"He's a boy no longer. And not only is he *not* King of Cornwall, he's still not King of Lyonesse, his homeland."

"Markion's only waiting until he's been battle-tested. Everyone knows it. Why else has he been training and schooling the boy himself these four years past? He's been grooming the lad for kingship. Mark my words, when we get home he'll make Tristan King of Lyonesse. You'll see. Tristan's lord of the land already in all but name. Everyone honors him there."

They trudged on, the mud sucking at their boots, past the cliff and into the rising woodland.

The veteran grunted. "You've been in Lyonesse. I've been at Tintagel and Dorr with Markion's troops. I've slept in their tents and heard their barracks talk. And I can tell you, you are dreaming."

The young soldier did not answer. The path rose steeply toward a narrow ridge. Their feet slipped on wet rocks, wet roots, soft earth that gave beneath their weight. Rain fell in a loud, steady hiss.

"Tell me, Kerro," the veteran continued between labored breaths, "just when do you think Markion will step aside, hand over his crown, and make Tristan King of Cornwall? When he dies, perhaps? But he's not yet forty; he's a man in middle years with a third of life ahead. And he has a son, Gerontius, eighteen, well trained and ready. He's here leading Cornish troops, representing his father as a son should who knows he is the heir. And when old Constantine dies, who will step into his shoes? Will it be young Tristan, firstborn of the rightful heir? Or Markion himself, with years of experience and a loyal army at his back? No, no, Kerro. You are dreaming. Your Tristan is unlucky. Bad luck his father died too soon, bad luck his uncle is ambitious, bad luck his cousin Gerontius is older and abler. He'll never see his birthright. Born between the stars, indeed."

"You're too hard on him. I tell you, it's a mistake to count him out. Look at him. A strong enough youth and shaping for a man. And quick-witted to boot. Would you have thought of that clever ambush? How did he know the Saxons would head this way? Eh? And now look, there's honor aplenty for all of us, thirty Britons killing a hundred Saxons, and not a man of us wounded. Except for scratches." He wiped his face again. "This boy will be somebody, I'll wager my life on that."

Haeric shrugged, hunching futilely against the onslaught. "Gods help the man who tries to build a fire on such a night!" He coughed and lowered his voice. "And gods help the man who ever tries to cross King Markion."

"Hey, Tris!" a voice called from the ranks. "Give us a song! We're freezing to death in this godforsaken wet!"

"By the blood of the Bull," Haeric grumbled as a chorus of voices echoed the plea. "Look how the ruffians treat him! In Arthur's day a prince was shown respect."

"They do him honor by asking him to sing. You don't know Tristan."

"Is he a commander or a bard?"

Kerro laughed. "Both. He's a wizard in his way. Listen."

Around them, dimly through the downpour, came the clear, melancholy tenor of the boy's song, piercing the curtain of rain, lifting their hearts and quickening their steps. At the top of the ridge the young commander raised his arm and halted the company, finishing the song with a deft rhyming couplet. Below them on the valley floor three bonfires burned, set well apart, the surrounding tents invisible in the dark.

"Wales on one side, Cornwall on the other, old Constantine in the middle to keep them from each other's throats," Haeric muttered. "But thank the gods for fire and food."

At the bottom of the hill a sentry met them, sword raised. Tristan gave the password and the men filed past, filthy and exhausted, to such comfort as they could find in the unrelenting storm.

Out of the dark a voice called in loud relief, "Tristan! Where the devil have you been?"

Tristan slid from his horse as a young man strode out of the shadows and punched him lightly in the shoulder. "I was beginning to give up hope. What happened? Let me guess—you thought of a new song and missed the turning."

"Oh, Dinadan, what a battle! And I *did* think of a new song. But it was the long climb up that sodden ridge that delayed us. And your company? How are Dorria's losses?"

"Light, thank God. Once we broke their line, they ran. Toward the cliffs and the river. At least two hundred got away."

"Not two hundred."

"What—you met them? You went that way?"

"It seemed the simplest route of escape. So we blocked it."

"By God!" Dinadan grinned and slapped his friend hard on the back. "However did you think of it? How many were you?"

"Thirty. But we took a hundred, easy."

"Christ, does Constantine know?" Dinadan threw back his head and laughed. "Your first battle, and by God, if you're not the fox set among the fowl! He put you on his flank so you wouldn't see much action, and you take out half the force that escaped him. It's too rich! Come on, get out of those wet things and let's split a wineskin. Come to my tent, it's hard by. I've news, but for your ears only."

Dinadan's tent was small and smelled of ill-cured skins, but it was dry. His servant had a small fire going, and a wineskin hung on its tripod stand above the flame. Dinadan poured the thin liquid into two horn cups.

"Hang your tunic there, it's your only chance."

"You've no kindling. It will never dry."

Dinadan grinned. "Dravic steals a log from the bonfire when my flame gets low. Go on. You'll freeze in those wet things. Shall I send him for your bedroll?"

"No need." Tristan tugged off his sodden boots and stripped down to his loincloth. The meager warmth of the fire met his icy skin, and he shivered. What a battle it had been! First the cold wet, biting into flesh, then the dry, icy prickle of fear when the Saxons burst through the underbrush, followed by the hot sweat of excitement and exertion, the exhilaration at such total victory, and lastly, the stab of dread at all the bodies. He laughed to himself. He had been more aware of his body's swift sensations than of the flow of the fight. And afterward, marching home in the glorious storm, he had heard around him the pleasant voices of men tired from battle, the comforting timbre of their speech, while the dark wind whistled in his ears and the rain hissed down. Now he could hardly remember the plan of battle or the moment when he had decided on the ambush—but he remembered every assault upon his senses, every touch upon his skin, every sound, every sight, every smell. Separate threads of his living spirit, they wove themselves, mingling and dividing, into the fabric of his memory.

Dinadan shook his head as he listened to Tristan's recounting of the ambush. "Tris, forget what it *felt* like. Who cares if it was cold or wet? How many Saxons got away? How many died? What were their numbers? You didn't count them?" Dinadan groaned at Tristan's sheepish smile. "I'll bet you named each raindrop that touched your face, and made a song about them. And yet you can't tell me how many Saxons died?"

Tristan shrugged. "One of the veterans counted a hundred bodies. Most of them fell into the river. Who cares, Din? They are dead. But what a glorious night for a battle!"

Dinadan handed him a winecup and raised a toast. "To your mysterious virtue, Tristan of Lyonesse. May you live forever."

Tristan raised his cup toward Dinadan. "To your unflagging friendship, Dinadan, Prince of Dorria. May you live beyond me."

The wine was only half warmed, and bitter. Dinadan wrinkled his nose and downed it, but Tristan held it on his tongue, examining the flavor, letting its sharp bite burn into his memory.

"Now, Dinadan, what's the news?"

"Trouble's brewing. I've been hearing snatches among the troops. And Constantine has called a council. Tonight."

"What's it about?"

"The men expect Wales to challenge the High King. They're all here, you know, the Welsh kings, or they've sent their proxies. They're presenting a united front. They must want something."

"What do they ever want but land or power? God knows they've land enough. They must be after the High King's crown." Tristan sighed and drank again from his cup. Awful as it tasted, the thin wine lit a fire in his belly that began to thaw his limbs. "Ever since Grandfather grabbed the crown at Arthur's death, it's been a burden to him."

"You don't see him offering to give it up, do you? It may be a burden, but he counts it worth the price." Dinadan grinned. "And you're the only one of his kin who will allow he grabbed it—most loyal Cornishmen are brought up to say Arthur bequeathed it to him as the rightful heir."

"They forget Mordred." Tristan waved the argument away. "I've thought of something else they might want, Din. They might withdraw from the alliance, as the northern kingdoms did when we were children. And if they go, what will happen to the High King? It would be no more than an empty title, a dead remnant from Britain's glorious past. His only troops would be us, his own Cornishmen. The dissolution of Arthur's Britain would be complete."

"Poetic, but not likely. If they wanted to withdraw, why did they answer his call in the first place? Why not stay comfortably in Wales and leave us to fight the Saxons? But they came, *all* of them."

"Thank God they did."

"Yes, without them it might have been a close thing. And I'm sure they know it. That's why I think they've gone together to demand some reward from Constantine."

Tristan frowned. "Were we invited to this council?"

"Are you jesting? I'm a lowly prince of a small subkingdom. All Constantine wants from Dorria is Castle Dorr. He knows our future is tied to Markion's, whether we like it or not. Have you heard my father on that topic? And *you*—he may be your grandfather, but he has little love for you. Markion is his darling, and you're the thorn in Markion's side."

Tristan shook his head. "Don't start that again. My grandfather may have blind spots, but he doesn't hate me. He's waiting, as I am myself, to see what kind of man I make. As for Markion, you wrong him. He's an honorable man, a fine warrior, and a steady Christian."

"And King of Lyonesse."

"As my guardian," Tristan said a little sharply. "Until I've proved myself. It was my father's wish. And he *is* our best hope for the future."

"Fah! He's a sneaky devil. I'd much rather serve you, Tristan, and I'm not alone."

"Look, Dinadan, I've spent the better part of four years in Mark's household at Dorr and Tintagel, learning all he has to teach me, learning to fight, learning to rule. I've even been included in his councils. Grant me that I know my uncle better than you do."

Dinadan extended his hand. "I'm sorry, Tris. Didn't mean to strike your sore spot. But you know as well as I do that sometimes you don't see the forest for the trees."

"I'm right about Uncle Mark."

"I yield. Have it your way."

"But I want to know what's going on in that council."

Tristan put down the winecup and slowly rose. Even naked, Dinadan thought, he was a regal figure, long-limbed and well made, with shoulders beginning to broaden and the strength of manhood beginning to mark his face. Dinadan, rising with him, felt somehow dwarfed, although he was a year older and dressed in princely clothes. There was something elemental about Tristan that cut through trappings, something simple and direct and open. It flashed through Dinadan's mind that this boy might not be made for kingship, with its daily battles between jealous lords and incessant demands for compromise. Was this what Constantine had seen? Perhaps he was, like the great Galahad, made for a single purpose, a deadly blade to cut a narrow swath, straight and deep, through his time. Dinadan shook himself and pushed those thoughts away. Tristan *had* to be king if they were ever to be rid of Markion.

"I want to know what's going on in that council," Tristan repeated. "Let's join them."

"And be publicly shamed when we're thrown out? I have a better idea. In this rain, there'll only be a couple of sentries, and they'll probably be guarding the entrance where there's shelter from the wet. Let's go around back and eavesdrop."

"I'm with you. You might as well undress and go as I am, unless you brought another tunic. We'll be lying in the mud."

No one guarded the rear of the High King's tent. The night was black. Torches seemed to shed no light at all. In the downpour they could hardly see their hands before their faces. Within minutes of lying prone in the mud their bodies were so filth-spattered they looked more like logs than human flesh. Lifting up the dirty canvas, they stuck their heads carefully inside the tent.

Warmth assailed Tristan's senses, the warmth of bodies pressed together in a small space, the musky stench of old sweat and unwashed men, steamy exhalations of bad wine and stale jerky, and above it all the sharp, acrid sting of firesmoke. He lay still and savored the rich heat while icy rain pricked his skin like needles and the thick, muddy ooze sucked him deeper into the earth. It was dark. He could hear the hiss of flames on wet wood, but something large and black blocked his view. Nearby he heard the steady suck and wheeze of an old man's breathing. His arm slid through the mud and nudged Dinadan.

"We're right behind Constantine," he whispered.

Dinadan's fist struck his ribs. "Shut up, fool." The words breathed on the edge of sound. "Behind his cot. Forgot to mention. He's wounded."

"Wounded!"

"Shhh! Not bad. Shoulder, I think."

As his eyes adjusted, Tristan could see a dull orange glow on the tent cloth and a darker shape that moved across the light, back and forth. But he found he could hear better if he lay still and closed his eyes.

A man was talking, a voice he did not know, low, clear, and melodic, with the unstudied authority of a commander. An older man, he decided, but still powerful. And by his accent, a Welshman. He was retelling the day's battle in a light most favorable to the Welsh, calling it a decisive rout. Well, a rout it had certainly been, but they'd been lucky with the terrain. Eight hundred fewer Saxons alive today than yesterday, but many thousands more where they came from, all along the Saxon Shore, the eastern territories, and more lately the rich lands of the southern Briton lords. He struggled to attend to the words, but the man's voice entranced him. There was something lyrical in it, the timbre both sweet and guttural, as if he tried to speak with a voice meant for singing. As if he tried to tell a tale with one harp string only and left all the others lying idle.

"Peredur," Dinadan whispered. "Leader of the Welsh kings. A gray-beard. Uncle to Percival, King of Gwynedd."

Tristan struggled to remember the map in Markion's workroom at Castle Dorr. Gwynedd was the largest and strongest of the Welsh kingdoms, and since their federation after Arthur's death it had been the leader. King Percival was a noble warrior, with many great deeds to his credit. Tristan remembered well the song the bard Hawath had sung about him. The prospect of meeting Percival was the reason he'd begged Markion so desperately to accompany Gerontius to this battle. But Percival had not come. Some excuse had been given about an Irish uprising in Demetia. It might even be true; Irish coastal raiders had kept Markion in Cornwall. Still, it had been a disappointment.

He heard the name Rhydderch of Powys. Where was Powys? For the life of him he could not remember the names on the map. But he recalled Hawath's tale, which interwove the lineages of all the great Welsh families, all Cunedda's children, and gradually the names of Welsh kingdoms came back to him: Gwynedd, Powys, Dyfed, Northgallis, and Guent. Rich names, rich heritage of heroes.

"Well, that's torn it," Dinadan whispered under cover of general conversation as the wine went round. "All the firebrands are here. Peredur's the only graybeard."

"Who's here? I didn't catch it all."

"Granach of Powys, Emrys of Northgallis, Llanyrr of Dyfed, and Marhalt of Guent, may he roast in Hell. He's the one who raped Granach's daughter as she was on her way to the convent her father promised her to. Year before last. Surely I told you that story. Strong as an ox he is, and just as bullheaded. Won't take no for an answer. He fancied her, so he took her."

"Did he kill her?"

"He married her, after."

In the dark Tristan grinned. "It was probably a plot cooked up between them."

Suddenly the voices quieted as Peredur spoke again.

"My lord King, as loyal Britons, we are concerned about the Kingdom's future. We have fought for you, all of us, these twenty years against Saxons and Anglii, against the Irish, even against the Picts."

Constantine stirred on the cot. "When it's suited you," he wheezed, but Peredur did not hear him.

"No High King can live forever, and there are those among us, and those back home whom we represent, who wish to preserve a united Britain. We wish to know who will be your choice to succeed you. Let us take council on it, and before we leave this battlefield, let us be certain of our futures that we may avoid bloodshed and warfare upon your death."

Constantine struggled to sit upright, his breath rasping in his throat.

"Bold!" Dinadan whispered. Tristan nodded.

"Sir," the High King rasped, "do you think age has blinded me? Am I without sense because I have lived beyond my youth? There will be no bloodshed. Your future is certain now. My son Markion is my heir. Who better than a proven prince of the blood royal to take my mantle? *When*," he snapped, "I am ready to pass it on."

Angry whispers snaked around the tent. "Blood *royal*? Who in God's creation does he think he is?" "The old goat thinks he is Pendragon! Listen to him!" "By Llud of the Otherworld, I'll have Percival before I'll have Markion!"

"No more dirty Cornishmen!" someone muttered a little too loudly, and everyone went still. The only sounds in the tent were the flames' hiss and the old king's breathing.

"My lord King." Peredur's cordial voice slid smoothly into the silence. "We Welsh dispute the choice."

"Go to Hell!" Constantine croaked, and men jumped from their seats, all shouting at once.

2 ✟ MARHALT

A mistake, thought Tristan. Outright defiance would gain Constantine nothing. He was outnumbered. The Welsh were ready, organized, and well led. Who would stand for Constantine? Gerontius, a good fighter but a poor substitute for Mark; himself; Dinadan of Dorria; and the princes of Dumnonia, who had served Cornwall for generations. They were, all told, perhaps five hundred strong. And it was foolishness, pure idiocy, to go to war with one another with the barbarian Saxons barely out of earshot.

No sooner had the thought passed through his head than Tristan heard it voiced aloud.

"My lords all, this is unseemly." Peredur's commanding voice cut through the protests. "We are allies, after all. We are all that's left of a united Britain. We were once great—some of us here can remember the days of Arthur and what it was like to live in peace. If we fight among ourselves, we do all Britain a disservice, for the Saxons wait poised to pick apart our leavings."

"How do you propose to settle this, then?" cried a Cornish voice. "Do you withdraw your insolent opposition?"

Peredur waited for silence. "That we cannot do. We oppose Markion because he has shown himself to be a greedy, selfish leader who thinks only of his own aggrandizement and not of Britain." He raised his hand to forestall the storm of protest. "I'm sure it looks quite different to you. You are happy to grow more powerful at our expense. But that is how it looks to us. And it is not, and never was, Arthur's way." He paused. "Many of us do not wish to serve King Markion. We want a leader who honors men beyond his own borders. We propose Percival of Gwynedd."

"Ha!" sneered Constantine. "Your own nephew, by all that's holy. What a surprise!"

"Yes, my own nephew," Peredur acknowledged calmly. "But a man who has seldom taken my own advice when I wished to see Gwynedd rise to prominence among the kingdoms. Instead of Gwynedd, he has always thought of Britain first. He remembers Arthur."

"Oh, certainly, and wants his crown!"

"No." Peredur spoke sharply. "That has never been his ambition. It is *our* ambition for him. He does not even know we propose him."

This news silenced everyone.

"Then how do you know he will accept it?" someone asked. Constantine snorted and fell into a coughing fit. Peredur waited until there was silence.

"If Britain chooses him, he will serve. I know him well. Not even his enemies doubt his prowess as a warrior. He was one of the Twelve who survived Camlann."

"My son Meliodas was another," Constantine spat. "There are heroes beyond *your* borders, Peredur!"

"My lord King, no one denies it. Had Meliodas lived to be your heir, we would not be here asking you to choose another."

In the dark, Dinadan's hand found Tristan's arm and squeezed it.

Constantine's breath was short. "I will not choose another. Markion is as able as his brother."

"We contest that choice," Peredur said gravely.

"How? If, as you claim, you do not want civil war?"

"We will select a champion to fight in single combat on Percival's behalf against anyone you put forward for your defense. If our man wins, we choose the heir; if he loses, you do. We are willing to swear, all of us, tonight, by whatever gods we each hold holy, that we will abide for all time by this decision." Utter stillness blanketed the company. "There are three conditions. Both champions must be kings' sons; both must be men of honor, Britons born. And both must volunteer." He paused. "Is this acceptable?"

"Grandfather," someone nearby whispered, "let me do it! Let me fight for my father."

"Hush, Gerontius," Constantine growled. "Have you forgotten your ankle? It's as big as a melon. You can hardly stand upon it. Damn Markion! Why isn't he here?"

"Is this acceptable?" Peredur repeated. "Or isn't there anyone who wants to fight for Cornwall?"

Tristan ducked out of the tent and pulled Dinadan with him. He shivered with excitement, breathing fast.

"Don't you want to see what happens?" Dinadan objected furiously. "Why, the future of Britain is up for grabs!"

"Quick! There's not a moment to lose. Will you do me a service, Din?"

"Certainly, but—"

"Run to the tent and fetch my sword."

Dinadan stared at him. Tristan scooped up great handfuls of mud and smeared it over his chest and arms and legs.

"What in God's name are you—"

"Quick! In another second it will be too late. I need my sword!"

"What on earth for?"

"Hurry, can't you? If I go myself, there won't be time."

Dinadan disappeared into the darkness. Tristan smeared mud into his hair until it was one thick, glossy mass, and tied it behind his head. He covered his face, his neck, his shoulders, then rolled to cake his back. He stood, rubbing the thick ooze well into his legs. Thank God he had come barefoot. When Dinadan returned Tristan was so dark he was invisible in the gloom, and Dinadan called his name aloud.

"I'm here, oaf, at your elbow."

"Good God!" Dinadan jumped. "What have you done to yourself? Have you gone mad?"

"I don't need the swordbelt. Just the sword." Tristan drew his weapon from the scabbard and hefted it in his hand, loving the way it felt, cool and balanced and familiar. "Promise me, Din, that whatever I say, you'll back me."

"First tell me what in God's name you're going to do."

Tristan smiled. His white teeth were the only part of him Dinadan could clearly see.

"I'm going to defend my uncle Mark."

"Dear God, no! Tristan, they'll kill you!"

"Listen." Tristan spoke gravely. "Do you think I don't know what they say behind my back? Do you think I'm deaf? Everyone, even you, thinks my uncle Mark has played me for a fool. This is my chance to do him the greatest service of his life, and to reclaim my birthright. If I win his battle for him, he must make me King of Lyonesse or be known all over Britain for a blackguard. It is his test as well as mine. We will know, after tonight, the kind of men we are."

Tears ran down Dinadan's cheeks. "You will be dead, Tris, that's what kind of man you'll be. Let Gerontius do it."

"He can't. He's injured."

"It's certain death! I know who they will choose—Marhalt the butcher!"

Tristan shrugged. "Every man has a weakness. I'll find his. And he has more to lose. I am unwed, unpromised, I have no kingdom. And even if I die, well—it will be something new I've never felt before."

"Oh, God!" Dinadan wept. "You and your damned sensations! Just once, why can't you think like other men? Let me do it, then. I'm older, I'm a king's son, I've as much right as you."

Tristan threw an arm around his shoulders and hugged him quickly. "Your heart wouldn't be in it, my friend. Mine is."

He turned and strode to the entrance to the tent. The sentries cried out in fear and drew their swords.

Tristan gave the password and pushed past them into the smoky light. Faces turned to him; eyes widened; men gaped. He stood still before them all, sword raised.

"I accept Peredur's challenge on behalf of King Markion of Cornwall!"

Someone laughed. Others grinned. But Peredur, standing alone in the center of the gathering, regarded him gravely.

"Are you a king's son?"

"Yes, my lord."

More laughter. "King of the swamp, that is!" "He's blacker than a Spaniard's whore! King's son, indeed!" "Worse, he's blacker than a Pict!" "Be gone, you savage!" "Go back to your cave, animal!"

Peredur raised a hand and stilled them. "Your father's name?"

"Meliodas of Lyonesse. King of Cornwall."

The laughter died. Peredur's blue eyes narrowed and a smile touched his lips. "He was a king, indeed. Your name?"

"Tristan."

Peredur bowed his head in greeting. "Welcome, Tristan. How old are you?"

"Age was not among the qualifications, my lord. I am a Briton born. Bred and raised by King Meliodas, trained by Markion. You will find me a man of honor."

Peredur eyed him thoughtfully. "I believe you." He turned. "King Constantine, is the lad acceptable to you?"

Constantine glared at Tristan, clutching Gerontius for support, but he said nothing.

"No one else," Peredur ventured quietly, "has volunteered."

Constantine nodded sharply. "He is my grandson. Of course he is acceptable to me." He shrugged. "If he's fool enough to take your bait."

"Very well, Tristan. I regret I placed no condition upon age, but as I did not, I must accept you as well." He turned and gestured behind him. "This is the man you will face. His name is Marhalt."

Out from the shadows stepped the biggest man Tristan had ever seen. Tall and thickly built, with arms and legs the size of tree trunks, and hands that could encompass a man's waist, Marhalt's blue eyes bulged as he stared at his young opponent. Tristan's first startled thought was to wonder what horse had been able to carry him from Wales, or had he walked? The irrelevance of his thought made him smile, and Marhalt frowned.

"Find me funny, do you, Tristan?"

"Not at all, my lord."

"Then quit your grinning. I'll make mincemeat of you."

Tristan turned to Peredur. "I make one condition, my lord." Around him men sniggered. Peredur raised a hand for silence.

"And what is that?"

"Sir Marhalt may choose the weapons. I choose the time and place."

"It must be done before we depart this valley and not three years hence."

"Agreed."

Peredur nodded. "Fair enough. Eh, Marhalt?"

Marhalt stared hard at Tristan and nodded. "Agreed."

"Very well. Marhalt—"

"Wait!" someone cried from the back of the tent. Gerontius hobbled forward into the light. "Tristan. Cousin. Please do not take this upon yourself. By rights this duty should fall to me. Let me fight him. It is my own father's honor that is challenged."

"You are injured, Gerontius. It would be unfair."

"Unfair!" Tears sprang to the prince's eyes. "Do you call *this* fair? My lords, my lord Peredur, he's only sixteen, only been a year in the army—"

"Thanks, cousin, for your praise of me," Tristan muttered between clenched teeth.

"And yet this very day, my lord," a voice cried from the tent flaps, "Tristan has slain a hundred Saxons with only thirty men!" Dinadan stepped forward, clad in boots and leggings, strapping on his swordbelt. "If that doesn't make him worthy to fight this lecherous dog, I don't know what does."

"Ha! Ha! Lecherous dog!" Cornish voices cried as the Welsh jumped to their feet.

"Silence!" Peredur bellowed. "We do *not* want civil war! Let Marhalt do the fighting."

"Please, Tristan," Gerontius begged, "you take on too much. You cannot defeat this man. It is better I should die than you."

"Certainly your father would not think so. Take heart, cousin. Perhaps I will defeat him."

Gerontius shook his head. "Tristan, how can my father ever repay you for this noble sacrifice?"

Tristan took his eyes off Marhalt and looked at his cousin. "If I die, he can give you Lyonesse. If I live, he can give it to me."

"It's yours anyway, Tristan. He was only waiting until you returned from this one battle. It isn't necessary to do—this." He gestured toward the Welsh giant.

"I'm doing it to prove that Mark is a man worth dying for. They don't believe that now. Many of our own men don't believe it. But after tonight, whatever happens, no one will be able to deny it. Don't you see? It's Cornwall's future that's at stake as much as Britain's."

Gerontius leaned forward and kissed him.

"All right. So it is decided." Peredur again commanded everyone's attention. "Marhalt, what weapons do you choose?"

Marhalt smiled disdainfully at the naked, mud-clad boy. "I choose one weapon only. The sword."

"And, Tristan? When shall this fight be fought?"

"Now, my lord. Here. Outside this tent."

"*Now?*" Marhalt stared. "In the pouring rain?"

"Now."

"But—" Marhalt turned toward Peredur. "Must I?"

Peredur glanced sharply at Tristan. "The time and place were of his choosing. Yes, you must fight now."

Marhalt's voice rose in agitation. "May I not even have ten minutes to don my armor?"

Tristan bowed. "I will give you five minutes for preparation. Meet me outside."

Another smile touched Peredur's lips, this time of admiration, as Tristan turned and strode out, Dinadan at his heels.

"Quickly!" Tristan whispered, dragging his friend aside. "More mud. Cover me with it, nice and thick. The rain has stopped and it's drying out. Pray, Dinadan, for a light rain, or a mist."

"By the looks of it, you'll get both. This is a night for fog if I ever saw one."

"I hope so. Marhalt's nearsighted."

"How do you know?"

"I watched his eyes. And he's left-handed. And he isn't very bright."

"Well, that wouldn't surprise me, but how on earth can you tell?"

Tristan grinned. "His wife leads him around by the nose, for one thing—oh, come, Dinadan, didn't you see that rape story for what it is? A woman's plan if I ever heard one. But if that wasn't clue enough, what commander worth his salt dons armor for a fight in the mud and rain?"

"He would be better off in nothing but a loincloth, like you?"

"Much better off."

"Tristan, one sword stroke will kill you."

"One of *his* sword strokes would kill me no matter what mail I wore. I might as well be naked."

Dinadan shook his head. "I'm damned if that sounds like a battle strategy to me."

"At least I'll be able to move. Just picture him in his leather tunic studded all over with brass, and leather leggings, too, with any luck. After today, they should be good and wet. What will they feel like to wear? He's probably had them drying before a fire, getting stiff. What will it feel like to move? He'll be as slow as a sea turtle in all that gear."

"God, Tristan, you're the only one who cares what anything *feels* like," Dinadan grumbled, slapping on the mud. "That bonehead won't even think twice about it. He'll just put it on and come after you."

"Let me live half an hour and his arms will feel it. And his legs. That's fine, Din, I'm coated all over. Now give me a moment to myself. I need to think."

Dinadan withdrew as Peredur emerged from the tent, followed by the Welsh lords, King Constantine leaning on Gerontius, and all the Cornishmen behind them. Twenty men lit torches and stood in a large circle outside the tent. The muddy turf was trampled and torn up from the passing of many feet. Puddles reflected the torchlight, dimpling as a steady drizzle began to fall.

While they waited, Tristan walked slowly around the circle, digging in his toes, testing the footing. Constantine scowled, Gerontius wept silently, and the Welshmen smiled and nudged one another, nodding at the witless boy.

Marhalt arrived in his damp leather armor, looking just as stiff and uncomfortable as Tristan had predicted, and just as oblivious of discomfort as Dinadan had foretold. He glared at Tristan.

"Don't yield to me, boy. It won't do you any good. We fight to the death."

Tristan raised his sword to his forehead in salute. "I have said my prayers. I am ready."

Peredur gave the signal and the fight began.

They circled warily. While his mind was on Marhalt, watching how he moved, timing his feints, gauging his nimbleness, Tristan's senses were alive to the thickening mist and the dim haloes around the torches. In another twenty minutes, if he could stay alive that long— The sword flashed, Marhalt lunged, Tristan leaped aside, blocking the blow. Marhalt whirled, struck out, barely missing. Tristan dove, somersaulted, spun, nicked the giant in the arm. Marhalt spat. He was fast for a big man, surprisingly fast. And unbelievably strong. Just crossing his blade had nearly torn the sword hilt from Tristan's grasp.

They circled again. Predictably, Marhalt lunged the other way. Tristan parried, dodged, cut him through the armor on the thigh, a light cut, but a bleeder. Given time— Again the blade came at him, hacking down. Tristan leaped aside; the giant's hand came out to catch him but caught a fistful of mud instead as the boy slithered free. The first fingers of mist drifted into the circle. Tristan heard the Welshman grunt, saw him shake his head. *Use your ears and nose,* he told himself, *not your eyes. Hear him, smell him! Listen to his feet!* The sword glinted, swinging sideways. He jumped back, staying balanced, knees bent, toes digging in for purchase. The sword swung up; Tristan darted in, hacked, then out, whirling away as the giant bellowed. Through the flickering mist he saw a dark rivulet run down the Welshman's arm from the shoulder. The great shadow loomed, coming fast, beating him back, right and left, beating him down. He backed, and backed again, hard up against the soldiers forming the circle. They retreated as the giant's deadly sword approached.

Gods of the high hills, gods of the moving deep. Tristan stumbled, rolled away as the sword fell. *Gods of the living forests.* Feinting, dodging, striking, twisting. *Gods of the burning sands.* Marhalt lunged, his thick boots sliding in the mud. Diving sideways, Tristan cut him well across the thick part of his arm. Blood soaked the giant's leather tunic, splashed upon the ground— how much, how quickly! Marhalt turned, hissing, and attacked. Tristan's sword was brushed aside, again and again, as if it were merely an annoyance. He could not stand against the giant, but circled backward, digging in his toes, nimble in retreat. *Gods of the birthless sky and deathless night, hear my plea!* Again and again the sword caught the light, flashed, came down. Again and again Tristan dodged, dove, leaped, and scrambled out of its way, now and then scratching his opponent, a nick here, a cut there. Would this bleeding ox never feel his pain? *Wonderful Mother, I am a mosquito!* Irritated, Marhalt rushed, slipped, and fell to one knee; Tristan landed a blow to his shoulder, but brass and leather dulled the stroke, and Marhalt came up swinging. He locked blades and with a mighty shove threw Tristan hard up against a soldier in the circle. The man staggered. Tristan fell. On hands and knees he crawled into the dark, beyond the reach of the smoking torches.

Marhalt bellowed, "Cheat! Coward!" and came after him. The circle shattered. Men began to shout. Tristan slithered in the mud, his face clogged with damp, struggling to stand. Damn the noise! He could not hear the giant. He rose. Marhalt was there, breathing fast in the night mist, staring about blindly, calling for light. "Coward! Devil! Show yourself!"

The giant could not see his mud-blackened body in the dark. *Mithra, Bull-Slayer, bless my sword!* Tristan braced himself and struck, slashing with all his might. It was like striking a stone wall; his whole body jarred, his wrist loosened. Marhalt gasped once and nearly tore the sword from his grip. He fell back, tripping on a tree root, whipping his body sideways as the Welshman's blade slashed down. Missed! He pulled himself to his feet, shaking, and leaned for a moment against the tree. He could not feel his hand.

"I knew you were a coward, you dirty Cornishman! Whore's son! You'll die for this!"

The voice was very close. Tristan gripped the sword with his other hand, and crept silently to his left. Lights were coming downhill toward them, singly and in pairs. Where was the giant? Light gleamed from a bronze stud—there! He dove, rolling on his shoulder, stabbing at the knee. Marhalt whirled, kicked out, caught him in the hip, and sent him flying, smashing up against a tree. Tristan cried out as the breath left his body. Marhalt shouted in exultation and came at him. Wrist and back screamed at Tristan— no time to listen! He threw himself sideways and clawed at the tree to stand. Dimly Tristan saw the blade coming, thrust his weapon out to block it, felt it give, twisting, wrenched away. He stepped back, too slow; the sword raced at him, something jarred him, freezing his breath. He crumpled, his body alive with pain, hot, searing, wet. His legs buckled. He fell hard against the unforgiving ground. His mouth gaped, breathless, sucking air. *Jesu Christ, who knows the pain of death, forgive me all my sins.*

"Aiiiii-eeee-aaaah!" Marhalt shrieked his victory, leaped forward, and slipped as his knee gave way. He fell hard against the boy's body, sword flying wide. Tristan screamed as the man's weight hit him. His eyes blazed with stars, blinded by fire and pain. He could not breathe. The big hands encircled his neck, slipping against the mud, squeezing hard. *Jesu God!* No time for prayer or breath; he could not move or think. His body hammered at his thoughts: *Do something! Act now!* Life was ebbing fast; he could feel his strength sinking, his youth dying, all his hopes unfathomed, all his songs unsung. The fleshy fingers slipped, he grabbed air, heard foul Welsh curses through the cold mist as the cruel hands found their grip once more. He had no strength, no hope, only dumb, blind terror. Deep within him, he revolted. It could not end like this. His fingers twitched helplessly in the mud,

groping for something, anything, while the light left his eyes and he struggled, desperate, against rising oblivion. There! The cold, firm feel of forged
steel. A sword hilt! Blind, breathless, he forced himself to hold hard with
both hands, slowly tighten every sinew, slowly raise his arms above his head,
and then strike down! Down! Down with all his might! The blade hit hard,
shattering his wrist, a dull thud followed by a loud roar, and then, on the
edge of sound, a scream. His scream.

3 ✟ SANCTUARY

From far away came the sound of water dripping. He imagined a still pool
deep in the forest glade, dappled sunlight, cool mosses soft against his
cheek. Up welled sweet water, cold and clear, lipping over mossy stones,
sliding silver-streamed onto rocks below. He shivered as the icy droplets
splashed against his face. He stirred, tasting water against his lips, feeling
flesh against his flesh, jarring and remote. Someone held him, someone
raised his head while he drank. The glade faded slowly, leaving nothing but
a shadowy mist behind. Where was he? Deftly, kind hands stroked his hair
and settled his head gently on something soft and sweet-scented—a bough?
A pillow? Slippered feet moved quietly on stone: sure steps, purposeful,
moving away. He was alone. He heard nothing but the sweet calling of a
meadowlark nearby, felt nothing beyond a breeze that stirred his hair, a seal
upon his eyelids and the deep satisfaction of a thirst refreshed. As he slid
again into senselessness he recognized the place, and rejoiced. *I am in
Heaven.*

Toward evening Tristan opened his eyes. He lay on a pallet in a small cell
with windows facing west and east. The golden light of late afternoon threw
a brilliant oblong across the slate floor. The walls were of wood and wattle,
mud dried and washed white with lime. On a plain wooden table he saw an
old clay pitcher, a horn cup, two jars stoppered with cork and labeled with
symbols, an unlit candle in a chipped holder, clean cloths neatly folded, a
thin-bladed knife, a mortar and pestle, and a fine ceramic bowl. The stone
flooring was swept spotlessly clean. Not a single dust mote danced in the
shaft of light. He could just make out the ragged tail of a straw broom in
the shadow of the low, curved door. The walls were bare of ornament but
were hung instead with bunches of dried herbs, blue, rose, brown, purple,

and faded green. It seemed to him he knew this place, recognized its quiet peace, the sharp herb scent, the moving air that smelled lightly, but so enticingly, of the sea. If he was not in Heaven, he was close to it.

He closed his eyes. He knew, without wondering at it, that he could not move, and he did not try to. It did not occur to him to wonder why or how he came to be there. Instead, he strained his ears to catch the sea sounds he knew could not be far away. It seemed to him he could feel the steady rhythm in the deepest part of his being, the incessant suck and thud of the mother deep, beckoning to him, her lost son, calling him home. With a sigh, he let his seeking spirit drift, to wash in and out with the moving tide, and fall toward sleep.

The door opened softly, and the purposeful steps he had heard before approached him. A cool hand touched his forehead. Struggling up from the mists of tide-borne dreams, he opened his eyes. A tall hooded figure in a gray robe stood above him, looking down. For a moment, terror stopped his breathing. There was no face inside the hood! The figure turned to the light, and Tristan gasped aloud. It was a death's head! *Dear Jesu God! If I am not in Heaven, am I then in Hell?*

"Be easy, boy. Jarrad, the cloth and cup." Strong hands lifted his head and shoulders with the utmost gentleness, while a youth, gray-robed like his master, approached with a healing drink. The cup was put to his lips. He drank, and breathed more easily. The hooded figure lowered Tristan's head onto the pillow and wiped his mouth with the clean cloth. Tristan could only stare at the hood in dread and fascination.

"Well," said the figure in a firm, familiar voice, "if you haven't returned to us at last." He pushed the hood back. The face, although thin and bony with deep-set, luminous eyes and close-cropped, graying hair, was a man's face, full of life, full of feeling.

"Uncle Pernam!" Tristan's lips struggled to form the words, but only the barest whistle of sound emerged.

"Don't try speech yet. It's enough that you've finally awakened. Do you know me? I see you do. Well, Tristan, welcome home to Lyonesse. You're in my house of healing. You've been here three months, and it's been touch and go at times, but heal you will."

Tristan stared. Three months?

Pernam nodded serenely, as if he had heard the thought. The boy Jarrad brought him the ceramic bowl. He dipped a cloth into fresh water, and cleaned Tristan's face and neck while he spoke.

"Yes, three months. It's hard to credit when you haven't seen or felt the time you've lived through. It's near midsummer. They brought you home the night of the equinox."

Tristan struggled to remember. Where had he been? Why was he in

Pernam's Sanctuary? Why hadn't they taken him on to his own home across the causeway, on the promontory? What was the matter with him?

Pernam signaled to the boy, who replaced the bowl on the table and pulled the stopper from one of the jars. The boy brought him the knife, the jar, and a new cloth.

"Pernam." He tried again and achieved a sound, a harsh, grating croak.

Pernam smiled. "Good. It's coming. Don't rush it. Your memory will return soon enough. Rest easy, listen to your body's rhythm. You'll heal faster if you obey your inner voice."

It was all Tristan could do to control his rising panic. Pernam and the youth were lifting a cover from him, washing his body with the wet cloth, *yet he could feel nothing!*

"Pernam!" he cried, and the word flew out, sharp and distinct. *"I am dead! I can't feel anything!"*

Pernam paused, holding the knife and jar. "The Good Goddess be thanked, you are very much alive. It is my doing you have lost your sensations. I gave you a potion with a drug to kill your pain."

Pain! The word struck with the force of truth. He had recently—but how recently?—suffered great pain. He seemed to remember it dully, from a great distance: mind-numbing, all-consuming, killing pain. "We have poulticed your wound twice a day," Pernam was saying, "but you have never been awake. I warn you, this might hurt, but it is necessary." He stuck the knife into the jar and withdrew a greenish paste. "Hold still." Tristan could not feel the touch of the blade against his skin, nor the application of the paste. Instead, he felt a thousand red-hot needles stab his side, from under his right arm, across his ribs, across his chest. Sweat broke upon his forehead; he gasped for breath. "There." Pernam handed the jar to Jarrad and wiped Tristan's brow with the cloth. "No more until morning."

"Twice a day?" Tristan managed in a whisper. "Pernam, what happened to me?"

Gently, Pernam drew the coverlet over Tristan, spoke in a low voice to the youth, and sent him from the room. Then he turned back to Tristan and mopped his brow again.

"You've been in a swordfight," he said. "You killed a giant."

Marhalt! The name sprang at him, and all at once memory flooded back, complete and in detail. The nearness of it shocked him. Unlike the pain, he remembered that fight as if it were yesterday. Marhalt dead? But Marhalt had killed *him*, not the other way around.

"Marhalt's dead?"

"Yes, that was the name." Pernam's eyebrow lifted. "You split his skull. Is that the way men fight nowadays? It sounded an unorthodox stroke to me."

Tristan tried to smile, but was not sure he succeeded. "He was five times my size and had his hands around my throat. You'll have to forgive me."

Pernam's smile transformed his long, thin face into the delighted visage of a child. "My dear, all Cornwall forgives you. You are everyone's darling. My father, Constantine, wept over you. My brother Markion kissed your brow."

"Mark was here?"

"For two weeks, while you raged in fever. He made you King of Lyonesse."

Tristan closed his eyes. *At last.* "I am sorry I knew nothing of it."

"He was sorry, too. He will come again when you are stronger and are able to receive him at Lyon's Head."

He looked up at Pernam's calm face. Ever since he could remember, this uncle, the youngest of Constantine's three sons, had been a solace to him, the only one, sometimes, who understood his songs and dreams. Pernam had always been as he was now, serene and whole, a man who had come to terms with life. There had never been a time when he could not talk to Pernam.

"Pernam." It came out a whisper. "I thought I was dead. The giant killed me. I remember it."

Tenderly, the healer's hands stroked the hair back from his forehead. "It was nearly so. He cut you well. You almost bled to death before they left the field. No one thought you would live. They bound your body as best they could and carried you home on a litter. They brought you to me, here in this room, more dead than alive."

Tristan watched his face, a noble face, with tanned skin, lightly lined, stretched across strong, well-molded bones. Although he could not feel their touch, he felt the strength that flowed into him through the deft, long-fingered hands. The dark eyes seemed to reach his soul. This man commanded power. He had suspected it in childhood; he knew it now.

"I have six new apprentices," Pernam said softly. "You trained them well, Tristan. Everything they know, you taught them. They were with me when I took the wrappings off your wound."

Tristan gulped. "Was it so awful?"

Pernam's thin mouth twitched into a smile. "The army physicians did their best, but they hadn't washed all the mud out. It festered."

"But it was the mud that saved my life. The oaf was strangling me."

"Ah, well. Suffice it to say I had to reopen the wound and let you bleed before you could heal. You were two weeks in a fever that might have killed you, and six weeks in chills and sweats. At one time we had four mixing tables in here. As you see, we are down to one. The numbing potion and the poultice. That and prayer and sweet rest are all that you need now."

"I remember—I think—he broke my wrist."

Pernam lifted Tristan's right arm so he could see it. Tristan gaped. Was that his own arm, that long shaft of bone and sinew? What had happened to his flesh? Had his whole body shrunk to no more than a pallid shroud upon his bones? Pernam was flexing his wrist for him, showing him that it moved.

"Not a bad break, really. It healed swiftly. You will have the use of it again."

"Pernam!"

"What is it, nephew?"

"Why is it I can feel nothing, not even the movement of my arm, but I can feel every inch of this burning wound?"

Something moved in the dark eyes, but Pernam said nothing, replacing Tristan's arm under the coverlet and taking care to adjust the pillow under his head. The light was failing. In silence, the room grew dark.

"Tell me."

Pernam's hands moved before his eyes, making a sign over Tristan's breast. Then he spoke.

"It is as I thought. I said nothing before because I was not sure. But if you feel it through the power of the drug, then it must be so."

"*What* must be so?"

"The sword that cut you was tipped with poison."

"Poison!"

"And no ordinary one. I have a large store of antidotes to poisons. I have tried them all. And the wound *has* healed, Tristan. For a long while it would not. We finally found a mixture of the right ingredients to heal the flesh, but I wondered if the wound was not deeper than the flesh."

"What do you mean?"

"I mean," said Pernam slowly, "that there was more on that sword than simple poison. There was enchantment."

Tristan stared at him.

Pernam sighed and looked past the window toward the lighting stars. "There are not many left nowadays who possess such power. In the old days, when my father was young, when Cador, my grandfather, served the High King Arthur, such power as this was given into the hands of men. The great Merlin commanded it—surely you have heard of him."

"Merlin the Enchanter? Yes, of course. But to me, he's a figure in a bard's song, like Kay the Short-Armed, Bedwyr of the Bright Sword, and the great Sir Lancelot of the Lake."

"And what do bards sing of but our glorious past? These men were real enough, like you and me. I saw Lancelot once myself as he passed through

Cornwall. And Merlin, though a servant of the god, was as much flesh as you are, while he lived."

"The bards say that, like Arthur, he never died."

Pernam smiled. "Well, bards do tend to stretch it a bit, don't they, bardling? But there is truth in much of what they say. Merlin was a great enchanter and always used his power for the good. Niniane of Avalon, Lady of the Lake, was another. And Morgaine the Long-Sighted, her successor. Some used their power for evil purposes: Morgan of Rheged, and the dread Morgause, Witch of Orkney. But they are all gone now. Even Avalon is only weeds and apple trees. Not all their secrets died with them, apparently. Someone cursed that Welshman's sword."

Tristan did not respond, and Pernam sat motionless beside him in the still summer twilight. Beyond the window a nightingale took up its liquid song. At length, Pernam rose and lit the candle. Dusk sprang to night when the flame was born. Now Tristan could see little else but his uncle's face.

"Will it always feel like this? Is there no help for it?"

"It will ease as you grow in strength. But I am afraid the pain will never wholly leave you unless the antidote, if I can call it that, is found."

"How do I find an antidote to enchantment?"

"Tristan, I do not know. Whoever cast the spell may have its cure, or know what paste to apply to draw the venom. I do not. But I am sure of this: Had you not killed Marhalt, you would have died."

"Of a certainty!"

"No, I don't mean by Marhalt's hands. Had he nicked you and done nothing more, the sword's curse would have killed you. You lived only because the sword's master died."

"What on earth are you talking about, Uncle?"

"There is no other explanation for your living through such bleeding, through such a journey, through such a fever. In a perverse way, the enchantment has preserved you, because Marhalt died."

"This sounds like madness."

"I have heard of such curses. The Druids used them in the days of their power. Someone with a knowledge of Druid lore may have cursed the sword, thinking to protect the swordsman. It would prove fatal to his enemies, and a boon to him, if he were a difficult man to kill."

"He was that, all right."

"Then as long as Marhalt lived, the sword would kill his enemies. But should he die fighting, the curse would preserve the man he struck. Although not without cost."

"Then I must find the man who gave the sword to Marhalt?"

Pernam nodded. "Or the woman." A scratching came at the door. "Ah, here is your supper. Come in, boys. I will raise you up, Tristan, and they will feed you. Allow them, if you will; it's part of their training."

In came six youths, robed like Pernam, each one carrying a candle and a basket. Pernam sat on the pallet and propped Tristan up against him.

"I can feel your hands!" Tristan cried in delight. "The drug is leaving me."

"Eat first. Then I will mix another potion."

"Oh, no! No. It is wonderful to feel again, even discomfort. At least I know I am alive. I don't want any more of the drug."

"It will be more than discomfort before long."

Out of the baskets came a clean linen napkin, which was tucked under his chin, a loaf of new bread still warm from the ovens, a flask of steaming soup, and a small glazed bowl. The boys poured the soup into the bowl, and one of them lifted it to his lips. It was hot but rich with flavor, warming his belly, sending heat and life into his limbs. He could not manage the bread alone—could not find strength to chew it—but another of the boys soaked it in the soup and he sucked it down. A third lad stood by with the horn cup of fresh water, while two more held candles high so they could see. The sixth sat on a stool by the window with a lap harp and gently plucked the strings, chanting in a clear, high voice words that Tristan did not know, but which seemed to ease his spirit and give him strength to eat.

"Are they not beautiful?" Pernam whispered in his ear. Tristan looked at their young faces, still rounded by childhood, at their flawless complexions, their clear eyes and serious, intent expressions.

"Pernam's angels," he whispered back, and heard his uncle's light laughter in his ear.

"They belong to the Goddess, not to me. Though Jarrad disturbs my sleep from time to time. . . . You were such a one as these, Tristan, when last I saw you. When Meliodas lived. You were this beautiful. And I daresay, when you have your health and we shave off that scruffy beard, you will be beautiful again."

"I didn't know I had grown a beard."

Pernam's fingers brushed his cheek, and he felt not the touch of flesh, but the stiff tickle of whiskers. "Four years of soldiering have made you into a man. Mark and Guvranyl, between them, stole your boyhood and remade you in their image. And now, see, you are a king." Pernam sighed. "It was bound to happen, I suppose. You are cut from Meliodas's cloth, not from mine."

The boys knew when Tristan had had enough, and stoppered the flask, folded away the napkin, and rinsed out the bowl. The singer brought his song to a close and slid off the stool. Pernam laid Tristan's head gently down on the pillow.

"I want to see Dinadan," Tristan said. "Can you send for him?"

"He is here in the guest house. He has been here all along. I will send him to you in the morning."

Pernam lifted a hand and the boys began to chant softly to a tuneless, rhythmic beat. Their odd music, formless, sinuous, curved into his thoughts, encircled the dull edge of pain, and bore him onward, away, into oblivion.

"Dinadan." Tristan grinned as the familiar face peered around the door.

"Tristan! Christ. You look like death."

In three strides Dinadan was beside him, grasping Tristan's hand roughly between his own as tears started in his eyes.

"It's good to see you, too. Din, don't cry. I'm going to live."

Dinadan laughed and wiped his eyes. "I should hope so, after all we've been through. God, Tris! I mean, my lord." He went down on one knee. "My lord Tristan, King of Lyonesse."

"Get up, idiot. You look a fool."

"Nothing new for me. First time of hearing it?"

"Yes."

"You'll get used to it. How do you feel? Or shouldn't I ask?"

"Like hell," Tristan said stiffly. "There's such a pain in my chest I can hardly breathe. But at least I feel it. Yesterday I felt like a waking corpse. Today I feel like a wounded man."

Dinadan shook his head. "Most men would take anything rather than feel it. But not you."

With an effort, Tristan raised a skinny hand and pointed to a linen bag tied around his neck with a silken cord. "See this? Can you smell it? It stinks of some magic weed my uncle knows, and as long as I breathe its vapors the pain will be bearable. He made me wear it since I won't take the drug. He says too much pain interferes with healing. He's brought me back from death, so I must obey him."

"Your uncle Pernam's a magician," Dinadan said fervently. "Do whatever he tells you. I can't believe half the things I've seen here. Although"—with a swift look away—"some of his ways are strange."

"All men are different. He is a healer in the Mother's service. His gifts are not those of a warrior."

"I know. But the boys—aren't they awfully young—"

"None of them is here against his will. Pernam doesn't take anyone but youths who beg to come and offer service, youths who dream not of killing men and leading kingdoms, but of something different." He paused. "He's a man of virtue. Else my father would not have let him live here. No one comes to harm under his care. Healing is everything to him."

"I've cause to know it." Dinadan hurried on in a lighter voice. "He's had me scouring the countryside for all kinds of plants, looking for a cure."

"You? You don't know one plant from another!"

"Didn't, you mean. I do now. Leth and Aran helped me—the gray-eyed twins. They taught me what to look for. Can you believe I rode halfway up the coast to Tintagel looking for just the right kind of fern? Half of what I collected they threw out, and once I nearly poisoned myself on the wrong kind of mushroom. Your uncle Pernam saved me. It's been an exciting visit here in Lyonesse."

"Dinadan, how ever can I thank you?"

"Let me serve you at Lyon's Head when you're well enough to go home," his friend said earnestly. "My father's given me permission to serve you instead of Markion, now that you are king."

"Why, I'd love nothing better!" Tristan exclaimed. He reached out his thin hand, and Dinadan grasped it. "Tell me about Marhalt. What I heard from Pernam only confused me. Did I really kill him?"

"Indeed you did. *Thwack!* Down the middle of his head with your sword. I was some ways off and heard the blow. It took two men to prize the thing out of his skull. And you ought to see the blade. I've got it in my chamber. I'd show it to you now if Pernam would allow weapons in the house of healing. A deep nick, right in the heart of the blade edge, to mark Marhalt's death blow. Wherever he lies now, he's got a piece of Cornish metal in his brains."

Tristan paled. "That was the sword my father gave me only a month before he died."

"Don't worry, the blade's as strong as ever. I've tested it against my own."

"Thank God for that. You know, Dinadan, since dawn I've been lying here thinking. If I had it to do over again, I wonder if I'd challenge Marhalt after all."

"Because you nearly died of it?"

"No," Tristan said slowly, holding his friend's hand, "because something tells me no good will come of it."

"You are King of Lyonesse, and the Welsh have been forced to accept Markion as High King of Britain. Isn't that what you wanted?"

Tristan sighed, his eyes on the cracked ceiling. A light sea breeze caressed his cheek. All of a sudden he was very tired.

"Maybe it's something I dreamed, maybe it's something Pernam said. But I've had this feeling that my fate is linked to Marhalt's. That someday he will repay me for the blow I struck."

Dinadan scowled. "Superstition born of pain and illness. You'll feel better when you're out in the light and air. Marhalt's dead. He can't touch you now."

4 ✠ ESMERÉE

Ly summer's end Tristan was strong enough to walk unaided. He delighted in this newfound freedom, and one morning, tired of walking
around the grounds of Pernam's Sanctuary, he crept out the gates and scrambled down the steep cliff path to the rocky beach below. He stripped quickly
and waded knee-high into the sea, his flesh tingling. Holding his breath, he
dove in, glorying in the rush of water, ecstatic at the sweet caress across his
skin. This must be, he thought, how a lover feels after a long absence. How
long since he had last been upon her, since he had last felt her great, enveloping embrace! He spiraled to the surface, blowing sea water from his
nose and mouth like the great fishes, and floated idly. The morning sun
kissed his face and breast, while the cool sea stroked his legs, tickling him
with her movement, buoying him lightly as a feather on her swells, up and
down, beguiling him ever farther out toward her deep domain. At last, as
his toes began to numb, he struck out for shore in long, smooth strokes. On
the beach he stood a moment, toes digging deep into the shingle, letting
the cool water stream from his body, the lover's last caress. On the thought
his loins awakened. Tristan laughed aloud and stretched his arms out toward
the glittering sea.

"Great Mother, giver of life, I salute you!"

"Tristan!" He turned. Dinadan was running down the beach. "There
you are! Pernam's looking for you. Why didn't you let me know where you
were going?"

Tristan shook the water from his hair. "I wanted to be alone."

Dinadan grinned and raised an eyebrow. "You don't need to be alone.
You need a woman."

Coloring lightly, Tristan reached for his leggings. "It's been happening
a lot lately. Often during rubdowns after exercise. Pernam says it's part of
healing, and not to worry."

"Well, I agree with him there. Worry's a waste of time. Just find a woman."

Tristan grinned. "Oh, aye, that's easy enough—there are so many of
them about." He eyed his friend. "And how do you know so much about it?
Last I knew, you had no use for girls, no time, no interest. What aren't you
telling me?"

Now it was Dinadan's turn to color. "I would have told you all about
it . . . but there wasn't time on the battlefield."

"You're serious? When was this?"

"Last winter. After Markion's council at Tintagel. You stayed; I accompanied my father home to Dorria."

"I remember. Before Christmas. Go on."

"What do you mean, go on?"

Tristan was lacing his sandals and looked up smiling. "Your face is the color of a ripe apple. You sly fox, keeping secrets from me. Tell me about it."

"Well, I, uh, her name is Diarca."

"Don't tell me her name, fool. She'd have your hide for that, and I wouldn't blame her. Tell me what it was like to lie with her."

Dinadan's face flamed. "For pity's sake! You can't expect me to tell you that."

"Why not? Oh, all right, forget it, if it's such a chore. I'm just curious, that's all." He tied the last lace and rose. He was taller than Dinadan by half a head. "Come on. Let's go."

"You'll find out soon enough yourself. Look at you, grown a head since winter, with the legs of a racehorse and the shoulders of an ox, and King of Lyonesse to boot. Before you're home an hour they'll be lining up outside your door."

Tristan smiled and slung an arm around his friend's shoulder. "With a red gash around my middle that will never heal. Pray I find a woman who won't mind scars."

Dinadan shook his head as they started up the cliff path. "More like it will endear you to them. You always were a lucky bastard."

At the top of the cliff they stopped for breath.

"Heaven help me," Dinadan gasped, "your wind is better than mine! If you're an invalid, I'm King of Rome. What are you waiting for, Tristan? It's time to go home and take up the kingship that awaits you."

"I'm waiting until Pernam tells me I can go. I owe him that."

"Well, I don't know why he keeps you here. You're strong enough now to return to Lyon's Head."

"He's found a new concoction for my wound. It's some deadly, bitter herb that he mashes up and makes me drink. I have to take it every morning." Tristan shuddered. "It tastes awful. But it does help."

They had come to the gates of the sanctuary, and the porter let them in. Pernam met them in the hallway, a basket under his arm. He bowed politely to them both.

"Good morning. You've been swimming, I see, Tristan."

"You're not going to tell me it's forbidden?"

"On the contrary, salt water has many curative powers. Swim as often as you like, but never alone. Surely someone raised on the sea as you've been knows better than that."

Tristan bowed his head and accepted the rebuke. "What did you want me for? More of that foul drink?"

Pernam lifted the basket. "I've something new for you this morning. Better-tasting. Come try it now and break your fast."

Tristan wrinkled his nose. "Nothing could make that vile herb taste better. What have you done, soaked it in spirits?"

But Pernam would say nothing until they were seated in Tristan's room around the little table. Leth came in with a pitcher of warm goat's milk and a plate of bread and honey, but this morning Pernam pushed the usual meal aside. From the basket he brought forth a dense round cake, studded with raisins and flecked with lemon rind. He cut a slice for each of them.

"Try it, my lord Dinadan. It won't hurt you. I want your opinion of its flavor."

Gingerly, they tried it. Tristan's features lit with joy. "It's wonderful! It's the best cake I've ever tasted. Are you sure the herb is in it?"

"Quite sure."

"And you've always said you had no skill at cooking. Modest man!"

"I did not do the baking. This was made for you by a friend of mine. A woman."

Both young men stared, and Pernam's lips twisted in a thin smile. "Do I surprise you? Then you do not know me as well as you think you do. Perhaps, Tristan, if you learn to broaden your mind, I will introduce you to this generous friend."

"I beg your pardon, Uncle. And please, take me to her that I may thank her for this marvelous cake. Will it be possible to get more of it when I return to Lyon's Head?"

Pernam frowned. "Probably not, unless you're willing to ride out here and fetch it. She's a local woman. But first things first. We must see whether the cake is as powerful as the drink. Perhaps the heat of baking weakens the herb's effect. We shall know in a week. If it works, I will ask her to bake you another. If you do not worsen over the next fortnight, I will send you home."

Dinadan smiled in satisfaction, but Tristan looked away.

"Have you a harp in the place, Uncle? Since I rose at dawn I have wanted to make music."

"As it happens, I do." Pernam signaled to Leth, who slipped out. "A very fine harp, although a small one. A traveling harp of horsehair, horn, and brass, said to have once belonged to Merlin the Enchanter."

"Indeed?" Tristan cried. "I have not heard that story. How came the harp into Cornwall? Merlin was a Welshman."

Pernam's deep eyes seemed to look through him to something beyond. "In those days Wales and Cornwall were friends. In the days of Arthur. Yes, and even before that, in the days of Uther Pendragon. This is the harp, they say, that Merlin used to weave a spell around the High King Uther, changing him into the likeness of Gorlois, Duke of Cornwall, so that he might lie undetected with the Duchess Ygraine and beget Arthur. And in the morning, when our ancestor Gorlois attacked the King's troops and was killed, Merlin hurried Uther out of Tintagel before the courier could bring the duchess news of her husband's death and the deception be discovered. In his hurry, he left behind his harp." Pernam's gaze returned to Tristan. "It's a pretty story, isn't it? I've no idea if it's true. Markion gave me the harp when he moved into Tintagel. The Goddess knows he had no use for it."

The boy Leth entered carrying a lap harp carved of horn, fitted with brass string shoes, and strung with horsehair. Tristan held it gingerly. It was very old. Settling it on his lap, he plucked it lightly, and its clear voice sang out sweet and true. "What a voice it has! Why, a breath will set it singing. It hardly needs a touch to tell its tale."

Pernam winked at Dinadan. "If I didn't know better, I'd say it was made for you. It's yours, Tristan. Take it with my blessing, and may it bring you joy."

"Mine?" Tristan swallowed. "Uncle, how can I ever thank you? This is—this is a treasure."

"You can start by taking yourself off somewhere private to learn the feel of it. Go on, bardling, I can see the longing in your eyes. And tonight, you can sing for us at supper."

When Tristan had gone, Dinadan and Pernam sat silently while Leth cleared the table.

"Did you see his face," Dinadan said, "when you spoke of sending him home? It was nothing like his face when you gave him the harp. Sometimes—sometimes I wonder if he really *wants* to be King of Lyonesse, and yet if he doesn't, why did he fight Marhalt?"

Pernam's eyes narrowed as he rose, straightening his robe with his agile, long-fingered hands. "He is a bard in a prince's body. Twenty, thirty years ago, perhaps, in the golden days of Arthur, he might have been celebrated throughout Britain. But he missed his time. He is caught between two natures. He was born between the stars." A deep sigh escaped him. "May the Mother forgive him."

Alone in the sunlit garden, seated cross-legged in the shade of a laurel tree, Tristan ran his fingers over the harp strings and closed his eyes for the sheer pleasure of their sound.

Coming down the path toward the gate with her servants, a woman heard his music and stopped to listen, waving the servants silent with a swift motion of her hand. She stood still a moment, leaning forward, hardly breathing, and then sighed in sudden exasperation.

"Why didn't he tell me? He has a bard here visiting, and he didn't tell me. Reatha, Lydd, take the baskets to the wagon and await me at the gate. I shan't be a moment."

She slipped into the garden and followed the liquid fall of sound to the laurel. When she saw Tristan she stopped and stared. So young! He sat in the grass bent over his harp, head cocked to the side, his ear near the sounding board, with such a look of perfect joy upon his face, a sigh rose to her lips and her eyes filled with tears. And the music! It flowed from his fingers without effort, a glorious river of sound, sweeping her before it, flooding her senses, drowning her breath. Even as she watched, he lifted his face to the morning sun and began to sing. She paid little attention to the words—it was a version of an old song she had heard often enough among the coastal fishing folk—but his voice! In a clear, haunting tenor it moved her with every syllable, sweet and melancholic, tragic and powerful. She listened, rapt, to the end of his song, unaware her pale cheeks were wet with tears. When the last note had faded to nothingness, he opened his eyes and saw her.

Her voice caught on a sob. "Who are you?"

Tristan froze. For a brief, panicked moment, he thought she was an angel descended on silent wings to fetch him from the world. With the sun behind her, her hair was haloed with light and her features shadowed. Then she moved and knelt beside him.

"Who are you?"

But his lips would not move. He could only stare at her in blank amazement. Fine brown eyes, liquid with tears, sweet trembling lips, skin dewy and pale as a lily at dawning—a rush of feeling swept him that set him shaking with the effort of control. His body whipped to life even as his will acquiesced.

"Lady," he fumbled, "I hardly know."

"Never mind. Do not tell me what they call you. I know your true name."

"How can you?" he croaked, blushing at his sudden stupidity and awkwardness, he who had never been stupid or awkward, even as a child. What devil had possessed him and stolen his wit and tongue?

She reached out a pale hand and brushed the hair from his brow. "You are Orpheus," she said with a slow smile. "For your song is a song of enchantment."

At the touch of her hand he closed his eyes. "Lady, if I am Orpheus, you are Eurydice." When he opened his eyes he saw her smiling.

"Thank you, young lord. That is a compliment indeed." She rose and paused. "How long are you staying with Prince Pernam?"

He swallowed hard. "A fortnight." He wanted to rise with her but could not. He was incapable of movement. He sat cross-legged in the grass as if he had grown roots there. His breath raced, and he could not slow it down. "Will I see you again?"

She nodded. "I come thrice a week." She turned toward the entrance to the garden, and the very way her head turned on her slender neck reminded him again of a garden, and of lilies upright in the sun. "The day after tomorrow," she said with a smile as she made him a reverence. "Wait for me, Orpheus."

He said nothing about her to Dinadan. Even had he wanted to, he could not have found the words. But Dinadan was busy in Pernam's stables, repairing the roofing, evaluating his stock of mules and horses, arguing about inbreeding, and teaching Jarrad the finer points of horseflesh. Left to himself, Tristan sought out a private corner in the garden or the orchard, in the rambling house, or in the low outbuildings that hugged the cliff. This was peace, he thought. Here, anyone could heal of any wound. Wherever there was sun and sea and wind, he could make a song.

This was how she found him the second time, bent over the lap harp, the sun on his face and the sea wind ruffling his hair. He looked up and saw her at the door to the washhouse, still and listening, her rich hair bound behind her head, shining like polished wood in the bright sun. He jumped to his feet, the song forgotten, the harp abandoned in the grass. She stood looking at him while Tristan's ears pounded with the silence and his throat went dry. Behind her something moved. Gray-robed Pernam stepped out of the building's shadow, eyes upon them both.

Pernam offered her his arm, and they both came toward him. The woman seemed to sail across the yard, proudly, fluidly, speaking to his uncle in her clear voice, gracing him with her glorious smile. They talked of mindless things, of wool and weaving. Impatiently, Tristan waved the words away with a flick of his hand. She filled his vision, the amazing warmth and fullness of her, the glowing flush of health under translucent skin, the vitality, the joy of living that lit her face, the wonderful, terrifying curves that strained against the lacings of her gown. Sweat broke between his shoulders and trickled down his back. For a moment he wished he could be as impervious to her as was his uncle Pernam; the next moment, he would not have traded places with his uncle for all the world.

She turned luminous eyes to him and smiled. "My Orpheus, we meet again."

He inclined his head politely and hoped she could not tell how he trembled.

"I think it's time I introduced you," Pernam said smoothly, watching Tristan with a light frown. "Tristan, this is your benefactress, the woman who has made your convalescence palatable. The Lady Esmerée. Esme, my nephew Tristan."

Her eyes widened, and a deep, glorious blush rose from her throat to darken her cheeks.

"Tristan," she whispered. "King of Lyonesse." And she made a graceful reverence to the ground. At once he put out a shaking hand and raised her.

"Lady Esmerée." He said it softly. It sounded like the night wind, the breath of the sea through winter grasses. "I have wanted so to meet you, to thank you for the cake."

"My lord, it was nothing. A small thing. I am glad it pleased you."

"It is not a small thing to me, who am faced with a lifetime of taking that vile herb. It means more to me than I can tell you."

She lowered her eyes. The wind had loosened her hair and blew soft, curling strands under her chin and across the bodice of her gown. One slender tendril lay on the soft white swell of her breast. Feeling eyes upon him, Tristan looked up at Pernam, who regarded him with both compassion and disapproval.

"Lady Esmerée helps us in other ways as well," Pernam said, retrieving the harp. He walked them both up the path toward the garden. "She and her women weave and stitch our robes, as well as the clothing we collect for the poor children hereabouts. We are all of us in her debt." They reached the entrance to the garden, where Pernam loosed their arms, handed the harp to Tristan, and bowed to Esmerée.

"Thank you, Esme. I should have the wool for you by the time of your next visit. When did you say your husband was coming home?"

A shadow touched her face and was gone. She stood very still.

"At week's end, the courier said." Her voice was low and small. "He will stay six days if he keeps to pattern."

Pernam glanced swiftly at Tristan, who stood rooted to the ground. "I'm in no hurry for the blankets. Before the snow flies is soon enough." And making a low bow to the space between them, he withdrew.

Esmerée turned toward Tristan, her lips lifting in a bitter smile. "Your uncle is a very kind man." She slipped her arm through his and drew him into the garden. "I owe him the life of my youngest daughter. He saved her from a snakebite when the priest had given her up for dead. He is the most powerful healer in all of Cornwall. I think it is because he does not give up. Life, mortal life, means more to him than it does to the Christian brothers. Their eyes are always on the next world."

A stone bench stood near the herb beds in the shade of the laurel. Esmerée sat down upon it and drew Tristan down beside her. His cheeks
flushed with color. She sighed.

"Since I first heard your music I have wanted to ask you, will you make
me a song for my daughter?"

He looked up at her then, with dark, tragic eyes. "I have made a song for
you." Color washed his face again. "I—I did not know you had a husband."

She took his hand and held it between her own. "And I did not know
you were a king's son, much less the warrior who saved all Cornwall, King of
Lyonesse and my sovereign lord. I thought you were a bard."

"Sometimes I am. Sometimes I don't seem to be the one who has done
those violent things."

"How old are you, Tristan? Sixteen?"

"Seventeen. In my illness I passed a birthday."

"Seventeen." She smiled. "A time of such promise for a man. You are
only getting the feel of your strength, of who you are and what you can become. You have many gifts. You are blessed with courage and with beauty.
Surely you were born to do great things."

Tristan shrugged, digging the toe of his boot into the soft earth. "And
you? Pernam said you were a local woman. But you are young and highborn
and beautiful. What are you doing *here?* Surely you should be wed to some
lord and be at court."

She was silent for so long Tristan raised his head to look at her. He saw
tears in her eyes.

"What have I said? I never meant to distress you."

She shook her head. "Thank you for those words, my lord. A woman
needs to hear them from time to time."

"I spoke only the truth."

She managed a smile. "I am not so young, three and twenty. And my husband is a lord who is often at court. I stay here because—I prefer it, and so does
he. I need space—wind and sea. I do not much like the company of men."

Tristan nodded. "We are cut of the same cloth, you and I."

She rose. "You are a king, Tristan. You must learn to like it."

He rose with her, silent, and followed her to the gate where her servants waited by her wagon.

"When do you come again, Lady Esmerée?"

"In two days. After that, my husband returns. By the time he leaves,
you will be gone to Lyon's Head."

At last he smiled. "Oh, no. I will wait. I dare not go without my cake."

But she clutched at his hand and held it hard. "Don't wait. Please. I
will send the cake. Don't wait for me." And before he could answer, she
was gone.

5 ⚔ SEGWARD'S WIFE

That evening he told Dinadan about her. His friend smiled as he listened to her praises, and teased Tristan that at last he had lost his heart.

"And about time, too. You are as ripe for plucking as this pear." He bit into the sweet fruit and let the juice dribble down his chin. Tristan laughed.

"An unpleasant comparison! Say, rather, that I am a nestling poised on the edge of flight."

"Fly, hawk, fly. I can't wait to see this vision of loveliness. Think of such a beauty visiting your uncle Pernam, who doesn't appreciate it."

"Think of her dolt of a husband, to leave such a woman behind. How could he do it? If she were mine, I would not let her out of my sight, much less leave her stranded here on the coast, alone and vulnerable."

Dinadan grinned. "Vulnerable, eh? Are you sure, hawk? Perhaps she loves him, perhaps he trusts her. Perhaps she is under Pernam's protection."

Tristan considered this thoughtfully. "Perhaps. I would like to think so. Despite his appearance, he's a powerful man. But I do not think she loves her husband."

"How could you possibly know that? Did you ask her?"

"Of course not. What do you take me for? It was something in her voice, in her bearing, when he was mentioned. That's all."

"It's not much. But you will find out soon enough if she is willing."

"Willing!" Tristan flushed crimson. "Is that what you think I'm after?"

"Of course. If not a bedding, what *are* you after?"

Tristan threw up his hands. "Sometimes, Din, you are like all the rest. You think with your manhood and not with your mind. What do I want of her? I want to look at her forever, to drink her in, every vibrant moment of her. I want to sing to her heart, to touch her soul. She feels my music the way I do; we share a language, we understand each other. I want—I want her companionship. Nothing more. But I want it every second."

Dinadan leaned forward into the pool of candlelight and scanned his face. "If you want nothing more, you're not human. Very well, deceive yourself. Perhaps it doesn't matter. But someday, Tristan, you might surprise yourself. Your feet, like mine, are made of clay."

Tristan rose. "I'm no longer free to lie with anyone I choose. I'm a king now, and what I do has consequences for my kingdom. This could never be some casual dalliance, not on her part, not on mine. And even to think of Esmerée as some—"

"What?" cried Dinadan, jumping to his feet. "What did you call her? I thought you said her name was Esme."

"Uncle Pernam calls her Esme and so, sometimes, do I. Whatever is the matter, Din? You look like you've seen a ghost."

Dinadan paced swiftly back and forth, wringing his hands. "I hope I'm wrong, I hope I'm wrong. But I'm certain I'm not. It's such an unusual name. God, Tristan, you have had another close brush with fate! Don't you remember the scandal? Don't you know who she is? She's Segward's wife."

"*What?*" Tristan's mouth fell open, and he sat down heavily in the chair.

"I remember her at Dorr," Dinadan continued. "I was fourteen, fifteen. You must have stayed at Tintagel with Guvranyl when Markion came to Castle Dorr to hold council. She was there with Segward. I remember the whispers about her, how lovely she was, how close Segward kept her, how suspicious and jealous he acted. All the women hated her for her beauty; all the men wanted just to breathe the air she breathed. Man or woman, the entire court could talk of little else. Segward was wild about it. Even Markion admired her too much for Segward's taste. One night Segward found a youth in her chamber and lost his wits, accusing him of rape and lechery, although the lady was well attended by her women and not yet abed. The very next morning they found the boy dead at breakfast. Someone had poisoned his gruel. Don't you remember it? Everyone knew it was Segward. At first he tried to defend himself, but it was beyond him—the lad was just a page the women had sent to fetch them wine. Don't you remember all the talk? Segward had to pay a heavy recompense to the boy's family, for he'd been no common lad, his father had some standing at Markion's court. It could have made trouble for all Cornwall, could have been a blood feud, but Markion settled it. Segward secreted his wife in some fastness and paid the blood price. Eventually it all blew over." Dinadan quit his pacing and came to where Tristan sat, leaning his hands on the table. "Except that now we've found where he hid her. Tristan, if he so much as finds you've held her hand, he'll kill you and worry later about Markion. That's the kind of man he is. You know that. Vengeful, full of hate."

Tristan cleared his throat. "Vengeful, yes. But not direct. That incident with the page was a little blunt for him; he must have been desperate. I know him well, Dinadan. He's Mark's chief advisor. He does not kill outright, in the open air. That would expose him to retaliation. He manipulates men like players on a board. Someone else always does his killing."

Dinadan shuddered. "He's a serpent in the grass. Beware of him. He's got spies planted in her household, I'm sure of it. I pray you, do not speak to her again."

"Of course I will speak to her again. Good God, if everyone thought as you do, she would have no friends at all."

"I'll wager he doesn't allow her any. Except Pernam, who, for all he's Markion's brother, is no threat. But you! You are King of Lyonesse and a potential rival for Mark's crown, however many times you deny it. Don't put yourself in a position where either one of them wants to get rid of you."

"I will try not to," Tristan said wearily. "I know it's good advice. Segward will be here by week's end. Should I greet him formally, perhaps, before I've received Markion and been anointed by the bishop? It would do him honor."

"For God's sake, no! Lie low and keep to your sickbed. Let him think you're at the edge of death. Whatever happens, he must not suspect you've laid eyes on his wife."

Esmerée brought Tristan two cakes on her next trip to Pernam's Sanctuary, enough to last him through her husband's visit. She stayed only a short time, and Pernam was with them both. She looked pale, Tristan thought, and did not smile much. He played for her the song he had made for her daughter, and she thanked him profusely, clasping his hand and drawing it to her breast. For the space of a lightning flash he saw in her eyes a sharp sorrow, a fathomless desire. Then she let him go, turning away, and gave her full attention to Pernam's conversation.

Tristan had little sleep during the next week. The cake proved efficacious. His wound bothered him little now, although it remained a red and ugly mark long after all his other scars had faded. He spent much of his time wrestling with Dinadan on Pernam's beach. The land along the cliffs for leagues in both directions belonged to Pernam; he was in no danger of being overseen. With the sun and steady exercise and long swims out into deep water, Tristan grew brown and strong and healthy. And with the return of health came impatience with inaction. At long last he spoke eagerly of returning to Lyon's Head, of sending for his uncle Markion, sending for the bishop, and getting on with the business of ruling his father's lands.

Dinadan was delighted. This was the fearless warrior prince he had met at Castle Dorr while they were still boys in training. This was the spirit of bravery and adventure that had won his admiration and his heart. This was the man who had killed the giant Marhalt.

Six days passed and Esmerée did not come. The first of autumn's storms assailed the coast, driving them all indoors to seek shelter from the rain and blowing spray. They shuttered the windows and lit fires against the seeking winds. Seven days passed. Eight. Nine. Pernam, calm-faced as always, took to walking out beyond the gate for an hour or so each day. Tristan lay awake half the night, tossing and imagining disasters, finally succumbing to the monotonous roar of crashing breakers.

On the tenth day the storm broke. Tristan awoke late and looked out sleepily on wet grasses sparkling in the sun. The sky was bright blue, the whitewashed buildings brilliant, every color fiercely and unnaturally intense. He rose and splashed cold water on his face and hair. The beach would be a wreck of driftwood, weed, dead fish, and flotsam. Still, it had been three days since he had felt salt water on his skin. He was wondering if he could persuade Dinadan to go down with him when his friend stuck his head in the door and whispered, "Tristan!"

"What is it?"

"I think it's Esmerée, but I'm not sure."

Tristan was at his side at once. "What do you mean, not sure?"

"Jarrad says at dawn the porter awakened Pernam. There was a servant at the gate with a wagon. Pernam went out and drove the wagon in, fast. He's been in a cell ever since with Leth, Aran, and whoever was in the wagon."

"And you think it's Esmerée? Is she sick?"

"I recognized the servant. I didn't see her, but Jarrad caught a glimpse. He says there was blood."

"Blood!"

Dinadan grabbed his arm and held it fast. "She may have been beaten, Tris. He says it's happened before."

"Beaten." The word escaped him in a whisper. Quickly, Dinadan slipped into the room and shut the door behind him. "Let me go!" Tristan cried. "I'll kill him if he's touched her! I swear I'll kill the bloody swine!"

"Shut up, fool! He's within his rights to do it, however base it is."

"If he's touched her, I'll have his life."

"On what grounds? She's his wife. Come on, Tristan, calm down. We don't know the truth of it yet."

"Take me to her. I've got to see her."

"Not until you're calmer."

Tristan dashed into the corner for his swordbelt, so long forgotten, and strapped it on. "Christ!" Dinadan cried. "Are you mad? He's not *here*! They'd not have brought her if he were still in Lyonesse. Have some sense."

Tristan looked up and met his eyes, man to man. "I'll find her myself."

Before Dinadan could move, Tristan was halfway down the corridor, shouting for Pernam. "Someday," Dinadan whispered through clenched teeth, "that fool will run headlong into death."

Tristan flew around a corner and careened into Pernam. The older man gripped his arms and held hard, stilling panic in one rough shake. "Silence!"

Tristan gasped, floundering, and looked up wildly at him. His uncle's grip was iron and his face as cold as slate.

"This is a house of healing. You will obey the rule of silence."

"But I—I—"

"Silence!" Another rough shake. "Do you understand me? If you disobey me, I will discharge you now. You will be at Lyon's Head by nightfall."

Tristan swallowed, and the fight went out of his limbs. Pernam loosed him.

"Try to remember who you are." Pernam's face was bleak in the morning light, and sweat glistened on his brow.

Tristan's fury contracted into a cold, dull pulse of hatred. "Take me to her."

Pernam turned on his heel. "Come with me."

At the end of the corridor a door gave onto a low porch overlooking the orchard, the outbuildings, and the sea beyond. Pernam leaned against a porch pillar, drew a cloth from his robe, and mopped his brow. "Praise be to the Great Mother, giver of life and all things bountiful," he murmured. "Praise the Good Goddess for the strength of women." He turned to Tristan, who had opened his mouth to speak. "Tristan, you are King of Lyonesse. You are king of the land we stand on. Your word is law. This is an obligation that constrains your actions. You owe it to your people to be generous, fair, and kind. Under no circumstances, ever, may you be hasty or quick-tempered."

Tristan's shoulders sagged. Finally he nodded.

"Take off that ridiculous sword."

Tristan unbuckled the belt and laid the sword aside. Pernam sighed and narrowed his eyes at the distant horizon, the thin, shimmering line where the brilliant blue of the sky met the dark blue sea. "I may be a fool to let you stay after what has happened. And if you were not king, I would not do it."

"But I *am* king," Tristan said slowly. "Take me to her."

Pernam shook his head, just a little movement from side to side. "Not until she allows it."

"But I—"

"Think of *her*, you selfish boy. Think of *her* and not your foolish, half-grown pride. A good king puts his people's needs before his own. Remember that."

Tristan exhaled and sat down on the still-wet timbers of the porch. "You are right again, Uncle, as usual. But I do so want to see her."

"What for?" Pernam asked softly. "To promise her protection? An empty promise. You cannot give it, even if you surround her house with guards. You cannot protect her from her husband."

"I can face him," Tristan began desperately. "I can fight—"

"What kind of king fights his own lords over something that cannot concern him? What kind of fool would you look? Your people would resent it. Who wants a king who pries into everyone's house at night?"

"She's not everyone."

"Ah." Pernam's voice changed. "So what you really want is to offer her words of love. To insult her with an affection she may not return, on pain of death. To put her in the impossible position of denying her own sovereign or cutting her own throat. You would place her in the gravest jeopardy for the satisfaction of expressing what you feel."

"No, no," Tristan protested, holding his head between his hands. "It's not like that at all."

"What is it, then?"

Tristan groped for an explanation. "I suppose I want to say I'm sorry. I'm sorry it happened, I'm sorry if anything I said or did made it worse for her. Tell me, am I the reason he did this?"

Pernam's lips twisted in a thin smile. "No. It's not you. It's drink and suspicion and bad temper. Nearly every visit ends this way. He seizes upon some excuse to beat her. He likes the feel of her flesh beneath his hand." Tristan writhed, and Pernam watched him sorrowfully. "Sometimes he's jealous of the shepherd boy, the stable hand, the gardener, the stray sailor, the new servant, the innkeeper's son—it hardly matters. He is easily angered in his cups."

"At Mark's court he never drinks."

"Perhaps not openly. You may be sure that in the wee hours, when he feels alone and safe, he drinks. He can't keep from it. In his soul of souls, he loathes himself."

"With reason."

Pernam sighed heavily. "Get away from here today with Dinadan. Come to me in the morning. You may see her then."

But it was three days more before Pernam would let him in. "She is angry you are still here," his uncle told him. "She does not want you to see her."

"I will not leave until she consents."

"You have put her in a dilemma already, Tristan. She would leave to be with her children, but she does not want you to see her bruises."

"I will go and bring her children to her."

Pernam laughed bitterly. "Segward would know of it before nightfall and be here by morning. You do her no favors."

On the morning of the third day Pernam came to Tristan's door at dawn and beckoned. Tristan splashed his face and hair with water, pulled on a clean tunic, grabbed his harp, and followed his uncle to Esmerée's chamber.

"Keep it short," Pernam snapped, and left him. Drawing a deep breath and letting it slowly out, Tristan pushed open the door.

She stood by the window in a gray gown, looking out at the gray light. Her hair fell in a dark torrent down her back. Tristan stood behind her, wanting to kneel, knowing it would only make her angry.

"Esmerée."

"Why are you here?" she whispered. "I wanted you gone."

"How could I leave?"

He wanted to touch her, to take her hand, but he feared that any man's touch might be repugnant to her now.

She turned slowly. Over her face she wore a white veil of mourning.

"You cannot help me by staying, Tristan. You can only do me harm."

"Then I will go. Tomorrow. But first, I have things to say to you."

"No!" The veil began to tremble. "I don't want to hear them." He took the edges of the veil in his fingers and slowly raised it. "You are cruel, Tristan."

"I want to see your face," he said gently. "Not because it is beautiful, but because it is *yours*." Even though he had braced himself for bruises, he stifled a gasp at the deep blue wells around her eyes, the purple ridges of her cheekbones, the bulbous swelling of her lips. She faced him defiantly, turning her face a little to the light so he could see the yellow-edged, greenish splotches on her cheeks. At the base of her throat were round purple stains where the villain's hands had been around her neck.

"Are you happy?"

"For this, he deserves death."

"No!" She grabbed his arm. "No. He has not killed me, or maimed me, or even permanently scarred me. He is careful never to leave a lasting mark. Everything you see will heal in time. He would do nothing to mar the value of his property. Sometimes"—her voice began to quaver—"I wish he would break my nose or tear my skin. Then perhaps he would not be so eager to come back." She straightened and looked at Tristan sternly. "Do you see now why I wanted to keep this from you? You will want to revenge yourself upon him because you are young, and kind, and high-minded, but the right is on his side, Tristan, not on yours. And you are his king. He must kneel to you and swear you service, and you must look him in the face and accept it. If you do not—" Here her voice broke, and she shook so hard he put an arm around her waist to steady her. "If you do not, he will set out to destroy you. If you so much as look at him with contempt, he will be certain we are lovers, and one night someone trusted, someone wholly unsuspected, will strike you in the back. For my sake, as well as your own, you must let him be and make your face a mask."

"I know. All this I know." But her slender body, trembling on his arm and half leaning against him, thrilled him with a powerful excitement. As if she sensed it, she gently pushed him away.

"So young you are, Tristan, and so innocent. Yet you must learn to practice deceit, and you have done nothing."

"Someday," Tristan said quietly, "he will die. Not by my hand, perhaps, but because of me."

She frowned, but something in her eyes told him she was not angry. "Is that what you came to say to me?"

He smiled. "No. Not that. What I want to say to you I cannot say in words. I have brought my harp."

Late that night Tristan lay sleepless on his pallet, staring at the shadows thrown by the full moon. There was an edge to the night air, a cold, salty hunger that signaled summer's ending. It was time, it was beyond time, to be going home. The shaft of moonlight struck the stone floor, harsh and bright, everything in its path brought into brilliant focus, the shadows beyond black and unfathomable. He watched that bright shaft slide slowly toward him, hour after hour, wondering if for her time passed as slowly, with shadows as still, as dead.

His ear caught the whisper of a movement. His eyes strained into the dark but saw nothing. Yet something, someone was there. He heard a step, lighter than a sigh, the gentle swish of cloth, and there in the moon's brilliant wake a robed figure stood, barefoot and hooded.

"Leth?" Tristan whispered, frowning at the delicately arched feet. "Aran?"

The hood fell back. Dark hair spilled unbound around a woman's face. In the unnatural light, she seemed carved of alabaster, pure, shining, unblemished.

"Esmerée!"

She lifted a finger to her lips and slowly smiled. The shock of that smile tore through his body. A sound like thudding hammers filled his ears. He jerked upright on the pallet. Moonlight lit the smooth curve of one bared shoulder. She came to him silently, from light to shadow, and knelt at his side. The hollow of her throat throbbed in steady time; her sweet breath blew warm against his cheek. As she leaned forward the robe swung open, revealing the dark, curving crevice between her breasts. A moan escaped him. She kissed his mouth, drawing his hands to her body, lifting them to her breasts, a mother's breasts, full and firm with nipples already erect.

"Why?" Tristan gasped. Under his hands her flesh was warm silk, smooth, glorious, and unbelievably soft.

She laughed, a low sound of joy deep in her throat, and then caught her breath as his hands moved, curving to her shape, caressing with a tenderness she had only dreamed of. "Oh, Tristan," she breathed, her lips against his ear, "I do this for myself as much as for you. I want, just once, to know the pleasure without the pain. And you, my sweet, my beautiful, generous boy, if you must live with his hate for my sake, let it at least be for a reason." She put a hand against his chest and felt how it pounded. "I am going to teach you how to love a woman. It is a gift worth having. If you learn well, you will thank me for it all the rest of your life."

She kissed him again, moving her hands on his body. Leaning into his touch, she shrugged off the robe.

PART II

6 ✟ MARKION

"Good hunting today, my lord?"

"Those are the last deer we'll get this season, Segward, unless we're very lucky."

"Aye, my lord, perhaps, but you're well known for your luck."

A company of men followed the king into the hall, stomping snow from their boots, blowing upon their hands, raising their voices in exaggerated retellings of the day's events.

Markion strode to the log fire and held his hands out to warm before the blaze. He was a tall man of middle years, with gray in his hair and beard and a body kept lean and hard with a soldier's discipline. Only at the neck and wrists did his leanness hint at the stringiness of coming age. He was plainly dressed in boots, leather leggings, leather tunic, and woolen cloak, but his cloak was pinned at the shoulder with the great enamel badge of Cornwall, the Black Boar with amber eyes, and around his neck he wore a golden torque. A servant approached with a cup of mead. Markion drank deeply, turned from the fire, and sighed.

"All in all, it was a good day. How was it with you, Segward? Where's Merron? Is there any news?"

The shorter man shook his head. "Not yet, my lord."

"Surely they've given the Saxons battle by now. It's less than a week's ride to the river mouth."

Segward shrugged lightly. "Perhaps the barbarians made it up the river to the high ground. Even so, it is possible Merron is right and Constantine has enough men to take them, even without the Welsh. But if they've made the high ground, it will take longer."

"And cost more." Markion frowned darkly. Behind him his hunting companions were sitting down to table as servants hurried in, laden with food. But although the meal could not begin until he took his place, he made no move to join them. Instead, he regarded his advisor. Segward was near his age, a little older, but there was nothing soldierly about him. Heavyset with flesh slack from light use, arms adorned with silver armbands and fingers thick with rings, swaddled in a soft woolen robe with a decorated border a handspan deep, he looked, Markion mused, like an old, fat peasant dressed in a rich man's clothes. Until you looked into his eyes. Those quick, sharp eyes missed nothing. They seemed to have the ability to see around corners and into the dark. It was for those eyes, and the sinuous subtlety of his thinking, that Markion employed him as political advisor. He dared not let him serve anyone else.

"Perhaps I should have followed your advice and sent for the Welsh," Markion said slowly, still frowning. "But you wanted Tristan there, and I could not do both." Segward said nothing. They had gone over the arguments a dozen times before. "The next time, Segward, I will go myself. I will not let you talk me out of it again. I'm too often at home. People say I leave the defense of Britain to my relations, father, son, and nephew while I hide at Tintagel. I cannot abide that."

"Someone must defend our homeland from the godforsaken Gaels. We know they fear you and keep watch upon your movements. If you leave Cornwall, my lord, they will be upon us like a swarm of biting flies."

Markion shook his head. "Let Gerontius handle them and make a name for himself among them. I should be out there in Britain, among the kingdoms, letting people learn who I am."

"Why?" Segward asked softly. "Your succession to the High Kingship is already ensured. You have little to gain by risking yourself against the Saxons, and perhaps much to lose. Give it time, my lord. Remember what King Arthur used to say. *All things come to him who waits.*"

Markion grunted. "And where is Arthur now? Dead these three and twenty years. Killed at forty by his own son. That's what comes of waiting. Come, Segward, more of this later. The men want to eat, and so do I."

After dinner the wine and mead went round. Men stretched out on the hearth, elbowing the dogs for a space near the fire. Some lay on the benches or sat in groups, idly talking, eyes sliding closed from time to time, bellies full of meat and wine, warmed by the log blaze.

Markion sat in his big chair, the king's chair of Cornwall, with his eyes upon the fire. Segward's mention of King Arthur still rankled. He was determined that one day his own fame would outshine that of Arthur, and *his* name, not Arthur's, would be remembered through the generations. Even now, so many years after Arthur's death, the memory of Pendragon had the power to infuriate him. Who had Arthur been to deserve such a legacy of admiration? A bastard born of rape and betrayal. A scoundrel's by-blow. Nothing more.

The tale of his begetting was the tale of Cornwall's shame. Uther Pendragon had no sooner been crowned High King of Britain when he invaded Cornwall, sneaked into Tintagel, and raped Ygraine, Cornwall's duchess, behind the old duke's back. Yet it was thanks to Duke Gorlois that Uther had a crown at all. Gorlois had been instrumental in enabling Aurelius Ambrosius, Uther's elder brother, to retake Britain from the usurper Vortigern.

Uther had owed allegiance to Duke Gorlois, who had made Ambrosius High King. Instead, Uther had killed Gorlois on the battlefield and raped his wife. And what had Uther done with the product of this criminal union? Instead of exposing him on a hillside or throwing him into the sea, he had handed the ill-begotten child to Merlin the Enchanter, to be hidden from his enemies, to be coddled, spoiled, and raised as a prince.

You would think, Markion brooded, that it shouldn't be difficult to outshine a man with such beginnings. But men had loved Arthur. He had possessed that most elusive of gifts, the ability to lead men by inspiring their love. And in his youth even Cornishmen had loved him, for he had made Cador of Cornwall, Gorlois's son, his heir. Had he stuck to that promise, Markion, too, might have followed him anywhere.

But the acorn never fell very far from the tree. When Cador's son Constantine reached manhood, had Arthur formally declared him? In a move that had shocked all Britain, Arthur had acknowledged a pagan bastard from the outland Orkneys as his own son and made the uncouth brat his heir in Constantine's place. A veritable outlander! A pagan as wild as the seas that raised him—and begotten on Arthur's own sister, if the tales were true, as evil a sorceress as ever blackened Britain's darkest haunts. *This* was the boy Arthur had chosen over Constantine, this demon's spawn, this witch's whelp, this incest-bred traitor, Mordred.

Markion's lips thinned in a bitter smile. For that, the great Arthur had deserved the fate that overtook him. The heir he chose had been his death. Markion himself could not have devised a sweeter revenge. He sighed deeply and signaled a servant to pull off his boots. Holding his feet to the fire, he rested his legs against the body of his favorite hound, sprawled asleep beneath his chair. To either side of him stood Segward, his advisor, and Merron, his seneschal, the two companions he was never without except on the battlefield. Sometimes he was tempted to think of them as gadflies. They never let him be, never stopped planning, never stopped plotting, never stopped goading him to action. But these were the men who shared his dream of a kingdom greater than Arthur's, of a legacy more enduring. Thanks to them, he had never been more powerful. His future as High King of Britain was ensured. Thanks to them and to his nephew, Tristan.

His fingers tightened on the arms of his chair. What to do about Tristan of Lyonesse? Surely God had blessed him, to let him live. Many of his own men believed that. The common people all over Cornwall loved him. Meliodas's son, they still called him, a good lad, noble, brave, and honest, the image of his father. Aye, that was the trouble. He was the image of Meliodas.

Growing up in Meliodas's shadow, Markion had seen at close range the spell his brother could cast over men. Like Arthur, he not only inspired them, he won their loyalty and worship, he seduced their love. To a man they would gladly have died for him. What Markion would not give for the secret of that magic! But try as he might, it had always eluded his grasp. Had Meliodas not fallen to an Irish sword, Markion would not be sitting in the king's chair at Tintagel with the crown of Britain within his grasp, and he knew it well. He wished heartily his success had not come at the hands of Meliodas's son. He hated owing so much to Tristan. There was no way to repay that debt, and people would remember it. The last thing he needed was a budding Meliodas in his kingdom, a man whom people could point to and say: *If it weren't for him, Markion would not now be king.*

"My lord," Merron murmured in his ear, "what dark thoughts are you thinking, to make you brood so? Have another cup of wine. The hunt was successful. Within the week we will no doubt hear of yet another great victory over the Saxons. Prince Gerontius will return home covered in glory. There is nothing to brood about."

"And Tristan?" Markion muttered, half to himself. "Will he come home, too?"

"Why, surely he will, my lord." Merron shot a swift look at Segward. "The men believe his sword is touched with magic. They are all eager to fight in his company. Thus he is surrounded by the best knights in Cornwall. Do not doubt he will come home safely."

Markion half turned in his chair to see Segward's face. "If he is so much as scratched by a Saxon weapon while I'm here in Cornwall, I'll not be able to ride abroad among my own people. Why was it, Segward, you so badly wanted him to go?"

"Does my lord not remember," Segward replied smoothly, "that young Tristan had lately been suffering from his moods? He penned himself too long inside his castle, and took to acting rashly—riding out alone at breakneck speeds in the early hours of morning, sailing alone in stormy seas out of sight of land. A call to battle was exactly what he needed to bring him to his senses. You know him, my lord. When once the soldier in him is awakened, he is unstoppable. Without doubt he has sent the Saxons fleeing. His exploits will be the talk of the army for months to come."

Markion barked a short laugh. "That I can believe. Have you been spying on my nephew again, Segward? Surely I must have foes more dangerous."

Segward's mouth slid into a mirthless smile. "I watch everyone, my lord."

"Fine, fine. Just remember this: I can't afford to have his death laid at my door. So let him stay in Lyonesse, why don't you? Out of danger. Let him play his harp and sing his songs. Forget him. He's spinning moonbeams, not plotting my downfall. He's a bard at heart."

Not a muscle moved on Segward's face, but his small eyes hardened. "He is the son of Meliodas. He must be watched."

Markion nodded slowly and turned back to the fire. "All right, then. Watch him if you must. But if he's wounded, just see that I'm not blamed."

The door flew open, and a cold gust of wind sent the flames dancing. A courier staggered in, numbed with wet. Merron hurried to his side as idle conversation died and the hall went still. Shrugging the snow from his cloak, the tired courier followed Merron to Markion's chair and went down on one knee.

"My lord king."

"Rise, Krinas. Do you bring us tidings of defeat or victory?"

The courier replied without expression, "We loyal Britons have defeated the Saxons in a rousing victory."

The room erupted with cheering as men awakened and harkened to the news.

"Five leagues from the river mouth we caught them, my lord. But there were many more than we had estimated. It took—"

"How many?"

A weary shrug. "Two thousand, roughly. Cynric himself was there. It took a week and every man we had. In the end, we drove them from the land and back down the river. But we could not hold the river mouth against them, my lord. They were so mobile; we were so few. We had to burn the land."

"Never mind," Markion said fiercely, so that all could hear. "We denied them access to the land they wanted. They will never settle their farmers on our soil. Let them go back out to sea and vent their rage. I care not if they own the seas—we own Britain!"

The soldiers cheered again, drunken and ecstatic, while Markion smiled wryly to himself. Not one of them reflected that Cornwall was a land bound by the sea, wrapped by coastlines, as vulnerable to sail as to horse. He was certain Segward was thinking of it, and of the Irish raiders who knew it, too.

Markion rose and lifted his goblet. "A toast!" he cried, and the men sprang to their feet, reaching for their winecups. "To the glory of Britain, and the glory of my father, the High King Constantine!"

The men shouted, stomped their boots and drank. "To Constantine!"

But the courier paled and again went down on one knee.

"My lord."

"What is it, Krinas? Tell me."

Markion raised a hand. The noise in the hall settled to a restless murmur. "My lord Markion, we paid a heavy price for victory. The High King Constantine—my lord, the High King is dead."

Silence fell. Markion did not move.

"Long live the High King!" someone cried wildly. "Long live Markion!"

"Long live the High King Markion!" they all shouted, grinning, slapping one another's backs, and finally kneeling before the new King. Markion watched them without expression, then turned back slowly to the courier.

"How did he die?"

"A broken neck, my lord. A messy skirmish—he was thrown from his horse. Sir Gerontius and Sir Tristan begged him not to ride, but he refused to take the field in a litter."

"An honorable death," Markion said calmly. "We will mourn him with a public ceremony. When does Gerontius bear the body home?"

The courier avoided his eyes. The hand that went to his pouch shook visibly, his fingers stiff as he withdrew a piece of parchment, much folded, unsealed.

"My lord King, my lord—" He forced himself to look up at Markion's frozen face. "My lord King, this is a letter from Sir Tristan, explaining and saying how sorry—" He gulped hastily. "—what a tragedy it was—Prince Gerontius was also killed."

The soldiers gasped. Merron clutched Markion's shoulder. The king himself did not move, could not move, but stared in disbelief at the trembling messenger. Segward bent and took the folded paper from the courier's fingers.

"My lord, he came to Constantine's aid, he and all his company. But it was an ambush, my lord. They didn't see the Saxons in the woods and were taken by surprise. They were all taken by surprise."

Markion's lips moved slowly. His voice was a bare whisper. "How did we ever defeat them?"

"Sir Tristan, my lord, your nephew. It was Tristan of Lyonesse who routed them from the woods and drove them to the river. He had circled behind the woodland, outguessing their strategy, and when they looked up from their slaughter, they found themselves surrounded. That's when they fled. They lost two to every one of ours."

"They didn't lose as much as we did!" Merron cried, gripping Markion's arm. "How could this have been foreseen? Cynric himself—he was reported in Saxony, my lord, a mere month ago. How could Gerontius—"

"Shut up." Markion's voice was cold and flat. Merron withdrew, wiping his eyes. Breathing hard, Markion turned to the room and looked into the stricken faces of his men. "Leave me." Heads down and eyes averted, they shuffled out. "Segward. Stay."

Markion stood before the fire. The hound pressed against his leg, tail beating a gentle rhythm on the floor. Segward saw the hard control that held in his grief, the clenched jaw, the upright body, the blank, icy stare.

"Go on, Mark," he said gruffly. "Let it out." And he turned away and crossed the room to stand before an old tapestry, worn with time, hung to keep out the winter drafts. He stood there a long time, listening to the awkward, broken sobs of a man familiar with pain, but not with its release. How much easier it would be if Markion had an enemy to fight, a miscreant to punish with his own hands, to reach out and grapple physically with the anger in his soul. What he needed, Segward thought, was a woman.

When the sound of weeping died, Segward turned. Markion sat hunched over in the big chair, his hands clasped, his beard wet with tears. Approaching in silence, Segward stoked the fire and pulled up a stool. He waited.

"Ah, God," Markion muttered. "I remember when Elisane died, I thought, *Go in peace, unhappy woman. You have done your duty, you have borne me three fine sons to build my kingdom on.* And now—" His eyes squeezed shut as he drew a trembling breath. "Now they are gone. All three. Constans but a baby, Gerfeint at seven. And now, my pride, my firstborn—*Jesu God!* What have I done to deserve it?"

"More to the point," Segward said quietly, "is what you're going to do about it."

The complete calmness of his voice struck Markion. He opened his eyes and straightened in the chair. "What do you mean? I'm going to bury him next to my father."

Segward shook his head. "Look ahead, Mark. What are you going to do about Cornwall?"

"What about Cornwall?"

"You are High King of Britain. But you still have Cornwall's future in your hands. Think about it, Mark. Think now. You need to let the people know. Who will be King of Cornwall after you?"

Markion's eyes narrowed as he frowned, searching Segward's face. "Do I have to decide this now? *Tonight?*"

"Yes."

"Why?"

"Because now is the time to act. Are you ready to make your nephew Tristan your heir? Are you ready to acknowledge him publicly when he returns? To let him take Gerontius's place? To promise him Tintagel?"

Markion's features hardened and he looked away. "Hell, no." He ran a distracted hand through unkempt hair. "But who else is there? My God, Segward, how Meliodas haunts me from his grave! First he takes back Lyonesse, and now Cornwall." He rose, his face haggard in the firelight. "Damn him! Meliodas's son will come into his inheritance after all, and I— I, Markion, High King of Britain, will leave nothing behind me."

Segward leaned forward, and his voice sank. "Not necessarily."

Markion's head jerked toward his counselor. Segward regarded him coolly, his bright eyes intent. *He looks at me*, Markion thought, *like a bird at a worm.*

"We have spoken before," Segward said softly, "about a dynasty. A line of Kings of Britain sprung from Cornwall's seed. A line of kings to reign forever, a royal heritage I can help you build. A line of kings, Mark, descended from you."

Markion stiffened and glared at him to keep his eyes dry. "My line is dead."

"If you give Tristan Cornwall, you give up that dream."

"I did not give it up! God took it from me!"

"And when the great wave crashes over your castle in the sand and destroys it down to the foundations, do you run weeping from the beach?" The corners of Segward's mouth twisted upward as his eyes glittered. "Or do you start anew?"

Markion frowned. He had the sense of slowly twirling, like a leaf in a rising breeze, unconnected to his past, free of his future, a plaything for dust devils and the wayward wind. "Start anew?"

Segward sat back, half smiling, and held Markion's eyes. "You are in your prime. With decent luck you'll live another twenty years. Time enough to raise three more sons to manhood. Time enough to get yourself another heir. It is the simplest solution, Mark. Remarry."

Markion shot to his feet and strode away. "Remarry! You talk like a madman. The last thing I want is another nagging, sharp-voiced woman at my heels, always trying to interfere in things that don't concern her. Heirs are one thing—I confess, I hadn't thought of that—but wives are quite another. Easy to get, perhaps, but difficult to keep." He stopped and turned, a malicious smile forming on his lips. "But of course you know that."

Segward's smile broadened, but his eyes grew smaller. "There is always a price to pay. But suppose I found you a wife both young and pretty, sweet-voiced and sweet-tempered, who regarded you more as father than as husband, and who never gave a thought to disobey? What would you say to that?"

Markion snorted. "You are dreaming. There are no such women."

"Suppose there were. Imagine it, just for the moment. The dynasty of Markion lies within her womb."

"It wouldn't bring Gerontius back."

"No. If that's what you want, I can't help you."

Grunting, Markion paced another length of the chamber. "Well. I suppose if such a maiden could be found, I would give it thought."

"And suppose," Segward continued, "that in wedding her you bound forever to Cornwall's side a rival kingdom and made a friend of a potential enemy, made a promise of a threat."

Markion stared. "Why, in that case, I would do it without thought. Is this a leg pull, Segward? Is there such a maiden?"

Segward rose, rings glittering on his small, fat hands as he straightened his robes about him. "Oh, yes, my dear Markion, there most certainly is. All I have told you is no more than the simple truth."

"Who's her father? Where is this rival kingdom?"

"Remember the Welsh?" Segward smiled in satisfaction at Markion's surprise. "Her father is the most powerful man in Britain after yourself. King Percival of Gwynedd."

"Percival's children are babies. I warn you, Segward—"

"I beg your pardon, my lord, but time has passed without your knowing. His sons are only a year or two short of warrior age; his daughter is just fifteen."

"Fifteen! Already?" He let out a low whistle. "Percival's daughter. Would he ally himself with me, I wonder? After Marhalt?"

"Now that you are High King of Britain, I have no doubt of it. He has always wanted peace through strong alliance. Marriage to Gwynedd brings you all of Wales. Percival has kin in Strathclyde; there's at least a hope of treaties in the north. The match can do you nothing but good."

"And she is not promised yet to anyone?"

"To my knowledge, no. But she is rumored to be a beauty, and we must make an offer soon. You must put the past behind you, Mark, and commit yourself to the future."

"Help me decide on the size of the offer, and I'll send a courier at first light."

Something close to a grin touched Segward's plump face. "No, no, my lord, a courier would never do. Nor such unseemly haste. Have you forgotten the Welshman's devilish pride? Send an advisor, a man you can trust, to negotiate the terms. Let it be done with subtlety and grace, with a minimum of fanfare, and let it take the long winter to unfold."

"You go, Segward. There's no one better. Be my ambassador and arrange it all. You're the only one who can."

Segward inclined his head. "Thank you, my lord. I would be honored."

"And in the spring I will go myself to fetch her."

Segward smiled and shook his head. "You are too much the soldier, my lord, and not enough the diplomat. You are far, far too direct."

"So? I *am* a soldier. The direct route is the shortest one."

"Ah, but now you are Lord of Britain. The direct route might make you enemies you cannot afford. Give a thought to the circuitous approach. There might be those in Wales, in Guent, say, who will howl at the very idea of your standing on Welsh soil."

Mark threw up his arms in exasperation. "Well, what would you have me do, then? Send for her as though she were my servant? Surely *that* would be a snub Percival could not ignore."

Segward paused, and Markion could feel his thoughts sharpening as surely as if he heard the scrape against the whetstone. "There is a middle road, my lord. A time-honored one. Used by Arthur Pendragon himself. Send a royal escort and a proxy to represent you. Have her escorted south in grandeur and ceremony, and meet her here at the gates of Tintagel. Percival will be impressed, honor will be conveyed, and you need not set foot in enemy territory."

"Surely once we are betrothed the Welsh will be our friends."

"Once the marriage is consummated and blessed with heirs, once a son of Wales is heir to the throne of Britain, they will love you well enough. But until then, you will be welcomed only in Gwynedd, and even then with reservation."

"If Wales is such a dangerous place for a Cornishman, how can I send you, Segward? I will not risk your life among them. I need you here."

"Percival is honor-bound to protect me during the negotiations. I'm hardly a warrior. I may be scorned and made the butt of jests, but I'm unlikely to be attacked. There would be no honor in killing me." Markion's face relaxed in relief. Segward leaned forward intently and placed a hand on his arm. "But neither can I be your proxy, Mark. I am not highborn. I am not of the blood royal. You would insult Percival to send me."

"Then who can I send?"

Both men went still, looking at one another. Stretched on the hearth, the dog raised his head and whimpered. Sweat broke on Markion's brow.

"There is only one man," Segward said.

Markion swallowed. His breathing quickened. He whirled away and strode down the length of the chamber. The dog rose from the hearth and watched him, whining.

"He may be the only one suitable, but Christ, Segward! He'd never go—I could never ask him. As it is, my remarriage robs him of his future. How could I possibly send him to fetch the bride? It's callous, it's cruel, it's beneath me." He stopped in midstride and suddenly laughed. "It's worthy of *you*." Segward inclined his head, accepting the remark as a compliment.

Markion resumed his pacing. "But it's too obvious. Everyone knows how dangerous it would be for him in Wales. Why, they'd kill him before he put a foot ashore! And how would I look, then?"

"They think he is dead." Segward's voice was a low, flat calm in the whirl of Markion's storm. "We started that rumor ourselves."

"They'll know he's living as soon as they see him!"

"They will *not* know. Peredur is dead. Percival has never seen him. The only men who can recognize him are Percival's soldiers, and they would not know him now. They only saw him covered in mud. He was sixteen then, still more a boy than a man. He's eighteen now, taller than you are, grown broad in the shoulder and lean in the face. No one who saw him then would know him now. And, of course, we will give him a false name. He will go as your cousin, Tantris of Caer Budeca, son of Rivalen, son of Constantine's brother Gerfeint."

"Rivalen had no son."

"The Welsh won't know that. He was a hermit. He could have had a hundred children unbeknownst to them. Or to us, for that matter."

"He was mad, Segward. He threw himself from a cliff at thirty."

"They won't know that," Segward repeated patiently. "What matters is that they will accept your proxy as a legitimate son of Cornwall's royal house. Since you cannot send your own son or your nephew, he will be deemed an acceptable replacement. That's all that matters."

Markion whirled and strode back down the room, the dog trotting after him. "It won't work, Segward. Even if he fooled them, even if he agreed to go, which he won't—what a halfwit I would look, sending him! Would you make me the scorn of all Cornwall? My own people will see the injustice of it, even if the Welsh do not. They'll think I sent him to his death on purpose. That's all I need, to drive a wedge between us. He's Meliodas's son and the people love him. Let me send him once into the lion's den, let me even *seem* to wish him ill, and no one in Cornwall will ever follow me again. They will despise me, down to the last goatherd."

He stopped before Segward, breathing hard, hands on his hips. "As it stands now, I've given him Lyonesse and I've trapped him there, if you'll only let him be. Let him stew on that godforsaken rock he loves so much. Let him stay there at the bottom of Britain, out of my way, out of the people's sight. For God's sake, let him stay there. I don't want to risk my kingdom for Meliodas's son."

Segward stoked the fire, unmoved, and then looked up. "You haven't heard a word I've said."

"I've heard everything. It won't work. They'll kill him and I'll be blamed."

"No. The danger is so obvious it will never occur to the Welsh to suspect him. They wouldn't believe the truth if he proclaimed it."

"Are you trying to tell me there's no risk?"

"Not precisely." Segward's voice went soft. "There is risk, of course. The danger is undeniable, given his utter lack of subtlety. Suppose for a moment that the worst happens. Think, Mark, of what it would mean for you."

"I tell you, I won't have his death laid at my door."

"But if it is laid at Percival's door?" The small eyes glittered; the soft body leaned forward. "If the Welsh do it for you?"

Markion frowned, biting his lip. "I will still be held to account."

"To what end? You will be the only one left alive who can lead Cornwall. You will be the undisputed rightful heir. You will have no rival. You can take your pick of Cornish maidens to found your dynasty. You can do absolutely anything you choose. You will be the only one the men can follow. Don't you see?" Segward's lips drew back, revealing small, even teeth. "You can't lose. You win either way." He chuckled silently, his cheeks creasing, his body fluid with spasmodic laughter. The hair rose on the back of Markion's neck.

In the long silence, the snap of the fire grew unnaturally loud. The hound, grown bored, slept again on the hearth.

"How will you get him to go?" Markion whispered at last.

Segward breathed a long sigh of satisfaction. "That is easy, really. He will want to go. He will volunteer."

"Are you mad? Whatever makes you think so?"

"It is part of his charm that he risks his life for you. He doesn't do it for the people's adoration; he likes to do it. I know him better than you think. He's a neighbor of mine in Lyonesse." Segward's voice had grown rough, and he paused to clear his throat. "Send him a letter and open your heart to him. Tell him about your plan to unify the kingdoms, to re-create the kind of union that existed in the golden days of Arthur. You know his great love for Arthur and the Companions."

"It's because he met Galahad once when he was a child. It made an impression on him."

"Explain to him that you have offered for Percival's daughter, although you have no desire to remarry, because you have a vision of uniting Britain once again under a strong king. Tell him your problem—war has taken all your relations from you, all but him and Pernam."

"Pernam!" Markion snorted. "The lover of boys. He hardly counts as a relation."

"Put it that there is no one but Tristan worthy to represent you. But you can't send *him* into Wales, for obvious reasons. Ask his advice on what to do."

Markion frowned. "He'll tell me to stop being so careful of my own skin and go to Wales myself."

"That is you speaking, not Tristan," Segward said calmly. "I know what Tristan will say. I know Tristan as well as he knows himself."

"You sound very sure."

"I am reasonably certain. And there is another reason he will want to go."

"Oh?"

"Percival himself. Since boyhood, Tristan has wanted to meet Percival of Gwynedd. He dreams about him sometimes."

"However do you know that?"

"I have my sources. However reluctant." Segward began to chuckle again, and Markion turned away.

"What if something happens, if he is discovered or kills one of them? The marriage is sacrificed and my dynasty is again in ashes."

"And we will have war with the Welsh." Segward watched him coldly. "It is a risk. But for great ambition, risks must be taken. If you win the war, any maiden in Britain will be glad to have you. Do you want to be the founder of a line of kings that will outshine the name of Arthur? Or do you want Tristan to love you until the end of your days, then succeed you and eclipse you? This is the choice before you, Markion of Cornwall."

Markion walked away and pushed open the shutters of the western window. The wind rushed in, clean and sharp with salt. Above his head clouds raced across the frozen, starlit sky. He drew a deep breath of the biting air and exhaled slowly. Life was short and often bitter. Would he be numbered among the thousands who lived and died without a trace? Or would he be one of a handful whose names were remembered beyond a generation, like Cunedda, like Ambrosius, like Lancelot, like Arthur?

"All right. I will do it."

They talked about Cornwall's offer late into the night. At last Markion stretched and drained his winecup.

"How you have the time to think of such far-fetched plans, I'll never know. But I'll bet there's something you've not thought of."

"Indeed? What would that be?"

"What if, as happened with Arthur himself, the bride falls in love with the proxy before she ever meets the bridegroom? Even so great a king as Arthur was bedeviled by that mistake until the end of his days."

"Not thought of it? Of course I've thought of it. Although, in truth, it hardly matters. She will go where she is promised, and bear you the sons she is required to bear. Do you care overmuch that she love you?"

"I hate discord in my house."

"Put yourself in her place, my lord. She is young and about to be forced to leave her home forever. She is far more likely to hate the very sight of your proxy than to love him, whoever he is. Unlike Guinevere, she has not been raised to revere the name of any king but her father. The very thought of Cornwall will be anathema to her."

"But if she hates Tristan for taking her away from her home, how much more will she hate me when she gets here? I am the very cause of her distress."

"By the time she gets to Cornwall, she'll be away from familiar surroundings and too frightened to show her temper. She's fifteen. It's unlikely she's ever been out of her own valley. Use your charm, Mark. You can be her protector, her guide, her friend. Be a second father to her; she will revere you. If we arrange things right, you have a very pleasant life ahead of you."

Markion stroked his beard thoughtfully. "For a time, perhaps, *if* we are successful. But have you forgotten the nature of women? Before she is twenty she will think she knows everything. Even kittens grow up to be cats."

"Give her a passel of children and by the time she is twenty she will have no time for you."

Markion smiled bleakly. "I suppose you are right." He rose and stretched again. "I'll sleep on this, and we'll talk again in the morning. Nothing can be done until the buryings are over." He sobered and walked to the door. As his hand touched the latch he turned back. "By the way, you never told me her name. The mother of my dynasty. What's her name?"

"Essylte."

"Essylte?" Markion frowned as he tried out the name. "Strange. But pretty."

"It's Welsh," Segward said, covering a yawn. "It means 'the fair.' I told you she was beautiful."

Markion grinned. "All women are beautiful at fifteen." He nodded good night, turned on his heel, and was gone.

7 ✝ ESSYLTE

"She's such a bothersome old witch! I wish she'd just leave me alone!" With a toss of her bountiful curls Essylte mounted the last step and motioned Branwen to come up beside her. "Remember, if she says *anything* about Palomydes, cough like the steam is getting to you, and we'll come away."

"Yes, my lady."

"All right. Here I go." The latch lifted at the touch of her hand, and the heavy door swung silently inward on oiled hinges. Together they walked into the damp heat of the queen's workroom. A tall window in the south wall, fogged with steam from the cauldron, let in a long, gray shaft of winter light. The queen herself stood at the mixing table measuring dark-colored powders from a collection of stoppered bottles at her elbow. Knowing better than to speak before they were addressed, the girls watched in silence as she deftly mixed the powders and funneled them into a blue-dyed linen bag. With neat, quick hands the bottles were replaced, the counter cleaned, the bag set in its place upon a shelf. The queen turned.

"Ah. Essylte. You've come at last." Faint lines tugged at the corners of her mouth and eyes, but Guinblodwyn of Gwynedd was still renowned for beauty. Such red lips, such coal-black hair, such an alabaster complexion were unmatched in all of Wales. She carried herself as if she knew admirers were watching.

Essylte made her reverence. "You sent for me, Mother?"

"An hour past. Where were you?"

"At lessons."

The queen's eyes narrowed, but she let the lie pass. She knew the tutor Paulus had been drunk since midday and that Essylte herself had brought him the wine. In the back of her mind Guinblodwyn was annoyed at such pointless deception, such lack of subtlety from a daughter of her blood. "No matter. It gave me a chance to finish my mixing. Next is the paste for ague." She pointed to a sheaf of dried herbs on the chopping block. "Why don't you start with those, both of you—save the seeds, mind, in the black jar, and throw the greens into the cauldron."

Branwen moved to obey, but Essylte demurred. "Do I have to, Mother? I *hate* mixing herbs and making drugs and powders—it's all right for Branwen, she likes it, but the smell of it makes me sick." She wrinkled her nose at the sharp, steamy herb scent. It was one of her earliest memories. All her life, it seemed, she had been made to come here, forced to feign an interest, obliged to learn this petty domestic witchcraft, and all her life she had loathed it.

"Foolish words from an empty head." The queen rinsed her hands in a glazed bowl with a gilded lip. She did not look at Essylte. "When you are queen and it falls to you to keep your husband healthy, and all his companions, and their wives and children—what will you do then?"

"Pooh. I will have others do it. Branny shall come with me, and she'll heal whoever is ill."

Branwen looked up, startled. The queen noted it. "Foolish girl. Never give power into another's hands."

"I don't care. I don't like it. Not all queens take that on themselves. Grandmother doesn't."

"Your grandmother Anet has other skills. She is a fine weaver, an artist of the first class. Her tapestries hang all over Britain." Guinblodwyn raised her head and looked directly at her daughter. "And you, Essylte? What is it you will do to distinguish yourself among your people? What do you offer back to the gods who gave you life?"

Essylte frowned. There it was again, the reference to pagan gods. Yet she was supposed to be a Christian queen. Everyone knew that for Percival's sake she had learned Christian teaching, and before Essylte was born had been baptized into the True Faith. But lately Essylte sensed her mother's Christian piety peeling off, like skin exposed too long to the sun, revealing an older, deeper self. Essylte shuddered. She preferred not to think about Guinblodwyn's side of the family.

"Well, Essylte?"

"I can sing."

The queen's lips twisted. "Excellent. I shall betroth you to a bard." She pointed to the table where Branwen was already at work. Reluctantly, Essylte joined her.

Guinblodwyn studied the girls. Not for the first time, she marked the likeness between these children of such different birth—the same height, the same slender build, near the same age, well featured, with the same wide forehead and the same firm chin. But there similarity ended. Like her peasant mother, Branwen's coloring was decidedly common—light brown hair, hazel-gray eyes, freckled skin. She faded into every background.

But Essylte! Young Essylte stood out among her peers, even among her family, like a swan among geese. Just to look at her, glowing like a rare jewel in the drab winter light, stung her mother with both pride and pain. Where had such coloring come from? Everyone in her own line, and most of Percival's, was dark. Yet Essylte's hair was a red-gold flame, alive and alight, rampant with curls. Her blue-green eyes, widely set and shadowed by incongruously dark lashes, changed their hue as often as the sea, and like the sea, shone deep, intense and clear. Her skin, which should have been marred with freckles, was so fair, so smooth, so flawless, so utterly without blemish, it had long been compared to Guinblodwyn's own. In a year or two, Guinblodwyn knew without a doubt, her daughter would outshine her. How could the child be so unconscious of her beauty? How could she show so little interest in such a powerful weapon?

"It is time, Essylte, you gave a thought to marriage. You must know your father and I have discussed it. Within the year, most probably, you will be betrothed."

Essylte shivered. "To whom?"

"To a fine man who will do you honor: Palomydes, Prince of Powys."

"Oh, no, Mother! I can't stand him!" Essylte shot a quick look at Branwen, who dropped the herbs into the cauldron. A thin curl of pungent steam rose from the roiling water. Branwen coughed. The queen looked at her daughter in irritation.

"A weak ploy, Essylte. Where is your subtlety? You will both stay."

Branwen curtsied. The queen came around the table and stood before her daughter. "What you can stand doesn't matter in the least. You will go where you are sent. But it will be easier for you if you consent."

Tears filled Essylte's eyes. "I couldn't bear Palomydes."

"Tell me why not."

"He—he smells."

"Powys is a wide land. Granach, the king, is failing. You will be queen there within a year or two. Surely for the promise of such power you can endure a man's scent."

"Not Palomydes! I hate the very sight of him. I would rather be abducted by the Irish and taken across the sea than lie with him!"

The queen's face darkened. "Nonsense. Don't be a fool. There is more to being queen than lying with the king. You will have power if you are strong enough to take it."

Essylte shrugged. Guinblodwyn drew a deep breath. "Now listen to me, Essylte, and listen well. I called you up here to let you know your future, and give you time to accustom yourself to it. Palomydes has courted you for six months. Half a year is a long time for such a prince to await an answer. Not only is he the heir of Powys and a good warrior with an honorable reputation, but he is in love with you. I might even say he is besotted. He will treat you well. Add to that, he is Welsh. You need not leave your homeland. You could easily do much worse, and are not likely to do better."

"I will never marry Palomydes."

The queen's nostrils flared. "If I accept his suit on your behalf, you will wed him whether you like it or not."

"What does Father say? *He* would not betroth me against my will."

At the mention of Percival, Guinblodwyn stiffened. Branwen tugged gently at Essylte's sleeve. For a long moment, no one spoke. Then the queen pointed to a stool. "Sit down. There." Branwen tugged again. Essylte sat.

Slowly, the queen began to pace around the spacious chamber. "Your father is perfectly willing to betroth you against your will. He is even now negotiating a match that will shame you in the eyes of all your countrymen."

"I know."

The queen whirled. "You *know?*"

Essylte gulped. "He is closeted every day with that ugly little foreigner. I know they're talking about me. Everybody says so. They say the foreign devil is driving a hard bargain."

To Essylte's amazement, the queen lifted a trembling hand to her brow and closed her eyes. "Great Mother, give me patience! It is impossible for such ignorant souls to know so much." She opened her eyes. Essylte quailed at the light in them. "And do you know who that ugly little monster is?"

"No, madam."

The queen spat the words out, one by one. "He—is—a—Cornishman!"

Essylte tilted her head to one side. "What prince does he serve?"

"It does not matter!" the queen cried, twisting her hands together. "Absolutely nothing could matter less. You are *not* going to Cornwall. I will not allow it. I will see you dead first."

"I will die before I marry Palomydes!" Essylte retorted, jumping from the stool. "And what makes you think Father is negotiating against my will? He asked me—*he asked me*—if I would go to Cornwall. He explained the importance of it to me—*he* thinks I am old enough to be consulted. You think I'm ignorant and helpless and will go wherever you send me. Well, I won't! I'm smart enough to know there's only one prince left in Cornwall, and that's the king. Markion, his name is. The High King of Britain."

The queen gasped. "Don't call him that! By rights, it is your father's title. *He* should be High King."

"And you High Queen? I know. I've heard the tale about a thousand times. At least Father had the grace to accept the Welsh defeat."

The queen shook so badly she leaned against her table for support. "Are you mad?" she gasped. "You can't mean you will take his part in this. Marhalt was my brother!"

"Uncle Marhalt," Essylte said firmly, shaking off Branwen's tugging hand, "lost the fight. You can't change that. And now, because you can't be

High Queen, you don't want me to, either. Is it because I would outrank you?"

"You are a child," Guinblodwyn whispered, staring at her. "You don't know what you are saying. The King of Cornwall is old enough to be your father. He is a selfish, vain, mean-tempered man."

"And Palomydes isn't?"

Branwen pulled at Essylte's arm. Slowly the queen straightened and her features hardened. "I will hear no more. You will do as I say. The Cornish envoy will not live to seal his bargain with Gwynedd. Come spring, we will be at war with Cornwall. And you will be wed to Palomydes."

"Never!"

The queen raised a white hand above her head and slowly brought it down. Essylte found herself sitting on the stool.

"I can make you do exactly as I wish," the queen said evenly.

"Oh, God!" Essylte cried, clenching her fists as tears welled in her eyes. "I'm so tired of all your witch's tricks! You can't run *everything*. Why can't you let me be?"

"I have found a place for you where you will be honored and cared for, cherished even, and given a measure of power and respect. I have done the best for you that I can do. Be content with that."

"I won't!" Essylte wiped her tears away with the back of her hand. "I'm no more to you than a prize cow, to be sold at market for the best price. Well, I don't care what you have arranged. I won't so much as speak to Palomydes. His family has been intertwined with yours for generations; it's not even exchanging masters. You would still be ruling my life."

The queen's red lips thinned into a smile. "You need ruling. You are hardly safe out alone."

Essylte rose, bracing herself against the witch's power. "I will die first."

The queen laughed. "You will not die. You will lie with Palomydes and bear him sons."

"I will tell Father you mean to kill the Cornish envoy."

The smile faded. Forcefully, Branwen pulled Essylte back onto the stool.

"Do that," the cool voice responded, "and I will tell Palomydes you have accepted him. As your betrothed, he has a right to your bed. He is a strong man; he will not be denied what is due him. You will *not* marry that filthy Cornishman."

Essylte leaped up, crying, "You would not! You would not! How could you? As God is my judge, I am not your slave! I don't care *who* has offered for me—I would marry a dog to get out of Wales! Away from you!" Sobs choked her as she struggled blindly for the door. "I will tell Father I wish to go—I will tell him to accept the envoy's offer—I will tell him about you and Palomydes—he will protect me! He has always loved me! And he hates you!"

"Essylte! I forbid you to go." The queen raised her hand above her head. Essylte's limbs grew heavy. Desperately she reached for the door as her vision faded. A small hand slipped into her own and with a firm grip led her from the room and down the stair. Branwen's gentle voice urged her to hurry. Behind them the queen's wail rose in the long, sharp crescendo of a Druid curse.

"Branny! Oh, Branny, why does she hate me so?"

Essylte lay prostrate across the bed while Branwen stroked her hair.

"That is easy, my lady. You are lovelier than she ever was, even in her youth, and her beauty is her pride."

"But even when I was little she wasn't kind to me. I never could please her, no matter how hard I tried."

"She always knew you would outshine her. She knew it from your birth. She looked into her crystal and saw what was to be."

Essylte shuddered. "I hate witchery. It serves her right, to have her whole life twisted by reaching for such power."

"Power is life to her." Branwen held a lock of Essylte's glowing hair across her palm and watched it as if she expected it to speak. "If you are High Queen of Britain, she must kneel to you. That is a thought she can barely live with. She has come a long way from her father's small subkingdom in Guent. She is queen of all Gwynedd. But High Queen of Britain! Imagine how she longs for that plum! And it was so nearly in her grasp. She did everything she could to arrange that it should fall to her, but instead it falls to you. No wonder she is angry."

Essylte raised her head. "What do you mean, she arranged it? She may have put Uncle Peredur up to the plan, but she could do nothing about the fight itself."

Branwen smiled, half to herself, and let the red-gold hair slip from her fingers. "Don't be so sure."

"What do you mean? Branny, what do you know?"

Branwen shook her head. "Nothing. Nothing certain. Nothing I can prove. And besides, it doesn't matter anymore."

"Nothing I can tell Father about?"

"Oh, no. And you ought not to taunt her about losing the king's love. From time to time, I think that is something she regrets."

"She ought to regret it. She ought to be ashamed everyone knows it.

Father has at least a dozen bastards that he cares for, and more than likely a dozen more he doesn't know about. Percival's bastards, people call them behind his back. I've heard them. Ceredig's one himself, did you know? Think of that—my own half brother, a house servant! It's all Mother's fault. Her cruelty and her witchery drove Father away."

Branwen looked down at Essylte's tear-marked face and said nothing.

"I don't know how you can spend hours in her workroom over those horrid pots. It would drive me mad. Sometimes I think I must be mad already, to stay here."

"I like herb lore. It's interesting. And useful."

"Sometimes I feel like I can't breathe, and I wonder if she has poisoned the very air of Gwynedd. How does Father bear it? Oh, Branny, I shall hate to part with Father, but if I don't escape from Mother, I know I'll die!"

"You will escape. You'll go to Cornwall. Lord Segward said so."

"Lord Segward?" Essylte sat up slowly. "You know the envoy's name?"

"From Ceredig, who waits upon them."

"He has heard them speaking? Oh, tell me what you know!"

Branwen glanced swiftly at the door and lowered her voice. "Only this, that what you told the queen was truth. Lord Segward serves King Markion, who has offered for you."

Essylte went still. "But why me? He must know that all Wales loathes him."

"That is the reason. He wants to heal that wound his nephew gave us. And for the same reason, King Percival listens to him. They both want a united Britain. They dream of the kind of alliance King Arthur had."

Essylte shrugged. "I don't believe half those old tales, anyway. Britain was never that united. Welshmen and Cornishmen and Lothians all drinking under one roof? These are fables."

"Fable or not, the dream is compelling. This is why King Percival considers the offer, and why he keeps it quiet the man is even here. No one knows outside Gwynedd; few know outside the castle. If the soldiers knew, there might be trouble. That's why they negotiate in secret. But Percival is at least listening." Branwen's eyes rested on Essylte's tousled hair. "Your son might be the next High King of Britain."

Essylte shook her head. "Pray don't talk to me about childbearing. I don't want any children."

"Even if it's Markion you marry? He will put you away if you do not bear. He *is* old enough to be your father, and his son was killed last autumn. He won't want to wait long to get another heir."

Essylte leaned forward and kissed Branwen's cheek. "You must come with me, Branny. I can't part with you, I really can't." She squeezed Branwen's hands and held them in her own. "You're the only one I can talk to, the only friend I've ever had. You'll come with me, won't you, wherever it is I go?"

Branwen lowered her eyes. "I—I serve the king, your father."

"Father can have no reason to oppose it. Why on earth should he care where you go?"

An ugly blush spread from the girl's throat to engulf her face. "Your mother needs my assistance in her workroom."

"Mother will have no choice. I'll ask Father to make it an outright order. He will give me anything I want as a guilt gift for sending me away. Just say you will come with me. What future do you have here, after all? Do you want to be my mother's drudge all your life? Come with me to Cornwall. We'll find a prince for you to marry, and you can be a lady with a house of your own."

Branwen steadied her expression as the flush slowly faded. "The king has promised to make me a good match."

Shaking her head, Essylte kissed her hands. "Dear Branny, if it were possible, he would already have done so. Most maids are promised, if not married, by sixteen. And if you are useful to my mother, she's as likely to poison you as let you go beyond her service. Please, Branny, come with me. We'll be homesick for a while, but we'll both be better off."

Branwen met Essylte's eyes, aglow with tears. Tears always came so easily to Essylte. "Is it so important to you?"

"Yes, Branny! Desperately important. Say you will. . . . It's settled, then."

Branwen withdrew her hands and slid off the bed. "I will do whatever the king commands," she said slowly. She went to the door and lifted the latch. "Keep your door barred and go nowhere without an escort. The queen means to prevent this match at any cost. And Palomydes is her tool."

Essylte shuddered. "That horrid creature. Surely Markion can't be worse. Where are you going, Branny?"

"To Ceredig. To beg audience with the king."

But as she turned to the door it opened in her face, trapping her behind it. A man stood on the threshold, tall and thickly built, richly dressed and adorned with silver rings and wristbands. His hair and beard were brown and curly; mats of curls grew along the backs of his hands and sprang from the throat of his tunic. Light blue eyes fastened on Essylte as he stepped into her chamber.

"Sir!" she cried, leaping to the floor and grabbing her jeweled dagger from the bedstand. Behind him, Branwen slipped silent as a shadow around the door and fled down the corridor. "Sir! How came you here? These are the women's quarters. Your presence here is forbidden."

White teeth gleamed within the beard. He closed the door softly and let the bar fall into place. "Others are forbidden, little beauty, but not I. Not now that you have accepted me."

"You are mad! I have *not* accepted you! If you have spoken to my witch-mother, you have heard nothing but lies. I detest you, Palomydes. I will never wed you."

He smiled again. "Such modesty is becoming in a maiden."

Shaking, Essylte raised the dagger. "You are dreaming. I would sooner lie with a toad. Get out!"

Palomydes grinned. "I do like spirit in a woman."

Essylte flushed scarlet and held the dagger firmly in front of her. "Don't come near me, you beast, if you value your life. My father has not approved the match. If you touch me he will kill you."

Palomydes shrugged. "I'm not worried about your father. Once you are taken he cannot wed you to another."

"Beast! Would you sink so low? And you a prince?"

"I will take what has been promised to me. The Great Mother knows I have waited long enough!" He pulled off his tunic and threw it aside.

"Ugh!" Essylte backed against the bed, wrinkling her nose.

"Put away your pretty blushes and that foolish dagger. Be sweet to me, Essylte, and I'll be gentle with you." He reached out a hand to her; she swiped at him with the dagger and missed.

"I *loathe* you! You smell worse than a midden. And so fat! So hairy! I loathe even the sight of you. Get out this minute or I shall call the guards."

He laughed. "There are no guards. Your mother has seen to that. Come, come, Essylte, your insults do not hurt me. You are only afraid. That will soon pass."

"Afraid? *You* are the one who should be trembling—my father will have your life! You're just a tool in my mother's hands—she wants to foil his plans for me, nothing more—yet you will die for it!"

He paused a moment; she slithered up onto the bed.

"I don't believe you. You speak from fear." He lunged. She dove across the bed and was on her feet in an instant, facing him across the fur-lined coverlet.

"Get out! Get out now!"

"Not until I've got what I came for." His thick lips curled into a smile. "By the Goddess! You are beautiful when you're angry."

"What a fool you are! Your feet are too big, and you smell like oxen. I would just as soon poison you as lie with you. Is that the kind of wife you want?"

He licked his lips. "Little hellcat, eh? That's fine with me. I'd rather fight than woo." He threw himself across the bed. Essylte dodged and struck down with her dagger, catching his arm.

"Bitch!" He landed heavily on the floor. She raced to the door and threw up the bar, but he caught her shoulder and spun her around, pressing against her and pinning her to the door. Turning her head, she sank her teeth into his hand. He wrenched away and slapped her lightly, flinging her head back. "Little bitch!"

Blood flowed freely from his wound. He did not even feel it. His hand gripped her wrist and the dagger clattered to the floor. Her arm burned, held twisted behind her as his lips sucked her flesh. Pinned, helpless, she drove her knee into his groin with all the force she could muster. He felt like steel.

"Damn you!" He fell against her, crushing her with his weight. "Bitch's whelp you are, right enough." He laughed into her face and kissed her. Weeping, she bit his lip. He hit her again. She screamed, tasting blood in her mouth. He shifted his weight, started pulling at her gown, sliding his big hands up between her legs, touching her soft flesh with blunt, questing fingers. She wriggled, freed her hands, tore at his face with her nails.

"Faaaa-therrrr!"

He ignored her and pulled at her underclothes. The fabric ripped. Coarse hands moved cold against her skin, prodded her, squeezed her, stroked her, forced her legs apart as his hot breath panted in her face. She beat her fists against his head, his shoulders, screaming, crying, cursing him wildly with every breath as he thrust himself forward.

Thunderous pounding filled her ears. The door behind her shuddered. Was that her father's voice? Palomydes, breathing heavily, backed away, pulling up his leggings. The door pushed open; Essylte fell to the floor.

"Palomydes! What in God's name is going on?"

Percival stood in the doorway. Branwen ducked past him and bent down to Essylte.

Palomydes bowed. "My lord king."

Behind Percival thronged the house guards, swords drawn. "What are you doing in my daughter's chamber? What have you done to the girl? Speak, man!"

Palomydes fell to one knee, groping behind him for his tunic. "My lord, I meant no offense. The princess Essylte and I are secretly betrothed, and I was, er—"

"What!" Percival's face grew dark. His body shook. The guards surrounded Palomydes.

"My lord, I have offered for your daughter these six months past—we are betrothed, my lord. I am within my rights."

"My daughter is not betrothed until I say she is. My consent is required, and you do not have it. But this you knew. You came to force yourself upon her, and force my choice."

"Oh, no, my lord!" Palomydes gulped. "No, never that. I assure you."

Essylte lifted her head. "Liar!"

Percival stared. Her hair, matted with blood, was stuck to her cheek, her face swollen, her lip split and bruised. For a long moment no one dared to breathe. Slowly Percival drew his sword and held it to Palomydes's throat. His voice shook. "If you have forced her, I will kill you. Now."

"My lord! I never—"

"Silence! Essylte?"

Essylte pushed herself to her knees and glared at Palomydes. Sweat broke upon his brow.

"I told you—I told you he would kill you," she whispered. "You wouldn't listen."

"Essylte! Tell him! Tell him I hardly touched you!"

"Liar!"

"But I didn't take you!"

"If I were half the liar you are, you would die."

"For mercy's sake, Essylte, tell him the truth! I never—"

"If my father hadn't come, you would have. Your leggings were around your knees."

"You filthy, double-crossing blackguard!" Percival breathed. The sword point trembled against the vulnerable flesh at Palomydes's throat. "I ought to kill you for so much as crossing her threshold!" He turned to Essylte. "You are whole, then?"

Essylte, still shaking, leaned on Branwen and struggled to her feet. Her smile was bitter. "Only just. Still negotiable."

"Essylte." Percival's arm slid around her shoulders and he pulled her to his breast. "My sweet little girl. I shall do with him whatever you wish— shall I unman him? Say the word." He kissed her swollen face.

"Oh, Father!" A sob welled in her throat, but she fought it down. "It would serve him right, but he's only her tool. This is Mother's doing."

"*What?*" His face lost color. The arm around her turned to iron. He glanced quickly at Branwen, who nodded. "My God!" he breathed. "Her own daughter!"

"And that's not all." Essylte drew a deep breath. "She plans to poison the Cornish envoy and so force us to war with Cornwall. I was to be wed to this—this monster and be well out of the way. If he died, then I would command all Powys, and she would command me."

Slowly Percival sheathed his sword and beckoned to the soldiers. "Take Palomydes to his chamber and see he stays there. I will decide later what to do with him. First, I will speak with the queen. Privately. Lleu, take a dozen men and fetch her. Yes, I said fetch her. Bind her and carry her if she won't come willingly." Percival wiped a hand across his brow. "This is the last straw. So help me God, I will put her away."

Essylte looked up at his pinched face. He smiled bitterly and touched his lips to her forehead.

"My lovely little girl," he said sadly. "If I have saved you from one fate, I have consigned you to another. This very day I have struck a bargain with Markion of Cornwall. You will be High Queen of Britain, Essylte, but I shall lose you to a man I do not trust."

"At least—" She gulped. "If I have to leave, at least it will be somewhere where I can bring Wales honor. And he—he cannot be as bad as Palomydes."

Percival's features hardened. "If I thought he were, I would not let you go at any price."

"Can I take Branny with me? Oh, Father, please let her come with me. If I am to live among strangers who hate me because I'm Welsh, let me take at least one friend with me."

Percival hugged her tightly. Over her head, his dark eyes met Branwen's. The girl trembled and dropped her gaze.

"Perhaps," the king said in a tight voice, "someone older would better serve you in a strange land. At sixteen, she can hardly be your guide."

"Oh, but she can!" Essylte cried. "She is my best friend, truly she is, in spite of her birth. And she is so wise, Father. Her advice is always good. She has served me since childhood. I couldn't bear to go without her. She has no kin, nothing to keep her here, no friends but me."

Percival cleared his throat. He was suddenly very pale. "Branwen? Are you willing? I will not keep you if you wish to go."

Branwen flashed him a quick look full of passionate emotion, then bowed her head and said in a smothered voice, "I will do whatever my lord thinks best."

Percival stood silent, staring beyond them to the wall. "Very well," he said at last, "I shall give the order." But his voice, low and weary, sounded like an old man's.

8 ✝ LYON'S HEAD

Down the long, rocky Cornwall coast the north wind swept, over barren moors, across frozen river valleys, howling through twisted forests of storm-bent branches. Down it blew in all its fury to the very end of Britain, across the breadth of Lyonesse to the edge of the Narrow Sea, and then across the tide-crossed causeway to the great promontory itself, rising black and solid in the storm's face.

At the sea's edge stood the fortress of Lyon's Head, foundations rooted in living rock that rose, fanglike, from the roiling ocean. Towers and battlements of stone overlooked the wide, heaving waters. Great walls enclosed a quiet village, sheltered a meadow and a wood, ran down the sloping point to solid iron gates, a guardhouse, and a long causeway to the mainland. At high tides and storm tides the causeway flooded, leaving the fortress unapproachable by land. And on this night the wild ocean, whipped into a frenzy by the wicked blast, rose to lick the rock roots of the guardhouse and spit spray high against the battlements, a warning to the men within of the precarious nature of their shelter.

Dinadan shivered and drew his cloak tighter around him. The log fire danced and snapped, but on such a night as this it gave only a feeble warmth. The wind was everywhere, whispering around the walls, lifting the heavy tapestries that hung there, sighing among the rushes strewn upon the floor.

"Damn, but I'm cold!" he muttered, shifting his shoulders. He shot a quick glance toward Tristan and shrugged. The King of Lyonesse sat crosslegged in the rushes, cloakless, his harp upon his lap, lost in song. Dinadan reached for the skin of spiced wine and let the hot brew slide down his throat. While it lasted, the heat in his belly quelled his shivering. He glanced down at the scroll before him, opened on the table, and sighed.

Since Tristan had taken up his kingship over a year ago, his moods had come more frequently upon him. No one complained—his people loved him unreservedly, the land was fertile, his rule benevolent, and his judgments fair. The Irish had risked landing twice, the Saxons once—all had been soundly defeated with barely a Cornish life lost. Markion had placed Meliodas's crown on Tristan's head with his own hands. The future was secure. He should be happy. Dinadan looked down again at the scroll with the High King's seal. Did Markion know Tristan was unhappy?

The last notes of the harp died as the sad song came to a close.

"For God's sake, Tristan, if I hear one more lament, or one more likening of the sea to a woman's breast, I'll fetch you a maiden myself. If you want Esmerée, go to her. If you don't, rest your soul in peace. I'm about to go out of my mind."

Tristan put down the harp and looked up. "Do I drive you to madness, Din? I don't mean to. It's this infernal, never-ending pain across my middle. What a magnificent storm rages outside! Just listen to it! But I can't enjoy them the way I used to—this burning, this gift of Marhalt, worsens in damp weather. On a night like this I can barely breathe."

"I'm sorry, Tris. I forgot. Live at Camelot or Dorr, then, instead of at the water's edge."

"I belong at the water's edge."

Dinadan scowled. "Stop talking like a bard. You know I was jesting. I've no desire to see you nearer Markion than you have to be. If the scar still pains you so, have her send you the cakes again. You don't have to see her; I'll fetch them for you, if you like."

Tristan slowly rose and picked up his harp. "He will kill you both. Her for baking them, you for coming near her gate. He has her watched."

"Ask her to send her servant with them. Or send one yourself."

"Then only she will die." Tristan shook his head. "I cannot so much as breathe her name aloud without being a danger to her. How do I know what spies he has planted in my household? He may not dare come against me, but he holds her life cheap enough." He sat heavily on the bench across from Dinadan and put his lap harp down next to the scroll. "After every visit to her he leaves a new mark upon her, just so I will know he has been there."

"How can you know this, if you haven't seen her since summer?"

"He makes certain I hear about it. One month it will be the talk of the marketplace; another, a courier will ride in with a piece of local news." Tristan slumped upon the table, head in hands. "Oh, God, Dinadan! What a hell has her life become since she met me! I cannot do anything to help her—everything I've tried has brought her fresh beatings. All I can do is nothing. It is pure hell to bear!"

"And this still goes on, so long after your parting?"

Tristan nodded. "On and on. Because she bore a daughter, because he thinks the child looks like me."

Dinadan leaned forward and lowered his voice. "*Is* she yours?"

Tristan looked up, wretched. "I don't know. Esme's sworn to him it's his. Segward doesn't believe it."

"What do *you* believe?"

"I think," Tristan said sadly, "she might be mine. Else Pernam would not be so afraid. He's angry with me; I expected that. But I can't think of another reason for his fear."

"Surely Pernam's medicine can help you. You took it, I remember, before you met her."

Tristan sighed. "I could. But I'd rather not ask him for it now. He probably regrets he ever healed me. He is certainly wishing he had never introduced me to Esme. And besides, I deserve the discomfort. For all the grief I have brought upon her."

Dinadan pushed the wineskin across the table to him. "It was *she* who came to *you*. You are doing all that you can on her behalf, and you are suffering enough. Drink up, Tris. Take a deep breath. We need to talk about Mark's letter."

Tristan shrugged. "I'd rather not."

"You must. I know you—you'll do as he requests just to change the monotony of routine. I won't let you. The gall of the man!"

"Get it out of your head I ought to be insulted. I've never wanted to be High King of Britain, or King of Cornwall, either. Let him get himself another heir. Poor Gerontius. I liked him, didn't you? He was good-hearted and brave, if slow-witted. I miss him." Tristan raised the wineskin to his lips and drank. "He would be near twenty now and looking for a wife himself. God, I wish he'd lived."

"But more to the point—"

"I know Mark, Dinadan. The last thing he wants to do is remarry. He likes women well enough, but not to live with. It used to be a joke my father told, how Mark hated to have women about him. He much preferred to leave Elisane at Tintagel and visit her there from time to time. Why do you think he took Castle Dorr from your father? To give himself someplace else to go."

"Whether he wants to remarry or not, he is doing it, and cutting you off from your inheritance."

"It's not an inheritance I want."

"Even so, it's your birthright. Not only does he wish to steal it—others resent that, Tris, even if you do not—but to ask *you* to steal it *for* him is the height of arrogance—it smacks of contempt and cowardice. How does he dare?"

Tristan smiled at Dinadan's wrath. "Be easy, Din. It's a simple matter, really. And the cause is noble. He knows I can do this for him; he knows he cannot do it for himself, and who else is there?"

"You're not falling for that nonsense about another golden age like Arthur's. Come on, Tris! That's so much chaff thrown in your face to hide his real intent."

"He wouldn't undertake marriage for a petty cause, or just to cheat me.

He hates the very idea of it. He hates the ritual and ceremony, he hates the formality and the fuss. All he wants is to lie with her and get her with child, and stick her in some fortress out of harm's way. That's all marriage is to Mark. In fifteen years he'll come back and claim his son. If you want to be angry, think of the poor girl." The smile died as a lock of dark hair fell forward to shadow his face. "Think of the young virgin, barely past childhood, raised by her parents for just such a sacrifice. All she will ever know of love is Mark's hot breath, his unwashed hands, his urgent need. Poor child. Like Esme." Tristan rose suddenly and strode away from the table. "Sometimes I think it is sinful, the burdens God makes women bear."

Dinadan shook his head and took another pull from the wineskin. "I've never heard such gibberish. Come on, Tristan, give your mind to this, if only for a moment."

"Never to know the unutterable sweetness of desire . . . I pity her from my heart."

Dinadan sighed and pushed the scroll aside.

"Why worry about the Welsh princess? We know nothing about her yet. Let's just hope she has no ambitions to power, or Mark will make her life a misery."

"He will do that in any event. Shall we pray the poor child is stupid and aims at nothing beyond breeding heirs? It's not a fate I'd wish on anyone I cared for."

"Is she worse off than the cook's daughter or the fisherman's girl?"

"God is cruel to women."

In exasperation, Dinadan waved the scroll at him. "Enough about women. Can you give a moment's thought to this important matter? The High King of Britain wants your advice."

Tristan shrugged. "I've already decided. I will go."

"No!" Dinadan slammed his fist on the table. "You cannot! Uncle or not, he is a villain to suggest it—"

"He doesn't suggest it."

"He asks you for help. For advice. A thinly disguised ploy."

"It doesn't matter."

"Do you value your life so lightly?" Dinadan took him by the shoulders and shook him firmly. "What about those of us who love you? What about Lyonesse? If you die, this too will belong to Markion."

"He is not sending me there to kill me. Mark wouldn't do that."

Dinadan's eyes flashed. "But Segward would. My God, don't you see? Tristan, open your eyes. This is his revenge. He might not come against you openly—it's just like him to get someone else to do his dirty work. And how clever to let it be the Welsh! It will look like revenge for Marhalt, a blood feud, pure and simple. No blame will attach to Markion, and certainly none to Segward. What a righteous little swine he is!"

Tristan frowned. "If it were Segward's plan to destroy me, then Mark would not approve it. So either Mark doesn't know or it's not as dangerous as you think."

"If it's not dangerous, why doesn't he go himself?"

Tristan sighed. "I've told you that already. It's anathema to him. Besides, he fancies himself a second Arthur, and that's the way Arthur did it. By proxy."

"And look where it got him. His bride fell in love with his proxy."

Tristan smiled. "That's the kindest compliment you've ever paid me, to compare me to Lancelot."

Dinadan scowled. "Will you attend to the point just for a moment? If it's not dangerous, why the false name? The invented heritage? If those are meant as true disguises, then *anyone* can wear them; it needn't be you. These are Segward's tricks to fool Mark into believing it's safe, but they don't fool me. You *can't* go into Wales, disguised, renamed, under any pretext, however noble. I know you, Tristan. You're too open for your own good. Before you've been there a week they'll find you out and kill you. Mark won't get his bride but he'll get Lyonesse, and Segward will be revenged."

Tristan's eyes narrowed thoughtfully. "Without the bride, Mark doesn't get the alliance he wants, the union with Wales. I believe that's more important to him than anything. No, Din, it won't wash. Mark has only Lyonesse to gain by sending me off to die, and all Britain to lose. Besides, if you can see the danger here, don't you suppose other Cornishmen can see it? Because of me, he's High King. If he betrays me, what will his knights do? Follow him loyally? You know they won't. No, Dinadan, he wouldn't risk it. Do not be afraid for me. Being High King is everything to Mark. He wouldn't risk both that and Cornwall, even for Segward."

"But don't you see? Segward has convinced Mark these childish ruses will guarantee your safety, even though he himself does not believe it."

"You think Mark's most trusted advisor has deceived him?"

"Yes! As he's done before, Segward is putting his own personal hatred before Cornwall's good."

"He's more intelligent than that."

"But when does passion overrule intelligence? When a woman is involved. You've betrayed his bed—he'll do *anything* to kill you. He'd deceive Mark, he'd deceive his own mother. Especially if he could arrange it so he was never blamed."

Tristan frowned. Dinadan grabbed his arm and held it. "Please, Tris. Please don't do it. Think of Lyonesse, of her future, of those you'd leave behind you. Mark has left you a way out, he's left it in your hands. Between us, we'll think of another way to satisfy his honor and bring home his precious bride."

Tristan met his anxious gaze. "What about *my* honor?" he asked softly. "There's only one reason I could give for refusing, and that's cowardice."

"Nonsense. It's not cowardice to refuse to walk into the wolf's den. It's sense. Everyone in Cornwall knows you're not a coward." He dropped his hand from Tristan's arm. "But you've never been worried about what people think. Not you. What's the real reason you want to go? It's bound to be something that touches your heart, not your kingdom. Something I'd never guess in a hundred years—to hear their bards? To get uncounted leagues between you and Esmerée? To admire the mountains of Gwynedd? To warn the fair Essylte? To satisfy your curiosity about—about anything at all? Or do you want to go because you've not been there before? Because it's something new to do? Tell me. I have to know. What makes a man with everything to lose and nothing to gain take such a risk?"

A puzzled smile crossed Tristan's face. He shrugged. "I don't know. But those are interesting guesses."

"What do you mean, you don't know? You *must* know. If you value our friendship and my service, do me the kindness to give me one good reason why you should risk your life in such a cause."

Tristan's eyes looked past him, past the stone walls and the dark night, to something beyond. "I want to meet Percival of Gwynedd."

Dinadan stared. "Why?"

"I've wanted to meet him since I was small. Since the bard Hawath came to Lyonesse to sing for my father. After 'The Lay of Arthur' he told 'The Tale of Parsifal and Galahad.' Have you never heard it? It stirred me to my soul."

"Are you serious?"

Tristan seemed not to hear him. His eyes were fixed on something in the distance. "Percival is one of those men blessed with both sense and vision. He fought with Arthur. Sir Galahad was his friend. They fought together. He has united the Welsh kingdoms under his leadership. He believes in a good larger than himself. Men like that are no longer born. Their time is past. I want to meet him before he, too, goes into the shadows. I have been waiting for the opportunity for years. Now it has come."

Dinadan passed a hand across his brow. "Fool! It will be your death. And all because of a tale told by a bard!"

Tristan smiled lightly. "And what do bards tell us but of our heroes? What do you want me to say, Din? If I simply wanted adventure, I would lie once more with Esmerée." He rose. "But there is another reason. I've been restless these six months past. I am driven by something I can't describe. I'm looking for something I must find. I don't know if I can explain it."

"Try. I beg you."

"All right." He paused. "I need to know what I'm made of. What's possible. What's missing. There's an emptiness in here"—he struck his chest—"that grows with time. I used to look forward to glory in war, to love of a woman. Lately, I just look down. There are moments—as scarce as rubies in the sand—when the truth flashes out at me, like the smile of God, and I see oh so clearly who I am and what the world is made for. I live for those moments. . . . Do you—do you understand at all?"

Dinadan shook his head. Tristan cocked his head toward the shutters, where the wind screamed for entrance and frozen rain beat like a shower of pebbles against the door. "Do you hear that? Can you feel that power? That menace? Wantonness, Esme called it once. How can you not marvel at it? The unthinking savagery, so total, so all-encompassing! Face it, defy it, it will take hold of you in a moment of surrender so complete, you are utterly lost within it. And when you are lost, you are found."

"What on earth are you talking about?"

Tristan sighed. "Maybe I'd better put it another way. Whether you like it or not, Dinadan, you know I'm not cut out for kingship. I know it, so you must, if you're honest with yourself." He waved away Dinadan's protest. "I don't mean I'm abdicating. I'm the rightful King of Lyonesse. This is my place. I'm competent to administer the running of this little storm-bound land. And I'll continue to do it." Seeing Dinadan's relief, he paused, half smiling. "But I'm dying here; part of me is dying, squeezed away by the everlasting pettiness and routine. I can't bear the daily squabbles among courtiers and petitioners, I've had a bellyful of other people's troubles and complaints. All day long I listen to the droning of sycophants, the honeyed lies invented to win my favor or sway my decision. Is this power, to have men grasping at my cloak to wring from me just a little more gold, a little more time, a little more of whatever it is they want? Is this kingship?"

Dinadan frowned. "Of course."

"Well. How Arthur bore it for twenty-six years I'll never know. I'd rather be fighting Saxons."

"From time to time fighting Saxons is part of it, too."

"I want, I long for the broad stroke, the great deed, the hard fight for glory and honor—not this daily diminution, this death by wearing down, like the sea that eats, year by year, at the roots of Lyon's Head. Give me something bold, something great to do!"

Dinadan frowned uncertainly. "You're bored?"

"I am like this winter gale outside!" Tristan cried, gripping his sides with both hands, "that rages and howls, seeking something beyond itself! Listen to it! Oh, to be one with such a driving force! To be vast and unmeasured. Limitless. Free from fetters. I tell you, Din, no one has less freedom than a king. I am hemmed about with ritual and regulation; I cannot speak without my words being written down as law. Sometimes I would trade my right arm to be a fisherman instead and spend my days in argument with the sea."

But Dinadan's anxiety was only increasing. "What is it you seek, Tristan? How is it to be found in Wales, if it isn't here?"

Tristan winced, gasping at the pain in his side. "It is found anywhere, everywhere, where it's least expected. There's that moment on the knife's edge, when anything could happen—when the great unknown swoops down, when the next breath could be your last, or first. In that moment you know things you never knew before. When you risk all, you find your center."

Dinadan frowned. "Is it excitement you want, then?"

Tristan cried out in pain and exasperation. "No, no! Look! I will show you what I mean."

He stepped to the outer door, unbolted the heavy shutters, and threw his shoulder against the studded oak. The storm's blast knocked him back into the room. With a defiant cry, he strode out to the battlement and was flung against the streaming outer wall, hugging the stone, gasping as the wind tore his breath from his body.

This, *this* was magnificence itself. Below him the sea thundered against the rocks. He could feel the vibration of the shock through the very walls, the foundation of the castle. Frozen spray whipped by the wind stung his face, blinded his eyes. Yet he pushed himself away from the wall and smiled into the wind's teeth. *This* was strength! *This* was power! Why could Dinadan not understand it? *This* was complete possession, to be overmastered by power he could not command. This was ultimate sensation, to stand, so small and weak at the edge of disaster, to yield to the fates, to laugh into the face of sudden death, to know that his soul was not his alone, but part of something wild and great and unknowable. The burning in his chest stopped his breath and he fell to his knees, gripping the parapet as a blast of wind flung him sideways. Damn the storm! Bless the storm! This was joy, this moment of complete surrender, this losing himself in the onslaught, a moment so brief, so intense, so prized! Felt only in the face of a great storm, in the heat of a deadly battle, at the striking of a pure note that sang of itself, and on entering a woman's body. To fight, to sing, to love, to truly live—for this, he would go anywhere, give up anything. For this, and not for Markion, he would go to Wales and face what awaited him there.

9 ✝ GWYNEDD

The prow of the Cornish ship nosed its way into the quiet harbor. All along the shore Welsh troops thronged under gently lifting banners, the Gray Wolf of Gwynedd stretching and hunching on his field of blue. At the end of the long quay Percival stood in a scarlet cloak, surrounded by his knights. Behind him foothills rose, awash with a thousand shades of young green on the lower slopes where the forest had awakened, and fading imperceptibly upward to the bare gray-brown of branches still asleep, shot here and there with dark pines and bare outcrops of rock. In a fold of hills above the harbor the gray stone towers of a castle hung between the trees. Atop the mountains the sun broke free of trailing clouds and flooded the hills with the pale yellow light of early spring.

Tristan stood on the deck beside the captain, the escort ranged behind him, and adjusted the fall of his cloak. On his shoulder he wore the Black Boar of Cornwall, not the Eagle of Lyonesse. He was quietly dressed, but his boots were of the finest doeskin and the hammered golden torque around his neck was Gerontius's own. His sword, his father's gift, he had refused to part with, but he wore it sheathed in a plain leather scabbard, so ancient and darkened with time it well hid the splendor of the weapon. He stood easily, his eyes traveling over the budding hills, the castle, the muddy harbor road, the roughly dressed soldiers, the formally clothed king.

Wales was not a rich land. Her shores were always open to attack by Irish raiders; her hills were steep and her soil thin and stony. Her great strength lay in her men and women, a fierce and independent people who prided themselves on their craftiness, their bold fighting spirit, and, beyond all else, their wonderful gift for music. Their greatest fault, Tristan mused, watching the land pull nearer, was one they shared with most other Britons: They valued independence above the strength of union. Only Arthur had been able to unite them all, not Maximus, not Ambrosius, not Uther, not Constantine. Only Arthur. And while he lived Britain had been a power to be respected, a light in the darkness, a bulwark against every foe from barbarian enemy to imperial Rome. Percival was a rare king, a Welshman with a vision, a man who looked beyond his own borders to a union such as Arthur had once achieved.

Tristan strained his eyes to see him better as the ship approached the quay. Percival was not a prepossessing man. He stood no taller than his companions, and shorter than some. He appeared to be slight of build, dark-bearded and dark-haired, a man more or less like any other. But it was clear from the way his companions stood and the way they bent forward as he turned his head to speak, he was held in high esteem among them. Tristan's heart beat faster. This was the man, if all the tales were true, who was the boyhood companion of that legend among men, Sir Galahad, in the days when Arthur reigned. What he would not give for an hour alone with Percival of Gwynedd! And now, as Markion's proxy, he would get it.

The ship sidled up to the quay, the hawsers were secured, the gangplank lowered. Percival led his companions forward as Tristan and his escort descended. They met halfway down the quay. Half a head taller, Tristan bent his knee and said in Welsh, "My lord King Percival. Greetings from my kinsman Markion, King of Cornwall, High King of Britain."

Percival's eyes traveled from the shoulder badge to the ancient scabbard to the torque and wristbands. Tristan glanced at the expressionless faces of the gathered Welshmen, wondering who among them was his foe. Finally, Percival nodded.

"Rise, prince. May I have the honor of your name and family?" He spoke flawless Latin in a musical, unhurried voice, a voice of authority and culture.

"My lord king, my name is Tantris of Caer Budeca. I am the son of Rivalen, son of Gerfeint, brother to Constantine and cousin to the High King," Tristan replied in Latin, keeping his eyes down. At Percival's silence, he looked up. The dark brown eyes were watching him warily. "I am the last living of Markion's relations," he said truthfully, "excepting only his brother Pernam, who is a healer and not a warrior. I wish I were higher born, my lord, to do you the honor you deserve."

This graceful speech produced a few murmurs among the men, and Percival allowed himself a smile. "You wear the Boar of Cornwall, sir. That is good enough for me." He spread his arms out to embrace the sea, the harbor, the hills. "Welcome to Gwynedd, Tantris of Budeca. May your stay here be a pleasant one."

A groom led horses forward, and he and Percival mounted for the ride up to the castle, the Welsh troops and Cornish escort walking warily behind. As they rode, Tristan gave Percival what news there was from Camelot, of longboat sightings and unrest along the ever-lengthening Saxon Shore, of Irish landings along the Cornish coast. In turn, Percival told him of tidings from the north, how the Picts had attacked all winter along the borders of Lothian and Strathclyde. Picts were a fierce and relentless people who feared nothing now that Arthur was gone from Britain.

"And how," Tristan ventured, "do the other Welsh kingdoms welcome my visit, and the marriage of your daughter to Markion?"

Percival's eyes crinkled in a smile, although his face was grave. "You are direct, my lord Tantris. A trait we Welsh appreciate. Most men would not ask such a question until we met in the council chamber, well after the feasting and the bard."

"I beg your pardon, my lord. I am not much used to diplomacy. But I have an interest in your answer, as I feel, even now, eyes upon my back."

Percival grinned. "You are observant as well, I see. But I doubt you are in real danger. Dyfed is with me, and Northgallis. Powys does not like it but will lift no hand to resist." He paused. "For obvious reasons, Guent is against it."

Guent. Marhalt's homeland. Tristan nodded. "You will not think me overly direct if I ask you, are there any men from Guent about?"

Percival chuckled. "I'm not fond of diplomacy myself. I'd rather say what's on my mind than feast and chat and drink and beat about the bush. No, there are no men from Guent about. I'd know if there were."

"My lord is gracious to be so patient with me. But if you don't care much for diplomacy, I fear we owe you an apology for the winter we've put you through." Percival shot him a quick look full of amusement. "I understand we sent you our finest expert on feasting and chatting and beating about the bush. Er, how did you like Segward?"

Percival laughed outright. "You put me in a difficult position, sir. I can lie like any diplomat and say what a Cornish prince must want to hear, or I can tell you the truth and insult my honored guest. Tell me, Tantris, which shall it be?"

Now it was Tristan's turn to smile. "In Cornwall, we call him the Snake. His mind has more turnings than a serpent's path." He inclined his head politely. "You cannot offend me, my lord. I am no ordinary envoy."

Percival's glance sharpened. "So I have perceived."

"I come out of allegiance to Mark, out of a strong desire to hear your bards and learn your music, and—" He paused and colored slightly. "Out of a lifelong desire to meet you, my lord."

Percival's gaze was direct. "Why?"

"I've heard so many tales of your exploits. All the bards sing your praises, even in Cornwall. And if they tell true tales, you knew Sir Galahad."

"I did."

"And do you know what became of him? Each bard I hear tells a tale with a different ending. Did he really die when he found the Grail?"

Percival's smile was enigmatic. "He always was a complicated man. Have you never been to Less Britain, Tantris?"

Tristan was about to tell him Lyonesse was not far from Less Britain, two days' sail in a stiff wind, but he remembered just in time to hold his tongue.

"I've never been anywhere, my lord. If my birth would allow, I'd be a bard. I'd rather spend my days harping and making music than riding to war."

"Ah," Percival breathed. "Then that's why we've never heard of you."

Tristan's lips twisted in a smile. "Not much fuss is made about anyone but Markion in Cornwall."

Percival lifted an eyebrow. "Why do you ask about Galahad?"

"Because he, like you, was among the last of the great warriors, the Britons the bards sing about. You both fought with Arthur. You lived in his time. You knew what it was possible for men to accomplish."

Tristan spoke with passion, and Percival grew grave. "Yes," he said slowly. "We know what can be done. And so does Markion, or you wouldn't be here." He turned in the saddle and looked hard at Tristan. "I love my daughter, Tantris, more than my wife, more than either of my sons. Melleas and Logren are good, ordinary boys. But my daughter is something special. I would not willingly part with her for any price. If I had not known Arthur, if I did not think Markion shared the dream I dream, I would never let her leave Gwynedd. Tell me, Tantris, if Segward the Snake spoke the truth of this, or no."

"Markion shares your dream," Tristan replied quickly, noting the fierce light in the Welshman's eyes. Here was a man of Mark's mettle. They had better be allies, or they would make deadly enemies.

Percival nodded stiffly. "It will be done, then." They passed through the outer gates at the head of the procession and into a large courtyard paved with stone. Percival brought his stallion to a halt as grooms appeared and took the reins. "Of course, her mother is against it."

Tristan swallowed. "She is? Why?"

Percival shot him a sharp look. "How not? She's Pelleas's daughter. Marhalt was her brother. But I've fought that battle for you. She will be tame about it." He slid from the saddle, unaware that Tristan was staring at him.

"The queen—your wife—is Marhalt's *sister*?"

Percival frowned. "Certainly. How could you not know? Lord Segward and I discussed how it was to be handled."

Of course Segward had known! Tristan recalled the parting ceremony and Segward's smug smile of farewell. But surely Markion himself could not have known it. He gulped audibly. "He probably told you the less said, the better."

"Exactly. His very words."

"Dear God," Tristan breathed, "have mercy upon my soul."

But the troops were coming up all around them and Percival did not hear him. Then, out of the din of murmurs, one voice rose loud above the others.

"I challenge you, you filthy Cornishman! I challenge your right to wed a Welsh maid!"

Heads turned. From the group of companions behind the king a large young man stepped forth, dressed for battle in a brass-studded tunic and leather helmet. His naked sword flashed in the morning light.

"Palomydes!" Percival thundered. "I'll have your tongue out of your head for this! Guards!"

But Palomydes did not waver. His sword pointed at Tristan's breast and his angry eyes never left Tristan's face. "I'm within my rights, my lord, as Essylte's suitor, to challenge this foreign bastard."

"You were sent home and forbidden to set foot in Gwynedd," Percival said acidly. "And you are not her suitor. She is promised to the High King of all Britain."

Still Palomydes ignored the surrounding guards. "The queen accepted my suit, sir, although you did not. I have the right to challenge this lowborn Cornish spawn. Look at your men, my lord. Look at their faces. See how many of them welcome this foreigner on our soil."

Percival swiftly surveyed his troops. Even Tristan could see they were reluctant to arrest Palomydes. Most of them looked eager for a good fight.

White-faced, Percival moved bodily in front of Palomydes. "By God in heaven, I will not stand for this. Arrest him, you cowards, or I'll do it myself!" He whipped his sword from its ceremonial scabbard and a collective gasp went up from the crowd. The King of Gwynedd had drawn his sword against one of his own countrymen to defend a foreigner. Tristan saw shock register on even the most loyal faces.

"Be easy, my lord king!" he called out, jumping down from the horse. "I recognize his right to challenge me. With your permission, we will settle this here and now." Gathering his cloak in his left hand, Tristan drew his sword with his right. Palomydes snarled in satisfaction. Percival glared first at Tristan, then at Palomydes, but it was already beyond his power to control. The Welshmen, cheering, cleared a large circle and waited, eager and expectant, for the fight to begin.

"Fools, both of you!" Percival snapped. "The future of all Britain lies in your hands today." A sharp look at Palomydes. "If you kill him, Palomydes, you will die."

"I won't kill him," Palomydes growled. "But I'll disarm him. And if I take his sword, then he goes back where he came from."

"You would start a war with Cornwall?"

"To keep your daughter in Wales, my lord, I would." Thin cheers rose from the soldiers, silenced as soon as Percival glanced their way.

"And if I take your sword," Tristan countered, "then you are the one who goes home."

"Agreed."

With a shrug, Percival backed away. Slowly, Tristan and Palomydes began to circle. The Welsh troops sang out encouragements and threats; the Cornishmen huddled silent on the edges of the throng. And everywhere men wagered coins, beads, rings, and buckles, whatever valuables they could lay their hands on, for or against one prince or the other.

With a flick of his wrist Tristan wrapped his cloak about his forearm. As he expected, Palomydes lunged. Dodging him neatly, Tristan aimed a thrust at the Welshman's waist; the blade struck a brass stud and slid off. The crowd roared at the first hit; wagers were paid in an undercurrent of furious cursing. Tristan emptied his mind of thought and let his body guide him, aware only of the firm courtyard stone beneath his boots, the wan warmth of the young sun, the cool morning breeze against his newly shaved cheek, and the familiar, welcome stretch and bunch of muscle beneath the soft slide of fabric. And, as always, the nagging burning in his side.

Within moments, he realized Palomydes was fighting not to disarm him but to cut him. The man hardly bothered with swordplay. He took every chance he got to lunge straight in. Blow after blow Tristan blocked with ease. For a swordsman, the big man was clumsy, and unlike Marhalt, he was slow. Tristan leaped and glided around him, avoiding his thrusts, landing cutting blows to his arm and shoulder, waiting for him to tire and yield. At last, blood streaming from his sword arm and sweat running from his helmet into his eyes, Palomydes cursed viciously and threw himself at Tristan. Tristan sidestepped and knocked the sword from his hand. Palomydes landed on stone and lay there, gasping. At the back of the crowd the Cornishmen cheered wildly.

Tristan bent to retrieve Palomydes's sword. As he lifted it into the light he saw a stain upon the tip, as if it had been lightly dipped in resin or painted with—He whirled to face Palomydes, who was pushing himself up. Palomydes, accepted by the queen as husband for her daughter. The queen, Marhalt's sister. Marhalt's sword, tipped with poison. He understood now who his enemy was.

In the silence Percival came forward, his eyes fastening on Tristan like an eagle's on its prey. Tristan realized the king was not the only one to have seen the flash of truth behind the disguise.

"You lied to me when you said you were no warrior. Who are you?"

They stood alone, face-to-face, in the middle of the circle. No one else had heard the question. Beyond them, still gasping, Palomydes pushed himself to his knees.

"Who *are* you?"

Tristan sheathed his sword and said nothing.

Percival's eyes slowly widened, and he paled. "My God."

Bowing, Tristan offered up the captive sword. "On Markion's behalf, my lord king, I give you back your dream. It does not matter who I am."

Percival hesitated, searching his face. At last he accepted the sword and nodded. "You are a brave man. You are welcome in my household. But I—"

A sharp gasp went up from the crowd. In the same instant, Tristan felt a searing pain between his shoulders.

"Coward!" "Blackguard!" "Shame!" the soldiers cried. Tristan staggered. His mind raced. He knew the feel of cold steel. He recognized that deadly burning. The man had thrown his dagger at his back. What was it Pernam had told him? There was no cure—the poison would have killed him had he not killed Marhalt.

"Great Mother!" he whispered. As he fell, he turned, whipping his dagger from his belt. It caught Palomydes in the throat.

10 ⚔ THE SICKROOM

Queen Guinblodwyn stood at the head of a narrow bed, looking down at the prostrate body of a wounded man. Sunlight flooded the little room. In a corner two servants had a fire going in the grate and a pot of water bubbling noisily on a tripod stand above the flames. Expressionless, the queen turned to the two girls at her side.

"It is my right to nurse him. As queen, it is my right." Essylte and Branwen nodded hastily. "But you heard the king's order. It is left for you to do." A thin smile crossed her lips. "He shames me by it, as this villain has shamed Wales by killing the Prince of Powys. Even so, I would have done my best for him. I would have cured him. But now—now I leave him to you, Essylte. We will see how much of healing you have learned."

"Yes, Mother."

"Branwen, you will report to me daily on his condition."

"Yes, my lady."

The queen turned to a small table where two jars had been set out, a mortar and pestle, a bottle of oil, and a small green linen bag. "I trust you remember how to mix the balm. I've had him stripped and washed. He will do better if he stays on his stomach. Oil his back daily to keep the skin soft. Remember, Essylte, first the hot cloth on the wound, as hot as he can bear. Don't be squeamish. Then the balm." Her hand dipped into her pouch. "I grant you access to my workroom to fetch any drug you need. Here is the key. Guard it well." Her lovely eyes narrowed in amusement. "May the Goddess be with you," she breathed, half laughing, as she turned and left.

Essylte looked at Branwen. "What's so funny?"

"She doesn't think you can do it. She thinks Percival's order will serve her own ends, not his."

Essylte looked down at the long body covered by a linen sheet. All she could see of his face was a tangle of dark hair. "It would suit her purposes if I failed? Then I *must* not fail. Father wants him to live so desperately. . . ."

"If he dies, you—we—will not go to Cornwall," Branwen said slowly.

"And then I'll be made to marry some Welsh prince five leagues from home. I'll be under her thumb forever." She gestured at the still body. "He's my pass to freedom. Will you help me heal him, Branny? You know much more of this than I."

Branwen nodded slowly. "I'll help you. If it can be done."

"Do you think he is past our help? He doesn't look it to me."

"I think your mother, the queen, is keeping some secret from us. A secret she doesn't think we'll ever guess."

"Well, that wouldn't surprise me. Do you think it's a secret we'll need to know to heal the Cornishman?"

Branwen shrugged. "I don't know. But it's odd, isn't it, that she said she could *cure* him, whereas when she spoke about you she spoke of *healing*."

Essylte frowned. "Are they not the same?"

"I'm not sure. Perhaps they are not."

"Well," Essylte said firmly, "I'm going to do my best. I've learned more than she thinks I have. But stand by me, Branny, while I have a look at his wound."

She walked to the head of the pallet and slowly pulled back the sheet. There, in the middle of his back, was a clean cloth, and underneath, a narrow, sharp-edged cut seeping dark red blood.

"It doesn't look so bad."

"But it's deep," Branwen said. "And we must get the heat and the balm down inside it."

"How?"

"Use your fingers to pull the edges of the wound apart."

Essylte shuddered. "Won't he feel it?"

"Not now. He's drugged."

Gently, Essylte placed her hands on the Cornishman's back. She was amazed at how hard his flesh was. It did not yield to gentle pressure. She had to force the edges of his wound apart. Blood oozed up, thick and glossy. "Ughhh!"

"That's fine. Nep, Lea, the hot cloth."

Branwen took the tongs from the servant and lowered the steaming cloth onto the wound. The stranger groaned.

"It's burning him!" Essylte cried, reaching for the tongs.

Branwen held her arm. "Let be. He needs the heat."

"But won't it scald his flesh?"

"Not much. The wound must heal from the inside out. We can't let his flesh close until the heat and balm have healed the inside. Otherwise he'll fester. Don't you remember old Finn the smith, who stepped on a nail?"

"I certainly do. It was disgusting."

"Your mother said that was the reason she could not save him. The flesh was healed, but the wound was still dirty. The festering spread all through him."

Essylte looked down at the inert man on the pallet, the tousled hair, the strong, wide shoulders, the long, muscled arm that bent to frame his face. "I want to save him."

"Then hold that there while I mix the balm."

Branwen went to the mixing table and began her preparations. Essylte dabbed at the bleeding wound with the cloth and used the tongs to keep the hot compress in place. The stranger had ceased his groaning and lay senseless beneath her hands. His dark hair was well cut and soft to the touch, thick and fine with a small curl at the ends. His face lay buried in the pillow, but the ear that showed was delicately scrolled and well set. The hand that hung over the pillow had long, lean fingers and a wide palm. The little finger wore a blue enameled ring. One long, well-muscled arm was gracefully flung—

"My lady, watch the hot cloth! What are you attending to?"

Essylte blushed as she retrieved the bloody compress. "Who is he, anyway? He must be highborn. He's too well made to be just anyone."

"Of course he's highborn. He's King Markion's proxy. It would be an insult to send anyone less than the foremost of his kin."

"I thought he had no kin. His father and his son and his nephew are all dead."

"This man's name is Tantris. He's the son of Markion's cousin, the grandson of Constantine's younger brother. A descendant of Cador of Cornwall."

Essylte ran her fingers tentatively through the dark locks that curled over his neck. "I wonder how old he is. He has earned my thanks forever for besting Palomydes." She shuddered. "May God forgive me for saying it, but I'm glad he's dead. The beast!"

Branwen came around to the other side of the bed with a cup of thin green liquid. "All right. Open the wound to let me pour this in. . . . There. Now, Nep, Lea, another hot cloth."

The stranger moaned again when the heat was applied, and drew a gasping breath.

"He's waking!" Essylte cried.

"Take the spoon," Branwen directed, "and when he opens his mouth, give him to drink of this. The queen left it. It's to dull the pain and put him back to sleep."

"Why can't he awaken? I want to find out who he is."

Branwen looked at her a long moment. "You know who he is, my lady. I've told you."

Essylte looked down at her patient, who stirred. Creases formed at the corners of his eyes and mouth. His breathing quickened. "I want to talk to him." She met Branwen's eyes defensively. "I—I want to know more about Markion."

Branwen spoke mildly. "There is time enough for that. Look at his face. He's beginning to feel his pain. He must sleep again until the wound heals enough that he can lie on his side. At least until tomorrow."

"Jesu Christ!" the man whispered. The long arm moved to brace against the bed.

Essylte poured the potion into the spoon and touched his cheek with a trembling finger. "Please, my lord, drink this."

He turned his head on the pillow. One brown eye looked dazedly in her direction. "Who. . . ?" Deftly Essylte spooned the medicine into his mouth. He swallowed and closed his eyes. "Dream," he sighed, and fell back asleep.

Essylte sat by his side until his breathing slowed to its former pattern and the arm hung limply from the bed. While Branwen tidied up the mixing table, Essylte found, to her own surprise, that she did not want to leave. There was nothing else for them to do. Healing needed time and rest, that she knew. She could do no more to help him than she had already done. But she felt a possessive affection for her patient, a joy in the knowledge that something she had done had helped him, and she did not want to stir from the source of this new satisfaction.

"You may go to dinner, Branwen, and Nep and Lea, too. I will remain here, in case—in case of anything."

Branwen's eyebrows lifted. "Alone?"

Essylte rose and made a pretty show of straightening her skirts. "And what possible harm can come of it while he sleeps?"

"There is nothing more to do."

"Then I will do nothing but watch over him." She nodded imperiously to the two servants. "You are dismissed." They rose, bowing low, and hurried out.

Branwen stood as still as stone, her eyes unreadable. "I will bring you your meal on a tray," she said in a flat voice, then turned on her heel and left without a curtsy.

Essylte frowned as the door closed behind her. Branwen hadn't wanted to leave, either.

Well past midnight Essylte awoke from her short slumber on the pallet. She knew instantly where she was—not in her own soft bed, but on the hard floor of the sickroom, with Branwen's vigil coming to an end. They had decided to take turns staying up and watching. Nep and Lea, too, were taking turns tending the fire. She could hear Nep's throaty breathing from the corner where he slept. They had given the wounded man two more treatments. Each time they applied the heat, he groaned and stirred, but he had not again awakened.

Essylte sat up and rubbed her eyes. The only light in the room came from the low fire glowing in the corner and the single candle burning by the bed. She could see Branwen's dim shape in the chair—no, not in the chair! Essylte jumped to her feet. Branwen sat on the bed itself.

"Branwen!" Essylte called out in a whisper. "I am ready. It's your turn to sleep."

Branwen jerked toward her, then looked quickly away, but not before Essylte caught a glimpse of her expression. Such intense tenderness and longing! In the next moment, Branwen had risen and tucked the linen sheet securely around the sleeping body. She yawned and rubbed her eyes. "There has been no change. He still sleeps. The wound is still seeping, which is a good sign."

Her voice sounded normal, but Essylte thought she trembled. In the wavering light she could not be sure. Essylte sat down in the chair and waited until Branwen lay down on the pallet. Then she unbraided her hair, combed it out, and moved silently from the chair to the bed. After checking for herself the condition of the wound, she folded her hands in her lap and composed herself to wait.

The night grew black as the candle burned low, but it was warm enough with the constant fire. Both Lea and Nep slept heavily. No sound at all came from Branwen's pallet. As Essylte stared down at the sleeping man a strange excitement took possession of her. She felt the way she imagined a newly hatched chick must feel: disoriented, unfettered, full of wonder at a world so completely new. Why she should feel so, she could not imagine.

Soundlessly, she drew the sheet down to his waist and, anointing her hands with oil, began to rub his back. His cool flesh was already smooth and supple—Branwen had thought of this before her! For a moment she paused, breathless with a pain so intense it paralyzed her. Fury, indignation, and wild, unreasoning hatred flashed through her and then passed away, leaving her scathed. She exhaled slowly. Her hands kneaded the yielding flesh with care, conforming to the shape of bone and muscle, sliding over the smooth skin with an unconscious caress. She smiled to herself. There was one thing that she could do that Branwen couldn't: sing.

Very softly, she began to hum an old Welsh lullaby. The words had long been lost, but the melody had the power to comfort. All over Wales it was sung by healers, wet nurses, and stablemasters alike. She hummed, and then softly sang, letting the notes fall singly, sweetly into the quiet dark. Slowly, it seemed, the living flesh grew warm and sentient beneath her fingers. He moved. She drew back hesitantly. His face was in shadow; all she could see was one dark eye, gleaming in candlelight, watching her steadily.

Essylte looked on in dread fascination as his naked arm extended and his fingers touched her hair. His hand lifted a long tress and pushed it away from her face. She sat very still, breathing fast, as his fingers slid up her arm to her shoulder, her neck, her throat, with a touch so gentle she could barely feel it, but with an effect so swift and so powerful she nearly gasped aloud. Ripples of excitement coursed along her skin, producing gooseflesh even where he had not touched her, until her whole body prickled with anticipation. She did not know what was happening to her. She seemed all at once so oversensitive that every breath of air sent a thrill of delight shivering through her. His dark eye regarded her. His hand lifted, paused, and fell away. She caught it between her own, gazed at it dumbly as if expecting to read in the palm the secret to its power, then brought it to her lips and kissed it.

"My lord." It came out a whisper.

The dark eye briefly closed. When it opened, its gaze was direct. A voice she had never heard before spoke clearly. "My love."

She rose unsteadily. Around her the room began to tilt and sway. She gestured once, futilely, in his direction, a gesture of supplication and denial, and fled from the chamber.

"Sweet love," he whispered to the empty night. "Don't go."

In the darkness, awake on her pallet, Branwen's eyes filled with silent tears.

For three days Essylte avoided the sickroom, yet the image of the darkened room, the bed, and the man in it swam before her eyes even in her dreams. This was a torture to her, but easier to bear than Branwen's hourly reports on his progress. Left alone to nurse the stranger, Branwen attended to his needs, fetched him water to drink, food to eat, blankets when he was cold. She opened the window for him every morning, dressed his wound, combed his hair, washed his face. Such service suited her, Essylte noted bitterly. Mild Branwen had suddenly bloomed. Against her will, Essylte listened to a wealth of intimate detail that tumbled from Branwen's lips, all told in such a tender voice that Essylte would weep in rage the moment she found herself alone.

The stranger had refused, Branwen told her one morning, to take any more of the painkilling drug, even if it meant he slept more lightly and less often. And while he usually ate very little of the soup and bread she brought him, that morning he had been ravenous. He had eaten three helpings of everything. He had asked to be shaved, and she had shaved him. He had asked for a bath—Essylte froze—but he had requested a bath slave. She had sent him two. Essylte exhaled.

"Even so," Branwen murmured, "I helped with most of the preparations. He has a horrid scar right across his middle. He wouldn't say how he got it."

"And how is his wound? Or have you been too busy gazing at his face to look at his back?"

The hint of a smile touched Branwen's lips. "Progressing well, my lady. No festering as yet."

"How soon will he be up and about?"

"At week's end, as the queen directs. Three days. But it will be another week before he can bear a tunic."

A week and three days. And then he would be back among his countrymen, feasting with Percival and beyond her reach.

That evening Essylte waited in a corner of the hall until Branwen went down to dinner with her patient's empty tray. Then, gathering her courage, Essylte entered the room again. The man was asleep. Lea, tending the coals, ducked her head in greeting. Essylte went to the small window, facing west, and looked out at the sea. It had been a cool day, and the salt breeze eddied against her cheek, damp and chill. The last rays of light shot gold across the glittering sea. Overhead, the first faint stars appeared. She reached out to close the shutter against the coming cold of night.

"Don't," a male voice said behind her. "Please."

She whirled. He had only been dozing. He pushed himself up on his elbows and regarded her. Now that she could see his face, she understood all too well Branwen's bloom. Here was nourishment for the daydreams of any lonely girl! Youth, strength, charm, virility, all were there in that serious face with its fine bones and clear, dark eyes. She hadn't known there were men like that in Cornwall. She had never seen such a man in Wales.

"I beg your pardon, my lord, I didn't mean to wake you."

"I wasn't asleep."

How direct, those eyes! He held out a hand to her, palm upward. Without willing it, she moved to his bedside and placed her hand in his. His face lit.

"You are the one!" he breathed, and brought her hand to rest against his freshly shaved cheek. "I've been waiting for you. Where did you go?"

He swung to a sitting position and gently took her arm, drawing her down to sit beside him. Essylte tried to look away. Heat rose to her face, but she could not take her eyes from his.

"You are the one who sang to me?"

"Yes, my lord." The words came out a whisper.

"You are the answer to a prayer." He touched her face. "I thought you were an angel. You disappeared. I waited days, weeks, years. I have been waiting my whole life for you, I think. Who are you?"

But speech was beyond her. She thrilled to his touch just as she had the last time, but now he was no longer weak and near sleep. Her pulse raced as his arm slipped around her waist and held her firmly. She closed her eyes as he bent his head and kissed her. His lips were soft, sweet, demanding, moving on her mouth as her budding passion rose in a sudden swell of unexpected force. She was in his arms, holding him, surrendering to his caresses without a thought beyond the wild joy of the next kiss. Flushed, they gazed shyly at one another. The light had gone from the room. The servant had slipped out.

"You are a sorceress!" he breathed. "I never meant to—but I—" He looked at her helplessly, his brown eyes huge and defenseless. "I love you from my soul," he whispered, "and I don't even know your name."

She slid to the floor, grasping his hand, clutching it to her breast as her tears spilled down.

"Sweet angel, what is it?" He pushed back the hair from her face and lifted her chin. "Have I frightened you? I'm not so bad when you get to know me. I'm rarely so impulsive. But I've been dreaming of you—it seems like forever I've been dreaming. Could you square it with your mistress and come to Cornwall with me? Would you? I will marry you tonight if you're willing, I swear by all that's holy. Say you're not promised to anyone. I'm a—a prince of sorts. I can give you a fine castle. Oh, sweet, say you are not wed to another! For as God is my witness, you were meant for me." He bent down to her and kissed her again. She slid her arms about his neck and wept against his shoulder.

The door opened and light came into the room.

"My lady!" Branwen advanced with a candle, followed by Nep and Lea. "Oh, no. Oh, no."

Essylte rose, wiping away her tears and struggling to compose her features, not daring to look at the Cornishman's face. "Go away, Branwen. What is it you want?"

Branwen stared first at one of them and then at the other. "You can't," she breathed, fastening on Essylte. "You can't. You will dishonor your father. Your mother will kill us all. For God's sake, Essylte, let him be!"

"You stay out of it! It's none of your concern."

"How not, when I serve King Percival, who arranged the match? His honor is at stake here. Do you care nothing for your father's honor?"

Essylte bowed her head and covered her face with her hands. Branwen turned to the bed. The Cornish prince stared at them both.

"Essylte?" It was a whisper, incredulous.

Branwen looked down at him. "And who else did you imagine she might be?" Her voice was bitter. "This is Essylte, King Percival's daughter. King Markion's bride. If the queen knew you had touched her, she would have your life, treaty or no. And so would the king."

The life drained out of his face. "Princess Essylte, I beg you will forgive me."

Essylte looked up amid fresh tears. "No!" she cried. "I won't. I can't." And she ran from the room.

Branwen set the candle down. "See what you have done, my lord. You've complicated everything. I told you this morning not to let anyone tend you but me."

"There must be—some mistake."

"No mistake. I have served her since I was five years old, and she four."

He shut his eyes tightly. "Oh, Branwen, I wish I were dead. Hell itself has no more pain than this."

Tears sprang to Branwen's eyes as she turned away. "Hell, my lord, has many gates."

11 ✝ PERCIVAL'S DAUGHTER

Essylte went back to him simply because she could not stay away. She would look at him, so near and so unreachable, and he would return her gaze with equal longing. The moment always came when she could not bear it a moment longer, and ran away. And then, alone with her thoughts, she would rant aloud and argue in circles, and weep and pray until she thought she would lose her wits. At such a moment, the torture of his presence was preferable to the torture of his absence, and she would go back to him. In such fits and starts they gradually became acquainted.

"Have you a harp?" he asked one day, when they ran out of small talk and could do little but gaze at one another. "Bring it to me that I may sing to you."

Branwen shot him a curious look, but Essylte thought nothing of it. Plenty of Welshmen plucked a harp at the end of a feast or on holy days, and sang to it, too—why shouldn't a Cornishman? She sent for a lap harp and both girls settled down to listen, hoping he had more skill than his youth promised. When he had tuned it, he turned to them and gravely inclined his head.

"This is for both of you," he said solemnly. " 'The Rose and the Wanderer.' " From the first touch of his fingers upon the strings they were enchanted, amazed at the glorious music that flowed from the instrument, enraptured by the ancient tale and the clear, melodic voice that sang as sweetly as the harp itself. He moved them first to laughter and then to tears, all the while watching their upturned faces, enchanted in his turn.

They left the harp by his bedside. Every time Essylte came to see him he played for her, or she sang to him, for while music filled the space between them, they could gaze at one another with better ease. His skill increased with practice. Essylte rejoiced, but Branwen grew thoughtful.

Tristan seldom spoke directly to Essylte but chattered constantly to Branwen, calling her by little endearments that sometimes brought a blush to her cheek. "My pretty Branwen," he would say, "my little gray-eyed nymph, my morning rosebud." He could always cajole her out of silence with his easy, graceful ways.

Essylte, hearing his flattery and seeing the blush on Branwen's cheek, found she did not mind at all. She saw Branwen for the first time as a man might see her: slender, pretty in a pale, faded sort of way, neat in her movements, with a quick grace and ready tongue. For the first time it occurred to her that Branwen might not always serve her, that one day soon she might find a husband of her own. Essylte frowned. It astonished her that she shrank from the idea. It astonished her that she had never thought of it before.

Although she could bear his compliments to Branwen with passable ease, Essylte trembled from head to foot and turned alternately hot and cold whenever Tristan looked her way. She knew he often observed her when he thought she wasn't looking, just as she stole glances at him when Branwen held his eye. Where, she wondered helplessly, would it all end?

One day she overheard her mother coldly inform the king that the Cornish prince was nearly healed. He could return to his countrymen the next morning and go back to Cornwall when he willed, the sooner the better, in her opinion. He would live.

Essylte hurried to the sickroom with the news. She stopped on the threshold. He stood at the window, in boots and leggings, shrugging off his tunic, while Branwen ran her hand over the flaming knife scar on his back.

"The flesh is closed, my lord, but it's no wonder it's so tender. The scar is still the color of blood."

He shrugged and bunched his tunic in his hands. "I know the feel of it. It will never heal. It's like the other." Then he looked up and saw Essylte.

She clung to the doorpost. It was the first time she had seen him on his feet. He was taller than Palomydes, with broad shoulders and a neat waist. The sheer animal beauty of him stirred her strangely. Even his scar—surely a battle wound—added to his allure. A purple slash across his flesh, it began on his right side, under the rib, and tore upward across his chest past the midline. How had he lived after such a blow?

He saw her looking and clutched the tunic tight against his chest. The desire to reach out and touch him was almost more than she could bear. Wildly, she cast about for something, anything, to say. "The scar will not heal, did you say? Why not?"

He held her eyes and slowly brought out the words. "I was cut, once, by a poisoned sword."

Her breath came fast, too fast. She gulped and tried to slow it. "Poisoned? Why, sir, you have come to the right place. We have balms that can heal any poison."

"I knew," he murmured huskily, "I had come to the right place."

Essylte turned and ran. She ran all the way to the queen's workroom, unlocked it with the key from her pouch, and searched among the shelves for her mother's special balm, the antidote to her pride concoction, devilsbane. The stuff was so powerful it could counteract anything. At the back of the shelf her hand alighted on the clay pot that bore her mother's seal. Here it was, at last. She hurried back to the sickroom to find the prince standing stiffly by the window and Branwen frowning by the brazier, nervously plucking at her skirts. Essylte approached and held out the pot of salve.

"Try this, my lord."

He drew a long breath as she came near him, and dropped the tunic from his hands. "You do it. Please."

Trembling, she dipped her fingers in the cool salve and lightly touched the scar over his breast. For a long moment nothing happened. Then he gasped. "Mother of God!"

Under her fingers the puckered, purple flesh faded to red, then pink, then pale, then disappeared altogether. Quickly, she applied the salve to the length of the long scar, and within moments his flesh was as new and whole as if he had never been wounded.

"It's a marvel!" she cried. "It's bewitchment!"

He turned. "Quickly! Try it on my back."

She did, and again the scar dissolved itself into new flesh. "How does it feel, my lord?"

He laughed aloud for joy. "Like heaven, you wonderful angel! The burning is gone, and all the pain—you have given me back my health and strength!"

He reached out to take her in his arms, unthinking, and they both froze as their fingers met. Branwen flung herself to the floor and reached under the bed, searching wildly for the swordbelt that had been thrown there with his boots when he had been brought in. She pulled it out and held the scabbard in her hand.

Tristan jerked toward her. "Branwen, don't."

Holding her breath, she drew the sword. "My God."

She met his eyes. He stiffened. "Don't."

"What's the matter?" Essylte cried.

Branwen began to shake so hard the sword waved wildly.

"Please don't," Tristan repeated softly.

"I should have known," she breathed. "I should have known when you played for us. I should have known by the tale, by the fight, by your scar, by your grace, your looks, your voice, by a thousand things—"

"Please, Branwen. Don't."

"Did you really think you could get away with it?"

"Get away with what?" Essylte demanded. "What is going on?"

Branwen's eyes never left his face. "You," she said slowly, lowering the sword. "You're the most notorious man in all of Wales. You are Tristan of Lyonesse."

For a long moment no one spoke. Essylte, eyes on his immobile face, laughed nervously. "Don't be ridiculous, Branny. Tristan's dead. Everyone knows that. Prince Tantris is his kin—of a certainty it is a family name."

Branwen held out the sword. "Look at the blade."

As Essylte stepped forward a shadow darkened the door. Branwen whirled and thrust the sword behind her, but too late. Queen Guinblodwyn stood on the threshold. Her sharp eyes flicked from the warrior's naked chest to the pot of salve in Essylte's trembling fingers, to the empty scabbard on the floor, and came to rest on Branwen. She did not move, but a sudden chill encased the room. Branwen shivered.

"Give me the sword."

"But my lady—"

Nostrils flared, the queen pointed a finger at her. "Give me the sword."

Branwen obeyed. The queen held the weapon in her hands, examining the blade. A third of the way from the hilt a small chunk of metal was missing, the jagged edges around the gap neatly filed to razor sharpness. Guinblodwyn reached into the bodice of her gown and drew forth a small square of folded silk. Within the silk nestled a little, shining metal chip. Branwen watched at her elbow as she slid the chip into the gap in the blade. It was an almost perfect fit. Slowly the queen raised her head. Branwen, hardly daring to draw breath, slipped out the door and fled.

"You killed my brother Marhalt." The words, spoken distinctly, dropped into the silence like icicles into still water.

Wearily, Tristan nodded. "In a fair fight."

She raised the sword and aimed the point at his breast. "You owe me a life."

"No!" Essylte threw herself in front of Tristan, holding him behind her. "It doesn't change anything—It was a fair fight—You *won't* kill him! He's Father's guest! You have no right! You gave me leave to heal him, and I did!"

Inexorably the queen approached, the sword held level. "Get out of my way."

Essylte burst into tears. "Kill me, then! Go ahead! I don't want to live without him, anyway!"

Guinblodwyn stopped, aghast. "Are you mad? You would die for your uncle's murderer? Where is your honor, Essylte? Where is your sense? This man has murdered, cheated, and lied—there is no honor in defending him. Let me have him and you shall marry whomever you will—I care not—*but get out of my way!*"

"Never!" Essylte cried, even as Tristan took her by the waist and set her down to one side. The queen lunged. Tristan, expecting it, dove, rolled, leaped to his feet, and snatched the sword from her grasp before she could gather herself for another blow. She screamed and flew at him with her nails, opening the flesh on his shoulder. Firmly, he held her off.

"My lady queen, I wish you might accept my apologies for something that I wish, I truly wish, had never happened."

"Fiend! Swine! Demon! I spit on the spawn who begot you!"

"I had nothing against Marhalt as a man. I never knew him. He was brave, and an excellent fighter. I was lucky, no more. It could have gone either way."

"You had the gall to come *here!* To *my* home! Who do you think we are, that we would stand for it?"

"I know who you are. You are the witch who poisoned Marhalt's sword. You wished me dead long before I wished any harm to Marhalt."

"What?" Essylte cried, pushing forward. "Is this true, Mother? You put poison on Uncle Marhalt's sword? And—and on Palomydes's dagger?"

"I put more than poison on that blade," the queen snapped. "I placed a curse on it as well. I did everything within my power to ensure Marhalt's success and your father's right to the throne of Britain. What did you expect? That with such power at my fingertips I should sit idly by and leave it for men to decide? All Marhalt had to do was nick the skin of his opponent. For a man his size, it should have been an easy enough thing to do." Her voice began to tremble as tears welled in her eyes. "He couldn't lose. I made sure of that. He couldn't lose that fight."

Tristan loosed his hold of her arms and spoke quietly. "It wasn't that kind of fight. Emotions were running high. Marhalt set himself to kill me. He warned me of it. He did more than nick me, as you saw yourself. He cut me well. If you had let him alone and trusted to his skill, I'd have died of that wound there on the battlefield. I was already blind and dying, with his hands around my throat, when I grabbed the sword and struck him. It was your curse on the sword that preserved me when he died."

Guinblodwyn shrieked and flung her arms into the air. She wailed and screeched in a tongue Tristan did not know.

"What's she saying?" he whispered to Essylte. "What tongue is that?"

Essylte gazed at her mother in bewilderment and consternation. "Mountain Welsh. I thought she'd given it up. . . . She's cursing the foul fates. And asking Uncle Marhalt's shade to forgive her. She's calling on the Great Goddess for revenge. . . . What did you mean, that the curse preserved you?"

"It was meant to make Marhalt's victory certain, so that even if we had the antidote to the poison, the curse itself would kill. But when Marhalt died, the effect of the curse was reversed, saving me. That's all I know about it."

Essylte shuddered. "That's the trouble with witchery—it's double-sided nonsense. Oh!" She clutched Tristan's arm. "She's just promised the Goddess my life for yours."

Guinblodwyn turned to them with narrowed eyes, dry now of tears.

"Hear this, demon spawn of Cornwall. If I cannot kill you, I will curse you. You can never, ever escape a Druid's curse."

"Druid!" He glanced swiftly at Essylte, who stared in horror at her mother and crossed herself fervently.

The low voice spoke levelly. The words echoed in the room as in a vast cavern, and a damp chill crept into Tristan's bones. "Five generations shall you father, and each of your descendants shall die before his time—a foul death, and without honor. Four women shall place their trust in you and live to see that trust betrayed. Three children shall your loins beget: a whore, a destitute beggar, and a murdering rogue. Twice will you swear before your God an oath you cannot keep—lies you will be called to answer for. And one day—" She drew nearer, her eyes burning in her drawn face. "One day, a man of your own blood shall avenge me, shall kill you when you least expect it, shall slay you with your own cursed sword! Yes, you shall die by the very sword that killed my brother. And in the hour of your death, Essylte, too, shall die. That is what I have promised the Goddess."

She laughed suddenly, shrilly, and, backing away, drew a dagger from her pouch. Tristan had her wrist in an instant and pulled her arm behind her. Trapped against his body, she spat in his face.

Feet ran down the corridor, voices sang out in the hall.

"Branwen!" the queen snarled.

The doorway swelled with people, soldiers, courtiers, servants. Percival stood in the center of the throng with Branwen at his side.

"Loose the queen!" he demanded.

Wrenching the jeweled dagger from her hand, Tristan let her go. Percival paled at the sight of the dagger and turned to his wife.

"You promised me."

Guinblodwyn straightened. "I did not know then, my lord, you schemed to give a traitor shelter under our roof." She spoke with a calm dignity and raised her voice that everyone might hear. "This man is no cousin of King Markion's. He is his nephew, Tristan of Lyonesse. The villain who slew my brother Marhalt. He has confessed it."

A murmur of protest swept through the throng of people. Percival's features hardened. "Whoever he is, he is here as Markion's proxy. We have only one choice before us: continue this blood feud and wage war with Cornwall, or put the past behind us and look ahead to a future as a united Britain." He looked around at all the nervous faces. "Let me remind you all, it was Wales that started this fracas. If my uncle Peredur had not been so ambitious for my honor, the queen's brother would be alive today and we could honor this prince as he deserves."

"Deserves!" the queen screeched. "You are mad! Kill him!"

Wearily, Percival signaled to his guards. "Remove her."

The room cleared rapidly once the queen had gone. Essylte helped Tristan into his tunic, and he strapped on his swordbelt.

"My lord," said the king, "it will be best if you leave tonight. Attend to your countrymen. They will be in danger even if I send extra guards. You will be safest on the ship. Essylte, Branwen, make ready at once. You will sail at dawn. We will forgo the ceremony." He kissed them both and sighed unhappily. "This is not how I would have it, but I see no other way. Be brave, my daughter. This is not farewell. When your son is born, I myself will come to Cornwall. Until then, remember the importance of what lies before you. Britain herself is in your hands. Let us pray to God that what starts ill ends well."

Late that night, when the moon had sunk into the sea, Queen Guinblodwyn summoned Branwen to her workroom. The girl had not slept. There had been far too much to do, and too little time. She found the queen alone in the dark chamber, a pair of candles on the worktable shedding the only light. The queen was robed in black. All Branwen could see of her was her cold, white face and her pale hands.

"Ah, Branwen. Thank you for coming so promptly."

"My lady."

"Sit down. I will not keep you long. No doubt the king wants to spirit you all away on the dawn tide."

"Yes, my lady."

Her lips thinned. "Percival thinks he is being clever." She studied the girl's face. Branwen found it impossible to meet her eyes.

"Tell me, Branwen, what do you want from life?"

Branwen looked up quickly. The queen's face was perfectly smooth, empty of expression. "Me, my lady?"

"I see behind your meek façade, my dear. You are intelligent enough to be ambitious. A woman of your mettle will not be content to be my daughter's handmaiden all her life. Don't deny it. Only a fool would want to serve Essylte."

"My lady does her an injustice."

"Do I? Perhaps. I confess she is a disappointment to me. You ought to have been my daughter. You have ambitions above your station, don't you, Branwen?"

Branwen's eyes were caught in the queen's gaze and held there. "Yes, my lady."

"Good. What is it you aspire to?" Branwen shrugged. "I knew your mother, Keridwen," Guinblodwyn mused. "When I first came to Gwynedd, she was tending the kitchen gardens. I brought her to help me in here. She was a magician with herbs. She healed anything she touched."

Branwen's eyes widened and her mouth went dry. She had not known her mother served Guinblodwyn.

"It's a shame she was not higher born. As it is, with your bastard blood, you can hardly hope to marry a lord in Cornwall. What, then, do you aspire to?"

Her face flaming, Branwen shrugged again.

The queen's voice sank to a gentle murmur. "You can't have *him*, you know. He loves Essylte and he always will. Don't grieve over it. It's a waste of your time. He's a simpleton, in any event. You deserve someone cleverer than that."

Branwen said nothing. Guinblodwyn rose and went to the shelf behind her, selecting three small dyed linen bags tied at the necks with silken cord.

"I am giving you three gifts before you go. Use them well. If you are as wise as I think you are, you will live a future that you choose."

She placed the first bag, a green one, in the pool of candlelight.

"This herb is the giver of sleep. One pinch in liquid, and whoever drinks it will sleep the sleep of children, deep, unwakeable, and long. Three pinches produce a painless death, five hours in coming. Save some for old age." A crimson bag dropped into the candlelight. "Loversbane. An aphrodisiac so powerful there is not a man on earth who will not be driven to consummation within an hour of taking it." The queen smiled. "Nor any woman. Remember this when you find the man you want."

Branwen hesitated. "Is that all it does? Does it not produce love?"

Guinblodwyn stiffened. "It's a distillation of nine herbs, not a magic potion. It will not produce passion out of nothing. It will intensify emotion. In some instances, that may be enough to bring forth love out of liking. But I advise you not to place much importance on love. It never lasts. You cannot afford to be romantic, Branwen."

A black bag was pushed into the light. "And this is my special gift to you. Witchbane. Deadly. Painful. Quick. Tasteless in wine or strong, hot tea. No one will know." Her voice sank to a whisper. "This is a key to the highest power in the land. With this, you control your enemies. But it does not come free. There is a price." She leaned forward until the circle of her white face shone fiercely in the light. "Kill him. I need his death. Kill him on the ship and they will not have the courage to face Markion. You will be back home, with no questions asked, within the fortnight. I will find you a suitor worthy of you, you have my word. Or kill him in Cornwall, and set them all by the ears. Let them accuse one another and fight among themselves. Let it be done where and when you choose. I don't care, Branwen, so long as he dies. But die he must."

Branwen reached out a trembling hand and took the linen bags, tucking them securely in her pouch. The queen sat back, a cold smile on her lips.

"And if I don't kill him?"

"Then I have misjudged you." The white face leaned forward again. "Don't cross me, Branwen. You will regret it. I curse you thus: While he lives, your children will be girls, heir to nothing. And it won't save Tristan. If you don't kill him, he will come someday to the fate he deserves. I have cursed him, and it will be so."

She paused. Her voice grew weary; lines appeared around her eyes. "I should be having this conversation with Essylte, not you. These should be her gifts, received from her mother on the eve of leaving home, as I received them from my mother, the Lady Niniane, when I came here to marry Percival. But my daughter, to my great grief, is a light-headed fool. She would not listen to a word I said."

"She would disdain your gifts, my lady," Branwen said slowly. "She would call them witchery and throw them in the sea."

Guinblodwyn rose. "That is why I gave them to you. Though we share no blood, you are more like me than she is. And you are royal." She smiled bleakly. "You see, Branwen, I know who you are."

The girl froze on her stool, afraid her next breath might be her last. The queen laughed lightly.

"Don't be so afraid. He lay with Keridwen before he married me. You are the only one of his bastards who is not a slap in my face. You have helped Essylte grow to womanhood, much good may it do her. I owe you something."

Somehow, Branwen found her voice. "How did you know?"

"Oh, I have always known, though he thinks he hides it from me. But tell me, brave Branwen, when will you tell Essylte you are Percival's daughter?"

Branwen swallowed. "Never."

The queen smiled. "Oh, yes. You will. I have seen it in my glass. Someday you will."

12 ⚔ THE STORM

Tristan stood on the slippery deck and frowned at the rolling horizon. In the west the sky was black. He turned around, catching hold of a hemp stay as the ship pitched wildly. There, faint through the cold, streaming mists, ever present like a vision in a nightmare, he could see the shoreline. Wales. The last place he could land. He scowled up at the small patch of sail, reefed down tight against the storm. Just his luck to have a coward for a captain. At this rate, they would be a month getting to Cornwall. Meanwhile, Essylte had not eaten in two days. He was tempted to raise the sail himself and send the small ship flying over the heaving sea, but he was in enough trouble with the captain as it was. Thanks to him, they had left on the wrong tide, just as bad weather threatened. He knew the sailors blamed him for it; so did his own soldiers. What did it matter? They were strong men all, and those who were sick would soon recover. All that mattered was that Essylte got ashore without delay.

He shut his eyes. He could not even think of her without feeling heat in his face. He could not bear to think of the future, could not bear to look even a week ahead. He shuddered at the thought of what she would be made to endure when she reached Cornwall—Mark's rough embraces, his crude jests, his boorish flattery. It was not possible to give that girl to Mark. He could never do it. And yet he must.

For the better part of two days and a night he had paced the fitful deck, unable to rest, but it had not helped. Nothing helped. Knowing the end— the inescapable end—made no difference. Some things, he swore under his breath, could not be reconciled with justice. Some things, however in-evitable, were simply wrong.

He opened his eyes to find Branwen at his elbow. The wind caught at her cloak and whipped it behind her. She gathered it up neatly in her small white hands.

"Ah, Branwen." He raised his voice above the wind's bellow. "I'm glad to see you."

The cool hazel-gray eyes met his own. "And I you, my lord."

"How is it below?"

The girl paused as she gathered the hood tighter around her face. "I have given her a sleeping potion. At least she does not suffer while she sleeps."

"Bless you for that. You are skilled with drugs?"

"My mother was skilled, my lord. I have inherited her interest."

"Modest girl. I wish you had a remedy for—all our ills."

She turned to him sharply but saw only his profile against the gray-green sea. "Your suffering will soon be over."

"Will it?"

"You will return to Lyonesse after the wedding. We will be at Camelot. It will be over."

He smiled bitterly. "Tintagel. You'll be at Tintagel. He'll never take her to Camelot. He doesn't like women there."

He saw her surprise, followed by disappointment, quickly masked. "And where is Tintagel?"

"Closer to Lyonesse than to Camelot, sweet Branwen. Oh, God!" He drew a long breath. "It doesn't bear thinking about."

They stood together and looked out at the distant shore, hidden inter-mittently by squalls of mist and rain. Beneath them the seas heaved and sank, and ran beyond them.

"We don't seem to be making much headway," Branwen ventured.

"What do you expect, with a sail the size of a washrag? By the Light! I've half a mind to cut that rope and haul it up myself."

"Won't the captain raise it?"

"Under no conditions." He pointed to the black sky behind them. "All he wants is enough sail to keep us from foundering in the sea. He's worried about his precious ship. Meanwhile, she sickens and starves."

"Well, my lord, if the ship founders, my lady is certainly lost," Branwen pointed out, "so perhaps you would do well to let the captain worry."

Tristan smiled, and for a moment his features lightened. "I *am* acting like a fool—I beg your pardon, Branwen. It's just that I'm responsible. . . ."

"My lord, I know the cause."

He stepped aside to let two sailors pass. They ducked their heads at him and began unlashing the thick ropes that bound the sail.

"What's this?" Tristan cried. "More sail at last?"

"Captain's orders, my lord!" one of the sailors shouted. "This looks to be a right wicked blow. We'll not try to ride it out after all. Captain says we'll go inshore and look for a safe harbor."

"Thank God!" Tristan crossed himself with fervor. "That's half my prayer answered."

Branwen looked up at him. "And the other half?"

"That we make it to the Severn estuary."

"The estuary? You don't aim for Caerleon?"

"No. Even though Markion holds it, it's too near Guent for safety. But if we can make it to the Dumnonian coast on the southern shore of the estuary, we might take shelter there with a lord I know. He's got a house on a point of land, a run-down villa from Roman days. But at least it's shelter. We could ride the storm out there if we make it in time."

They watched the men hoist the sail halfway up the mast. The ship sprang to life, bucking in the wind like a green horse, flying forward, flung on her beam at every wave crest, wallowing unsteadily in every trough. Tristan began to feel uneasy; Branwen went white. The captain himself approached and bowed, hiding a grin.

"Best go below, my lord. It'll be rough work on deck. And wet."

"I can see that. At this rate, how long until the Severn?"

"Nightfall, if we're lucky. It's a race against that storm. If she hits first, I'm heading for a harbor, I don't care whose land it is."

You will, Tristan thought, *when they cut our throats,* but he did not say it.

An hour past nightfall they raised the Severn estuary in a sheet of rain and a rising wind. Scudding like a leaf in a stiff breeze, the ship tore inland before the westerly gale, jerking in her rope stays, careening from crest to trough, her sail half in shreds, four strong men hanging on the tiller. At last, a low cliff jutting well out into the estuary afforded them protection in its lee. They dropped the anchor and swung to, riding heavily in the swells. Above them on the cliff shone the dim lights of a villa. The captain grumbled that they'd better try their luck with whoever lived there, as the ship had taken on water and if the crew did not spend all night bailing, she'd sink to the bottom and they could walk the rest of the way. Taking the hint, Tristan ordered his men ashore to commandeer whatever boats they could find and take the women off. Essylte, deep in her drugged sleep, could not be awakened. Tristan wrapped her well in cloaks and blankets and carried her in his arms.

The path up the cliff face was steep, slippery, and guarded. At the top three sentries challenged them. Tristan peered through the rain at one of them.

"By God, Blamores, is that really you? Is this Rook Point?"

The man gasped. "*Tristan? Tristan of Lyonesse? You're alive!*"

"It will take more than a Welsh sword to kill *me*! But a cold night in a Cornish storm might do it."

"Come with me, my lord. I'll take you in myself, and all your company. There's room aplenty since my lord Guvranyl's away."

"Guvranyl's not here? Where is he? With Mark?"

"Aye. Awaiting the Welsh princess."

Tristan grunted. "I have her in my arms."

Guvranyl's house was of stone and wood, patched with plaster, a long, low, rambling building that enclosed a courtyard where a garden had once stood. A high wall protected its landward approach; guardhouses stood along the edge of the cliff. Secure from thieves, Tristan noted, but not from Saxons. Easy to take from the sea if you had numbers.

Old Junius the caretaker met him at the door, grinning his toothless grin of welcome.

"By the blood of the Bull, if it isn't young Tristan, alive and hearty! Just look how you've grown."

Branwen shot him an amused glance as he colored briefly. "Not now, Junius, I beg you. The lady is ill. We'll take Guv's chamber, since he's left it for us. We'll need a fire and hot water and hot broth. Does the roof still leak?"

"In places. But not in the master's chamber. Come along, come along. You remember the way."

Guvranyl, Tristan explained to Branwen as they followed the old servant through tiled passageways, was Markion's chief swordmaster, and Meliodas's before that. From childhood, he had taught Tristan everything he knew about fighting, riding, wrestling, and battle tactics. "He must be old as the hills, fifty if he's a day, but still as nimble as a cat. He still teaches the more talented recruits. I was hoping he'd be here; I haven't seen him since we buried Constantine. And Gerontius . . . Ah, here we are."

Guvranyl's chamber was large, simply furnished, and swept scrupulously clean. The walls were patched, the cracked mosaics on the floor carefully mended, the narrow windows shuttered well against the storm. Everything in the room had an obvious use; nothing was ornamental. A broad oak bed stood against the wall near a pine clothes chest and a double-flamed lamp. In one corner sat the metal tub for bathing and the covered waste pot; in the other, a small brazier. A hanger for a Roman sword hung on the wall above the bed. There was nothing else.

"A chair," Branwen murmured. "Can I have a chair brought in, to sit beside her?"

"You may have anything you like." Tristan sat on the bed and let Essylte slide gently from his arms. Her pale face looked serene and peaceful, surrounded by her turbulent, blazing hair. He glanced at the one blanket of fine-combed wool neatly folded across the foot of the bed. "We'll need more blankets, Junius. Furs if you have them. And another brazier. And food, for God's sake. Branwen, how long until she wakes?"

"By midnight the drug will leave her, my lord, but if she's warm and comfortable, she may not wake. Don't worry. Sleep is the best thing for her."

"I wish," he whispered, "I wish I had a magic salve to give her, as she gave me." His finger traced a gentle line from ear to chin, then slowly he withdrew his hand and rose. "Junius, have a pallet made in here for Branwen, and send a servant to attend the princess."

"My lord—" she began, but he shook his head and smiled.

"You must sleep, too. And she must not go untended."

"And you, my lord?"

He shrugged and gestured vaguely toward the door. "I'll be nearby."

"Try to sleep, my lord." Branwen laid a gentle hand upon his arm. "You have not slept since we left Wales. You look like death. What good can you do her without rest?"

"If I do, will you rouse me when she awakens?"

"As soon as she gives me leave."

He glanced again at the bed and then nodded. "All right. After I've seen to the men, I'll try. I can't promise more."

Late that night the wind rose to a screaming pitch, hurtling rain at the shutters, battering the doors. Tristan lay awake on a narrow bed, staring at a ceiling he could not see, listening. The unrestrained fury of the storm filled him with excitement and foreboding. His body lay taut as a drawn bow, refusing to relax toward sleep. He had felt like this, he remembered, that day his father rode away to fight Irish raiders in spite of the soothsayer's warning, and again, on the eve of his first real battle, where he had expected to meet Percival and had met Marhalt instead. He knew what such a dreadful thrill betokened. Something was coming, something that would change his life forever. The shadow of its approach already lay across him.

Toward dawn the wind died to a fitful howl, and rain fell in a steady roar. Someone tapped lightly on his door.

"She is awake, my lord, and taking broth. She is not ready yet to see you. Wait until midday, she begs you, if you please."

Tristan sighed, his eyelids suddenly heavy. "Thank God," he whispered, and was asleep.

He awoke to the opening of his door. Junius himself entered with a candle and lit the lamp at the foot of his bed. Through the open doorway Tristan saw a servant trimming the wicks and lighting the lamps in the hall.

"Junius?"

"My lord?"

"It can't be the time of lamplighting."

Junius grinned, showing gums. "Can't it?"

Tristan pushed himself up. He did not feel slow and leaden, as he usually did when he had slept too long; he felt refreshed, awake, eager. The familiar pain in his side was gone. He realized with surprise that he had not felt so wonderful in a very long time.

"Tell me the truth, you old pagan devil. What hour of the day is it?"

Junius laughed. "I swear by Lord Mithra Himself, young master, it is the hour of sunset."

"No wonder I feel so good." He swung his feet to the floor, but Junius went to the door and clapped imperiously. Three bronze-skinned boys entered carrying a tub, ewers of hot water, and armfuls of towels. "Not now, good Junius, although I'm sorely tempted—I must see to the Princess Essylte."

"Oh, aye, your solicitude is understandable enough," Junius agreed, directing the bath slaves to a spot in the corner. "There's not a man on Rook Point, warrior or slave, who hasn't been charmed out of his shoes by the Princess Essylte."

"She is up, then, and well enough to walk about?"

"Oh, I'd say so." Junius chuckled, unfastening Tristan's tunic. "She and that quick-eyed maid of hers, who's no servant born, if you ask me, have explored the house from kitchen to stables. Talked to everyone, they have, asked a million questions—mostly," Junius said with a grin, tucking Tristan's dirty tunic beneath his arm, "about you. What a pretty pair they are! Did you bring the brown-haired one for you?"

"Bring the—oh! You mean Branwen. No, of course not. They've been raised together, she chose to come. And Essylte is well? No fever? No pallor?"

Junius raised an eyebrow. "It was only seasickness. A good sleep and a hot meal, she's right as rain. What a blessing youth is! Now stop dawdling and get in that bath."

"I don't have time—if it's already lamplighting, I have to see to dinner—"

Junius grinned. "It's been seen to, young master, while you were sleeping. Didn't I tell you they'd been to the kitchens? Dinias showed them all through the storerooms. They're preparing a feast for you, to thank you for their safety. I'm to take you to them as soon as you're clean enough."

"In that case," Tristan replied, smiling, "I think I'll bathe."

The hot water felt glorious on his skin. The fresh tunic Junius brought him had to be the best in the house—soft, combed wool, bleached white, with a wide blue border. Junius found oiled sandals for his feet, and a blue robe of good thick wool.

"A proper prince you look now, my young lord." Junius nodded in satisfaction.

Tristan smiled. "Your Roman blood is showing."

The rain had stopped. He pushed open the shutters to drink in the rich, earth-laden scents of evening. Stars, clean-washed and bright, swarmed overhead in thick profusion. Somewhere, a nightingale was singing. All his senses seemed suddenly alive and heightened, just as on the night he had met Marhalt. Time slowed down. Each passing moment brought him its own gift to savor and enjoy. He wondered if this was how God felt always, if this was what the Sacred Scrolls meant by "the fullness of time." It was, to him, the blessing of all blessings.

"What a night!" Tristan breathed. "Tonight I believe I could conquer the world."

Watching him, Junius chuckled. "Settle instead for a maiden's heart."

Tristan paled. "God keep me from it!" He crossed himself quickly. "I swear before Christ I will not touch her. She is Markion's bride."

Junius gaped at him, then cleared his throat awkwardly. "I was talking," he said, "about Branwen."

Guvranyl's chamber was so completely transformed that when Tristan stepped across the threshold, he doubted for a moment he had opened the right door. Skins on the floors, old tapestries on the walls, silken cushions on the bed, the chairs, the floor; polished candlesticks of pewter and bronze, a small table beside a low Roman couch—where on earth had they found that old couch? He vaguely remembered it in the back of the hayloft with broken saddles, cracked reins, and assorted junk thrown upon it. Here it was, cleaned and dusted, the rents in the fabric newly stitched, looking only a quarter of its age. The general effect was startling. The old soldier's room was now a luxurious bower, simplicity and order overcome by rampant finery.

"Well! That's much better." Branwen looked him up and down. "Now I can believe my lord is King of Lyonesse." And she made him a low reverence.

Tristan smiled and raised her. "Don't judge a scroll by its seal. I'm the same man I was before I bathed and shaved."

"It's the sleep more than hot water. You look . . . well, you look ready for anything."

"Perceptive of you." Tristan glanced appreciatively around the room. "What have you two been up to? And where's Essylte? Where did you get all this stuff? Did you bring it with you from Wales? How ever did you get it off the ship?"

"Please, my lord, one question at a time. We brought very little from Wales and all of it's still on the ship. These furnishings we found here, in this house."

"In Guvranyl's house? I don't believe you. He'd never allow such trappings. He's a hard man who believes in hard beds, cold baths, and early rising. I know. I was under his tutelage for long enough."

"Then you did not know he had a wife?" A soft voice spoke behind him. He whirled. Essylte stood in the doorway, holding a wineskin. Tristan's breath caught in his throat. She wore a white gown, cut low across the breast and belted high. Around her shoulders she wore a russet cloak, dark enough to make the white dazzling and red enough to set off the flame-red highlights in her hair.

"A wife?" he croaked, furious to find he could not speak. "Not Guvranyl."

Essylte smiled. "Well, a woman, then. Someone's been living in the south wing in a style more comfortable than Sir Guvranyl's, and according to Junius, it was his wife. A brief marriage. She died a year ago in childbed and he hasn't been here much since then, but her rooms are kept just as they were. I had to promise we would put everything back before we left."

While she spoke, he watched the candlelight play on her lovely features, the thin, firm nose, the rounded cheek, the wide eyes, green in the shadows, blue in the light. The gown set off the perfection of her smooth, glowing skin, the long, graceful curve of neck and shoulder, the quick, quiet pulse at the base of her throat. The ache to touch her grew into a pain. As if she sensed his thought, her eyes met his and held them.

Tristan bent his knee and bowed his head. "My lady Essylte."

She put out a hand to raise him, and he held it firmly.

"Don't, my lord," she said softly, her voice sounding strained. "You are a king. You needn't kneel to me."

He rose, still holding her hand. "Let me choose to whom I kneel." He lifted her hand to his lips, kept it there, and let it go.

"Is that the wine?" Branwen came between them and took the wineskin. "Allow me, my lady. I'll set it to warm." She lowered her voice to Essylte. "Is my lord still standing?"

"See what we have found, my lord," Essylte said shyly. "A Roman couch. Won't you sit down?"

Tristan eyed it doubtfully. "Is it safe? Last time I saw it, mice were living in it."

Essylte flashed a smile. "We turned them out and restuffed it with straw. It's not so bad. I tried it myself."

Gingerly, Tristan sat. It wasn't uncomfortable, and Essylte looked so delighted, he pronounced it perfect. But when he offered her the seat beside him, she shied away, taking instead a chair across the table.

"You know," she said slowly, keeping her eyes lowered, "this is the first time I've seen you that you look like a king. It's—it's kind of like meeting you all over again."

"I'll do my best to make a good impression."

"I mean—if I had seen you before as you are now, surely I would have guessed who you were. You don't look like some lost cousin."

He smiled. "Then lying naked on a sickbed was a good disguise."

She blushed brightly, but her eyes were laughing. "If you are truly King of Lyonesse, why did you come to Wales at all? You must have known your life would be in danger. How could you risk it so?"

He regarded her thoughtfully. There was no point in telling her his suspicions of Mark. He must tell her only what he knew for certain.

"All my life I have wanted to meet your father. The chance came to go to Wales—I volunteered. It was a risk, but I thought it a small one. Thanks to Segward, everyone thought I was dead. No one who suspected I might live would believe me foolhardy enough to go."

"And yet," she said quietly, "you were discovered."

"By my bright-eyed Branwen," he said lightly, looking over his shoulder to where Branwen warmed the wine above the fire. "It's hard to get much past Branwen."

Branwen colored. "It is my fault, my lord, that the queen discovered you, and you got no chance to speak with Percival. I beg your pardon for it."

Tristan waved away her apology. "What's done is done. And after all, I got away with both my life and the princess. I was even cured of Marhalt's poisoned stroke. And as for Percival, perhaps he will pay us a visit next year in Cornwall." It was on the tip of his tongue to finish, *To see his grandson*, but he kept it back. Even so, Essylte looked away.

A heavy silence followed, broken only when servants entered with the meal. They set a veritable feast on the little table: fish stew, steaming hot; crusty bread fresh from the ovens; a fowl roasted in its juices and stuffed with dried spiced meat; grilled sausages; currants set in jelly; honey cakes studded with raisins; dried apples baked in the oven and swimming in cream; and combs of honey, warmed to dripping point. Tristan was amazed at such a spread, and said so.

Essylte and Branwen both looked pleased.

"Most of it was standing ready in the pantry or the storerooms," Essylte explained. "The fowl was killed in the storm when the henhouse collapsed. The fish were caught by local boys, who know the ways of the sea. The sausages are the gift of a neighbor who heard you were here. So you see, my lord, you have the storm to thank for this feast. Not us."

"There is more here than we could eat in a week."

"When you are done, Junius and the staff will have the rest," Branwen said. "It is a feast for everyone."

"And you, too, Branwen," Tristan said quickly, rising to place a chair firmly between him and Essylte. "We three will eat together."

"Three," Branwen murmured, "is a crowd."

Essylte looked up with beseeching eyes. Tristan pointed to the chair. "We wish to be crowded," he said. "Come, sit down."

Obediently, Branwen sat. While they ate, Essylte plied Tristan with questions about Lyonesse, and he regaled them with stories of his home-land, of Dinadan and his uncle Pernam, of sea adventures and wild rides over the midnight moors. In turn, Essylte responded with tales of evenings spent in her mother's workroom bent over the witch's cauldron, hating the stink of brewing herbs, secretly terrified of her mother's pale oval face, so beautiful in the moonlight, an unearthly spectral visage whose watchful eyes always found fault.

Branwen watched them feint and parry, using words to keep their de-fenses up, all the while dancing slowly around the central truth neither wanted to acknowledge. When they stumbled and let a silence hang, their eyes met with an intensity that frightened them both. Then they turned to her, helpless and beseeching, and she found a new topic for them. On it went, and on it would go, until the parting came and they sent him away. Essylte would weep all night, that was sure. And the night after, and the night after. What would Tristan do? Pace all night and drive himself half mad, as he had on shipboard, or take his frustrations out in a fierce gallop over the hills? Or worse, in swordplay? She thought of the small linen bags tucked in her pouch. There was more than one way out of their dilemma, but she had to think carefully. There was her own future to consider as well as theirs.

Servants returned to clear the meal away. At Essylte's bidding Tristan reclined upon the couch. She sat beside him on a cushion on the floor. Branwen brought them each a goblet of warmed wine.

"My lady, why don't you sing for us?"

"Yes, do," Tristan seconded.

"If you will not think it presumptuous of me," Essylte responded shyly, looking up at him. "I will give you the song of Enide, who pined for her lost love when she could not find him."

"A good tale," Tristan whispered, "if it ends happily."

Essylte shrugged. "Bards don't tell tales that end happily. I learned this one from Rhydderch the Elder."

"He is a master. Go on, then."

He reclined in unaccustomed comfort and let the sweet notes fill his ears. Her voice was clear and true, the voice of his dreaming. He could not take his eyes from her, but reveled silently in the sheer beauty of her nearness, the wild red-gold hair spilling over her shoulders, the soft swell of her young breasts rising with each indrawn breath. He closed his eyes. She was so young. So unworldly. Not like Esmerée, who understood the power of beauty and knew how to use it to suit her ends. Essylte had no more idea of her effect on him than a swallow did of the wind under its wings. She simply sailed on, innocent and unknowing, while he lay rigid beside her, sweat springing on his brow, trying to slow the racing of his heart.

When the last note ended he raised his cup to her and drained it.

"Sweeter than honey, fair Essylte. Give us another, I pray you. Don't stop now."

"It's your turn, my lord," she responded, flushing at his praise. "You're the one with the bard's gift. We have no harp, but surely you can give us a tale without it."

So near, her eyes, now blue, now green, made his head swim. "I will pay you back in coin, pretty princess. I'll give you the tale of the ill-fated love of Lancelot for Guinevere."

As he sang, he watched her face. She would not meet his eyes but kept her gaze in her lap, her face still. Only the faintest quiver at the corner of her mouth gave lie to her emotion. As the last note died, she looked up swiftly at him. She was trembling. Surely he did not misread it.

"My lord," she whispered, and raised her winecup to him.

"Now it's your turn again."

Branwen rose and took up their empty cups. While Essylte began another song, she refilled them. She looked back once at Tristan. He was watching Essylte, transfixed, hardly breathing, every fiber of his body attuned to her every movement, and the silly girl did not even know it. Or did she? Did she tremble, or was it the flickering candlelight? Branwen shut her eyes, bowing her head. *You can't have him; he loves Essylte. Don't grieve over it. It's a waste of your time.* Slowly, from under clenched eyelids, two large tears squeezed out and slid down her cheeks. She held her breath, fists bunched tight against her sides, and steadied herself. From her pouch she pulled a linen bag, loosed the cord around its neck, and dropped a pinch of powder into each goblet. Wiping her cheeks, she watched the grains dissolve in a sparkling shimmer and sink invisibly into the wine. She tucked the bag away and picked up the goblets.

"My lady. My lord."

With an effort, Tristan glanced away from Essylte. "Thank you, Branwen. Why don't you join us?" He offered her his cup.

"Thank you, my lord. But I don't sing. If my lord will forgive me, I beg to retire. I'm suddenly very tired."

"Surely not. The night is young yet."

"Yes, my lord. Give me leave to rest for an hour or two, and I shall be ready when my lady wishes to retire."

"Very well, then, if you must."

She met his eyes directly. "Shall I send a servant in to attend you?"

A shadow of a smile touched his face. "No need. We will attend ourselves."

The door closed behind her. Tristan turned to Essylte and raised his winecup. She touched her cup to his. They looked at each other a long time.

"Fair Essylte, long life and great happiness."

"Tristan of Lyonesse," she whispered. "My happiness is in your hands."

She lifted her cup and drank deeply. He did the same, letting the warm, fragrant liquid slide down his throat.

"Sweet Essylte."

"I think," she said firmly, "you had better tell me about Markion."

He nodded reluctantly. "What do you want to know?"

"What does he look like?"

He smiled. He hadn't expected it, but of course it would be the first question a girl would ask. "He's taller than most men, brown eyes, brown hair graying at the temples. He wears a beard but keeps it trimmed. He has good teeth. He's lean for a man his age, fit, strong, healthy. He likes drink, but he's not the brooding type. He's a soldier, all in all. There's nothing about him that's not explained by that."

He stopped. A tingling sensation rose from his toes to the top of his head. Something inside him seemed to swell and rise, pushing against his throat, against the back of his eyes, against the flesh of his chest and groin. His sight grew sharper. He could see the soft blond down along the base of Essylte's ear. He could see in great detail each one of her dark lashes. He could hear her silent breaths, quickening ever so slightly. He could smell the scented wash she had used on her hair; the thin, acrid burning of coals in the brazier; the glorious, God-given fragrance of her young body underlying it all, bringing to mind wildflowers on a sun-bright hill. Something magnificent was happening to him. Every sense had sharpened to dagger point, and the desire to touch her had grown into a need. He burned for it.

"My lord!" She looked up at him, wide-eyed. "My lord, I am ill, I think." He saw the light film of perspiration along her upper lip and, reaching out a hand, slipped the cloak off her shoulders. His hand rested on the warm flesh of her upper arm.

"It's grown warm in here, that's all."

She rose to her knees, her face on a level with his. "Tell me," she said fiercely. "Tell me about my husband. Is he a kind man?"

Tristan almost smiled. She was a brave girl, and he admired her attempt to fend him off by thrusting Mark between them. But he had no energy for the game. Every ounce of strength and concentration he could command was focused on fighting down an overwhelming urge to hold her in his arms. The room had grown unbearably stuffy. He would die if he did not get some air. He fumbled with the clasp of his robe and shrugged it off.

"Kind? That depends on whom you ask. Guvranyl would say yes. Elisane no."

"Who's Elisane?"

"His first wife."

She clasped his hand. "What do *you* say?"

His fingers closed around hers and tightened. "I—I—I've always thought so. But sometimes I am not sure."

"Do you trust him?" she cried, holding hard to his hand with both of hers and drawing it to her breast.

Tristan could not breathe. She filled his vision. He was going up in flames and he could not breathe.

"Not anymore," he whispered. Her silken skin rose against his fingers. He bit back a groan, his entire being, mind and body, straining for release. She loosed one of her hands and laid it gently against his cheek.

"I don't want to marry him."

"Then don't."

"I can't when you look at me like that." She collapsed against him and kissed him roughly, releasing in an eye blink the pent anguish of an hour's desperate struggle for control. He drew her up onto the couch, his fingers moving deftly on the laces of her gown, working with a will of their own, finding her sweet flesh, feeling the wild racing of her heart beneath his hands.

They clung together, moved together, speaking with hands and lips and bodies, alive, alight in a world aflame. And in the wild heat of their conflagration, something new was forged; their separate selves dissolved and melded into one, stronger together than each had been before, unbreakable in union.

Outside the shuttered window the wind rose, sighed, and passed by.

The liquid song of the nightingale stirred his dreams. He lay listening, wrapped in inexplicable euphoria, wondering through the fog of sleep if this was heaven, this sweet-scented bliss. He heard a sigh and felt the warmth of a living body against his own. His eyes opened. The room was dark and still. He lay in Guvranyl's bed, and this woman who lay softly breathing in the crook of his arm, this was the beautiful Essylte. How had it happened? He remembered every moment, but it seemed, somehow, to belong to another life. He turned his head to look at her, hardly daring to believe she could be real. He touched her hair and her cheek, running his fingers lightly down the white curve of her neck to her throat, to her breast. Her breathing quickened. He ran his hand along the curving contours of her body, enjoying the smooth slide of her skin, the generous response his touch evoked.

"Tristan . . ."

"Essylte, my love?"

Her eyes opened and her lips parted in a smile. "I wanted to hear you say it."

"I will say it a thousand times. I love you more than life. I always will."

"Oh, sweet, you say it well." She kissed his lips, her shyness gone, all her hesitance behind her. "And I love you beyond life, beyond death. Tristan, what will happen to us?"

He drew her closer, his lips in her hair, needing to feel the touch of her body's curves, needing every yielding inch of her again. "You will be beside me, forever. I will never let you go."

She moved in his arms, willing, ready. "I am yours, always, always. But tell me that again in the morning."

He laughed lightly, but she kissed him wildly, in desperation, and he lost his laughter in her heat.

13 ⛨ THE BARGAIN

It was dark when Branwen slipped inside the room. She leaned her back against the door until the latch slid softly home, shielding the sound with her body. She could see nothing. She waited, listening intently, as her eyes adjusted to the darkness. The silence seemed as thick and as impenetrable as the night. Beyond the shutters even the birds were still.

Gradually dim objects began to appear out of the dark and take on vague, insubstantial shapes. Against the far wall she made out the columns of bedposts. With the return of sight came the return of sound. From the bed she heard the light, slow, steady sigh of breathing. Moving with a noiseless tread, one arm outstretched for the unseen obstacle, she inched toward the bed. Her foot slipped on a white mass on the floor—she drew a quick breath and then relaxed, weak with relief. Essylte's gown! Carefully, she stepped around it. Two paces from the bed, she stopped

They lay entwined in each other's arms, still, after so many hours. Tristan's long body dwarfed the girl's. Even in sleep he held her with care, one arm bent, cradling her head, one arm draped across her, his face buried in her hair. Her head nestled in the hollow of his throat; her breasts, half hidden by the blanket, pressed against his body. Branwen's lips slowly twisted. They could not let go, even in sleep.

Inching forward, she leaned closer and strained through the dark to see his face. A lock of hair had fallen across his brow. His eyelids, curiously full like a child's, reminded her of seashells. She reached out and lightly brushed the hair from his face. He stirred, his lips moving against red-gold curls.

"Mmmmmm." He shifted, drawing the girl closer.

Branwen backed away until she was in deep shadow. She pulled the hood of her cloak tighter about her face and stood, a watching statue, as the man awakened.

His hand moved along the girl's back, sliding under the blanket. "Sweet Essylte. Sweet wife. My beautiful love." His lips brushed her face and sought her mouth. She curled an arm around him and opened her eyes.

"Tristan. Oh, Tristan, say it again."

"Marry me, Essylte. Come with me to Lyonesse. You are mine forever. It was meant to be. And I cannot live without you."

"Nor I without you," she breathed, yielding to him.

They whispered together, laughing lightly, while his hands moved and she responded with small, secret sounds of satisfaction. Their delight filled the darkness, reaching out even to Branwen standing stiffly in her corner, enveloping her in their overmastering joy, sharing with her the sweet secrets of unbearable desire.

Furiously she fought to look away, to close her eyes, but it was beyond her power. She could not help but watch his hands on the girl's supple body, could not but feel his tenderness as if it were her own flesh he stroked. Well she remembered the feel of that long back beneath her fingers on the sickbed in Gwynedd, alone in the dark. She could almost feel it now, moving between her hands, as he took the girl in his arms and began the long, slow dance of love. In spite of herself her breathing quickened. That was her own ear he bent to whisper into, her own throat his lips caressed with such soft care, her own sweet sighs, so eager, so alive—*Ahhh, God!* She shut her eyes, too late. Her own body, lit by his fire, blazed beyond her command and she was trapped, burning alive, as they took flight together, rising without her, soaring beyond the reaches of her imagination into a joy she could not alone possess.

In the cold, silent dark Branwen stood alone and still. Silence encased her like a shroud. One by one her stiff fingers unlocked from fists and stretched at her sides. She inhaled slowly. Straightening, she stepped forward and forced herself to look again at the great bed. The lovers lay in each other's arms, entwined, limb indistinguishable from limb, their breathing slowed again toward sleep. She looked down at Tristan. Never had she seen a face in such repose, a soul so at peace. *So, wanderer, you have found what you seek. You count it worth the risk. And so must I.* With dry eyes she turned away and walked to the door, lifted the latch, and let herself out.

It was dawn, and cold. Branwen stood before the door and gathered her cloak around her. In the kitchens the slaves would be stoking the oven fires, but here no one else was up and about. Taking a deep breath, she lifted the latch and went in.

Essylte, in the white gown with the russet cloak about her shoulders, sat on the Roman couch and wept. Tristan stood frowning beside her. He looked up as Branwen entered and met her eyes. She curtsied low.

"Good morning, Branwen."

"Good morning, my lord, my lady. I beg your pardon for oversleeping." She glanced briefly toward Essylte. "Why is my lady weeping?"

Tristan half smiled. Reaching for Essylte's arm, he drew her into his embrace. "Why do you think? You needn't play the innocent with me. You know well we have been the night together."

Branwen colored at the direct look in his eyes. "My lord?"

"You left us for the purpose. Do you deny it?"

She hesitated only a moment. "No, my lord."

"I thought so. For that, you owe us the use of your wits to help us find a way out of my lady's dilemma."

"What dilemma is that, my lord?"

Tristan's arm tightened around Essylte's shoulders but his eyes never left Branwen's face.

"What do you think?" he repeated softly. "She is torn between her promise to her father and her promise to me." Tristan touched the tangled red-gold curls that tumbled down her back. Branwen, watching, could almost feel the infinite tenderness of the gesture. "With her lips she has promised Percival to marry Markion; with her body she has promised to marry me. Either way, she will disappoint someone she loves."

Essylte, her arms around Tristan's waist, looked up at Branwen with reddened eyes. "Oh, Branny! Whatever shall I do? Father will be so angry. I cannot leave Tristan, and yet, and yet— Don't you see? The peace between the kingdoms depends upon it."

"You can't leave me." He kissed her warmly. "You are mine now. Your father will come to understand it."

"He never will. He will invade Cornwall, he will attack Lyonesse to get me back. You don't know him when his passions are aroused."

With a glimmer of a smile, Tristan bent and whispered in her ear. She colored, smiled, and kissed him quickly. "Stop, Tristan. Please, stop just a moment and give this thought." She glanced beseechingly at Branwen. "Please help us, Branny, won't you? Help us decide what's best to do?"

"I think," Branwen said calmly, "we had better put the chamber back to rights, light the fire, break our fast, and then sit down to conference."

"Yes," Essylte agreed at once. "And I must change my gown, and do my hair—I look a fright, I'm sure. Please, Tristan"—this as his arms tightened and pulled her closer—"we cannot think straight now. Everything will be clearer after breakfast."

"After breakfast will make no difference. You are mine, Essylte." He kissed her again.

Branwen walked him to the door. "Go stealthily and make sure no one sees you," she said in a low voice.

Tristan raised an eyebrow. "Are we keeping this a secret?"

"It's for the best, my lord, at least at present. It gives you both more choices."

"There is only one choice." Branwen did not reply, and Tristan shrugged. "Have it your way, then. I'll be discreet."

Back in his own chamber, Tristan dressed slowly, changing Junius's fine wool tunic and cloak for the leather tunic, leggings, and boots he had arrived in. Someone had closed the shutters since he'd stood gazing at the stars last night. He pushed them open. It was a fine morning, quiet and cool. A gray-pink mist lay on the estuary, steaming upward as the sun slowly strengthened. The glorious joy that had possessed him all night long still sang loud in his soul; he could hardly keep from smiling. But a shadow tugged at the edges of his happiness, a nameless dread that touched him with a cold, fleeting finger. He shivered.

Behind him the door opened.

"Good morning, my lord." Junius bowed. His quick eyes glanced at the bed, neatly made, and the face he raised to Tristan held no expression whatsoever.

"Don't worry," Tristan said lightly, "it was innocent enough. Thank you for the loan of those clothes. We had a wonderful evening."

Junius bundled the garments under his arm. "On occasion, the company of young ladies can be delightful indeed. Shall I bring you breakfast, my lord? One of the stable lads caught three fine fish at dawning. They're roasting now on the spit."

"Thank you, no. I'm breaking fast with the Princess Essylte and Branwen. But you can bring me a bath slave and a razor."

Amusement lit Junius's features. "My lord was shaved last night."

Tristan smiled. "My lord will shave again."

Junius grinned. "Women do love a smooth cheek." He chuckled, nudging Tristan. "What did I tell you, eh? Pretty as a picture, she is, and soft on you, although she hides it. You had no trouble, I'll wager."

Tristan colored, unable to speak.

"A word of advice, my lord." Junius was peering out the window into the lifting haze. "Don't let her mistress know. There'll be trouble later, at King Mark's court. There always is."

He was speaking of Branwen! In the midst of his relief, Tristan felt again the cold finger of dread. *I swear before Christ I will not touch her. She is Markion's bride.* He stifled a gasp as the witch's curse came back to him. *Twice will you swear before your God an oath you cannot keep—lies you will be called to answer for.*

"Dear God!" He sank to his knees. "What have I done?"

"There, there," Junius said kindly, dropping a hand onto his shoulder.

"You can hardly be blamed. A young man in the prime of life, a pretty maiden who is willing—just see it doesn't continue past arrival at Markion's court. Everything will be all right."

Tristan looked up, unseeing. "How can it?"

"Come, my lord, pull yourself together. I'll send you a bath slave. And after breakfast, we should send a courier to the king."

"To Mark?" Tristan blinked. "Why?"

"Why, to warn him of your coming. As far as he knows, you're still in Wales. There are preparations to be made for receiving the young princess. And for the wedding. You'll be there before the week is out. You must send the courier without delay."

Tristan rose, struggling to think straight. "Yes, yes, of course. But not yet, good Junius. I'm not sure yet where—when we leave. Let me speak once more with Princess Essylte. Surely tomorrow will be soon enough."

Junius frowned. "Today is better. If the ship is ready."

"Just so," Tristan countered smoothly. "I must inspect her and talk with the captain. She was damaged in the storm. It may take time to put her right. I will let you know, Junius, when to send the courier. Later."

"Very good, my lord." Junius bowed, and Tristan began to pace back and forth across the room.

Branwen opened the door to Tristan's knocking. The chamber he entered was Guvranyl's once more, simple and unadorned but for the little table, all signs of last night's revelry gone without a trace. As if it never had been.

Essylte stood by the window in a dark gray gown, her red-gold hair alight with the morning sun. She looked, Tristan thought, like a flame new-sprung from ashes. When she turned to him his breath caught in his chest, struck again by the arrow of desire. In three swift strides she was in his arms, holding him with all her slender strength, whispering the words he wanted most to hear.

"An hour away," he breathed, his lips on hers, "is a year of agony. Sweet Essylte, I cannot part from you."

They were interrupted by servants entering with breakfast: willow tea, freshly baked bread, bowls of raisins and warm honey. Reluctantly, they came to table at Branwen's bidding, eating little, but holding hands throughout, as if each touch might be their last. Branwen served them silently and tended to the coal fire in the grate.

"We are ready for a conference," Essylte said, pushing away the food.

"Tell her, Branwen," Tristan pleaded. "Tell her she is only leaving her father for her husband. She needn't be afraid. It will be all right."

Branwen looked up. "Will it, my lord? Essylte knows what her father's reaction will be."

"Can't we reason with him?" Tristan turned to Essylte. "Your father honored me in Wales. In Cornwall, I'm second only to Markion. You would be nobly wed. Won't that be honor enough for him?"

Essylte gulped. "Tristan, he has this dream of uniting all the tribes of Britain under one High King, of making us strong again, as we were in Arthur's time. He—he will sacrifice anything to this dream."

"He has already sacrificed his daughter to it," Branwen murmured.

"If Mark does not wed, I will be his heir. Is that not good enough?"

Both women stared at him. Branwen was the first to speak. "And yet you came to Wales to fetch his bride?"

"I never wanted to be High King of Britain," he said levelly. "Until now."

"Surely Markion will wed another in my lady's place," Branwen pointed out. "Had he been content to leave the Kingdom in your hands, he would not have sent Lord Segward in the first place. So you cannot fulfill King Percival's ambition unless you can prevent your uncle's marriage. You must kill him, then. By war or by stealth."

Tristan rose in agitation. "I will not kill him. I have sworn oaths of fealty to him, and he has done nothing to wrong me." He turned to Essylte. "I would be the rogue your mother thinks me, to do such a thing."

"Don't bring dishonor upon yourself," Essylte begged. "Not for my sake."

"Then," Branwen said calmly, "there seems to be no way for Essylte to wed you without angering her father."

Tristan stood behind Essylte and cupped her shoulders in his hands.

"How angry will he be? Surely he remembers what youth is like. I have even heard that he married for love against his family's advice."

"Yes," Branwen said softly. "And look where it got him."

"He will never forgive me," Essylte said, shaking. "I know well what he will do. He will demand justice of Markion. Nothing will content him but—but your death, and my return. At first he will think I was abducted, and will raise an army himself to get me back. But when he learns I broke my promise to him of my own will, he will—he will consider I have betrayed him, and shamed him before Markion." Her voice began to quaver. Tristan gripped her shoulders firmly. "My mother will drive him mad. She will taunt him with it endlessly. She will dangle Palomydes's memory in his face. She will never let him forget it. He will be so miserable! He will never forgive me."

"Yes," Tristan murmured, "but will he bring his army south? Without you, there is no treaty between the kingdoms. Will he join Markion against me?" Essylte shuddered but did not answer. Tristan looked at Branwen. "What do you think?"

"What choice will he have?" she said softly. "He must do something to redeem his honor, even if his dream is denied him."

Tristan shrugged and began to pace the room.

"As for my uncle Mark, it is perfectly clear what he will do. I am the only man in Cornwall he has reason to fear, and I have slapped his face. Mark's always been touchy about his honor. He wouldn't be Markion if he didn't come after me. There is only one thing he can do: marshal his forces and take back what was promised to him." He turned sharply on his heel as Essylte began to weep silent tears. "When I lay with Essylte, I betrayed Mark. He must kill me now. He will publicly accuse me of treason and rape, and then he will attack me."

"Oh, no!" Essylte cried. "Not on my account! Let this not happen all on my account!"

Tristan knelt beside her chair and clasped her hands. "My sweet love, you cannot help who you are. And neither can I."

"Oh, Tristan, can't you send to him and speak privately with him? We need his help with Father. Wouldn't he understand? He must have been young once."

"He will understand no better than your father," Tristan said gently. "Mark never loved a woman in his life. And my dearest, you are not just any woman. You are Percival's daughter. Marriage to you means something for Britain's future. No one else would serve his purpose. To take you from him is to challenge his authority, his future, his very rule. At least, that is how Mark will see it. In his calmer moments. But he is not a reflective man and will be furious at my betrayal. He will come against me openly to satisfy his honor. He must."

Branwen spoke quietly. "Can you withstand him? If Percival doesn't join him?"

Tristan shrugged. "Lyonesse is a tiny kingdom, hard against the sea. Even if only Cornishmen come against me, there will be more than enough. Even many who love me, like Guvranyl himself, the lords of Dumnonia and Dorria, will likely join Markion against me in this cause." He paused, holding tight to Essylte's hands. "I have betrayed him. Last night I—I didn't see it so, God knows. But that is the way everyone else will see it. And it is true."

Essylte bit her lip hard against fresh tears.

"Lyon's Head, my fortress, is impregnable. It cannot be taken by sea, and two men can hold the causeway against an army of any size. But Lyonesse herself is easy enough to overrun. All Mark need do is sit down outside my gates, cut off my people from me, and starve me out. And what he will do to my people while he is waiting . . ." His voice shook. "He will burn their homes and ravage their lands, and lay it all to my account. The coward king, trapped inside his fortress—" He turned away sharply and rose. "That," he said angrily to Branwen, "is what Mark will do, with or without Percival beside him."

"And if he kills you," Branwen said evenly, "what will happen to Essylte?"

Tristan stared at her, breathing hard, and then lowered his eyes. "I don't know. It's—it's unlikely Mark would settle for my—my widow. He would probably—I don't know—send her home to her father in disgrace. I couldn't—I wouldn't allow that to happen."

"But how could you prevent it?" Branwen asked mildly. "Unless you jump together into the sea?" Tristan did not answer. "It seems, my lord," she continued, "that you cannot go to Lyonesse. It isn't safe for my lady."

"Oh, God!" Essylte buried her face in her hands. "Where can we go, then?"

"Not to Wales. Not to Cornwall. Not to Lyonesse." Branwen ticked the places off upon her fingers. "Not to Strathclyde, ruled by Percival's kin; not to Rheged, bound by treaties to Strathclyde. Not to Lothian or Elmet—the whole northern alliance is bound by treaty to one another. They are more likely to see this as a chance to force Percival to their side, a thing he has long resisted. They can't wait to make war on Cornwall. He alone has held out for years, hoping for unity and peace. Wherever you go, they will use this as an excuse to seduce Wales and start the war they have always wanted, Briton against Briton."

Essylte sobbed openly. "That is my father's nightmare! I have destroyed his dream. It is all my doing."

"No," Tristan said gravely, "I brought this calamity upon us both, upon us all. Because I love you." He squared his shoulders and looked into Essylte's eyes. "Whatever happens, you belong with me. We will leave Britain, then, if there is no place for us here. I can commandeer the ship and sail to Less Britain, or Gaul, or Ireland. I will take service with some king . . . we may not live as king and queen, but at least we will live together."

Essylte clutched at his hand. "Where, Tristan? Where can we go that no one will know you? All of Britain will be looking for us. You can never put your hand to a harp, or sing aloud, or talk in your sleep. Or wield a sword. Where will we be safe?"

"Somewhere. Anywhere! It *must* be possible."

"The High King will get word to all his allies," Branwen said quietly. "You must seek refuge among Britain's enemies. Saxons? Franks? Alemans? Who will shelter you and risk war with Britain?"

"Oh, no!" Essylte pleaded, looking up at Tristan. "I couldn't do that to my father. Seek shelter with his enemies? Oh, don't ask it, I pray you, Tristan. If you love me, don't!"

Tristan looked down at her. "Where, then? Shall we disguise ourselves as beggars? Shall we live in caves in the wilds of Rheged? You can no more hide your birth, Essylte, than a swan can pass for a goose. And I would not foist such a life upon you, when but for me you might have all of Britain at your feet."

"I don't want all of Britain. I want you."

"O God, deliver us! Is there no way out?" Tristan fell to his knees, and Essylte slid from the chair into his arms.

Branwen watched them, unmoving. They were circling, slowly but inevitably, toward the center of the web she had so carefully designed. All that was required of her was patience. Soon, very soon, they must do her bidding. Their tenderness, their very devotion to each other, would be their own undoing. She schooled her face as they embraced before her, ignoring her presence. Once—how recently!—their whispers and their cruel kisses had struck at her like knives. Now she had armor against them. She rose and stood at the window, looking out. If Tristan truly loved the girl, he was trapped. If not, she herself had risked little, lost nothing. But how long would it take them to decide to do what they must do?

The sun rose high, and then began its long descent. Still Tristan paced back and forth across the chamber; still Essylte wept and wrung her hands. Again and again they went over all the possibilities, but they came no nearer a solution. To live, they must separate, and separation to them meant death. Essylte lay upon the bed with a headache from so much weeping. Tristan drank a skin of wine. Branwen said nothing but had fruit and bread brought in, which no one touched. Junius came twice to beg Tristan's attention, and twice was sent away. The third time, he had the ship's captain with him, who wished to report to Tristan on the readiness of the ship. Glaring at Junius, Tristan strode out to hear him. The damage to the ship's hull had been repaired, and the sail mended. If Tristan wished, they could sail on the morning tide. Tristan nodded curtly, turned on his heel, and returned to Guvranyl's chamber, shutting the door behind him.

Dinner was brought in. No one ate. Finally, dry-eyed and exhausted from weeping, Essylte spoke.

"Tristan, there is only one choice before us. You see it as clearly as I."

"No."

"My love, I must marry Markion. If I don't, you will die."

"What is death? I will not give you to him."

"Let me do it, Tristan. It's the only way for us."

"For *us*? What is left for us if you marry my uncle?"

"We will live. You will live, and I will see you from time to time. We may at least have speech together."

"Speech." He spoke bitterly. "This is a life of torment you doom us to."

"But it is life. Who knows what might happen? Markion will not live forever. You said yourself you would not wish death or shame upon me. Yet any other course will bring us to such straits."

"God forgive us, there must be some other way."

"God will not forgive us for a sin we don't regret and would do again. There is no other honorable end for us."

"Oh, Essylte! How can I give you to him?"

"Because I ask it of you, love. Because it has to be."

"Sweet Christ. To have brought you to such a pass."

"Is there any other way? Tell me, and I will do it."

A long pause. At the window, Branwen hardly breathed.

"No." His voice was weary, defeated. "I would rather see you High Queen of Britain than disgraced for my sake. If it must be so, so it must be."

"Thank you, Tristan."

Branwen turned. They stood together, arms about each other, lips joined in a sensual kiss. Her fingers dug into the window ledge. They were almost there.

"But my dear love," Tristan whispered, "we have forgotten something. You are no longer maiden. He will know I—someone—has been with you. There is no getting around it. Even drunk to the point of senselessness, Mark will know."

Essylte closed her eyes and leaned against him. Branwen let out a long, silent sigh.

"I would not turn time back, even if I could," Essylte murmured. "Oh, Tristan, I can't bear this any longer! Let us choose death together if there is no other way."

Tristan's arms tightened about her. "If only—if only there were some way to fool him."

At last Branwen stirred. "Perhaps there is."

She had been silent for so long, her words had the effect of a thunder-clap. They both jumped.

"How?" Tristan asked eagerly. "You have a plan?"

Branwen held herself very still. "The king must be deceived for only one night."

"Yes. One night."

"Then you need someone to take my lady's place. For one night."

"Take my place?" Essylte looked quickly at Tristan. "Is this possible?

Can it be done? Would he not know, by her shape or voice, that it was not me?"

"He would know," Tristan said, "by the hair alone."

"Not everyone looks at me with the eyes of love," Essylte replied with a ghostly smile. "Perhaps it could be hidden somehow?"

Branwen stepped closer to them. "I think, my lady, that if the imposter were of your age, your height, your shape, and knew you well enough to imitate your ways, it might be done. Markion will not know you well. The room will be dark. We can find a way to disguise the hair."

"But where can we ever find such a maiden? How could I ask it of her? Who would want to make such a sacrifice for me?"

Branwen took a deep breath very slowly. "I would."

Essylte gasped. "*You?* Oh, Branny! No! I daren't let you."

Tristan rose. He took both of Branwen's hands and searched her face. "Are you serious? Would you do it? Why?"

Branwen dropped her gaze. "What reason could I give that you would believe, my lord? Because Essylte and I are, well, almost as sisters? Because I see no way out of this dilemma except death? I don't want either of you to die."

Tristan said nothing; neither did he let go of her hands. She smiled bitterly and looked up at him again. "What do you want me to say? That I don't want her to die because my future is tied to hers and I don't want to go to Gaul? It's true. I will live better, and find a nobler husband, in Markion's court than in any other. If she is shamed, I am shamed with her. If she is sent home in disgrace, what happens to me? . . . Now do you believe me?"

"You can't know what you risk. It is your own life, if you are caught, as much as ours."

"I know."

Tristan looked at her a long time. He dropped her hands.

"We owe you much for this. It is—a lifelong obligation. What can we give you in return?"

Branwen managed a small smile. "When I find the lord I wish to marry, you will approve my choice and help me to my desire. Both of you. Whoever he is."

Tristan did not hesitate. "Agreed. But that is little enough to do. Surely there must be something else?"

"Nothing. Except—except if I should conceive a son by Markion, Essylte must agree to raise him as her own. Neither of you must tell the truth of his parentage until I give you leave."

Essylte looked bewildered. "But is it possible to keep that secret? Markion will guess all on his own. You will be with child, and I will not."

"It is an easy thing to fool a man about pregnancy," Branwen said. "You can safely leave that part of it to me."

Essylte shrugged. "Well, it is an honorable enough request. It will be Markion's child, after all. As long as my father thinks it is mine, all will be well."

Tristan frowned but raised Branwen's fingers to his lips. "I owe you service, Branwen. You have saved Essylte's honor and her life. You are a noble woman."

"Oh, Branny!" Essylte cried suddenly. "Are you sure? He's old enough to be your father—you can't guess what it might be like."

"Can't I? Anyway, it doesn't matter."

"But he might be—ugly or cruel." Essylte blushed scarlet.

Branwen half smiled. "I don't much care what he is like. It doesn't matter. All that matters is that he thinks I am you. I trust Tristan to get him drunk enough."

"Nothing easier. But Branwen, think carefully. This is sin, this is a stain upon your soul. We two are already guilty, but you are not. This is not a thing that will lightly wash away."

"But it is my soul, my lord. Let me sin where I choose, as you did."

Tristan reached down and lifted Essylte into his arms. "Though I am damned to let you do it, Essylte will die if you do not. I must accept damnation."

He looked out Guvranyl's narrow window to the oncoming night. Was it only last evening he had looked out upon a world full of promise and delight? Now the future stretched out before him, fearsome, comfortless, dust and ashes on a bed of coals. How it was to be borne he could not guess. And all his life, every waking moment, he would owe Essylte's life to Branwen.

PART III

14 ⚜ THE CLIFFS OF CORNWALL

M arkion stood on the dais in the great hall of Tintagel and raised his tankard.

"To Essylte of Gwynedd, the loveliest maiden in Britain!"

Servants scurried everywhere with skins of wine and pitchers of mead as the press of men below him raised their cups to the king.

"To Essylte!" they shouted, and drank.

"To the fair Essylte, Percival's daughter!" Mark lifted his tankard a second time.

"To Essylte!" The echoing roar reached to the rafters.

"To my Essylte, soon to be Queen of Cornwall and High Queen of Britain!"

The hall erupted with cheering as the men toasted and drank and stomped their boots upon the floor. At the back of the hall, unnoticed in the commotion, Tristan upended his winecup and spilled the final portion of his wine upon the floor, where one of Markion's hounds eagerly licked it up.

"Segward!" Markion shouted, grabbing his counselor and pulling him forward. "You're a genius, man! You're to be commended. By God, if she isn't an unholy beauty!" The rest of his remarks were lost in the boisterous laughter and ribald jests of his courtiers. Segward bowed, unsmiling.

"Calm down, Tris." Dinadan nudged him gently. "You look ready to cut someone's throat. Ease up, man. You won, and Segward lost. You're alive. You've covered yourself with honor. You've returned to Cornwall. Let him stew in those juices awhile. Isn't that revenge enough?"

"Damn Segward. I wouldn't waste a moment's thought on him."

Dinadan watched him worriedly. He could see that Tristan's mind was somewhere else, and he recognized the symptoms that usually preceded the blackest of Tristan's moods. Ever since morning, when the Cornish ship had sailed into the narrow, cliff-crowned harbor, bearing with it the Welsh princess and every man of the escort alive and well, all Tintagel had celebrated the triumph of Tristan of Lyonesse. Everyone except Tristan himself.

Dinadan had been ecstatic with relief. The courier they'd had three days ago had told a harrowing tale: The Welsh had seen through Tristan's thin disguise and attacked him, whereupon he'd killed one of their princes in a swordfight and been cut himself. Dinadan had seen with his own eyes the satisfied smirk on Segward's face when he heard this news. But the courier had continued: Tristan had nevertheless managed to escape Gwynedd with the promised princess and Percival's blessing, only to be shipwrecked on the journey home. Again Segward's eyes had lit, as Dinadan's hopes plunged a second time.

Dinadan had accompanied his father to the harbor that morning in Markion's train, not truly believing anyone could survive such a journey against such odds. When he saw the battered ship, her sail patched in fifty places and her hull hastily repaired, he knew the courier's tale was true. Not since that summer morning in Pernam's Sanctuary two years ago had he been so happy to see Tristan.

But Tristan had not seemed happy to be back in Cornwall. Throughout the disembarking, the greeting ceremony, the presentation of the princess to Markion, the ride up the cliffs and along the high moor from the harbor to the fortress, Tristan had been at his formal best, cool, distant, but very, very pale. The only person he had spoken to willingly had been the little mousy girl who attended the Welsh princess and who had ridden at Tristan's side during the long procession north.

If Tristan's formal demeanor had puzzled Dinadan, it had puzzled Segward, too. Dinadan had seen those little sharp eyes studying Tristan's face, and he had seen Segward frown. Something was amiss. It crossed Dinadan's mind that the wound Tristan had received in Wales might be mortal, and that he strove to hide this from everyone at court. It was the only reason he could think of for Tristan's black humor and odd aloofness.

"Tristan! Tristan! Tristan!" The cry filled the hall. Heads turned, searching for the King of Lyonesse, as hands clapped and boots stomped to the rhythm of the swelling cry. From the dais, Markion's gaze found Tristan, and the King beckoned to him. Dinadan grabbed his arm as Tristan tried to turn away.

"What ails you? Go on, get up there. This is your triumph, Tris."

Strong hands steered Tristan across the room. Men thumped him lovingly on the back and called out his name. Stone-faced, Tristan was pushed and led to Markion, who slung an arm around him and kissed his cheek.

"Here's the brave son of Cornwall who carried out Lord Segward's plan and made our great union possible!" Flushed with wine, Markion waved his tankard in the air. "My nephew, the brave and honorable Tristan of Lyonesse!"

The room roared.

"Ah, Tristan." Markion hugged him roughly, "I couldn't have done it without you. For this you will be remembered long in Cornwall, and honored well."

Tristan looked into his uncle's face and saw there his emotion, his gratitude, even his admiration. But he saw no more than the plain, open face of a commander, pleased with victory and acknowledging his thanks to the troops who had brought it to him. There was no trace of deceit or hesitation in Mark's manner, no scent of shame. He couldn't have known what a death trap Gwynedd had been. He couldn't have known about Marhalt's sister. *He could not have known.*

With an arm around Tristan's shoulder, Markion faced the crowd. "Let us today proclaim, this wedding will be the biggest celebration Cornwall has seen in a hundred years! This is the start of our own golden age! Merron, let the word go forth—we invite everyone in Britain to attend. I set the date a month hence, that all have time to come. Ask all the lords of Cornwall, and all my noble companions from Dumnonia and the Summer Country round about Camelot. Send couriers to the north, to Rheged, Strathclyde, Lothian, Elmet. And to those lords left in Logris, whose lands we will yet reclaim from Saxon hands. Let them all receive my personal greeting, and let any who will, come into Cornwall and celebrate this union with us!"

The great hall erupted with wild cheering.

"Eh, Segward?" Markion grinned at the little man. "What say you to that? Let's have everyone witness this bedding!"

Segward's eyes glittered in amusement. "Wedding, you mean, surely. A slip of the tongue, my lord, but a revealing one. With such a woman, a month is a long time to wait."

Markion laughed. "Aye, it is indeed, when I think I might lie between those soft white thighs tonight!"

Tristan froze. The hall rang with laughter. Markion's arm around his shoulder clamped him to the king's side, yet he began to tremble and could not still it.

Markion looked down at Tristan and hugged him hard. "Come, come, Tristan. Do I offend the poet in you? Would you rather sing about her hair and eyes? Ha! Ha! Where's the red-blooded man in you, nephew?" He drained his tankard and staggered a little sideways. "My nephew disapproves of me." He grinned to his men. "He would rather sit at his harp and sing her praises than lift his spear to her! Ha! I shall serve you well, Tristan. You will sing us to bed at our wedding feast, an ode of your invention. How's that, then, my lad? Show us what you can do."

Tristan did not move. He looked at the throng of grinning, eager faces, seeing in them a wolf pack salivating for the kill. But Markion, pleased as punch at doing him honor, was waiting for his reply. He struggled to make his lips form the words.

"I would be honored, Uncle." A low bow hid his face.

Markion thumped him on the back. "She is my betrothed, I have a right to her bed. Yet I swear before you all that I, like Arthur, will forbear to touch the maiden until I wed her. I will prove to all my people, to all of Britain, that I am a man who can command his appetites. I can wait patiently, when necessity demands, and I am a man of my word. She is safe from me until we are married." He threw back his head and laughed heartily. "But then, let her look to her skirts! I'll make up for lost time!"

The men roared with laughter, slapping their thighs and cheering the king on. Unobtrusively, as slowly and carefully as he could, Tristan disengaged himself from Markion's embrace and made his way to the door. Segward's eyes, narrow slits in his pudgy face, followed him with an eager look of speculation.

Dinadan met him on the threshold but, seeing his face, stood aside to let him pass. Tristan strode down the wide hallway, up a winding staircase, and out onto the battlements of the northwest tower. At Dinadan's sign, the sentry saluted and retreated, leaving them alone. The two men stared out at the quiet sea, stretching unbroken from the cliffs to the horizon in a blue sheet of unfathomable dimensions. Overhead, seabirds wheeled and called to one another, high, mournful cries carried away on the ever-moving air.

Tristan slammed his fist against the stone. "Damn him! What a swine he is! Oh, God, Dinadan, this is impossible."

"Listen, Tristan, so he's coarse in his speech and his ways? He has no grace about him. You knew that. You've known him all your life. Markion hasn't changed."

"He's a pig in human garb."

"I thought he showed commendable restraint, promising not to touch the girl until they're married. It was a noble impulse. He must be in awe of her."

Tristan turned to face him, his dark eyes enormous in a pale, drawn face. "Dinadan, there's something I should tell you."

Dinadan's breath stopped. "I knew it. I knew it the moment I laid eyes on you."

Panic flickered in Tristan's eyes. Dinadan grabbed him and embraced him roughly. "The courier told us about it, the fight in Wales. It's mortal, isn't it? The wound the villain gave you."

Tristan's eyes widened. The corners of his mouth lifted briefly. He gripped Dinadan's arm and kissed his cheek. "Yes. But not in the way you think."

He paced back and forth across the battlement. "You were right, you know, about the danger that awaited me in Wales. You can't know how right. More than once I wished I'd listened to your excellent advice. The man I fought was a rejected suitor of Essylte's. After I disarmed him he threw his dagger at my back. A poisoned dagger."

"Poisoned! You mean, like Marhalt's sword?"

"Exactly like Marhalt's sword. It was the same poison. It came from the same hand."

Dinadan licked dry lips. "Whose?"

Tristan stopped his pacing and faced his friend. "The Queen of Gwynedd. Essylte's mother. Percival's wife. Marhalt's sister."

Dinadan staggered. *"What?"*

Tristan nodded, resuming his pacing. He sketched briefly the events that had followed, ending with the queen's discovery of his name, and the flight from Wales.

Dinadan paled. "Wait—you go too fast—do you mean to say she *made* the poison? And the princess found the antidote? Are you healed, then?"

Tristan shrugged off his tunic and showed his astonished friend his unmarked chest and back.

"My God!" Dinadan cried. "There's not even a normal scar! But how can that be?" His face lit with joy, and Tristan could not help a smile.

"Maybe Pernam could tell you. All I can say is that the Queen of Gwynedd has some very odd and very old powers."

Dinadan grinned. "I'm beginning to be glad you made that trip to Wales, in spite of my advice. But if you didn't suffer a mortal wound, why did you say you did? You scared me to death."

Tristan dropped his eyes. "I know. Forgive me. You see through me too well. And your guess was almost right. I do suffer from a wound that's likely to be mortal, but no villain gave it to me."

Dinadan frowned, but Tristan had raised his head and was looking beyond him into the distance, a look of longing on his face. Dinadan turned. Far to his left he saw two figures walking on the battlement of the southern tower. One was the princess. He recognized her green gown from the morning's presentation. She had doffed her golden veil, and now her radiant curls fell loose around her shoulders. Her companion walked beside her, demurely dressed with her mousy hair bound in a plain scarf. They walked arm in arm, looking out to sea. Even as he watched, they paused, and the princess turned his way. For a long moment she stood perfectly still. Then slowly she placed her right hand over her heart and extended her arm toward him, all in one graceful motion. *Yours forever!* Pain caught at his chest. Wasn't that how Diarca had saluted him as he rode away from Castle Dorr? He glanced behind him. Tristan's arm was outstretched toward the girl, desperation, devotion, agony, adoration plain upon his face.

In a flash Dinadan understood. How could he not have guessed? He remembered well the awe, the admiration that had struck his own breast that morning when Markion raised the girl's veil and they all beheld her face. To a man like Tristan, so sensitive to beauty and sensation, two weeks in her company would be enough to destroy him. A heaviness gripped Dinadan's heart. Of course the girl was in love with him. Ask Esmerée if he couldn't charm birds to his hand, songs from the sea, and hearts from their moorings. What chance had the poor princess had? A handsome stranger sweeping into her father's castle and carrying her away—it was the stuff of daydreams.

In silence, Dinadan slipped his arm across Tristan's shoulders and turned him away.

April slid swiftly into May, the earth warmed and sprang to life, decking the open moors with wildflowers and the forests with a hundred hues of green. Day by day lords arrived with their trains of knights to pay homage to King Markion. Tents sprang up everywhere. By day the country around Tintagel was filled with the sounds of warriors' greetings, their hunting calls, their games. By night their cooking fires lit the gullied headland and their music rose to the stars.

In all this time Tristan did not see much of Mark, who was kept busy overseeing the arrival and welcome of his guests. Although no one came from the northern federation or from Wales, three lords came from Logris, two with news about recent Saxon encroachments and the sack of Amesbury, one with nothing but bitter complaints about the hopelessness of fighting an enemy whose numbers increased by thousands every year. But every man of standing in the Summer Country, Dumnonia, and the heart of Cornwall came. The most important kings had to be well entertained. Mark dined with them and drank with them, gleaning what information he could about the state of things in their homelands and trying to judge their true feelings about his marriage to a Welsh princess. For this he kept Segward always near him.

With Segward occupied, Tristan slipped away more and more often to the company of Branwen and Essylte. There Dinadan would find him, in the garden or the bower, wrapped around his harp and singing to them, or sitting in silence, gazing into the girl's face, while Branwen chattered on between them and the servants went about with lowered eyes.

"Come away, come away," Dinadan begged. "They have more than enough to do, there are a thousand preparations, look how their fingers fly at their needles—you hinder them, Tris, but they'll never tell you so."

On most days Dinadan was adept at getting him out of Tintagel on one excuse or another: hunting, patrolling the coasts for signs of Irish raiders now that the seas were open, leading an honor guard to welcome the wedding guests, who began to arrive in increasing numbers. Even so, Dinadan could not be with him every minute. Sir Bruenor, his father, had arrived with all his knights from Dorria a fortnight early and commanded much of his time. But whenever he was free from his father's service, Dinadan hauled Tristan off to another gallop over the open moors.

One day he came upon Tristan at the foot of the stairs to the women's quarters.

"Tristan." Dinadan pulled his friend aside. "You'll never guess who's coming from Lyonesse. I overheard Merron giving orders to the chamberlains—your uncle Pernam is coming, and he's bringing Esmerée."

"Esmerée! Pernam I can understand, but why would Esme come? Is something wrong?"

"Segward must have sent for her."

"He never would!"

"Well, she'd never come unless commanded. And he'd never bring her to court again, not without a damned good reason."

"What reason could there be?"

Dinadan met his eyes. "Either it's a test for you, or for her, or both . . . or he's learned the truth and seeks to taunt her with it."

"Taunt her? How?"

"I wish," Dinadan said with a half smile, "you could see your face whenever you look at Essylte. If *I* can see your heart so plainly, what will Esme see, who knows you even more, uh, intimately?"

Tristan flushed. "Do you mean Segward expects her to be jealous? And has brought her here to inflict that punishment upon her?"

"That is exactly what I mean."

"The poor fool. She won't be jealous. Segward misunderstands our friendship."

"She's more than a friend, surely." Dinadan lowered his voice to the barest whisper. "She lay with you for a year and bore you a child. How can you think she won't be jealous? She wouldn't be a woman, else."

Tristan shook his head. "If she were to wed a man who made her heart sing, I'd be the happiest man in Cornwall. I'd come to celebrate the marriage and honor the man who pleased her so. I'd never be jealous of him. I'd only be happy for her. And she will feel the same for me. Wait until she gets here. You'll see."

"But it's not you who's getting married."

Anguish flared in Tristan's features, and Dinadan cursed himself for a fool. His friend turned away and slumped against the stairwell.

"I'm sorry," Dinadan said swiftly. "Forgive me. But you've got to be more careful, Tristan, and guard your face. Segward already suspects there's something going on. I think he's bringing Esmerée here to make sure of it."

Tristan shuddered. "That man can't live without suspicion." Then his voice softened. "But don't worry about Esme. She isn't stupid. She'll protect me."

"Pray God she can. Because this castle is a trap. Once you're in, there's no way out. And it's a long way down."

Essylte sat on a velvet stool while Branwen braided and bound her hair. She gazed out the unshuttered window at the violet evening sky, strewn with stars springing to life in the wake of the dying sun.

"Tell me, Branwen," she said slowly, "do you think the sun wheels across the sky, as the Romans believed, unharmed by the dark? Or do you think, with the Ancients, that he meets his death each night in the western sea and is born again each morning in the east?"

Branwen looked down at her sharply. "I believe the sun rises each morning and sets each evening. The why of it matters not to me. What makes you ask?"

Essylte shrugged. "If he dies each night in the sea, then a new beginning is always possible. It would give me hope. But—my whole life I have watched him sink into the sea, and never have I seen the steam arise. I fear the Romans have it right after all."

"What nonsense to bother so about! You are out of humor, that is all. I will be finished in a moment, and we can go down to the hall. You should eat more than you do; you have lost flesh since we've been here."

Essylte shuddered. "How many days are left?"

"Five."

"Oh, God! Why did I ever agree to this? Tristan was willing to go anywhere in the world."

"But this is the only place you will be safe. Let's not go through it all again, for both our sakes."

Essylte turned on the stool and grasped Branwen's hands. "Oh, Branny, I beg your pardon. That was selfish of me. I forgot what you have promised on my behalf."

Branwen half smiled. "You act like I am going to my death."

Essylte colored. "No, but—if there is not love between you . . ."

"Never mind," Branwen said gently. "It will all be over soon."

Essylte cast her glance around the small antechamber, which held the chests of clothes, the tall polished bronze that gave back her reflection in the lamplight, the table with her jewel box and comb, the gilded chair in the corner. Beyond a thick silk curtain lay her chamber, luxuriously appointed with skins upon the stone floor, triple-flamed lamps on bronze stands, two braziers kept heaped with coal, two great windows opening onto the unending vista of the western sea, a great tapestry on the wall depicting the death of Uther Pendragon, and the huge bed, piled with furs and blankets. Ygraine herself, they said, Uther's wife and Arthur's mother, had lived most of her long life in that very room. In that very room was Arthur himself begotten and Gorlois of Cornwall betrayed. She shivered. She was terrified of that room, full of ghosts as it was, signifying power and betrayal. She much preferred Branwen's room, which opened off the antechamber through a low door opposite the curtain. It was small, with one lamp and one brazier, no tapestries at all, but a comfortable bed and a window looking south along the coast. Most nights she could not abide the queen's bed, but halfway through her sleepless vigil crept into Branwen's, and finally fell asleep to the gentle rhythm of her steady breathing.

What would her father think of such cowardice? She straightened her shoulders and looked up at Branwen. "I'm ready to go down."

Branwen nodded. "Remember, keep your eyes down when he addresses you. Offer nothing. It's gone well so far. He knows next to nothing about you, perhaps not even your voice."

"Have more people arrived today? I seem to hear noise from every landward window, and the moors are filled with tents. Will there be new faces to greet and try to remember?"

"No doubt. We'll go over their names and ranks when we get back here. You've done brilliantly so far. Everyone is impressed."

"If I don't concentrate on that, all I see is Tristan. I don't dare look his way, I don't dare. But he's all I think about."

Branwen took her hand. "Be strong, Essylte. Segward's always watching. Both of you. Ah, I hear Sir Merron at the door."

As they had done every night for three weeks past, they descended to the great hall on the arms of Sir Merron and Sir Guvranyl. Everyone rose as they entered, bowed as they passed, only taking their seats again when Essylte had made her reverence to King Mark and been handed into her chair. Then the meal was served and conversation resumed.

Essylte concentrated hard on listening to everything and saying as little as she could. The hall was warm, even though the windows were unshuttered and open to the sea air. The smoking torches, the close-thronged men, the stale smell of sweat, old wine and leather clogged her throat and killed her hunger. It seemed like only yesterday she had been at Guvranyl's house eating fresh fish stew, Tristan as young, handsome, and sweet-scented as these men were old, ugly, and foul. Her hand shook as she reached for her winecup. Seeing it, Markion grinned. His hand slid under the table and squeezed her thigh.

"Only a few more days, Princess. Be patient."

Essylte gagged on her wine and pressed her hand to her mouth. At that moment, a horn sounded, and the door swung open. A courier strode in and bent his knee to the ground.

"My lord king. Your brother Prince Pernam has arrived from Lyonesse with two servants and Lord Segward's wife. They are in the forecourt now."

"Well! They've made good time. I did not expect them until tomorrow. By all means, beg them sup with us. I will see them at once."

When the courier had gone, Mark turned to Essylte. "I expect you haven't heard much in Wales about my brother Pernam. When you see him you'll know why. He's hardly a warrior. Truth to tell, I'm surprised he came. He's never been in a hurry to do me honor. Perhaps he came as escort for Segward's wife."

"And why, my lord, does Lord Segward not keep his wife at court?"

Markion grinned. "He can't stand other eyes looking at her. Afraid someone will take her from him. She's a beauty still, although she's past five and twenty. So he hides her away in Lyonesse."

"Lyonesse? Does Sir Tristan protect her, then?"

Markion smiled slyly. "Indeed he does, although it's not the kind of protection I think Segward has in mind."

He laughed shortly, and Essylte looked puzzled. "Does your nephew know her?"

"Oh, aye!" Markion hooted. "Rumor has it he knows her very well indeed."

Essylte's eyes flew to Tristan's face as the guards at the door announced the guests and Markion rose to greet them. A hush descended on the throng. Pernam stepped into the hall in a gray robe, a black cloak slung around his shoulders, hood thrown back. He wore no sword, nor even a dagger in his belt, and from the thong around his neck hung the symbol of the Good Goddess, the Mother of men. Yet no one, not even Segward, dared a sneer. The healer carried himself with authority, a certainty that belied any need for weapons. His close-cropped hair, bony face, and deep-set, piercing eyes made an indelible impression. He was not a man, once seen, to be forgotten.

Essylte watched him approach the king, but it was the woman on his arm who absorbed her attention. Segward's wife kept her eyes down, her hood forward, her face hidden.

Pernam's eyes flicked once toward Tristan, then twice more in quick succession. A light frown creased his brow. Then his fierce, assessing gaze slid in turn to Segward, Markion, and Essylte. A faint smile touched the long, thin mouth, and Essylte smiled back.

"My lord king." Pernam bowed to Markion. "You do me honor to receive me here."

"Well, well, Pernam." Markion shifted uncomfortably. "You do me honor to come to Tintagel. It's been a long time. You look—the same."

Essylte was sure Prince Pernam's eyes were laughing, but his face was grave. "And you, Mark, are looking well. I was grieved to hear about Gerontius. He was a fine lad. I have asked the Good Goddess to protect his spirit."

"We've been Christian here for three generations, brother. He's in Christ's Heaven if he's anywhere. Put your pagan ways aside while you're in our midst."

Pernam bowed again. "Let me present Lady Esmerée."

At last the woman let her hood fall back. Essylte caught her breath. How could this lovely woman be Segward's wife? She was stunning, with dark, shining hair and flawless skin, lovely eyes that met the king's with calm certitude, delicate fingers that accepted his kiss without a tremor. More striking even than her beauty was her poise, her graceful bearing, her serene calm.

"My lord king."

"Lady Esmerée. How good to see you back at court again."

"I am delighted to be here, my lord. I congratulate you on your coming nuptials. No one expected them so soon."

Markion was thrown into confusion, and Essylte hid a smile. She spoke out of two sides of her mouth, this lovely woman, and to the High King's face. She had courage.

"My dear," Segward interrupted in an icy voice, "you must be tired from your journey. How delighted I am to see you so early in the evening. It will give us time to talk later."

For the first time Essylte saw her tremble, and then still herself. Did she fear her own husband? Essylte looked at Segward with new eyes.

Esmerée made him a low reverence. Unobtrusively, Pernam's hand shot out to steady her. "My lord, I look forward to it. I hurried on the road for the purpose."

Markion cleared his throat. "Er, you remember my nephew Tristan, I think."

For a brief moment, no one moved. Essylte saw Segward flush and pale, Esmerée lift her chin, Tristan shift from one foot to the other.

Esmerée curtsied low to Tristan. "Of course. My liege lord, Tristan of Lyonesse. A pleasure to see you again, my lord."

"And I you, Lady Esmerée." The tone of his voice was barely cordial, but it burned into Essylte's heart. Segward, too, looked short of air.

Esmerée paused. "My lord looks—hard used. Do you suffer from old wounds, or was your journey into Wales a danger to you?"

"I am recovered from my old wounds," Tristan said quietly.

Segward had opened his mouth to speak when Pernam intervened. "I will have a look at him later, my lady, if he will permit me. He's young yet. Whatever ails him will heal in time."

Markion was clearly at a loss to understand what had been said. "Well," he grumbled, "enough of that. Let me present to you my betrothed, the Princess Essylte, daughter of Percival of Gwynedd."

Essylte rose as Markion took her hand. Esmerée's eyes widened, and she made her reverence very low.

"Princess Essylte."

"Lady Esmerée. Prince Pernam. I am honored to make your acquaintance." She extended her hand to Pernam but found it grasped by Esmerée, and held between her hands with a firmness and warmth that surprised her.

"How beautiful you are! And so young. You must miss your homeland terribly. Have you seen much of Cornwall since you've been among us? Or just the environs of Tintagel?"

Essylte blushed. "Not even that, my lady. Mostly just the inside of the castle, and the sea."

"Oh, my dear, I beg you will let me come to attend you later. I can help you through the days that are to come." She smiled a little bitterly and let go of Essylte's hand. "I was married at your age. I remember what it was like."

Essylte's hand grew cold, released from that warm grip. "Oh, I wish you would!" she cried with more vehemence than she intended. "Please, come to me after hall. I would so like to have someone to talk to."

Esmerée smiled. Mark grumbled and cleared his throat. Pernam looked pleased, Segward annoyed, and Tristan startled. Beside her, Essylte heard Branwen's stifled laugh. She turned to Markion. "And now, my lord, may we not find these honored guests some seats among us? They have traveled a long way and we keep them standing."

Back on solid ground, Mark nodded and clapped his hands for servants. Everyone began moving, and the hall once again filled with the clamor of voices. Essylte felt eyes upon her and looked up. Tristan, smiling, stood gazing at her with his hand over his heart.

* * * *

Late one afternoon as the sunlight waxed golden and gilded the sapphire sea, Pernam descended the cliff path that twisted down the headland opposite the great rock of Tintagel. He walked slowly, frowning, scanning the broken shore. At last, reaching the rock-strewn beach, he heard the sound he sought: the loud *slap-slap-plop* of a flat stone thrown hard against the incoming tide. He paused a moment to whisper a quick prayer and smooth away his frown. Then he climbed over a wall of tide-washed boulders and stepped lightly down the other side, choosing a flat rock near the bottom for his seat.

Scowling, Tristan sent another stone flying into the sea—three skips and smack into a wave, startling a seabird, who flapped away in noisy protest.

"What do you want?" He spoke belligerently.

Unruffled, Pernam arranged his robe about him and did not answer.

Tristan flung another stone, missing badly, and swung around. "I suppose you'll never forgive me for Esmerée."

"There is nothing to forgive. You gave her what she wanted. You've protected her as best you could. What he does to her, you cannot prevent. . . . Did you think I was angry about the child?"

Tristan flushed suddenly and looked away. "Yes. But I'm not even sure she's mine."

"She most certainly is yours."

Tristan's eyes flew to his face. "Truly? How do you know?"

"She told me. . . . You ought to come visit me when you're next in Lyonesse. I'll have the child with me, like as not."

"What—what is her name?"

"Aimée. It means 'beloved.' "

Tristan's features softened, and to cover, he bent for another stone. "Odd name."

"Frankish. Like Esmerée."

Tristan looked startled. "Esmerée's a Briton."

Pernam's long mouth twisted in a half smile. "Is she? Then her father wasn't killed at Autun, fighting for Childebert with Arthur. Then she wasn't orphaned at three, raised by her brother, promised to a nunnery at twelve to ease the burden on his family. Or rescued from that fate by Segward, who saw her as she traveled with her brother to that impoverished convent, and who, seeing her promise, outbid the Christians for her services."

"My God," breathed Tristan, staring. "Twelve?"

"He used her as his bath slave for the first two years—"

"The monster!"

"And only forced her when she had turned fourteen. He considers he has done her greater honor than she deserves by making her his wife. Here in Britain, no one can prove her father once served a long-dead Frankish king. She must be forever in Segward's debt for whatever standing she has."

"That demon's spawn!"

"She's never had anything to call her own," Pernam finished gently, "excepting only her children. And of them, only Aimée was conceived in love. It is a great gift, Tristan. No, I do not hold the child against you."

Tristan sat heavily on the shingle near Pernam's boot and wiped the back of his hand across his eyes. "I never knew." Pernam watched his dark hair ruffle in the wind. "I apologize for my rudeness to you," Tristan said, looking up. "I've avoided you for four days, and all to no account."

"I know."

"I thought you sent Esme to Essylte to keep me away."

"No. That was her own idea. Don't look like that—you would only bring tears to that pretty child. The girl needs her, Tristan. Esme can give her a strength that you cannot."

"But I—I need to see her. I have so much to say, and there is so little time!"

Pernam watched his face carefully. "Yes. Tomorrow she marries Mark."

"Oh, God!" The cry was wrenched from Tristan. He bent forward, burying his face in his hands.

Pernam laid a hand upon his shoulder and felt him shake. "Tristan. You must be strong."

The dark head shook from side to side. "This is beyond my strength."

"You only think so." Pernam sighed. "How did it happen?"

"One look!" came the muffled cry. "One look at her face, and I knew. I knew in my soul. Clearer than I've ever known anything. Dear God, Pernam, I would give up anything I possess to make her mine. I would give up my name, my crown, my birthright. If she—if she—there's no hope of rescue, Pernam. I shall die tomorrow."

Pernam looked sadly down at him. "Is that how you see it? As all-encompassing disaster?" He sighed again and stared out across the sea as the sun sank, flaming, toward the horizon. "You are only a man, Tristan. How do you know what the gods hold in their hands for you? You see a maelstrom all around you, but it is a matter of perspective. With distance, with clearer sight, you would see the ebb and flow of divine purpose. You would see not only the storm's face but the quiet waters, the eddies and still pools where peace reigns, where wisdom takes root and grows—these also surround you, although you see them not. With patience, you will come upon them. Patience and time."

"Is this meant as comfort?"

Pernam's hand fell firmly on his shoulder. "You have always been a restless soul. Since your youth you have been seeking something beyond your reach. It is what makes you such a daring warrior, and what makes your music so poignant and profound. Can you not see in this 'disaster' the touch of the god's hand? You ache to possess this woman. Yet what would such possession bring you? The fulfillment of all of your desires? Nay, Tristan, it would only bring you a moment's respite from your seeking. Yours is a nature destined to reach beyond your grasp. If she were yours, you would reach beyond her, too."

"Never!" Tristan cried. "How can you think it? You don't know her—she's quick, changeable, alive. Vivid. She belongs with me. We are right together. Mark is—Mark is all wrong."

"Nevertheless, the gods gave her to him. There is a reason."

"What reason? Am I doomed, then? I warn you, Pernam—"

Pernam shrugged. "No. I meant only that, being human, we cannot guess what the gods have in store. All we can do is take what we are given and do our best by it. The acceptance and the striving are what make you the man you are. To succumb, either to love or to despair, is death."

Tristan shot to his feet. "What nonsense! To succumb to love is the purest joy I have ever known."

Pernam's brows lifted.

Coloring, Tristan turned away. "I didn't mean—it doesn't matter. Never mind. Tell me, Pernam, why you have come all this way to see me."

Pernam paused. "You face a wall too high to climb, too far to go around, too strong to batter. There is only one thing to do. Yield. Turn away, and get yourself gone from here."

"You understand nothing if you think I can leave."

"Come, Tristan, use your wits. What can you do to prevent it? If you are wise, you will not make it harder for her, but will take yourself away and bide your time. Go home to Lyonesse. Go back to Dorria with Dinadan. Take up your sword and fight some Saxons. Leave the girl alone to work out her fate. It is the only way she will get from one day to the next."

"And leave her here alone?" He looked toward the fortress, visible beyond the nearest cliff. Tintagel stood on a great rock rising from the sea a stone's throw from the jagged coast. A narrow neck of land connected the fortress to the shore. Like Lyon's Head, the place was easily defended. Approach from the sea was impossible; the sheer sides of the castle grew straight from the vertical tower of living rock. The causeway, guarded at both ends by gates and troops, could be held by a handful against an army of thousands. Tristan had spent much of his life at Tintagel, both when his father held it and after Markion took over his education. Still, he shivered whenever he rode under the great gates. To him it was a prison. He could not forget poor Elisane: Not once after she married Mark had she set a foot outside it. No wonder she had gone half mad before she died. It might well be impossible to capture, but it was certainly impossible to escape.

"I can't leave her here to wither away like Elisane. It's cruel. It's impossible."

"You only think so. But you will have to do it. The sooner you face that, the better off you will be." Pernam rose and looked hard at his nephew. "Come, Tristan. You are a king. Kings have no easy choices."

Closing his eyes, Tristan drew a long breath and exhaled slowly. "What I wouldn't give for your cool sense, Pernam. Don't you ever want what you can't have, so desperately you can think of little else?"

Pernam's lips twisted. "From time to time."

"Do you? And do you ever lie awake possessed by a fever only love can cure?"

"Often."

Tristan smiled bitterly. "And Mark thinks you a weak man. All right. If I can bring myself to it, I will do as you advise. After it is over—if I can—I will leave with Dinadan and not come back."

"Do not wait," Pernam urged. "Go now. I will square your absence with Mark."

"You forget the High King's command. I am to sing at supper, a merry song to send them off to bed." He shuddered. "I can't desert her before that. I have to stay until—it is done. Come morning, I will go. That's the best I can promise, Pernam. Don't ask for more."

Pernam bowed slowly. "I cannot ask for what you cannot give. But I have your promise. Thank you, Tristan. In time, perhaps sooner than you think, you will see the wisdom of it." He raised his hand in blessing. "May the Goddess watch over you and guide your steps."

15 ✝ THE PLEDGE

At midmorning King Markion wed Essylte of Gwynedd with all his nobles in attendance. The Bishop of Dorria pronounced the words that bound them one to the other in the eyes of God. Markion himself placed upon his bride's head the silver crown studded with amethysts that Queen Guinevere had worn so many years ago, and Ygraine of Cornwall before her.

From then on, until day darkened into night, it was a time of feasting and games for the pleasure of the wedding guests. At dusk, fatigued from exertion, or ceremony, or drink, everyone gathered inside the great hall at Tintagel for the long-awaited wedding feast.

Essylte sat beside Markion, slim and straight, clothed in a golden gown. More than one guest remarked to his neighbor that the new queen had not smiled all day, not even once, not even to Markion. But others shrugged, winked, and put her solemnity down to her maiden's modesty. Look at Markion, they said—half drunk before the feast even began. What untried virgin wouldn't fear a night in *his* bed, wild as he got in his cups? Look at Tristan, some observant souls whispered. What ailed the man? He drank nothing but water, and kept himself as far from Markion as he could get. Ah, replied others with knowing nods, but he always was a strange one, brooding over his music when he wasn't killing heathens, always restless, that lad, always moving on. What Tristan needed, they laughed to one another, was a woman of his own.

So they drank, and ate, and toasted the king and queen, and drank some more. Two boys from Logris played duets upon the lute; people danced and sang, the dances and songs growing bawdier as the hour grew late. Markion, flushed with wine and straining at his tether, began to kiss his young bride's fingers, then her cheek, then her neck. For as long as blushes and coy protests could hold him off, she checked his advances. But when his hands began to grope her under the table, she pushed him away.

"My lord king," she said firmly, "isn't it time for the bard?"

"The bard? What bard? Oh, yes. Tristan. I nearly forgot."

At his signal, the great harp was carried into the hall. Men quit their dancing and made room, respectfully, for the bard and his instrument. Tristan strode to the center of the gathering, pale-faced and solemn. He bowed once to Markion. "My lord King and uncle. Queen Essylte. My lords and ladies all. In honor of my uncle's wedding I have written him a song of celebration, to honor his ancestors and his descendants. I give you 'The Glory of Cornwall.' "

Markion looked delighted and settled back in his chair to listen. Tristan seated himself on a stool, leaned the harp against his shoulder, and, closing his eyes, let his fingers stroke the strings. The notes spun golden to every corner of the great hall, enthralling, compelling. One by one, heads turned, conversation died, until they were all caught in the web of his music, expectant and intent.

Tristan lifted his head and began to sing. His tale recounted the stories everyone loved best, of Cornwall's past glories and the men who had led her. But in each case the hero had fallen because he had lost the love of the woman he took to wife. The great Gorlois had made Cornwall first among all the kingdoms in the time of Ambrosius, but his wife had loved Uther Pendragon, and Gorlois fell. He sang of the golden age, of Arthur and Guinevere, of Lancelot, Gawaine, and the justice of the Round Table. Whatever men believed about Lancelot, no one could deny that Guinevere had long loved King Arthur. While she stood behind him, his power lasted twenty-six years and peace reigned throughout the land.

Tristan's melodic voice ensnared his listeners. He wrapped them in his song, binding their wills to his. Through him they saw the great battlefields of the past come to life before them: Doward, Caer Konan, Caer Eden, Calidon, Agned, Badon, Autun, Camlann. Through him they saw faces many of them had never seen in life: Vortigern, Ambrosius, Gorlois, Uther, Arthur, Lancelot, Gawaine, Mordred, Percival, and Galahad. They saw as well the women who stood by them, or deserted them, or were left behind, neglected, as each king crafted his own fate. Most of them knew from their own lives what it was to have the comfort and support of a loving woman, or to want that if they did not have it. Not a single heart was left untouched as the music sang to them of promise, of what Cornwall could become, of what Britain again could be, if Markion could win Essylte's affection, as Arthur had won Guinevere's.

Now a new age was dawning. Would Markion rise to take his place among the great Kings of Britain? It would depend, it would all depend, upon whether or not he earned the love and respect of his young Welsh wife. For the heart of all lasting glory, Tristan sang, his clear voice rising to the rafters, was lasting love.

As the final notes whispered around the walls, all eyes turned to the High King's table. Esmerée and Branwen had kerchiefs before their faces; Essylte's eyes were swimming. Markion himself, grave and excited, rose slowly and bowed low to Tristan.

"My thanks, nephew, for a moving tale. It is excellent advice. And I shall take it."

The hall exploded with noise as men cheered and clapped. "Tristan! Tristan! Tristan!" They brought him wine from the High King's table, and he drank deeply of it. They lifted him upon their shoulders and paraded him around the hall. Markion raised Essylte, apologized for his impatient advances, and bade her lead the ladies out. He would come to her, he said gravely, at midnight. Essylte made him a deep reverence, and in her wake the women left the hall. Tristan was deposited at the High King's table, toasted thrice, and begged for another song. He gave them a rowdy one, an old favorite about the fisherman's daughter and the wandering knight, and everyone joined in. Soon the hall was full of laughter and singing, drinking and dancing, ribald jokes and betting on the birth date of the coming heir.

Tristan, pleading fatigue, asked Markion for permission to retire. Mark gave it to him willingly. Segward's eyes followed Tristan to the door, but when he was joined there by Dinadan, who threw an arm around him and walked out at his side, Segward shrugged and went back to his winecup.

In the dimly lit hallway Dinadan stopped. "Well, I'm to bed. I've not much of a head for wine. Are you coming, Tris? We should be off early if you want to be clear of the headland by dawn."

"Soon, Din. I'm going to walk a while on the battlements and get some night air. I need to clear my head. Don't wait up."

Dinadan smiled. "That was one hell of a tale. Do you think it will work?"

"I pray so. But I don't know."

"A stroke of genius to make Markion think the attainment of his dearest dream depends upon gentle treatment of Essylte. I salute you, Tristan."

Tristan shrugged. "It's all I could think of to do for her. But you know, Dinadan, it's not just a tale. It's true enough."

"Aye. I don't doubt that it is. If Markion could only be that kind of man ... Well, good night, then, Tristan. Be at the gates an hour before dawn."

"Good night, Din."

When Dinadan had gone, Tristan slipped silently through the dim corridors to the stairs leading to the women's quarters. Few men stood guard tonight. Mark had given everyone light duty on this night of celebration. At the foot of the stairs Tristan waited in black shadow. There was a guard at Essylte's door, standing beneath a lamp, but the lamp burned low and flickered dangerously. He waited. Time dragged by in silence. The guard shuffled once, yawned, leaned against the wall. From far away came the faint sound of singing, off-key and raucous, the riotous celebration of drunken men. Tristan waited, palms sweating, growing ragged with impatience. What if Mark, eager for the release of his singular, self-imposed restraint, could not wait much longer and cut short the celebration? It could not be much shy of midnight—how could he explain his presence here? If he went openly up the stairs, what excuse would the guard believe? His hand slid to his sword hilt; the feel of cold iron gave him courage. Just as he stepped forward from the shadows, the lamp flickered wildly and went out, throwing the stairs and the landing into darkness.

The guard swore aloud. "Damn lazy house slaves! There's no oil in this lamp. What were they doing at lamplighting? Playing dice? Sweet Christ, and with the King due here any minute! Oh, yes, *I* know who'll be blamed—not the house slaves, God forbid. It was Kellis's post, it was Kellis's duty to check the lamp. Kellis will be blamed, sure as God loves kings." Tristan flattened himself against the wall as the guard felt his way down the stairs, still mumbling. "Might as well be a house slave myself. Have to do all the work anyway. Watch now—as soon as I'm well away fetching the oil, the King himself will come and find no one at the door. I'll be on border patrol by dawn, see if I'm not."

Smiling bleakly, Tristan slipped silently up the stairs, felt for the door, and tapped gently on it. Instantly it opened onto blackness. A hand grabbed his sleeve and pulled him in.

"Name?" Branwen's voice breathed in his ear.

"It's me. Tristan."

A sigh of relief. "Safe, Essylte." A sliver of light grew into a shaft as a the curtain parted and Essylte stepped forward, light from the room behind her throwing her shadow forward at his feet. He caught a glimpse of the great bed, piled with furs, and wine set to warm for the coming King.

He took Essylte in his arms and kissed her. It seemed the most natural thing in the world. Her slender body shook uncontrollably, and he pulled her hard up against him to still her fear.

"Essylte. My sweet love. Be strong. Be patient. I will not leave you."

Branwen beckoned them into her chamber. "Come in here. Hurry, do. The guard will be back any moment and he must not hear you."

They followed her into the little bedchamber. Here, the light from a single candle filled the space and warmed it. Essylte, her arms around Tristan, laid her head against his chest.

"You brought your sword." Branwen spoke flatly.

"Yes. If we are discovered—well, at least we can choose how we will die."

"Please," Essylte whispered, "don't talk of death. I am responsible."

"Don't be ridiculous. If anyone is to blame—"

"I am the one who should lie with him. I—I am the one who made the vow."

"If you keep your vow," Branwen said calmly, "Tristan dies."

"I know!"

"And you as well, my beautiful angel." Tristan's arms around her tightened. "We have been over this a thousand times. There is no other way." He looked at Branwen, standing straight by the door. "Are you ready, Branwen?"

"Yes."

"I honor your courage. Tell me what preparations you have made."

Branwen took Essylte by the hand and drew her away from Tristan until they stood side by side. Tristan's jaw dropped. They wore identical bed-gowns of cream-colored silk, intricately embroidered with blue and green threads upon the bodice. Their hair was dressed the same, braided with thick cream-colored ribbons and wound upon their heads. The effect was astonishing. In the candlelight, he could hardly tell them apart.

"Amazing!" he breathed. "What's the secret of it? Am I bewitched?"

They both smiled, the same smile. "We are much the same height and build," Branwen explained, "and but for our hair and complexions, similarly featured. People have remarked upon it all our lives. So I bound up our hair, and hid my freckles with a bleaching cream. We've made a pair of nightcaps to cover our hair. Essylte will tell Markion, or, rather, I will," she colored quickly, "that these caps are the custom in Wales. No woman sleeps without them for fear the beauty of her hair be ruined. If he doesn't see my hair, I may go undiscovered."

Tristan walked up to her, still staring. "The effect is magical. Why, in this light your eyes look green, like hers."

She looked up at him. "Is it enough, my lord? Will it work? Will Markion be able to tell us apart?"

"Never. Not in his state. He won't see you both together?"

"No. Essylte must be there when he comes in; the place is lit well. She must blow the lamps out, and make some excuse to come out for a moment. Then I go in."

Tristan nodded. "And in the morning?"

Branwen met his eyes with barely a tremor. "I'll come out before dawn and help her dress. She must be gowned for day when she sees him, so he will know the night is over and not grow amorous."

Essylte shuddered. Tristan slipped an arm around each girl's shoulder. "We three are in this together. We must keep each other strong."

Essylte nodded. "If Branny can lie with him, I—I can bear his kisses."

Tristan touched his lips first to her forehead, then to Branwen's. "We do it for each other, that we may all three have a future." Branwen shot him a quick look, passionate and fierce, but he was turned to Essylte and did not see it.

A scratch came at the outer door.

"My lady Branwen!" a man's voice called. "Bid the Queen be ready. The King is on his way."

"Kellis," Branwen whispered. "Quickly, Essylte, into the Queen's chamber with you. Tristan, close that door and stay behind it. Be sure you keep still."

Tristan stood for what felt like hours near the window in Branwen's chamber, looking out at the night sea. How fathomless she seemed, robed in endless black, yet in a few short hours she would be all glittering surface, all shallow glory in the dawn. The sea was always spoken of as if she were a woman—why was that? What if women were really so changeable? Here he was, risking everything—his honor, his name, his very future—for a girl just turned sixteen he had known two months. And yet just the thought of Mark's arms around her was enough to—

The door opened quietly and Branwen came in. "You are safe. Kellis suspects nothing. The lamps are all refilled and rekindled."

Tristan made an effort to think of nothing but her words. "You did well, my pretty Branwen, to steal the oil. It worked perfectly."

She smiled lightly. "I like it when you call me that, my lord. I always have."

He reached out an arm to her, and she hesitated a moment before she walked into his embrace. "You have more courage than many men I know. I like that best about you." He held her lightly. She slipped an arm about his waist.

"It is only a bedding, my lord. It is not a battle."

"There are beddings and there are beddings. If you have seen sheep rutting in the field, you have seen Mark's idea of making love. No, forgive me, sweet Branwen, I did not mean to speak so crudely. Soldiers celebrating a victory is one thing; a king with his young bride may be quite another. Must be. I've seen Mark at one, but not the other."

Branwen drew a deep breath. "Others have survived it. So will I."

"That's the spirit I like so well. You will survive it and save us all." He looked down at her upturned face. "Tell me," he said lightly, "what you want from me. In exchange for our lives. A good marriage? A kingdom of your own? I know more than one prince who might provide that."

She gazed up at him, a light flush warming her features. "In time, my lord. When I am—ready."

He hugged her gently. "What do you think of Dinadan? Is he comely enough? He's heir to Dorria, unpromised, and he's a good man. Moderate in his habits, steady and good-humored."

Branwen smiled. "I pray you will not try to sell me a horse, my lord, until I am in the market. At the moment, I am content to go without."

Tristan's smile faded. "What if you should get with child?"

"In one night? It's unlikely."

"But if you do?"

She looked up at him swiftly. "What is it you want to know? Which horn of the dilemma shall I choose, the hasty marriage or the bastard child? I can't tell you that, because I don't know." She paused, and lowered her eyes demurely. "I did not mean to be insolent, my lord. I beg your pardon. But—surely we need not think of that tonight."

Tristan dropped his hands. "But I believe you have already thought long about it, Branwen. I know you've already worked it out in clear detail. Tell me what your plan is."

Branwen turned sharply as the sound of voices reached them, soldiers' voices, raised in shouts and exclamations, coming up the stairs. "He is here!"

Tristan was already at the door to the antechamber when Branwen caught his arm. "No! My lord, stay in here! Keep the door closed. They must hear nothing." She pushed by him firmly, pulling a dark robe over her bedgown. "Don't worry. Essylte knows what to do. We have talked of little else for a solid month. Now close the door and await me."

Tristan stood with his ear pressed to the crack in the door. He was scarcely aware he breathed. He heard the King's men sing Mark to the door of the Queen's chamber, and then, amid much shouting and laughter, descend the stairs to their own rest. He thought he heard the soft, unintelligible music of Essylte's voice. Certainly, that was Mark's baritone, imperious, importunate. He inched open the door, hardly knowing what he did, just as the curtain parted and Essylte stepped into the antechamber, wide-eyed and shaking.

"I've blown out the lamps," she whispered, clutching Branwen. "But the braziers are lit. He's abed and drunk, but—but not near sleep. He—he did not want to let me go. You'd better hurry. Oh, Branny!"

Branwen squared her shoulders. "Not now, Essylte. It's too late for regrets. Is my cap in place? Very well, stand aside."

"Oh, Branny, I can't let you!"

"Don't fret so. My fate is in my own hands. I prefer it that way." With a quick shrug she was free of Essylte's restraining hand and gone through the curtain into the darkness beyond. Tristan stepped into the antechamber and Essylte collapsed against him. He held her tight, his lips pressed against her hair. Together they stood, hardly daring to breathe, listening to the man's low laughter, the girl's soft replies, the creak of the ancient bed, and then, unmistakably, the sounds of love. Essylte drew away without looking at him and ran into Branwen's chamber.

He found her lifting the wineskin from its stand above a flame. She filled a winecup and downed it all in one breath.

"Oh, Tristan, I am evil to let her do such a thing on my behalf. I know it is a sin. It must be. It feels like one."

"You have not forced her," he said quietly, taking the winecup from her shaking hand. "She does it of her own will, for her own reasons. And it is not all on your behalf."

Essylte's eyes widened. "What do you mean? If not for me, for whom?"

"For herself," Tristan replied, lifting a hand to her hair. But she shied from his touch and backed away. "For the chance to be the mother of the next High King."

Essylte grimaced. "Let her. I do not envy her that."

"Don't you? Are you certain? You are Percival's daughter; can you be without ambition?"

She smiled at him and set his heart singing. "You are the son of Meliodas and grandson of Constantine. Can *you*?"

He laughed lightly. He was her instrument, he thought irrelevantly, and she could play him like a bard. "We are cut of the same cloth, you and I. I knew it the moment I saw you. We take little joy in power." He took a step forward. "We take joy only in each other."

She backed against the door. "Tristan, I beg you not to touch me. You know I love you with all my heart, and I always will, but—but I—today I vowed before God, and now it is a mortal sin."

He took a deep breath and let it out slowly. "I have not forgotten. I want only to comfort you. I promise you by the blood of Christ, Essylte, I will not lie with you again. I cannot. It would mean damnation for both of us."

She nodded, calmed a little. "If we are not already damned. And whom can I confess it to? Not to the bishop, who is my husband's friend."

"Don't call him that."

"My husband?" Anger flicked her voice. "He *is* my husband. We can't undo it now. And while we speak, he lies with my servant instead of me. I have made him an adulterer, though he knows it not."

"He is no innocent in fear for his soul. What Mark is doing now he has done a hundred, a thousand times before." He smiled sadly. "Did you think him faithful to Elisane? Not a day of their marriage. Nor will he be to you. He takes his pleasure where he finds it, and always has."

Tears edged Essylte's eyes. "This is the man my father chose for me?" she whispered. "It's not fair! Men do without a backward glance what they would kill a woman for!"

Unable to help himself, Tristan stepped closer. "Yes, sweet, but you know the reason as well as I. Let him plant his seed where he may; only you can bear the High King's heir." Tristan cupped her shoulders in his hands. "The heir must be his, and no one else's. So no one cares who lies with Mark, but it is Cornwall's, nay, Britain's business who lies with you."

Her eyes, green in the candlelight, gazed into his. "Then get you away, Tristan!" she whispered. "For when you touch me, I am afire!"

He retreated at once, his breath fast and light, and gripped his sword hilt. "My lady, I am going."

"Going?" She quailed. "But I did not mean—going where?"

"Away. To Dorria. To Lyonesse."

She cried out, and covered her mouth with both her hands. "So far away? But why?"

"To stay would only endanger you. You know that. I *must* leave."

"When? How soon?"

"Before dawn."

"*Tonight?*" She gasped, and clutched at his hand. "Tonight? Oh, my love, don't go! I pray you! Not so soon! What shall I do tomorrow night, when—when—" She fell to her knees, pressing his hand to her lips.

His fingers closed around hers. "Essylte, my Essylte, take courage. I will be back. God knows I could not be long away from you. But we—we must be careful. There is no reason I can give for staying that Segward would believe. As it is, he already suspects me."

"How do you know?"

"Dinadan is certain of it."

She rose, smiling up at him. "My source is better informed. Lady Esmerée told me his suspicions all run another way."

"What do you mean?" Tristan sat on the stool beside the bed as Essylte paced back and forth across the little chamber, her eyes bright with excitement, her hair springing loose, here and there, from its tight bonds about her head.

"It's amusing, really. You'd never guess—Segward thinks you burn for Branwen. It is a rumor Sir Guvranyl has spread, in perfect innocence. He got it from the courier we sent before we sailed from the estuary, who got it from old Junius, no doubt. He thinks, they all think, you are lovesick for the Queen's maid. Lady Esmerée said we should do nothing to dispel the rumor. It is a perfect cloak to hide behind."

Tristan stared at her. "Branwen? Is this a jest?"

"Certainly not. You may ask Esmerée yourself if you doubt me."

"No, no, I don't doubt you. It's just—"

"So you see, you can stay on and everyone will put it down to love for Branwen. You *will* stay, Tristan, won't you? You said you wanted to offer me comfort."

"Yes, but I won't endanger you to do it. This is not a lie Segward will long believe. I can't hide my heart. It's a cloak made of netting; it will not bear inspection."

"I will need an oceanful of comfort tomorrow night!"

Tristan closed his eyes to blot out the thought. "But Essylte—I can't be here tomorrow night."

"Why can't you? I must."

He opened his eyes and looked at her. "Because," he said evenly, "if I am within reach of him when he touches you, I will kill him."

She said nothing, but all the defiance drained out of her and she sank to the floor at his feet.

Tristan glanced quickly at the window to see how high the stars stood. He had hours yet. She was trembling like a leaf in a tempest; he could not leave her. But he could find nothing to say. All his concentration was bent on ignoring her nearness. The cream-colored ribbon that bound her hair had slipped its knot. The end of the silk lay against his leg—so slight a touch, so insignificant an encounter—yet the storm within him swelled into a rage, driving him toward the edges of control. He felt sweat break on his brow and drew a long breath to calm himself.

Essylte's voice, low and curious, broke in upon his thoughts. "Lady Esmerée knows a lot about you."

"We are old friends."

"Friends?"

"We met through my uncle Pernam when I was recovering from the wounds that Marhalt gave me."

"She is a friend of Prince Pernam's, then?"

"Yes. And of mine." Part of him was amused at her jealousy. How quickly she had smoked that out! He knew Esme had told her nothing, that Essylte must have read it in the tone of her voice or the tilt of her head, or a silence held a beat too long, or a laugh a shade too forced. Women seemed to share a language mysterious to men. Some secrets could not be kept from them.

"Esmerée knows the truth about us," she said softly. "She knew at once, there in the hall. She knows you very well, Tristan."

"Is that what she told you?"

"No. But it was obvious. She knows you even better than I do. Her distress at our—predicament was clear. And it was not on my behalf."

Tristan managed a smile. "Some of it was. She has a heart that can hold the world's grief."

"She is the most beautiful woman I've ever seen."

"She is very lovely. But there is one who is lovelier."

Essylte did not smile. "Why did she ever accept a man like Segward?"

"She had nothing to say in the matter."

Essylte trembled. "She called you 'Orpheus.' What hell did you rescue her from?"

Tristan looked down at her upturned face. Her heart spoke in her eyes, willing his love from the depths of her uncertainty and fear. He clenched his fists to keep his hands still. How he longed just to run his finger along the fine, curving line of her cheek! His will was fast dissolving. He had to get free of her soon. "What is it you want to know, Essylte? Ask me. I will tell you the truth."

"Did—did you love her when you lay with her?"

He drew breath sharply. He found himself on his feet, and Essylte beside him, a hand on his arm. Her sweet scent filled his head until he could think of nothing else. His arms found their own way around her waist, his hands slid of their own accord along her back. The pain of wanting her began to beat at his temples, hot and insistent. "Did I love her? I thought so, then. But . . . it was nothing like this."

"Are you certain? Think. Did you not once love her as much as me? Tell me, Tristan. I need to know if this is a thing that will someday fade and desert me, or if I will feel like this forevermore."

He nearly laughed, to hear his own thoughts echoed so precisely, but the laughter caught in his throat. "Never. God, it was never like this."

Holding her in his arms was like holding a living flame. She quivered, alight with desire, her bright hair dancing free from its ribbons, her glowing eyes burning into his will. "Never like this," he whispered, finding her lips, drinking her in. She responded to his touch, firing like kindling in a blaze, breathing with him, moving with him, already one with his unspoken need.

Beside them the candle guttered for a moment in the night wind, then blew out.

He awoke to darkness. For a moment he did not know where he was. Then he felt the girl's silken skin against his body, felt the tickle of her hair against his arm, smelled the sweet warmth of her flesh, rich with the scent of love. He pulled her closer. A deep peace took hold of him, a glorious contentment, a sense of things being at last where they belonged.

"Essylte," he murmured sleepily. But the sound of his own voice awakened him, and in midbreath it all came flooding back. He froze. In his arms the girl's warm body stirred.

"Tristan."

Twice will you swear before your God an oath you cannot keep—lies you will be called to answer for! Twice he had sworn—*sworn!*—not to touch her. In God's name, what was left for them now?

"God help me," he breathed, holding tightly to her, "God forgive us both."

She grew still. Around them the silence was complete. The only sound was the half-heard sigh of the sea against the fortress stone.

Her voice, when it came, was hard. "I don't care. I'd welcome even Hell so long as we could be together."

"Essylte—"

"Hell for me is life without you, Tristan." Her lips moved against his throat. "We are one. Now and forever. If God condemns us for it, then—then I am willing to be condemned."

"Essylte, my bright angel—"

"*You* are my husband, Tristan. Not Markion."

He drew her closer and buried his face in her hair. "Dear Christ, I would that I were!"

"You are. The words I spoke before Markion did not make him my husband. Words are nothing. It is by our deeds that we are judged. And by our deeds, he is Branwen's husband. You are mine."

"I am yours forever, sweet Essylte." He kissed her softly. "But you are still Mark's wife. We have not the power to undo that, however strong our love."

"Listen to me. There is no marriage without consummation. It has *always* been thus. Listen, Tristan." The hard note still rang in her voice, and he listened to it fearfully. She fought with all her strength and wit against damnation, but something in her had already changed, and it was his doing. "As long as you and I are faithful to each other, we are more closely wedded than Mark and I will ever be, no matter what words the bishop pronounces over our heads. If we are true to one another, it is all that matters. Oh, Tristan, pledge to me, and I will pledge to you, that we shall never, ever lie with anyone else. That we shall be faithful to our love all our lives."

His heart ached at her mighty struggle. He could not bear to tell her it was a dream built on dust and ashes, that he had doomed her to perdition, in all her innocent splendor, for a passing ecstasy. "My magnificent woman," he whispered, hugging her close. "Think on this a moment. Is it possible? What about Mark?"

Essylte began to tremble. "To lie with Markion would be adultery."

"But is it possible to avoid him?"

"If Branny is as ambitious as you think, if she continues to take my place. . . . Somehow we will manage it—it *must* be possible to avoid him."

"Sweet Essylte—"

"And you, Tristan? Why do you hesitate to pledge to me?"

"I would not have you make a promise you cannot keep."

She moved against him, her lips warm and demanding, drawing him out of his despair into the unruly heat of her desire. "Either I am damned now or damned later. Let it not be now. Come, Tristan, make me your promise if you love me—why do you shy away?"

He gripped her hard and kissed her. "I swear by everything I hold holy that I shall never lie with any woman but you. You have my heart, Essylte, and no one else. And if it comes to damnation, we shall walk through the gates of Hell together, arm in arm."

He pulled the blue enamel ring from his finger and pushed it onto hers. "This is a token of our promise. Remember, when you see the eagle carved upon the crest, that you are Queen of Lyonesse, and my wife." He kissed her again, pushing the shadows away, enchanted by her warmth and her reborn desire. "Maybe you're right. Maybe it is possible after all. God in His wisdom has given Branwen ambition. Let's hope He has given her enough."

The stars outside the window had dimmed to pale, glimmering ghosts of their midnight glory before Tristan slid out of Branwen's bed and crept stealthily down the stairs to Dinadan and the waiting horses. The guard Kellis, half asleep in his corner, opened an eye as he passed and watched him go.

16 ⚔ THE HEIR

Old Talorc, King of Elmet, sat on horseback on the crest of a low hill. Below him in the valley a battle raged, hotly fought and impossible to predict, between Briton troops still in ragged formation and a wild, cutthroat, desperate barbarian horde. The river plain was soaked in blood, churned to mud, thick with bodies. The din of battle—the thud of hooves, the smash of spears on shields, swords against axes, screams of pain, of warning and command, victory paeans—floated up to the king and his escort, but softly, no louder than the cries of hopeful ravens circling overhead.

The old king, white-bearded and frail, his long nose red with cold, although it was April, lifted a hand and beckoned his captain closer. "Pylas, my eyes are failing. What in the name of Mithra is going on?"

"Your noble son Prince Drustan leads the center, my lord, which is holding. Uwaine of Rheged's on the right flank—it's still intact but wavering. They've been hit hard."

"And the damned Cornishmen? Markion's idea of reinforcement?"

"Bruenor of Dorria leads the left flank, my lord. It's holding well, despite their numbers. I've never seen so many Anglii, my lord—they must be in federation—ten tribes at least."

"Humpf," Talorc snorted, pulling his thick cloak tighter about his thin frame. "They unite when it suits them. I know the chieftains in their fed-eration. Do you think I don't have spies? But they never dared test us until they treated with that filthy Saecsen, Badulf." He hawked, turned his head, and spat. His gaze ran down the river to the score of high-prowed, shallow-bottomed sailing craft that lay along the shore, each one bearing Badulf's emblem, the white sea dragon. "Sea power," the old king muttered. "Once the wretched Anglii have that kind of sea power . . ."

The captain cleared his throat tentatively. "My lord, some among the men said that Tristan of Lyonesse thought the Saecsens might—"

"Hah! Tristan!" Talorc laughed rudely. "Oh yes, by all means, tell us what young Tristan thinks. By the Bull, Pylas, how did Markion have the nerve to send him here? He belongs in a holy house, chanting prayers, not on a battlefield."

"My lord, his reputation as a warrior is unsurpassed—"

"In Cornwall, perhaps. I spit on Cornishmen. If he were any good, he'd have *led* the troops Markion sent. He's his nephew, after all, and heir to the High Kingdom, such as it is. It is his right. But no, Markion sends one of his sycophants who isn't even kin. By the blood of the Bull, I was ashamed to receive him—and wouldn't have, but I needed the men he brought." The king's thin body trembled. The captain signaled his attendant, who ap-proached with a skin of warmed wine.

While Talorc refreshed himself, Pylas scanned the battlefield. "Look, my lord! Smoke!"

Talorc strained forward. "Where?"

"On the river. The Saecsen keels are burning! Set adrift and burning!"

"Burning! How? Who fired them?"

The captain grinned. "That was Sir Tristan's plan, my lord, if I under-stood the gossip. To come up behind the Saecsens and burn their means of escape. Watch the field. As soon as their rear guard spots the smoke, the Saecsens will desert the Anglii like a false friend in bad weather. They'll risk anything but their boats."

No sooner had he spoken than a cry went through the troops. Men broke and ran toward the river. The charge wavered, confused. Immediately the Briton left flank pushed forward, trapping the barbarians between the center of the Briton line and the water.

"So," Talorc said softly, "Bruenor knew the plan."

"Aye, my lord. It would seem so."

"How many keels are burning? Are they all destroyed?"

"All but one, my lord, and that one seems to be drifting back downstream."

The sound of the Elmet victory paean floated up to them as the flanks of Britons closed around the Anglii like the inexorable jaws of a great fish. Talorc smiled.

"Here, Din! Quickly!" Tristan shoved his dagger between his teeth and jumped out of his makeshift coracle into waist-deep water. He threw his shoulder against the bow of the Saxon keel.

"Tris! What are you doing?" Dinadan paddled closer, a torch ready in his hand.

Tristan beckoned sharply. "No, don't fire this one—let's take her! Help me get her off the beach before they see us."

Dinadan doused the torch and slipped into the water. Between them, they pushed her prow out of the mud. Once free, she slid sweetly back into the river, light and silent. Tristan hoisted himself up, swung a leg over the gunwale, and clambered aboard. "Call the men—six of us could handle her, maybe fewer. Come on! Any minute now they'll see the smoke and be on to us! Get Brach and Harran and Borsic—"

"Whatever *for?*"

"We'll take her! We'll sail her. She's our prize!"

"You're out of your mind." But it was too late to argue. Tristan was already unshipping the oars. Muttering under his breath, Dinadan retrieved his coracle and paddled to the nearest burning boat to drum up a crew.

A wild yell jerked Tristan's attention to the shore. A young Saxon lookout had seen the smoke. He stared, unbelieving, at the burning fleet, and then at the last keel drifting slowly from the reeds into the current, Tristan in the prow. He threw down his ax and began to run. Tristan watched him come. He was young and fast. He dove into the water and swam with swift, clean strokes for the slowly moving keel. Tristan glanced wistfully at the oars, but until he had another rower he could do nothing to speed the keel's progress. Dinadan was summoning the men, but they would be minutes getting to him, and the blond Saxon boy was an oar's length away. Tristan drew his sword and backed up to the widest part of the deck. This was a needless death; he did not want it laid to his account. But he knew Saxons. They fought from passion, not from sense. Nothing would prevent that boy from boarding.

He heard the gasping breaths, saw the strong young hands on the gunwale, a leg kicked over, two. The boy landed heavily, rolled, sprang to his feet. Tristan stepped forward and touched his sword point to the boy's naked breast. For one long moment they looked at each other. The Saxon was no more than a beardless youth, fifteen at most. Rage and fear swept across his features. He clutched at his dagger, then let it drop as he stared at Tristan, tears misting his light blue eyes.

It was cruel to make him wait. Such bravery as his deserved a merciful death. "Go to your gods, Saxon," Tristan grunted, and thrust the blade between his ribs. He caught the body as it crumpled and for a moment held it close against him. His voice fell to a whisper. "May they keep your spirit from harm."

A chorus of shouts and curses lifted his head. Sixty Saxons came racing toward him, brandishing short swords and two-headed axes. Beneath him the keel began to gain speed as it felt the current's pull. He withdrew his sword from the youth and dumped the body overboard, crossing himself quickly. A brief glance ashore assured him that most of his men had already joined the Cornish forces under Bruenor. Dinadan and four others were paddling madly for him. The Saxons threw themselves into the water. Three of them made it to the craft before the Britons. The first Tristan slew as the man pulled himself from the water. The second hauled himself aboard and had raised his arm to hurl his ax when Tristan's sword slashed across his waist, spilling his innards in a great, glistening pool upon the deck. The man made a croaking sound, staring down in horror, and died before his body fell. The last Saxon threw himself at Tristan, flinging him down and knocking the sword from his hand. He was a big man, heavy with muscle but blue with cold. Tristan slipped the dagger from his belt and plunged it upward into the Saxon's belly. The man grunted, trying to lift himself away. Tristan twisted the dagger hilt and pushed, kneeing his attacker hard in the groin. Pain and cold made the Saxon slow. He bellowed and grabbed for Tristan's throat, but Tristan, soaked in his attacker's blood, slithered from his grasp, crawled to his sword, whirled, and brought the blade down hard across the Saxon's neck. He stood above the body for a moment, gasping for breath. "God damn you to Hell, you heathen bastard!" Lifting the head by its hank of yellow hair, he flung it far out into the river.

"Tristan! Behind you!" Dinadan shouted, swinging a leg over the gunwale, pointing to the bows. Ten more Saxons fought to climb aboard. Tristan attacked, joined by his companions, and gradually, as the boat responded to the current and picked up speed, they fought off their pursuers. Four of them manned the oars and sent the shallow-bottomed craft flying downstream.

Tristan loosed the rope that bound the sail, and tossed the lines to Dinadan. "Here, raise the sail. I'll have a go at steering her."

The keel proved an easy boat to sail, responsive to every breath of wind, quick to Tristan's hand upon the tiller. He was amazed at her speed and stability. In all the years he had spent on the waters around the coast of Lyonesse, he had never handled a craft so swift, so sweet to steer, so alive beneath his hand. The shore seemed to fly past, thick with hardwoods just leafing out in the late, cold spring. The sounds of battle dwindled into silence.

"Where are we going?" Dinadan asked anxiously.

Tristan grinned and pointed to the Saxon bodies piled in the bows. "Strip those men and let's have their clothing. Leave them their jewelry— it's primitive stuff. Then send them overboard to their water god. But one or two have tunics I'd kill for just now. I'm half frozen."

Dinadan tied down the sail and bent over the bodies, wrinkling his nose. "They're soaked, Tris."

"I don't care. It's only water. My tunic reeks of blood." As he spoke he stripped off his tunic and leggings, preferring to stand naked and feel the cold bite of the wind on his flesh than bear another moment with that filthy barbarian's blood sticking to his skin. He shuddered. For a moment, with those hands at his throat and the wind knocked from him, he had panicked— it was Marhalt all over again, the nightmare returned in daylight. He still felt sick from it.

Dinadan hurried back with a bundle of Saxon clothing under his arm. "Here, half-wit, take what you want." He lowered his voice. "My God, Tris, you're nothing but skin and bone. What ails you?"

Tristan looked up, eyes full of grief. "You know what ails me." He pulled a tunic from the bundle and gestured to the rowers. "You'd better change, too. Everybody'd better. In an hour we'll be at the river mouth, and we don't want to be taken for Britons then."

"Why not? All this land belongs to Elmet. Talorc's an ally."

"Then where did this landing party come from? This is a river keel, not a longboat. She's not fit for the open sea. The Saxon Shore's a long sail from here. So where did the keels come from?"

Dinadan frowned. "You mean, they have a base somewhere? On Angli ground?"

"Indeed, and if all this land is Elmet's, someone is betraying old Talorc and dealing with Saxons. I want to know who."

The men looked at one another. "What are we looking for? Longboats?"

Tristan nodded. "Or a Saxon camp. Or a fleet of river keels. Somewhere where the natives raise a hand to wave us welcome."

"But," Dinadan said slowly, "we are one keel, and they are many. We can't outrun a well-manned Saxon craft if they give us chase."

Tristan looked up at the coarsely woven brown sail with the white sea dragon painted on one side. "Don't be downhearted, Din. I have an hour to learn how to sail her."

Men crammed into the feasting hall that night, vying for a seat on the crowded benches, standing pressed three deep against the walls. Badulf was dead, and everyone wanted to see for himself the Cornish prince who had, in one afternoon, freed Elmet from a decade of Saxon trouble. Servants scurried everywhere. Meat and wine were placed on the tables and passed freely among the standing men. The king wanted no one to go hungry or thirsty on this night of celebration.

On the dais with King Talorc, Prince Drustan, Sir Uwaine, and Sir Bruenor sat the men responsible for the Saxon ambush: Tristan sat the king's right hand with Dinadan beside him, and beyond Dinadan the four Cornishmen who had manned the oars in the Saxon keel.

Talorc rose, splendidly dressed in a fur-trimmed scarlet robe, and hushed the crowd. He raised a formal toast to his Cornish guests. Not only had their combined forces won a great victory against the Anglii, Elmet's ancient enemy, they had also routed the hated Saecsens from their land. The old wolf himself was smoked from his lair and killed, all by the clever ruse that Sir Tristan had devised. By stealing a keel and disguising himself and his brave companions as Saecsen thegns, he had discovered the Saecsens' sea lair and had drawn seven of their fearsome longboats upstream in hot pursuit, where the Briton army, still on the field, had surprised them and demolished them with fire arrows. Badulf was killed, and his son with him. The good Briton villagers had arisen and burned the Saecsen base. Those who were left had taken to sea in whatever craft remained.

Dinadan looked up during this speech and winked at Tristan. Talorc made the victory sound inevitable, but it had been a close thing. Tristan and his companions had been nearly overtaken by the longboats. It had needed courage and a neat bit of sailing to evade them. A great risk, but it had worked. Tristan raised his winecup to Dinadan and drank.

Thanks to Tristan of Lyonesse, Talorc finished, thanks to the brave Cornishmen sent to Elmet by the High King Markion, Elmet was free of the Saecsen scourge upon her shores for the first time in ten long years.

Every warrior in the hall rose to his feet, stomping his boots and clapping his hands in thunderous applause. Tristan bowed low, and when at last they hushed to let him speak, he thanked them gracefully, in the accent of Elmet, for the opportunity to come to their country and slay their Saecsen dogs. It was sport he liked well; he was honored to have been of service to the great king Talorc. If ever they found another warren of such foxy devils, he would be pleased to join them in their hunt again. They laughed and applauded. He had copied their speech exactly, they marveled to one another. He sounded just like a Parisii of the tribe of Drustan. He must have the ear of a bard.

Talorc slid a gold wristband, heavy with gems, from his own arm and pushed it onto Tristan's.

"You do us honor, my lord Tristan," he said gravely. "Take this as a sign of my respect. In all my life I have met only one man as brave as you. And that was Galahad of Lanascol, a Breton born, but a Briton to his soul. My father, Drustan, lived in Arthur's time, a time of heroes. You belong, if you will pardon my saying it, to such a time, a time of brave men and noble deeds, a time that is already past, and lives on only in the songs of bards."

Tristan bowed low. "They have a saying in Lyonesse, my lord, that I was born between the stars. I do not live in that world; I do not belong in this. They say that I belong"—he gestured vaguely toward the door—"beyond. That I am a wanderer."

Talorc's eyes narrowed. "May Mithra guide your steps. It is a hard fate. I would not have that on my back for all the world."

At that moment a horn sounded, the doors of the hall swung open, and a courier strode in. He wore the royal badge upon his cloak, a sign that he came from the High King Markion. The man strode to the dais and went down on one knee before Talorc.

"My lord Talorc, King of Elmet, greetings from Markion at Camelot. I bring good news to all of Britain. Eight weeks ago the High Queen Essylte bore a son to Markion at Tintagel. The babe thrives and grows strong. The union of Cornwall and Wales is now complete. In token of this, King Percival of Gwynedd plans a visit at midsummer to Camelot and Cornwall. We invite you to join us, my lord, if the wars allow, and help us celebrate the union of Britain by pledging your kingdom's support to Britain's higher cause, and by lighting a bonfire to celebrate the birth of Britain's heir."

Expressionless, Talorc nodded. "Elmet thanks Markion for such welcome news. We'll be pleased to light the bonfire. A healthy prince is a good omen for any kingdom. As for traveling to Camelot at midsummer to join Markion's alliance, we will take counsel first, and send our reply later. Now come, man, sit down and take refreshment. And give us the details. What's the boy's name? Constantine?"

"No, my lord. The High King named him after his nephew, who won him his throne and his wife. Tristan the Younger, they call him."

Dinadan turned to Tristan in time to see color wash his face and drain away, leaving him paler than before. "What's the matter, Tris?"

Talorc frowned at them both. "My lords, what is amiss? Sir Tristan, the Queen of Cornwall has borne a son with your name. Your uncle Markion has done you a great honor."

"Who named him?" Tristan leaned over the table, his voice shaking. "The Queen? Lord Segward? Mark himself?"

The courier looked blank.

"What does it matter who named him?" Talorc wondered. "Your uncle consented to it. He honors you by it. I raise a toast in your name. Long live Tristan of Lyonesse!"

The hall resounded with cheering. The courier was given a seat at the king's table, and everyone plied him for news.

"Were you at Tintagel?" Dinadan asked. "How fares the Queen?"

"Aye, my lord, I was there for her lying-in, with all of Markion's court. A healthy boy she had, may God be praised, born at midwinter. The image of the High King. By the time the King left for Camelot, the Queen was up and well enough to sit with us at dinner. Lovelier than ever, if you ask me. Which is saying something."

The men grinned and Talorc nodded. "Aye, I've heard of her beauty. As who has not? Markion's a lucky man."

Tristan passed a hand before his eyes. The courier, having refreshed himself with wine, settled down to give them all the gossip. "The Prince of Cornwall's not the only addition to the nursery," he said with a sly look at Tristan. "The lady Branwen's heavy with child as well and due to bear—probably has, by now. I've been gone over a fortnight." Eyes turned to Tristan.

He looked up. "Branwen? Branwen, too, did you say?" His face was ghostly pale and his eyes glittered. The men smiled among themselves. "What was it? A son or a daughter?"

The courier cleared his throat. "Forgive me, my lord, I can't tell you that. By now she must have been delivered, but when I left Tintagel she was still cursing the day she ever lay with a man." All the men laughed heartily, except Tristan, who looked away in anguish.

"Dinadan," he whispered. "Let's get out of here."

"You can't leave now. You'll insult Talorc—this feast is in your honor. You'll start a war if you leave before the king."

It was late before the men would let Tristan go. He and Dinadan, both unsteady from the liberal supply of rich, unwatered wine, stumbled arm in arm after the page to the rooms King Talorc had prepared for them. Compared to Tintagel, the king's fortress was a primitive place, with floors of hard-packed dirt and walls of wood and wattle. But the bedchamber was hung with tapestries, strewn with straw, and lit with four triple-flamed lamps. The bed, although uncarved and plain, was huge, and richly adorned with skins and cushions. A wineskin warmed near the brazier. Silver goblets stood on a low table. Tristan went right to the wineskin, filled a goblet, and drained it.

Dinadan turned as the chamberlain shut the heavy door. "What in God's sweet name is the matter with you tonight? You're drinking as heavily as Segward."

Weaving on his feet, Tristan met Dinadan's eyes. "I didn't know—she never sent me word—God, Din, I never knew she was with child." Tristan clutched his winecup until his knuckles whitened. "How long have I been away? Six months in Dorria and Lyonesse before coming to Elmet—plenty of time to send me word. Why on earth didn't she let me know?" Tristan hiccoughed and stared miserably into his wine. "Unless, after all, it is not mine."

Dinadan gripped Tristan's shoulder. "Be easy, Tris. Of course the child is yours. Everyone in Cornwall knows it." Tristan blanched. "But she's a proud girl. Perhaps she didn't want to force your hand."

"Force my hand? There's nothing I could have done."

"Well, then, there you are. Why would she send to you? She knew, no doubt, you'd find out in time."

Tristan stared miserably into his winecup. "I wonder. I wonder if she's been able to be faithful."

"Of course she has. She's been in love with you since before you brought her to Cornwall."

Tristan flushed. "But is she still? Oh, God, Dinadan, I wake up some nights in a cold sweat, thinking of her with Mark—"

"With Mark? Why would Mark—"

"What if he's not my son?"

"Son? The child is—"

"Didn't you hear? The Prince of Cornwall has my name."

"—yet unborn . . ."

Silence fell between them. Tristan replaced his goblet on the table with extreme care. Dinadan's eyes widened, and his breath whistled sharply through his teeth.

"We are not talking about Branwen?"

Tristan shook his head.

Dinadan stared at him unblinking. "Are we—are we talking, then, about the High Queen of Britain? Markion's wife?"

Tristan nodded.

"Are you telling me—" Dinadan gulped. "Are you telling me the Prince of Cornwall might be *your* son and not Markion's?"

Tristan shrugged. "Possibly. Probably."

Dinadan gaped, unable to speak. He grabbed the bedpost for support and sank heavily to the bed. Tristan said nothing but stood still, straight as a spear, waiting for what was coming.

Dinadan's eyes were full of fear. "You've lain with Essylte? That's what you're telling me? Jesu God, Tristan. You're a dead man." Dinadan spread out his hands in a gesture of helplessness. "I wouldn't have believed it of you. You, of all people, to cuckold Markion." He looked away, avoiding Tristan's gaze and twisting his hands together. "I know you're infatuated—that's not hard to understand—but to betray Markion for her! You have put her own life in danger, I hope you realize. And for what? This isn't a secret that can be kept. Markion—or Segward—is certain to find out."

"It isn't infatuation."

Dinadan looked up, startled at the irrelevance of Tristan's response. His friend's face was no longer a mask, but an open window to his heart. Tears welled in Dinadan's eyes. "Oh, God, Tristan. No. She is *not* your true love, the heart of your heart, the soul thrill you've been seeking. She can't be. She's your uncle's wife. Your sovereign. To lie with her is treason."

Nothing changed in Tristan's expression.

Dinadan reached for a winecup and drained it. "How long has this been going on?" When Tristan did not answer, Dinadan rose unsteadily and faced him. "You're going to shut me out, too? You don't trust me to stand by you? You've changed, Tristan. I wouldn't breathe a word of this to any living soul. I wouldn't dare. You have my word. But get it through your thick head that Essylte is Markion's wife and High Queen of Britain. She is not, and cannot ever be, your lover."

Tristan flushed and gripped Dinadan's arm. "Thank you. You're a good man, and I need you." Then he turned and began to pace. "You're wrong about Essylte. But how can I explain it? If you've never felt what it's like to die as a single individual and be reborn, in a hail of light, as a whole person, complete, in need of nothing—if you haven't been wholly overmastered by a woman who loves you, then I have no excuse to offer that you would understand."

Dinadan shook his head. "Is this your justification for betraying Markion? May God forgive you."

"It wasn't preventable," Tristan flared. "I tried everything I could think of to prevent it. To stay away. It was beyond my strength. Some things are impossible. Some things are meant to be."

"Meant to be." Dinadan regarded him unhappily. "If that's how you felt, why in God's name did you bring her back to Cornwall? And stand by while Markion wed her?"

"What choice did I have?" Tristan cried.

Dinadan slung an arm around him. "All right. At least you saw that. You had no choice unless you wished to spend your life in exile. Hang on tight to your love of Lyonesse. Now, explain to me, please, how it is possible this child of Essylte's could be yours? You've spent very little time with her, she's been attended every minute, if not by Esmerée, then by Branwen. And how did you manage to get past Branwen? It struck me last spring that she had all her wits about her. No one got in to see Essylte without going through Branwen first. And you'd be the last person she'd let in alone."

Tristan drew a deep breath. "Wrong again, my dear friend. Branwen is part of the plan."

As Dinadan listened to Tristan's full confession, a weary numbness grew around his heart. He grew less and less able to think clearly, to make sense of what he heard.

"But you can't know if this boy is yours," he protested finally. "We've been gone almost a year. Your sweet Essylte must have lain with Markion a hundred times since then."

Tristan paled. "She swore she wouldn't. But I don't know if—it was possible to keep that vow. So you see why I must go back. Tomorrow. To find out if he is my son, or Mark's."

Dinadan passed his tongue over dry lips. "What do you mean, she swore she wouldn't? How could she avoid it?"

"If Branwen agreed to take her place."

Dinadan exhaled slowly. "Jesu God! *Permanently?*"

Tristan nodded.

"How could you? Two innocent maidens—you've ruined them both."

"What if neither of them has ever lain with a man except the man who took her maidenhead? Isn't that fidelity?"

"But you've been in Branwen's bed—it's all over Cornwall—"

"Yes," Tristan said softly. "But not with Branwen."

It took Dinadan a moment to understand. "Dear God. Then *Mark* is the father of Branwen's child?"

"He must be."

Dinadan's lassitude left him, and he began to pace feverishly about the room. "What if it's a boy? Your life's in her hands, Tristan, and so is Essylte's, if she tells Mark the truth."

"That's why I want to get back to Cornwall."

Dinadan nodded. "We'll leave at first light. Talorc will let you go. My father can finish the mopping up with the men he has." He paused. "It's not possible this can all be true. How could Mark not know?"

A ghost of a smile crossed Tristan's lips. "He's seldom there. And he's easy to fool."

"Segward's not."

"Like all of Cornwall, Segward thinks I pass my time in Branwen's bed. I'm safe, so long as Branwen is my shield."

Dinadan shook his head. "Why, Tristan? Why do you take the risk? And you, a Christian, how do you justify it to yourself?"

Tristan shrugged unhappily. "I don't. I can't. . . . Sometimes I—I want so much to die, to release her from this cursed bond between us, I put myself in the way of death, hoping it will take me."

"Today in the Saxon keel you did that. And nearly succeeded."

"Yes. Selfish, to risk all your lives as well. If I had the courage, I would take my life by my own hand. But I'm a coward." He turned away, reaching for the wineskin. "When I am away from her, it is all I think about—death, sin, misery, damnation."

"And so you drink."

Tristan filled and drained another winecup. "When I am with her, Din, it's as if a great cocoon is spun around us, holding us safe and close in a world of our own, in a time of our own. When we are together, nothing else matters. Nothing can touch us. It is the closest thing to Heaven I've ever known."

Dinadan gripped his arm. "Tristan, this is more than foolhardy. It's suicidal. There must be an end to this, a way out."

"Besides death?"

A scratching came at their door. Dinadan shook him lightly. "Here is something better than wine to make you forget, if only for a while. Prince Drustan said he'd send us a gift tonight. Mind your manners, now, and be polite."

"Oh, no," Tristan groaned. "Not again."

A servant stood at the door with two young girls, one dark, one fair, clutching their robes about them.

"Sir Tristan, Sir Dinadan, my master Prince Drustan sends you these maidens as his gift. They are village girls, but they've been washed."

"Please," Tristan said quickly, "thank Prince Drustan for us, but we don't—" Dinadan elbowed him sharply as one of the girls looked up, fear in her eyes.

"My lord," the servant said nervously, "it is an honor for these girls to serve you. And for their families. They've been chosen with some care. If you reject them, they will be sent home in disgrace and never get husbands." He took the fair girl by her thin wrist and pushed her toward Tristan. The robe slipped, revealing a small white shoulder. Head down, the girl trembled until her pale hair shivered. Tristan put a hand under her chin and lifted her head. Enormous dark eyes looked back at him in a face already familiar with suffering. Gently, Tristan drew her robe tighter around her and pulled her to his side. Dinadan breathed a sigh of relief and took the hand of the other girl. The servant smiled and bowed low. "When you are done with them, my lords, send them out. They know where to go."

When the door closed behind them, Dinadan shot Tristan a sharp glance. "Are you mad, Tris? You'd insult Drustan to his face? Our host and the future king of Elmet? Over a girl?"

"No, over a pledge." Tristan looked down at the girl held tight against his side. "What is your name?"

"Farra, my lord," she whispered.

Tristan poured wine into a goblet and handed it to her. "My name is Tristan."

She smiled shyly. It lit her face. "My lord, I know."

Across the bed, Dinadan winked at him and took the dark-haired girl in his arms. Tristan tossed some cushions off the bed, piled them on the floor, and threw a wolfskin over them. He sat down on the makeshift pallet and held out his arms to the girl. After a moment's hesitation, she slid to the floor. He pulled her onto his lap, an insubstantial weight, her body light and fragile beneath the woolen robe, all arms and legs. He guessed she could not be much past thirteen. She trembled violently. He hugged her and pressed his lips against her ear.

"Farra, what is it I am required to do to satisfy your honor? Don't be shy. Tell me straight out. What were your instructions?"

She turned in his arms until she faced him. Spots of bright color appeared on her cheeks. "They said I must please you—my lord, I am sure it was understood that—" She gulped. "My lord, I must lie with you."

"Will they require proof?"

Her face flamed. "I don't know what you mean. . . ."

He smiled briefly and touched his finger to her lips. "Of course you don't. Forgive me, sweet child, but I cannot lie with you."

"Wh-what?"

"Shhh." He indicated the bed, where Dinadan and the dark-haired girl were busy amid the blankets.

Farra's voice voice sank to a whisper. "But you *must*, my lord! I—I am not afraid!"

"I know. You are a brave girl, Farra. But that is not the reason." He ran a finger down the childish curve of her cheek. "I was hoping for some way to compromise. I do not wish to shame you."

Tears sprang to her eyes and her lower lip trembled. She tugged at her robe until it fell from her body and she sat naked on his lap. She slid her slender arms about his neck. "Why don't you want me, my lord? Do I not suit your taste? Prince Drustan chose me himself."

Tristan groaned. "Prince Drustan has an eye for women. You are very lovely, with a shape beyond your years." He reached out and brought her hair forward until it hung in two long, glimmering sheets over her shoulders and hid her breasts. "Do you think I don't desire you? I want you more than I have any right to. But I am bound by a pledge."

"What pledge?"

"I have promised a woman, a woman I dearly love, that I will hold faith with her, and she with me. For as long as we live, we will lie with no one else but each other."

"Oh!" Farra quavered, her eyes shining. "How noble! Is she highborn? Is she very beautiful?"

"Very highborn and beautiful indeed. But this is a secret, Farra. Will you keep it for me? Her, uh, father does not favor my suit."

"How can he not? Everyone says you are the finest knight in all the land."

"I would that he thought so, too. Promise me, Farra, to keep my secret?"

"I promise it, my lord."

"Now pull your robe up, little vixen, and do not tempt me from my vow."

"But my lord, I will be sent home in disgrace."

"Don't despair. We'll find another way to please your father."

The girl wriggled back into her robe. Tristan glanced up at the groaning bed. Dinadan and the girl were completely absorbed in the intensity of their exertions. Tristan pulled off the golden wristband Talorc had given him and slid it up Farra's arm. The gems winked in the lamplight, bloodred, blue, and green. The girl gazed at it in wonder. Never in her young life had she seen such wealth so near.

"It's yours," Tristan whispered, amused by the expression on her face. "You deserve it for your service to me this night."

"But my lord, I have done nothing for you tonight!"

"Shhh. That is not so. You have done all I wanted. What lord could ask for more? Take this home to your father and show it to him. He will not doubt its source. Half of Elmet saw King Talorc take it off his wrist and give it to me. Your father will need no other proof." He smiled at her disbelief. "Who will believe I would give you such a gift, except in exchange for pleasure? Say nothing, and let them draw their own conclusions."

"My lord," she whispered, clutching the wristband, "you are a noble prince. I don't have to earn it? I don't have to"—she gestured toward the bed and wrinkled her nose—"do that?"

Tristan laughed lightly. "Indeed, you do not. Now hush, and lie down here with me and shut your eyes. We, too, will fall asleep. No one will know what we have not done."

Happily, she snuggled against him. "Oh, my lord," she breathed into his ear, "I shall have such sweet dreams."

"Yes," Tristan whispered. "And so shall I."

17 ⚔ TINTAGEL

It was easy going cross-country. Although they often skirted Saxon lands, they met no one who challenged them. Past the Giants' Dance they ran into two of Markion's scouts and learned that the King was still at Camelot and expected to remain there until King Percival's arrival at midsummer. Well east of Camelot they turned south, and by the middle of May they stood on the Tintagel headland, looking at the dark stone fortress silhouetted against the sun-bright sea.

"Well," said Dinadan. "There it is."

Tristan stroked his chin. "I must be shaved before she sees me. I've been a year away at war—she won't know me with this beard."

Dinadan laughed. "Oh, aye, isn't that like a woman? Not to know a man but by his chin?"

Tristan managed a smile. "Go ahead, have your sport. I'll be shaved anyway. Guvranyl's a man who loves a razor. I'll borrow his servant for an hour and have my hair trimmed, too."

They turned their horses down the slope and galloped to the causeway. The guards recognized Tristan and saluted smartly, calling out congratulations. Guvranyl himself greeted them in the forecourt.

"Tristan! Dinadan! My scouts sent word you were on the road. I hear you did old Talorc a better turn than he expected, and rid his land of all his enemies at once. That's my boy! Come on in and tell me all about it. How was it in Elmet?"

Tristan saluted his old arms master, then hugged him. "Touch and go, Guv. A risky business. I should have let the Saxons have Elmet. It's cold as a witch's tit up north. Thank God I'm back in Cornwall, where the land is green and the wind soft."

"Then it's just as well you returned in springtime. The winter was a hard one."

Tristan glanced anxiously at his face. "Is all not well, then? Who's fallen ill?"

"Not to worry. The Queen and all her ladies are fine. Some of the men had fevers. Too much food and wine, if you ask me, and not enough hard living. Segward was abed six weeks. So ill his lady wife came north to tend him. Nothing but soft flesh, that man. Why Mark loves him, I'll never understand. He's recovered now—but you'll know that; you'll have seen him at Camelot."

"Er, we didn't stop at Camelot." Tristan was busy adjusting his sword-belt, and spoke casually. "We thought Mark might be here, with his wife and heir, and didn't hear differently until we were well into Cornwall."

Guvranyl chuckled. "You never were a liar, Tristan, God be thanked. Don't bother to try to fool me. I know well why you've come back."

Tristan looked up sharply. "You do?"

"Certainly. But it's not my place to give you the news you came to hear. Get yourself a wash and a shave, and I'll send to the Queen." Tristan froze. "She can tell you all about it herself."

He turned and led the way into the castle as Dinadan came up and took Tristan's arm.

"Don't panic, ass," he whispered. "He's talking about Branwen."

Tristan exhaled in relief. "My conscience is quicker than my wits. He must think I came to learn about Branwen's child."

"Well, didn't you?"

Tristan stood nervously in the great hall, waiting with Dinadan and Guvranyl for the coming of the Queen. Long shafts of light fell slanting through the tall, unshuttered windows, illuminating in sharply defined rectangles the cracked mosaics on the floor. A young spider swung on a slender thread into the sunlight and stopped in his descent, basking in the heat. Outside, the cries of wheeling seabirds pierced the silence like the mewling of a human babe.

At last they heard her footsteps. The sentries snapped to attention, flattening themselves against the doorpost as the Queen swept by. She wore a spring-green gown trimmed in gold. Her hair was pulled back from her face, tightly braided and bound in a golden net. Her ears, throat, and wrists were adorned with jewels, and around her brow she wore a thin circlet of beaten gold. She walked with a measured step, holding herself straight and tall. Three of her women attended her, all wearing the unbound hair of maidens. They were only a year or two younger, but next to the Queen they looked like children.

Coolly detached, she stood before Tristan and Dinadan while they made their reverences and watched them without expression. Behind her, her girls peeked around her skirts, eyeing the two knights and smiling shyly.

"My lady Queen," Guvranyl began. "Your husband's nephew Tristan of Lyonesse and Dinadan of Dorria are just returned from their travels to Elmet, where they have put down a great rebellion among the Anglii there."

"And among the Saxons, too, I understand. My lords, I congratulate you on your brave exploits." Her voice was formal, cold and correct.

Tristan found himself tongue-tied, unable to frame the words he knew he ought to speak. Could this be his fiery Essylte, this cool queen who looked at him with a stranger's eyes? What had happened in a year's time to take the passion from her?

After a moment's hesitation, Dinadan stepped forward. "My lady Queen, it is we who have come to congratulate *you*, on the birth of your son and the Kingdom's heir."

A light flush spread across her cheeks. "Thank you, my lord."

"I didn't know—" Tristan whispered, and stopped.

She met his eyes at last. "My lord king is a superstitious man. He wanted no one told until the prince was born and pronounced healthy and likely to live."

Dinadan nodded. "Of course, of course. Not an uncommon practice. And—is the child still healthy? May we see him?"

Something flashed in the blue-green eyes, something that set Tristan's heart beating painfully, but her answer was still cool. "Indeed, I should be happy to show him off." She paused. "There is another child in the nursery besides my own, Sir Tristan."

Dinadan nudged Tristan sharply. Tristan cleared his throat. "Er, my lady, I beg your pardon. . . . We have traveled so far and so fast to see for ourselves. . . . How does Branwen? Had she a son or a daughter?"

Guvranyl smiled. Essylte's features softened. Tristan received the distinct impression that he had at last said the right thing. "She had a daughter, my lord. Three weeks ago. After you have seen the child, I will take you to see the mother."

"Thank you, my lady. I see she does not attend you. Is she ill?"

Essylte smiled briefly and her three attendants exchanged knowing looks. Tristan realized with a rush of relief that all of it was pretense, her coldness, her distance, her disinterested speech, this meaningless conversation. It was all pretense for the sake of Guvranyl and the girls.

"She does not feel as she ought, and keeps to her chamber a good deal. The midwife says there is nothing wrong. I thought perhaps a visit from you might do her good."

"I should be delighted. But first—first I should like to visit the nursery."

Guvranyl smiled and nodded his approval. Essylte turned to him. "I will take them there myself, Sir Guvranyl, if you do not need them?"

"No, no, go right ahead, my lady. It's what they came for."

Essylte led the way through the corridors, Tristan and Dinadan following at a respectful distance, and her three maids behind them. At the nursery door she dismissed the girls, who curtsied prettily with smiles and blushes for the two knights, and hurried away giggling among themselves.

"Half-wits!" Essylte hissed under her breath, then pushed open the door.

The nursery rooms opened onto a walled garden, with a fine lawn between old apple trees, and roses climbing rampant over the nursery door. Tristan was flooded by a wave of memories. He had been a child here once, had played on this very lawn with Gerontius. He had stayed here whenever his father had come north from Lyonesse. He had never stopped to wonder, until now, why Meliodas did not leave him at Lyon's Head. Perhaps, with his beloved wife dead, he had been reluctant to part with the child who was her pledge of love to him. Tristan turned slowly. He remembered these walls, this very woven hanging depicting ships upon the sea. There in the corner stood the old chest full of knights and horses carved of wood. The battles he and Gerontius had waged! He remembered round, full-breasted Gurna, who had tended them, healed their hurts, listened to their woes, fed them, clothed them, and rocked them to sleep upon her bosom, crooning in her gravelly voice. He remembered Gerontius's bony arm clutching him in the bed they shared, spilling his awful childhood secret—he had wished Gurna was his mother, instead of the sad and distant Elisane.

Here was another Gurna, kind-faced and placid, who handed a swaddled bundle into the waiting arms of his beautiful Essylte. Tristan was transfixed by the change that came over her as she took her child in her arms. Her cold demeanor melted before his very eyes. A solemn, quiet joy diffused her features as a tiny hand clutched her finger. She seemed to glow, alight with wonder and happiness.

"So this," Dinadan said softly, "is your son Tristan. What a handsome babe he is. Tris, come look."

Tristan looked down at full, pink cheeks, mud-colored eyes, a tuft of dark hair, and a red, toothless mouth gaping like a wound. The baby had eyes only for Essylte. He would not be distracted, but looked up at her adoringly, openmouthed, emitting urgent noises from his throat. Essylte smiled down at him in delight, but Tristan frowned. Something must be wrong. He felt nothing, looking at the child, not a twinge of tenderness or recognition. Was he Mark's son after all? Mother and child seemed to share a means of communication that was denied him. They were in a world he could not enter without a key.

"Come," Essylte said softly. "He is hungry." She walked out into the sunlit garden and beckoned them to follow. "Wait here, Brenna," she said to the nurse. "They will want to see Keridwen next."

Essylte seated herself on a bench beneath a budding apple tree in a pool of dappled sunlight, undid the laces of her bodice, and put the baby to her breast. She looked up to find Tristan watching.

"Come," she whispered, smiling. "Sit here beside me, and look."

Nervously, he sat down at her side and looked over her shoulder at the smooth curve of her breast, the baby's rounded cheek, the full eyelids closed in ecstasy, the thin seal of milk at the corners of the busily sucking mouth, the tiny fist held motionless in the air. A sudden wrenching deep inside him forced out a sigh.

"How I envy him!"

Essylte turned and smiled. "He takes after his father."

His chest tightened until he could not breath. "He looks like Mark."

"No, no," she breathed, "he looks like you."

Tristan bowed his head. He found he was trembling uncontrollably. She leaned gently against his shoulder and his arm slipped around her waist. Only Dinadan was near enough to see them, and he had found something interesting to examine in the grass.

Tristan looked up to find his son regarding him, lazily content, his mother's nipple resting in the corner of his mouth. The little hand waved. Tristan put forward a tentative finger; the baby grabbed it and pulled it toward his mouth. Tristan laughed. "What a strong little fellow!"

Essylte smiled and lifted the baby to her shoulder. "Like his father."

Tristan gazed at the child, who would not let go of his finger. "Essylte— I'm sorry I wasn't here. I didn't know. . . ."

"It's just as well you weren't here."

"Was it hard for you? The birth?"

She was silent a little while, patting the baby on his back. "It was the hardest thing I've ever done. It took a long time. I'm glad you weren't here. You'd have given us away."

He nodded, running his hand over the baby's oval head, the firm skull, the thin, silky hair. "More than likely."

Essylte lifted the child down, cradled him in the crook of her arm, and offered him her other breast. He accepted greedily, closing his eyes and making soft, contented noises as he sucked.

"Great Mother!" Tristan whispered. "What joy!"

"He brings me unimaginable joy," Essylte said softly. "Every day is new."

"How old is he now?"

"Three months."

"As Queen, surely you are entitled to a wet nurse."

"What for? I'm not traveling. No one comes to visit. And I wanted— from the start, all I wanted was to hold him in my arms. I look at him, and I see your face." Her voice began to tremble. "I wouldn't give this up for anything. Only you—" Her eyes met his, alive, burning. "Only you have ever brought me pleasure so intense."

Tristan looked away, afire in every sinew. He had his answer now. She had given him the key, she had let him in again, yet his joy was bittersweet. He was no longer foremost in her thoughts. Here was a helpless infant whose need of her was greater than his own. Who would have dreamed love could have such consequences?

"Who gave him my name? Did you?"

She shook her head. "No. It was Mark's idea. I wouldn't have dared. But it pleased me greatly, and he saw it." She paused. "He likes to please me. . . . He is not a bad man."

"No. I never thought he was."

"There is another reason I sent away the wet nurse," she continued in a level voice. "As long as I nurse the child, Mark will keep his distance. He wants nothing to do with babies. He could hardly bring himself to come for my lying-in. He came only because it was expected of him, because the birth had to be attested to and the child formally acknowledged." A smile crept into her voice. "He saw me nursing once. I thought he was going to be ill. He will not come back to Tintagel until the baby's weaned. You were right, you know. He wants a broodmare, not a companion."

"He'll be back for your father's visit, won't he?"

"My father?" She turned to him in surprise. "My father's coming?"

"That's what the courier told us in Elmet. At midsummer. There's to be a big celebration in Young Tristan's honor. An attempt to draw more kingdoms into the alliance. Didn't you even know?"

"No." She gazed off into the distance, the tenderness gone from her face. "No, he didn't tell me. It's just like him. Percival's not my father anymore, in Mark's eyes. Now he's the High King's kin." She glanced down at the sucking baby, and her features softened. "It doesn't matter. Celebration or no, I will nurse him and Mark won't come near me."

"Is it—is it that bad?"

She looked up at him briefly. There was more in her face than he could read. "You don't understand. You can't. You're not a woman. I live a lie. It has changed me." She shrugged and pulled the sleeping baby from her breast. "Anyway, I must nurse him until Branwen gets her health back."

"Is she really ill?"

"I don't know what's wrong. Maybe you can find out. She's not confined to bed, but she hardly stirs from her room. She has a wet nurse for Keridwen, poor little child."

"Essylte . . . is Keridwen Mark's daughter?"

She turned to face him. "Of course."

"Was Branwen happy to be bearing? Or upset?"

Essylte regarded him curiously. "Content. Esmerée was here this winter to nurse Segward through a fever. She helped us both a great deal. She told us what to expect. And she brought her children with her."

Tristan hardly breathed. "Her children?"

Essylte smiled. "Three little girls. Perfectly beautiful and well behaved. The youngest is the sweetest child I've ever known. Not yet four and already sings like a lark. Little Aimée."

"I—I—I am glad for your sake Esmerée was here."

"So am I. Branny was fine about it all until the birth. I was with her most of the time, to help her through it. I don't know what happened. When it was all over, she just withdrew into herself. She wouldn't even hold the baby in her arms. Why, I spend more time with Keridwen than she does. *Someone* must be a mother to her. See what you can do, Tristan. If Branny's not back to normal by the time young Tristan's weaned . . ." She began to tremble. Tristan took her hand and held it hard.

"Then you have done it? You have kept your promise?"

Her eyes widened. "Did you doubt me?"

He flushed. "I thought Mark might have caught you unawares and forced you—"

She straightened. "Mark *never* caught me unawares." She sank back against the tree a little, holding tight to the baby. "I have become expert in deceit. I'm an excellent liar."

Tristan pressed her fingers to his lips. "I know it must be difficult. I bless you from the bottom of my soul."

"And you?" she said, withdrawing her hand. "Have you kept your promise? Branny told me it would be impossible for a man, that every time you survived a battle, young girls would be thrown into your bed as a token of gratitude. Is this true?"

"Yes, my dear love, it is true. But I took none of them. I did not want them. I want only you."

Her face lit. "Oh, Tristan."

Dinadan coughed warningly. Tristan looked up to see Brenna through the doorway, pacing back and forth with an infant in her arms. Essylte handed the child to Tristan and began to lace up her gown.

"Don't be afraid," she laughed. "He won't break. Hold him tight. You won't wake him. After a meal he'll sleep through anything."

Tristan marveled at the light, warm weight he held. The boy's face against his cheek was smoother than velvet. This undeniable life, this solid flesh, was the result of that last, wild night of love in the tower of Tintagel. He could not believe it, although he knew it was so. For the first time in a year, he felt like singing.

Aware of eyes upon him, he looked up. Essylte was smiling at him. Her eyes were wet with tears.

* * * *

Kill him. . . . Kill him. . . . While he lives, your children will be girls, heir to nothing. . . . Die he must.

Branwen groaned and turned her head on her pillow. Beads of sweat formed along her brow. Her damp hair, unbound and straggling, clung to her pallid cheek. Slowly she rose from the depths of sleep, fleeing from the witch whose burning eyes and hollow voice haunted her dreams. Always, always the same voice calling through the mists, the same refrain pounding in her ears: *Kill him. . . . Kill him. . . . Die he must.*

Without warning, someone took her hand in a warm, strong grasp and led her firmly, step by step, back into the light. She opened her eyes. Tristan sat beside her, his hand in hers, his beautiful brown eyes studying her face. She shook herself to be sure she wasn't dreaming.

"Tristan?"

He raised her fingers to his lips and kissed them. The last shreds of nightmare dissolved in the warmth that seemed to flow from him as from an open blaze. He reached out and brushed damp strands of hair from her face.

"My pretty Branwen," he said softly. "I never thought to see you ill."

She struggled to sit up. His strong hands slid under her arms and raised her with ease. She gazed at him, remembering all the times she had pictured him, all winter long, through interminable pregnancy, discomfort and cold, pictured him here, alone in her chamber, waiting only for her. And here he was, larger than life and more vivid than any daydream, his strength, his warmth, his passion, his physical beauty so near he was overpowering. She had no more resistance than a summer moth, hopelessly drawn to the flame that was its doom. She could not keep her eyes from his face. Slowly the heat of life returned to her and a rosy flush spread over her waxen skin. She managed a smile. The smile he flashed in return set her heart beating wildly.

He brought her hand to his cheek. "That's better. That's the fighting spirit I remember. You've had a hard time of it, haven't you, little Branwen?"

How wonderful to hear his voice again, so vibrant, so melodic! The voice of a thousand daydreams. "Hard enough."

"I'm told you don't sleep well."

She shivered. "I have bad dreams."

"Many women do, after bearing. They will fade."

She smiled. "And how do you know so much about bearing, my lord?"

Tristan grinned. "Not on my own account, of course. But I have a friend who is wise in woman-lore."

"You mean Esmerée. . . . Tristan, I am your friend. I will keep your secrets."

"It doesn't seem to be much of a secret."

Now it was her turn to squeeze his hand. "But it is. Even Essylte doesn't know about Aimée."

"How did *you* know? Did she tell you?"

"Of course not. But I watch and observe. One woman can always tell where another loves."

"You exaggerate. It was years ago. We are friends now, good friends. Nothing more. Ask Esmerée."

Branwen watched him look away, his fingers plucking at the wool of her blanket. She remembered only too well Esmerée's face when she spoke of Tristan, and the affection in her voice. Was it possible he did not guess at his power over women? Those who loved him loved him unreservedly and long, as she herself knew as well as anyone. She closed her eyes to hide her thoughts from him. The woman he loved could never be his—*she* could be his, but he would never love her. She could not have invented a sadder tale.

"Branwen," he whispered. "You have gone quite pale. What dark thoughts disturb you?"

She forced herself to smile. "Secrets, my lord."

Tristan drew a long breath. "You are a storehouse of secrets."

She pulled aside the blankets and reached for her woolen robe. Tristan wrapped it around her. "They are safely kept, my lord." She made her way to the window, where the golden light of afternoon slowly faded into cool, dusky shadows. "Everything is going well. All of Cornwall thinks I've borne your child, and Essylte Mark's."

Tristan followed her to the window. "I've seen your daughter. She's a pretty little thing. She looks like you."

Tears crept to her eyes. "Don't be kind. Don't. She's scrawny and ugly and underfed. I know it, and I'm helpless to prevent it. I've not an ounce of mother love in me. I don't know where it went. I hope she dies. She'd be better off."

"Don't say such a thing." He drew her into his arms and held her tightly, stroking her tousled hair. With her face pressed against his chest she wept, shatteringly and beyond control, thinking not of the bony baby in the nursery, but of the man who held her in his arms, this man of daring and fearless deeds, whose strength and beauty were all she wanted, whose heart she could never have.

At length Tristan lifted her and sat down with her on the bed, cradling her like a child. "Little Branwen, I take it on myself. I have asked too much of you. You have lived a lie and borne a child to a man you do not love. Shall I take the child away and have her tended elsewhere? No one will think it strange. My uncle Pernam runs a house of healing. He will love the girl if you cannot. He is Mark's brother; it is even fitting."

Branwen lay still, her head against his chest, listening to the slow, strong beating of his heart. "No," she whispered. "There is no need. Essylte loves the child. She is mother enough for both of them." She looked up into his face. "Without Keri, what excuse would you have to visit the nursery at Tintagel? You would never see your son." The light in his face was a dagger in her heart, but she smiled. "He is a beautiful boy, young Tristan. Strong and healthy. Everything a prince should be. I congratulate you."

"Thank you, Branwen."

She pulled herself up and slid out of his arms. "And you are wrong, you know, about Mark. I like him well enough. He's no more than a big, selfish boy. He's teachable. And he loves me." She smiled bitterly. "He thinks he loves Essylte. He is charmed by her beauty and her pretty ways. But I'm the one he talks to and shares his problems with, alone in the dark. It's me he really loves."

"I don't doubt it," Tristan replied. "But isn't that a nettle shirt that rubs on tender skin? To do so much, yet go so unacknowledged?"

"If and when I bear a son, I'll have acknowledgment enough." She watched her words strike home, saw his newborn father-pride spark his anger, saw the flame of indignation at the thought that his son, the Prince of Cornwall, should be set aside and bastardized for a child of hers. And then she saw him sober, and swallow his resentment, and slowly nod.

"If it happens, so it must be. I accept it."

She reached out to him in compassion, against her will, when the door opened and Guvranyl appeared on the threshold with Dinadan behind him.

"Sir Guvranyl!" She clutched her robe tight to her body and made him a quick curtsy.

Tristan rose from the rumpled bed. Guvranyl winked slyly at him; Dinadan stared in surprise. "My lords, is anything amiss?"

"Nothing's amiss," Guvranyl assured him. "It's time to eat, and no one could find you. We asked the Queen and she sent us here. We had a bet laid on. Dinadan bet we wouldn't find you here; I bet we would." He grinned at Dinadan. "That's a silver coin you owe me, my young lord."

Wooden-faced, Dinadan pulled a coin from his pouch. "I seem," he said slowly, "to have been wrong about a great many things."

Tristan sighed. "Appearances will be the death of me. Come on, Din, let's go down together. I'll try to explain it to you."

"The lady Branwen wishes to see you, my lord," the page whispered at his elbow. Tristan nodded. Guvranyl and Dinadan were half asleep, stretched out in cushioned chairs by the fire, an empty wineskin on the floor between them. The Queen and her women had taken themselves off after dinner. Hours ago. But Tristan had been unable to drink wine with his companions and enjoy the talk of men. All he could think of, as he fidgeted in his chair, was the soft evening breeze that set the lamplight trembling, the whispering of the sea beyond the windows, the midnight fires burning in the heavens, the banked fire in his body. Beautiful Essylte was somewhere within these walls, listening as he was listening to the sea wind, watching the wheeling stars, waiting for the moment when he would find his way to her.

He rose. "Sir Guvranyl." Guvranyl waved a lazy hand and yawned.

"Good night, Tristan."

"Dinadan."

"Humpf," Dinadan grunted, and yawned.

"In the morning, my lords."

He let the page lead him, although he knew the way. At the top of the stairs, Kellis barred the door.

"Who goes there, in the King's name?"

"Tristan of Lyonesse. Good evening, Kellis."

"My lord Tristan. By all means, enter. The lady sent for you half an hour ago."

Tristan smiled. "Never keep a lady waiting." He put his hand to the door and walked into the antechamber. Branwen stood at the narrow window, gowned and waiting. The door to her chamber was open. The curtain to the Queen's chamber was closed. All this Kellis saw before he smiled and withdrew. "Lucky devil," he whispered under his breath. "A talent of silver he doesn't come out before dawn."

Tristan waited until the door had closed behind him. "Well, Branwen, you're looking better. There's color in your face."

"Your visit helped." She made him a reverence and nodded toward the curtain. "I wish you joy, Tristan. Go on in. She's waiting."

Branwen turned and walked into her room, shutting the door firmly. Tristan paused at the curtain. His heart pounded, his hand trembled on the silk. He had waited so long, he had desired this so much—and yet part of him wished to be away, anywhere else, killing Saxons in Rheged or Elmet, somewhere where red blood flowing could wash away the stain of his precious sin. He took a deep breath and parted the curtain.

Triple lamps and candlesticks flooded the chamber with light. Essylte stood at the end of the big bed in her green gown, as cool and calm as he had seen her first that morning. The bed was piled with furs and cushions, velvets and silks of scarlet, purple, and gold. Color, light, and warmth engulfed him. It was like walking into the heart of a fire.

"Essylte."

She did not move, but followed him with eyes that betrayed no feeling.

He walked up to her and took her by the waist. Still she stood, cold, dispassionate, a woman carved of stone. Around her brow she wore the gold circlet of her rank. Mark's gift. He lifted it off her head and let it fall to the floor, where it rolled crookedly into a corner. A smile touched the corners of her mouth. He pulled the golden netting from her hair and took out, one by one, the pins that held her tresses. His fingers worked the braiding loose, and at last her glorious fire-gold curls fell into his hands. She closed her eyes when his lips touched her face and his hands slid beneath the laces of her gown. She held out against him to the limit of her strength, refusing to gasp, refusing to return his kisses, refusing even to touch him.

"Vixen," he murmured in her ear. "You are no ice queen. Why do you tease me so?"

She trembled but kept her eyes fixed on the wall behind him. "Discipline. Control. It's part of deceit. It's what keeps me alive. I practice it daily."

He kissed her roughly and pulled her hard up against him. She knew it angered him to be reminded of Mark's presence, of Mark's rights, of the lie they all three lived in order to deceive Mark, but it angered her, too, that deceit should be a part of her daily life, when all Tristan had to do to avoid it was ride away from Tintagel in the open air. But although she was master of her voice and her expression, she could not control her body's responses to Tristan's touch. Heat rose to her face and her pulse quickened as his hands slid over the soft fabric of her gown. And, like any woman whose anger springs from hurt, she was defenseless against compassion.

His grip slackened and he slid to his knees, pressing the palm of her hand against his cheek. "I'm sorry, Essylte. It's my fault you live a lie. If I had been able to resist you that night at Guvranyl's house, if I had done my duty to your father and to Mark, you would have no need to lie. I am ashamed I have forced this fate upon you."

Tears welled in her eyes. She sank to the bed and cradled his head in her lap. "You never forced me, love. Don't you remember that night? There was no power on earth that could have kept us apart. And if you had done your duty, I would never have known the joy of love. Nor the pleasures of the body."

He raised his head at the tenderness in her voice, saw the flush in her face, the brilliance of her eyes, the quick rise and fall of her gown with every indrawn breath, the firm swell of her mother's breasts straining against the soft silk of her bodice.

"Branny knows nothing of such pleasures. I've asked her. Mark's bed is a place of labor and exertion, but not of joy. At least, not for her. All this you saved me from, that night at Guvranyl's house. Never be ashamed of it. I am not."

"Oh, Essylte."

She gazed around the room, and a small smile formed upon her lips. "I have loathed this room from the moment I first set foot in it. It's a chamber of births and deaths and unrequited loves. It's filled with ghosts. When I am in it, I light all the lamps to banish the shadows." She smiled down at Tristan and began to draw the braided laces from the bodice of her gown. "If you would do me a service, Tristan, you will banish them from my heart, as well."

At dawn, as she fell at last into delicious sleep, she reflected that Tristan had done what she asked of him. During all the hours of darkness she had not once thought of Mark, or Branwen, or the future. He had narrowed her focus to immediacy, to lips on flesh, to hands on skin, to the quickening friction of body against body, to the intense appreciation of each single, separate moment, full to bursting with emotion, until all ability to think was swamped in a rising sea of sensation. And she knew, as she sank toward sleep with her lips against his hair, that when they awakened and consciousness threatened to return, he would save her from it all over again.

18 ⛨ PLAYING WITH FIRE

Tristan floated idly on the gentle swell of the sea. Above him the sky blazed with the light of midday; below him the sea's cold caress cooled his skin, tempering the sun's power. When he closed his eyes he saw Essylte's image against his fire-shot lids, her beautiful body stretched pale and taut against the purples and reds of the royal bedcovers. With motherhood she had lost the last traces of her girlish shape. She was everywhere curves and firm, warm, yielding flesh between his hands. She had grown in power, too. A smile of hers could rob him of thought.

"Tristan, don't you think it's time to leave? We've been here a week already. It's long enough." Dinadan sat on a boulder at the sea's edge, letting the hot sun dry the water from his body.

Tristan opened one eye and looked at him. "Do you miss home? Why? Who's waiting for you?"

Dinadan hesitated. "Actually . . ."

At once Tristan righted himself and stood waist-deep, pushing his wet hair from his face. "There *is* someone? Not—what was her name? Diarca?"

Dinadan colored. "The very same. However did you remember?"

"She was your first. You wouldn't tell me about it. I remember that well."

"You had no right to know."

"I was only curious. You didn't often do things before me."

"You've made up for lost time."

Tristan grinned. "How prickly you are! It must be serious."

"Serious enough. Before we left for Elmet, my father began negotiations. I don't expect trouble on that account. She's been—fond of me a long time."

"Why, Dinadan, you never told me." Tristan sobered and walked out of the sea. "All these months together, fighting, sharing the same tent, the same fire, the same platter, you never said a word. I had no idea."

Dinadan shrugged. "You're prickly yourself sometimes, you know. Sometimes you close up, clamlike, and there's no getting at you. Ever since Markion's wedding, and that's a year ago now, you've been fierce and temperamental. And drunk."

Tristan glanced away unhappily. "Why are you telling me now?"

"For one thing, because you can hear me." Dinadan rose and pulled on his tunic. "Whatever else she has done, Essylte has released you from your private hell. In fact," he said, regarding his friend's tanned body, sea water glistening on him like a shining skin, "you've never looked better. No more hollows under your eyes or your ribs. I've never seen you happier. More satisfied with life."

"I am alive again. I was dead, and now I am alive."

"Well, you're a different man from the Saxon-killer who rode in a week ago. And you've started singing. The warrior is sleeping; the bard is back."

Tristan smiled. "Let him sleep forever. He'll get me killed someday, with his foolish stunts."

Dinadan laughed and tossed him his tunic. "It *was* close, wasn't it? Here. Get dressed. It's time we got back. I won't wake the warrior, I promise you that. But Tristan, it's time for the lover to leave."

"I suppose it's selfish of me to keep you here, when at home you might have Lady Diarca to warm your bed."

"It's not just that. It's time for you to leave Essylte alone. Do you think you can visit here forever? It's suspicious enough we've stayed beyond three days. My father must be in Camelot by now, and Markion has discovered we left Elmet early. If he doesn't guess at once where we went, Segward will. Get home to Lyonesse and safety. You're playing with fire to stay."

"Let them come. I'm ready to take on any man who dares to challenge me."

"Markion won't challenge you, fool. He'll have you killed. And you know damn well he's within his right."

The joy drained from Tristan's face, and he stood, naked and defiant, at the edge of the sea. "I'm not an evil man, Dinadan. I would know if this were mortal sin by the heaviness of my spirit. But my spirit soars."

"You knew it well," Dinadan replied evenly, "in Elmet."

"I was in darkness then. Away, far away from the light that gives me life. She is my sun, my spring, my starry night, and my brightening dawn. Oh, God, Din!" Tristan's hands bunched into fists. "Would you send me back into that cold hell already? Would you drive that knife into my heart? It's beyond my power to leave her." He stilled himself with an effort and managed a smile. "Don't be in such a hurry, my poor, lonely Dinadan. You've forgotten what it's like to be with a woman. It's ambrosia, it's a bed of clouds, it's enchantment and delight. I've lost the power to deny her anything. You'll have to drag me away yourself if you want me to go."

Dinadan met his eyes with a worried frown. "That's the difference between your love and mine. I'm still my own master with Diarca. She casts no spell. We're the same together as we are apart. It's an easy, comfortable kind of love. The kind that lasts."

Tristan stiffened. "What do you mean? That ours is not?"

"Tristan, you are possessed. She owns your very spirit."

"And I hers."

"Beyond a doubt." Dinadan's voice grew sad. "I wish you could see—I wish there were a bone of moderation in you. Or in her. I'm afraid of where it will end."

"End?" Tristan forced a smile. "Why, Din, I will die before it ends."

Dinadan nodded abruptly and started up the path from the beach. "Exactly."

King Markion halted his horse at the bend in the cliff path.

"Ho!" called the captain of his escort, raising an arm. The troop of cavalry pulled up sharply. Segward, shifting uncomfortably in his saddle, kicked his horse up to Markion's side. Before them the towers of Tintagel rose beyond the rolling turf, a dark giant squatting in the sea.

"Krinas!" the King said to his captain. "You've given orders to the scouts?"

"Yes, my lord. No one has reported your approach."

Markion surveyed his castle. The westering sun cast shadows across the landward cliffs, but he could see no movement anywhere. No cooking fires, no banners, no flurry at the gates, no sign that anyone knew he was anywhere about.

"All right, Segward," he said evenly, looking straight ahead and avoiding the small, bright eyes of his companion. "You've got what you want. A surprise it will be. Although God only knows what you expect to find."

"My lord." Segward licked his lips. "I expect to find evidence of treason. There is no other explanation for their refusing to stop at Camelot. Your nephew is after your Queen."

Markion snorted rudely. "Hogwash."

"My lord will see—"

"Damn right I will. I warn you, Segward, you are biting off more than you can chew. That business with your wife has turned your wits."

"I am content to face your wrath if I am wrong, my lord."

"As indeed you will." Markion glanced at him, saw the fevered eagerness of his expression, and paused. "Segward, you have served me well, and I will indulge you this. But this is all. What will I tell Guvranyl when we return with no notice given? He'll leave my service for Tristan's. It's where he'd rather be, anyway. In his heart he's still Meliodas's man."

Segward shook his head impatiently. "Irrelevant. He'll stay."

Markion grunted. "Well, let's get on with it, then. It means hard riding between here and the gates. Get to the rear where you won't get run over."

As he spoke he put spurs to his stallion. The captain brought his arm down, and the escort thundered away in the King's wake.

The sentries at the causeway gate stared in shock as horsemen galloped across the headland. One lifted a horn to his lips to sound the alarm, but the other grabbed him. "Be still! It's the King! Look!"

"Quick! Send to Sir Guvranyl! Something must be amiss."

"The devil take those drunken scouts! The King in Cornwall, and no one to let us know!"

Markion rode through the gates to smart salutes and slid from his horse as Guvranyl, breathless, ran into the yard to greet him.

"My lord Markion!"

Markion nodded. "Be easy, Guvranyl. You're not to blame. We come unannounced on purpose. Tell me quick: Is my nephew here?"

"Aye, my lord. And Sir Dinadan of Dorria."

"And whereabouts might I find him?"

"Tristan?" Guvranyl, rattled, looked about as if he half expected the two knights to appear out of the stonework. "Or Dinadan?"

"Tristan, of course. Where is he?"

"Why, my lord, he's with the Queen."

Markion drew a long breath. "Where?"

"I—I don't rightly know. They were—a little while ago they came in from a walk along the shore. Shall I send to find—"

"No," Markion snapped, pushing by him. "I'll find him myself."

He strode through the castle with Guvranyl at his heels, scowling darkly, flinging open doors and curtains, his face growing more pinched and pale from one empty chamber to the next. Finally he came to the nursery.

The King strode past Brenna before she had time to bend a knee, and paused at the garden door.

Essylte sat under the apple tree, clapping her hands and laughing. Tristan frolicked on the lawn with a naked infant in his arms, raising the baby over his head, calling out, "Fly, hawk, fly!" and emitting a series of screeches from his throat. The child waved his arms and shrieked in delight, and Tristan laughed. "What a fierce little eagle you are, indeed!"

"Tristan."

Essylte whirled. "Mark!"

Tristan turned and stopped with his little eagle in midflight. "My lord King."

"Whose child is that you brandish about so roughly?"

Tristan bent his knee to the ground, then rose and brought Mark the baby. "Why, my namesake, Uncle, the Prince of Cornwall. The handsomest lad in all the kingdoms. I do congratulate you. He looks just like you."

Markion did not take hold of the proffered baby, did not even give him a second glance. Essylte hurried to Mark's side, making her reverence. At the sight of her he softened, slid an arm around her, and kissed her briefly.

"Little beauty, still nursing, are you? That's a pity. But you're looking well."

"Thank you, my lord. I'm sorry you had to find me here, so unready." She straightened her gown nervously. It was stained with salt spray and muddied from her game of tag with Tristan on the beach. "I should have been prepared to greet you, but—I'm sure Sir Guvranyl told me nothing about it."

"No matter. He couldn't. I didn't let him know." He turned to Tristan, who handed the baby to Brenna along with its swaddling clothes. "I came quietly to find out what you were up to, Tristan, passing me by in Camelot to come to my Queen."

Tristan looked up slowly and met his eyes. "To see your son, my lord. That's why I came. Although your lovely Queen is well worth paying homage to in any season." He bowed formally to Essylte.

Markion studied him. "Paying homage, is it? All the rest of my commanders managed to follow orders and report to me before asking permission to go home."

"Aye, my lord, but Sir Bruenor commanded in Elmet. He gave us leave. As you are my uncle, and this young man my cousin, I considered our bond of kinship as permission. And as you are a merciful man, my liege lord, I thought you might forgive me."

Markion frowned. "You don't really expect me to believe you rode all that way, in such haste, and risked insulting me, for a mewling babe? You're not a fool. You must know he alone stands between you and my crown."

Essylte gasped. "But Mark, he loves the child! He would never wish him harm!"

Both men ignored her. Tristan's features hardened, but when he spoke his voice was soft. He met Markion's eyes. "I have no designs upon your crown, Uncle. You must know that by now. If I had, I'd never have gone to Wales."

Markion scowled, at a loss to reply. Where was Segward? When would that fat peasant learn to ride a horse? It was true, all Tristan said—without Tristan, he would have no wife, no son, no dynasty. He knew it well. But he hated hearing it.

Essylte pressed his arm and put her lips to his ear. "My lord, be easy with your nephew, I pray you. He has done us both such honor through his attentions to our son. And he has made such a difference in poor Branwen."

At the mention of Branwen, Markion brightened. "Well, Tristan, I mean no insult. God knows I owe you much. If you *really* think the child so irresistible—but in that case, why aren't you playing with, er, Branwen's daughter?"

"She's asleep," Tristan replied evenly.

Markion looked first at Tristan and then at Essylte. Both their faces were turned to him, hers innocent and pleading, his a mask. Markion shrugged. "Very well, then. Give us a song tonight at supper, nephew, to show there are no hard feelings."

"My liege lord, I would be honored."

Markion shrugged again, turned on his heel and left.

When the door had closed firmly behind Markion and Brenna had withdrawn from sight, Essylte glanced quickly at Tristan. "He knows. He knows! Who told him? How could anyone suspect?"

Tristan took her by the shoulders and shook her gently. "Hush, sweet, hush. He does not know. He cannot. He's not a subtle man, Essylte. He can't mask anger, and his anger's gone. Be easy, now."

"Someone's been talking to him, then. What shall we do? Oh, Tristan!"

"The Snake, no doubt, has been at work. Oh, my sweet darling, how you tremble!" He slipped his arms about her and held her close.

"Tristan, I am so afraid! Until now he has suspected nothing."

"From now on," Tristan whispered, "he will always wonder. The seed of suspicion, once planted, takes root and thrives in almost any soil. And in a man past forty, with a wife of seventeen, it is certain to flourish."

She rested her head against his breast and closed her eyes. He pressed his lips into her hair. Out of the corner of his eye he caught movement. A man stood in the shadows of the nursery, half hidden by the open garden door. Tristan waited, unmoving. The figure slid slowly into the doorway until his face was in the light. Segward's eyes met Tristan's and locked. Tristan tightened his hold on Essylte and drew her closer. Segward's lips thinned into a smile. With a flourish of his ringed hands, he bowed his most courtly bow and silently withdrew.

Markion hurled a flagon of mead against the wall. It shattered into a thousand pieces, a golden shower of liquid froth and baked clay shards. The sentry poked his head around the door.

"Get out! God damn you, get out!" The man fled. Markion collapsed in his chair. The misery on his face aged him twenty years. "How do I know it's true? You accuse him, but you hold a grudge against him. I won't be the tool of your revenge."

"I tell you, I've seen them with my own eyes."

"Prove it to me. If it is true—*if* it is true, mind you—then I will punish him."

"How?"

"Exile. I will send him home to Lyonesse and make him stay there."

Segward drew a measured breath. "The punishment for treason is death."

Markion snorted. "Did Arthur kill Lancelot? I will banish him to Lyonesse. He will see her no more. That should suffice."

Segward's eyes narrowed in his pudgy face, and his voice sank to a snarl. "You can't even be sure the boy she bore is yours."

Markion slumped, closing his eyes. After a long silence, he pushed himself up out of the chair and walked to the window. For as far as he could see, the rugged coast of Cornwall ran northward, defying the summer sea like a firm brown fist. This land, like her kings, had withstood the test of time. Born of giants, blessed by gods, guarded by the stern strength of her warriors and the wisdom of her kings, she, above all else, must be preserved. Cornwall was what mattered. But he must be sure. To act in haste might destroy what he sought to save. His fist closed around his sword hilt.

"Prove it to me," he said slowly, "and I'll kill him. But give me proof."

Segward exhaled in a long, silent sigh. "Very well, my lord. I have a plan."

19 ✝ THE BOWER IN THE WOOD

"I don't like it," Dinadan grumbled, packing his saddle pouch. "An outing to the Morois Wood? If he wants to hunt, why is the Queen in attendance? If he wants to picnic, why so many men? It doesn't ring true. It's not like Mark. He's up to something."

"You always think he's up to something," Tristan replied, checking his stallion's girth. "What could he be up to? Maybe he just wants a chance to escape the castle. And Segward." He grinned. "Now, if Segward were along, I might agree with you. Everyone knows riding is no pleasure to him. But he stays, so be easy, Din. Mark's nothing without him. And it's a beautiful day to be out in the open air, with the sky above alive with birdsong, the meadow grasses thick beneath our feet, the forest in full leaf—perhaps even Markion is moved by the richness of life and wants to be part of it."

"I'll believe that when he takes up a harp and sings. No, Tristan, there's something in the wind besides birdsong."

"Well, friend, let it be. Essylte is coming, that's all that matters to me. Between her and nature's glory—what a beautiful day it will be!"

Branwen put the last pin in Essylte's hair and fastened golden netting around the braiding. She glanced quickly at the Queen's bed. Only one head had left an imprint on the pillow, only one side of the coverlet had been disturbed.

"Tristan's been shy of you lately, I see," she murmured. "That's wise."

Essylte lowered her eyes. "Mark has him watched. If he stirs from Dinadan's side, he is followed."

"You see him only in the nursery, then?"

Essylte smiled bitterly. "I see him everywhere. No restraints are put upon our meeting. I think they are trying to catch us out." Her smile softened. "It's best in the nursery. He holds Keridwen while I nurse Young Tristan. We can say what we will there." She took Branwen's hand. "Don't look like that, Branny. Tristan truly loves her. She's a sweet little thing. And growing stronger."

Branwen regarded her a moment in silence. "Wait here," she said, and disappeared behind the curtain. When she returned, she held a small silver flask. "Now listen, Essylte, and do as I say. You are right to be suspicious. Segward *is* trying to catch you out. And this frolic of today, which is so unlike Mark, may be nothing but a trick."

Essylte's smiled died. "How?"

"I don't know exactly what is planned, but I can guess. Now listen closely. If ever they leave you and Tristan alone together, drink one swallow of this potion. One swallow, no more. For the sake of your son."

"What is in it?"

"An herb that will keep you safe. If you do as I say, you will be protected, and no harm will come to either you or Tristan."

Essylte's fingers closed around the flask. "I will obey you, Branny. Thank you. And I will be on my guard."

"No, no, be yourself. Let Mark see no difference in your manner. With this drug you are safe from him, so be easy and lighthearted. Let him see you suspect nothing." She paused. "Whatever he has planned, it is Lord Segward who did the planning. Do not be shy of Mark. And tell Tristan nothing of it."

"Why not?"

"His manner to Mark must also be unchanged, and he is not so—practiced in deceit."

Coloring brightly, Essylte turned away. "I don't like keeping secrets from Tristan."

"You have learned to keep so many secrets," Branwen said evenly, "and all for his sake. You can keep one more."

Markion and his company of chosen companions cantered across the flowering moor and over the rolling hills to the dark Morois Wood. The edges of Morois, Markion explained to Essylte as they rode along at a comfortable pace, afforded the best hunting in all of Cornwall, but the depths of the forest were to be avoided. Time out of mind, the heart of the forest had been held sacred by village folk, the haunt of gods and the spirits of departed souls. No one had ever gone deep into the forest and returned.

"Does no one live there?" Essylte asked. "In Wales, the wild lands are full of holy men."

"It's rumored that Morois hides a hermit," Mark conceded. "But no one's ever seen him. He's likely a phantom, like all the others."

When they reached the forest outskirts the path narrowed and they rode in silence, single file, deeper into the woods, where cool shade fell around them like a cloak. Narrow shafts of sunlight pierced the interwoven branches overhead, making a dappled mosaic of the forest floor. From everywhere around them rose the voices of a thousand birds, accompanied by the furtive rustling of small creatures scuttling to safety underfoot. Alive to every woodland scent and melody, Tristan began a song in praise of the magnificent Creator, who, with a stroke of His hand, brought forth such wonderful bounty from the rich brown earth, from the cool glades, the bright meadows, the shimmering sea, and from the wombs of women. His clear voice floated through the shadows to the treetops, enveloping the entire forest in his joy.

Mark turned in the saddle and saw tears glinting in Essylte's eyes. He looked away quickly, his heart growing heavy. But a vow was a vow, and doubt was something he could not live with. They reached a sunny clearing and he pulled up. "Krinas."

"Here, my lord."

"We take this trail north and east into the deer thickets. Are the men ready with their bows? Quivers full?"

"Yes, my lord."

"Good. I'll be very much surprised if an afternoon's hard hunting won't get us a buck or two. My lady Essylte." He beckoned her to ride closer. "I will leave you here. I imagine you must be weary, with so much exercise after a long winter of staying in. Will you give us leave to part with you, that we may bring you back the makings of a feast? You're in no danger, my dear. We're a stone's throw from the moors."

Essylte bowed politely. "Of course, my lord. I shall not be sorry to stop and rest a while. And I am not afraid of the forest."

"I'll leave you guarded, of course—"

"Sir Dinadan," Essylte proposed quickly. "I beg you, my lord, leave him with me. He is a friend to me and we might pass the time in cheerful conversation."

Markion forced a laugh. "I'll do better than that. I'll leave you guarded by the finest swordsman in all Cornwall, the noblest warrior in my kingdom, a knight of the blood royal whom no one will dare attack."

"No," Essylte whispered breathlessly, but Markion went on loudly in an enthusiastic voice.

"My own kin, no less. My royal nephew, Tristan of Lyonesse. Tristan, attend me."

Tristan rode near and saluted. "My lord King."

"We have lately had words, sir, that I am ashamed of. I would show you now in what high esteem I hold you. I leave you to guard the Queen while we are hunting. Find someplace out of the sun and bid her rest until we return."

Stone-faced, Tristan met his eyes. "Whatever my lord wills. But I assure you, Uncle, you have nothing to prove to me."

"Well, well, I'm glad to hear it. Come, lads, let's be off."

"May Dinadan stay with us?" Tristan asked quickly as Markion moved to go.

"Oh, no. He comes with me. He's too fine a shot to leave behind." With that, the King cantered out of the clearing with all his men in his wake.

Their hoofbeats had hardly faded when Essylte turned to Tristan. "Love, I fear him! He means us harm. He'll have us watched, for certain. Branny warned me of it. Take me back to Tintagel. Now."

Tristan dismounted and came to her side. "I cannot disobey his direct order. Not unless you are ill. Come, Essylte, don't shake so. We are in no danger except from ourselves."

She laughed miserably and slipped from her horse into his arms. "Except from ourselves. Oh, Tristan." She held him and rested her head against his shoulder. Her voice sank to a whisper. "Beloved, you have been so long from my bed. . . ."

"Don't," he said gently. "Not now. You know my heart, Essylte. It is only fear for your safety that has kept me away."

She looked up at him with burning eyes, her body warm and alive in his hands. "We have so little time," she breathed.

He let go of her and stepped back. "I'll hobble the horses and leave them in the clearing, where they can graze. Then I will obey my uncle's orders and find you a shady place to rest. Are you hungry?" he asked, unstrapping his horse's girth. "I'm famished. I'll bring along my pack. I wish Dinadan had left me his wineskin. All I have with me is water."

"I prefer water."

Tristan hung the bridles on a low branch and slung the saddle pack over his shoulder. "Then we shall be content enough." He reached out and took her hand. "Come with me. I know a place not far from here where we can sit and eat and talk."

She gazed around at the thick undergrowth. "We won't get lost?"

He grinned. "And be eaten by wicked hermits? Don't be afraid. I know this part of the forest like the back of my hand. I used to hide out here to escape Guvranyl and his endless exercises when I wanted to make a song." He nodded to a narrow opening in the bushes. "It's up this deer trod a ways. A pretty place to sit in comfort. A bower in the wood. Come on."

Tristan tugged gently at her hand and she followed. After a hundred paces they reached a stand of pines, where the forest opened up and a soft carpet of needles hushed their steps. Beyond the pines the land rose gently and then fell gradually away. In a shallow valley a brook ran noisily through a sun-flecked glade. Tristan stopped and pointed. At the edge of the glade a standing stone, man height, stood in dark silhouette against the summer leaves.

"Oh!" Essylte gasped. "Whose is it?"

Tristan shrugged. "There's no way of knowing which god it belongs to.

The inscription has long been worn away. All you can see are a few hatch marks. The local people say they are the marks of giants. The giants who made Cornwall."

Essylte's eyes grew wide. "Do you believe this, Tristan? You are a Christian. Surely you don't believe the world was made by giants."

Tristan smiled. "Before the one God there were many gods, and before them, who knows? Folk memories go a long way back. Who's to say God never took another form to inspire men's awe?" He paused. "Whatever the truth of the stone, I've always felt this valley to be a safe, protected place. Come. We're almost there."

Off the deer trod the land dipped slightly, forming a little hollow. Three hazel trees grew close together, with climbing ivy entwined so thickly among their branches that the boughs hung low, shading the hollow.

"Here we are." Tristan led her inside the bower. "Long ago I pulled out all the rocks and stumps. The bedding of leaves and needles is ten years thick and softer than your bed at Tintagel." He smiled quickly. "As I have reason to know."

Tristan spread a cloth upon the ground, and Essylte sank gratefully onto the sweet-scented cushion of leaves and bracken. From where she sat she could see the glade and the standing stone and could hear the brook. But she was nearly invisible to anyone beyond ten paces from the bower. She looked up nervously at Tristan.

"This is a perfect place for a tryst."

"Isn't it?" Tristan bent over the saddle pack. "It's too bad I didn't know any girls back when I used to—" He turned suddenly and saw her face. "Essylte. I promise you. I promise you I will not."

Tears sprang to her eyes, and she bowed her head. "Oh, God, it's laughable! You will not, and I want nothing more. I am alive only in your arms. How unbearable it has all become!"

He unbuckled his swordbelt and, drawing the blade, laid it down on the ground between them. "Let this be as a wall between us. We may speak across it, but nothing more. Our lives depend upon it, Essylte."

She nodded quickly and wiped away her tears with the back of her hand. He handed her the waterskin and lifted from her saddle pack a linen cloth tied with ribbon and a silver flask.

"What's this?"

"Meal cakes and raisins, and a honey drink Branwen made me." She avoided his eyes and tucked the flask away out of his sight. "But I am not hungry."

"Well, I am." Tristan sat down beside the sword with his own ration of jerky, olives, and bread and began to eat. "I have been wanting to talk to you, Essylte, about our future. Now that we have a son. I never thought about it before, but I see things differently now that I'm a father."

Essylte sat very still. "What do you see, Tristan?"

"I want my son to grow up in Lyonesse."

She paled. "And how can that be, without betraying our secret?"

"Perhaps Mark can be brought around."

"You misjudge him if you think so. He has only one thought in his head, and that is his dynasty."

"Sooner or later Branwen will bear him a son. And then she'll tell him the truth."

Essylte crossed herself quickly. "If she does, he will kill us all. He will kill her first."

Tristan shook his head. "Perhaps not. Perhaps once he has a son of his own on whom to found his dynasty, he will let you and young Tristan go. Lyonesse is the boy's birthright. Not Tintagel. Not Camelot."

Essylte began to tremble. "He thinks he has a son of his own *now*! Tristan, only your dreams father these beliefs. You do not know Mark—don't you remember that morning in Guvranyl's house? You knew him well enough then! *Never* tell him. You can't believe he would countenance such deception. He would never accept as heir a bastard boy, born of a bastard serving maid—" She shuddered. "If he ever knew that all this time he has lain with her instead of me, he could not forget it or forgive it."

Tristan reached out a hand over the sword, but she shrank from his touch. "Essylte, I want to make you mine in the eyes of God. I want our union to be a formal one, and our son acknowledged. You deserve no less from me. I want to do you honor. I'm so damned tired of skulking around behind my uncle's back. It's demeaning."

Her head whipped up. "*You're* tired!" she cried. "*You're* demeaned! Why, you've only been to Tintagel once since I was married! *I'm* the one who must begin and end each day with a barefaced lie. *I'm* the one who's left here in this cold prison to rejoice at his departure and grit my teeth at his return, and scheme how to betray the High King's bed. O God, grant me patience! How do you *dare* consider yourself demeaned for a few small hours spent conniving against your uncle? It is my *life*! Do you hear me, Tristan? It is my life." She turned away and covered her face with her hands.

"Essylte, I—"

"Do you know what he did to me three nights ago? He burst in upon me in my chamber. It was the evening of his return, after he had found us in the nursery. He demanded to know what there was between us. He asked me outright—outright, with my hand upon the Book of God—if I had ever been your lover."

"Christ!" Tristan was ashen. "Why did you not tell me? What did you say?"

Essylte struggled hard to still her tears. When at last she spoke, her voice was low. "I told him that no man had ever had me except he who had my maidenhead. Then I—I asked him if he did not remember that night, for I remembered it well."

Tristan exhaled slowly and shut his eyes.

"Do you see the woman I have become? With my lips I told him truth," Essylte went on, "but God knows that in my heart I lied. I shamed him, Tristan. He knelt on the floor before me and begged my forgiveness. He promised me that he should make it all up to me when the baby is weaned. I—I was ashamed." Her voice grew bitter. "He would not forgive us, Tristan. He will never forgive us, once he knows. I thank God he is so seldom at Tintagel, and that Branny conceived when I did. We must be careful about that. Every day that passes we must plan how to deceive him. He is back before his time, and now we are unready. Every day he begs me to quit nursing, that he may come to my bed. But Branny's not well enough yet to take my place, so I must stall him a little longer. But this is certain—by the time my father comes to visit, Branny must be ready. Mark has ordered me to find a wet nurse."

Tristan reached out a hand across the sword but then withdrew it. He could find no words to say.

Essylte wiped tears from her eyes. "Thank God he finds childbearing repugnant, and everything it entails: milky breasts, swaddling clothes, babies' cries. Blood on a battlefield may be no more than a day's work to him, but blood in a woman's bed is more than he can bear."

Tristan swallowed. "Essylte, I'm so—"

"*Don't* say you're sorry!" she snapped. "I'm not sorry. It's the way it has to be."

"But it's my fault it's the way it has to be. I *am* sorry about that."

"Oh, Tristan." She cast him a sad smile. "What could we have done to prevent it? I have asked myself this a thousand times. It's pointless to go back. Let us look only toward the future. I do not care if my life is a short one, so long as I can see you from time to time. You give me such joy—I love you so dearly—let me hold you in my arms from dusk to dawning, and I am content to suffer our separation. Until the next time."

"But it drives me mad! You were meant for something better. Let me take you and our son to Lyonesse. Let Mark do what he wills against us."

"No. Please, Tristan, if you love me, let things go on as they are. Don't talk again about Lyonesse. As you value the baby's life." Her fingers gripped the silver flask. "Promise me. Promise me, Tristan, you will not tell Mark."

He knelt down next to the sword and kissed the blade. "I promise, Essylte."

With a sigh, she lifted the flask to her lips and swallowed.

"What is that you drink?"

She smiled wearily. "Only a potion Branny made me. To keep me safe from you."

Tristan rose as she settled herself for rest on her side of the sword. He leaned against the trunk of a hazel tree and peered out at the sunlit glade. When he turned back she was asleep. A bright tendril of hair had escaped her net to frame her face. Dark lashes brushed the high curve of her cheek. She wore the same look of innocence he had seen on the baby's face only that morning.

He swung away and glared out at the quiet forest. He must do right by her, whatever the cost. Either Mark must know the truth and set her free, or he himself must leave her. And he had promised her he would not tell Mark.

He knelt by the sword. "After today, my dear heart, I cannot come near you again. Dinadan is right; it will kill us both."

The silver flask had slipped from her fingers and lay on the ground cloth. He picked it up. "Sweet sleep, let me stay by her a little longer, for tomorrow hope is ended."

Lifting the little flask to his lips, he drank.

"You, Krinas. And you, Dinadan. Attend me." Markion wheeled his horse and pointed. The two knights turned from the knot of men busy with the deer's carcass, and bowed. "Get your horses and follow me. Brychan!"

"Yes, my lord?"

"Three is enough for today. When you've trussed them, take them home. I'll meet you all at dinner."

"Very good, my lord."

Markion spurred to a fast canter down the forest track, the two knights riding hard to keep up. Dinadan frowned, crouched over his gelding's neck to avoid whipping branches. They were riding not for Tintagel, but deeper into the forest. He hoped Markion knew what he was doing, with only two knights as escort. They rode for an hour before the undergrowth thinned and they trotted into a clearing. There was Tristan's bay and Essylte's gray mare. Dinadan looked swiftly about.

"You won't find him here," Markion said evenly, swinging down from his horse. "But he can't be far away."

Dinadan and Krinas dismounted and tethered the horses.

"Hanno!" the King called softly. "Stand forth!"

A minute passed and Markion called again. Leaves rustled, the bushes parted, and a youth appeared, dressed in green-dyed tunic and leggings. "Here, my lord. At your service."

"Did you follow him?"

"Nothing easier, my lord. I hid in a pine tree. Neither of 'em ever saw me."

"What are they doing now?"

Hanno grinned sheepishly. "Why, my lord, they're sleeping."

Markion paled. "Are they indeed? After a hard afternoon's work, I don't doubt." Krinas and Dinadan exchanged glances.

"No work that I saw," Hanno said. "Unless you mean arguing."

Markion grunted and pointed down the path. "Unlikely. Lead the way. And go quietly."

Krinas bowed quickly. "My lord, shall I stay with the horses?"

"No. Come with me. Both of you. I want witnesses."

"What does he take Sir Tristan for?" Krinas breathed, as he fell in step behind Dinadan. "A half-wit, like Hanno?"

Dinadan did not answer, but prayed silently and fervently to God to deliver Tristan from the trap his uncle had set him. "Let us not take him unawares," he whispered to himself over and over again with every step. "Let him hear us. Let him flee. Let him not be taken."

Soon they came to the pine ridge and the sunlit valley. Hanno stopped and pointed toward a wooded glade. "In there, my lord."

Markion grunted and drew his sword. "An excellent place for a tryst. Draw your weapons, men, and follow me. If he has so much as touched her, I will have his life." He shot Dinadan a fierce look. "You will not warn him."

"No, my lord."

With a nod, Markion led the way to the bower. Under the ivied boughs, he stopped. His sword point dropped. His whole posture slackened. Dinadan crept closer and peered around his shoulder.

Tristan and Essylte lay asleep on the forest floor, as innocent as two children. They faced each other, an arm's length apart, with the sharp, shining blade between them. Nothing about her gown was wrinkled; nothing about his tunic was disarranged. Except for the tendril that caressed her cheek, even her hair was in place. They slept the sleep of the innocent, deep and dreamless, with such a look of peace on their faces, even Markion was moved.

"Praise God," Dinadan whispered.

"I knew it," Krinas sighed.

"Well." Markion straightened and sheathed his sword. "They argued, you say, Hanno?"

Hanno, who had crept up behind them, nodded brightly. "Aye, my lord. She was right angry at him."

"What were they arguing about?"

Hanno lifted his shoulders in an eloquent gesture. "Couldn't say, my lord. They was talking about food. Sir Tristan, he was hungry, and the Queen wasn't."

Markion knelt at Essylte's side. He withdrew a heavy gold ring from his hand and slipped it on her finger, then raised her hand to his lips and kissed it. "He's overreached himself this time," he said slowly, rising. Dinadan dodged out of the King's way as he swung around. "Krinas!"

"Here, my lord."

"I want Segward brought to me as soon as we return. Dinadan, stay here with Tristan and the Queen until they awaken. Tell them I have ordered a feast tonight in their honor."

"And Lord Segward, my lord?"

Markion's voice was cold. "Lord Segward will not be there."

Part IV

20 ✝ THE BONFIRE

Dinadan stood at the unshuttered window and gazed out at the wide blue sea. West, south, and east it stretched limitless to the horizon, glittering like metal in the midday sun. Here in Lyonesse, at the bottom of Britain, he thought wryly, water turned to gold. And the man who commanded such magnificent wealth? Away in the distance a small bleached square of canvas inched across the deep, dipping in and out of view in the gentle swells. Dinadan sighed once in exasperation. A servant scratched at the door, and he turned. "Come in."

"My lord, a messenger for Sir Tristan."

"Whose courier is it, Malken? I'll see him myself if he's from Dorria or Camelot."

The servant hesitated. "Not a courier, my lord."

The door swung open and a woman curtsied prettily. "And not from King Markion, my lord Dinadan. At least, not directly." She met his eyes and smiled.

"Lady Esmerée!" Dinadan hurried to her side, waving the servant out of the room. "What are you doing here at Lyon's Head? This is the last place you should be. Did anyone see you?"

Esmerée smiled and laid a hand upon his arm. "Do not fear for me, good Dinadan. I come openly. My husband sent me."

Dinadan stared. "Whatever for? Is this a trap?"

He led her to a chair, but she would not sit. Instead, she walked to the open window and lifted her face to the sea breeze.

"No, it's not a trap. He no longer counts me sufficient bait. King Mark has orders for Tristan, and Segward decided to let me bear the message."

"But—why on earth?"

"Because he knew it would give me pain."

Dinadan came to her side. "He's not here, you know. He's out there. Sailing."

"Yes. I recognized the sail. He was off my coast this morning. To be honest, that's why I chose this time to come."

"I'm sorry."

"Don't be." She shrugged lightly. "I owe him a great deal. More than I ever could repay. I never thought it would come to love, with a boy of seventeen." Her chin lifted. "But I do not want his pity."

"Part of him will always love you, Esmerée."

She squeezed his arm. "You are a gentleman, Dinadan."

"I mean it. If he had never gone to Wales, perhaps—"

"Shhh. Do not even think it. He would never be mine, even if I were unwed." Her voice sank to a whisper. "They were destined for each other, those two. Surely you can see that."

Dinadan shifted uncomfortably. "I don't know about destiny. She has cast a spell upon him, sure enough."

"And he upon her."

"He cannot get free of it, whatever oath he swears."

"Neither can she."

"Look at him out there. He won't come in for meals. He won't come in at sunset. He'll drift all night with the sea currents and sail back when his waterskin runs out and he's nigh dead from thirst. He'll push it to the edge. He's lost flesh; he's losing his wits. She is driving him mad."

"I know."

"He will ride up and down the coast road on a wild, unbroken colt until it drops to its knees. Or he'll swim straight out to sea until he's out of sight. Day and night he tempts death. That's why I came down from Dorria, to see if I could save him from himself."

"Pity the woman who has no horse to ride, no boat to sail."

"He's been moodier than ever. He will do anything so long as he risks his neck doing it. All his songs welcome death. He's become a danger to himself."

Esmerée moved away from the window. "He won't die. Not while Essylte lives. But his sanity is quite another thing. Tell me, Dinadan, why has he spent these last months here in Lyonesse? Is it at Mark's command?"

Dinadan shook his head. "He swore an oath never to see her again."

Esmerée sank into a chair. "For her sake, no doubt. Poor, sweet Tristan. What a dreamer he is."

Dinadan looked at her more closely and saw lines at the corners of her lovely eyes, the drag of weariness at the corners of her mouth, a hint of fatigue in the pale skin of her throat. For all that, she still had a face that turned every man's head. "Would you care for wine or water? You must be tired from your journey."

She smiled. "I would take some tea, if you have it. Thank you, Dinadan. It was a long walk and roads are dusty in summer."

"Walk! Surely you didn't walk all that way? Segward owns horses and mules; why doesn't he use them?"

"He sold the mules. His horse he keeps with him. He wants us to till the land with the tools God gave us. For the improvement of our souls." She lifted her welling eyes to his. "I think it's to keep me away from Prince Pernam, my dearest friend in all the world."

"The black-hearted bastard!" Dinadan cried. "May he roast long in Hell." He shouted to the servant for willow tea. "I'll not permit you to go home on foot. We'll loan you a mare and a wagon—"

"No, no, my lord," she protested with a sad laugh, dabbing at her eyes. "Do you think he will not hear about it? You will only make it harder for me by your kindness."

"You will *not* walk home. I'll send you home on a mare, Tristan's gift to his uncle Pernam. Tomorrow, you can ride it to Pernam's Sanctuary. He can take you home from there himself. How's that? It's only common courtesy. How is Segward to know we did it to foil his cruel restrictions?"

"He always knows."

Dinadan paced back and forth across the chamber. "Is Segward back in power, then? Last May he fell out of favor with the King. I know. I was there."

Esmerée nodded. "When Markion returned to Camelot he left Segward at Tintagel. But now, with Percival coming, Markion must rely upon him once again whether he likes it or not."

"Percival is coming? Good heaven, I'd forgotten."

"In response to Markion's invitation to the kings of Britain when his heir was born. He will hold a great celebration at midsummer on the cliffs of Tintagel in honor of the child. The unification of Britain, he calls it. My husband has arranged the ceremony. They will kneel by the light of a great bonfire and swear oaths of fealty." A smile touched her lips. "To Tristan's son."

Dinadan grunted. "You knew?"

"How not? I was all last winter in Tintagel, nursing Segward."

"Do you know the other half—the dangerous half—of this deadly game they are playing?"

"I know who fathered Branwen's daughter, if that is what you mean. Essylte is such a trusting innocent. There is not much I don't know about them." She paused. "I fear for her. The future cannot hold much joy for either of them."

A servant scratched at the door and entered with a clay jug of willow tea and two painted goblets. Esmerée drank thirstily of the brew and sat back with a deep sigh. "Thank you, my lord. That was wonderful. Now it's time to give you my message and be going."

"I am all ears."

"The High King Markion commands Sir Tristan, along with all the lords of Cornwall, to attend the presentation of the next High King of

Britain on midsummer eve at Tintagel. You must be there, too, my lord.
And so must I. Segward wants Tristan to be my escort north."

"Damn his black heart. Let *me* escort you, Lady Esmerée. Only give me
leave, and I shall take you to Dorria tomorrow, and we can both go to Tintagel with my father."

Esmerée shook her head and rose. "Thank you again, but no. Although
I should like to meet your betrothed. Will she be coming to Tintagel with
you?"

Dinadan colored lightly. "Not this time. We will be wed at summer's
end, and she is too busy with . . . with . . . well, with whatever girls bother
about before a wedding."

Esmerée laughed. "With her bridegift, no doubt. I wish you well, Dinadan. Tristan will mourn the loss of your company, I am sure of it. You are
the reason he still has his wits about him."

"If he does."

Esmerée lowered her eyes. "I have a reason for declining your kind offer. I want Tristan to come to my house to collect me. I want him to see my
children."

Dinadan took her hands. "You mean his daughter, don't you? Has he
never seen her?"

Her lips trembled as she tried to smile. "No. But I hardly expected it.
He cannot treat her any differently from the others or Segward might judge
it proof of his suspicions and do her harm. But I want him to see her. At
least once."

Dinadan raised her hand and kissed it. "You are a woman in a thousand, Esmerée. We will all come to your house together, Tristan, Pernam,
and I. And now, let's go see about that mare."

The midsummer sun had already begun to throw their shadows long when
the men of Lyonesse topped the last low ridge and looked across the ragged
moors to the castle of Tintagel. Tristan raised an arm and halted his troops.

"My God," he breathed. "Is there anyone who hasn't come?" Thousands of tents dotted the headland, hundreds of banners lifted lazily in the
fitful breeze. On the outskirts of the encampments the horse lines seemed to
stretch for miles.

"Every lord in Dumnonia is here," Dinadan said, shading his eyes.
"And the Summer Country. Half of Logris, by the look of it. I don't see any
of the northern lords. I don't think Elmet is here. Wait, what's that banner
yonder, hard by the causeway?"

"Wales," Tristan said flatly. "In the place of honor. Percival's men." He turned in the saddle and surveyed the rest of his company. "Once, I'd have been overjoyed for the chance to talk with Percival."

"You're not looking forward to it now?"

Tristan shrugged. "It doesn't matter. Nothing much matters anymore. There is no happiness left in anything."

"What has happiness got to do with it?" Dinadan whispered fiercely. "Look there! We've been spotted. They're lining up to greet us. Give the signal, and let's get going."

"Tristan! Tristan of Lyonesse!" The cry rose triumphant in the evening air, echoing across the moors, through the unshuttered windows of the castle, to the farthest reaches of the fortress: "Tristan of Lyonesse!"

Percival turned from his window and grinned. "It's young Tristan, at long last. Now there's a brave lad, Brynn. Straight and honest as the day is long. A poet in his soul."

"Yes, my lord."

"And not afraid to risk his skin when it matters. Sometimes I wish—if only my uncle Peredur had never challenged Constantine, I might wish to see my daughter wed to Tristan rather than Markion. And that stays within these walls."

"Of course, my lord."

Percival shrugged. "Perhaps it was a mistake, this alliance. She's unhappy. She hides it, but I can tell." He stroked his beard, and his eyes softened. "But she loves the child, God bless him. And Branwen seems content. Perhaps in time Essylte will come to like Mark better."

Markion sat in his carved chair while his servant struggled to pull on his boots. Segward stood at the window.

"Your nephew has decided to grace us with his presence after all. At the last moment. How he loves an entrance!"

"You leave Tristan alone," Markion growled. "He's worth three of you any day of the year. Find out where he's camping and send him our greetings. See that he knows we have a room ready for him here. And Sir Dinadan." He flicked a malicious glance at Segward. "*And* Lady Esmerée."

Segward stiffened. "She comes at your invitation, my lord. Not mine."

"Essylte is fond of her. Why shouldn't she come?" His boots on, the King rose and adjusted the crimson cloak his servant laid across his shoulders. "Has Merron doubled the guards outside the Queen's rooms?"

"Of course. And he will let Tristan know that if he wishes to renew his ties with Branwen, she must come to him. No man enters the Queen's rooms but the King."

"It's unnecessary, you know. Your distrust of my nephew has tainted all your thoughts. I'll indulge you because it can do no harm and you've been of service to me. But, Segward." Markion's look was cold. "Don't push it too far."

"Perhaps," Segward continued lightly, "Tristan ought to marry Branwen. He's just turned twenty. It's high time he was wed."

"My nephew wed a serving maid?" Markion snorted. "You let Tristan be. He can pick out his own bride when he's ready. He needs no help from you." Mark reached for his crown and placed it on his head. "And if he never marries, I'll be all the happier. No heirs but mine will ever hold Cornwall."

"Look, Branny, he comes!" Essylte strained to peer past the wide stone sill down into the courtyard. "Why, he's got a woman on his arm! I thought Sir Dinadan was to be his companion. Who is she? Why did he bring her?"

Branwen came up beside her. "Back up a little. You mustn't be seen staring out of windows. Let me look, I'll tell you who it is."

Essylte stood behind her, gripping her shoulders, standing on tiptoe.

"Look how she leans on him. What a pretty mantle! How graceful she is. And not a hair out of place, although they've just ridden in."

"Essylte, do be quiet. You're acting like a—"

"Oh, Branny! See how he smiles at her. How does he dare, when he knows I am within? I will have her eyes out, the brazen—"

"It's only Lady Esmerée. See? Lord Segward is coming forward to take her arm. No doubt Tristan served as her escort. That's all it is."

"All?" Essylte cried. "She's traveled all the way from Lyonesse with Tristan. Next you'll try to tell me that they haven't seen each other all summer long, and I *know* she lives only five leagues from Lyon's Head."

Branwen drew Essylte away from the window. "Come, Essylte, such jealousy is unbecoming. Do you doubt him?"

"I must see him, Branny!"

"I'll think of some ruse to get you near him, and you can satisfy yourself your fears are false. Just give me time."

At sunset Markion addressed the gathering of lords from a great rock near the edge of the headland. Queen Essylte brought forth her son, a sturdy babe beginning his sixth month of life, and displayed him before all the gathered kings. Percival swore an oath of fealty, as did Tristan, Bruenor, Pernam, and all the lords of Cornwall. Other men followed, one by one, pledging their united service to the child. When it was done, Markion set torch to a great bonfire amid thunderous shouting and stomping. Someone struck up a lute, another a lyre, the cooks hurried to lay meat upon the flames, and the celebration rapidly turned into a feast, with singing, dancing, and dicing that would last well into the night.

Essylte and her women returned early to Tintagel with the baby. Tristan stayed by the bonfire long into the night, drinking with Markion, talking to Percival, trading jests with the visiting lords. It was well past midnight before he could escape unnoticed into the castle. He strode through the deserted corridors to the stair below the women's quarters. Three guards stood outside Essylte's door.

"What's this, Brychan? Pwyll? Kellis? Is anything amiss? Do you anticipate an attack upon my lady's quarters?"

Brychan grinned. "Indeed, my lord, I believe Lord Segward does. And you might be the very one he anticipates."

Tristan stopped halfway up the stairs. "Me? You are jesting!"

"Oh, no, my lord. Our orders were quite specific."

Tristan laughed and came up to them. "Well, then, I might have saved myself the climb and got drunk with the others out on the moor." He elbowed Brychan discreetly. "But I've a longing to taste a woman's lips, and hold a soft body in my bed. Would you deny me my pretty Branwen?"

Brychan shook his head. "Surely there must be a thousand maidens, my lord, who would lie with you for the asking."

Tristan laughed lightly. "You think so, do you? You are a credulous fellow indeed. I am not such a butterfly, Brychan. I am more like a tree. Where my seed falls, I take root. And stay."

Brychan grinned. "More like a blackthorn, my lord, if you'll forgive me. Sharp, and dangerous to the unwary."

"Nay, Brychan, more like ivy. I persist, especially when unwelcome. The less I'm tended, the wilder I become. I will have my way in the end; I will cover what I will."

Brychan threw up his hands. "You're too many for me, my lord! You may have your sport, and I'll not keep you from it. But by King Markion's orders, she must come to you. Shall I send her?"

"And deny me the pleasure of whisking her away? Certainly not. I pray you, scratch upon the door and announce me."

"But my lord—"

"I won't go in, if that's my uncle's order. Although I can't see what it gains him. Bid her open the door and come out to me."

Brychan did as he was commanded and Branwen opened the door. Essylte stood behind her, still in the golden gown of the presentation, her riotous curls, recently unbound, falling about her shoulders in a tumult of vivid color. She glared at him and the smile died on his lips.

Branwen curtsied low. "My lord," she murmured. "We are glad to see you safely come from Lyonesse."

"And I—I am glad to see you, too, Branwen. You've got your life back in your cheeks."

Branwen flushed. "I am recovered, my lord, thank you."

Tristan glanced quickly at Essylte and offered Branwen his arm. "Come spend an hour with me, pretty Branwen. Let me sing you a song."

The guards chuckled and winked at one another. Branwen hesitated, glancing discreetly toward the queen's chamber. Tristan shook his head lightly.

"I'd have been here before now, sweet Branwen, but my uncle and King Percival kept me long in talk and drink. They are making a night of it, as the air is so fine. I'm afraid my lady Queen will have hours to wait for her King. I'm sure she can spare you for a little while."

Branwen curtsied obediently and took his arm. "Very good, my lord. If it's not for long."

Tristan smiled knowingly at the guards. "Don't worry, little vixen. It doesn't take long."

Under the cover of the guards' laughter Tristan led Branwen down the stairs. "Take no offense, Branwen. But I know these men—if I touch the right strings, they will play my tune."

"Indeed," Branwen returned coolly. "My lord is a master musician, as everyone knows."

When they were safe inside Tristan's chamber, he lit a single candle and closed the shutters on the windows. The room was simply furnished, with a stout oak bed, a pallet hastily made up against the other wall, and a table with a single candlestand and a shallow bowl of water. Dinadan's bedroll had been thrown on the pallet, but he was not there.

Tristan gestured toward the bed. "As there is no chair, the bed will have to do."

Branwen looked angrily around the room. "This is the meanest chamber in Tintagel! No doubt Lord Segward chose it for you himself. I will have chairs and lamps and hangings brought in here tomorrow."

Tristan raised his eyebrows. "Will you, indeed? Do you have such power here?"

Branwen smiled and sat down on his bed. "This is a women's fortress, my lord. Men are seldom here. And among the women, I am second only to Essylte."

Tristan bowed. "How have you both been, Branwen? How are the children?"

"You have seen your son. As healthy a child as ever drew breath in Cornwall. Keridwen lives and thrives, although she is a small, weak thing and probably always will be. Mark has made Essylte quit nursing, and Brenna has hardly enough milk for two."

She spoke lightly, but Tristan fidgeted uncomfortably.

"Has he—"

"Not yet. Tonight is to be the first time since her lying-in. That's why she's so frightened. Tonight we begin again the old charade."

"She didn't look frightened to me. She was ready to eat me alive."

"Oh, yes," Branwen agreed. "She is furious enough with you."

"But why, in God's name? What have I done?"

"She saw you walk in with Lady Esmerée. She saw you smile at her. She saw her hand upon your arm, she saw her glances, your parting kiss."

Tristan colored. "Esme is my friend. I owe her a great deal. She has borne much on my behalf."

"I know what she has borne, my lord. But there is no reasoning with a jealous woman."

Tristan exhaled in relief. "Jealous! The little fool. Give me five minutes with her alone and I will teach her to doubt my love."

"In her heart she knows it. She has not gone a night without weeping since you left. And I ought not to tell you this, but she has cursed the vow you made."

Tristan looked away. "Does she? So do I. I would give my kingdom, I think, for another night with her."

"It won't be possible this time. Segward watches your every move. That's why I asked Mark to send for Lady Esmerée. She is adroit at watching him, and we might be able to find out what he's up to."

"*You* asked Mark?"

"Yes," Branwen said evenly. "Of course, he thought it was Essylte. He will do almost anything to please her."

"This is power," Tristan breathed. "I congratulate you, Branwen. Is there any chance I can see Essylte alone? I must at least have speech with her."

"It will be difficult. There are guards on every chamber, the grounds are thick with guests. And you, Tristan, *you* won't be allowed to relieve yourself in private."

"But I *must* see her!" Tristan grabbed her hands. "There must be somewhere—the beach, the woods, on a horse, in a boat—it *must* be possible. I cannot come all this way and not speak with her alone."

"Well . . ." Branwen hesitated, looking down at their clasped hands. "There is one place. Men will not go there, but it's natural that *you* should."

"Where? Where!"

"The nursery."

"Of course." In his joy, Tristan bent and kissed her. "Sweet Branwen! I should have thought of it myself. We will go to see our children, and no one can think ill of us for that."

"Indeed. But there is danger, my lord, if you stay too long. Even there, you will certainly be watched."

"How soon can it be arranged?"

"I will send you word, or come myself, when it looks safe."

"Bless you." He went to the door. Reluctantly, Branwen took his arm again. "I will await your signal," he said. "Here, let me ruffle your hair a little. The guards will look for it." She closed her eyes as his hands touched her hair. When she opened them, he was looking at her gravely. "Do you hate me for this deception? For the lies you must tell on my behalf?"

"No, my lord. I don't hate you."

"You're a brave girl, Branwen."

"I'm a woman now, my lord," she whispered. "When you bid me good night at my door, you must kiss me. A real kiss." She smiled up at him. "The guards will look for it."

Every minute of the next day took years to pass. It seemed to Tristan that the world was watching him wherever he went, whatever he did. Dinadan slept in his chamber and ate at his side, Pernam and Percival sought him out for private speech, half the lords of Logris approached him to offer him marriage to their daughters and thereby secure his fighting arm against the Saxons. Markion himself was often near, and Segward, it seemed, lurked behind every door.

Finally, when the heat of the day was past and the sea breeze blew cool across the moors, Markion got up a hunting party and half the lords went with him. Tristan declined the invitation and waited in his chamber, pacing nervously. Just when he thought he could bear the waiting no longer, someone knocked softly on the door. He whipped it open.

Branwen curtsied low. "My lord."

"It's about time. I am half mad with waiting. What kept you?"

"Markion spent most of the day with Essylte," she replied evenly. "She is not in the best of tempers."

"Take me to her. At once."

Branwen's eyes flashed. She turned on her heel and led him through the corridors to the nursery. No one paid much attention to them. The few who did hid indulgent smiles. "Remember," Branwen warned outside the nursery door, "you're here to see my daughter."

As they entered the long, cool room with cradles at one end and toy chests at the other, the nurse, Brenna, rose from her low chair with a baby in her arms and made them a low reverence.

"My lord Tristan. Mistress Branwen. She's just been fed. Hungry today, she was. Would you like to hold her, my lord?"

Tristan accepted the sleeping bundle. "May I take her outside?"

"Not in the sun, my lord. There's a bench beneath the apple tree. Queen Essylte is there now. That's the best place, and cooler, too."

"Thank you, Brenna."

Tristan walked slowly across the lawn toward the tree. Essylte held her baby sitting in her lap, supporting him with her hands, tickling him and making faces at him, her glowing hair bound tight around her head under a jeweled net. Young Tristan laughed and giggled, waving his arms in excitement. As Tristan approached the child caught sight of him, raised a fist in the air, and gurgled.

Tristan laughed. "He knows me!"

Essylte did not look up. "You are a stranger to him."

Branwen moved to Essylte's side, screening her from Brenna's inquiring gaze at the nursery door.

"I am not. He waved at me."

Essylte shrugged, coolly avoiding his gaze. "He waves at everyone."

Tristan sat down on the bench beside her, tucking Keridwen in the crook of one arm and slipping the other unseen around Essylte's waist.

"Let me go. I did not give you leave to touch me. I did not give you leave to sit."

Tristan pulled her closer and touched his lips to her neck. "That it should come to leave-giving between you and me," he breathed into her ear. "My sweet love, it has been a thousand years since I saw you last."

Her lower lip began to tremble. "You have passed the time agreeably enough, I don't doubt, in the company of the beautiful Esmerée."

Tristan's lips slid along the line of her jaw and kissed the edge of her mouth. Branwen coughed discreetly. "Esmerée is a bright star in the firmament of beauty. But you, Essylte, my only love, you are the sun. You are heaven and earth to me. You know that. Don't torture me with phantom jealousies. You will drive me to indiscretion—shall I kiss your feet right here in the orchard? I will do it—only say the word."

She turned to him suddenly, her resistance gone, her blue-green eyes enormous with tears.

"Oh, Tristan!" she whispered. "It's not you, it's Mark. I—I feel unclean.

He has kissed me and held me—he found me alone in the tower and he trapped me—his lips have touched me, and his hands—as if I were a serving wench! He all but lay with me, right there on the tower stairs—if Merron had not come by, I would be this minute in the sea!" A tear slipped down her cheek and the baby began to whimper. "I can't bear it, Tristan, I can't bear it. Take me away from here."

Tristan extended a finger to his son, who wrapped a chubby fist around it, instantly delighted, and drew it to his mouth. Essylte leaned her head on Tristan's shoulder. Branwen bent over her, pretending to adjust her net, while Tristan kissed her lips, drawing her grief out of her.

"I want nothing more," he whispered. "And one day, I will. But it must be planned carefully, or it will result in all our deaths. Yours, mine, Branwen's, young Tristan's. You were right, you know. When I take you away, it must be done with Mark's consent."

"But when can I see you alone? Only you can make me feel clean again."

Tristan cast a swift look at Branwen. She frowned lightly. "This is the only place, my lord."

Tristan nodded. "Very well, then it will be here. Attend me now, Essylte. Come here again this evening. An hour before midnight. Use any pretext you like—it's the only place to take the air in solitude. Come out here and wait for me by the apple tree."

"Here? With Brenna watching? Will it be safe? How will you get in?"

"Leave that part of it to me. She will see no one but you. When you hear the nightingale's song twice repeated, go to the lower edge of the garden. See that ancient apple tree, all gnarled and bent? I will be under it, waiting for you. Its sheltering boughs will give us privacy, at least for a while. No one but you will know I'm there."

Essylte brightened and sat up. She leaned forward and placed her lips against his cheek. "Bless you, Tristan. I'm sorry I ever doubted you."

He took her hand. On her finger she wore his ring, the golden Eagle of Lyonesse soaring against a blue enamel sky. He raised her hand to his lips. "I forgive you anything."

"It's time to go," Branwen urged. "Brenna is coming out the door."

"Ow!" Tristan exclaimed sharply, pulling his hand out of the baby's grip. "He bit me!"

Essylte laughed outright, her eyes shining up at him. "Don't take it to heart so. He bites everyone."

21 ✝ THE APPLE TREE

"Where are you going?" Dinadan asked. "You ate nothing at dinner and now you're calling for your horse. What's afoot?"

"I'm riding down to the Lyonesse encampment. To see the men."

"At *this* hour?" Dinadan pulled him into a nook in the courtyard wall. "You're a pitiful liar, Tristan. You always were. What's in that sack?"

"Provisions."

"For what?"

"Look, Din, you're better off not knowing. Don't make me tell you."

"It's Essylte, isn't it?" Dinadan whispered. "You can't be going to see her."

"This is Tintagel. Mark's men are everywhere. This escapade will mean my death if I'm caught, and yours if you know about it. So I'm not going to tell you."

"What's in the sack?"

"A rope and a hook."

Dinadan let his breath out slowly. "Her window is at the top of the castle. With a sheer drop to the sea below. I don't see why you're worried about Mark."

Tristan smiled. "I'm not climbing to her window."

"What, then?"

"An old trick remembered from my boyhood. That's all I'll say. If you want to help me, tell anyone who misses me I've gone to see my men. And I *am*, first."

A groom led Tristan's horse into the courtyard. Dinadan clasped Tristan's arm. "If I can't stop you, then I wish you success."

Tristan cantered down the footpath the locals euphemistically called the coast road until he reached the Lyonesse encampment. Most of the men were drinking around a fire or dicing in the tents. He had a few words with the commander, then turned back toward Tintagel. Just before he came in view of the postern gate he dismounted and led his horse onto a narrow track that wound steeply down the cliff. Slipping and sliding, they descended to the beach, where Tristan tied the horse to a thwarted tree and threw his cloak over the animal's flanks. It was a warm night with a calm sea, but the breeze blew cool. Grabbing the sack, he ran along the shingle to the very roots of the castle walls.

Markion seldom posted sentries on the western walls, except for the lookout on the tower who scanned the sea for Irish raiders or Saxon longboats. As boys, Tristan and Gerontius had prided themselves on finding a way to sneak inside the impregnable Tintagel. At low tide they could make their way past the roiling currents to the base of the great rock. The footholds in the rock face were just where they had been ten years before, only smoother, and so were the footholds in the more friable fortress wall above. Within minutes Tristan was on the battlement and running silently along the outer wall, ducking past narrow windows until he came to a high stone wall between two towers. Opening the sack, he tied the rope to the hook, held his breath, and heaved the hook over the wall. It caught fast. The rags he had wrapped about the prongs muffled the clang of impact, but he waited and counted to ten. No one came, no one called out. He swarmed up the rope, threw a leg across the wall, and dropped twenty feet to soft grass with a solid thud.

It was very dark. No light showed within the nursery, and the orchard was deserted. Crouching, he ran to the ancient tree and climbed up into its lower branches. The orchard remained perfectly still. Tristan settled himself to wait.

Before long he saw the flicker of candlelight in the nursery window and heard the soft chime of women's voices. The door opened.

"Pay me no mind," he heard Essylte say. "I only want a breath of solitude. There are too many people about. And the night is so fine. Go back to your bed, Brenna. I will let myself out in a bit."

She wore a dark cloak over her gown, and when she stepped out into the orchard she seemed to disappear. Brenna, in her nightdress, came partway out across the lawn, holding her candle high, ostensibly to light the Queen to her seat, but Tristan saw her eyes flicking all about. At length, as Essylte reached the bench, she dipped a curtsy and returned indoors. A few moments later the light went out.

Essylte sat on the bench with her cloak wrapped around her. Tristan waited. She began to hum softly, and he saw her pale arms moving. He stared through the dark until his eyes ached and smiled to himself. She was taking down her hair. Once he thought he saw the nurse's round face at the window, but then, after a while, nothing moved anywhere. In the still night the only sound was the sweet melody of Essylte's soprano.

Slowly Tristan let himself down to the ground, cupped his hands, and let fall the liquid notes of the nightingale. Essylte's song cut short. She waited a moment, then began to hum once more. Tristan repeated the call. Still singing, she rose and began to stroll across the lawn, back and forth, in apparent aimlessness. With each traverse she came a little closer to the orchard wall. Tristan stared hard at the black square of nursery window. He saw nothing. Essylte reached the old tree as her song ended. She ducked under the boughs and found herself in Tristan's arms.

"Oh, Tristan!" she whispered between kisses, "how my heart has longed for you!"

He held her tight, glorying in the feel of her body against his, in the sudden blazing of his long-dead soul. "At last," he murmured into her unbound hair, "the pulse of life returns. Beloved, this is happiness."

They embraced, their lips and hands eloquent with longing. At last Essylte pushed him away. "Tristan, I must lie with you or I must leave you. This wanting cannot be endured!"

He sat at the foot of the tree and pulled her down onto his lap. "But we must endure it. We cannot lie together. Not here. And I have sworn, not anymore."

She slipped her arm around his neck. "You swore it for me. But I cannot endure this abstinence. I absolve you of your oath."

He laid his head against her breast and drew a trembling breath. "Would that I could obey without dishonor! Nay, Essylte, let us sit quietly together and talk—about our son, about our future—and let our consciences be clean at the hour's end."

"My conscience is already clean," she whispered.

"Last time we met you were full of recrimination."

"I was not burning alive with a desire so long unrequited!" she cried, half weeping. "Oh, I am as changeable as the sea! One day it is all despair, the next withering desire, the next dying by degrees of loneliness. Only in your arms can I find peace."

He laughed softly. "It is the same with me." Against his head the silken fabric of her gown rose and fell with each quick, indrawn breath. He closed his eyes. He was alive again, resurrected by the warmth of a woman's body. Here was the central truth he had sought for in heaven's storms. To live again on the blade edge of ecstasy! His arms tightened about her. "Sing to me, sweet Essylte. Surround me with your voice. Penetrate my heart and let my spirit soar. We will live forever, joined together, in your song."

In the middle of the night twelve days later, a scratching came at Segward's door. Cautiously he arose from bed, lifted the latch without a sound, and inched the door open.

"Brenna?"

"My lord."

"Keep your voice down. Have you news?"

"Yes, my lord." She looked behind her nervously, but the corridor was dark. "I believe they are meeting. In the nursery garden."

"Ahhhh." Segward's sigh was rich with satisfaction. "Go on. How do you know?"

"For twelve nights now, excepting only the night of the storm, my lady has come to take the air alone. Once, Branwen came with her, but she stayed indoors. She didn't tend the babies. I think she was watching me."

"More than likely. What did Essylte do?"

"She sat on the bench beneath the apple tree. At first. And then, when the nightingale started singing, she began to pace, or sing, or walk about. Then she disappeared."

"Disappeared?"

"Yes, my lord. I dared not light a candle. I dared not go out and call her name. I could not discover where she went. But tonight—tonight I saw her."

"Yes? Go on."

"There was a moon tonight, my lord. I saw them both come out from beneath the old apple tree at the bottom of the garden."

"Both? Give me names, woman, and be quick about it."

"Sir Tristan, my lord. He climbed up that stone wall as nimble as a spider. I never saw anything like it. One minute he was there, and the next, gone. And my lady was humming to herself and lacing up her bodice, bold as brass, as she came back."

Segward chuckled. "Very good, Brenna. Very good indeed. When did this start?"

"Twelve nights ago, my lord. The night after the bonfire."

"Day after tomorrow everyone goes home. I have but one night, then."

He reached into his pouch and counted out three silver coins. "There. Tell no one what you have seen, or that you have spoken to me, until I give you leave to tell the King. Or I shall see you hanged for stealing."

She clutched the coins and hurried away. Segward laughed softly to himself and closed the door.

Behind him in the dark, Esmerée lay on his pallet with her face against the wall. Her eyes were open.

The final day of celebration was a day of games and contests, with horse races and footraces over the moors during the morning, and swimming races along the seashore in the afternoon. As the heats progressed, the wagering grew fast and heavy as each kingdom bet on its own young men to win the day. Tristan brought joy to Cornwall by winning the final swimming race three lengths ahead of everyone and causing more than one bystander to remark that he must be part fish to beat them all so handily.

"Well done, Tristan." Dinadan waded into the shallows and threw an arm around Tristan's shoulders. "Well done indeed. You've beaten them all: Logris, Dorria, Dumnonia, the Summer Country, even Gwynedd. I congratulate you."

All along the shore the Cornish lords cheered and applauded, while the defeated swimmers sat catching their breath on the pebbled beach. Tristan stood knee-deep in the sea, bronze-skinned and naked, with water streaming from his hair. He bowed in acknowledgment of the applause and grinned at Dinadan.

"Thank God there's no one else. I'm about done in."

"You don't look it. You look like you could race all day. They're all gasping, and you're not even out of breath."

"I've spent half the summer in the sea."

"When we left Lyonesse you were thin as a rail. You didn't sleep. Now you're as fit as ever. You've put on flesh and you've found your smile. And your songs are no longer all about death."

"Well," Tristan said with a brief smile, "you know the reason."

"But you've hardly seen her, Markion keeps her so close."

Tristan bent sideways to clear water from his ears. "Haven't I?"

Dinadan looked at him sharply. "Have you? How? I've shared a room with you. What haven't you been telling me?"

Tristan laughed and waded toward the beach. "If I keep secrets from you, Din, it's so you can swear in perfect honesty I've been in my own bed every night."

"I'll be damned—you *have* seen her."

The crowd of onlookers began to break up as they walked out of the sea. Many of the swimmers came up to congratulate Tristan on his victory.

"Where's Mark?" Tristan asked Dinadan. "Has he gone in already?"

"He left after the third heat, when he was certain of your victory. You fattened his purse for him today. No doubt he'll reward you publicly at the feast tonight."

Tristan toweled himself dry and pulled on his tunic. "What a day!" He gazed westward toward the dark blue horizon. "On a day like this, I feel I could live forever."

"In that case," a deep voice said behind him, "I pray you have not gone near the Queen."

Tristan whirled. Pernam sat on a boulder at the foot of the cliff path, his short-cropped silver hair brilliant as a jewel in the sun.

"Uncle Pernam! Where have you been keeping yourself? I've hardly seen you since we rode in two weeks ago." Tristan embraced him warmly and Pernam smiled.

"I've been given a room in Tintagel, but I prefer a tent on the open moors. That place"—he nodded toward the brooding towers of the castle—"has more the feel of a prison than a fortress. It pens my spirit in. Besides," he added, the corners of his eyes crinkling in amusement, "I prefer the tent for more practical reasons. My brother Markion disapproves of my friends."

Dinadan fidgeted. "He disapproves of most things, it seems to me."

Pernam rose. "But not of Tristan. Not anymore. Tristan is his golden boy at the moment. He can do no wrong."

Tristan raised an eyebrow. "What's this about, Uncle? If you came down to the beach for more than a greeting, now's the time to tell me."

Pernam spoke in his calm, unhurried voice, collecting them both with his gaze. "Esmerée sent me. She has a message of some urgency for you, or she'd not have ventured from the castle without Segward's leave. She wants to speak to you in person." He paused. "I must tell you, Tristan, that my only interest in this affair is in protecting Esmerée. She has taken a risk on your account. I hold you responsible for seeing no harm comes of it."

"Yes, Uncle," Tristan said meekly. "I will do my best."

"She is in my tent. Come with me, both of you."

Pernam's tent was pitched on the open moor behind the Lyonesse encampment, not far from the horse lines. A startlingly handsome youth guarded the entrance. Although he carried a polished dagger, it was clear from both his stance and his nervousness that he was no warrior. Joy flooded his face when he saw Pernam, and after bowing low and showing them all inside, he left them alone and went to tend the cooking fire.

Esmerée rose from a cushion at their entrance.

"Thank you, Pernam. You are too good to indulge me. Much too good."

Tristan noted her pale face, and instead of taking her hand, he drew her into an embrace and kissed her cheek. "Sweet Esme, don't risk yourself for my sake. It can't be so important it could not wait."

"But it is," she said gravely, gently pushing him away. "I came as soon as Segward went to Markion. It can't wait, Tristan. He means to have your life."

Dinadan started. "Who does? Markion?"

"Why don't we sit," Pernam suggested, "and I'll ask young Arthur to bring us some willow bark tea." They obeyed, and Pernam went out to his beautiful assistant.

Esmerée did not wait for his return but said at once to Tristan, "Segward has been spying on you through Brenna, the wet nurse. With my own ears I heard her report to him that she had seen you with Essylte in the nursery garden, an hour before midnight, every night but one for a fortnight past. Is this true?"

"So *that's* where you've been!" Dinadan groaned. "I should have guessed it. Sir Grayell didn't know where on earth you'd gone."

"Hell and damnation," Tristan grumbled. "Doesn't anyone have anything better to do than meddle in my affairs?"

"But *you* are meddling in Markion's affairs," Pernam said gently, coming in with four clay cups of tea. "Had you done as you ought, none of this would have happened."

"I know, I know." Tristan bowed his head and ran his hands distractedly through his hair. "But I've only had speech with her, Uncle, nothing more. I've barely touched her. We've met, we've talked. It was all so innocent, Mark himself could have watched us without blushing."

"I hope you're right," Esmerée said quietly, "because tonight he *will* be watching."

"What?" Tristan paled.

"Segward took Brenna to Markion. What else can that mean, but that he has told the King all he knows? That you are here with us now means that Markion does not believe him. If I know Segward," Esmerée said slowly, "he will not rest until he convinces Markion of your guilt." She gazed into Tristan's eyes. "And your guilt is your death."

Tristan nodded.

"Knowing the time and place of your tryst, I believe he will make Markion a witness to it."

"Yes," Dinadan put in quickly, "Markion believes what he sees."

"But how?" Tristan whispered. "Where will he be? Waiting in the garden?"

Esmerée leaned closer and lowered her voice. "Not where you can see him. Most probably he will be in the apple tree."

Tristan grimaced. "It was foolish of me to think we could meet unobserved, even for private speech."

"It was foolish of you to meet with her at all," Dinadan breathed. "You can't go tonight, Tristan, you *can't*. Now that you know about the trap, avoid it."

Tristan shook his head. "A trap that misses its prey once is still set for another day. I must try to spring the trap but catch Segward in it instead of me."

Esmerée agreed. "It is easily done if you and Essylte have the courage for it. Meet as you have been meeting. Change nothing. Only let him witness a meeting between two true and loyal subjects who are driven to secrecy by Segward's devious behavior, and who have the best interests of the kingdom at heart. Discredit Segward, and you will be safe from Markion."

Tristan took her hands in his. "Can you get this message to Essylte?"

"Yes. If not to Essylte, to Branwen."

"Good. Tell her to follow my lead. I will play her the tune to sing."

"I will."

He lifted her fingers to his lips. "Thank you, Esmerée, thank you again for the gift of life."

She smiled at him, unaware that her features were alive and glowing, that her heart could be read upon her face. "My lord is most welcome. I only return the gift that you gave to me."

When she hurried away moments later, the three men stood outside the tent and watched her go. Pernam raised his hand in blessing. "There goes the most noble heart I know." He looked at Tristan. "You realize what will happen to her if you succeed in discrediting Segward. . . . He'll be banished to Lyonesse, and in his fury he will beat her every night."

The night was dim enough. Thin clouds shrouded the waning moon and a seaborne haze hugged the cliffs, breathing damp against the castle walls and throwing haloes around the torches. Tristan landed on the soft turf with a light thud. The old apple tree looked spectral in the mist, and he hesitated for a moment, heart pounding, before he slipped beneath its branches. He knew at once Markion was already there. It wasn't anything he could hear or see, and he dared not look up into the branches, but he had the distinct sense of being watched. The hairs rose on the back of his neck and his shoulders itched.

"This is foolishness itself," he murmured firmly. "I'm glad it's almost over."

Soon he saw lights in the nursery windows, heard Brenna's smug voice and Essylte's brave one. Essylte waited on the bench until he called her down the garden with the song of the nightingale. She came directly, without subterfuge, and slipped under the branches of the tree. Tonight she wore the circlet of gold around her brow.

"Sir Tristan."

"My lady Queen." He bowed. "How does your son, the heir?" He made it sound like a ritual question, and he was glad to find her quick to take up the same bored tone.

"Fine. Fine. Keridwen was a little better today. I believe her teeth are coming in. That's what makes her so fussy."

"I wish I could see her more often, but Branwen advises against my going too much to the nursery. She doesn't trust that nosy nurse. Branwen thinks that Segward pays her to gossip about us."

"About *us*? But why?"

Tristan shrugged in annoyance. "He's never liked me. I think he'd like to blacken my name, if he could."

"What a small-hearted man he is. My lord Markion never smiles when he's about. It makes me wonder why he keeps him in his service."

"Oh, he's a very clever man," Tristan said lightly, "but he hasn't Mark's judgment. That's why we must meet like this. Although we have been friends since I brought you home from Wales, Segward would like to see in it something more than friendship."

The frightened quaver in Essylte's voice was real enough. "What do you mean, something more?"

"Don't upset yourself, I pray you," Tristan said gently, taking her arm and seating her on the soft grass between the roots of the tree, where they had been wont to sit together. "You know the king has doubled the guards at your door and forbidden entrance even to me, so that Branwen must come out to me, through the very corridors of the castle, and endure the stares of the sentries, their winks, their sly jests"—his voice grew warm with indignation—"just to spend an hour with me in, er, talk."

"I know how Branwen spends her time with you, my lord." He heard the smile in her voice. Above their heads a branch shook momentarily.

"Well, then, perhaps you know that the guards are Segward's doing. My uncle Mark can have no reason to doubt you, or to doubt me either, for that matter. Everyone seems to know about me and Branwen. But if Segward can once plant the seed of suspicion in my uncle's heart—"

"Suspicion of what?" Essylte said quickly, the tremor in her voice unfeigned.

"Please don't distress yourself, my lady. That's why I first suggested this meeting place. I've known for some time that Segward wants my uncle to believe we are lovers."

"Don't be ridiculous!" The arrogance in her voice gave way immediately to shame. "I'm sorry, Tristan, I mean no insult to you. You're my good friend. I hope you always will be. I meant that it's ridiculous that Mark should believe such a thing. You're being overcautious, surely. I don't see why we can't walk and talk in the sunlight together. Mark would never mind. Why should it be different with you than with Dinadan, or Prince Pernam, or a hundred others?"

Tristan sighed. "You don't understand the nature of suspicion. It's an evil seed. Once it takes root in the mind, it colors all thoughts, desires, beliefs. Nothing looks the same as it once did, although nothing has changed. It's a dark veil that falls before your eyes. Once in place, it is there forever, impossible to remove of your own will, very often impossible even to see. It destroys trust, breeds jealousy and contempt. It takes a strong mind to recognize the harm it does, and put it away."

"Markion is strong," Essylte said softly. "And I know he loves me."

"Men are most vulnerable to suspicion where they love. If he did not care for you, only his pride would be at risk."

Essylte sighed unhappily. "But don't we risk the very suspicion that you fear by meeting so secretly?" Her pale arms moved in the dark, gesturing to the small space that enclosed them both. "This looks like nothing so much as a tryst."

"We are hiding from Segward, not Mark." He paused. "Don't worry. Tomorrow I go home to Lyonesse, and Segward can do as he pleases."

"I shall miss you, Tristan. It's lonely here when all the men are gone, and there's only Branny to talk to. I miss your stories and your songs." Again she spoke with the ring of truth.

"You have your son," Tristan said gently.

She looked up at him, the pale oval of her face just discernible against the dark tree trunk. "Yes. And Markion wants another."

He froze a moment. His own heartbeat thudded in his ears. "Another? So soon?"

"He had three sons before," Essylte whispered, "and he outlived them. It is a dagger in his heart. He wants to be certain of an heir. He wants to found a line of kings. It is a noble ambition, after all. My father wants the same."

Tristan nodded nervously. "But what are you telling me? That the royal nursery is already growing?"

"Not yet," she said quickly, "but it must happen, sooner or later. I am telling you what to expect."

"Well," he managed, struggling to hide his relief, "bridges can't be crossed until you come to them. I hope Mark *does* found a line of kings. He's been a good steward to Cornwall, and if the Saxons would let him be, he could take his place beside Arthur as a great High King of Britain."

"There are those," Essylte said slowly, "who suspect you of resenting his kingship. They think you want his crown, because it belonged to your father before Markion."

"You've been listening to Segward's lies, my lady Queen. I've no desire to rule beyond the boundaries of Lyonesse. Ask my uncle Pernam, or ask Dinadan. When I dream, it is for music or for love, not for power. As far as kingdoms go, I will do everything I can to further Mark's ambition. He has always been good to me."

Essylte extended her hand; Tristan took it and raised her. "And you have done more than duty requires for him. How I wish he had you as his advisor, instead of Segward!"

Tristan bowed politely over her hand. "All things change with time. Be

patient, my dear Ess—my lady, and maybe one day—how did you put it?—
we can walk openly in the sun."

Essylte squeezed his hand, made him a quick reverence, and departed.
Tristan waited until she had disappeared inside the nursery doors, then went
to the garden wall and, using the crevices and footholds he and Gerontius
had used as boys to escape their nurses, climbed straight up the wall and
slithered down the rope on the other side.

Markion balanced in the branches of the tree, tears flowing un-
checked into his beard. Segward had made a fool of him again. He had
heard it now from their very mouths. They were friends, no more—and
why not? They were much of an age and united in their admiration of
him. *And I believed that jealous, two-faced snake! He shall not spend another
day in my employ. I'll send him packing, and invite Tristan to stay another
week. I'll make sure they are not watched. My beautiful Essylte, how could I
have doubted her? If it's the last thing I do, I'll tear the veil of suspicion from my
eyes and bury it forever.*

22 ✝ CASTLE DORR

On a hot day in September Tristan and his company of soldiers cantered up the long, winding approach to Castle Dorr. The castle stood
on a hilltop less than a league from the coast, surrounded on three sides by
the eastern fringe of Morois Wood. Guard towers faced west to the heart of
the forest and east to the sea. Built of gray, roughly quarried stone, the castle
had a cold, forbidding aspect. Tristan remembered well the searching bite of
the east wind that no tapestry yet woven could keep out. Still, he had
passed some of the happiest days of his boyhood in Castle Dorr, and he
looked around in satisfaction at the rich country they rode through: flocks
of sheep dotting the open hillsides, orchards ripening toward harvest, hay-
fields alive with the steady susurration of swinging scythes, pens full of low-
ing cattle, dusty yards where chickens, goats, children, and dogs milled and
played under the watchful eyes of village women. He could almost believe
nothing had changed from the days when Meliodas had brought him to
Dorria on his visits to Bruenor. Then, Dinadan had been but seven or eight
years old, full of boyhood mischief, and now—now Dinadan was getting
married. Tristan smiled wryly and set spurs to his horse.

Sir Bruenor himself met them at the gates. "Tristan! How glad I am to see you! You are welcome, my boy, and your men with you. It was good of you to leave your beloved Lyonesse for me. I trust the journey was an easy one?"

"Thank you, my lord, it was tranquillity itself. Good weather, dry roads, and the certain knowledge of good food, good wine, and good conversation at the end—who would *not* travel in such a circumstance? And I would not miss Dinadan's wedding for any price—all my life I've waited to see him run when a woman calls."

Bruenor laughed and slapped him on the back as the groom led his horse away. "Dinadan will certainly be glad to see you. He's been suffering a bout of cold feet, I think."

"With the wedding tomorrow? I can cure him of that, my lord. I'll sing him a little ditty that reminds him of the joys of married life." He winked. "The sailors' favorite."

Bruenor chuckled. "Speaking of music, I'd be proud if you'd sing to my guests, Tristan. And the girl herself, Lady Diarca, is afire to meet you. You're one of her heroes, you know. Because you slew Marhalt and saved Cornwall."

Tristan coughed gently. "Nowadays it's considered a breach of manners to rejoice in the slaying of Welshmen."

"Ha-ha! So it is indeed, ever since the bonfire! Just the same, it was a noble deed, and nobly done. She is right to admire you for it."

Tristan accepted this praise with a modest bow as Bruenor led him through the outer courtyard and into a small garden.

"You should think of marriage yourself, Tristan. You're only a year younger than Dinadan—just twenty, aren't you? High time to be wed." He grinned at the younger man. "And don't tell me you haven't met the right woman. Everyone knows you have."

Tristan paled. "They do?"

"Of course. Do you deny it?"

"No," Tristan replied uncertainly. "No, I can't deny it."

"No one ever expected you to marry for political considerations, so go ahead and marry for love. Why wait?"

Tristan stared at him in confusion. "Well, sir, um, the lady is not free at the moment to wed me."

"Not free!" Bruenor laughed aloud. "That is a weak excuse indeed for such a man as you! All you have to do is ask her, I'll be bound. I don't know a woman alive who wouldn't trade a mistress's service for a husband's." He turned away, laughing, and shouted for Dinadan. Tristan leaned against the wall, limp with relief.

Dinadan greeted him warmly. "Tris, thank God you've come. You've got to keep me steady, friend, I'm as edgy as a cat in a fire. Now that the day is nearly upon me— Is something amiss? You look like you've seen a spirit."

Tristan laughed weakly. "Your father gave me the scare of my life. He didn't mean to, he didn't know it, but I damn near fainted right here in the garden." He took Dinadan's arm. "Come on, let's share a wineskin. I've a powerful thirst."

"Let's go down to the sea, as we used to do as boys. Just for an hour or two—you remember the place. We'll drink our troubles away and make life simple again."

They followed a long descending trail to a deep bay ringed with sand and found again the small cave at the foot of low cliffs where, as boys, they had hidden so often from their duties. Dinadan took a swig from his wineskin and passed it to Tristan. "It's smaller than I remember. I don't think I've been here since we were last here together."

"We used to look for pirates, remember? But we never saw any."

"Now we look for Saxons. And we *do* see them from time to time. But they don't land often in Dorria. The coast is too well defended."

"Or they're just scouting. There's little point in taking Dorria before they've settled Dumnonia and the Summer Country. They'd be too easy to drive out."

Dinadan grinned. "All right, all right. You're a bucket of cold water on my vanity. I'm in charge of the shore defenses, you see. Pass me back that wineskin. Jesu! You drink like a fish!"

"You've got another. I saw it."

"Lucky for me I do."

"I told you I had a powerful thirst." Tristan paused. "Nowadays it never leaves me." Dinadan avoided his eyes, and Tristan squared his shoulders. "So what's all this I hear about your getting cold feet?"

"Damn my father. He's been talking to you already?"

"You can't be seriously uncertain. You've loved her since before I went to Wales."

"Maybe I'm worried about the kind of husband I will make. I don't want to be like Mark, whose affection wanes and waxes with the strength of a woman's beauty. And forgive me, Tris, but I don't want to be like you, bound hand and foot by a cruel passion that won't give you any peace. I suppose I'm wondering if there's really a middle ground."

"If I could marry her," Tristan whispered, "it wouldn't be a cruel passion. It would be heaven on earth. To spend the rest of my days in Lyonesse with the sweet Essylte? Christ, I burn for it." He looked away quickly. "You either love or you don't. There's no middle ground between loving and not loving. Mark's never loved anyone except himself. He's the only one he makes sacrifices for." He took his eyes off the sea and glanced at Dinadan. "You've loved her for years and you know it. What's this really about?"

Dinadan shrugged. "We had an argument. Our first."

"Saints preserve us all!" Tristan grinned. "Not an argument!"

"About you and Essylte." Dinadan saw the smile die on Tristan's lips. "She's more on your side than I am. She thinks Essylte ought to run away to Lyonesse to join you, and let Mark annul the marriage."

"And you?"

Dinadan drew a long breath. "I think you ought to give her up. You know that."

Silence fell between them. Shoulder to shoulder, they stared out at the cloudless sky and the blue incoming tide, wave following wave in unending, steady rhythm.

"Well," Tristan said at last in a flat voice, "you will be glad to learn that I have taken your advice. I have put her out of my life. I have sworn never to see her again."

Dinadan took another pull at the wineskin and let the silence hang. Finally he said in a neutral voice, "When I last saw you at midsummer, you were delirious with joy at foiling Segward's plan and fooling Mark. He all but gave you his blessing to bed her, as I recall."

"There is very little joy in fooling Mark. The more often we succeed, the more we suffer for it. However easy it is to do, betrayal itself leaves its mark upon us both. To be apart is torture; to be together stains us with dishonor. There is no peace left for us. We must either stay apart and try to let time dull the bright edge of our affection, or cast caution to the winds and escape somewhere together. Essylte's choice, like Diarca's, was for the latter, even if it meant quick death. But now I have the child to think of, too. They will live only if Mark protects them. I made her stay with him."

Dinadan clasped his arm. "You have done the right thing, Tristan. I knew you would. You always were courageous."

Tristan forced a smile. "Say, rather, I wish to be. Every hour of every day my soul strains toward Tintagel and Essylte, locked in her prison. If you were with me, I'd be sure I would not waver in my resolve. As it is, you'll have to come and visit from time to time and keep me steady on my course."

"Stay on here, why don't you, after the celebrations, when everyone else leaves? Stay on until winter, and we'll drink together and remember the old days when women mattered less to us than swords and horses."

Tristan laughed and slung his arm around Dinadan. "I doubt very much your bride would welcome my staying on. She may have other ideas about how you should spend your evenings."

"She does indeed," a cool voice said from above them. "Nevertheless, she endorses the invitation." With a shower of pebbles a neat-footed moorland pony slithered down the steep path to the beach. The girl who sat astride him smiled at them both. She was dressed like a boy in tunic, leggings, and boots, but she was in no danger of being taken for one. Clear brown eyes looked out of a pretty face, and rich, dark hair fell in a thick braid over her shoulder. She threw Tristan a charming smile, and he smiled back at her.

"Diarca!" Dinadan wriggled out of the cave and rose hastily, dusting the sand off his clothes. "Diarca, meet my dearest friend in all the world. Tristan of Lyonesse."

Her smile broadened as she cast Dinadan a look of affection. "I thought it might be. No one's talked of anything but his arrival since he came in. But then you disappeared. I volunteered to fetch you both." She slid off the pony and made a deep reverence before Tristan. "I am pleased to meet you, my lord. It is an honor I have long looked forward to."

Tristan raised her and touched her fingers to his lips. It was impossible not to smile at her. She had the gift of lightheartedness, an eagerness to please and to be pleased, a spirit that saw the sun behind the clouds.

"Thank you. I am honored by your esteem. Dinadan has talked about you for years, and I am very pleased to meet at last the joy of his heart, the grace of his hopes, the light of his tomorrow. Words cannot do justice to your beauty or your charm. I begin to wonder that he ever leaves Dorria."

She laughed and colored lightly. "My lord has a bard's tongue, that would make a golden castle of a morning's digging in the sand."

"Diarca," Dinadan interrupted, "if you heard what I said about horses and swords, I didn't mean—"

She turned to him and smiled as she took his hand. "Of course you did. But you don't need to apologize. Do you think that I haven't wished myself back in my safe girlhood a thousand times this summer?"

Dinadan's look lightened, and he kissed her quickly. "You're an angel."

She wrinkled her nose at him. "You're drunk, and it's an hour before dinner. Shall I send for horses, or can you make it back afoot?"

"Tristan's drunker than I am."

She glanced at Tristan and smiled. "So he is. But he's had more practice, I think." She dipped them a quick curtsy. "I will leave you to your reminiscences, my lords. I only wanted to meet Sir Tristan before his public greeting in the hall. Women do get lost in a crowd." She leaped upon her pony and turned his head back up the hill. "If I were you, I would start back soon. Sir Guvranyl wants to greet Sir Tristan before dinner." She clucked to the pony; with a leap and a bound they were up the rocks and lost in the trees.

"Well!" Tristan exclaimed, slapping Dinadan on the back. "I salute you, Din. You never told me she was so—resourceful."

"Willful and headstrong, her mother calls it." Dinadan smiled. "You like her?"

"I do, indeed. That's a woman a man can be a friend to."

"She's been my friend a long time. I guess I'm just wondering if that's love."

"You've spent too much time running about with me. Spend a year in her company and you'll be in doubt no longer." They started back up the long hill to the castle. "You didn't tell me Guvranyl was coming. I haven't sat down and talked to him in years. I remember he used to drill us on the beach not far from here. Is his chamber near mine? Have you put me with Mark's company?"

"Hell, no. You're next to me. And Guvranyl *is* Markion's company. He's the King's proxy, that's why he's here."

Tristan stopped in his tracks. "Mark didn't come himself?"

"Sent to say he couldn't—off fighting Saxons in Logris. If you ask me, the old soldier seems right pleased to be free of Markion."

They climbed in silence for a while. "My father employed him before Markion did," Tristan said finally. "There was friendship between them. I believe Guvranyl's still loyal to his memory. He's that kind of soldier. Old-fashioned. True. Men aren't made from that mold nowadays."

"Markion's not the only one to send a proxy. Prince Pernam sent one as well—remember Jarrad? Apparently there's some sort of plague among his boys that Pernam must stay and tend to, but whether he sent Jarrad here to serve as proxy or to save him from infection, I couldn't say."

"Probably both. Have you spoken to Jarrad? Is Pernam himself afflicted with the plague?"

"No, no, apparently not. But he misses the help of Esmerée. In the past, when so many have fallen ill together, she has helped him with the nursing. But now, since Segward is banished to Lyonesse and keeps her so close at home, he dare not send for her. It would only make things worse. Segward would beat her just because she was wanted elsewhere."

Tristan shut his eyes tight. "The day is coming when the earth will open and swallow his black-hearted soul. I can feel it in my bones." He opened his eyes and smiled bleakly at Dinadan. "Either that, or I shall kill him myself."

"You promised Esmerée you wouldn't."

"That is the only reason he is still alive."

* * *

The feast that night lasted long past moonrise. Young Hebert, a Breton bard, gave them lay after lay until his voice grew hoarse. When the company clamored to hear Tristan, Hebert graciously offered him his harp. Tristan gave them the tale of Diarmaid and Grainne, an ancient favorite about lasting love in the days when the world was young, and gods walked among men. Not an eye was dry as he finished. Hebert went down on one knee.

"Nay, Hebert," Tristan said quickly, raising him, "do not kneel to me. I have only a smattering of training. I have none of your technique and nothing of your memory. If I move them, it is because they love me. I can sing of love well enough, but mine is a poor skill beside yours. I thank you for the loan of your harp; she has a true voice."

Hebert smiled. "My lord, you underestimate your gifts. A bard is nothing without passion behind the words. You have hold of the central secret—and the gods have blessed you with a voice."

"Cursed me, more like, with a voice and no one to sing to." Tristan sank onto the bench between Dinadan and Guvranyl as Bruenor signaled the wine bearers for another round.

Guvranyl embraced him, and Tristan was astonished to find his beard was wet. "Wherever did you learn such music? I never heard anything so beautiful in all my life, and I know I never gave you time or leave to learn it."

Tristan smiled and hugged the old man, feeling the lean bones, the stringy muscles of age beneath the fine cloth of his robe. "You'd be surprised, Guv, at the things I learned when you weren't looking."

The old soldier's eyes misted. "I miss the sound of music. Your father Meliodas always had the finest bards in Britain come to Lyonesse, and paid them well. The army went without new saddles and once without new swords, so Meliodas could have his music. I thought it was foolishness then. Now I'm not so sure."

"Surely Markion has bards in Camelot? It's been a tradition since Arthur's day, to host the best bards in the land."

Guvranyl shook his head. "Markion has no ear for music. Camelot was once a civilized place—none more so—but now it's just a collection of fighting men. Dinner is meat, wine, dogs, drunkenness, fighting, and sleep. I am glad to know that in Dorria and Lyonesse the light of civilized life has not gone out."

"Why, Guv!" Tristan cried. "Have you changed so? You disdain the company of fighting men? An odd sentiment for a master-at-arms."

Guvranyl drained his winecup. The gaze he fixed on Tristan did not waver. "Times have changed. Markion is not Meliodas. Tristan, we are losing Britain. It is even possible—if we take no steps—that in my lifetime we will lose Cornwall."

Tristan stared at him. He took Guvranyl's arm and felt how it trembled. "Easy does it, Guv. No more wine."

Guvranyl's lips stretched in a thin smile. "Wine or no, it's true. This heir of his changes nothing. At the rate Mark is losing men, that babe will never live to see his birthright." The smile broadened. "Or should I say, *your* birthright. It's you who should be King of Cornwall, Tristan, and High King of Britain. If you were leading those blockhead Logris lords, we could put the fear of Almighty God into those pagan Saxon bastards!"

"Hush, you old fool. You're speaking treason."

"Am I?" Guvranyl shrugged. "Then so is half of Mark's army." The soldier's eyes flickered and his voice went low. "The time is coming, Tristan, when you could take it from him. No one would stop you. Let him lose one more major battle, or do one more mean thing—"

"Guvranyl, I beg you to be quiet. You're drunk. You don't know what you're saying. You've served my uncle Markion for nigh on eight years, and you're the most loyal man I know."

Guvranyl rose, staggered, and leaned against Tristan. Unsteady as he was, his speech was perfectly clear. "I serve Cornwall. Markion will bring us all to ruin. He should never have been King. Meliodas only took the shore patrol that day because Markion feigned illness. It was Markion's duty, but he always was deathly afraid of Gaels." He hiccoughed once, straightened, and walked in a straight line out the door.

"My God, Tristan, what are you gaping at?" Dinadan elbowed him in the ribs. "Your jaw is on the floor."

Tristan turned to him, his eyes wide and unfocused. "I've just learned— if I understood him aright—that it was Markion's fault my father died."

Dinadan sobered instantly. "It wouldn't surprise me."

"And he sent me to Wales. I didn't believe, then, that he meant me harm. But now—he must have hoped the Welsh would do to me what the Gaels did to my father."

"Of course he did. I've told you that a thousand times."

"But why, Dinadan? He knows I don't want his throne. Why should he fear me so?"

"Because so many others want it for you."

A distant trumpet sounded. Heads turned toward the door. A few moments later a page entered, knelt at Bruenor's side, and whispered a message in his ear. Bruenor leaped to his feet.

"Noble guests!" he cried. "Here is a most welcome surprise! I have the honor to announce the arrival at Castle Dorr of our young Queen, Essylte of Gwynedd."

The guards snapped to attention as a hooded figure in a dark green cloak swept into the room and made a graceful reverence to Sir Bruenor. In the stunned silence, her pretty voice reached to the back of the hall.

"My dear lord Bruenor, I pray you will forgive so sudden an intrusion into your company. I should have sent ahead to let you know. I have come to represent my husband at the marriage of your noble son, Sir Dinadan. The High King is away at the wars or he would have come himself."

Sir Bruenor smiled down at her in some confusion. "I thank you, my lady Queen, for such a thoughtful gesture. You are always welcome at Castle Dorr, for any reason. But—er—Markion already sent his excuses with Sir Guvranyl, who serves as his proxy."

The hooded figure went very still. "Sir Guvranyl is here?"

"Aye, my lady. He arrived three days ago."

Essylte pushed her hood back. Her hair was braided tight against her head and bound with a net of tiny pearls. Across her brow she wore a thin silver circlet, symbol of her sovereignty. Sir Bruenor bowed.

Essylte looked calmly up at him. "How odd. He has sent two of us, then, for the same purpose."

"No matter, no matter," Bruenor returned easily. "You are welcome at Dorr and always will be. You've been traveling late, my lady. Have you eaten? Let me send to see if the kitchens are still open."

"We pressed on as fast as we dared to get through Morois before dark. As for me, I am not hungry. But I would appreciate some provision for my men."

"At once. I will see to it." Bruenor nodded to his seneschal, who slipped discreetly out the door. "You are welcome to join us, Queen Essylte, but as you see"—he gestured toward the benches and tables—"we are all men here, getting as drunk as we can as fast as we can, to celebrate Din's last night unwed. Lady Diarca and her women retired some time ago."

Essylte turned and briefly surveyed the men. Everyone knelt. Tristan trembled as her glance touched him and passed over. No more than a moment's contact, the briefest recognition, mild as the breath of May, yet his soul lit and his body fired to life.

"My lord, I thank you for the invitation, but I am tired from the journey. As soon as a bed can be prepared I will go to it."

Dinadan stepped forward. "My lady Queen, I would be honored to escort you. Diarca has taken charge of the women's rooms and can find a space for you, I'm sure. She has long wanted to meet you. You can bide with her while a chamber is prepared."

Essylte made him a reverence. "Thank you, Prince Dinadan. That suits me well."

"Excellent—" Bruenor began, but stopped as Tristan came forward.

"And I." Tristan found himself standing at her side without knowing he had moved. "I will come with you." All eyes turned toward him.

Essylte smiled. "Very well, my lord. Markion's honored nephew is always welcome."

She lowered her eyes discreetly and took Dinadan's arm. Unable to speak, unable to prevent himself from following, Tristan tagged along in silence until they reached the women's quarters. Diarca greeted Essylte warmly and with affection. They sat together on a cushioned couch and chatted amicably while servants hurried to make tea and warm wine for the men. There was plenty of room for her and any companions she had brought with her, Diarca assured Essylte.

"I have brought no companions with me," Essylte said quietly, her hands folded tightly in her lap. "I came at the last moment and my companion is ill. I didn't like to leave her, but it was necessary."

She never turned to him or spoke to him, she never so much as cast a glance his way, but Tristan knew her message was for him.

"Do you mean Branwen?" Dinadan asked. "Is it serious? I thought she had recovered from her childbed."

"She has," Essylte responded. "In a month's time she will feel better, but just now she is too ill to travel."

Diarca nodded knowingly, but Tristan was at sea. What on earth was she telling him? Whatever ailed Branwen? What was he supposed to do about it?

Diarca rose and took Dinadan's hand. "Come with me, my love." She beckoned to the old nurse who attended her. "Come, Lenore. I must have speech with Dinadan and you'd best attend us." The nurse cast a quizzical glance at Tristan and Essylte. Diarca shook her head lightly. "They are old friends," she whispered. "There is nothing to fear."

Out in the corridor Dinadan bent down to her. "Are you mad, leaving them alone together?"

"Of course not. But she has come all this way, through Morois in one day, to tell him something. I must give her the chance to tell him or she'll never sleep." She shivered. "Could you feel the fire in that room, Din? I know now what you mean. They will consume one another if they continue as they are."

"He had sworn," Dinadan said slowly, "never to see her again."

"But *she* came to *him*. He could not prevent that."

"God," Dinadan breathed, "must weep to see them."

* * * *

Essylte stood at Diarca's window, hands clasped tight, and stared out over the dark forest she had just ridden through. Tristan watched her from across the room.

"What is wrong, Essylte? Have you come all this way to tell me Branwen's ill? Should I go to Tintagel to see her? What do you want me to do?"

Essylte drew a deep breath. Lamplight glittered off the silver circlet on her brow, trembling as she trembled. "She's ill only in the mornings. She's with child."

Tristan frowned to hide his relief. Relief was clearly not the right response. "Indeed?"

Essylte turned toward him. "So I have come to beg you to break your vow. My life, and Young Tristan's life, depend upon it."

He could see the tumult of emotion breaking through the hard edges of her control, but his wits were useless. He could not guess the cause of her despair. "Break my vow? But—"

"Tristan!" The cry was wrenched from her. She ran across the room and flung herself at his feet, her hot tears splashing over his hands. "Don't you see? Don't you see what is ahead?"

He raised her and took her in his arms, cradling her head against his chest. "I'm afraid I don't, sweet. Calm yourself, Essylte, and tell me what's amiss. I promise you I will protect you." He led her to the couch and sat her down. She struggled to collect herself, and at last, looking down at their hands clasped together, she spoke.

"Last summer—Midsummer's Eve—you remember. Young Tristan was presented. And afterward—that night—Mark lay with Branwen. He lay with her every night for a fortnight, and she conceived."

"Yes. I understand."

"She is nearly two months gone. Two months!"

She began to tremble, and he pulled her closer. "My dearest love, why does it frighten you so? Why does it mean all our deaths?"

She pushed away and faced him. "Can't you count, Tristan? Everyone at Tintagel has ten fingers. Just because Segward's gone doesn't mean his spies aren't there."

"So? Next spring Branwen will bear a child. Everyone will think it's mine. Why do you worry?"

"May God restore your wits! What happens when Markion comes home at Christmas? What happens when he sees Branny with a swollen belly and me without? He will know which of us is in his bed. I—I—I will have to lie with him." Tears spilled down her cheeks. The hand that gripped his was ice. "I will die first."

He kissed her wet cheeks, and then her lips, and drew her onto his lap. "I see. So what must we do? Keep Mark away until Branwen bears?"

"Longer. She gets weary and low after bearing. He cannot come to Tintagel until she is able to lie with him again. A year, at least. And—I fear she will not want to lie with him anymore."

"Why? Has she said this to you?"

"Not outright. But I think this child she carries is important, even decisive in some way."

"I doubt very much I can keep Mark away for an entire year."

She looked up at him, green eyes swimming. "Lie with me, Tristan. I am begging you. If I conceive now, I can fool him at Christmas about the size of my belly. And I can keep him from coming back until well after Branny is healed. You took the vow for my sake—now you must break it for my sake."

Tristan shut his eyes. "But I swore it upon my love for you," he whispered. "It is not such an easy vow to break."

Essylte leaped to her feet. "Cruel heart! Would you deny me? When it means my life? Oh! You are tired of me already! Is that it? You have been all summer in Lyonesse with Esmerée, and you—"

Tristan grabbed her hand and pulled her hard onto the couch, pinning her against the cushions as his lips sought hers. "Stop. Stop now. You break my heart, I will hear no more of it. *Not want you?* O God! Do you think I am made of stone?" His hands slid over her gown. "There is not a bone in my body that does not want you. Every fiber of my flesh aches for your touch. Did you really come all the way from Tintagel for *this?*"

Half laughing, half sobbing, she hung on his neck. "I dared not go to Lyonesse—on what excuse? This was the perfect place, the perfect time. No one will suspect. Everyone knows Dinadan is my friend."

Tristan bowed his head against her breast as her hands slipped under his tunic. "No. Sweet. No. I mean, not here. Not now. Diarca's only gone for a moment. Let me think. My darling girl, be still a moment." He pushed himself upright and straightened his tunic. "There is only one way to do it. As soon as the feasting is over, I will escort you back to Tintagel. I'll send my own men home to Lyonesse. How much of an escort did you bring?"

"Twelve."

"Good." He paused. "How much time do you need? I mean, er, how long will it take?" He colored lightly at Essylte's puzzled frown. "I know it takes longer for some women than for others. Last time," he said, clearing his throat awkwardly, "it needed only a single bedding. I need to plan for the time. How long should we be together?"

She slipped off her silver circlet and placed it around his head. "Give us a fortnight, and all will be well. If God smiles on us."

"A fortnight might be difficult, unless your men are fools."

"They're Markion's men, my dearest. Not mine. What do you plan to do?"

He shook his head. "Don't ask me. It's better you do not know. Secret some extra waterskins among your belongings, and beg a day's rations from the kitchens. Ask for a litter, not a horse. If Bruenor questions you, which he won't, tell him you are with child."

She sucked in her breath and looked up at him uncertainly. He took her hands and held them. "Essylte. Are you certain this is what you want? Let me go to Tintagel and get our son, and take you both to Lyonesse. The time may be ripe to test Mark's resolve."

"No, no!" she breathed. "I'm not ready to die yet, Tristan. If we can keep going just a little longer—who knows? Maybe the Saxons will kill him in battle and he'll die a hero's death. That would solve everything."

She smiled up at him, but Tristan flinched. "What has Markion done to us that we should wish him an early death? What if our wish is granted? Will we be happy then?"

Essylte covered her face with her hands. "Are we damned, then? What have we ever done but love each other?"

Tristan swallowed. "What indeed?"

23 ✝ LOST IN MOROIS

The Bishop of Dorria married Dinadan and Diarca at midmorning. The day was warm and dry, and the wedding feast spilled out the doors of the hall into the garden and even beyond the courtyard onto the cleared hillside. There was food enough for an army, and wine enough to put every man in a stupor. Hebert was in perfect voice. Men sang and danced and ate and drank until the afternoon was well advanced. Of them all, only Tristan and Essylte drank nothing, and barely touched their food. At dusk the women led the bride away. An hour later, staggering on his feet, supported by his companions, Dinadan was led away to join her. In the feasting hall the drinking went on and on. Men slid senseless from their seats and lay snoring where they fell. Those who were left crowed in victory and called for another round of wine.

Tristan drew Sir Bruenor aside and thanked him for his generous hospitality. At dawn the next morning, he planned to escort Queen Essylte back to Tintagel, and he begged leave to go.

Bruenor tried hard to focus on his face. "Of course I give you leave, of course I do. God, you look like Meliodas! I wish he were here. Sonofabitch's whelp never touched wine, but when he did he could drink me under the table. Ha-ha! But what's the hurry? Stay with us awhile, my boy. Queen's welcome to stay, too. We'll be celebrating all day long—there will be races, contests, songs—and you just got here yesterday!"

Tristan explained carefully that Essylte wished to leave as soon as possible, that neither she nor Markion had known, when he sent her to Dorria, that she was with child, but that he would be furious to learn she had risked traveling in her condition. It was best to get back without delay.

Bruenor grinned in delight. "Again? That randy old goat! Who would have thought he had it in him? Bless the girl, she may leave when she chooses. Yes, yes, by all means escort her yourself. Markion will thank you for it. I hope little Diarca will prove such a breeder of sons!"

They left at dawn, with a cool mist rising from the dewy grasses. A league east of the looming forest the road forked. Tristan sent his own men home along the south road, which ran through the lower reaches of Morois at its thinnest point, and then on down the peninsula to Lyonesse. Bleary-eyed and nursing headaches, they were only too willing to part from their sober commander and return home at their own pace. Tristan led Essylte and her twelve men straight into the forest.

He had ridden through Morois often enough, both in Meliodas's train and in Markion's. The road between Tintagel and Dorria was considered safe for travel, at least for a group of armed men. It was well worn and easy to follow, except in a mist. But in the heart of the forest even bright sunlight dimmed to dark, and an eerie stillness carpeted the land, so that no one, not even hardened soldiers, passed through without making signs against enchantment, or clutching amulets, or whispering prayers of protection. Here and there throughout the forest, tracks branched off the main road, some no more than deer trods, some clearly the work of men. No one Tristan knew had ever ridden down one of those tracks to see where it led. No one had ever dared even step off the road. Legend held the heart of Morois was haunted by Faerie folk. In the broad light of day no one believed in Faeries, but the heart of Morois Wood was another matter. Since his boyhood, when Tristan had first seen those branching forest tracks, they had beckoned to him, calling to him from their mystery, but he had never been in command of his movement, had never had the power to follow their call. Until now.

As they rode, Tristan scanned the forest for signs of life, but nothing moved in the dappled light and shadow. Shafts of bright September sun pierced the leafy canopy here and there, throwing the ragged undergrowth into sharp relief. But they traveled alone. Nothing moved, nothing watched, nothing threatened from the tangled verge. For the thousandth time Tristan racked his memory. He knew the place he sought, but he was not sure how late they would reach it. Thank God Essylte had agreed to the litter. It forced them to move slowly, and they would have to set up camp somewhere for the night.

In late afternoon the forest thickened around them and the men, still edgy from last night's drinking, began to look nervously about. Tristan raised a hand and halted the procession. They had come to the place he sought. On the southern side of the road was a little clearing in a thin stand of pines. Ten minutes' work in the underbrush would give a company of men space enough to set up a dozen tents. As it was, they hobbled the horses, tossed their bedrolls on the ground, and rigged a small pavilion for Essylte from skins and blankets and the litter cloths. The men felt better after they built a fire. They had all packed their saddlebags with leftovers from Bruenor's generous table, and Tristan had brought three extra skins of wine. They cheered his foresight, and cheered again when he bade them finish it off to clear their headaches, and cheered him a third time when he volunteered to stand the first night watch. By the time the thin moon rose above the pines, they were all twelve fast asleep and snoring. Tristan lifted aside the skins of the pavilion and peeked inside. Essylte was ready, wrapped in her dark green cloak and hood. She had bundled together armfuls of gathered bracken, her saddle, and her litter cushions and tucked a blanket around them to form a long, lumpish bundle. Tristan nodded his approval. If it was merely glanced at, not inspected, it gave the impression of a sleeping body. He pointed to her candle. She blew it out and reached for his hand. Together, as silently as thieves, they crept over the carpet of pine needles and out onto the road.

It was so dark they could see nothing at first. They faced away from the fire until their eyes adjusted and they could see the lighter darkness of the road against the deeper black of the forest on either side. Side by side, holding tight to one another, they walked down the road into the heart of Morois Wood. As time passed they found they could see well enough to distinguish the trails that intersected the road at odd intervals.

"What if they wake up?" Essylte whispered. "They will come after us, surely. Shouldn't we hide away well off the road?"

"Few men are brave enough to ride into the depths of Morois at night," Tristan replied. "And none of them is in Markion's service. Besides, they won't know this is the way we've come. They'll scour the forest within light of the fire, then wait for morning and look for tracks."

"Will they track us this far?"

"I doubt it. The road is dry and hard. And even in daylight this part of the forest is always dark. They'll be so frightened by the time they get here, they'll hardly take their eyes from the trees. We have plenty of time to hide, my love. I'm only looking for the right path."

"The right path? Where does it lead?"

"I mean, the one I'm looking for. It's at the top of a low rise and heads due north, I think. Come on, it can't be far."

Another hour of walking brought them to the place Tristan remembered, and they left the road for a narrow track that ran straight through the undergrowth for a hundred paces, then snaked eastward and wound slowly uphill. Essylte clung to Tristan's hand as they climbed, feeling their way. The forest here was alive with night sounds, the low call of owls, the distant throaty howl of a beast more formidable, the beat of wings, more felt than heard, erratic rustling in the undergrowth, and now and then a shriek, bitten off.

Essylte shivered. "Tristan, are we in danger?"

He squeezed her hand. "No, love."

"Where are we going, then? Where does this path lead?"

She heard his soft laugh. "I've no idea."

Her instinct was to panic—two people alone in the middle of Morois Wood, on a night so dark they could hardly see a step before their faces, and they didn't know where they were or where they were going. But, oddly, she felt safe. The night seemed a blanket drawn down to hide them, the forest an old friend who pulled them to its bosom with the promise of protection. Surely the forest itself, so mysterious, so feared, would shield them from pursuers. She understood there would be pursuers. The knowledge did not trouble her at all. She did not care what happened to her, so long as she shared her fate with Tristan.

She smiled to herself as her breathing quickened. Ever since he had vowed not to see her again she had hungered night and day for the touch of Tristan's hands. Her desire was a living pain that swelled with every step into the forest, more real, more compelling even than her fear.

The path ended abruptly in a circular clearing at the top of a hill. They stood hand in hand, awed by the beauty of the place. A thin slice of moon burned overhead, shedding silver shadows on the gray grasses. The night air moved around them, cool and free. A ring of stones marked the center of the clearing, and in the middle of the ring they could see the scorched earth that signaled a recent fire.

"It's a sacred place," Essylte breathed. "It must be. I can feel it."

Tristan nodded and bent to touch the ashes. "Aye. Look yonder, under the trees. Can you see the standing stones? This is a Druid grove."

"Druids?" Essylte shuddered and looked quickly about. "Here?"

"Don't be afraid, Essylte. Last night, the night of the new moon, there was a ceremony here. The earth is still warm. Modron, the three-in-one: Virgin, Mother, and Crone, unless I miss my guess. You have no need to fear; she is your protectress."

"But I'm a Christian. I don't worship the Mother."

He smiled at her. "Then this is not a sacred place."

But she knew it was. Something powerful presided in that clear, open space—not the familiar power she worshiped in the chapel at Tintagel, with its cross of beaten silver and its chalice of studded gold. Christ spoke to her of mercy and forgiveness, of beauty in squalor, of joy in submission and of life everlasting. This power was different, older, cruder. It made no promises. An ancient, hallowed stillness crept into her bones, a driving joy suffused the very air she breathed. Her feet were rooted to the earth. She had grown there, anchored in timelessness. But she was a fragile, hollow reed, void of content. Her body ached the ache of emptiness, of the fallow field. Her blood beat with the desire to blossom, to bloom, to bring forth life. A low moan escaped her. Her eyes widened as she recognized her yearning, and Tristan smiled.

"Standing there in your dark cloak with your bright hair, lit by a moonbeam with the night behind you, you are light and shadow, truth and mystery; a woman as fair as a star of the heavens, and as unknowable. You could be the Goddess Herself, my sweet Essylte."

"I am only a woman," she whispered. "But I am half myself without you."

Tristan shifted his saddle pack off his shoulders and spread a blanket on the ground within the ring of stones. From his wineskin he poured a libation into the waiting earth, then took a long pull and offered it to Essylte.

"Drink." She obeyed. He pushed the hood off her head and undid the clasp that held her cloak.

"Tristan!" she breathed. "Do you feel what I feel?"

"Do I not!" he whispered back. "My blood beats in my ears! Tonight I am emperor, conqueror, King Stag himself in earthly form."

One by one, he loosed the braids that held her hair, until the bountiful curls fell into his hands. She pressed against his strong body, wild and alive, wondering whether this stirring need that drove her was his magic or the Mother's.

"Oh, Tristan, at last we are free!"

He lifted her in his arms and knelt on the blanket. "Tonight we will worship the Good Goddess, the giver of life. Together." A quick smile. "I wager the Mother will be pleased with our offering."

She laughed. "But we are Christians—we don't know the ritual."

He bent over her and touched his lips to her face. "Christian or pagan, Druid or renegade prince, it is all the same. This ritual is as old as time."

Essylte sang as they walked through the forest and plaited a crown for her hair from the hanging vines. In the hood of her cloak she had gathered pine nuts, acorns, and berries. The forest in October proved a generous host, ripening fruits for them, sending deer, fox, and rabbit across their path. Tristan had taught her how to set a rabbit snare. There was nothing easier, really. She wondered why no one taught girls this fundamental skill. Rabbit stew flavored with pine nuts was a nourishing and tasty dish, especially as it was the first one she had ever made with her own hands. And if they had missed onions and bread, neither of them had said so. Of course, they had only made stew when they stayed at the woodcutter's empty cottage, where there was a cooking pot. Most of the time they stuck the meat on a barbed stick and roasted it over a fire. It was still nourishing but took time and energy to chew.

Twice, Tristan had killed a deer. He had fashioned a spear from a stripped sapling and bound his dagger to the end of it to make a killing weapon he could throw. More than once he had regretted not raiding the weapons room at Castle Dorr. A bow and a quiver of arrows would make a big difference now. But such weapons were difficult to hide, and he could not have carried them openly without raising a host of questions. Deer were nearly impossible to kill with a single spear strike. It was a primitive art, Tristan told her. No doubt their forefathers, who had peopled Cornwall in the wake of the giants who had fashioned the land, had mastered that art, but to a modern, civilized warrior used to more deadly weapons, it was an arduous and chancy way to hunt. Once he had been lucky, when a deer ran across their path at dusk. But the second time, when they were hungry, he had waited at a salt lick, sitting perfectly still for hours on end, until two young bucks appeared. The skins were not cured, of course. They had neither the tools nor the time. Tristan used them for carrying deer flesh or for sleeping on at night when they were out of meat. If they were rubbed with ashes from the fire, the smell was bearable.

There were certain advantages, Essylte thought, to a wanderer's way of life. Her legs had grown strong with constant walking, her feet tough. She had lost flesh, she knew, because her gown, torn by brambles and in need of patching, hung loose about her, but her body was stronger, more agile, able to perform feats she had never dreamed possible for a woman. She had crossed streams by leaping from boulder to boulder, had crossed a chasm by swinging on a vine, had climbed trees for apples, for concealment, or purely for the pleasure of knowing she could do it. She had clawed her way up a cliff to hide in a cave the day they heard hunting dogs. She grinned. If her mother could see her now! This ragged, unkempt girl with tangled hair, lean and strong as any boy, was a far cry from the gowned and pampered Queen of Powys Guinblodwyn had envisioned! The thought of it made Essylte laugh in sheer delight.

She bathed in rushing streams and washed her hair with soaproot. She enjoyed standing naked in the cold water, with the warm sun on her back, and Tristan—always Tristan—there at her side, smiling at her, alive with delight, making her feel the most beautiful woman in all the world. She no longer feared the forest. She felt at home now in its branches and its bowers, its hills and hollows. The only thing she feared was being caught.

It had been a close thing at the woodcutter's cottage. They had come across it at dusk, only days after their escape. Tristan had been reluctant to approach it—it meant some village or hamlet lay nearby, and it wouldn't be empty long; this was the time of year for getting in wood for winter burning—but a storm was brewing, so they took shelter in the cottage. How wonderful it was to lie in a bed again, warmed by a leaping fire and Tristan's arms around her, while outside the wind raged and the rain beat furiously down.

Nostalgia for the settled life had hit her like a blow. She begged Tristan to stay another day, and another. He indulged her against his better judgment. He held her, and whispered to her, and made sweet love to her to dry her tears. But on the morning of the third day he had taken her hand and led her firmly away. Smoke from their fires had surely been noticed in the village, and sooner or later someone would come by to investigate. How could they be certain no messenger from Castle Dorr had reached the village? Whether Tristan was regarded as victim or villain, the disappearance of the Queen of Cornwall, the High Queen of Britain, was a catastrophe large enough to be bruited about the entire land.

That very afternoon, from their hiding place in a pine tree, they had watched and listened as the woodcutter and four men from the village searched the woods below them. They were armed with axes, cudgels, and a sword, but thank the Good Goddess, they did not have dogs. They knew whom they sought. The tallest of them held one of her hair ribbons in his hand.

"Green, they said she were wearing, eh, Birn? A green gown and cloak? I wager this be hers, then."

"Yes," another had replied. "We'll send to Dorr when we get back. Pray the bastards don't take 'er into Black Hollow. She'll never come out from there alive."

"Then we'd best be quick about it," the woodcutter had cut in gruffly, "if you want to search the woods from here to there and be back by dark."

Tristan had marked which way they went, and after they returned at dusk, hurrying in the failing light, he followed their trail. Black Hollow turned out to be no more than a bog with chancy footing. With the help of a long stick to probe the bubbling mud, he had led her safely through the marsh grasses, from tuft to tuft, until they reached firm ground on the other side. Thinking she was being clever, she had pulled out her remaining hair ribbon and tossed it into the thick, black ooze.

But that had made Tristan angry. "We don't want them to think you're dead," he said. "That way, you can never go back."

"Good!" she had returned defiantly. "Let Mark put aside the marriage and wed another. Then I am yours forever."

Tristan's eyes had flashed in the dark. "And what happens to our son?"

It was the only time in the whole six weeks they had mentioned the future. It was safer just to go on from day to day, hoping the future would never come. Sometimes at night, with the warmth of Tristan's body against her own and his lips against her cheek, she wished for death. She knew she would never be happier than she was now. Whatever it was that lay ahead would be immeasurably worse, could not help but be worse, than wandering through Morois Wood with her lover at her side.

But Tristan himself was changing. It wasn't the drawn look about his face or the leanness of his body that worried her. It was the look in his eyes. Except when he was loving her, which was still, as always, a joyful celebration of desire between them, he wore a haunted look. He put her in mind of a hound who had misbehaved; his eyes spoke of mute suffering, of shame, and even of regret. At first she thought his love had cooled, but the heat of his denial, and the proof that followed, convinced her she was wrong. Nor was he sorry he had rescued her from death. He would walk into the jaws of Hell for her, he told her, and she believed him. But he could not live from day to day, as she could. The past lay heavy on his shoulders, and the dreaded future just around the corner. He was waiting for the second shoe to drop.

Essylte shook her head impatiently. It was the Christian in him that made him so gloomy, so conscious of sin. Christ, like Mithra, was a man's god, with a man's understanding of the world. But the Power she had met on that Druid hilltop was a different sort of Power altogether. As ancient and fundamental as the earth itself, it spoke to her in a language she understood, a mother tongue of mysteries profound. It had claimed her soul on that sacred hill in the white moonlight, and it protected her still. The Goddess—if one could use such a term for a Presence undivided into gender, a spirit both male and female, both spear and vessel, both driving force and receiving joy—the Divine, the wellspring of holiness, had been there on the hilltop with them, sweetening their union with a silver shower of moonlight kisses, inflaming their desire with the heat of the earth itself. That Spirit had entered her body with Tristan. It had kissed her with Tristan's lips, touched her with Tristan's hands; it had driven them, whipped them to urgent frenzy, to fierce rejoicing. It had cried out in ecstasy with Tristan's voice, and as the stars exhaled, it had slept pillowed on her breast with Tristan's dark head. There on the bright hill, with the warm earth below them and the starlit sky above, the Spirit of the Mother had blessed their union and breathed the breath of life into Tristan's seed.

Essylte's hands met instinctively over her flat belly in a protective gesture. She had not told Tristan. This was her secret, shared only with the Mother, a blessed gift, a warm nugget of joy she cradled with a fierce, possessive love. It gave her the secret strength to laugh when Tristan frowned, to see the sun behind the clouds, to regard each morning as blessed renewal and the coming of night as a lovers' celebration, full of mystery and delight.

She had not told Tristan because she did not want to lose this magic. She did not want to return to Tintagel and part from him again. She did not want to hear any more oaths. Tristan, worried about the coming of winter, wanted to be out of Morois before the first snows fell. He waited daily to hear that she had conceived and his duty was done. She shuddered. He would do what it took to protect her, even if it meant sending her back to Mark. But the thought of Tintagel and its cold, encasing walls terrified her after the freedom of the forest. She wanted never to go back.

Wind stirred the treetops, and a shower of leaves drifted down across her path. There was a definite chill in the air, and now the nights were growing cold. When the wolves came down from the heights she and Tristan would need a bonfire to keep them off—and the smoke from a bonfire could be seen for leagues. Essylte looked around at the forest about her. Half the hardwoods still bore their leaves, and the sky was more blue than gray. Surely winter was at least a month away. On the thought, the treetops rustled and swayed, and a gust of cold air touched her cheek. The sky was darkening swiftly. Up ahead, Tristan stopped and cocked his head to listen.

"What do you hear?" she called, running to catch up.

"Rain." He sounded edgy. "In the west. Coming this way."

As hard as she tried, she could hear nothing. "Nonsense. It's a beautiful day."

He jerked his head down the path. "This trail was made by men. I'm going to follow it over that ridge. Perhaps there's a farm or a village on the other side."

"A village! Then we ought to go the other way."

He gazed at her darkly. "Essylte, you need food and rest. You ought to see your face. No one would know you. This is the heart of Morois. If anyone is there, they won't have heard about us. No one comes this deep into the wood. Not alone."

"Perhaps only Druids live here, or Faerie folk, or giants! Oh, Tristan, let's go another way!"

"I'm going to find out. Listen—do you hear? That's thunder. We were lucky with the last storm, we found an empty cavern. But I don't want you spending a night out in the wet, not as thin as you are."

"Oh, I see," she returned bitterly. "Now that my curves are gone, you have no more use for me. When my breasts were full of milk you were attentive enough, but now—"

He stopped her with his lips upon her mouth and drew her so roughly to him that she could not breathe. "Such nonsense!" he whispered. "Such foolish prattle." He kissed her again and held her head against his breast. "You can't seriously doubt me, Essylte. I have never given you cause. If you die, I will die with you. This I swear. But I want you to live. You are not as strong as you think you are. I want a decent shelter from this storm, that's all. Will you condemn me for wanting as little as that?"

She blinked away tears and looked up at him. "I'm stronger than you think. I'll never die while you live."

His hand caressed her cheek and lifted her chin. "What's the matter? Is something wrong?"

She shook her head quickly. "No, no. Nothing at all is wrong. I am happier than I have ever been." Hope lit his face, and she pushed him gently away. "Go ahead, look for your shelter. Don't worry. I'll follow you faithfully."

He pointed up the path. "An hour's walk, I wager, to the ridge. We'll climb a tree and look for firesmoke. But it may rain before then. You'd best put on your cloak."

Long before the hour was up the swift-flying storm came upon them, broke the heavens open with thunder and blinding fire, and drenched them to the skin.

24 ⊕ THE HERMIT

Cold, slanting rain drove them down from the ridge into a hollow dell. There, a low hut hunched among the pines like a wounded animal trying to escape notice. Huddled against the trees, well off the path, it looked an odd-shaped shadow in the blowing dark. Tristan drew his sword, but he knew before he entered it was empty. It had the feel of solitude.

"Come on in, Essylte. It's safe." Her hand was freezing, and her whole body shook with wet and cold. Inside it was so dark they could see nothing. His foot touched a stone. He dropped to his knees and explored the dirt floor with his hands. There was a ring of stones in the center, hearthstones, almost certainly. Overhead rain dripped through a hole cut in the thatch to let out firesmoke. He searched eagerly beside the stone and found flint and tinder, and nearby a basket of kindling.

While he bent over the flint he whispered a prayer of thanks, to Christ, to Mithra, to the Great Mother, especially to the Mother, who seemed to have taken Essylte under Her wing. Even from where he knelt he could feel Essylte's shivering, the cold that pierced her to the bone. In the past month they had grown so close, he seemed to have entered beneath her skin to share each of her sensations. He thought what she thought, felt what she felt, dreamed what she dreamed. Their physical union was not that of two separate bodies meeting, but of two seeking halves of one self, one hope, one dream, one flesh, complete only in the sweet, fierce mystery of joining. She was his breath of life, the melody of his harper's song, the flashing blade of his warrior's spirit: his soul. He could no more part from her than he could leave his bones behind.

A spark struck, the tinder caught, a wisp of flame curled upward and blossomed into fire. He added kindling and watched as the flames sucked and sighed, snatched at the dry sticks, and settled down to burn. He rose and looked around.

They stood in a circular dwelling with a domed roof of thatch, built in the beehive, pre-Roman pattern of Druid days. There were no windows and only one door, low and curved, made for a smaller man than Tristan. The hut was scrupulously tidy. A bed of bracken and straw lay snug against the wall, covered in skins, with an old wool blanket folded carefully at its foot. Near the hearth he saw a short, three-legged stool, a cooking pot, and a tripod. An odd assortment of wooden bowls, spoons, and cups were neatly stacked on a low shelf beside crude clay oil jars stoppered with rags. An ax hung in its sling behind the door, its edge bright with use. Underneath it was a small locked chest.

"Whoever lives here left without his ax," Essylte observed, her teeth chattering. "Whose place could this be? It's not a woodcutter's cottage."

"Of a certainty," Tristan agreed. "For one thing, there's no wood." He took her by the shoulders. Her lips were blue with cold. "You're soaked to the skin. Come, let's get these wet things off you." Her fingers were stiff and unmanageable; she could not even undo the clasp to her cloak. Gently he did it for her, drawing off the sodden garment, unlacing the ragged gown and lifting it over her head. Even her shift was wet, even her undergarments. He reached for the woolen blanket on the bed and wrapped it tight around her naked body. Then he took her in his arms and clutched her to his breast, stilling the upwelling of desire. Always, always, whenever he looked at her, the fierce yearning for her struck at his soul.

"My sweet Essylte, you will soon be warm enough. Sit here on the stool and feed the fire with kindling. I'll take the ax and bring back enough wood to get us through the night."

"Be careful, Tristan." She drew his head down and kissed his lips. "I will be with you."

Wood was easy to find. An hour's work in the pelting rain yielded him more than enough, but he didn't want to stop. The labor relaxed him. The swing of the ax stretched and bunched muscles stiff with cold, the sweat worked loose the hard knot of fear that ate at him like a canker, and cooled the longing that still pulled at his body. He smiled to himself. She had only to look at him with those dark-lashed blue-green eyes to stir the very fibers of his being. Dear God! To think that he had lain with her every night for two months and still she was not with child! Was there magic in Morois? Were they under some evil spell? Even as he thought it, he dismissed it. Nothing could be evil that so clearly pleased Essylte. She was like a child in her delight, carefree, glorying in every moment. Knowing what she had been through, fearing what might yet come to her, he did not begrudge her her joy. To love without secrecy, to love with abandon—it was clearly heaven to her. Why was it not heaven to him?

He piled the logs on one of the deerskins and dragged it back to the hut. He knew the answer to his question. He was responsible for the way she looked: the ragged gown, the slippers nearly in shreds, the wild, un-combed hair, and worst of all, the way her collarbones and hipbones stood up from her flesh. He was the reason she risked her life in Morois. But for him, she would be safe in Tintagel, dressed warmly in rich furs and velvets, sitting in the Queen's chair by an open blaze, her hair dressed with pearls and ribbons. For all their love, he was a curse to her, he thought bitterly, and always had been.

"Your mother cursed us, sweet Essylte," he muttered to himself. "And cursed we remain." He shuddered as he remembered her words: *Four women shall place their trust in you and live to see that trust betrayed! Three children shall your loins beget: a whore, a destitute beggar, and a murdering rogue!* But this was witchery. No one could possibly know his fate. He didn't have three children, at least not yet, and only two women had ever put their trust in him. Three, if one counted Branwen.

A thought struck cold at his entrails. Why had Branwen not told Essylte of her conceiving? If Branwen should waver, if Essylte should ever be forced to lie with Mark . . . Tristan stood rigid in the rain, shaking. Clear in his mind's eye he saw Mark's lean, stringy hands on Essylte's body, his dry lips against her face, his drunken, grunting lust, his impatient, driving need between her soft white thighs . . . He bellowed aloud, filling the forest with his cry. His chest heaved for breath. He fell to his knees on the sodden forest floor, nauseous to dizziness. He waited, head down, until his breathing slowed and all that remained was a bitter cramp in his gut and the taste of bile in his mouth.

Essylte stood in the doorway, looking out. "Tristan? Tristan! Are you there?"

He forced himself to calmness and pushed himself to his feet. "I am here," he called. He grabbed the end of the deerskin with trembling hands and dragged it to the hut. "I am coming."

She gasped when she saw him in the light. "Tristan, what has happened? What's amiss? You look like you've seen a spirit from the Otherworld!"

He smiled weakly. "Nay, not that. Be easy, sweet. I'm all right."

She clutched the blanket tighter around her. "I felt fear suddenly, as I sat by the fire. As if something crept up close and touched me with a slimy paw. Something horrible!"

He dragged the logs inside and shut the door behind them. "We are one soul, you and I. Yes, I was afraid. But it passed."

"What was it?" Her drawn face looked up at him, her eyes enormous. "Is there something out there?"

He shrugged and forced a smile. "No, love. Not out there." He touched his breast. "In here. Don't ask me what it is."

She smiled, to his surprise, and sighed in relief. "It's only your silly fears. You're the bravest man in all Britain, and the best warrior, too—why do you torture yourself with worries? Come, take off those wet clothes and sit by the fire with me. You're too cold for me to touch, now that I'm dry."

He stripped quickly and laid his wet clothes next to Essylte's on the other side of the hearth. The heat of the fire met his skin like a caress. Or was it Essylte's gaze? He looked up. She knelt by the fire, stirring the cooking pot, her eyes fierce with desire. Life stirred his loins, and he laughed out loud. "Witch woman! What will you do to me? I am your slave, Essylte. Have you not had enough of me yet?"

"I will never have enough of you." She smiled. "But I will feed you first." She had arranged skins on the floor beside the stool, and she beckoned to him. "Come. I've put some deer meat in the pot with the nuts I gathered. It's a poor excuse for stew, but at least it's something."

"Let me add a good log to that fire, and it will cook faster."

The fire hissed and spat in protest at the wet wood, but the resulting steam was hot and welcome. He pulled the door tight and stuffed handfuls of grass in the ill-fitting space around it. The hut warmed quickly. Essylte's shivering diminished, and warmth returned a little color to her cheeks. She sat on the stool with Tristan at her feet, his head resting against her knees.

His quiet voice split the silence. "Tell me now about Branwen."

"I told you. She's sick as a dog."

Tristan paused. "That's not what I mean. You told me you felt this child meant something important to her. Did you mean she planned it?"

"I'm not sure," Essylte said thoughtfully. "It's odd that she didn't tell me, isn't it? If I'd known at midsummer what she intended, we could have lain together under the apple tree and perhaps all this could have been avoided."

"Yes," Tristan replied evenly. "That's just what I was thinking."

"She knows how to prevent bearing, yet she didn't."

Tristan looked up quickly. "She can prevent it?"

Essylte nodded. "Mother taught us. I wish now I had listened better, but at the time I couldn't see the point."

"Are there really such herbs? I know every village midwife claims such power, but I've never seen it work when it was wanted."

"It's three herbs, mixed in proportion, boiled over fire for the time it takes to chant the spell, and then set to cool under the waxing moon. I know the herbs, but I can't remember the amounts or the words of enchantment." She grinned. "As a sorceress, I'm hopeless."

"Thank God for that."

Her fingers stroked his hair and tickled the new beard on his chin. "Why did you ask about Branwen?"

"Oh," he said slowly, "I wondered if she has a plan she hasn't shared with us."

"What do you mean? What kind of plan?"

Her lovely eyes narrowed in a frown, and he was relieved to see it. She had worried about it, too.

"Think back to the plan we made that day in Guvranyl's house. Look at it from Branwen's point of view. What does she stand to gain?"

Essylte began to tremble. "She is my dearest friend in all the world, Tristan. She has served me since we were children. She did it for me."

He shook his head gently. "No, my dear. Servants, even dear ones, are not such friends as that. She may have felt for your distress, but she did it for herself. For the same reason she agreed to lie with Mark beyond the wedding night."

Tears brimmed in Essylte's eyes. "Why, then? To bear the King a child?"

"To bear the King a son."

"Let her. What difference does that make? She can't ever let him know it's his, or he will kill us all."

"Perhaps. He will kill *us*, that's for certain. And our son. But whether he kills Branwen or marries her in your stead depends upon several things."

Essylte gasped. "She would never! And Mark would never marry a lowborn girl—it would insult his pride."

Tristan paused, watching her face. "Who are her parents, Essylte?"

Essylte gaped at him. "Her mother was a common house servant in my father's castle. *In the garden.* Later she served my mother. No one knows who her father was."

"Someone knows."

"Well, Branny doesn't, or she'd have told me. Her mother died when she was little. How on earth would she find out unless her father revealed himself to her?"

Tristan shrugged. "If you are right, then we have nothing to fear. And this pregnancy of hers was a mistake. Perhaps she didn't remember the words, either."

Essylte shook her head. "Branny never forgets a thing. Perhaps the herbs don't grow in Cornwall. Oh, Tristan, now I am afraid. Ever since little Keridwen was born, things have not been quite the same between me and Branny. Now you tell me you suspect her of some kind of treachery. Can it be possible she means us harm? After all she has done for us?"

Tristan pulled her off the stool and onto his lap. The blanket slipped from her shoulders as he bent his lips to the warm skin of her throat. "I only suspect her of having a double purpose. What she has done for us, she has done also for herself. That's all. Don't go making phantoms where none exist. I'm sorry I spoke."

She shrugged off the blanket and pressed her body against his. "Tristan, Tristan, take me to Lyonesse. I am ready to go. I can't be parted from you—not again, not ever again. Death is better."

"First, Tintagel," Tristan breathed, his mouth against her breast, "to get our son. And then I will shelter you both in Lyonesse. It is time. And if

Guvranyl is right, we may have more backing than I thought. We may even live through it."

"Do you promise, Tristan?"

"Yes, my love. We will make our stand in Lyonesse. I swear it on our lives."

Their lips met, their arms entwined, their bodies sought each other without thought, joining with the firm familiarity of a handclasp as they began again the slow, sweet, urgent dance of love.

Tristan awoke in the middle of the night. For a moment he did not know where he was. The fire had burned to embers. He could see no walls, but neither could he see stars above him. Then he saw his clothes, and Essylte's, spread out on the hearth to dry, and he remembered. Wondering what had awakened him, he rose from the bed of bracken and picked up his sword, listening hard. The rain had stopped and a small wind had sprung up, blowing the grass from the cracks around the door. Moving air brushed his cheek as gently as a sigh. The fitful rustle of leaves and the whispering pines were all he heard. The hut still glowed with warmth; he added wood to the embers and teased them into flame. He peered into the cooking pot. There was plenty of stew left for breakfast. They had eaten little, their hunger for one another displacing their desire for food.

His gaze fell on the dirt floor by the stool, which bore telltale signs of recent disturbance, and he smiled. Who would have guessed such passion lurked in Percival's lovely daughter? Had he suspected, there on his sickbed in Gwynedd, what feverish energy lay within her heart, what buoyant joy drove her loving, he would never have been able to resist her. He would have succumbed to her in her father's house, and died in Wales.

Laughing silently at himself, he stooped to pick up their discarded dinner bowls, and froze. Someone groaned. He whirled. Essylte lay still under the blanket, fast asleep. There was no one else in the hut. He walked to the bed and knelt down. "Essylte?"

She did not move. He reached out a hand to touch her and gasped aloud. She was burning alive! He snatched the blanket off her. The skin all over her body flushed pink, hot to the touch. Around her brow her hair clung in damp tendrils. As he watched in horror, her head swung toward him listlessly and her eyes fluttered half open. Her dry lips barely moved. "Water."

He jumped to his feet. "Yes! Yes! Water—the waterskin's right here. There's a little left. Here you are. Drink." But she had not the strength to rise. He propped her up against his shoulder and held the skin to her lips. "Drink, Essylte! Please, drink."

Some of the water got down her throat; some dribbled from her chin. She was a dead weight in his arms, too weak to support herself. He held her and kissed her and stroked the hair back from her face. "Please, Essylte, tell me what is wrong. Tell me what to do." But her eyes closed and she did not speak. Tristan looked around wildly. "O ye gods, hear my plea! Come to me in this hour of my need. Heal her! Save her! I will pay any price for her life. Great Mother of men, the land from which we spring—Lord Mithra, the Light, who spilled the blood of the Bull—Yahweh of the burning bush, Jesu Christ of the empty tomb—Llud, Llyr, Eroth, Myrddin, Cerunnos the Horned One—hear my plea! I am your servant. Have mercy upon me and let her live!"

He soaked his tunic in the last of the water and pressed it to her brow, to her glowing body, to her burning cheeks. She sighed once but did not respond to his pleadings or open her eyes. He knelt by her side, praying, racking his brains for something to do. He knew no herb lore, nor any healing arts save those of the battlefield. He could bind a severed limb and slow bleeding from a sword cut, but a fever! He gazed helplessly at Essylte. Women could die from fevers; children often did. Even men, if a wound went bad. What was it Pernam had done for him? Plenty of fresh water, plenty of cool compresses. But he had no more water.

He staggered to his feet and grabbed the waterskin. Outside the night was black, but the storm had cleared. Faint stars shone above the pines. He could see his way about well enough to know, after an hour of searching through the woods, that there was no stream, no spring, no well. The best he could do was to soak his tunic in the wet grasses and cover her with it. But as time passed she grew worse. She tossed fitfully, moaning in misery, her breathing shallow and swift. When he lifted the tunic off her, it was dry and warm. Fighting back tears of panic, he went to the door of the hut and threw it open.

The woods outside gradually took shape out of the dark as night dimmed to the cold gray of dawning. Tristan fell on his knees on the threshold and buried his face in his hands.

"God forgive me for my sins! I care not what becomes of me. But Essylte is more than life to me. Spare her, for my son's sake if not her own. Show me the way to heal her." His breath caught on a sob. "Help me! Spirits of the sky, of the rivers and crossroads, of the land and all it blessings, spirits of the souls of men, come to my aid! Whoever hears me—help me! I beseech you!"

"Give me one good reason why I should." A deep voice, thick with suspicion, echoed from the woods. Tristan leaped up, staring. A small man in a gray cloak, ghostly in the rising mist, stood fifty feet away beside a donkey.

Tristan blinked twice. "Who are you?"

"Who are *you?*" the apparition replied sourly. "Why are you here? Leave at once."

"Leave! How dare—give me your name, sir!"

"Nonsense. Get out. Who gave you leave to go inside?"

"I cannot leave. Are you a healer? My—wife is ill."

The gray figure snorted. "Next, I suppose, you'll be asking me for spells. Off with you, before I lose my temper. Get out. Get out of my house."

Tristan gaped. "*Your* house?"

"He has ears," the stranger muttered to the donkey.

"Sir, I beseech you, for the love of Christ, tell me where I may find water to bathe her brow."

Through the lifting mists black eyes glowered at him from beneath thick black brows. "I do not serve Christ. Tell me who you are."

"I am a traveler, sir. If I have trespassed, I most humbly beg your pardon. We took shelter from the storm, but not soon enough. The lady Ess— my wife is ill with fever. I fear—I fear for her life."

The little man watched him for a moment, then pulled at the donkey's lead and turned away. "A traveler, is he? From the Blessed Isles, perhaps, where clothes are of no consequence. What does he think a rain barrel's for, I wonder?"

Tristan looked down at himself in some surprise. He had forgotten he was naked. When he looked up, the man and donkey were gone into the mist as silently as they had come. Tristan rubbed his eyes. A rain barrel stood between the trees and the hut, twenty steps away and brimming with water. Had he missed it in the dark? Had the mist cloaked it? He grabbed his waterskin and raced to the barrel to fill it.

Essylte sighed, senseless, under the fresh compress. Tristan, hastily dressed in damp boots and leggings, built up the fire to warm the stew, and knelt by her side with the waterskin in anxious impatience. He was dimly aware of sounds outside the hut, but he could spare no thought for anything but Essylte's uneven breathing and the undiminished burning of her skin.

He turned when a shadow fell across the door. The gray-cloaked figure stepped across the threshold, glared at him, then stooped to pick up the unwashed dinner bowls. Tristan colored and opened his mouth to speak.

"Don't bother," the other said, gathering the bowls and righting the overturned stool. "It's your house, obviously. Pay me no mind." He looked at the stack of firewood, fingered the edge of the ax, and grunted. "Right at home, indeed." He leaned over the stew pot and sniffed delicately. "Poisoned her, did you? Fool." He lifted the pot from its stand, and with the dirty bowls underneath his arm, disappeared outside.

Tristan stared after him. Poison? He turned back to Essylte. After a moment of panic, he steadied himself. He had eaten what she had eaten, and more of it, besides. It might not have been the tastiest meal they'd ever had, nor the most nourishing, but it had served them well enough for six weeks now and this stew had been no worse than the others.

The little man returned with pot and bowls scrubbed clean. He put the bowls on the shelf and set the pot of fresh water over the flame. Gathering firewood under his arm, he nodded angrily to Tristan. "With your permission, of course, master, I'll take some of this wood my ax has chopped and start a fire in the bake house."

"Please—" Tristan began, but the stranger was already gone. Bake house? Had he missed that, too, in his search for a spring? And where had the donkey gone? He stared miserably at Essylte. Without her he had lost his bearings and gone adrift in a maelstrom of confusion. "I swear by the blood of Christ," he said slowly, "that when she is recovered I will take her out of Morois to safety, whether or not she is with child."

When the stranger returned, Tristan rose and bowed to him.

"Sir," he said, "please excuse my hasty—"

"Traveler." The black eyes looked up at him from a brown, wizened face. "I want none of your excuses, and I want none of you." He knelt by the chest, unlocked it, and withdrew a roughly woven bag. "Until you go and leave me and mine in peace, you may call me hermit." He reached into the bag and sprinkled an aromatic herb into the cooking pot. "Which I was, until you came, and which I will be again." He gathered up their clothes from the floor, shook them forcefully, and carried them outside. When he returned he carried a grain sack stuffed with straw. "By your leave." He walked past Tristan and slipped the rough pillow under Essylte's head.

"Thank you," Tristan whispered. "Do you know aught of healing, hermit?"

"Traveler," the deep voice growled, "you presume too much."

"I beg your pardon."

The black eyes regarded him gravely. "You owe me service for all your presumptions."

Tristan nodded. "I acknowledge it. As soon as my wife is—"

"Now." The fierce black brows met in a frown. He pointed to the ax. "Three trees you will fell and chop for me. Arm-length logs. Before the sun sets."

"But I—" Tristan glanced wildly at Essylte. "I cannot leave her."

"You can," said the hermit. "And you will." He lifted his cloaked arm and pointed out the door.

Tristan found himself standing in the forest with the ax in his hand. He blinked twice. He had no recollection of walking there, nor of taking the ax. He looked about frantically, but the hut was gone. In its place stood a rough-hewn lean-to where a donkey gazed at him quizzically, munching hay. For an hour he searched everywhere for a path back to the hut, but he found nothing, not even an animal trail. Finally he shouldered the ax.

"Your master is either a madman or a magician," he said levelly to the donkey, "and he will join his ancestors tonight if he has harmed Essylte. But I will obey him."

The moon had risen silver in the frosted night by the time he finished. He loaded the wood onto a rude donkey cart he found stowed in the lean-to, and hitched up the donkey. Although he was still dressed only in leggings and boots, and his breath hung frozen in the frigid air, he was warm enough as he strode through the forest at the donkey's side. The animal seemed to know where he was going and, as Tristan did not, he let the beast have his head. Eventually he saw the domed hut huddling black against the moonlit forest. A thin stream of smoke issued from the roof. Tristan unloaded the cart and stacked the wood as fast as he could, unhitched the donkey, and slapped him on the rump to send him on his way. Then he put his shoulder to the door and pushed it open.

Warmth, fragrance, light assailed his senses. His eyes flew to the pallet. Essylte lay motionless and pale, as cold and still now as she had been burning and restless before. He fell to his knees and reached for her hand. It lay in his, lifeless and unresponsive. "Oh, dear Christ! Essylte!"

"Hush. The Queen sleeps. Don't wake her."

The hermit sat on his haunches by the fire, sipping from a wooden cup. The black eyes met his, man to man and unafraid.

"What have you done?" Tristan breathed. "If this is your doing, I swear I will—"

"She sleeps, fool. She lives. The fever broke."

Tristan knelt at her side and put his ear to her breast. There, faint but discernible, he heard the rhythmic sounds of life. He exhaled, whispering a prayer of thanksgiving. The hermit pushed a cup into his hand.

"Drink this."

The hot liquid slid down his throat, fragrant and sweet. He looked up and met the black eyes. "Thank you. Thank you, hermit. Is this your doing?" He nodded toward the pallet.

The hermit scowled. "No doing of mine, traveler. I gave her a mustard poultice and a strong tisane, not a whit more. I can't spare the stores." Tristan began to smile as the hermit turned away, still grumbling. "Let it not be said I steal credit from the Divine. I'm no thief, unlike some I could name."

"I've paid for what I've taken," Tristan replied. "You've seen to that. And I would bless your name, if I knew it, for your ministrations. When will she awaken?"

"She will wake when she's strong enough to wake." The hermit dipped his ladle into the cooking pot and handed Tristan a bowl full of mushrooms, wild onions, and bits of dried meat all swimming in a thick, hot porridge. Then he brought over a plate of meal cakes, newly baked, studded with nuts and raisins.

"This is wonderful," Tristan managed between mouthfuls. "Don't tell me you made all this yourself."

"Certainly not. What could a poor lowborn hermit do that couldn't be done better by a king's son?"

Tristan's head flew up. "What makes you think I am a king's son?"

The bright black eyes met his. "Your size, of course. Only in a king's house could you eat enough to grow that big."

Tristan laughed. "And I've lost flesh this month past. But I'm no giant. There are plenty of men my size in any village: woodcutters, peat diggers, plowmen."

"But none with your sword arm." Nothing moved in the hermit's stony face, but intelligence gleamed in his quick eyes. "You've a fighter's build. And your right arm's larger than your left."

"And my sword lies here beside the pallet. So much for your deductions," Tristan scoffed. "But men may wield a sword and not be kings' sons, just as men may eat well in a lord's house and not be kings' sons."

The black eyes flashed. The hermit pointed to Tristan's boots. "Such fine doeskin is not the common garb of warriors."

Tristan smiled. "I'm not a common warrior. I confess it. I'm particular in my tastes."

The hermit's eyes slid to the pallet and back. "Indeed."

Tristan flushed lightly. "How do you dare?"

The hermit rose suddenly and pointed a finger at him. "Arrogant prince! I'm no subject of yours. Your power is no more to me than smoke in the wind. You are a guest in my house. Before you will speak to me so, you will take the woman and go."

Staring at the dark, ferocious little face, seen in light for the first time, Tristan slid to his knees and made the ancient sign of propitiation. "You're one of the Old Ones, aren't you?" he asked softly as the hermit stiffened. "You're descended straight from the ancient Britons, without a drop of Roman blood. I've heard about your people, of course. Bards sing of your heroes and your gods, and tell the tales your ancestors wove. But I've never met one of your kind before." He paused. "Is that why you live here all alone? To avoid my race of men?"

"To avoid men altogether!" the hermit spat.

"Let me beg your pardon. You saved her life. I owe you for that."

The hermit acknowledged his submission with a slight nod of the head.

"I will name a service you can do me." Reaching into Tristan's pack, he drew out his lap harp. "Listen to bards' songs, do you? Let me hear one, then, Tristan of Lyonesse."

Tristan stared at him and paled. "How—"

"By the rings on her fingers," the hermit snapped. "If you have wits, use them."

Tristan groaned. On her right hand Essylte wore Cornwall's wedding band, and on her left, the ring he had given her with the Eagle of Lyonesse. If even this hermit knew that they had disappeared together . . . "So that's why you called her Queen."

"King Markion has men all over Cornwall searching for her," the hermit said gruffly, watching his face. "And looking to kill you."

Tristan bowed his head. "I thought as much."

"You must count her worth the price."

"She is beyond any price." He looked up at the hermit with drowned eyes. The little man had pushed back his hood and squatted by the fire. His weathered skin was stained the color of walnut by age, hard use, and sun. His hair, roughly cropped close against his head, was black threaded with silver, like his beard. The hands and wrists that poked out of his sleeves were wiry and strong, ageless hands that worked to live from season to season with nothing to spare. But his fearsome eyes, black as night pools, were pits of infinite sadness.

"You loved a woman once," Tristan whispered, wondering at his own temerity, but emboldened by those eyes. "You will understand. She is the breath of life in my body, the beat of blood in my veins, the sweet summation of all that is good in me. I cannot part from her."

The hermit pointed to the harp. "A man with a bard's soul draws beauty out of pain. Let me hear your music and I will judge for myself what is in you."

Tristan took the harp and pulled it onto his lap, adjusting the string shoes and tuning it carefully. "You ask much, hermit. My voice has been still a long time." He closed his eyes and exhaled, listening with his spirit to the inner stirrings of his soul. His fingers moved against the strings, tentatively at first and then, as the inner springs of feeling began to flow, with the familiar assurance of a lover's touch. Music floated free; chords and notes fell sweetly into the silence, beguiling the heart in liquid song. Tristan bent over the harp, remembering Dinadan's wedding at Castle Dorr, with the bright sun shining from a cloudless sky and food stacked high on groaning tables, and the harp sang of it. He thought of the dark night in the forest when he and Essylte, hand in hand, had crept from their escort into the fastness of Morois, and the harp sang of it. He saw in his mind's eye the starlit hilltop within its circle of standing stones, the rain of moonlight, the blossoming of desire as Essylte succumbed to the Mother's call, melting against his body like a second skin, and the harp told the story. The days they had spent wandering, in laughter and joy, in fear and worry, in cold discomfort and in the blessed warmth of their embraces, all passed before his memory and the harp rejoiced. He pictured Markion and his army, urged on by Segward, scouring the edges of Morois with raised swords, crying out for Tristan's blood. The harp trembled, raising the hair on his neck. He thought of precious Essylte, her innate sweetness, her wonderful laughter, her quick teasing, her trembling fear, her tenderness, her girlish anger, her hot bloom of passion beneath his hands, and the harp sang it all, movingly, sweetly, sadly. Finally, Tristan envisioned the future that he dreaded, death or exile for himself, wretched imprisonment in the cold rock of Tintagel for the beautiful Essylte, with no lover but the greedy Markion, and no one at all to share her soul. The harp wept.

Tristan's fingers stopped moving. The last vibrations circled around the hut and faded to nothing. The hermit rose and came to where Tristan sat slumped over the instrument. Slowly, he bowed from the waist.

"Tristan of Lyonesse, my name is Ogrin. I offer you the use of my humble house for as long as you like to stay. The ancestors have honored you. They have blessed you with the ancient gift of Speaking Without Tongue, as I—" He paused, and something like a smile creased his lined face. "I have the gift of Seeing Without Eyes."

Tristan looked up uncertainly, blinking at the firelight as if he had just entered the room. "Oh, how the harp hurts me. . . . What did you say, Ogrin? Blessed? If I am blessed, why is my heart so heavy? Why can't I sleep? Why do I dream about wolves when I do?"

"The Queen and her child lie on your conscience."

Tristan brushed tears from his eyes. "The Queen, yes. But not the child, thank God. He is safe in Tintagel."

Ogrin paused. "I speak of the child she carries in her."

Tristan's head whipped up. "She is with child? How do you know?"

"Don't believe me, then," Ogrin returned sourly. "If you'd listened with your bard's ears to the rhythm of life around you, you'd have known it two months ago."

"Two months!" Tristan turned to Essylte and gently touched her face. "Sweet child, the Mother did indeed bless you. Why didn't you tell me? Once I was in tune with the beat of life, the storm winds and the sea's song. But I have been deaf a long time now."

Ogrin raised a hand over his head and spoke quickly in a tongue Tristan did not understand, a guttural chanting that wound into his mind and closed his thoughts, dragged at his eyes, pulled him to the earth. He yawned and curled up next to Essylte on the pallet.

"Sleep comes upon you," Ogrin sang in a low voice. "No dreams disturb your rest. No worry for the morrow. The Queen's child shall be safe—" Ogrin paused. "Although his face you shall never see. Peace will find you, my friend, when your lover lies beside you and the ivy twines thrice around the hazel."

Tristan, pillowed on Essylte's breast and already sinking toward sleep, did not hear him.

25 ✝ TRIALS OF THE QUEEN

Essylte sat outside the hut in a warm pool of sun, stitching a length of russet fabric, her red-gold curls falling in a thick curtain around her face. She coughed once and clutched her chest, but then relaxed. It was a dry cough and the hollow pain that had racked her body in every coughing spell for the last three weeks had at last diminished to no more than a catch between her ribs. She looked up quickly, feeling Tristan's anxious eyes on her. He stood by the woodpile, ax in hand. She smiled and waved. He nodded, hefted the ax, and went back to work.

She watched him a moment, admiring the play of muscles across his back and shoulders as he bent, straightened, swung, and bent again. He moved fluidly, as graceful as a dancer. Desire stirred, and she smiled to herself. Wanting him was as easy as drawing breath. She pressed one hand against her belly and fancied she could already detect the hard, growing presence of her child. Tristan had sworn last night that he could feel it, that he could hear the pulsation of its life within her life. It was the first time since her illness he had come to her bed. She sighed and closed her eyes, remembering with a warm flush of pleasure his gentleness and power. He knew her body better than she did herself. He knew how to blow upon the sparks of her desire, fan them to flame, then bank them and stoke them at his will, using lips and words and hands, until she was well nigh wild with wanting. It was that wildness he waited for. Then, with the world trembling on knife-edge, his dark shadow swooped over her, filling her vision. She felt again the strength of his arms around her, carrying her in glorious flight to those precious, fire-struck moments when the world dissolved and released them, free, a single spirit in the soaring light.

She opened her eyes and found Tristan watching her, the ax slipped from his fingers, a light sweat filming his brow.

"Hem, hmmm." Ogrin, come from the bake house with a basket of new bread, stepped between them. "Not safe alone." Essylte smiled and bent over her needle, sewing to the steady *thunk thunk* of Tristan's ax.

When the sun swung behind the pines, the air grew chill. Ogrin called them in to dinner as dusk settled early in the woods. They ate together while the blaze warmed the hut. A month of Ogrin's cooking had put flesh back on Essylte's bones and a bloom back in her cheeks. In return, Tristan had cut enough wood to last the hermit through three winters and had gathered enough wild hay to feed his donkey until the snowmelt. And if the hermit turned his head away when the heat between them grew beyond their power to control, so they ignored his strange rituals with snakeskins, bird beaks, knives, and animal innards at the stone cairn by the hidden spring.

"His people were Druids," Tristan had explained. "But he is the last of his family. Among his own kind he is highborn, learned in the folk wisdom of his clan, a seer, a judge among men. How he reached his present state, he won't say, but it's possible that there just isn't anyone left."

"Isn't he the Hermit of Morois you once told me all the people feared?"

"People fear what they don't know."

"You said he ate men for breakfast. He'd be hurt if he heard that."

Tristan had grinned. "Hurt? Contemptuous, maybe, at what he considers to be the startling ignorance of modern men. We're a fly-by-night race of beings, in his opinion, always at war with one another. He fully intends to outlast us all."

Essylte shook her head as Ogrin ladled more of the rich stew into her bowl. "Oh, Ogrin, I can't eat another mouthful. I'm full to bursting."

The lines in the hermit's face relaxed into a smile. "One for you. One for him." He pointed to her belly.

"Him?" she asked quickly. "Are you certain?"

Ogrin nodded. "Him."

Tristan slid an arm around her waist. "Mother of my sons," he whispered in her ear, "try to eat a little more. We want him to be strong."

As she ate, Ogrin brewed his strong tisane and Tristan plucked at his harp, picking out a new melody, finding the chords to enfold it and bring it to life.

"How lovely that is," Essylte murmured.

"It's for you, my love. It's 'The Lay of Essylte.' One day it will be sung all over Britain."

She smiled at him. "My mother once told me in jest she would marry me off to a bard."

Tristan winked. "She should have had more faith in the power of her own foretelling."

As he played, her hands rested against her belly and she thought of the baby there, so fragile and so innocent, a son of Tristan born into a world ruled by Markion. It wasn't fair to deceive him about his father. More than that, it was wrong. She shivered, and Tristan broke off his song.

"What is it, love?"

"Tristan, must we leave? Is it necessary?"

Tristan forced a smile. "Ogrin's a hermit, my dear. He can hardly keep up that game while we're here."

"Was it necessary to negotiate with Mark? Wasn't it possible we could just sneak away?"

"No, sweet, it wasn't. Not once he put two and two together. I had hoped the Saxons would keep him busy and our disappearance would be brief, but as things worked out," he shrugged and Essylte dropped her eyes, "his concern for his honor outweighs his concern for Britain. I hate to think what the Saxons are doing while Mark's army scours the moors for me."

"He must regard you now as his foremost enemy. How do we know that he won't kill you?"

Tristan grunted. "That's what we're negotiating for. If Mark wants you back, he must promise to forgive us and harm neither of us. Those are the terms of your return."

"He will never agree to it. Never."

"Guv thinks he will. Reports from Logris are dire and growing worse. If he doesn't return soon, he will lose those rich lands to the Saxons, and what will his kingship be worth then? If he beats them back and proves his power, he might win the respect of the northern lords. If he wants to be a King like Arthur, he must have their backing. But Logris is on fire. He doesn't have much time."

"And how do you know this?"

"Guvranyl told Ogrin at their last meeting outside the village. He was there in Mark's camp when the courier brought the news. Guv's reliable. He was loyal to my father, and he's loyal to my father's son."

"How do you know they won't follow Guvranyl to Ogrin, and Ogrin to us?"

The hermit's face turned to her, his black eyes contemptuous.

"Don't worry about Ogrin. He has powers you don't suspect. No one can see him unless he wishes to be seen. He can't be followed."

"And when he brings Guvranyl here tomorrow?" She shivered, and Tristan drew her closer. "Guvranyl has no such powers."

"Ogrin will draw a veil across this valley, so whoever tries to follow will be lost within a mist. Or some such trick." Tristan winked at Ogrin. The hermit ignored him and went back to stirring his tea. "Don't worry, sweet. Guvranyl wouldn't be coming if negotiations hadn't reached the last stage. We'll be safe. We won't be killed. Ogrin's seen it in the flames."

"I don't believe in such nonsense," Essylte whispered, leaning her head on his shoulder. "If Mark hates you enough, he will break his word once we're in his power. He will never let us go to Lyonesse."

"If he tries it," Tristan whispered, "his own army will rise against him. He will have no choice."

"I wish I were as certain as you are."

Tristan drew her shift off her shoulder and brushed his lips against her skin. "I will never leave you. Never." The hard knot of anxiety began to melt within her breast. She sighed with pleasure as his fingers worked the laces of her gown and his hands slid under the fabric. She glanced swiftly at Ogrin. He had already turned his back and pulled his hood close around his face.

"Tristan!" Guvranyl slid off his gray gelding, his arms thrown open in welcome. "By God, I thought I'd never see you again!" He embraced Tristan warmly, pounding him on the back. "You look good, lad. In fine fettle. How've you kept so fit?"

"Oh," Tristan replied lightly, "wandering around Morois."

Guvranyl laughed and wiped a tear from his eye. "I never thought you'd last a week in this damned enchanted forest. You've given old Markion a devil of a time!" He sobered as his gaze fell on Essylte. His eyes widened. "Is this the Queen?" He bent his knee to the ground. "Queen Essylte. Royal lady, I hardly knew you, you are so changed."

Standing at Tristan's side in her patched green gown with her hair unbound around her shoulders, Essylte extended her hand and raised him. "How changed, Sir Guvranyl? Is it the gown? Or the hair? The informality of the setting?"

"No, no, my lady. None of those. It's hard to put a finger on it. You look different, stronger, more finely drawn. Even more beautiful. A regal woman. You're not the young girl I knew as Markion's wife."

"You *have* put your finger on it," Essylte said softly. "For I am not, nor ever was, Markion's wife."

Guvranyl frowned, and Tristan slung an arm around his shoulders. "Come, Guv, and I'll explain it to you. But it's a long story. You must swear faith with me first."

Inside the hut the men sat before the fire and Essylte served them tea and meal cakes.

"Bring me up to date on the state of things," Tristan began. "When did you last see Mark?"

"Yesterday," Guvranyl reported. "He and his men are camped upon the moor at the edge of the forest."

"Have they tried to follow you?"

"Oh, yes," Guvranyl grunted. "They've tried. But I always find them sitting on the roadside in a stupor when I'm making my way back. I don't know what it is that knocks them from their horses and steals their wits. But whatever it is, it's useful."

Tristan winked at Essylte. "How was Markion when you saw him? Will he come to terms?"

"He has done, I think, as much as he is able. He's mad as a hornet, but he's in a corner and he knows it. Bring her out and he'll agree to take her back to wife. As for you, he'll guarantee you safe conduct through his lands to anywhere you want, excepting only Lyonesse."

"Tristan!" Essylte knelt at his side.

He waved away her protest. "Does he promise not to harm Essylte—ever?"

Guvranyl nodded. "For the rest of his life he will protect her and hold her harmless, if you will give her back."

"No!" Essylte cried, clutching Tristan's arm.

"How long is my safe conduct good for?"

"One year. After that, he will hunt you down. And if you set foot in Britain, he will kill you."

"Or I him."

Guvranyl shrugged. "What will you do?"

"Does Segward know the terms? Does he agree?"

Guvranyl grimaced, as if he had a bad taste in his mouth. "Nothing will please Segward but your death and the Queen's disgrace. But Mark has agreed to the terms in spite of Segward."

"Oh, Tristan! You can't do it!" Tears sprang to Essylte's eyes. "Remember your promise to me."

He turned to her. "I remember," he said softly, clasping her hands. "And I will keep my promise."

Guvranyl's eyes flicked from one of them to the other, but his face gave nothing away. Tristan looked at Guvranyl directly. "Does he trust you, Guv?"

"He does. I have never given him cause to doubt me."

"If you wish to continue to serve him, you had better stand outside while I speak to the Queen. If you can break faith with him and serve me, I will tell you the truth of how things stand."

Guvranyl rose from his stool, bent his knee to the ground and inclined his head. "You are the only man who can save Cornwall, Tristan. I have known you from a boy; I have had the training of you. There is not a dishonorable bone in your body. I forswear my oath to Markion and I swear my faith to you."

"Thank you, Guv," Tristan said gravely. "But do not yet resign from Mark's service. Not until I give you leave. He would kill you before he would let you go, and I need you living."

Guvranyl nodded slowly. "What are you planning, Tristan?"

Tristan loosed one of his hands from Essylte's grasp and drew Guvranyl toward him. "Listen," he said, "and I will tell you."

On a gray day in mid-December, Markion sat upon his bay stallion and stared at the rutted road leading into the Morois Wood. Behind him, rank upon rank, stood the men of Cornwall, ten companies at attention. Snow drifted lazily from leaden skies. Horses stamped impatiently on frosted ground. The jangle of bits and swish of tails played a steady accompaniment to Segward's fierce whispers.

"He's turned Guvranyl against you, my lord King, that's certain. He'll never come out on his own. He's loved her since he saw her first in Wales. Ask Percival if he did not bed her then! What can she look like, after three months in Morois? He's afraid of what you'll do to him when you see her. It's a thin ploy, a plot, a—"

"Silence!" the King snapped. "Whose idea *was* it to send him to Wales? If you speak again without my leave, Segward, I will strip you naked and flay the flesh from your back." Segward flushed and sullenly withdrew.

Bruenor and Dinadan, mounted on Markion's right, waited, stiffening in the cold, as Markion's anger grew with every minute that passed. Finally a gray horse appeared on the road. Snow swirled around it, thickening.

Markion leaned forward in the saddle. "Is that Guvranyl?"

"Yes, my lord," Sir Bruenor answered, at his elbow. "And there's someone coming behind him. On foot."

Everyone strained to see. Gradually two figures appeared out of the darkness of Morois, walking together behind the horse. A man and woman, royally clad, walking serenely, as if the armed force they approached was their own escort.

"By God!" Dinadan whispered. "If it isn't Tristan!"

As they neared the army the snow stopped and a weak sun pushed out. Markion stared. Essylte wore a russet gown, trimmed with fox, and new boots of soft worked leather. Her dark green cloak of good Welsh wool he thought he remembered, but now it was lined with rabbit pelts and trimmed in gold. Her hair under the warm hood was braided about her face, the way he liked it best. In spite of his anger, his heart lifted at the sight of her, and he nearly smiled. She was even lovelier than he remembered—too thin, perhaps, but with fine bones, translucent skin, and glowing eyes lit from within, an astonishing, ethereal beauty that was new. In all his life, he had never seen anyone like her.

"My lord King Markion!" Guvranyl reined his horse to a halt and saluted. "In accordance with the terms discussed between us and agreed to, I bring you your nephew, Tristan of Lyonesse, and Essylte, your Queen, whom he has rescued from death, and who carries in her your second son."

A low murmur raced through the troops like wind through a hayfield. Markion snorted. "A likely story."

Bruenor coughed. "Indeed, my lord, it may be true. At my son's wedding Sir Tristan told me of the High Queen's pregnancy. And that was before, they er, disappeared."

Markion frowned. But Essylte faced him boldly and did not drop her gaze. "Is this true, Essylte?"

She made him a low reverence. "As I am your obedient servant, my lord," she replied coolly.

Markion bit his lip, aware that more was going on than he understood. "Bring her a horse," he commanded. A trooper led forward a black mare, and Tristan lifted her up into the saddle. At Markion's signal she rode up to his side. He searched her face but could make nothing of her contained expression. "I welcome you back, Essylte."

"I thank you, my lord."

"Have you fared well?"

"I have been ill, my lord. But I am recovered."

"Where were you?"

"At a hermit's house, my lord. Well tended."

"Were you all of the time with my nephew Tristan?"

She turned on him her blue-green eyes and her lips lifted in a small smile. "All of the time, my lord."

The King's face hardened. "Put him on a horse," he snapped. But as Tristan mounted, Markion turned to the captain of his guard. "You, Melcor, take the reins. Two men on either side and three behind. I'll take no chances."

Guvranyl's face darkened. "You promised him safe conduct. You gave your word!"

Markion smiled thinly. "He'll be safe enough. A royal escort befitting my royal nephew." He laughed as he whirled his stallion, grabbed the bridle of Essylte's mare, and gave the order to march.

* * * *

Markion led Essylte to her chamber with a firm grip on her arm. Outside her door the sentries snapped to attention but their eyes slid sideways, watching. Markion pushed Essylte before him and closed the door firmly behind his back.

"Well, lady, you are home at last."

She faced him, trembling visibly, but held herself erect. "Thanks to your graciousness, my lord, and to your nephew's courage."

Markion's lips twisted in a sneer. "Ah, yes, it always comes back to my nephew, doesn't it? The time has come to be honest with me, Essylte of Gwynedd. What is there between you and Tristan? Are the rumors true?"

"Of what does my lord accuse me?"

"Don't play the innocent with me. You're as aware of the talk as anyone else. I've promised to spare your life, but I want the truth. You've been gone three months and now you are with child. By your own lips you've been all the time with Tristan." He approached her, pulled off her cloak, and pressed his hand against her hard belly. "Is this my son or Tristan's?"

Essylte stilled a shudder. "My lord accuses me of adultery, then?" She raised her face to his, so near, and called tears into her eyes. "I swear by Almighty God I am no adulteress. Every minute since my marriage I have kept faith with my husband, the bravest and strongest of men." She lifted a hand to his tangled hair and pushed it back from his brow.

Markion's features softened and he grunted, pulling her hard up against his body and kissing her fiercely. "I'd give anything to believe you," he growled, pulling away. "Why do you shake so, if not from fear?"

"My lord, I am weak from the journey and from—my ordeal."

"Ordeal, was it? You didn't look so when you walked at Tristan's side."

Essylte's eyes flashed. "My lord sees what he wants to see!"

Markion laughed. "I like your spirit. Well, I will learn the truth from you before I leave. I'm tired of words—yours, Segward's, Tristan's. I'll have the truth out of you for everyone to see. Then I'll know." His hands cupped her breasts and slid to her waist, her hips, her thighs. "You tempt me, lady, almost past bearing, but before I lie with you again, I'll be certain of your virtue. Until then, this chamber is your prison. You will not pass beyond its walls." His hands fell to his side. He turned on his heel and strode out the door, leaving her standing by the bed.

Essylte grabbed the bedpost for support. A prisoner! He had promised Guvranyl not to harm her, he had promised to take her back to wife, but had he promised freedom? At the moment, she hardly cared. Her relief that he had not forced her outweighed her fear. For a long moment she had thought he meant to insist upon his right. Just the touch of his hands on her gown revolted her. Genuine tears welled up and spilled down her cheeks. "Tristan," she whispered, "how much better it was in Ogrin's hut!"

The curtain parted. Branwen stood on the threshold, neatly dressed in a gray gown, her hair pulled back from her face and covered by a kerchief, her hands folded below the gentle swell of her belly and her gray eyes lowered submissively. "My lady. May I come in?"

Essylte bit her lip. "What do you want?"

Branwen knelt at her feet. "If I've offended you, Essylte, I beg you will forgive me. All this time I've—I've feared for your life. I realized what you meant to do, but—it was dangerous, and I thought it was my fault you decided to risk everything that way. I was afraid you would die in Morois and it would be my fault."

Essylte fell to her knees and embraced her. "Oh, Branny, don't say such things! It's true I've doubted you, but I never held it against you. It's not your fault, and I wasn't in any danger. Tristan kept me safe, dear. He was with me all along."

"You should have told me you were going. I could have helped you."

"It turned out well enough. I thought you might try to stop me."

"But why?" Branwen's eyes met hers. "I want what you want, Essylte."

Essylte hesitated. "Why did you wait so long to tell me of your pregnancy? If you'd told me sooner, we could have planned it differently. As it was, I had no time. I had to act at once."

Branwen blinked. "I was trying to decide whether or not to keep it."

Essylte stared at her in silence. "You would kill the King's child?" she whispered.

Branwen nodded. "If bearing it would put you—us—in jeopardy. I wasn't sure. I didn't know when Mark planned to return to Tintagel. When I heard he'd be coming at Christmas, I took the poison, but—" Her voice quavered. "It didn't work. I was too far along. That's when I told you. The next thing I knew—you were gone."

"Oh, Branny!" Essylte breathed. "You took poison?"

"When I heard you had disappeared, I knew why, of course, but it was too dangerous, Essylte! Too easy for Mark to figure out. If I had come with you, I could have arranged it all at Castle Dorr. I have potions. It would have been easy. And safe."

"But it would have put Sir Bruenor and Dinadan in jeopardy if Mark ever counted back upon his fingers." Essylte shivered. "Did you hear what he said to me just now?"

Branwen nodded. "I was listening behind the curtain."

"He doesn't believe me, and he says I am a prisoner. What does he have planned, I wonder? He said he would learn the truth."

"I don't know now, but I will before long. Those of the house servants who are not in Segward's employ are in mine. Before nightfall, I will know."

"And where is Tristan?"

Branwen's eyes widened. "Did he not come back with you?"

"Not freely. He was brought back with the kind of escort a prisoner warrants. I don't know where he is now, or what Mark is doing to him."

"By nightfall, I will know that, too." Branwen squeezed Essylte's hand. "Don't worry. Mark can't afford to harm Tristan. Half of Cornwall would leave his service if he did." She hesitated. "Will you tell me what happened in Morois? Did you manage to get with child?"

Essylte smiled briefly. "Oh, yes. And without potions. I'm nearly three months gone."

"Three months! Then why did you stay so long in Morois? Were you lost?"

"Lost? We did not care where we were. It was a time of freedom and utter happiness in solitude—so remote now it all seems like a dream." Her voice faded as her focus drifted away. "I would give anything, even this child, to be able to do it again."

Branwen regarded her gravely. "In three months of solitude you must have talked about the future. What does Tristan plan?"

"When he can, he will take me and Young Tristan—and you, of course, Branny, and little Keridwen—to Lyonesse. No more lies, no more deceptions. We are done with that now. We will go to Lyonesse. Sir Guvranyl thinks the army will rise for Tristan."

Branwen walked to the window where the west wind whistled through the shutters. She stood still a long moment, letting the cold sea breeze dry the sweat on her brow. "Does he, indeed?" Her hands slid protectively over her little belly. "So the time has come to tell the truth? We are to make our stand against the King?" She closed her eyes, as if to listen to the beat of life within her. The time was coming when she must decide between them, Markion and Tristan. But she would not be ready until the spring, until this child was born. Tristan was forcing her hand—intentionally, perhaps?—and if she could not stall him, she must be ready sooner than she wished to take the final step, make the final choice, from which there was no return. She drew a deep breath and opened her eyes. Would she have the courage for it when the time came?

* * * *

Three days later Markion held a Council meeting with a group of hand-picked nobles and the Bishop of Dorria in attendance. They met to decide the fate of Tristan of Lyonesse and Sir Guvranyl, Tristan's accomplice in the abduction and ravishing of the Queen. Branwen and Essylte waited in the Queen's apartment for news of the decision. Essylte paced back and forth the length of her bedchamber in open agitation. Branwen sat at the antechamber window, as still as a cat, watching a gray December fog creep toward her over a gray December sea. One of Mark's chamberlains shared a bed with one of her own maids, and the girl would get news of the decision to Branwen before the men even left the Council chamber, before anyone else in Tintagel could know, before Segward could get word to his informers, before Dinadan could get free of his father and sneak into the women's quarters, and long, long before Markion would deign to officially notify his wife.

Time passed, the day dragged on, the fog drew nearer until all but the immediate coast was lost to sight. Essylte lay curled on her bed, exhausted with pacing, giving vent alternately to panicked rage or silent tears. Branwen remained by the window, a thick shawl drawn tight across her shoulders, until the sea fog wrapped the coast in its impenetrable embrace and began to lick the stones of the fortress wall. Then she sighed, pulled the shutters closed, and rose.

A swift, light tapping came at the outer door.

"Who comes?"

"Regan, my lady. I've brought a flagon of mead for the Queen, with the King's compliments."

Recognizing her maid's voice, Branwen opened the door. Five guards stood on the landing outside Essylte's door, but as she had anticipated, they would not prevent a serving maid from bringing a gift from Markion to his wife. She shut the door firmly behind Regan and dropped the bar silently across it.

"What news?"

Essylte pushed past the curtain, her eyes puffed with weeping. Regan made her a quick reverence and put down the heavy cup of mead. She turned to Branwen.

"Council's about to break up, my lady, but Treffor came out to me early, as instructed—"

"Oh, for pity's sake!" Essylte cried, twisting her hands together. "Give us the ending first! Is Mark going to kill him?"

"Don't mind the Queen," Branwen said smoothly to the wide-eyed girl. "Her journey through Morois was a hardship that has turned her wits. It happens to everyone who stays in the forest three nights running. Now, Regan, tell me the decision first, and afterward how they came by it. As much as you know."

The girl nodded nervously. "Exile. Banishment. For life. For both of them."

Essylte sank against the wall and covered her face with her hands. Regan shot a quick glance at her.

"Keep your eyes on me," Branwen said evenly. "Go on."

"The Council—Treffor said the Council voted death for Sir Tristan, but King Markion commuted the sentence to exile. Because he had brought the Queen back. Because he is the only son of the King's brother Meliodas, and the last left but one of Constantine's line."

Branwen's lips twisted. "Poor Segward. Will Sir Tristan be allowed to keep Lyonesse?"

Regan shook her head. "He and Sir Guvranyl have a month to get out of Britain. After that, they will be hunted down and killed if they set foot anywhere on British soil. Including Lyonesse."

A wounded sound, part groan, part sob, came from Essylte. Branwen put a hand on Regan's shoulder, turned her around and steered her to the door.

"I must tend to my lady now. Come to me at bedtime. I would like to hear everything else you have to say."

Regan clutched her arm, glancing swiftly at the huddled agony crouched against the wall. "Please, mistress, there is only this: Once Sir Tristan and Sir Guvranyl are sent away, the King will put my lady the Queen to trial as well."

There was no reaction from Essylte. Branwen said quickly, "What kind of trial?"

Regan shuddered. "I don't know. It's not decided yet. But Treffor said the tests they talked about to prove her guilt were the kind of things—" She swallowed audibly. "The kind of things no one could survive, even in innocence."

Branwen's lips thinned. "Was Lord Segward at this meeting?"

"Oh, yes, my lady. More, he met privately with the King and the Bishop of Dorria before the Council meeting."

Branwen nodded, her face tight, and gave the girl a copper coin from her pouch. "Well done, Regan. Let Treffor discover as soon as he may what Markion has in mind, and he shall have that silver torque he's been longing for."

When the girl had gone, Branwen replaced the bar against the door and turned to stand with her back against it. Her knees shook so hard she did not trust herself to stand. Essylte had sunk into a lump of colored cloth on the antechamber floor, her sobs ragged and hoarse.

"For God's sake, Essylte," Branwen said roughly, "control your grief. He will live. Tristan will live. You've got something much bigger to worry about now."

* * * *

A mailed fist beat upon the chamber door.

"I have come for the Queen!" a stern voice demanded.

Branwen hid the jar of salve and took the empty flask from Essylte's hand. "Don't be afraid," she whispered, "the charms will work. The potion will protect you from pain. Be brave, now. And remember what you have to do. Look for the pilgrim in an old brown cloak patched with green. That's Tristan. Guvranyl will be beside him, with the swords. If anything happens, stay with them. Their horses are hidden on the beach. With Dinadan."

White-faced, Essylte stood still as stone. "If it comes to that, I am already dead. He will kill us all, the children first."

"Don't think such thoughts, Essylte. Concentrate, please, on the task before you. We have done nothing but plan for this trial for five interminable days. We cannot fail now."

"Tristan and Guvranyl should have left Britain when Mark first banished them. It is death to them if they are discovered."

"They will not be discovered if you remember what to do, and do it," Branwen retorted. "Now, think! Don't dwell upon your fear. This is a public testing, and you are High Queen of Britain. There's not a man in that crowd whose heart won't melt when he lays eyes on you." Branwen regarded her shrewdly. "Why is it that fear and pain make you more beautiful and me plainer? Never mind, it's a blessing, really. It's like being handed an extra shield. Are you ready? Take a deep breath and let it out slowly." She reached for the latch and swung open the door. "The High Queen is ready, my lord."

Two guards stood outside on the landing. They bowed low at the sight of the Queen. Dressed in a plain bleached shift, wrapped in a white wool cloak lined with white rabbit pelts, her red-gold curls tumbling unbound around her shoulders, and the silver crown of Britain across her brow, Essylte stepped forward and placed her hand upon the foremost soldier's arm. "Let us go."

They walked solemnly down the stairs, through the corridors of Tintagel, and out into the frigid stillness of the courtyard, where a company of troops fell in behind them. The procession snaked across the causeway where the winter wind bit at them, danced and swirled around them, making the torches smoke and the men pull their cloaks tighter. The Queen paced on, oblivious to the cold, toward the great crowd on the cliff and the bonfire that awaited. The guards they passed crossed themselves and made the sign against enchantment behind their backs.

The great gathering of onlookers hushed as they approached, and parted to make a path for them: soldiers, servants, beggars, farmers, goatherds, shepherds, whole families from the villages round about, pilgrims, priests, wise women with amulets about their necks and fingers weaving spells, children staring openmouthed. A sea of faces turned toward her, curious, unbelieving, full of pity, full of morbid excitement, even full of lust. She looked at none of them, but put all her concentration into walking, one foot before the other, keeping herself upright and calm.

At the center of the crowd a great bonfire blazed. Essylte could feel its heat even from where she walked. Three men stood silhouetted against its ferocious light: Markion, Segward, and Donal, the Bishop of Dorria. Against her will she began to tremble. Her foot caught on a tuft of dead moor grass and she nearly stumbled. The crowd gasped; the guard caught her arm. Coolly, she thanked him for it.

The stumble brought her back to herself and she remembered Branwen's words. She searched the crowd for the cloak she sought, but there were so many, the day was cold, and the people poor; so many were patched, it was difficult to tell the colors against the raging light. And then she saw it. It was a ragged cloak, unevenly patched, and its wearer had yet to turn around, but she would recognize that back anywhere. As she got closer the cloak half turned. She saw a hideous face, discolored like a leper's, with warts on the chin and a misshapen nose. The face lifted and a pair of warm brown eyes met hers. She caught her breath and looked away.

"Don't look, my lady," the guard murmured gently. "Such ugliness ought not to be allowed in the Queen's presence."

Was this the same guard who had hammered on her door with such malignant authority? She began to see the truth of Branwen's words. The leper's cloak brushed her foot. "I can't abide it," she whispered as her eyes rolled back into her head, and she fell. Tristan caught her. For the first time since they had walked out of Morois they were face-to-face. Her eyes fluttered open, and she breathed in his warm, familiar scent. For the briefest moment she relaxed in his embrace. Then the guard bent down and grabbed her as the crowd cried out in horror.

"Away with you, filthy leper! Unhand the Queen!" The guard pulled Essylte to her feet as the leper and his companion disappeared into the crowd. The guard held tightly to her arm. "I beg your pardon, my lady. If you feel faint, lean on me."

"He touched me," Essylte quavered.

The guard's voice was heavy with pity. "Trust in God, my lady Queen, and all will be well."

A small dais had been built before the bonfire. Markion, Segward, and the bishop stood beside it. The guard led her to Markion and bowed. But Markion made no move of greeting. He did not even look at her.

Segward stepped forward with an unctuous smile. "This way, my lady Queen." He reached for her hand but she turned her shoulder.

"Don't touch me, Snake. I will go up of my own accord."

She climbed the three steps to the dais and faced the crowd. A wild cheer arose as the people stomped and waved in greeting, in adoration, in compassion and support. She made them a low reverence, and the din doubled. Out of the corner of her eye she saw Markion's commanders standing nearby, grave and disapproving. Sir Bruenor, foremost among them, had a look of constrained horror on his face. Dinadan was not there. She gazed out past the crowd toward the moor. He was with Tristan and Guvranyl, somewhere.

The bishop raised his arms, and slowly the people quieted to hear him.

"Markion, High King of Britain, has called us all together to bear witness to the trial of his Queen, Essylte of Gwynedd, whom he accuses of adultery with his nephew, Tristan of Lyonesse."

A few people stomped and clapped, but a loud hiss issued from the general throng. Essylte bowed her head in acknowledgment.

"To this end"—the bishop glanced nervously at the King and raised his voice—"I am bidden to subject the Queen to trial by fire, as our ancestors did of old, to test the purity of her soul. Thus will the Almighty God who made us all reveal to us either the unblemished virtue or the tainted wickedness of her soul."

"I object!" a voice cried. Essylte saw Sir Bruenor step forward and face Markion. "My lord King, it ill becomes you to treat the Queen so. You have her back. You promised Sir Tristan, in front of us all, that if he brought her to you, you would keep her from harm and restore her to her honor. You have done neither. And while we sit here in Cornwall putting the Queen to trial, she who is not your enemy but your sworn companion, the Saxons are rampaging across Britain, burning towns and villages, laying waste the land! I beg you, my lord, let the Queen go! Whatever her sins, they are behind her, and are between her and God. Lead us out to fight the heathen Saxons and drive them from our land! In such pursuit lies glory. In this," he said with a grimace, extending his arm toward the bonfire, "in this lies only shame and degradation."

The commanders raised a cheer, and behind them, the troops. The people took it up, crying, out, "The Queen! The Queen!"

Segward leaned forward and spoke frantically in Markion's ear. The King's face hardened.

"Sir Bruenor, I have heard you, and I mark well your words. If the Queen proves her innocence, I will fulfill my promise. But do not ask the High King of Britain to take a wanton to his bed. If she proves worthy of me, I will take her back. But if she is evil, she must die. And as Lord Segward reminds me, it was on her way back from your own fortress that the Queen went missing. Were I in your boots, my lord, I would be more careful of my tongue."

Sir Bruenor flushed with anger. "I speak the truth, Markion, and every man here knows it!"

Markion looked at him coldly and turned to the bishop. "Go ahead," he snapped. "Get on with it. Put her to the fire."

Essylte raised her eyes to heaven and prayed silently. The weak December sun filtered gold through pewter clouds. Behind her the fire roared and scorched her back, even through the cloak.

The bishop cleared his throat uncertainly and lifted up his arm. "In the name of most Holy God, I sanctify this blaze as the Lord's holy fire—"

Essylte smiled to herself. The bonfire was lit every year on the winter solstice in honor of a service older than the Christian God's. She thought of the Divine Mother and the new life that grew inside her. She wondered if the bishop knew he was blaspheming.

"—a refining fire," the bishop intoned, "to separate the pure from the dross, to purify the iniquities of sinners. *I will come near to you to judgment,* saith the Lord, *and I will be swift witness against the sorcerers, and against the adulterers, and against false swearers.* Lo, this is the Refiner's fire, which shall purify the children of the earth."

The bishop turned, picked up an unlit torch, and lighted it from the bonfire. Then he climbed the dais and stood next to Essylte. She looked at him in some surprise. He sweated furiously, and the hand that held the torch shook visibly. "Essylte, Queen of Britain, the Lord sees your heart. The Lord hears your words. Answer this question truthfully, as you value your life. Have you ever betrayed your husband's trust? Have you ever, on pain of burning, lain with any man but him?"

Calmly, Essylte raised her voice into the waiting silence and said clearly, "No, my lord bishop, I have not."

A great sigh swept the crowd. Markion stepped forward. "You are too easy, Bishop!" he barked. "Ask her again, and name me!"

"Essylte, Queen of Britain! Have you ever, on pain of burning, lain with any man but Markion?"

Essylte straightened. Over the crowd of people silence hung heavy as a weight. "My lord Markion," she said, looking at him, "my lords all, my people of Cornwall and of Britain: This I swear. Since I left my father's house, no man has ever held me in his arms but Markion—" She paused and pointed vaguely into the crowd. "—and that man there, that leper, who caught me when I fell."

The crowd cheered.

"Liar!" Segward cried.

"Go on!" Markion growled. "Test her!"

The bishop turned to Essylte. She could smell his fear. She could see the driving excitement in his eyes. "Queen Essylte," he began, "I beg your forgiveness for what I must now do—"

She smiled gently at him. "I forgive you, Father. I do not fear the fire of God." She loosed her cloak and let it fall. The people gasped. She wore only a plain linen shift, and the unbound hair of a maiden. The heat of the fire brought a flush of warmth to her face. But the crowd, huddled together in the winter cold, whispered, "Miracle" and "Innocent."

"Go ahead, Father," she repeated, seeing Markion's frightened stare. "Test me."

The bishop held the torch between them. "Essylte of Gwynedd, pass your hand through the flame. Slowly."

She drew a long breath and let it out easily. Raising her arm, she passed her right hand slowly through the flame, letting it rest for a moment in the fire until the people wept and cried for her to stop. Her flesh sizzled and smoked, but all she felt was a tingling sensation up her arm. The bishop yanked her hand from the flame and gasped aloud.

"My lords," he squealed excitedly, "she is unmarked! It is a miracle!"

"Let me see!" Markion snarled. The bishop held her wrist and showed him both sides of her white, unblemished hand. "Do the other one!"

"But my lord!"

"Do it! Now!"

Essylte met Markion's eyes. "You are beneath my contempt," she said levelly, and put her left hand into the flame. Markion took her arm and held it there, while the crowd began to hiss and jeer. At last, his nose wrinkling at the smell, he pulled it forth. It was unmarked. He touched his hand to her palm and jerked his fingers away. He blinked and stared first at the bishop, then at Essylte, the whites of his eyes showing.

The people cheered and pushed forward to the foot of the dais. Segward slipped silently away.

"Essylte," Markion said uncertainly, "I beg your pardon. I was so sure— but I see I have listened to poisoned tongues. Will you, could you ever, find it in your heart to forgive me?"

Essylte pointed to her cloak, and Markion stooped to retrieve it for her and lay it carefully about her shoulders. "That depends," she said stiffly, "on several things. But this I require of you, Markion of Cornwall, if I am to stay here and not take my sons home to Gwynedd—"

He paled and nodded obediently. "Anything. Name it!"

"You will stay away from my bed until I send for you. You will ask my leave before you lay a finger on me."

Markion opened his mouth to protest, saw the dark looks on the faces of the bishop and his commanders, and nodded. "Be it so, lady. I swear I never meant you harm."

Essylte shuddered, drawing her cloak closer about her as her arms began to burn. "You have wished me in my grave. And publicly at that. Do not lie to me anymore, Markion. And I will not lie to you."

She stepped down from the dais and strode through the crowd, which parted eagerly and reached out to touch her cloak. An hour, Branwen had told her, that's all she had. She hurried as fast as she dared toward the causeway. An hour to get back and reapply the salve to keep the blisters down. Her hands would be unusable for three days. But by that time, God and the Mother willing, Markion and all his men would be back in Logris. And Tristan could come out of hiding.

PART V

26 ✟ KING'S RANSOM

"S o this is Lyonesse."

Essylte sat on horseback beside Tristan and surveyed the rich and thriving land spread out before her. Guvranyl and Dinadan followed in their wake with fifty troops and a litter for Branwen and the children. Essylte preferred to ride at Tristan's side, since the weather held fair. The three-day trip from Tintagel had been easy going, mild for the time of year and with dry ground for the horses. They had passed through moor, forest, bog, and meadow as easily as on a summer day, and now stood on the narrow neck of land that connected the kingdom of Lyonesse to Cornwall and to Britain.

Essylte lifted her chin as wind fluttered the edges of her hood. It was a southwest wind and unexpectedly warm. "How green the land is! Compared to what we've come through, it's like a different country. Or does spring come early in Lyonesse?"

Tristan smiled. "Some call it an enchanted land. I'd be the last to argue." He gestured to the long, narrow neck of land on which they stood, the sea visible on both east and west horizons. "Every year, it seems, this strip gets narrower. Either the sea is rising or Lyonesse is sinking. It's true the sea wind is warmer here than in the rest of Britain. And the sea, too. I swim in it year-round."

"That's because you're crazy." Dinadan rode up to Tristan's side and smiled at Essylte. "He swims and sails in all weather. You can't get him out of the water. His mother was a mermaiden."

Essylte laughed. "I knew there was something different about him the minute I set eyes on him."

Dinadan sobered. "Tristan, it'll be dusk in an hour. Do you want to camp or push on to Lyon's Head?"

"The moon rises early and full tonight. Let's push on. How are Branwen and the children?"

Dinadan shifted in the saddle. "Branwen would rather get behind a thick stone wall with an army at her back. She keeps watching the horizon behind us."

"She needn't. Markion's in Logris. By the time he gets word of our escape, he will be ten days getting back. Filas, Regis, Dynas, and the companies they lead will break from his army to join us. That leaves him less than three-quarters of his force. He can't bring all his men south or he'll lose Logris forever. Tell Branwen not to worry. At least, not yet."

"I've been through the numbers and so has she. She's still unsettled." Dinadan paused. "And so am I."

"Then let's push on. I'll send a courier ahead to let them know we're coming. And one to my uncle Pernam to bid him attend us at Lyon's Head." Tristan paused. "Where is Segward?"

Essylte shrugged. "No one knows. Not with Markion, that's certain. He left Tintagel the night of the bonfire and hasn't been seen since."

"Then he must be at home." Tristan signaled to his captain. "Grayell, we ride for Lyon's Head directly, and I want couriers sent ahead. And I want you to lead a company of men to Segward's house and arrest him. Take him to Lyon's Head, in chains if he doesn't come quietly enough to suit you. Escort his lady and his children with all the dignity they are due. They will be my guests."

A smile tugged at the corners of Grayell's mouth. "Yes, my lord. With pleasure."

Tristan gazed at the fertile land around him, which his father, Meliodas, had called "the land of promise." He had been in love with the daughter of a bard when he said so, and it must have seemed to him that his future—as King of Lyonesse, King of Cornwall, and heir to the High King of Britain—held nothing but promise. But that promise had never been fulfilled. He had lost his young wife in childbirth only a year after their marriage, and in his grief had never taken another. He had kept his young son by him ever afterward, wherever his travels took him, as a token of the companionship he could not do without. Twelve years later he had lost his life to Irish raiders, and both his kingdoms to his brother Markion. Now, poised on the edge of an act that would settle so many fates, Tristan wondered if this land of promise, this green and fertile Lyonesse, had something better or worse in store for him.

"The time of reckoning is upon us," he said slowly. "And upon Segward. We will all be judged by what we do in Lyonesse."

"What will you do?" Essylte asked. "Kill him?"

"That depends upon Segward. And, I suppose, upon Esmerée. But I will see justice done."

When the orders were given and the couriers sent, they moved off at a brisk pace into Lyonesse. Essylte gazed in admiration at the country they rode through, orchards and meadows, woodland and rolling pasture, well-tilled land, well-tended roads, gentle hills cupping fertile valleys in a protective embrace. Even deep in winter's sleep it was a rich and enticing land. She noted the fortifications standing everywhere along the shore, ready to light their signal fires at a moment's notice to warn of Saxon longboats. A land so rich in gifts must be costly to defend. How different it was from stony Wales! Yet for the first time since she had left Gwynedd, she felt at home. It was a land of light and song compared to Cornwall. Even the seabirds wheeling overhead seemed less shrill than those that circled so endlessly above Tintagel. And the moon! Lifting like a giant's lantern above the eastern sea, the moon looked twice its normal size, a huge bronze globe hung on the horizon, almost close enough to touch.

Well past nightfall they came to a set of double gates set in rock at the edge of a cliff. Below them the winter sea sucked and thudded against cruel rocks. Above and beyond the gates loomed a shadow darker than the night sky, a giant standing stone thrust from the sea, pierced here and there by the light of flaming torches. Guards at the gate saluted, exchanged passwords, and swung the great gates open. Half a league away Essylte saw the fortress on its rocky promontory, and in between, only the sighing sea. "Tristan, how do we get across?"

He smiled. "Follow me."

They started forward across an unbelievably thin, dark ribbon of rock, so narrow that in places two could not ride abreast. She dared not look down, but clutched her mare's mane and kept her eyes on Tristan's back until the road widened, a second pair of gates passed overhead, and she was in a torchlit courtyard full of people calling greetings to Tristan and bowing in her direction. She slid off the mare into Tristan's arms.

"Welcome to Lyon's Head, my lovely Queen," he whispered into her hair. "We are home."

Later, they stood together on the parapet outside Tristan's chamber. Overhead, the moon sailed brilliant in a starry sky. Below, the restless sea lapped at the fortress foundations. Essylte breathed in slowly and exhaled on a sigh.

"This is happiness," she murmured. "This is where I belong. Between the stars and the sea, on the edge of land. Not at the center of things, as my father wanted, but at the edge. Here. With you." His hand came down upon her shoulder. "The wind is so warm. Standing here in this light robe, with my arms bare, I'm not cold at all. It's so strange. It's like magic."

"The west wind always blows soft, even in winter. But it's cold enough when it swings north and east."

His hands slid down her arms and across her hips, coming to rest on the firm swell of her belly. She leaned back against him. "I used to wonder, when I sat in my mother's workroom boiling her horrible herbs, what it was I wanted to do when I was grown." She spread out her arms toward the sea.

"I have found the answer here." She smiled as his lips touched her neck. "What more could I ever ask for, except to be safe forever?"

"No one is safe forever."

"I know," she whispered. "I know."

"I'll protect you as long as I live, Essylte."

"I know you will." She turned to him, her eyes dark in the moonlight. "That's not what I'm afraid of. And I'm not afraid of death. But I don't want to outlive you, Tristan. Whatever happens, I don't want to live in this world without you."

His hands pressed gently against her belly. "If it comes to that, you *must* go on. For our children. I don't want my sons to lose you." He touched his finger to her lips to still her protest. "We have grown, you and I, beyond just ourselves. We've made ourselves a family, sweet Essylte. Let Lyonesse serve as a nursery for the future of Cornwall, whatever becomes of us."

"Is that why you sent for Esmerée?"

"Partly. I want her children here. They will not be safe outside the gates of Lyon's Head once Mark arrives. That's why I sent for Pernam, too. But I must speak with Esme about Segward before I take my vengeance on him."

"And when will Mark come?"

Tristan shrugged. "A fortnight. A month. Two, perhaps, if he's smart. Why should he hurry? We're not going anywhere."

They stood together and listened to the sighing of the sea. The castle walls were invisible in the dark, but sea foam glimmered phosphorescent around the roots of the fortress, licking into crevices and swirling into eddies far below.

"With how many men?"

"More than I have. But not as many as he thinks. There will be deserters to my cause. After his cruel treatment of you, half his army would defend you against him, if it came to that."

She turned her head and looked up into his eyes. "Will it come to that? Tell me the truth."

Tristan shrugged. "I don't know. That depends upon Mark."

"You won't fight him, Tristan, will you? Promise me you won't. That will bring my father down upon your head."

"I will do whatever it takes to protect you."

"And if I can't be protected?"

Tristan shivered and pointed out to sea. "Less Britain is that direction. It shouldn't be more than a two-day sail in the boat I've built. You must see her to believe her, Essylte. I built her myself, along the lines of a Saxon keel I once commandeered. And I copied the rigging, too, for better maneuverability. She's sweet to sail; I've practiced all summer. In the next two weeks, while we gather stores from all over Lyonesse, I'll fit her out with provisions. If it comes to a war I know I can't win, we'll sail away. All of us. But if we do, we can't come back."

Essylte embraced him. "I don't care. You are all that matters. I loved living in Ogrin's hut with only rags to wear. I don't need to be a queen, Tristan. But I need to be with you." She pulled his head down and kissed him fiercely.

Tristan bent and lifted her in his arms. He carried her inside, where the warm breeze stirred the lamp flames and threw their shadows shimmering on the wall. Above the bed hung an old silk banner with the Eagle of Lyonesse on a field of blue. Time passed, the moon swung westward, the shadows of the lovers quivered on the wall, moving, entwined, to the beat of life that gripped them. The banner lifted in the light wind and rippled once; the eagle stretched its talons and raised its wings, straining toward the stars.

"Don't kill him, Tristan, I beg you."

The great hall echoed the whispered words. Floored in stone, pillared in marble, hung with tapestries and banners, adorned with twelve double-flamed bronze lamps, man height and burning sweet oil, the king's audience chamber at Lyon's Head stretched the breadth of the fortress, from the north face to the south. Narrow windows looked north over the causeway and the gates. To the south, morning sun fell in great shafts through wide windows open to the sea, flooding the hall with light and throwing the dais, the king, and the kneeling supplicant into sharp relief.

No one looking at Tristan now could call him a boy. Stern, grave, and still, his face was the visage of a king. His glittering crown, his ring of office, his golden torque etched with eagles, his robe, his tunic, his sword—all were regal, but nothing proclaimed his sovereignty so much as the carved solemnity of his face.

All around him his men fidgeted in suppressed excitement. Soldiers crowded at the door and thronged in a semicircle around the dais. Their air of expectation was a living presence in the room, a great hawk restless in its jesses, waiting for the moment when the hood was drawn.

Tristan looked down at the kneeling woman at his feet, whose hands were raised in supplication. He sighed heavily. "In God's name, Esme, why not? After what he's done to you, again and again? And to Essylte? He's as much as admitted that he put Mark up to the trial by fire. How can I not?"

"Please," she whispered, raising her eyes to his. "He does not deserve your mercy, my lord, but I beg you for it on his behalf. It is beneath you to kill him."

Tristan leaned forward and lowered his voice. "How can you say that?

Do you love him, then? Can you love the man who has treated you—and your daughters, too—worse than I treat my dogs?"

Esmerée began to tremble. "No, my lord," she breathed. "I do not love him. I loathe him."

"Then how—"

"None of his schemes have come to fruition. He is banished from King Mark's presence forever. He is without power. Let that be his punishment."

"Banished to live freely in Lyonesse? To stay safe at home under *my* protection—dear God!—where he is free to beat anyone he chooses? It is not punishment enough!"

"He values public status and the King's favor above all else, because he could not come by them by birth. He will suffer cruelly from banishment. Eventually, he might take some action that would justify your vengeance, but until that time, Tristan, my lord king, I beg you to spare his life. I do not want his death upon your hands." She glanced quickly at Essylte, sitting beside Tristan in the queen's chair of Lyonesse, and lowered her eyes. "And he is the father of my children."

Tristan paused. When he spoke his voice was low and grave. "Even so, Lady Esmerée. He has already taken action against me. He has put the Queen's life in jeopardy. He cannot go unpunished."

"That was an action against the Queen—against Markion's wife," she breathed, her gaze nailed to the floor. "Not against you."

Tristan reached down and grabbed her hands. "Esme! If you had seen it! A public bonfire on the cliffs of Tintagel—a public burning if she had not passed the test! It was an affront to her honor, and to the honor of all Cornwall."

The soldiers nodded to one another and murmured their assent.

"Yes, my lord. It was an evil thing he did. But—" Esmerée raised her eyes to his and looked at him directly. "Whatever his intention, he has not harmed you. It is not your right to punish him. It is Markion's."

Dinadan, at Tristan's elbow, drew breath sharply. The room went still. Essylte looked at Guvranyl, at Grayell, at the gathered courtiers, at the soldiers standing at attention by the doors. Every one of them looked away.

Tristan spoke formally and rather stiffly to Esmerée. "Very well. If you think that I, as the High King's nephew, have no right to protect the woman he calls his Queen, the woman I myself brought out of Wales for him—if you think that Markion has any right to call himself her husband after the way he has treated her—then I will do as you wish. Markion is coming. I will leave him to Markion."

A light flush spread across the pale cream of Esmerée's complexion, and she bowed her head. "I thank you, my gracious lord. You are generous indeed."

Tristan regarded her sadly. "No, no, lady, it is you who have been generous to me, and to Essylte. Many times. If you would let me, I would repay you by ridding you of this scourge of a husband, but I will do your bidding. I owe you that much. You have pleaded so eloquently on his behalf."

Color flooded Esmerée's face until it was crimson. When she could speak, her voice shook. "Repay me, Tristan, by being careful of your honor." She sank stiffly into her reverence and turned away without looking at the king. All eyes followed her as she left the chamber.

Essylte said bitterly, "Even in Lyonesse they think I shame you."

Unsmiling, Tristan took her hand. "Not so. Here you are the Lady of Lyonesse. Esme has a tender conscience, and it pains her."

Dinadan coughed lightly. "My lord, Sir Grayell informs me your uncle Pernam has arrived. Will you see him here?"

Tristan's gaze swung to the door and met the carefully neutral stare of the guards. "No. Let him rest from the journey and bide a while. I'll see him at my leisure. Guvranyl, how stand the shore defenses? Have the people been informed? Are many seeking shelter in Lyon's Head?"

"Aye, my lord, the word's got about. Most folk are hiding their valuables and preparing to shelter here at the first signal of Markion's approach. As far as I can tell, they are behind you, Tristan, man, woman, and child. They are proud you've rescued the High Queen. They feel, as I do, that Markion usurped your place when your father died. It is your crown he wears. You are Meliodas's son. *You* ought to be High King, and Lyonesse first among the kingdoms."

Guvranyl did not trouble to lower his voice, and the cheers of the gathered warriors filled the chamber at his words. Tristan looked around at the faces of his men. Without exception, he saw hope, pride, and banked excitement in their eyes.

"So." He exhaled slowly. "Is this what you want? Shall I fight my own uncle, kill my own kin, dishonor my name for the crown of Britain? Shall I sink to the level of barbarian? Is that what you have come to see?"

One of the older soldiers cleared his throat. "My lord, it has long been known among us that it was on account of Markion that our lord King Meliodas died. *You* carry the true strain of the noble House of Cornwall, Sir Tristan. We would rather follow you." Heads nodded eagerly. All the soldiers muttered in agreement.

Tristan rose and faced them. His features hardened, but his eyes grew sad. "Markion did not kill Meliodas. Irish raiders did. No one forced my father's hand. Do not forget I have knelt at Markion's feet and sworn him fealty. I do not take that oath lightly. And neither should you. We are men of our word in Lyonesse. I am sworn to Markion, as you are sworn to me." One by one they lowered their eyes or looked away. He paused. "But before

Markion, I am sworn to Lyonesse." Instantly he saw hope rekindled in their faces. "Markion may banish me from every corner of Britain but this. He has no right to rob me of Lyonesse. Here I am, and here I mean to stay, and the Queen with me."

All eyes turned to Essylte. A few men cheered; gradually others joined; soon the hall was filled with shouting. Tristan lifted a hand for silence. "I will raise no hand against him. But if he comes to me looking for war, well then, we shall give him what he wants!"

A great cheer rose to the raftered ceiling. Soldiers yelled wildly, grinning, stomping their feet and raising paeans of victory. "Tristan the High King!" they cried. But Tristan's face, when he turned to raise Essylte and lead her out, was as cold as slate.

Pernam crouched beyond the seawall below the postern gate, gathering kelp stranded on the rocks by the receding tide. Tristan, coming upon him unawares, watched in silence for a moment, then pushed up his sleeves and joined him. When the healer's basket was full of the dagger-edged strands of blistered, green-brown weed, and Tristan's unpracticed hands were sliced and bleeding, Pernam straightened.

"Enough. I thank you, Tristan. You have saved me an hour of toil."

"What do you want these slimy things for, anyway?"

Pernam smiled. "With a little preparation, they yield a powerful medicine. They're also nutritious."

"You *eat* them? Ugh. Will they heal my hands?"

"A soak in the sea and a night's rest is all you need to heal your hands."

Tristan rinsed his hands in the sea, wincing at the sting of salt water, while Pernam swung his basket over the wall. They sat together on the seawall, watching in silence as the warm wind slid over the cooler sea, drawing from its heaving surface a thickening shroud of mist.

Pernam stared thoughtfully into the moving fog. "So, nephew, why did you summon me? What is this all about?"

"Do you have to ask? He tried to burn her. Alive. In public."

"I heard."

"He dares to call himself a Christian and her husband. He's gone too far this time. I will not forgive him for it."

"Forgiveness is a tricky thing. So difficult to come by when it's wanted. You abducted her to rescue her?"

"Be more careful of your tongue, Uncle. I love you well, but those are treasonous words."

Pernam's face remained impassive. "But treason is the issue, surely."

"It is not. I don't want his crown. God knows I have none of his ambition, even though everyone in Lyonesse seems to think I ought to. They would have me break my oath and kill my uncle—do they believe they could follow a man capable of such treachery? I told the men I would not do it. If Mark strikes the first blow, I'll fight him. I'll have no choice. But I'll not attack a man I've sworn fealty to."

Pernam exhaled slowly. "Tristan, you don't know how glad I am to hear you say that."

Tristan shook his head angrily. "And I did not abduct her. But, dear God, Pernam! I couldn't let her stay penned in Tintagel after the monster tried to burn her! You'd be closer to the truth if you said she ran away with me. After such humiliation, she would throw herself into the sea before she'd spend another hour under his rule."

"So this is not about the Kingship, then, but only the woman?"

"Of course it is. That and his order banishing me from Britain. Lyonesse is mine."

Pernam regarded him gravely. "Leave aside the banishment for the moment. Would you wage war, and risk your future, Essylte's future, and the futures of Lyonesse and Britain, for one woman?"

Tristan picked up a pebble and hurled it into the sea. "Over *this* woman. Yes. I would and I will."

"Then you are no king."

Tristan shrugged. "I told you that myself once before." He looked up at his uncle swiftly. "And would you not, for Jarrad? Or for Arthur?"

Pernam's nostrils flared. "The case is not the same and you know it. I am no warrior. They cannot bear the High King's heir. Even so, Tristan, the answer is no. I would not. A man's honor, and certainly a kingdom's, is more important than the satisfaction of desire."

"And is that all they are to you?" Tristan said softly.

Pernam turned away. For a long moment he gazed into the oncoming mist. "Of course not. Even so. Britain comes first."

"For Britain, then, he must give her up to me. That's all that matters, now. It's the only way there can be peace between us."

"Mark cares less about peace than you do."

"She is mine, Pernam. In body and in soul. She has never been his."

Pernam looked at him gravely. Tristan flinched at the steady stare of those still, gray eyes. "In the eyes of your own God they are man and wife. If you are a Christian, Tristan, you must hold that vow holy."

"She is his wife in name only," Tristan whispered. "Not in the way that matters. They have no union. Her heart and soul are one with mine. She is the breath of life to me, flesh of my flesh, bone of my bone, for she carries within her—" He broke off, too late, and watched Pernam's eyes widen.

"Nephew, what have you done? You are not such a fool!"

Tristan managed a small smile. "Three months in the Morois Wood is a long time."

Pernam looked away, breathing audibly. "Even Markion can count on his fingers. How can you deny the charge of treason?" Pernam pushed back his hood. The bones of his skull showed beneath his close-cropped silver hair. In profile he looked lean and predatory as an eagle. "Ours is a family cursed with essential flaws. Even back to Gorlois of Cornwall, an old man driven by vanity to marry the girl Ygraine, who betrayed him with Uther Pendragon. My father was ambitious beyond his station. Markion is greedy beyond his means. You are no different, Tristan. You have betrayed your kinsman and shamed your name. Worse, you have led that pretty child down the same dark road. She is Queen, and she has committed treason against her King. You are responsible for that."

"He is not her king."

"Markion is her lord by all the laws of Cornwall. Tristan, Tristan." Pernam's head slowly sank into his hands. "What has happened to your honor? Have you lost all sense of proportion in your love for this woman? You would have done better to let her be."

"*I couldn't,*" Tristan whispered. "God knows I tried. Again and again. *I could not.* It is—it is like trying to do without one's breath. You can stop it for a while, but then the body's need for air and the spirit's need for life overrule the will. You may grow faint, you may fall senseless to the ground, but you will breathe again."

Pernam rose and picked up his basket. His face was cold. "Why did you bring me here?"

Tristan rose to stand beside him. "To keep you behind the fortress walls so Markion can't burn you out and take you hostage to use against me."

Pernam snorted. "I can handle Markion without your help."

"And to—to get your advice."

"My advice is to give him back his wife."

"And to comfort Esmerée—and her children."

"They are here?" Pernam asked quickly. "In Lyon's Head?"

"Yes. And Segward is in the dungeon."

Pernam set down the basket with careful deliberation. "Then I will stay. You'll kill him, I suppose."

"God knows I want to. The burning of Essylte was his plan from the beginning. But I have this very morning agreed to abide by Esme's wishes, and she has begged me for his life."

Pernam exhaled slowly. "Wise woman," he breathed.

Tristan scowled. "Idiocy, to my mind. I've agreed to let Mark decide his fate. So now we are all waiting for Markion."

Pernam nodded slowly, his eyes narrowing. "And what will happen when he comes? Have you asked yourself that? Can you put yourself in his place and look ahead?"

"What do you mean?"

"How can he let you take his wife without appearing to suffer great insult at your hands? Do you think he will listen calmly to your pleadings and just hand her over? You can't be such a fool. He will want something for her, something more valuable in the world's eyes than any woman, so that he will have gained in the exchange." Pernam's voice grew strained. "Think, Tristan. What have you got that would be worth his while to get?"

Tristan glared seaward. "No," he said. "No."

Pernam shouldered his basket again as the fog rolled in over the seawall. "In Mark's eyes, the only thing you've got worth having is Lyonesse. That's why he banished you. He hoped he could get it by declaration and not have to raise a sword against Cornwall's champion. No doubt that's still what he's after."

"Lyonesse is mine."

Pernam nodded and turned away. "So is the woman. But for how long?"

27 ✠ OATH UNBROKEN, VOW UNKEPT

Wrapped in a thick wool robe with a shawl about her shoulders, Essylte pressed her face hard against the shutters and strained to peek through the cracks. "Did I ever say it was warm here?" She shivered as the wind whistled past her cheek. "Why, it's colder here than it is at home!"

"What do you expect at winter's end?" Branwen muttered, hunched over her spindle.

"Come, Essylte, sit by the fire. It's warmer here." Esmerée rose from her stool by the brazier and made room for Essylte, but Essylte only shook her head and paced back and forth before the window.

"No, no, Esme, you sit there. You're the one with the cough. I'm healthy as a horse." She laughed and ran her hands over the curve of her belly, noticeable now even under the voluminous robe. "And nearly as heavy. This one's going to be bigger than young Tristan. A fighter, I think. He kicks at me day and night."

Branwen said nothing, but her hand stole under her robe to rest on her own bulging belly. Esmerée cast her a worried glance, caught Branwen's defensive eye, and went quickly back to her needlework.

"Tristan rests his head on him at night," Essylte continued, unheeding. "He loves to listen to his movement and sing to him of the great deeds he will one day do." She smiled to herself and turned, her unbound hair shimmering about her shoulders. "How eager he is to see this boy born! Did I tell you he wants to be with me this time? Can you imagine it? Me, the midwife, and Tristan of Lyonesse!" She laughed, and her laughter rang like silver bells in the cold stillness of the room.

Esmerée smiled up at her. "You are lucky, Essylte, to bear children with such ease. It is more difficult for some."

But Essylte missed her warning glance at Branwen and continued in her merry voice. "I let him tend the children in the nursery—he is so fond of them all, even yours, Esme. Young Tristan took his first steps yesterday, did you hear? Holding on to Tristan's fingers. Tristan was so pleased he ordered a celebration, and we all had raisin cake together. Young Tristan got more of it on his cheeks than in his mouth!" She laughed. "It is such joy, being all day with Tristan. Part of me wishes it would never end. But the other part—"

"Essylte, hush a moment, do." Esmerée reached out and placed a hand on Branwen's knee. "How do you feel this afternoon, my dear? Any better at all?"

Branwen shrugged her thin shoulders and went on with her spinning. Essylte came away from the window and laid her pretty hand against Branwen's head.

"Branny hates pregnancy," she said lightly, stroking the mousy hair. "But her children are beautiful. You will count it worth your while in the end, Branny."

Esmerée frowned. Branwen's skin looked yellow next to Essylte's rosy flesh. Her cheekbones stood out from her face, and her eyes were sunk in hollows. "Let me send Pernam to you," Esmerée whispered, leaning toward the girl. "He can ease your pain without hurting your child. He's a wizard with medicines."

Branwen shook her head stubbornly. "I'm fine. I don't want any medicines. It's as Essylte says. I'm not fond of pregnancy, but I'll survive. Only six weeks now."

"Six weeks!" Essylte sighed heavily. "Oh, let this awful waiting be over before six weeks have passed. Let me stand in the light and call Tristan my husband in the eyes of God." She went back to the window and peered through the cracks. "Whatever is keeping Markion? I can see all the way to the foothills, but no sign of him yet. You don't suppose he'd come by sea, do you?"

"Certainly not," Esmerée replied firmly. "He'll come overland with his army if he comes at all. You'll hear the lookout's warning before you see so much as a banner out that window."

Essylte turned. "If he comes at all? What do you mean?"

"Only that it's three months since the solstice and we've seen nothing of him. He's off fighting Saxons. That's all I meant. He'll come for Tristan as soon as things are calm in Britain."

"He'll come when it suits him," Branwen muttered.

Esmerée looked at them both and put down her stitching. "He will come for his son, whatever he decides to do with his wife. Have you thought of that? He will want his heir back."

Essylte shivered. "He won't take young Tristan. I'll tell him the truth before I'll let that happen."

Branwen's head shot up. "You will do no such thing! I have your oath, and Tristan's, that you will tell him nothing without my leave."

Essylte paled. "Whatever do you mean, Branny?"

The spindle fell to the floor and Esmerée stooped to pick it up. Branwen trembled from head to foot. "You promised in Guvranyl's house, the morning after—you promised me you would not reveal without my permission that it was I who lay with him."

Essylte swallowed and nodded slowly. "Yes. All right. We will not tell him that. But since Morois, he already knows that Tristan is my lover. We will just admit that—it has been so longer than he thought."

Branwen closed her eyes and swayed on the stool. "Not yet. Not the truth about the children. Not yet."

"All right. All right, Branny. Be calm, now. I'll do as you wish a while longer. Don't excite yourself."

Esmerée, reaching for the spindle, happened to nudge the edge of Branwen's robe. She gasped. The rushes on the floor beneath her skirts dripped dark red. "Branwen!" Half rising, she caught the senseless girl just as she slid from her stool.

There on the floor, hidden before by the fall of Branwen's robe, was a great, glistening pool of blood.

All night the east wind howled around the fortress. Snow sifted through shutter cracks and spilled onto the cold stone floor. Heavy tapestries shivered on the walls as gusts whistled by. Everywhere in the castle people huddled together for warmth, under blankets, under skins, hard by a flame. Near the great log fire in the King's hall men gathered around Tristan, as they always did, but conversation was subdued. Tristan sat in his carved chair with the Queen upon his lap, her face buried in his cloak. Her violent weeping had subsided. Now she lay in his arms like a dead thing, pale and still, while he stared moodily into the leaping flames.

After a solemn meal and a flagon of ale, most of the men drifted away. As the night wore on, only Dinadan and Guvranyl remained, feeding the fire themselves, keeping the wine warmed and the cups filled. They talked fitfully of horses, weapons, and battles, averting their eyes as Tristan kissed Essylte's tear-ravaged face and murmured into her ear.

"Don't let her die," Essylte whimpered, hooking her arm about Tristan's neck and pressing her lips to his throat. "She's my dearest friend. Don't let her die."

He stroked the long fall of her hair and pulled her closer. "If she can be saved, Pernam will save her."

"But if he can't?"

"Hush, Essylte. It does no good to fear it. It will come, or it will not."

"Oh, God!" She hiccoughed once. "I have such a dire foreboding! Sing to me, Tristan. Sing me a song to drive this fear away."

He cradled her in his arms and crooned her a lullaby. Soon her breathing slowed and she sank swiftly into an exhausted sleep. Dinadan pushed a cup of hot wine into Tristan's hand.

"Drink, Tris. You've had nothing for hours. You must be half frozen."

Tristan drained the cup and thanked him. "Listen," he said, cocking his head. "The storm has passed its peak. It's dying. Tomorrow the weather will break and the sun will shine."

Guvranyl grunted. "It's as strong as it ever was. Don't you hear that wind?"

Tristan smiled lightly. "Nevertheless, the worst is passed. I know storms. Ask Dinadan."

"Aye," Dinadan groaned. "Believe him. He listens to storms the way most men listen to bards. He can judge a storm to a hairsbreadth."

"Well," Guvranyl conceded, "I'll be glad to see the end of this one."

"Not I," Tristan said slowly. They both gaped at him. Tristan gathered the sleeping Essylte closer in his arms and sighed. "When the wind dies, the weather will turn. Within a fortnight the seas will open."

Guvranyl frowned. "Saxons?"

Tristan shook his head. "Mark."

"Markion doesn't need to wait until the seas are open," Dinadan objected. "It's a straight ride down from Cornwall."

"If he were willing to come alone, he'd have come by now," Tristan replied, still stroking Essylte's unbound hair. "He's waiting for his allies."

What allies?

Before Tristan could answer, the door pushed open and Pernam entered, his hands, face, and hair wet from a recent washing. Tristan stiffened and Essylte awoke. "Prince Pernam!"

Dinadan and Guvranyl made room on the bench and pushed a cup of wine into the healer's hand. Pernam accepted the hot drink and sat wearily next to Tristan.

Essylte laid a pleading hand upon his arm. "Please—please—tell me she is alive."

Pernam smiled kindly and took her hand in his. "I am happy to be able to do it. Branwen lives, my lady. It was a close thing, but we were able to stop the bleeding in time. She is very weak. I've sent to the kitchens, Tristan, to have marrow broth warmed for her. I didn't think you would object."

"Of course not." New tears spilled down Essylte's pale cheeks. Tristan pulled her head to his shoulder and looked at Pernam. "And the child?"

Pernam shook his head. "It died days ago. Even so, it fought against leaving her body. Poor, brave Branwen. Nothing to show for such a night of agony. She is rid of it now, but it nearly cost her her life."

"A son?" Tristan asked, and Essylte looked up, blurry-eyed.

"No. A daughter." Pernam stared into the fire, his expression carefully neutral. "She should have no more children. The next one will kill her, almost certainly."

Tristan said nothing. Essylte leaned toward Pernam eagerly. "May I see her? May I stay with her until morning? Lady Esmerée must be weary with nursing. I would be happy to take her place."

Pernam's eyes widened in surprise. He inclined his head. "My lady is very gracious to make the offer. I'm sure both Esmerée and Branwen would be most grateful for your attention. But you yourself, my lady Queen, look a little fatigued. Branwen has asked to see you, but it is not necessary that you stay."

Essylte smiled. "Branny doesn't care what I look like. I'm all right now that I know she will live. For a moment I—" She looked around at the men with a hunted expression. "I'm all alone here, except for Tristan. Branwen has been my companion since I was four years old. She's like a sister to me." She slid off Tristan's lap and took his hand. "Come, Tristan. We'll go see Branwen and make sure she takes her broth."

Branwen lay on a pallet under four thick wool blankets. Three braziers warmed the room to sweating point, and Esmerée, who rose to greet them, looked flushed with heat. Most traces of blood had been washed from the room, and Esmerée herself had clearly bathed and changed her robe. Essylte hugged her and thanked her warmly. At Pernam's nod, she withdrew gratefully to bed. Pernam spoke with Branwen, took her wrist in his hand, touched her forehead and her neck, then gave Tristan and Essylte permission to approach.

Tristan could not conceal his shock at the change in the girl. So wan, so wasted, she looked as if she had lost half her spirit as well as half her bulk. Essylte slid to the floor beside her and pressed Branwen's thin hand to her lips.

"Branny! Oh, Branny! Thank God you did not succumb with the poor little child. I will stay and nurse you until dawning. I don't want to be parted from you."

Branwen's mouth twitched in an attempt to smile. "And Tristan?"

Essylte glanced up at him and smiled. "He can wait. This time you come first. Do you remember the last time I nursed an invalid? I cured him of his sickness and his wounds, only to fall ill myself from love."

Branwen's eyes, dark in the shadows, gazed up at Tristan. "I remember."

"Well, I love you already, Branny. I need you. You will face the future with me, a new future, without Mark in it. We shall grow old and happy together."

"I doubt that," Branwen whispered, her eyes still on Tristan. "Your mother cursed me, Essylte."

"What?"

"Her curse has followed me like an arrow homing all these years. It nearly killed me. I must end it somehow."

"Branny, what are you talking about?"

Branwen sighed a shallow sigh and closed her eyes. "In a week's time I will be strong enough. In a week I will tell you. You and Tristan."

Essylte looked up at Tristan. "What is she talking about, do you know?"

"No. I know nothing about a curse."

Pernam stepped to the bedside and raised Essylte. "No more tonight. If you wish to nurse her, come to me after you've had rest and breakfast. I will tend her now. She must be still." He looked down at Branwen. "May the Mother guard her spirit. She is asleep."

By morning the storm had tailed away to breezes, and as Tristan had predicted, the weather turned. The west wind blew again, mild and fair, melted the snow and sent green shoots bursting from the mud. Branwen gained in strength day by day, until by week's end she could stand on the parapet in the sun for an hour at a time. The gowns she had worn before her pregnancy hung on her like someone else's clothes, but her cheeks were fuller, and the hollows above her collarbones less deep. Essylte delighted in her progress and spent hours each day at her side. There was no more mention of curses between them. Essylte had almost forgotten it when, on the evening of the sixth day, Branwen spoke.

"Tomorrow," she said, "at midday, I will come to Tristan's chamber. Let you both be there."

"She is so serious," Essylte told Tristan as they lay abed that night. "But I don't know what she wants or fears. It's odd, isn't it? All these years she's never said anything about a curse. Do you think—I've heard that people who undergo horrible pain can lose their wits—"

"Hush," Tristan said, pulling her closer. "Branwen's wits have always served her very well. I don't think she's mad. I think she has a plan."

"A plan for what?"

"Ah, sweet, that I don't know. But it strikes me that, since I've known you both, Branwen has never been without a plan."

The following day dawned cool and brisk, but out of the wind it was warm enough to sun without a cloak. Essylte rose early, but Tristan rose earlier, leading a party of his men to hunt in the hills. They returned near midday with two bucks and a young boar. Tired of cabbage, fish, and mutton jerky, the soldiers raised a cheer. Tristan slid into the sea to bathe, then hurried to his chamber. He found Essylte there before him, waiting on the parapet in a blue-green gown with her hair coiled neatly on her head and a slender golden torque around her throat.

"What's this? Dressed for a royal audience? It's only Branwen."

"Then why did you bathe and soap your hair?"

Tristan grinned. "I was filthy with boar's blood. We found a young male enjoying a good roll in the spring mud. We also got a good look north of the hills. No sign of Mark."

"Let me help you dress, Tristan. She'll be here soon. I don't want anyone but I looking on your nakedness." She came toward him, and he took her in his arms.

"You are spring itself, Essylte. With your sea eyes, your milk skin, your glorious curves"—he placed his hand upon the swell of her gown—"and this strong, energetic life growing within you, how could a man look at you and not want you?"

"Not now, Tristan. If Branwen finds us in each other's arms, she will be cross."

"Why should she? God in heaven, all the world knows of our love, and Branwen knows its strength better than most. Let her wait an hour." He kissed her hungrily.

"Wasn't it you who said," she managed between kisses, "that waiting intensifies the pleasure? Let *us* wait an hour, until she is gone."

A tap came at the door. Tristan released her, and Essylte tossed him a robe. "Quick! A robe, at least."

Tristan pulled it over his head. "Enter!"

A page peeked around the door. "The Lady Branwen," he announced, and disappeared.

"The *Lady* Branwen?" Tristan's eyebrows lifted.

Branwen walked in. She wore a gown of pale yellow, taken in to fit her slenderness. Her light brown hair, half coiled and braided, half hanging loose like a maiden's down her back, was dressed with ribbons and held with two pearl clips. Bracelets of etched gold adorned her wrists. She moved slowly, but there was dignity in her step. Weak as she was, she gave the impression not of frailty, but of strength. Both Tristan and Essylte stared openly at her.

"Branwen." Essylte stepped forward and took her hand. "Branny, you look lovely. And so richly dressed. Pray, what is the occasion? Are you celebrating something?"

Branwen's cool eyes met Essylte's. "The end of deceit, perhaps. As you told me yourself not long ago, the time to tell the truth is at hand." She looked at Tristan, standing barefoot in his robe, his boots and his hunting clothes in a clutter on the floor. "Have I come at an awkward time?"

"Not at all," Essylte said quickly, flashing Tristan a look. "Tristan was late getting in from the hunt, that's all. Come out into the sunshine, Branny. I'll bring a stool for you."

"Thank you, but I need no stool."

They stood on the parapet with the salt breeze in their faces, the silence between them growing awkward the longer it continued.

Tristan cleared his throat. "I'm amazed at your progress, Branwen. Are you feeling well?"

"Not well, my lord, but better, thank you." Branwen lifted her eyes to him. "I hear your hunt was successful and there will be fresh meat at dinner."

"Yes, we were lucky."

"Did you see any sign of Markion?"

"No. I kept lookouts posted. No sign."

"It is partly about Markion that I wish to speak with you. Are you prepared to kill him, Tristan?"

Tristan frowned. "Not unless he forces me to it."

"The fortress is alive with rumors that a fight between you is the only permanent solution, that it is what you aim at. That your abduction of the High Queen was the first step toward making yourself High King."

Tristan passed a hand across his eyes. "I have no ambition beyond Lyonesse. My break with Markion was over his treatment of Essylte and nothing more. I have told my men so."

"Then tell me, both of you, who know Markion nearly as well as I, if we tell him the truth, will he put Essylte aside and make me his Queen?"

Essylte gasped. "Branny! If only he would!"

Tristan frowned. "It's barely possible he may put Essylte aside if he thinks her too soiled now for his bed. But the other . . . No. Never."

Branwen nodded. "I agree. It might be different if I had borne him sons. But your mother cursed me with daughters, Essylte, and as a result, I have no claim on Markion."

"Is *that* what her curse was? But why did she curse you, Branny? Whatever did you do?"

"She wanted me to kill Tristan, and she gave me the tools to do it." Essylte cried out and reached for Tristan, whose arms accepted her without thought. Branwen regarded them without expression. "While he lived, she promised, all my children would be daughters. And so they have been. Now I can have no more." Her voice shook. "Every time you hold each other in your passion, or share a kiss in tenderness, you have me to thank. You have me to thank for Young Tristan, and for that boy in your belly. Every moment you have spent together since we left Gwynedd is my gift. I have sacrificed my future for your pleasure, because I loved you both."

Essylte began to weep, her arms around Tristan's waist. "Oh, Branny! My mother sent you to kill him? Then she would kill me as well!"

"Indeed, Branwen, we owe you everything." Tristan's lips moved stiffly. "So great a debt is impossible to repay."

Branwen's gray eyes darkened. "Nevertheless, the time has come to repay it. In the crisis that is coming there is only one way out without death, without dishonor. *You* will have to make the sacrifice this time. Both of you."

Essylte's weeping stilled. "What sacrifice?"

"Remember your vow to me, Tristan of Lyonesse." Branwen looked up at him defiantly. "Remember the vow you swore in Guvranyl's house as the price of my complicity in your deception. You vowed that when I found the lord I wished to marry, you would approve my choice and help me to my desire. Both of you. Whoever he was."

Tristan frowned. "I remember."

"No!" Essylte choked, reddening. "No!"

"Have you found him, then?" Tristan asked. "Who is he? I will do everything I can to arrange it for you."

Branwen squared her small shoulders and smiled lightly. "I am glad to have your word on it, my lord, for you are the man."

Essylte slid to the stone floor, sobbing. "Never! Oh, God! I knew it! I knew it all along!"

Tristan looked blankly at her. "Me?" Branwen's gaze did not falter. "But I am bound to Essylte."

"Only by love, and love does not come into this matter." Branwen smiled bitterly. "Oh, it is true enough that I have loved you, Tristan, since I first tended you in the sickroom in Gwynedd. And all these years I have watched Essylte touch you and kiss you and claim you for her own. I have hidden in the background, stifled my despair, and waited upon events. I have spared your life, and because of me you have known the love of this woman you cherish; you even have children by her. What more can a man ask than that, except perhaps for a glorious death?" At the dawning anguish in Tristan's eyes, her voice hardened. "You know perfectly well, both of you, that Markion will never let you marry. He would sooner kill you both than live with the name of cuckold whispered everywhere behind his back. He comes to kill you, because he knows you have betrayed him. Marry me, and you can yet allay his fears. Marry me, and let Essylte go back to him. All the children will be safe. Your son will live to be High King of Britain. The alliance with Wales will stand. It is easily accomplished. Mark will ask no questions because he won't want to know the answers. You have everything to gain and nothing to lose, except sole possession of Essylte's body. And you have had that long enough."

Essylte clung to Branwen's gown. "Don't, Branny! How could you ask it? Ask the sun for his light, ask the earth for her stone, before you ask such a thing of us."

Branwen looked down at her. "You are selfish, Essylte, to want more from this man than you've already had. Think of your children, whom Markion will kill when I tell him whose they are. Think of Tristan, who will die for your unbecoming greed. And if it is the thought of Markion's bed that stirs such terror in your soul, it is not something you can avoid in any case. I can bear no more children. There can be no more pretense. You will live through it. As I did."

"Devil! Demon! Witch! How can you be so cruel? You ask for more than I can give!"

"Nonsense. It's a lot less than I have already given. It is my turn now. And you have sworn it. Before God. Would you break your vow?"

Tristan stood as still as stone. On her knees, Essylte clasped her hands together and raised them to Branwen. "But he and I—we have sworn faith with one another. On our very lives. I cannot break that oath either."

"But you must. All our lives depend upon it."

Essylte leaped to her feet. "I will not! Who are you to demand this of me? I will keep my oath to Tristan and break my vow to you. I would rather leap into the sea than let you lie one night in Tristan's arms. Death is preferable to infidelity."

"Then die," Branwen snapped. "But that is the choice before you."

Essylte stamped her foot furiously. "You are not worthy of him!"

"No? For years everyone in Cornwall has thought him my lover."

"Worthy enough to warm his bed, perhaps, but not marriage. You— a serving maid, and a bastard one at that—you have no right to wed a prince."

"Hush, Essylte." Tristan reached for her hand.

Branwen's voice softened dangerously. "I wondered when we would come to that. You have always taken great pleasure in your superior birth, haven't you, Essylte? What a comfortable feeling it must be to have a low-born companion as your friend. How confident of your elevation it makes you feel! But I am not as lowborn as you like to think. Like my half brother Ceredig, I am one of Percival's bastards. I am the first of them. Your father is my father, Essylte of Gwynedd."

Essylte stared at her. For a long moment she could not breathe; then her breath exploded in a shriek. "You lie!"

Branwen reached into her pouch and drew forth a golden ring etched with the Gray Wolf of Gwynedd.

"That's my father's ring!" Essylte cried. "Where did you get it?"

"He gave it to me the night before we left. When he bid me farewell."

"He never did! You stole it!"

Branwen reached into her pouch again and withdrew a small folded paper. She handed it to Tristan. "Read this to her."

Tristan glanced at the writing and the seal. "Essylte," he whispered. "Percival himself verifies it. Branwen is your sister."

"No," Essylte cried, clinging to him. "It cannot be!"

"My sweet, it explains the likeness between you. It explains her fidelity, her willingness to link her future with yours, her ability to fool Mark. It explains everything. It must be true."

"Even so," Essylte wept, "she is not trueborn! She is not worthy to be your wife! Oh, Tristan, is there no way out? I will surely die if you marry anyone but me."

With one arm around Essylte's shaking shoulders, Tristan looked gravely at Branwen. "What you ask is difficult to accept. But I do not deny you have the right to ask it. Can you give us time, Branwen, to talk it over and thrash it out?"

Expressionless, Branwen nodded. "You have until Markion arrives. If you refuse me, Tristan, then you must kill him. There is no other way."

"Either way I am dishonored," Tristan whispered.

Branwen shrugged. "It is too late to think of honor. It was already too late that morning in Sir Guvranyl's house." Taking back her paper and her ring, she tucked them into her pouch, turned silently on her heel, and left.

"Tristan!" Essylte cried against his breast. "Don't ever leave me. I cannot be parted from you."

"My sweet Essylte." His lips came down on hers as his fingers pulled the pins from her hair. He held her as tight as he dared and pressed his cheek hard against hers. "I will never leave you. We are one. That cannot change."

"Swear," Essylte quavered. "Swear you will never wed any woman but me. Swear it now."

He lifted her in his arms and carried her to the bed. "We are fated, Essylte. We are two sides of a single coin. If ever I marry, it will be to no one but you. This I swear."

28 † STORM WINDS

Three hundred horsemen thundered down from the hills in the cold, gray dawn. They heard nothing over the steady drumming of hooves as they raced toward land's end, for fog lay thick upon the sea, stifling even the thud and hiss of breakers. Mist skulked along the valley bottoms, snaked into crevices and gullies, writhed in pale, twisted fingers across the road to cloak their way. At the last moment they saw the ragged cliff edge. The dark gates of Lyon's Head sprang out at them. The horses screamed, rearing, as blasts sounded from the lookouts' horns.

"Beware! Beware! Horses!"

"Ho, there! Grayell! It's me, Regis of Caer Conan! Open the gates, for God's sake!"

Sir Grayell fought to recover his wits. The horsemen had come out of the mist between one breath and the next, like nightmare apparitions, and it was moments before he recognized the voice. "Dornal, Geoff, Hargas, to the gates! Quick, lads! Ho, Regis! How many are you?"

"Three hundred. Filas and Dynas have brought their men with mine, and we've fifty archers with us."

"Oh, good man!" Grayell slapped the neck of Regis's sweated horse as the gates opened. "Best dismount and lead him across. The road's only wide enough for one at a time, and if he spooks at the mist, you're lost."

Regis grinned as he slid to the ground. "Oh, aye, I remember the first time I crossed it. So precarious a stretch of rock—I wonder the sea hasn't beaten it down."

"God is holding it up for Tristan," Grayell replied solemnly. "God loves that man. There's no other explanation for the fact that he's still alive."

Regis grunted. "He'd better love him well, or we're all dead men."

"Trouble?" Grayell frowned. "Were you followed?"

"No, no. We sneaked out in the wee hours, but Markion knows well enough where we've gone."

Halfway across the rock bridge, Grayell turned and looked swiftly behind him. "So the High King's in Lyonesse at last?"

"Camped just beyond the hills. Be here tonight."

"So," Grayell breathed, "the confrontation has finally come. Tristan wants no bloodshed, but me—I think a hard, cleansing battle is what we need."

"Well, you're likely to get your wish."

"You've got to help us convince him, Regis, to take Markion's crown. It's his by right. You've got to make him see that."

"Why else am I here?" Regis cried. "You don't mean that Tristan doesn't want the Kingship?"

"That's exactly what I mean."

"Hold up, man! Are you jesting? Why else did he take the Queen and all her household to Lyonesse, if not to force Cornwall to that choice?"

"He loves her," Grayell replied levelly. "That's what this war is all about, to Tristan. The Queen. Nothing more."

Regis snorted. "Isn't that just like him? It's a mood. It will pass."

"I'm not so sure."

"Well, put it to him thus: Markion's her husband. If he wants her, he'll have to kill the old bastard and take his place."

"How many of Markion's men are loyal? I mean, truly loyal? Would fight for him to their death?"

"A handful. The rest will fight for the High King. Whoever he is."

"Then our course is clear," Grayell said slowly. "We must persuade Tristan to kill Markion."

"My God," Regis breathed. "I can't believe it will take persuasion. You'd think he'd jump at the chance."

The fair-haired guard unlocked the dungeon gate and let Branwen in. She shivered as she entered and pulled her cloak tighter. All about her, stone walls sweated moisture. She could feel the damp chill in her bones.

"Where is he?" she demanded, using anger to keep fear at bay.

The guard gestured. "Over here, my lady. He's the only one we've got."

He unlocked a low door and pushed it open. Light from a high window fell on the cracked stone floor, throwing half of the small cell into shadow. Something scurried in the corner. Branwen jumped. A squat figure rose from a bench and came toward her.

"Well, well. Good morning, Branwen. How good of you to visit me."

Branwen shuddered as Segward stepped into the light. He had dropped flesh in his imprisonment, and his mottled, livid skin hung in folds from his jaw. His small eyes had lost their greedy glitter and stared at her devoid of all amusement, hard and mean.

"You know why I came," she answered coldly.

His lips drew back from his teeth in a mirthless smile. "Pretty Branwen." He lifted a pudgy finger to her cheek, and she jerked away. "Not so lovely anymore, my dear. Too thin. Too pale. Too hard a life, is it, for such a delicate flower? Too stifling for you, pet, to serve such witless beauty day in, day out?" He chuckled wickedly. "You're worth three of her any day. We both know that."

Branwen kept her eyes on the shadowed corner. "You threatened Esmerée. You told her you would kill her daughter if I did not come."

"Not any daughter. Just the youngest. Tristan's brat." A shadow of amusement flicked across his face and was gone. "And what is it to you if the child dies? One bastard more or less can make no difference."

"You're a bastard yourself, Segward."

He laughed. "You're worth ten of them, you are. You've been studying me, haven't you? And you've had me watched since first you came to Cornwall. I knew that. I admired it. We're two of a kind, you and I."

Branwen shuddered. "Never."

"Ah, but we are." He settled himself on the bench again, and Branwen breathed more easily. "You've been my only opposition worth the name. And I may say you've been a masterful foe at times. We *are* alike. I, too, have wasted years in serving a brainless prince who listens with half an ear to my advice. I did it for power. I admit it. Why did you do it, Branwen?"

"Is this why you brought me down here? To ask me questions? Make me your proposition, Segward, and have it over. I'm cold and the stink of this place is making me sick."

He stiffened. "I'm not fond of the climate, either. But you've borne worse." His voice sank, and the hairs stood up on the nape of Branwen's neck. "You've held that scarred old ox in your pretty white arms, when he came to you straight from the drinking hall, stinking of dogs and mead. You've seen him so drunk he could only stagger, you've seen him with vomit in his beard. He's not your husband and he never will be, but you let him put his hands on you, you let him use your body, you let him pound you like one of his ewes in heat. And you've never uttered even a single word of complaint."

Branwen stared at him. Her throat went dry. She put out a trembling hand and felt for the wall behind her.

Segward nodded. "I know you've been in Mark's bed. You've been there from the beginning and she has not."

"Who told you?" Branwen croaked.

"No one. No one else suspects. I worked it out myself."

"How?"

He showed his teeth in a smile. "Close, steadfast observation."

Branwen leaned against the cold stone wall as beads of sweat formed along her brow. Her voice came out in a whisper. "You're very clever. For a bastard."

"Yes. I am. But then, bastards have to be. Don't we?"

Branwen clutched at her cloak. "What do you want of me?"

"First, I want to know why you've put up with serving that royal bitch all these years. Then I'll tell you what I want of you."

"There's no need to malign her. I don't hate her. It's not her fault her mother was married to Percival while mine was not. She may be unthinking, but she's not mean."

Segward whistled. "So *that's* who you are. I ought to have guessed. That's how you were able to fool Mark."

Branwen nodded. "But no longer."

"Oh, no. The game's up. Still, you haven't told me why you stay in the Queen's shadow when you could push her aside with a word and stand in the sun."

"Could I?" Branwen smiled bitterly. "Like you, Segward, I wanted power. And even you don't know how much power I had. He talked with me, you know, as he waited for sleep. He told me all his plans. And I advised him. He valued my advice as much as yours—more, at times." She looked away, and her lips compressed in a tight line. "And he never realized, when he spoke to Essylte in daylight, that she had not the faintest comprehension of his meaning. He never could see beyond her skin, her eyes, her hair."

Segward's cold eyes gleamed. "If she was in your way, why didn't you destroy her? Disfigure her? Dishonor her? Tell Mark the truth?"

"I was waiting—until I bore him a son."

"Of course."

"And now—" She cleared her throat as her voice grew tremulous. "Now I never will. What use has he for a bastard daughter? If he learns the truth, he will kill us both."

"So," Segward suggested in a soft voice, "we must be careful that he does not learn the truth, mustn't we?"

Branwen looked at him steadily. "What do you want?"

"In exchange for your life, my pretty princess? What price to place upon your freedom? A very big price, certainly."

"I can get you out of here."

Segward smiled gently. "I am all but out already. Esme, bless her naive and honorable soul, got the naive and honorable King of Lyonesse to promise me a hearing before Markion. I trust my wits to win my freedom after that. No, no, I am thinking along the lines of something a priest once read me, about taking vengeance, about demanding a life for a life."

"An eye for an eye," Branwen whispered. She swallowed in a dry throat. "You want me to kill someone?"

Segward's smile slid into a snarl. "Who has been the bane of my existence since Markion became High King? Who is the only man who can oust Mark from Cornwall? Who was brazen enough to seduce Esmerée behind my back, and foist his bastard on me?" His voice rose. "Who slipped out of every trap I set him? Who turned Markion against me? Who stuck me in this godforsaken hole? That fornicating hypocrite! Damn him! I won't rest until I dance upon his grave!"

Branwen turned away. Tears slid down her pale cheeks as her eyes stared unseeing at the wall. "Tristan," she whispered, clutching at her cloak with trembling fingers. "It is you, again. It has always been you. I can't escape it. I have known it from the start."

Esmerée curtsied to the floor. "Tristan, I am at your service."

Tristan waved his chamberlain away and smiled as the door closed. "Esme, thank you for coming so promptly. I knew I could rely on you." He took her hands in his and lifted them to his lips. "You know that Mark is here. In Lyonesse. That he is coming this evening to Lyon's Head."

She met his gaze steadily. "The castle is afire with rumors. I am glad to have this news confirmed."

"I've spent all morning with men who have come from his camp. Things are moving swiftly now, and I may not have time to speak with you again. That's why I sent for you."

Her grip tightened on his hands. "Pernam says the soldiers want to make you High King in Markion's place. They want you to kill him."

"Some do."

"Tristan—"

"No, Esme, I won't. It's not Mark's crown I want, it's his wife. We will see when he gets here what he'll ask for in exchange."

Esmerée's eyes filled with tears. "You think Mark will *negotiate*? Tristan, when did he ever? He's come to punish you, nothing more."

"And to get his wife back."

"Only to punish you," she whispered. "He cannot want her now."

"Yes," Tristan said softly, "I count on that."

Esmerée looked quickly away. "Fool's dreams. My dear love, what are you thinking? What can you offer Markion in exchange for Essylte that he cannot take by force? Oh, Tristan, escape now, while there is still time! He will never let you live!"

Tristan walked to the chest where his swordbelt lay and solemnly buckled it about his hips. "If it comes to force, there's not a swordsman in his army who can best me. He will have to kill me if he wants her."

Esmerée smiled bitterly as tears slipped down her cheeks. "You young fool! All he has to do to best you is hold a dagger to Essylte's throat. And he will if you do not crawl on your belly and beg his forgiveness."

"Is that what you want me to do?"

"No. No. Of course not." She closed her eyes and exhaled slowly. "I don't see any way around it, Tristan. He is your liege lord, your uncle, and High King of Britain. You cannot kill him; he cannot let you live. You must escape or die."

"I have a plan," he breathed. "This is the service I need of you. Go to Dinadan and tell him to have the boat made ready. It is all but done—they are only awaiting my final order. If we need to, we will flee from here tonight, Essylte, the child, and I."

"Boat? What boat?"

"I thought you must have seen it. I sailed it all along your coast last summer. It's faster than anything Mark can put to sea. I've had it readied for a sea voyage, as a last resort."

Her eyes widened. "And you would trust Essylte and the child to such a craft?"

He nodded. "You're no sailor, or I'd tell you why. It doesn't matter, Esme. But I've no time now to get Dinadan alone, and this must be kept a secret. I spent most of last night explaining it to Essylte. She is ready, and she will have our son ready if the time comes. Just tell Dinadan to oversee the preparations of the boat himself. Can you do that and not be overheard?"

"Of course I can." She took his face in her hands and gazed into his eyes. "So that is what you meant when you said you might not have time to speak to me again. You meant, ever again."

"Yes." He drew her into his arms. "Lovely Esmerée, you know I hold you in my heart and always will. If I leave—before I leave—I will rid you of your husband. I have had my scribe prepare a document that grants you all his lands. Pernam has it now. If I leave, I will see that Mark vouchsafes that promise. You and your daughters will have a place to live. I've given Pernam some things of mine for them, and gold for their dowries. They are a king's granddaughters, after all."

Esmerée pressed her face into his tunic, trembling with unvoiced sobs. He touched her hair lightly. "There is another service I would ask of you."

"Anything," she whispered.

"Attend Essylte. Since her break with Branwen she has had only house servants by her, and none of them is a confidant. She is frightened, Esme.

For me, she puts on a brave face, but it is only skin deep. Stay with her until all this is settled. Give her what peace you can."

Esmerée pulled away from him and lifted her face to his. "I shall comfort her as if she were my sister. Oh, Tristan, my dear friend." She pulled his head down and kissed his lips. "My prayers go with you always, gentle Orpheus. Take her safely out of Hell if it is in your power. I wish you both safe passage to a better world."

"In Heaven or in Hell, she will be with me. This Mark cannot alter. Alive or dead, we will be together."

At dusk the lamplighters went out from Lyon's Head to light the torches along the narrow, rocky causeway connecting the island fortress to the landward cliffs of Lyonesse. From her chamber window Branwen looked across the watery chasm at the gathered armies on the cliff. The darkening mass of men and horses quivered and writhed like a live thing, breathing torch flames, stuck all over with banners and spears. She shut her eyes to block out the image. So many men, all come against Tristan. Thanks to that narrow causeway, they could come at him only one at a time. But the reverse was also true: He could attack them only one at a time as well.

She turned from the window and lifted the candle stand from the table. Drawing a deep breath, she walked to the small chest in the corner of her chamber. Amid the intricate curling vines carved upon the lid was a wolf's head, fangs bared. The Gray Wolf of Gwynedd. The chest had accompanied her all the way from Wales. It contained everything she owned. Essylte had three of them twice as large.

She lifted the lid and knelt down beside the chest, bringing her candle closer. At the bottom, tucked under her neatly folded clothing, was a small carved box inlaid with mother-of-pearl. She opened it and drew out a soft leather bag tied at the neck with a golden cord. With slow, deliberate fingers she untied the knot and drew out three small linen bags, one crimson, one green, one black. She sat back on her heels and considered them carefully. The cold voice of remembrance whispered in her ear: *Use them well. If you are as wise as I think you are, you will live a future that you choose.* Segward. Mark. Esmerée. Tristan and Essylte. She closed her eyes and let her breath out slowly. Two large tears crept from under her lids and slid, one by one, down her wasted cheeks. After a moment she opened her eyes and tucked one of the bags in the breast of her gown.

Horns sounded at the gate. King Markion and twelve companions rode forward from the armies, stopped before the drawn swords of Tristan's sentries and dismounted. Sir Grayell gave the signal, and the gates of Lyon's Head swung open. Markion stared at the guards. No one met his eyes; no one saluted. He lifted his hand and led the twelve men through the gates in single file, across the causeway, through the open gates at the other end, and onto the island fortress of Lyon's Head. A company of soldiers closed ranks around them, bearing torches, and lit their way through the curving streets and paved courtyards to the very doors of Tristan's castle.

Once inside, Tristan's seneschal led them to the great pillared hall, now lit by a hundred torches and filled with men. Markion searched the sea of faces as the crowd parted to let them through. A few of the soldiers bowed; some only inclined their heads. Most stood unmoving and looked away. With his head high and his face stiff with the effort of control, Markion walked across the room to the dais where Tristan waited for him.

Standing alone, dressed simply in dark cloth and boots, wearing no ornament but the slender crown of Lyonesse and no weapon but his father's sword, Tristan reminded Markion so forcibly of Meliodas that the High King unthinkingly slowed his step. Tristan came down off the dais, and with every eye upon him, bent his knee to the ground and bowed his head.

"Welcome, my lord and uncle, to Lyonesse."

Markion stared down at the dark head for a long moment. "I banished you, Tristan. You and that old goat Guvranyl. What are you doing here?"

Tristan rose. "You cannot banish me from Lyonesse. It is not yours to give or take away. It was my father's gift."

"I am your King," Markion snarled softly. "Or have you forgotten the oath you made me?"

"I've not forgotten. I owe you service."

"Wise man," Markion snapped. "You've not enough men to defy me."

"I have more than you think," Tristan replied softly. "And some of them ride under your banner even now. Think twice, Uncle, before you try to oust me from my birthright."

"Do you dare to threaten me?"

For answer, Tristan shrugged.

"What are you doing holed up in Lyonesse with my wife and my son? Why have you defied me?"

"I will see justice done."

"Justice!" Markion looked around defiantly at the sea of hostile faces. He glanced behind him at his twelve cloaked companions. "Justice for whom? Who has been unjustly treated? Besides me?"

Tristan's gaze turned so suddenly fierce that again Markion was brought up short. But the reply, when it came, was whisper soft. "Queen Essylte."

Markion stiffened. For the first time he noticed the small group of women standing to one side. Essylte herself stood at the edge of the dais, hands folded demurely under the curve of her belly, the sweep of her sea-green gown accenting the color of her eyes, her bright hair braided in a halo around her face and bound with a royal band of silver across her brow. Although she stood perfectly still as she met his eyes, he had the impression of whirlwind movement, of fierce emotion, sharp as a knife thrust.

"I did not come here to talk about women," Markion growled.

"In that case," Tristan replied easily, "we have no argument between us. Put the Queen formally aside and I am yours to command."

"You are mine to command in any event!" Markion flared. "I am your King! That woman is still my Queen. I have no intention of putting her away. But I want her gone from this hall while I speak with you."

Tristan beckoned to Essylte, who came forward to stand at his side. "But she is what we have to speak about. Understand me, Mark. I did not bring her here from Tintagel to defy you or to grab your power or to start a war between us—"

"As if I would fight over a woman!"

"I brought her here for safekeeping. To protect her. From you."

Markion barked a short laugh. "False words from a false heart! She is safe enough from me. I've told her so." His eyes narrowed. "*You're* the one who can't leave her alone. Give her to me, give me back my son, and prove to me you don't want my crown."

Tristan's hand leaped unthinkingly to his sword hilt, but Essylte touched his arm quickly and he paused.

"Raise your sword against me, would you?" Markion cried. "Segward was right about you after all, Tristan of Lyonesse! You're a traitor in your soul." He flung back the edges of his crimson cloak and held his arms out. "See? No sword, no dagger. The High King of Britain comes naked into your stronghold."

Tristan's hand relaxed to his side. "You're in no danger from me. Nor from my men."

"You abduct my heir, you steal my wife, you turn half my men against me, and you expect me to believe you don't want war?" He gestured to the sea of soldiers. "Why are *they* here, then? I know them all. They used to serve me. You're just like your father—what you have is never enough!"

"I tell you, I don't want war. I don't covet your lands. I don't covet the crown of Britain. Do these soldiers frighten you? I will send them away. I want only one thing from you, Markion—"

"Yes! Segward warned me! You want your birthright back!"

Utter silence followed. Markion's face flamed as he realized what he had said.

"You admit it, then. You admit you stole my birthright when you stole my father's crown."

Markion's glance flicked swiftly from side to side. "I admit nothing. A king is moved by necessity."

Tristan drew a long breath and let it out slowly. His features hardened. "This king is moved by necessity as well. I will not return the Queen and her son. By your own hand you put them in jeopardy. I have saved them from it. Now they are mine to protect."

"No, son." A voice spoke behind Markion, and everyone turned. "They are mine."

One of Markion's companions stepped forward and dropped his cloak. Essylte gasped and sank to her knees. "Father!"

"So that's who you were waiting for," Tristan breathed. "Percival!"

29 ⊕ TRISTAN'S LEAP

"I think," Percival of Gwynedd said quietly, "it would be best to clear the hall."

Tristan nodded and gave the order. Grudgingly, the crowd of men filed out until only a handful remained: Guvranyl, Dinadan, Pernam, Loholt the seneschal, Grayell and two of his lieutenants, and the men who had marched in with Markion. A few women huddled by the door next to the servants.

The two factions faced one another. Bruenor scowled at Dinadan, who would not meet his eyes. Percival stood between them with his arm around Essylte.

"Now, my lords, it is time for talk." Percival dragged a chair from the dais, settled it among the rushes on the floor and sat Essylte upon it. "Let's have no talk of banishment or treason. We are all honorable men. Let us discuss this matter with calm and decorum." He looked at Tristan. "You said, my lord, there was only one thing you wanted from Markion. What is it?"

Tristan swallowed. "My lord . . ."

"Well?"

Tristan spread his hands out helplessly. "Does my lord have to ask? I want your daughter."

"Of all the—" Markion began, red-faced.

Percival held up a hand and silenced him. "You want my daughter, Essylte? Markion's wife and High Queen of Britain? What gives you the right to ask for such a gift? Or to take it without her husband's leave?"

"She is a daughter of your royal house, my lord, not a thief, not a traitor, and yet he treats her like mud beneath his boots. He treats his dogs with more compassion! He has shamed her publicly, he who should hold her honor dearer than his own."

Percival's face was grave. "I have heard you deny you want his crown. And yet you must know that Markion's marriage to Essylte has brought him alliance with all Wales. If he gave her up to you, what do you think would happen to that alliance? Who would be High King of Britain, then?"

Color washed Tristan's face. "My lord," he said earnestly, "let him keep the crown. Let him marry a daughter of Strathclyde, of Lothian, of Elmet. Let him form what alliance he will. I tell you truth: I do not want to be High King."

"Yet you would wed the High Queen. Like it or not, you would be Markion's rival outright. He would have to kill you, or you him, before the land could be at peace. Britain would be split right down the middle. Is that what you want?"

"Of course not. Britain would not be split if Wales—if you ally yourself with Markion for the kingdom's sake. Nothing has to change."

"Ahhh," Percival said softly, glancing at Essylte. "Then she agrees to leave her son behind?"

Essylte shot a desperate look at Tristan. His face had gone white, his eyes enormous. Percival continued in his gentle voice. "Why do you think I am allied with Markion? Why do you think Powys, Dyfed, Northgallis, and Guent follow my lead? You have eyes, lad. Surely you can see. They have no love for Markion. They live for the day my grandson, a son of Gwynedd, becomes High King of Britain. He is the legacy I leave behind me. Take that from me, and I am your sworn enemy, not your ally."

Tristan passed a tongue over dry lips. "I'm not an ambitious man, my lord Percival. Ask anyone who knows me. I've no wish to diminish Markion. Let your grandson be High King. Let Markion rule until his dying day. But let his mother raise the boy, and let her live with me." He met Percival's gaze directly. "I love her more than life, my lord. That is what drives me. Not ambition."

"I knew it!" Markion cried, raising a fist in the air. "I knew it all along!"

Percival looked at him coldly and touched Essylte's hair. "My daughter is precious to me. But she accepted Markion, without condition, and a man may treat his wife how he will. I cannot countenance your desire, Tristan, much as I understand it. I—"

"My lord!" Tristan cried. "He put her to the fire! At the winter solstice! In public!"

Percival stared at him blankly. "He *what*?"

"Did you not know? Did Markion not tell you that when he called you south against me? Did he fill your head with lies about my villainy and hide the truth of his? *That* is why I took her from Tintagel!"

The blood left Percival's face. "Essylte, is this true?"

"Yes," she said evenly, looking straight at Markion. "It is true. He himself held my hand in the flame until the flesh stank. Until the bishop wept."

Percival took her hands and lifted them into the light. "But they are perfect. Unharmed. Unblemished."

She looked up at him. "That's Branny's doing, Father. She gave me a salve to protect me when we discovered what the vicious brute meant to do."

Color returned to Percival's face. "Branwen!"

"A trick!" Markion cried excitedly. "It wasn't a true test after all! She tricked me!"

"Damn you!" Percival roared, dropping Essylte's hands and whirling on Markion. "How dare you treat my daughter so? I've killed men for less, and so have you. Is *this* how the High King of Britain treats his Queen? You *burned* her? As a *test*?"

"She's *not* burned," Markion retorted. "She tricked me. She's told me lie upon lie for years. There's no truth in her, my lord! All I wanted from her was truth."

Essylte bowed her head and wept. Tristan stepped to her side and took her hands in his. She pressed her face into his tunic to hide her tears.

"Look at them!" Markion shrieked, pointing. "If they are not lovers, I am King of Rome!"

Percival turned and regarded them. "Essylte, my daughter," he said softly.

She raised her face to him, eyes swimming. "I love him, Father, I love him more than life."

"I told you! I told you!" Markion sputtered, beside himself. "Your bitch of a daughter has made a cuckold of me!"

Percival's hand flew to his sword hilt and stopped, shaking. "Guard your tongue, Cornishman! My men lie between you and Britain. If I join forces with Tristan, you'll be trapped between us. So speak my daughter fair. Without me, you're just a prince of Cornwall."

Markion gulped hastily. "But they've both been false from the beginning—your daughter and my nephew. Segward has known all about it for years. He warned me a thousand times. Where's that fat peasant when I need him? He's had them watched—he can tell you the truth of it."

Percival hesitated, glancing from Tristan to Markion to Essylte and back again. "Where is Lord Segward?"

"At this minute, in my dungeon," Tristan said slowly. "It was his idea to burn the Queen alive before her subjects. When she foiled his plans and defied the flames, Markion banished him to Lyonesse and I imprisoned him. I will send for him if you like, but do not expect to hear truth from his lips. He is not called 'the Snake' for nothing."

Percival's hand, still trembling, fell slowly to his side. "Nevertheless, I will hear what he has to say."

Tristan nodded. Sir Grayell signaled to his lieutenants, who left just as the door opened to admit the wine bearers.

"Father," Essylte whispered, holding hard to Tristan's hands, "I am no adulteress! Segward the Snake will tell you so, but it is not true. I am clean of that sin."

Percival frowned. "I am aware of Lord Segward's motives. As now I am of yours. Let me listen to him. Then I will listen to you."

Before long they heard the guards returning. Segward bowed low in the doorway, his small eyes flicking around the hall.

"My lords! What a mighty gathering is this!" His lips stretched in a smile, but the watchful expression in his eyes did not waver. "King Percival, I am honored to bask in your presence once again, and hope your journey south was an easy one. My lord Markion." He knelt stiffly on the ground as he reached for Markion's hand and kissed his ring. "Too long a time, my good lord, we have been parted. Ah, but your nephew is an unforgiving man! This long winter in the dungeon has frozen all my joints. I can hardly move. And I wonder, as I weep my way to sleep, whatever have I done to offend the good Sir Tristan? Kept my wife under lock and key, perhaps?"

Tristan said nothing but looked pointedly at Percival.

"Tell him," Markion growled, raising him. "Tell him all you know about Tristan and my Queen."

Segward's smile broadened. "Oh, no, my lord! Not now, surely. It would take more than a night to tell it all. And here they both are, who would blush to hear told to others what they have so long kept a secret between themselves."

Percival stiffened. "I'm afraid we must hear it, Lord Segward, if you can discipline yourself to be brief about it."

Segward grinned as he bowed. "I am so afraid, my lord king, that the tale of Tristan and Essylte does not lend itself to brevity. But if you like, I shall begin."

A cloaked servant stepped into their midst with a tray bearing six cups of wine. Essylte, blurry-eyed, waved the woman away, but Tristan reached for the two nearest cups and pushed one into Essylte's hand. She accepted it meekly. Percival glanced at the servant in annoyance and then froze. Two cool hazel-gray eyes looked up at him from inside her hood. She glanced, once, down at a golden cup. He took it. She nodded, just a dip of the chin, as she turned away. Markion lifted the nearest cup without even looking at it, his eyes fixed on Tristan. Two cups remained on the tray as she approached Segward, one of carved horn, the other of beaten silver. Segward squinted at the face inside the hood and raised his eyebrows.

"I do like your spirit," he murmured, too low for the others to hear. "But you have to get up early in the day to get the better of me. I suppose mine is the silver one?"

She lowered her eyes demurely. "Whatever my lord wills."

"Who's the other cup for?"

"For me, my lord." Her eyes flicked momentarily to his. "I have a right to it."

Segward grinned and grabbed the horn cup. "Go on, then. Take it." Her hand shook as she took the silver cup and Segward smiled.

Percival raised his goblet. "Let us all drink together to Britain's future."

"To Britain!" Markion and Tristan echoed his cry and drank. Segward paused, his eyes fastened on Tristan's face. Tristan's eyes narrowed. His lips pursed. He shuddered and stared down in consternation at his winecup. With a silent chuckle, Segward raised his cup to the cloaked woman and downed his wine.

"The wine's amiss," Tristan warned, taking Essylte's cup from her hand. "Don't drink it."

"Mine was all right," Markion declared.

"And mine." Percival pointed. "What's the matter with Segward?"

Everyone turned. Segward staggered, clutching at his throat, his eyes bulging. He gagged once and fell to the floor. His limbs convulsed uncontrollably, heels drumming on stone. Froth formed on his lips as he stared wildly up at the cloaked woman with the silver cup. "Bitch!" he croaked. Urine spread in a dark stain across his leggings, and Segward lay still.

"My God!" Markion cried. "What ails the man?"

Tristan frowned. "He's dead."

Everyone crowded around. Someone shouted for the physician, others shouted for a litter, for water, for guards. In the confusion, the cloaked servant withdrew. Women pushed through the throng, led by Esmerée.

"He is mine to tend," she said, dry-eyed. "Put him on the litter and follow me. I will prepare him." The guards obeyed, and soon the hall emptied for the second time.

"What happened to him?" Markion wondered, standing over the soured straw. "I've never seen such a fit come upon him. Was he poisoned? Where's the maid who gave him the wine?"

Percival, moving slowly like a man in sleep, lifted the horn cup from the floor and sniffed it. "There's nothing here but dregs. It smells all right.

He chose the cup with his own hand, Markion. I saw him. The maid never poisoned him. He probably fell ill from vapors in the dungeon."

"Yes," Tristan agreed coolly. "It's always damp. What a pity."

Markion shot him a swift look. "He's been in the dungeon all winter, he said. But he didn't take ill until he was about to reveal what he knew about *you*! Vapors be damned! You killed him."

Tristan stared at him blankly. "I? How?"

"That girl—there was something familiar about her. She served your ends—she served *you*!"

"If I had wanted to kill Segward," Tristan said evenly, "I could have done so anytime this winter. No one would have missed him. Not even you."

"He knew the truth about you!" Markion cried. "You have been lying with my wife behind my back!" Markion's fists bunched. Sir Bruenor laid a hand upon his arm, but Markion shrugged him off. "It's been your plan from the beginning—I see it now. Too cowardly to challenge me outright for my crown, you bed my Queen—the two-faced little bitch—to plant your seed in *my* garden, to foist your ill-begotten brood upon *me*—"

Percival's hand dropped to his sword hilt as Tristan's blade whipped from its scabbard. Markion stopped in midsentence, the point of Tristan's sword at his throat. The harsh slither of metal echoed around the hall as ten swords lifted in Markion's defense. Tristan's guards ran forward from the doors, drawing their weapons, and Sir Grayell and his men raised their naked blades at Tristan's side.

"Be still about the Queen." Tristan's voice trembled. "If another slander passes your lips, uncle or no, King or no, I will kill you and take what comes to me. Do you hear me?"

Markion's eyes slid left and right. "So this is how you treat the High King of Britain. I came unarmed into your stronghold as your guest. I might have known that a son of Meliodas would care more for a woman than for honor."

At the mention of his father's name, Tristan's sword point pressed against Markion's flesh. "You tread on dangerous ground, Uncle. More than one man in this room knows why my father died."

Markion's face flushed a deep, dusky red. "Lies! Slander! I was abed with a fever when Gaels attacked him. Do not lay his death at my door! Look to your own honor, Tristan, before you seek to tarnish mine."

Tristan withdrew the sword, and Markion bent quickly, a hand to his boot. Essylte screamed. Tristan twisted away as the hand came up, blocking the knife thrust with the hilt of his sword. "Take that!" Markion bellowed, striking again. "You stinking traitor!"

Everyone shouted. Blades flashed openly. Percival fought desperately to get between the angry men. Without warning, a torch appeared, thrust between the sword blades, blinding the combatants. Everyone backed away a step.

"Gentlemen," Pernam said gravely, "this is not a contest of champions. Put up. Put up."

"You heard him!" Markion screamed. "He's betrayed me!"

"Yes, and I heard you, too, brother, admit how you treated the wife who brought you your kingdom."

"Tristan!" Essylte wailed. "Tristan's wounded!"

Heads turned. A dagger protruded from the fleshy muscle of Tristan's upper arm. Essylte lifted a hand to the hilt, but Tristan stopped her.

"No, heart, it's little more than a scratch, but let Pernam do it. Knife wounds are child's play to him."

Pernam ripped a strip of cloth from his robe and bound Tristan's arm as he pulled the dagger out. He hefted the blood-bright weapon in his hand. The handle was black enamel chased with silver in the shape of a boar.

"I know this dagger of old." He looked up at Markion. "It is yours, brother. Do you deny it?"

"Certainly I do not," Markion retorted. "He attacked me. He had his sword point at my throat! After I showed him I was unarmed. He invited me into Lyon's Head and then attacked me—I, his sovereign lord. He deserves a slow, cruel death. He's betrayed me. He's betrayed Britain."

Pernam's eyebrows gently lifted. "Unarmed?"

"He didn't know I had it! Yet he attacked me!"

"Perhaps," Pernam replied softly, "he knows you well enough not to trust you. We've had enough argument for one night, I think. Let us go to our rest and let our tempers cool. I have a feeling the situation will be clearer in the morning." He handed Markion the dagger. "Shall I send for torchbearers to light you on your way?"

"No need," Markion growled. "We are not leaving the fortress. We'll stay the night in Lyon's Head. And I'll keep my wife with me."

"Never!" Essylte cried, backing away. "Father, don't let him touch me! You have seen the kind of man he is! He would slay his own kinsman, who protects me. Tristan did not attack him—do you see a mark on the King? A drop of blood? But look!" She gestured toward Tristan's bloody sleeve as her tears began to fall. "Look how my lord bleeds from his wound! I swear before God I will throw myself from the tower before I consent to be alone with Markion."

Percival scowled at the High King. "Until I have the truth of it, let no one lie with the Queen." He glanced sternly from uncle to nephew. "Not Tristan. Not Markion. Swear your oaths on it."

Markion's face was red with anger. "You can't rely on words! He has no honor—he promises one thing and does another. He'd sell his very soul for a night in her arms."

Percival's lips thinned. "Very well. I'll station one of my men outside her door, and another outside his. You do the same. In the morning we will sit down together, without weapons, and discover the truth." He looked around doubtfully at all the angry faces. "If we can behave like civilized men."

Clouds covered the stars and the moon had set. The sea heaved and thrashed against unseen rocks, a vast, seething presence unlit by a single reflected glimmer. The great fortress melted into the surrounding dark, more felt than seen by the dozing sentries on the battlements. High above their heads, pressed hard against the cold, unforgiving wall, a shadowy human form inched across the seaward rock face.

Tristan dared not look down. He focused every fiber of his concentration on finding the next toehold, the next finger grasp, the next outcrop of undressed rock that would support a man's knee and grant him time to regain his breath. He recognized the foolhardiness of his endeavor. No one in his right mind would attempt it in daylight, never mind at night. But he also recognized that what drove him would not be silenced, could not be denied, was blind to reason and deaf to argument. There would be no peace for him in life if he did not reach her window.

Essylte knelt by the edge of her bed, hands clasped tight together. If he did not come, she would never see his face again. If he did not come, she would lose her wits by morning or she would die. What would death be like? Was it so greatly to be feared? Perhaps it was only a dark night wind that lifted the soul and swept it out to sea, light as a feather on an angel's wing. If he did not come, she would weep until the stones crumbled into the sea in their grief at hearing her, until the stars drowned, until the earth spread wide her arms and the Great Goddess took her in.

In her womb the unborn baby kicked, and a tear slid down Essylte's pale cheek. She could not wish for death without wishing for his death, too, this poor child of Tristan's who had never looked upon the light of day. All the world's pleasures would be denied him, all its beauties and its joys, if she died tomorrow. Branwen was right. She was selfish to think only of herself. She would have to wait until she could leave her infant prince safely in other hands. Only then would she be free to welcome death, if Tristan was not with her, if he was exiled, or dead. She shivered at the thought and wondered if she could find the servant who had poisoned Segward. If only, if only the stupid girl had given that cup to Mark!

She rose quickly and strained to hear. For hours, the perfect silence of the moonless night had throbbed against her ears. But now—was that a scrape of boot on stone? Was that an indrawn breath? She turned and looked toward the window, an inky blotch in the black wall, invisible when she looked directly at it, visible only when she looked away. Something moved, something quivered in the dark. She reached out; a hand caught hold of her arm and pulled her hard into waiting arms.

"Tristan!" she breathed, alive again against his living flesh.

His finger pressed against her lips. "Hush, love. It is death if we are caught."

"But you came to me!"

He laughed silently. "I had no choice."

"Nor I." She drew his face down and kissed his lips. "I am wild with waiting!"

His breath caught in his throat. She had shrugged off her nightdress, and her lovely body shone in the darkness, as if she had gathered light into her flesh and allowed it to shine from her breasts, her hips, her thighs. She knelt on the old bed, arms outstretched. "Come to me, Tristan."

The ferocity of his desire frightened him, and he concentrated on moving slowly, on touching her fingers, her arms, her shoulders with consummate gentleness. "Silence," he breathed into her hair, taking her body carefully into his arms, striving for control of the whirlwind conflagration that consumed him. "Absolute silence."

Her lips pressed against his ear as she wrapped her arms about him and drew him down to her. "I am queen of the firestorm," she whispered. "Let go, let go. Tonight we will burn alive, but no one will hear."

"How is it," he whispered as they lay entwined, waiting for their breathing to slow, "that you always know what I am thinking?"

She pushed a strand of hair from his face. "Because I *am* you. And you are me. It's a truth you know well enough when we are joined. Why do you forget it when we part?"

"You are right," he answered. "But it always amazes me."

"Tristan." She hesitated. "Do you feel what I feel?"

"That our fate is upon us? Yes."

"Will we die in the morning?"

His hand slid from her breast to her belly and rested there. "*You* cannot die. You have a child to protect."

"If I cannot die, you cannot either, Tristan." She raised herself on an elbow and strove to see him in the dark. "If we—if we are separated—if they force us—as long as one of us lives, the other must also. For as long as we both live there is hope that someday—"

"Yes," he breathed, pulling her close. "Someday!"

"Tristan, if my father sides with Mark—I cannot withstand him. What shall we do?"

"We'll escape in the boat if it comes to that."

Her tears fell on his shoulder and she struggled to hold them back. "But they'll come after us to get Young Tristan. Both of them. Unless I tell them the truth. Oh, Tristan! Mark's words to me were like a knife in my heart. It is true I have lied and lied, when he has asked me again and again for the truth."

"If Mark learns the truth, he'll kill the boy."

"Not with my father there. He's still his grandson. He might side with you instead of Mark if he knew. I've thought of nothing else all night."

Tristan said nothing but gently stroked her hair. "And what about Branwen? She's risked death to keep our secret dark."

"Only by accident. She never intended to miscarry."

"No, no, my heart. I mean, she poisoned Segward to keep his mouth shut."

"Branwen?" Essylte squeaked. Tristan clapped a hand over her mouth and they lay frozen, listening hard for any sound of movement from the door. At length they relaxed and Tristan withdrew his hand.

"Yes," he whispered. "It was Branwen who served the wine. Percival recognized her. So did I. So did Segward. That was why I wouldn't let you taste it."

"What do you mean?"

"Don't you remember what she told us? Your mother gave her the means to kill me. And kill me she must, to be free of the Druid curse. Unless I wed her, what use am I to her anymore? So I thought she might have added something to the wine." He wrinkled his nose. "My cup tasted bitter. But it must have been imagination, since no harm came of it." He paused, frowning. "Or Branwen made it bitter deliberately so Segward would think she had poisoned me and his cup was safe."

"But Father said it couldn't be the wine. Segward chose his cup himself."

"Your father was protecting Branwen." This silenced Essylte. "Segward met his match in Branwen. She outsmarted him at the end. She knew which cup he would choose. Either that or she poisoned them both."

Essylte shuddered, and Tristan pulled her close and kissed her. He was startled to find he could see the dim outline of her face. "Love, it's nearly dawn. I must go."

A tremor shook her, but she kept her voice calm. "How does your arm? Does it pain you?"

He smiled. "Until you asked, I had forgotten all about it. Pernam came to me in my chamber and dressed it with a balm. It's sore, but it will heal. I was lucky I twisted, or he'd have struck my chest."

Tears filled her eyes and slid slowly down her cheeks. "He is not fit to wipe your boots."

"He's High King of Britain, with a thousand troops outside to prove it. We have—what? Five hundred? Six?"

"But not all of his are loyal. You said so yourself."

Tristan brushed his lips against her hair. "I lied."

"Oh, Tristan!"

He rose from bed and dressed. Essylte covered her mouth with her hands to keep from sobbing. The dark relented, and gradually the objects in her chamber took shape in the gray light. "Tristan, your arm is bleeding!"

"No matter. It will serve me."

She flung herself out of bed and into his arms. "I will never see you again! My heart has been heavy with the fear all night."

"Nonsense," he whispered. "I promise you, Essylte, I will see you again." He kissed her slowly, memorizing the sweet taste of her. "I will kiss these lips again. I must. Nothing can part us. You said yourself, we are one."

A heavy fist pounded on the door. "Lady Essylte! Are you awake? Are you alone?"

"Quick!" Tristan pushed her away. "Put on your nightdress and pretend you're asleep. Keep them guessing, if you can. I need time!" He slithered out the window as Essylte dressed and huddled among the bed skins, shutting her eyes tight and fighting sobs.

The door opened. "Aye. The Queen's abed. Alone."

"Send for one of her women. King Markion's orders. He's on his way."

The door closed. Essylte gasped. Markion! She choked back a sob and fought to think. Why Markion? Why now?

Before long she heard the shuffle of boots and the door pushed open again. Someone touched her shoulder with a gentle hand.

"Essylte. Wake up, my dear."

"Esmerée!"

"So. You were feigning sleep. Tell me quickly—has Tristan been here?"

Essylte nodded, eyes brimming. Esmerée's eyes darted quickly about the chamber. "However did he manage it? Well, no matter. King Markion is coming and you must be dressed." She flung open the clothes chest. "Do you care which gown you wear?"

Essylte shook her head. "Why is he coming? Is anything amiss?"

Esmerée lifted a gown from the chest and shook it out. "I know nothing about it, my dear. I was awakened and told to attend you. But the guards seem to think the King is angry."

"Oh, God!"

"Hurry now. Arise and let me have that bedgown."

Essylte sat up slowly and swung her feet to the floor. "We must—we must make him wait—we must go as slowly as we can. Time is important."

Esmerée looked at her closely. "Why?"

"Esme, he's only just left."

Esmerée looked about in bewilderment. "How?" Essylte pointed to the window. "Not the window? Why, it's straight down!"

Essylte shuddered and Esmerée's gaze returned to her. "What's that on the shoulder of your bedgown? Essylte—it's blood."

Essylte jumped up, and the two women stared in consternation at the bedsheets. They were smeared all over with fresh blood, even the pillows. Essylte's hand flew to her mouth. Esmerée gripped her arm.

"Are you bleeding? Is it the child?"

Essylte shook her head. "No," she quavered. "It's Tristan's."

"Dear God!" Esmerée pulled the bedgown off Essylte. Her smooth flesh was streaked and stained with light smears of blood. Esmerée grabbed the clay pitcher of water from the nightstand and emptied it over her.

"Esme! What are you doing?"

Frantically, Esmerée rubbed her body clean. "Stand still. Dry yourself with one of those skins. Help me with this gown—oh, my poor Essylte, Mark will have your life if he sees this!"

Frightened into silence, Essylte obeyed. There was no way to clean the sheets, no place to hide them, no way to procure fresh ones. They covered the bed with skins and coverlets as best they could and hid the stained bedgown in the bottom of the chest. Essylte was sitting on the chest with Esmerée behind her, combing out her hair, when the door flew open and Markion strode in unannounced.

He glared at her, hands on hips. Esmerée stopped her combing and curtsied, but Essylte made no move to rise. She stared back defiantly at Markion.

"Where is he?" he breathed, scanning the room. "Where is my traitorous dog of a nephew?"

"How should I know?" Essylte asked coldly.

"He is not in his chamber," Markion growled, "nor has he been, this hour past." He drew his sword. "I'll find him. I'll find him before I slit his throat!" He thrust the sword under the bed, once, twice, thrice.

Essylte whimpered. Markion whirled. "Get off that chest! I'll have it open!"

Esmerée pulled Essylte to her side and Mark flung the chest open. He did not bother to search among the clothes, but plunged his sword straight down, again and again. "Damn him! I'll split his brains when I find him!"

The two women clung together. Essylte forced her voice to calm. "I want my father here."

"He's coming," Markion snarled. "I've sent for him. God knows why. I should know better than to trust a Welshman."

"You have no right to speak so!"

Markion laughed aloud. "Do I not? We'll see about that! He's been here, hasn't he? My fornicating nephew. I know he has."

Essylte returned his fierce gaze in silence. Markion spun furiously, his sword whistling in the air. "Tri-i-sta-a-an!" His bellow echoed off the stone walls, hollow and cold. Boots clattered down the corridor. Markion slashed at the bedcovers in his fury, flinging the furs around the room.

"Markion!" Percival shouted from the doorway.

Markion froze. Then he turned, breathing heavily, and pointed with a shaking finger to the bed. "Look at that. Look at that, my lord. *That* is your daughter's bed."

Percival came forward slowly. The bed was a mess of slashed blanket, torn furs, and rumpled, bloodstained sheets. Percival turned to Essylte, who gazed blankly at him. "Is it the child? Speak, Essylte." But Essylte said nothing.

"It is not her blood. Nor the child's." Markion's voice trembled with rage. "It is Tristan's!" He faced Percival, his features distorted by his wrath. "He bleeds from my knife cut! O God! Not deep enough! Who else—who else in Lyon's Head bears such a bleeding wound?"

Percival took Essylte's hands. "Tell me truth, daughter. The Kingdom depends on it. Was Tristan here with you?"

Essylte said nothing. Esmerée slipped a trembling arm about her waist, but Essylte stood perfectly still.

"Your silence will do the lad more harm than good," Percival implored. "Speak, Essylte, if you value his life."

Essylte's eyes brimmed with tears, but her tight-lipped expression did not change. Percival shut his eyes and dropped her hands. Then he turned to Markion.

"My lord—"

He stopped at the sound of booted feet pounding down the corridor. "My lord King!" A breathless face appeared in the doorway and a guard saluted hastily. "My lord, we've got him! He walked into the hall as cool as ice. And dripping wet. He said he'd been bathing in the sea." The guard snickered. "In boots and leggings."

"Hold him!" Markion exploded. "Hold him fast! Kill him if he makes a move to flee!"

"Aye, my lord." The guard disappeared.

Shaking violently, Essylte slumped against Esmerée's shoulder.

"Markion," Percival said wearily, "let us all go back to the hall together. Do nothing hastily. More than your honor is at stake here. The future of Britain is in your hands, as well."

Markion signaled to the sentries at the door. "Take these women to the hall. Carry them if you have to."

Dawn broke over the eastern sea. Long rays of early light angled through the windows and pierced the cold gloom of the king's hall. Twenty of Markion's men held the doorways. Sir Grayell and the rest of Tristan's guards stood in a tight knot, disarmed, surrounded by more of Markion's troops. Markion stood on the dais with Percival, Essylte and her women, and Sir Bruenor. Tristan, still dripping, dressed only in leggings and boots, stood at the foot of the dais, held fast between two guards. The knife cut on his upper arm bled sluggishly, dripping from time to time on the rushes at his feet. Each of the guards held a dagger to his ribs.

"Well." Markion smiled down at Tristan, his voice rich with satisfaction. "I've caught you this time. You've played me for a fool one time too many, Tristan. I've got you now."

Tristan shook his wet hair from his face and smiled back. "Only with my consent. I yield, Uncle. For the moment. I've let you take my fortress. I gave Dinadan and Grayell orders to disarm my men and let fifty of your soldiers in. I've given you Lyon's Head. Until noon. Then, if we have reached no solution, I will take it back. And we shall have our battle, after all. But for the moment, Lyon's Head is yours. As a token of my good faith."

Markion's expression turned from surprise to bitterness. "Oh, aye, you yield now that you have no choice. It will avail you nothing. I'll kill you and take pleasure in doing it."

Tristan inclined his head. "Whatever serves your ends best, Uncle. But what will my death gain you?" He smiled lightly. "You'll have a wife you can never turn your back on." Markion colored quickly, and Essylte nodded. "She'd as soon stab you in your bed as lie with you. Do you want such a wife? Put her away. That's all it takes to be rid of me. Put her away and let us go."

"Never." Markion's features hardened. "On my life, never. I would rather see you dead. Both of you."

"You will not harm my daughter." Percival's hand rested on his sword hilt as his arm slid around Essylte. "It's your life if you do, and to hell with Britain—I promise you that."

"If you kill her," Tristan continued calmly, "you destroy Britain and give up your dream of kingship. And any hope of a lasting legacy—except as a villain. Percival will not stand by and see his daughter slaughtered. If you touch her, you will be at war with Wales within the hour. And within the year, Britain will be in Saxon hands."

Markion glanced quickly at Percival, who returned his gaze with a stony glare.

"And if you kill me, you will have to kill her to prevent her from killing you. You are safe from her only if I live."

"I can't keep her and let you live!" Markion cried. "You will cuckold me again!"

"Then let her go."

"And reward you for your betrayal? Never. I must kill you, Tristan. There is no other way."

"Give him to me." A firm voice spoke from the doorway. Everyone turned.

Branwen stepped out of the shadows and into the light. Her yellow gown, the yellow flowers wound in her braided hair, caught the morning sun and warmed, like a bud opening into bloom. She walked across the hall and stepped up onto the dais with all the dignity of a queen.

She curtsied low before Percival. "Greetings, Father."

He cleared his throat awkwardly. "Branwen. My daughter."

"Your daughter?" Markion repeated stupidly. "She can't be your daughter. She's the Queen's companion. A serving maid."

"*Was* the Queen's companion," Branwen corrected him gently.

"Yes," Percival said slowly, his expression a mixture of sorrow and admiration. "She is my daughter. I acknowledge it."

Everyone stared at Branwen as she made her reverence to Markion. "I am not trueborn, my lord King. I tell you myself what my father prefers not to mention. Yet I am not without power." Her eyes flicked once to Tristan, who had gone pale. "I will marry your wandering nephew, my lord, if you will grant me leave. The kingdom will be intact. You will bind my father's loyalty to you twice over. You can build your dynasty of kings. And I can promise you"—her eyes glinted metal-hard—"that I will keep Essylte out of his bed."

Markion's lips slid slowly into a smile. "Well, well, this is something to consider. My lord Percival, will you give your blessing to such a match, knowing what a scoundrel my nephew is?"

Essylte laid a beseeching hand on Percival's sleeve, but Percival did not move. His eyes were on Branwen. "Why, Branwen? Do you say this because you wish to wound Essylte? Or to sacrifice yourself for the kingdom's good? Or do you love this man?"

"Oh, she has loved him long," Markion said easily. "Everyone knows it. She has been in his bed a hundred times. She has borne him a daughter."

Branwen lowered her eyes modestly as Percival drew a long breath. "Is this so? Well, then—"

"No!" Essylte's shriek rent the sunlit morning. "It is *not* so!"

"Essylte!" Tristan cried quickly.

"Silence!" Markion roared. The dagger points pressed against Tristan's ribs and he went still.

Essylte shrugged off Esmerée's restraining hand and stepped before Markion. "The girl-child is not his. She has *never* lain with him. It was a ruse only, to get him into my quarters. Tristan is my husband, Mark, as you never were!"

"Be still, Essylte!" Branwen grabbed Essylte's arm. Essylte thrust her away.

"You are not my son's father!" Essylte shrieked at Markion. "Tristan is!" Everyone gasped. "You are not the father of this child I carry! Tristan is! You are not my husband, Markion of Cornwall! Tristan is! I have loved him since I met him with a love stronger than the bond of life—I would kill you, and myself, before I would let you harm him. If you take his life, I will take yours. If you force him to marry Branwen, I will kill you or die in the attempt. But if you let him live . . ." Her voice quavered. "If you let him live unwed, then I will—I will submit to your will." She squared her shoulders bravely. "But be warned: I will *never* bear you sons. I take my oath on it. If you do not put me away, your dream of a dynasty is dust and ashes."

The blood drained from Markion's face. He stared at her in dumb confusion.

"Royal brat!" Branwen wailed. "Oath breaker!"

"I am beyond caring!" Essylte cried. "Last night he said he wanted the truth from me. Now he has it. See how pleased he is!"

For a moment no one moved. Essylte stood before them all in her golden gown, her hair alight in the sun like a living flame. Tristan opened his mouth to speak, but the daggers bit into his flesh and stopped him.

Markion was breathing heavily. Sweat formed in beads across his brow. "I am your husband," he managed. "You married me."

Percival stepped forward and took Essylte firmly by the shoulders. But she would not move. "I was never in your bed. Not once. A marriage unconsummated is no marriage at all."

Color washed Markion's face. "*Someone* was in my bed! Someone with your voice, your body, and your scent! If not you, you Welsh witch, who was it?"

No one spoke. Branwen moved slowly to the wide, unshuttered window and stood facing out to sea. After a moment she turned back to the king. "It was I, Markion." She watched indignation swell his features and smiled bitterly. "You are not as dishonored as you think. I, too, am Percival's daughter. A moment ago I was good enough to wed your nephew. Whether you believe it or not, marriage to me would have brought you your heart's desire. Marriage to Essylte never will." She paused. "I am the one who has listened to your dreams, your plans, your regrets. I am the one who has given you advice worth more than gold. In your heart, you know my value. You have spoken words of love to me that came from your soul. Yet now you regard me as if I had snakes growing from my head. Can true birth mean so much?" She lifted a silver winecup from the window ledge and turned it slowly in her fingers. "I will give you one last word of advice, my royal lover, because I honor you. Whatever happens now, you have lost your dynasty. If you put Essylte away, you lose Percival's alliance and thereby the kingdom. It will take time to form another alliance with another lord and win another bride, and you are not young. And this time, Tristan will not be your giant-slayer. He stands to gain so much more if you do not wed. I advise you to keep Essylte and the alliance with Wales. You will be High King of Britain to the end of your days. And if it's Tristan's sons who sit in Camelot after your death and not yours, well, they are Meliodas's heirs, and it is fitting that they should. Don't you agree?"

"Whore!" Markion croaked, pale as death.

"As for Tristan, whether he likes it or not, I am the one who shall determine his fate." She beckoned to the guards. "Let him come to me."

The guards looked at one another. The only doors in the hall were behind them, and well guarded. They looked at Markion, who shrugged. Tentatively, they withdrew their daggers. White-faced, Tristan approached Branwen, his eyes on the silver cup. He recognized it.

"Tristan!" Essylte sobbed. Percival pulled her roughly away.

Tristan looked down at Branwen. "My life has been in your hands from the beginning," he said slowly.

Branwen smiled. "You don't regret it, do you? I've given you everything you wanted."

"I acknowledge it."

"Will you—could you bring yourself to marry me, Tristan?"

He shook his head slowly. "I ought to. I owe it to you. But I cannot. And I believe you would come to regret it if I did. My heart would always be Essylte's."

Branwen looked up at him calmly and kept her voice low. "He will not harm her. Did you see his face? He wants the Kingship more than anything. You must trust me. I know him. He will not harm her. Percival will not let him harm the children. But you, Tristan, you must go. Forever. Now." Her eyes slid toward the window. "Dinadan guards the coast road and Pernam waits by the boat. Go now."

His eyes widened. "Then the cup is not for me?"

A brief smile touched her lips. "Never you. I love you."

"Blessed Branwen," he breathed, bending down to kiss her cheek. "May I not take her with me? Is there no way?"

"Not now that she has told the truth. He would follow you to get her back. He will want his own son from her."

"I can't leave her to Markion."

"You must." She drew his head down and softly kissed his lips. "She will be safe. She will bear your son. One day you will see her again. Don't ask for more. But go now, my dear, before they suspect. Go now."

"God grant you long life!" He looked back once at Essylte, put his knee to the window ledge, and leaped.

Markion gasped, guards started forward, Essylte saw the silver cup in Branwen's hand and cried out, "My sister! Don't!"

Branwen turned, met her eyes with a sad smile, and raised the cup to her lips.

Essylte screamed.

Part VI

30 ✝ RYOL THE GIANT

Hot sun glittered hard on the tranquil sea. From horizon to horizon nothing moved on the burning deep but a single square of bleached canvas. The sail flapped from its spar as the boat rose and sank on the sea's swell. Tristan lay curled in the shadow of the sail, his eyes bloodshot from sun, his head splitting from thirst, his arm hot and swollen, his body shivering with fever. As he lay he slept, and as he slept he dreamed. Sometimes he was a flying fish, arcing upward toward the great light in the sky that beckoned him to eternity with his father's voice. Sometimes he was an eel, writhing toward a giant maw at the bottom of the sea, enchanted by the siren's song that sang with his mother's voice. But most often he was an eagle flying high above the great blue waste of ocean, swooping down to the dying man in the lonely boat, talons outstretched, ready and eager for the kill.

Now and then in moments of lucidity, memory returned. Dinadan on the coast road with Tristan's sword, his dagger, and, God bless the loyal fool, his crown. How heavy they had seemed to carry; how utterly useless in a boat. Pernam in the sea cave where the keel was hidden, holding a basket of food, a cloak, a tunic, and skins of fresh water. He had frowned at the cut in Tristan's arm, kissed him on both cheeks, and bade his God go with him. The keel, slipping across the sea in the bright of early morning, the sail filled with the offshore breeze, while gulls wheeled overhead and a shower of arrows fell into the water far astern.

Tristan groaned. Squinting hard, he opened his eyes and shut them again at once, blinded by the sea glare. Reason returned long enough to whisper a prayer for rain. *Send me a storm wind. Send me a blessed storm!* He looked down and was an eagle again, seeing between his outstretched talons the burning, fevered body of a lone sailor, drifting on the sinking swell toward eternity. . . .

He awoke with a jolt. It was dark, but stars shone overhead and there, against the darker shadow of the shore, a line of breakers glimmered on a beach. With the scrape of wood on stone the boat lifted, swung landward, and jolted a second time against the unseen rocks. Shoals! Tristan pushed himself up and reached for the stowed oars, amazed at how little strength he had. In the time it took him to set the oars and pull himself off the shoal, a fitful breeze sprang up, rain pelted lightly on his back, and the stars disappeared behind a great, silver-edged cloud. He slid out of the boat when he felt the keelrib scrape the pebbled beach, but he found he had not the strength to pull the craft to safety on the shore. He took down the sail and used the stays and steering ropes to tie the bow to the nearest stout tree, anchoring the stern with the heaviest stone he could lift. Exhausted, he sat sweating on the beach to catch his breath. How long had he been at sea? He remembered little of it. His throat ached with a desperate thirst, but he seemed always to have lived in that condition. He rose shakily, retrieved his sword from the listing keel, strapped it on, hooked his dagger in his belt, placed his crown on his head, wrapped his cloak under his arm, and started up the beach to look for a stream or a spring.

An hour later he staggered across a small stream and fell to the ground. He buried his face in the cool water, thanking God. He lay there, trembling, unable to drink more, his raging thirst still unsatisfied. After a while he felt better, drank more, and pushed himself to his knees. He smelled woodsmoke. Struggling to his feet, he followed his nose to a clearing in the thick woods where a group of men huddled around a cooking fire. At the smell of roasting meat he hunched over, clutching his stomach. They had posted no lookouts, for, unsteady as he was, he got close enough to hear their conversation. When he looked around at their firelit faces, he understood. They were only boys.

"We've *got* to wait for reinforcements, Kaherdyn. Have some sense. We can't storm the place ourselves."

"We have to try. If she never reached Brittany, then she's been there *days* already—a week, even!" This voice sounded desperate, close to tears.

"We'll only die ourselves unless we get some help," a third voice pleaded. "What good will that do her, to be the cause of her brother's death?"

"*She* isn't the cause!" The boy called Kaherdyn spoke in bitter anger to keep tears at bay. "None of this is *her* fault. She didn't go there willingly— she was abducted!"

None of the young men looked at him. "Why won't your uncle Gallinore loan us men? Brittany's not at war."

"I've sent to him. He will, he will, I know he will. But until then, I *can't* just sit in Benoic and wait while Iseulte—" He gulped hastily. "While my sister lies a prisoner in the giant's lair. For all we know, every single hour we delay is an hour of torment to her!"

Tristan stared at the boy who spoke so bravely and so eloquently. His head ached as he straightened. He staggered dizzily and put out a hand to a nearby tree to steady himself. Then he squared his shoulders and thrust through the shadows into the circle of light. The boys shouted and scrambled for their weapons.

"Do not fear me!" Tristan cried, swaying on his feet. "I've come to help you. Let me do it. I will save the fair Essylte."

A circle of bright sword tips wheeled across his vision, his knees buckled, and he fainted.

When he awoke he found his headache gone, his throat dry but no longer afire, and the fierce pain in his arm dulled to a steady ache. He pushed himself up from his bed of leaves and bracken and looked around. He lay in a clearing of grass and scrub surrounded by towering pines and hardwoods just leafing out. The golden light of late afternoon slanted through the branches, casting dappled shadows over the uneven ground. Within the circle of firestones banked embers still burned. He shut his eyes, opened them and stared again. He recognized nothing.

His sword, his dagger, his crown, his cloak, and his tunic lay beside him, the clothes neatly folded, the crown placed carefully on top. His arm was freshly bandaged and bound with a leather thong. He flexed it carefully. It was sore enough, but the throbbing pain had gone. A waterskin lay beside his clothes, and he drained it thankfully. No water had ever tasted so sweet. Scanning the trees for movement, he rose, donned his tunic, and buckled on his swordbelt. A twig snapped. Tristan whirled, sword up, as a group of boys appeared at the edge of the clearing, all of them dressed for battle. They stopped when they saw him. One of them pushed forward from the others, a fair-faced lad with thick chestnut hair and a beard just beginning.

"Who are you, sir, and why do you draw your weapon? We do not threaten you."

"I told you, Kaherdyn! I told you not to leave him his sword," another muttered. "But you wouldn't listen."

Kaherdyn signaled to the boys, who fanned out right and left around the clearing and drew their swords.

A smile tugged at the corners of Tristan's mouth. "Never mind who I am just now. Who are *you*?"

The chestnut-haired boy regarded him solemnly. Alone of them all, he had not drawn a weapon. "I am Prince Kaherdyn of Lanascol," he said quietly. "We saved your life. We fed you and gave you water while your wits were wandering these two days past. Why do you threaten us now? We mean you no harm."

"As if you could do me any. Tell your lads to keep their distance. They don't know much of swordsmanship, and I've no wish to hurt them." He stood perfectly still, facing Kaherdyn. The boy met his gaze steadily. Tristan's lips spread in a slow smile. Without warning, he whipped around. Metal clashed, sunlight glinted off a flying sword as it fell, spinning, in a

great arc to the forest floor. The black-haired youth who had crept up behind him now stood weaponless, holding his wrist, Tristan's sword point at
his throat. "You mean well," Tristan said to them all, looking at their frightened faces, "but you're untrained. Put up your swords, and I will mine." He
sheathed his first. One by one, they all obeyed. The black-haired youth ran
to tug his weapon from the ground. Tristan turned back to Kaherdyn. "A
trick, prince? I thought more of you than that." He paused, and when he
spoke again there was awe in his voice. "Lanascol, did you say? I've heard of
Lanascol before. . . . Are you kin to Sir Lancelot of Lanascol, who served
King Arthur?"

Kaherdyn inclined his head politely. "His grandson."

Tristan fell to one knee. "A thousand pardons, Prince Kaherdyn. I wish I'd
known. But I've been wandering witless, I don't know how long. My past is
gone, and my future with it. Let me serve you however I can, and I will be content to live out my days in the kingdom Lancelot himself once called home."

Kaherdyn looked down at him in confusion. "But my lord," he said
plaintively, "who *are* you?"

The dark head came up. The man's brown eyes met the boy's gray-
green ones. "My name is Tristan. My father was Meliodas, King of Cornwall. Markion the High King is my uncle."

Kaherdyn's jaw dropped. *"Tristan of Lyonesse?"*

"At your service."

Kaherdyn raised him quickly. "Don't kneel to me, my lord. You are a
king, and the savior of Britain besides."

The boys crowded around him. "You slew the giant Marhalt!" they
cried eagerly. "King Markion owes his crown to *you!*" "How many Saxons
have you killed, my lord?"

Tristan laughed. "Thank you, young lords, for your praises. I will answer
all your questions in good time. But first—where are we? How long have I
been here? How did I get here? Who healed my arm?"

"I will answer your questions," Kaherdyn offered as his companions
quieted, "if you will answer two of mine."

"Fair enough."

"We are hard by the stronghold of a murderous brute known as Ryol
the Red. He's a giant. He used to serve my father until—" The boy gulped
and hurried on. "He betrayed my father's trust. His lands, such as they are,
run with ours. At the present moment, we are still in Lanascol, on the outskirts of the forest of Broceliande. As for you, you came ashore two nights
ago. You probably blew in with the storm—"

"Storm? There was a storm?"

The boys nodded, wide-eyed.

"Oh, yes," Kaherdyn replied. "A very great storm. We were nearly killed. Three ancient father-trees came down in the forest near our camp. And the sea! Breakers above the height of a man's head! How you survived it in that shallow craft I've no idea."

"And yet," Tristan mused, "I believe I prayed for that storm."

"We've found your boat and stowed her safely, but"—Kaherdyn's chestnut brows met in a light frown—"she looked to us like a Saxon craft. It gave us a start at first."

"You were right. I built her myself along the lines of a Saxon keel I sailed once. She's quick as a knife through water."

"That explains it." Kaherdyn eyed him curiously. "You sailed her all the way from Lyonesse?"

Tristan shrugged, half smiling. "I must have."

The boys looked at one another. "You were ill with fever," Kaherdyn continued, "and we could get no sense from you. As for your arm, the worst was already over. I only sealed the wound."

"How?"

Kaherdyn pointed to the circle of stones. "With fire."

"I thank God I do not remember that!"

The other boys grinned, but Kaherdyn gazed at Tristan solemnly. "Why are you here, Tristan of Lyonesse?"

Tristan gazed down at the strong young face, the clear-eyed virtue of youth too young to know sin. "Kaherdyn of Lanascol," he said softly, "that way lies madness. Do not ask me that. What is your second question?"

Kaherdyn straightened. All the boys went still. "A moment ago you offered me service. I would take help gladly from any man at all, but from such a man as you, it would be a gift from God. But I must know, before I accept your offer, how you knew my sister's name."

Tristan frowned. "I didn't know you had a sister."

Silence followed. The boys stared gravely at Tristan.

"You spoke her name," Kaherdyn said evenly. "You stepped into this clearing wearing a crown upon your head and offered to rescue the fair Iseulte. I only want to know how you knew her name."

Tristan blanched. "*Essylte?* Is that what you said? *Essylte?*"

The boys glanced furtively at one another.

"My sister, the Princess Iseulte," Kaherdyn repeated quietly. "Three weeks—no, a month ago she was abducted by Ryol on a journey through Broceliande to my uncle Gallinore in Brittany. If—if she is still alive, we must get her back." Tears rimmed the boy's gray-green eyes, and he did not bother to wipe them away. "Whatever has been done to her, it—it matters not to us, to Mother and me. We must have her home again at any cost."

Tristan began to tremble. One of the boys reached out a hand to support him.

"Your sister's name is Iseulte?"

"Yes," Kaherdyn replied patiently. "She's nineteen and unwed. Ryol—Ryol had the gall to—to send a message to my mother that he had—saved her from spinsterhood." The boy's eyes swam, but he faced Tristan bravely. "He's only raped her, not married her. I know her well—she'll kill him if she gets a chance. If she does, if she even tries, they'll kill her. We must get to her before that happens."

Tristan stared at him blankly. "Her name is Iseulte?"

Again, the boys glanced at one another. Kaherdyn frowned darkly. "I've told you twice. Her birth name was Elen, but since childhood everyone's called her Iseulte because she was so fair. She's known throughout Less Britain for the beauty of her hands."

Tristan made an effort to collect himself. "And why are boys sent to rescue her? Where are your fathers? Uncles? Brothers? Where are the men?"

"A hundred men have already died trying," one of the boys piped up. "Kaherdyn's sent to his uncles for help, but no one's come yet."

"Uncles? Where is your father, Kaherdyn? Does he live?"

Quick pride flashed in the boy's eyes. "Indeed, my lord, I daily pray he does. He's on a pilgrimage to Jerusalem. He's been gone two years."

"Why so long? Has there been trouble with pirates?"

"Oh, no. Not any trouble that we know. But he didn't go by ship, my lord. He walked."

Tristan stared at him in astonishment. But the reverence on the faces of the boys dried his laughter in his throat. "I see. That's quite an undertaking. Who holds Lanascol in his absence?"

"My mother, the queen, of course. She sent our troops to attack Ryol, but they died, every single one of them. Now we're shorthanded at home in Benoic, and she's sent to my uncles for help. But until the men come, I—I just can't do *nothing*."

Tristan nodded quickly. "I'd feel the same in your place. Well, show me the way to this wonderful fortress and let me think how it may be taken by a wandering harper and a handful of brave, beardless youths." He smiled at their grim faces.

Tristan lay on his belly in the sand behind a gorse bush. Beside him, clear-eyed Kaherdyn pointed wordlessly seaward. Tristan nodded. There was no need to speak. In all the wide blue bay, in all the golden stretch of sand, there was only one possible place the boy's sister could be. Rising from the empty sea like the broken fang of some strange, primordial beast was a circlet of solid rock, ringed by cliffs, bound by water, crowned by a crude fortress of wood and stone.

"The fortress doesn't look like much," Tristan muttered, squinting.

"No, but there's a good, solid tower of dressed stone behind it," Kaherdyn said. "Probably Roman. They can see everything for leagues. The only approach to the beach is the one we took, because the forest comes down so close. Getting from here to there is the problem."

"I see the problem very well. There must be a causeway of some kind. How do they get supplies in?"

"There is at low tide, but it's well guarded. They say you can ride two abreast most of the way, but it's treacherous, and if you put a foot wrong, there's quicksand all about. Even Ryol loses men that way."

Tristan grimaced. "Not a hero's death. What about boats? Do they use them?"

"Very small craft. Little more than coracles. It's so shallow, you see. Sandbars everywhere. And when the tide comes in, it races. They often find their boats on the beach in the mornings."

"What's on the backside of the island? The seaward side?"

Kaherdyn raised his shoulders. "No one knows. I don't know anyone who's ever seen it."

Tristan grunted. "That's my best chance. I'll row in on the last of the tide and sail out at the turn. Let's hope there's someplace at the back of those cliffs to stow the keel safely."

Kaherdyn shook his head. "You can't do it by sea. It's too shallow. Except at the very height of the tide, and then the current's too strong. Ryol bragged to my father once that the place was impregnable. I heard him."

Tristan turned his head in the sand and looked at the boy. "When was this?"

"Three years ago," Kaherdyn said steadily. "They were allies then."

"And what changed that?"

Kaherdyn looked away. Already Tristan recognized the firm set of the jaw and the thinned lips that signaled private ground. When he made up his mind to be obstinate, the boy could not be moved.

Tristan put out a hand to his shoulder. "Prince Kaherdyn, it may be no business of mine, but if this man took your sister as some sort of revenge when your father was away, then it might help me to know what he wants revenge for. Don't send me in there blind."

Nothing in the boy's face moved. "What you have guessed, you have guessed aright, Sir Tristan. More than that I cannot say. It is not my secret to share."

Tristan sighed. "Well, he was probably boasting, anyway, about the inaccessibility of the place. It can't be any worse than Lyon's Head. Every fortress has its weak spot, if you can find it. I'm willing to wager this one does, too. I only wish I didn't have to find it in the dark."

"God will guide you," Kaherdyn said gravely.

Tristan forced a smile. "Don't be too sure. The Great Goddess may be pleased with me, for all I know, but Christ is most certainly disappointed."

Kaherdyn's eyes widened. "Are you a pagan?"

"I'm a little of everything. My parents were Christians and I was baptized. When I was a boy, the Christian God spoke to me. But lately, I've heard other voices."

Kaherdyn smiled in evident relief. "All men sin," he said easily. "Don't worry. God is with you even when you doubt."

Tristan smiled at the youth in his voice. "Would it make a difference, Prince? If I worshiped Mithra, or Yahweh, or Cerunnos, would you let me die to save your sister?"

Kaherdyn's untroubled gaze met his. "Of course I would," he said at once. "My father once told me not to mind if my soldiers had feet of clay, or if the workmen I employed to build my house had dirty hands. The important thing is that the battle is fought bravely and the house built well." He smiled quickly. "Does that make any sense to you?"

"Your father sounds like a wise man." Tristan turned and stared back out at the lonely island. "My keel draws no more water than a coracle. At high tide, I'll make it to those cliffs. Pray for me that I find a place to land without smashing the boat against the rocks. Pray I can find your sister without being killed. Pray that I can get her down to the boat unseen. Pray that I can sail out of the range of fire arrows before they see me."

Kaherdyn grinned. "That's a lot to ask of prayer. We'll create a diversion on the shore with torches and smoke. They'll never think to look behind them."

Tristan laughed softly. "I like you better, Kaherdyn of Lanascol, every day I know you. What did the bishop once tell me at Castle Dorr? Ah, yes, I remember. God helps those who help themselves."

The night was dark with a fair wind. Clouds scudded across the stars, blowing unseen shadows across the sea. Tristan sat at the helm, racing in on the pull of the tide, scanning the shore for lights that would mark the island. He had spent the afternoon well out to sea, only drifting landward as the sun set and the tide came in. At dusk he had hoisted his dark sail. Kaherdyn had thought of that trick, smearing charcoal on the sail to make it more difficult to see. Tristan was not yet afraid of being seen; he was more afraid of sailing by the island onto a sandbar in the dark.

At last he saw a light, but it was high above him. He dropped the sail and leaped to the oars, pulling hard. He was nearly on the island! He could hear the crash of waves on rocks. How had he come so far so fast? The tide must be at full race! He pulled hard against the current to slow his approach, but it was like trying to hold back the wind. He saw the white froth of breakers ahead, then the boat lifted on a swell and darted past the rising wall of rock. The tide was sweeping him around the island! Desperately he pulled for the rock face, no longer caring if he smashed the boat. If he missed the island, he would beach on a sandbar and end his life in quicksand trying to escape. All at once, the pull of the tide released him. He lost his balance and fell to the floor of the boat as it was swept into an eddy and spun around, oars bobbing in the water. He sat up. The boat rocked gently, bumping the cliff face, at rest in a calm pool. Above him rose the sharp finger of rock that stuck out from the cliff and created this eddy behind it. The swirl of water, circling in the reverse direction from the tide, would hold him there forever unless he thrust himself out into the racing current.

"God is with you even when you doubt," Tristan whispered. "Who *is* that boy's father, anyway?"

He scrambled out onto the rocks and searched for footholds, toeholds, any way to climb the cliff. To his amazement he found a path. Drawing his sword, he crept stealthily up the steep, twisting trail, expecting any moment to come face-to-face with an armed guard. But he met no one. At the top of the cliff the trail turned again and ran along the cliff face. But Tristan, ducking low, ran toward the lights of the fortress. Out of the corner of his eye he caught movement. Flames showed on the distant shore, moving everywhere, thirty or forty separate flares. These must be Kaherdyn's troops, lighting fires as well as torches to give the impression of greater numbers. That single-minded boy would burn down Broceliande itself to get his sister back. Ahead, Tristan saw three men with their backs to him, silhouetted against the raging light. He prayed Ryol would be as curious about the fires as his night watch.

Ryol's fortress proved to be little more than a ruin of rubble patched with wood and roofed with thatch. Tristan slid in shadow from window to window, from knothole to crack, and peered inside. He saw a great room full of drunken men, some slumbering, mouths slack with snores, some weaving unsteadily in the dim light of smoking torches, a few villains stealing coins from their sleeping comrades, a few men alerting to the lookout's warning cries of fire. But no sign of a woman, and no Ryol. He continued from wall to wall until he had circled the fortress. He found the cookhouse, the barracks (if he could use such a term for a single room strewn with bedrolls and hammocks), the storehouse, and the waste pit, but he found no woman. To the west rose a square tower, solidly built of stone, with two lookouts at the top, both eagerly watching the shore maneuvers. He approached cautiously, sword raised, expecting it to be well defended, but found no one at the entrance. Either everyone was out on the southern cliffs enjoying the show on the beach or Ryol thought his tower too secure to worry much about its capture.

Tristan put his shoulder to the door. Inside, a stair twisted upward and vanished into the dark. He paused, listening hard. He heard nothing. Cautiously he ascended the stairs until he came to a landing where a torch burned sullenly. Two doors faced him, one large, curved, and ornately carved, the other small and ill-fitting but serviceable. He inched open the smaller door and saw, as he expected, stairs leading to the upper battlement. With his sword he cut a swatch from his cloak and wedged it into the doorjamb until the door stuck so tight he could not budge it. Then he put his hand to the latch of the other door and lifted it slowly. Someone whimpered. He pushed hard and the door swung inward on oiled hinges.

He stood in a large room, richly furnished with tapestries on the dressed stone walls, rushes on the floor, furs and stuffed cushions on the huge carved bed, a double-flamed lamp on a bronze stand, a silver candle stand on a marble-topped table beside a gigantic chair. He wrinkled his nose. The place was luxuriously furnished, but it stank. It reeked of sweat.

A breeze blew softly through the window and set the lamp flames dancing. It was then he saw the woman. She stood perfectly motionless by the edge of a tapestry on the other side of the bed, as much a part of the furnishings as the bronze winestand at her elbow. If the wavering light had not swept a shadow across her alabaster flesh, he might not have seen her at all. But once he saw her he could not take his eyes from her. She took his breath away. Eyes of vivid blue looked straight into his own. Raven hair shimmered in the lamplight against skin so pale, so smooth, so unblemished, it cried out to be caressed. As the thought crossed his mind her eyes flashed and her lips lifted in a snarl.

He cleared his throat. "Princess Elen of Lanascol? My name is Tristan. I am sent by Kaherdyn, your brother, to take you home."

For a moment nothing happened. She looked at him with eyes full of malignant, unwavering hatred. Then she shook her head, once, and he gasped. With the movement of her head her hair swung aside and he saw that she was half naked, her gown ripped so badly only a ragged skirt remained. She had smooth, rounded shoulders, full, firm breasts, and a narrow waist he could encompass in his hands. He tried to speak but found he could not command his voice. The longer he stared the icier her cold blue gaze became. Slowly, she raised her hands before her face to ward him off. Slender, long-fingered, classically elegant, they were the most beautiful hands he had ever seen. Iseulte of the White Hands. He had heard of her before. Surely some bard at Lyon's Head had sung her praises once.

"Lady Elen." He cleared his throat again, annoyed to find his voice a whisper. "Lady Elen, come with me, quickly! I'll get you off this island and away—back to your family. But there isn't much time."

She shook her head again and then bit off a cry as a loud thud sounded on the stairs. Tristan whirled. The door slammed open. Ryol the Giant filled the doorway, breathing hard. He had long, stringy red hair and small, light eyes. Once he had been a warrior, perhaps, but his flesh had grown slack from lack of discipline and use, as his vigilance had grown slack from lack of challenge. He grinned when he saw Tristan and showed a mouthful of rotten teeth. He spoke a broken pidgin of mixed Breton and Latin, with an accent so outlandish Tristan could barely make out the words.

"So. Here is hero. You brave man, eh? Rescue maiden? Go home, laddie. You too late. She be no maiden now!" He bellowed in laughter, his great belly jiggling in waves. He had already unlaced his tunic and loosed the cord that bound his leggings in anticipation of the evening's entertainment. His arms and legs were as thick as tree trunks. He stank of sweat.

Tristan backed slowly. If only he had more room! The giant filled the chamber; it was impossible to get past him. To be caught in those fists meant death. A sword thrust would do the monster little harm, with all that flesh, unless . . . Tristan leaped onto the bed, picked up the cushions, and threw them at his face. Ryol caught them in his hands and laughed. With his sword held low in a dagger grip, and while Ryol still had his hands full of cushions, Tristan lunged and stabbed his sword hard upward, deep into the giant's throat.

He pulled the sword out as Ryol staggered toward him. Bright blood splashed down the giant's chest, onto his tunic, onto the rushes on the floor. Ryol bellowed again, this time in rage. He lifted a mammoth leg to kick Tristan across the room, but Tristan dove under the bed. Ryol drew his own sword and thrust it after him. It missed Tristan by a hair. He wriggled out from under the bed near Elen's feet. With a roar, Ryol threw himself across the bed. Tristan grabbed the woman and pulled her hard against the wall. Ryol landed on the bed with a crash. The wood splintered and the bed collapsed. Ryol grunted, head down, his sides heaving as he sucked in air. Blood spurted rhythmically from the gash in his neck, pooling in a dark, glistening lake on the stone floor.

Tristan raced for the door, found his cloak where he had dropped it, reached for Elen's hand, and pulled her after him. He wrapped her in the cloak. "Stay there," he commanded. She did not even look at him. Her gaze was fixed on the writhing, bleeding mass of fatted flesh on the broken bed.

Tristan walked up to the dying giant, raised his sword above his head, whispered, "Go to your gods, Ryol," and brought the blade down as hard as he could. Even so, it took five hacking swings to sever the giant's head. Grabbing it by the lank, red hair, he lifted the head and ran for the door. "Follow me!" he cried. But the girl froze, staring at the headless corpse. "Elen! Listen! The alarm has sounded. We have no time! Follow me now." She turned away from him and walked slowly to the body. While he stood there, helpless, listening to the sentries pound at the wedged door and shout for help, the black-haired beauty walked calmly to the double-flamed lamp and pushed it over. Instantly the rushes ignited and the room filled with smoke. "Elen!" Desperate, Tristan sheathed his sword, grabbed the girl by the waist, and dragged her out of the room and down the stairs.

Outside the tower Ryol's men had gathered, alerted by the sentries' shouts and by the smoke. Most of them had swords, a few had knives. One of them carried a Saxon ax. Tristan stopped. He could not take them all on, even if his hands were free. If they did not kill him, they would surely kill the girl. He stood still, one arm locked around the rigid body of his captive, and faced them all.

"I am Tristan the Giant-Killer," he announced, projecting his harper's voice to the back of the crowd. "Tonight I slew the giant Ryol. Let me pass and I will do you no harm. Stop me and I will destroy you." The men grumbled but no one came forward. In the dim light of smoking torches he saw their stupefied, half-comprehending stares. Slowly he raised the dripping head into the light. The sight produced instant silence. He walked through the crowd unhindered, dragging the girl and holding the head high, and they made a path for him.

"Quickly!" he muttered to her when they were back on the cliff trail. "Use your legs, can't you? One or two of them will come to their senses shortly, and then we'll be for it." But he got no response from her. She remained a dead weight on his arm. In the dark he sought for the finger of rock that marked the eddy, but nothing looked familiar, and he could not find it. "God of Kaherdyn," he breathed angrily, "if you're still with me, show me the way!"

"Halt!" a voice cried abruptly. A shadow loomed ahead, holding a sword. Tristan whirled, flinging the girl and the head aside and drawing his sword all in one motion. The guard leaped for him. Tristan dodged, plunged his sword into the man's belly, and kicked him off the cliff face onto the rocks below. And there, where the guard had been standing, a narrow path branched off and wound down toward the sea.

Tristan retrieved the head and bent over the princess he had thrown to the ground. "I beg your pardon, my lady. I had to do it—it was him or us. But look! He has shown us the cliff path, so it was not in vain. Come with me now to the boat. If Kaherdyn's God is with us still, we might even make the tide."

Halfway down the trail he heard the pounding of feet behind them. He dragged the unwilling girl to the edge of the path, clutched her close against the rock, and waited. Three men half ran, half slithered down the steep trail, swords drawn. He let two of them go by, then swung his sword into the body of the third. With a whistle of escaping air the man collapsed. Leaving the girl alone with the head of her tormentor, Tristan hurried silently down the path behind the others. He heard them reach the boat, grunt in dismay, call out to their companion, then turn and start back uphill. Again he hid, let the first man go past, and attacked the second. But this time they were walking, not running, and the leader heard his companion fall. He turned and faced Tristan on the path. He was not a big man, but he was a fighter and in good trim. Tristan knew, as they dodged, struck, and parried, that this would take time he did not have. He backed slowly over the body of the dead man. Down they went together toward the water, step by step, until Tristan heard the sea behind him and the gentle scrape of the boat on rock. He cried out and fell, twisting sideways as the sword came down. It just missed him, tearing the edge of his sleeve. He kicked out at the soldier's wrist. The sword spun away and the man staggered. The man staggered. In that instant Tristan leaped up and swung his blade, catching the fleeing soldier between the ribs. He died silently halfway to the ground.

Gasping for breath, Tristan ran back up the path. He found the giant's head where he had left it, but there was no sign of the girl. "Damn her lovely eyes, where did she go?" he whispered furiously. "What a family they are! Both of them, stubborn as oxen. He wants her back, she doesn't want to go. I'm blessed if I know what to make of them."

Then he heard the splash of oars in water. He turned and raced back down the path. A cloaked figure sat in the boat, struggling with the oars, while the craft spun slowly in the eddy.

"Wait!" he cried. "Wait for me!" He swore under his breath, flung the head into the keel, and leaped, catching the gunwale and falling heavily on top of his grisly prize. "Damn! Ugh! What a filthy mess! And you! What do you think you're doing? Let me have those. Go sit in the bows—there's a bench and a skin of water. Get out of my way now and be still."

But of course she went rigid as soon as he made it into the boat. She did not move or speak. He had to lift her and carry her forward to where he wanted her to stay. He rowed the boat to the edge of the eddy and watched the moving sea. He had not left it too late after all. The tide had turned and was on the ebb. He pulled hard out into the current; the boat swung, lifted, steadied, and slid silently past the towering granite walls. He thought he heard shouts from atop the cliff, but he hardly cared. He was nearly out of bowshot and heading fast for the open sea, and, most important of all, Kaherdyn's God was with the silent black-haired beauty in the bows. Ryol's men were powerless against him now.

At dawn he sailed past the breakers into the little bay where he had first landed in Lanascol. Kaherdyn and his friends waited on the shingle in subdued excitement. When he felt the keelrib scrape the sand, Tristan stepped out into knee-high water and carried the girl ashore. She stood on the shingle before her brother, wrapped in Tristan's cloak. This time her brilliant eyes were firmly on the ground.

"She has not said a word since I first saw her," Tristan told Kaherdyn. "She has not touched water. Or food. And she needs a tunic." He lowered his voice. "In truth, Kaherdyn, I believe she is not well. She has been hard used. The man—the man was a beast."

Kaherdyn put his arms around his sister. "Iseulte, Iseulte. It will be all right now. Everything will be all right." But she shrank from his touch and clutched the cloak tighter around her. He frowned. "What happened, Sir Tristan? How did you get her out? How did you find her? Where is Ryol now?"

Tristan beckoned him closer to the keel. "I found her in his bedchamber, half dressed, and took him as he prepared to lie with her. Do not fear, he is dead." He reached into the keel and drew out the head by its lank red hair. Time had done nothing to improve its appearance. Two of the boys gagged; even Kaherdyn turned green. "I've brought a trophy home to give the queen, your mother."

Kaherdyn was startled. "How did you know?" he whispered. "How did you know he took Iseulte as revenge against my mother?"

Tristan smiled gently. "I didn't until I met him. Then I guessed. He was, er, a man of appetites."

Kaherdyn's face went white. "My father fought him and took his lands. All but that godforsaken island and a strip of beach. But he didn't kill him because Ryol begged his pardon and swore an oath of fealty."

Tristan laid a hand on his sleeve to stop him. "It's all right. You don't need to tell me. Just take this giant's head to your mother and let her do with it what she wills."

Kaherdyn nodded. "Maybe now she will sleep at night." He turned to his sister. "Come, Iseulte. It's all over. All of it. Forever."

He stretched out his hand to her, but she stood motionless in the sand, head down, as rigid as a tree.

Tristan shook his head. "Give her time. Get her home to her mother as fast as you can. I don't think she wants men around her. Not even boys. Did you bring a horse for her?"

Kaherdyn looked desperately at Tristan. "You'll come with us, won't you? You've got to—I can't manage her alone."

Tristan bowed. "I am at your service, Prince Kaherdyn. Give me the horse and I'll carry her home." He smiled wryly. "I've dragged her down the giant's tower and across half his island. She's used to my gentle touch by now."

31 ✠ THE QUEEN OF LANASCOL

Hidden deep in the Wild Forest of Broceliande, the green clearing of Benoic shone like a rare jewel. A slow river curved around fields and meadows dotted with cattle and standing stones, only to disappear again into the impenetrable forest. In the middle of the clearing rose a low hill ringed by a thick wall of wood and stone. Within this encircling wall the town of Benoic grew and thrived. From the main gate a broad road, paved with stones, swept uphill to the king's house at the top.

Tristan looked about him with interest as Prince Kaherdyn led his troops through the gate, past saluting guards, past staring townspeople, up the curving ride to the fortress on the hill. He was not sure what he had expected of Lancelot's birthplace, but it was not this tiny jewel embedded in the wilderness. The king's house, part dwelling, part fortress, was made of wood and wattle. He had imagined something more like Camelot, large, impressive, built of dressed stone in the Roman style, built to last. But when they rode into the paved courtyard, where sentries stood at attention with polished swords, where grooms ran out from nowhere to take their horses as soon as they dismounted, where the captain of the guard embraced Kaherdyn with tears in his eyes and barked orders that were instantly obeyed, his sense of disappointment faded. Small and simple it might be, but it was a fortress nonetheless, with a pervading sense of order, calm, and discipline.

His last doubt died when the great bronze doors swung wide and Queen Dandrane herself came out to greet them on the steps. Her skin was the pale cream of her daughter's, but her face was Kaherdyn's, even down to the gray-green eyes, the tilt of her lips, and the bountiful chestnut hair. She was dressed plainly in a gray shift with an etched copper belt, but she needed no adornment. Age had lent majesty to her beauty. Her eyes flew to her daughter, standing between Tristan and Kaherdyn with head bowed low, but the queen greeted her son with only a tremor in her voice, thanked Tristan warmly for his help, and begged his attendance at a feast to be held that night in his honor. She sent for servants to show him to his quarters, asked if he required a razor or a bath, and ordered water and mead sent to his chamber, along with a wreath of wildflowers to sweeten the air.

As Tristan turned away to follow the servant indoors, he saw the queen take her daughter in her arms. For a moment, the wide gray-green eyes lifted to his. They were swimming with tears.

The feasting hall was large, Tristan noted in surprise, nearly as large as his own in Lyon's Head, but it was only half full, and half of its occupants were women. Everyone rose when the queen entered. Tristan hardly recognized the plainly dressed mother he had met that afternoon. She swept into the hall like a ship into harbor, royally adorned with gold at ears, throat, waist, wrists, and fingers, her rich hair bound in golden netting and a band of beaten gold across her brow.

She stood at Tristan's side and raised her winecup. "Tristan of Lyonesse," she said, smiling, "a toast in your honor." The hall erupted with cheering. Everyone drank to him again and again, calling out wishes for health and long life.

The queen lowered her voice and leaned toward him. "You must be wondering why we are so many women. Ryol himself is the reason. Nearly all our fighting men outside the house guard have died trying to bring my daughter home. Their widows are here, for the feast is held in honor of all those who risked their lives for her, and for me." Her kind face grew sad. "These women have lost nearly as much as their husbands, and more than you. They have lost their livelihoods. I maintain them now."

"My lady queen is very kind," Tristan murmured.

"It is only just. Why should they starve because their husbands died in my service? They are not much of a burden. In Benoic, everyone works together."

Servants swarmed around them with baskets of bread, platters of roasted meats, and bowls of dried fruits and nuts. Tristan's cup was refilled as soon as it was emptied with a neat wine far richer than any he had tasted in Britain.

"I owe you my son's life, as well as my daughter's," the queen said gravely. "It was against my will he led that band of children out of Benoic. I ought to punish him for disobedience, but I cannot. I am too happy to have him back. I thank you for that, too."

"He's a brave lad," Tristan replied, "and a determined one."

Her lovely mouth widened. " 'Stubborn' is the word I use."

Tristan grinned. "It ill becomes me to disagree with my host while I drink her wine and eat at her table."

She laughed lightly. "I like your manners, Sir Tristan. I thank you also for the giant's head. I've had it stuck on a spike at the main gate. The villagers have built a bonfire and are dancing around it." Her smiled faded. "As hideous as it is, I thank you for bringing it back to me. Now, perhaps, we can begin to put this horror behind us."

"And your daughter?" Tristan asked gently, seeing the despair behind her smiling eyes. "How does she fare now that she is home?"

"Iseulte is ill. He has damaged her spirit far more than her body. Her body will heal, but . . ." She turned away as her lips quivered. "The brute has robbed her of her innocence, of the person she used to be. At the moment she is no one. It is too soon to know who she will become."

"Let time pass."

"Indeed. It is my only hope."

Silence fell between them. All around them people ate and drank, talked and laughed and jested, but the queen sat quietly and stared at her plate. Her sorrow fell like a shadow across Tristan and stilled his appetite.

"My lady Queen of Lanascol," he said formally, "I have come a long way without knowing my destination, yet God has washed me ashore on your doorstep and shown me how I may be of service. Kaherdyn has told me your husband is away on a pilgrimage. If you would do me the honor, allow me to stay in Lanascol and serve you, at least until he returns."

Her eyes widened in surprise. "The honor is mine, Sir Tristan. You offer me a service I could not buy with all the gold in Lanascol. And you want nothing in exchange but to live in Benoic? What does a man like you want with a place like this? We are too small for your scope."

Tristan shook his head. "Nay, lady. There is something about this place—I have wanted to see it since my boyhood, when my father told me tales about his campaigns with Lancelot and Arthur. In a way, it's like Camelot to me. Some of the old magic of those golden days still clings to it."

A quick smile lit her lovely face. "I understand you. I, too, would have liked to know those men. But Lancelot died before I was married to his son, and I never met him." She hesitated, lowering her gaze. "We were married beside his grave on our way home from Wales. That's as close as I ever came to him."

"From Wales?" Tristan said quickly. "Are you Welsh, then?"

"Indeed. I grew up in Gwynedd. King Maelgon was my father."

Tristan stared at her openmouthed. "But Percival of Gwynedd is Maelgon's son!"

The queen's features lit with joy. "Val is my brother. My twin. Oh, I have not seen him for so long! Tell me what you know of him, I pray you."

Tristan's head reeled. "I have been sent here," he whispered. "Indeed, I have been sent." He steadied himself with an effort. "Percival is the greatest king in Britain. He holds Wales together in the only unity that embattled kingdom knows."

"I meant," she said gently, "tell me about *him*. When I left his wife had just borne him a son. She was a beautiful girl, if a little vain. King Pelleas's daughter Guinblodwyn. She disliked me, but that was only natural. Being twins, Val and I were so very close. We shared everything. I hoped that when I left they would grow closer and come to friendship once again." She looked at him expectantly.

"I don't know what their past has been," Tristan said evenly, "but they are hardly friends now. When I was in Gwynedd they did not speak or share a bed. She's widely considered a witch, I gather, and has gone back to the pagan practices of her childhood."

"I am so very sorry to hear that. Poor Val . . . You were in Gwynedd?" Tears misted the queen's eyes. "How I envy you. I have so longed to see my homeland again. How have the children fared? When I left—let's see— little Essylte was two and Melleas a baby. They must be grown by now. Are there any others?"

Tristan's throat tightened. "Percival has two sons living. Melleas and Logren."

"Two boys, how wonderful! And what became of young Essylte? She promised fair, as I recall."

Something struck in Tristan's chest and he could not breathe. He saw the queen's gaze sharpen. He struggled hard to find his voice. "Have you not heard? Percival married Essylte to my uncle Markion, King of Cornwall. Now she is High Queen of Britain."

"My niece Essylte?" She paused, watching his face. "So that's who it was. We get news from time to time here in the Wild Forest, but rarely is it recent. I knew Markion was High King, as I knew it was you who made him so. I had heard he took a Welsh princess to wife. But I did not know it was Essylte. Has she borne him a child?"

Tristan cleared his throat. "There is a son. Yes."

"Then Percival's grandson will be the next High King. What an honor she has brought to our house! And to yours."

"Yes," Tristan whispered. "Everyone who knows her honors Essylte."

He looked away as he said her name, and Dandrane watched him thoughtfully. "I will accept your offer, Sir Tristan. You are welcome in Benoic for as long as you like to stay. No, don't thank me. I will get more benefit from it than you, I have no doubt. But answer me a question, if you will.

Why is the Lord of Lyonesse, and Markion's honored nephew, willing to hide himself away in Broceliande?"

Tristan glanced at her nervously. "I am here because I cannot go home. My uncle the High King has banished me from Britain."

She searched his face. "Is there a price on your head?"

"No. He doesn't care if I live, so long as I don't live in Britain."

"And your lands?"

"Are in his hands."

"You are the man he owes his crown to. Is Markion a tyrant, then? Or do you deserve his judgment?"

Tristan hesitated, but the clear gray-green eyes, Kaherdyn's grave eyes, compelled the truth. "In his place I would have done the same. Or worse."

"I see." She looked around the hall. "I regret we have no bard to entertain us, but so few bards are left who remember the old tales, and fewer still who care to come through the forest to Benoic. When I was a girl in Gwynedd, we had the best bards in Britain. Ah, well. Time passes." She rose, and the hall rose with her. "It's time to lead the women out. Will you stay drinking with the men, Sir Tristan, or can I beg your company a little longer?"

He bent over her hand. "I am at your service, Queen Dandrane."

She led him down a corridor flagged in stone to a large, square room with cushioned chairs and a thick woven mat upon the floor tiles. She dismissed the women who attended her and lit the lamps herself. Then she walked to the window and pushed open a shutter, breathing in the scent-laden air of a soft spring night. Candlelight glimmered like rainwater over the gold of her gown.

"I want you to raise me a fighting force that can protect Lanascol from men like Ryol. He was the worst, but there are other such men about. Men of ambition, but without honor. Our army died at Ryol's hands. You're a warrior; men will follow you, men will come to you to learn. My husband would do it if he were here. But I cannot gather the men I need myself. Will you do this for me, Tristan?"

"I will, my lady."

"You must start from scratch, almost. There is no one left."

"I will ride around Lanascol, from household to household, and seek out the young men. Let me take Kaherdyn with me. We will have you the makings of an army by summer's end."

He was rewarded by a smile of relief. "Thank you. I'm sure Kaherdyn would love to go." She moved away from the window. "I also have a favor to ask you."

"Ask, lady, and I will do it."

"When you rescued Iseulte—when you found her in Ryol's chamber—

she was disheveled, Kaherdyn tells me, and needed your cloak to cover her nakedness. You, who saw her there, know what the brute used her for. I know it, and Kaherdyn, but—"

"Your secret is my secret," Tristan said softly. "No one else in all the world need know what happened to your daughter. If you are worried what I might say as I travel about your kingdom, don't be. I shall say nothing."

"Thank you, but you know what wings bad news has. Everyone in all of Less Britain already knows. I ask for more than that." She walked again to the window and looked out. "When he comes, he will come down that road and through the gate. Every day I watch for him. For the past month I have feared he would come before Iseulte came home. Now I am afraid he will come before she heals."

"You don't want your husband to know?"

She turned to him, her eyes bright with tears. "It is surely impossible to keep the truth from him. But when he learns it—" She shivered, and Tristan stepped closer.

"Will he blame her?"

The queen's lovely eyes widened. "Quite the reverse. He will forgive Iseulte, he will forgive me, in time he will forgive even Ryol. But he will never forgive himself. He will take all our sins upon himself, and blame himself for being away. It is himself he will punish, not us."

Tristan frowned. "What do you want me to do?"

"If he blames himself, Iseulte will not be able to support it. I fear she will throw herself in the river, or cut her wrists, or harm herself in some other way. She cannot bear to disappoint her father. I cannot protect her, Tristan, and protect him, too. This is what I ask. Protect my daughter from herself, while I protect my husband. You see," she said, smiling even as tears welled in her eyes, "it all started with me. He had planned this pilgrimage for years, but he only undertook it after— Well, there is no reason you should not know. Ryol came upon me alone once, when Galahad's back was turned. He tried to rape me, and would have succeeded but for Galahad's opportune return. They fought, and with Galahad's sword point at his throat Ryol submitted and swore faith with Lanascol. He gave us no trouble for years. Until this. Galahad felt responsible for my ordeal—my shame became his shame. He determined to walk all the way to Jerusalem in expiation. Imagine, just imagine, what he will do when he finds that Ryol ravished his daughter in his absence!" She buried her face in her hands while Tristan stared at her in disbelief.

"Galahad?" he whispered. "Sir Galahad? *The* Galahad? Your *husband?*" It was barely possible to believe a single warrior had fought Ryol and disarmed him without killing him, but if it was Galahad. . . . What had Percival said to him in Gwynedd? *He always was a complicated man.* Did that mean he lived? Surely Percival would have told him if Galahad had married his twin sister! But they hadn't had much time to talk. Tristan gulped and put out a hand to a nearby chair to steady himself. "It can't be," he breathed. "It can't be the same man."

The queen wiped tears from her cheeks. "Have you grown up on bards' tales of his death before the Grail?" She smiled bitterly at his expression and gestured at the chair. "Sit down, Tristan, before your knees give out. You're not alone. Few outside Lanascol know the truth about Galahad. His fame tore across Britain like a comet across the night sky, and then he disappeared, utterly and completely. Hence the legends that grow like moss all about his name. But he is a man, for all that, like any other."

"*Not* like any other," Tristan croaked, struggling to find his voice. "He was different. Stainless. Virtuous. Holy."

Dandrane watched him with compassion. "It is much more complicated than that," she said softly, moving to a seat opposite him. "What is holiness? Is the hermit holy who cuts himself off from his fellow men and dedicates his life to God's worship, an act by which no one benefits but himself? Or is the man holy who lives in the company of sinners, shares their joys and sorrows, and even their sins, yet loves them more dearly than himself and sheds his blood on their behalf? Which man would you rather serve? Which man would you go to in your hour of need?"

Tristan nodded. "You are right."

"When I was a girl in Gwynedd they used to say that saintly men were all wicked children. There is some truth in that, I think. A man who has been wicked knows the pain of doing evil, knows suffering, dishonor, degradation. Such a man knows the true value of virtue better than one who has never erred. Look at Arthur. Was there ever such a leader among the Britons? He is remembered and revered for his goodness, his kindness, his forbearance, his justice, as much as he is remembered for his prowess as a warrior. Yet as a young man he slaughtered innocents, and lay with his own sister to beget his bastard son. Perhaps evil in a human soul is like a refining fire; striving to free oneself from its power reveals the essence of a man."

"Are you telling me that Sir Galahad was a great sinner?"

Gentle amusement narrowed her eyes. "I am. He has done things he did not believe any God-fearing man capable of doing. Ask him yourself. Every day he draws breath, he errs."

"In that case," Tristan breathed, "there is hope for me."

The queen smiled. "There is hope for us all. Surely that is the truth Christ died to teach us."

Tristan watched her gravely as the lamplight played over the lovely contours of her face. Here was a woman whose beauty went to the bottom of her soul. He wondered if she had ever been wicked in her youth. He found it difficult to imagine. "Is there no Grail, then? Was that, too, a bard's invention?"

"Oh, no," she said quietly, "there is a Grail. But it has nothing to do with holiness. That is blasphemy."

"What is it, then? Can you tell me?"

"Part of an ancient treasure long lost to Britain's kings. There were three treasures once: a Sword, a Spear, and a Grail. Merlin found the Sword for Arthur, who named it Excalibur and used it to save Britain from the Saxons. But Merlin did not find the Grail and Spear. No man had seen them for over a hundred years when Arthur sent Galahad to find them." She smiled suddenly. "And find them he did. Many years later and when he least expected it. But they are not holy, Tristan, no matter what the bards say. They are sacred to Britain, perhaps, belonging to her kings. Arthur himself certainly thought of them in political terms. But to bards truth is a fabric easily embroidered. From time to time a few reach us through the Wild Forest and, unaware of who their host is, take up their harps and sing to us of how Galahad the Virgin Knight, alone of all Arthur's valiant Companions, achieved the Grail and died in its blessed light." She winked at him. "How it amuses him to hear it! He was fourteen when Arthur died and was never one of his Companions. As a youth, he feared women, hence his reputation for chastity, but like all men, he outgrew it. The Grail itself was an emperor's feasting krater, buried by his wife to keep it out of Saxon hands. But nowadays bards endow every tale with Christian meaning, they are so afraid of offending the bishops."

Tristan shook his head. "The bards I know believe the tales they tell of Galahad."

"Consider this a moment. All his life, because he was Lancelot's son, Galahad has been a figure of importance. He was tall for his age and had his father's skill with a sword. He was raised in Camelot by Arthur himself. And he did, as a young man, blaze a trail of glory across Britain. You will find him spoken of with awe in the northern kingdoms, in what remains of Logris, throughout the Summer Country, and of course in Wales. Every Saxon knows his name. His loyalty could not be bought, nor the service of his sword. Thanks to him, the Saxons and Anglii retreated for a space of time. And then, at the age of five and twenty, he disappeared from Britain." She smiled shyly. "I am the reason for that. No one knows it because when we left Britain, we came here. Benoic is small and unimportant in the scheme of things. Although Galahad and his brothers have protected Britain by fighting to keep Less Britain a united buffer against the Franks, the Burgundians, and the Alemans, Galahad has dropped out completely from affairs in Britain. It is no wonder, really, that everyone thinks he is dead. All the bards have done is to put an ending on a story they had no ending to."

"I will make you a song," Tristan offered, "that tells the true tale of his deeds."

She reached out and warmly grasped his hand. "That would please me greatly. But get to know him first. He will not deny you anything you ask— you have rescued his daughter, who is precious beyond words to him." She paused. "That is, if you will stay until he returns. I am afraid I can't tell you when that will be."

Tristan rose and lifted her hand to his lips. "You are graciousness itself, my lady. I would be pleased to raise an army for you and to serve you for as long as Lanascol needs my service. You do me great honor by letting me stay. This place has the feel of a sanctuary. Perhaps I, too, can begin a new life here."

Dandrane rose quickly from her chair and clasped his hand. "I do hope so, Tristan. There's no need to speak of the tragedy behind you. I can see well it is death to you. That is why you risked your life for us—you valued it no longer. I know well enough what is in your heart. It was in mine once, too." Her kind face drew closer and she touched her lips to his cheek. "And I saw your face when you spoke her name." She squeezed his hand. "Stay here with us and heal. Let time pass."

32 ✝ THE RETURN OF THE KING

Tristan sat on the garden wall one warm September afternoon, bent over his harp. He plucked the chords gently, eyes closed, as the melody took shape in his moving mind. It was another bittersweet love song, he noted wryly, even as the notes flowed from his fingers. And it would sound better on that old harp of Merlin's he had left in Lyonesse. This new harp had an airy sweetness to it that did not suit his melancholy mood. But at least he could sing. In the two years he had been in Lanascol, his spirit had remained so long grounded, wings clipped by grief, he had lost all hope of ever finding his voice again.

Like Marhalt's scar, the aching for Essylte was always with him. But for this agony there was no antidote. He was bereft; worse, she was bereft on his account. He shuddered involuntarily, and the harp howled. Quickly he stilled the strings with the flat of his hand.

Iseulte looked up from her seat upon the nearby bench. Tristan smiled apologetically. "A thousand pardons, Elen."

The clear blue eyes read his perfectly. "A calm soul, Tristan. All is not lost. She lives. Hold on to that."

He let his eyes linger on the sheen of black hair that fell like a cloak over her shoulders. "I will try."

She smiled and returned to her needlework. "Have you not told me, day after day, for two eternal years, a calm soul, a calm soul? And see, my soul is calm. I can speak again."

He ran his fingers along the harp strings in a gentle cascade of notes. "And what a beautiful voice it is. Well worth waiting for. I should teach you to sing."

She shook her head. "Not I. But let me hear the song again. The melody is enough to break the heart."

Tristan closed his eyes, seeing in his mind's eye that last dawn in Britain, the beautiful Essylte held close within his arms, her red-gold hair soft against his skin and her warm, sweet scent filling his nostrils.

> *Like a bird on the wing*
> *Like a bud on the bough*
> *Like a shiver of wind*
> *Or the shape-shifting cloud,*
> *Like the first bloom of beauty*
> *The first sigh of spring*
> *The leaf in the storm*
> *On a gossamer string.*
> *Quicksilver madness*
> *Strikes white to the bone*
> *As I cry in the dark:*
> *Love is here, love is gone.*
>
> *In my storm-ravaged midnight*
> *She's a fleet lightning dream.*
> *Her love's like a shadow*
> *Forever unseen.*
> *Despair stains the moonlight.*
> *Bereft of her heart,*
> *No nightingale sings*
> *In the sweet, empty dark.*
> *I would sail on the tide*
> *Toward the birth fire of dawn,*
> *But grief stirs the night wind*
> *And drowns my love song.*

Iseulte turned her head away to hide unexpected tears. "Truly, you are a master, Tristan."

He shook his head. "I am a bard only when the spirit moves me. I do not practice enough." He smiled. "I don't know all the genealogies, either. Until I came to Lanascol, I never knew Sir Percival had a sister."

Iseulte smiled, and Tristan regarded her with pleasure. How far she had come! But it had not been an easy journey. She had lain for a month in her bed, blankets drawn over her head although it was high summer, her body curled, knees to chin, in a protective stance against the entire world. When by autumn she had progressed no further than to lie on her back and stare wordlessly out the open window, Queen Dandrane had begun to despair for the recovery of her wits. True to his promise to the queen, Tristan had done what he could for her daughter, sitting with her when his travels allowed, telling her bards' tales, tales of ancient gods and heroes, tales of his own youth, tales of Lyonesse. Once or twice he had wept as he spoke, for the thought of his lovely Lyonesse, for remembrance of all he had lost. And once or twice he had seen tears in the vivid blue eyes and on the alabaster cheeks. But he said nothing. He let her rest within her shell and did not try to coax her out.

By midwinter she could rise from bed to sit for hours by the unshuttered window, covered in blankets and surrounded by braziers, staring wordlessly out at the snow. Come spring, she could walk on his arm to the garden. He remembered well the first time he had led her from her room. Until then she had not allowed a man to touch her, not even Kaherdyn. She had looked away, shaking so hard she could barely stand, as though the pressure of his fingers against her arm might burn her flesh. But she had withstood it.

Six more months went by before she could walk on her own, taking the initiative to go where she would. But still, she would not speak. Queen Dandrane, worn thin between the worry for her husband and the worry for her daughter, spent long hours in the chapel on her knees.

And then, last Christmas, Queen Dandrane had learned from Kaherdyn that Tristan could play and sing, and she had given him the new instrument that had reawakened his long-dead voice. For hours he sat with it in his chamber, getting the feel of it, holding it like a lover in his embrace, singing the sea songs that had once so infuriated Dinadan. The next thing he knew, Iseulte was at his door, her face wet with tears. She pointed to the harp and, for the first time in twenty months, spoke. "Don't stop," she said. "Don't ever stop."

Since that day she had talked to him often, but although she had wept in her mother's arms a hundred times, she had spoken only to Tristan. For his part, Tristan found himself able to tell her things he could share with no one else. Eventually he even told her about Essylte, and was surprised to find that she had already guessed something near the truth. She alone had heard the screaming of his heart in his music, a cry so bitter and so deep he would hear its echoes all his life.

As spring lengthened into summer, little by little she began to tell him about her abduction, clasping his hand as she spoke, her eyes dark with terror. One by one, she won her battles against fear. There was a resilience in her he admired and a strength he trusted. She was healing before his very eyes, and he envied her for it.

He slid off the wall and sat beside her on the bench. "I leave tomorrow to inspect the shore defenses. We've destroyed Ryol's stronghold, leveled the outbuildings, and strengthened the tower. The causeway to the beach is a wide one now and shored up with rock. Kaherdyn believes it's impregnable. Would you like to see it? You'd hardly recognize it. I'll go with you. It might help."

Iseulte paled. "No. Not yet. Please." She dropped her eyes. "Take Mother instead. She has never seen the place. She will go if you ask her. She owes you much for rebuilding Lanascol's defenses."

Tristan shrugged lightly. "She owes me nothing for that. I asked to stay."

Her head flew up. "You did? I did not know that."

"Why not? I cannot go home. Where better to live what life is left to me than here, in the place Sir Lancelot and Sir Galahad both called home?"

"Yes, we breed strong men in Lanascol," she said softly. "But you, Tristan, you will go back. Someday. I know you will."

A horn sounded, shattering their peace. Once, twice, three times. Iseulte rose. "A courier! Oh, Tristan, go see what he wants! It could be Father."

He extended a hand. "Come with me."

"Oh, no! I can't—I—"

But he took her trembling hand and gently led her forward. "Yes, you can. The queen will receive him privately, to get his news. Court won't be assembled. You won't have to appear publicly. Come, you'll see."

They found Queen Dandrane in her antechamber, attended only by her women. A courier knelt at her feet, the dust of travel still in his clothes and hair, his message pouch slung loosely around his shoulder. Queen Dandrane bent her head over a short scroll, reading so intently she did not hear them enter.

At last she looked up, blinking back tears, and signaled them to approach. "Tristan. Iseulte, my dear. A letter from your uncle Galahodyn.

Your father is on the road home. He has spent a fortnight with Hodyn in Neustria. Hodyn says—Hodyn says he is not well. He was wounded in the East, it seems, and the wound has festered. He has been ill a year, and the journey home has been a slow one. But—but he is coming."

Iseulte crossed herself quickly and sank to her knees.

The courier went pale as he stared at Tristan. "Tristan? You can't be Tristan of Lyonesse? Who disappeared from Britain these two years past?"

Tristan inclined his head. "At your service. How long is the journey from Neustria? When should we expect Sir Galahad?"

The courier gulped audibly and fought to collect his wits. "My lord, I cannot say for certain. It is a week's ride on horseback, but he travels in a litter."

"A litter!" Dandrane pressed a hand to her mouth.

"Yes, my lady. I was held up a day when a storm flooded the river and the fording place washed out. He may be a day or two behind me. He may be hours."

Tristan, with his hand on Iseulte's shoulder, felt a tremor go through her. He frowned lightly. "What news is there from Britain?"

The man's eyes flitted nervously between Tristan and Iseulte. "Recent, my lord? Not much."

"In the last two years."

"In two years, my lord, much has happened. What is it—what is it my lord wishes to know?"

"What of my uncle and his Queen?"

"Er, um," the courier stammered, "God has not smiled on King Markion, my lord, since, uh . . . you, er . . . since, that is to say—"

"Go on. Out with it."

"Since you ran away," the courier finished on a gasp.

Tristan flushed darkly. "Ran away? Is that what they are saying?"

"Some call it that. Markion's men, mostly. But others just—others just say you disappeared."

"Go on about Markion. What's happened to Britain since he lost the willing service of half his commanders?"

The courier steadied himself. "Well, my lord, the Saxons have been gaining every season. Last spring the High King lost a battle at the Giants' Dance. The Saxons overran Amesbury again and all the land around. Drustan of Elmet was killed by Anglii invaders, and the northern federation is split into factions over the succession. Only Percival of Gwynedd has kept faith with Markion. Only the west stays strong."

"Thank God for Percival. Now, tell me what you know of the Queen."

Iseulte looked up at him and reached for his hand. Dandrane rolled up her scroll and tucked it away, watching from the corner of her eye.

The courier hesitated, licking dry lips. "What about the Queen, my lord? I have not much news of her."

"You know well enough what I want to hear. Is she well? How fare the children?"

The courier pulled anxiously at his beard. "Both boys are well. About the Queen herself, reports vary. After Ysaie the Sad was born she was ill for months. Some say she has been low-spirited ever since, but others say her health has been perfectly fine. I know not which tale is true."

"Ysaie? Why did she give the child so dolorous a name?"

The courier shrugged. "Perhaps because the High Queen wept for two months before and after he was born. Perhaps because the birth was over-hard. He's a big lad for his age, and was so when he was born. She'll have no more, they say, although she's young enough and Markion himself is strong as a horse."

Something near a growl issued from Tristan's throat. His hand slid to his sword hilt.

The courier bent his forehead to the ground. "Forgive me. My lord asked me for the news."

"That's not news." Tristan spun on his heel and strode away, then turned and came back again. "Is that all you can tell me about her, man? Did you see no one who had been at Tintagel?"

Sweat beaded the courier's brow. "Well, my lord, we had a bard once. Hebert of Aquae Sulis. Said he knew you."

Tristan nodded. "He does."

"He sang us a song in your honor, my lord, full of the tales of your exploits. That's how most of us learned what was going on in Britain. He said you came three steps shy of death to gain King Markion his crown, and risked your life in Wales to bring his bride out. But for all your bravery and daring, Markion defeated you in the end, by denying you the only reward you wanted. Your life is forfeit now in Britain." The courier lifted his head to glance at Tristan and quickly bent it once again. "It is not always wise to help kings to their desires, my lord. So Hebert said. Obligation makes them irritable."

"Irritable!" Tristan laughed, but there was no mirth in it. "As a starving wolf is irritable. Hebert has eyes in his head. If he's been to Tintagel, he sang of more than that. How does the Queen? Does she smile? Dance? Sing? Surely she cannot pass every hour of the day in misery."

Iseulte squeezed his hand. The courier's eyes flicked uneasily from lord to princess. "Hebert never mentioned Tintagel, my lord. But, um, he did say, uh, that without her faithful companion—I forget the maid's name, but you know it well enough, my lord, if the tales are true—without her Welsh servant, the High Queen is most unhappy. 'A rudderless ship on a stormy sea' was the bard's way of putting it. I suppose that—"

Tristan's face lost color. Iseulte slipped an arm about his waist. His voice was a whisper. "Branwen? Do you mean Branwen? Branwen is gone? Where?"

The man's brow furrowed. "Gone, my lord? Aye, to the Otherworld. The lass is dead."

Tristan closed his eyes.

"How?" Dandrane asked quickly. "By disease, by accident, or at another's hand? Quick, man. Speak."

The courier turned to her and ducked his head. "Yes, my lady. I thought you knew already of these events. The maid has been dead two years. She died the day Sir Tristan disappeared from Lyonesse."

A cry escaped Tristan, and Dandrane spoke fiercely. "How? Who killed her?"

Confused, the courier shook his head. "Nay, lady, no one touched the maid. She took the poison draught herself, and by her own will she died."

Tristan staggered, his eyes blind with tears. "That cup was meant for me. Oh, God, how I am damned! But I never knew she meant to take it. Oh, Essylte, forgive me! I have robbed you of everything dear to your heart."

Dandrane rose. "Thank you for risking the hazards of the road," she said firmly to the courier. "My servant will show you to the kitchens, where you may wash and have a meal. I will send for you later to hear more news about my husband."

The courier bowed low and hurried out behind the servant. Dandrane turned to Tristan and Iseulte. "Take him to the chapel, Iseulte. It is the best place for such grief." She hesitated. "Stay with him and bring him what comfort you can."

The girl's lips worked, but no sound came out. Her brilliant blue eyes gazed longingly into her mother's face, then shuttered closed as she turned away and nodded. Dandrane stood watching the empty doorway for a long time after they had gone.

Galahad came home at sunset three days later. Queen Dandrane waited in the forecourt of the king's house, with Kaherdyn on her right hand and Tristan and Iseulte on her left. Flanking them on both sides stood two companies of Lanascol's young army and behind them the house guard, boots and buckles polished until they gleamed in the dying light.

From the king's house they could see the slow procession, thirty horses coming two abreast behind a litter. Torches lined the steep, ascending roadway, forming a tunnel of light for the returning king.

Tristan stood with his arm around Iseulte's shoulder. Beneath her robe she felt as still and rigid as an oak.

"He already knows," Tristan said quietly, pulling her closer. "Your uncle Galahodyn told him. He's had time to come to terms with it. There is no need to be afraid."

She did not respond. Her eyes remained fastened on the roadway and Tristan sighed inwardly. *He absorbs sin as a sponge does water,* she had said to him once. *He believes himself the father of sins. And I—I will add another to his burden.* Unconsciously, his fingers tightened around her shoulder. Iseulte's sin had been thrust upon her, but his own—his own had been fashioned by his own hands, with hardly a regret. . . .

Six quick blasts on the horn signaled the approach of the procession. As they crested the hill Tristan saw a man walking before the empty litter. He wore an old bleached robe and sandals, and leaned heavily upon a staff. He might have been a beggar, he was so plainly dressed, but there was no doubt who he was.

Queen Dandrane stepped forward. Tears misted her eyes. "Galahad! My dear lord, welcome home!" She embraced him quickly and then knelt at his feet. He raised her, took her by the shoulders and spoke softly, then held her in his arms and kissed her. Iseulte drew a long breath, and Tristan felt her shoulders soften.

Kaherdyn stepped forward, and as Galahad greeted his son, Tristan watched the great knight in fascination. His head was bare—no crown, no circlet, no helm, not even a hood against the sun—and raven-black like his daughter's, flecked with gray only at the temples. But his beard was white. He wore no ornaments—no torque, no wristbands, not even a swordbelt— yet he was by reputation the deadliest swordsman living, and a powerful king besides. His face was tanned and weathered by years in the sun, and he moved like an old man, but his eyes! Tristan quailed momentarily as Gala- had's gaze slid over him and fastened on Iseulte. His eyes were as brilliant blue as his daughter's and alive with the intense vitality of youth.

Iseulte began to shake as he approached. "Elen, Elen, Elen," Tristan hummed a ditty under his breath, "beautiful Elen of the west, whom we all love best, sing me a sweet song as you send me to my rest."

He knew by the catch in her breath she had heard him, and for a mo- ment he thought she would step forward of her own accord into her father's arms. But instead she sank to the ground, lifted the dusty hem of his coarse robe, and pressed it to her lips. Galahad knelt stiffly beside her and lifted her chin so their eyes met. For a long moment they gazed at one another.

"I left a child," the king murmured, "and return to a woman grown. I hardly know you, little Elen. Be patient with me. I love you so."

Tears splashed down the girl's face as she fell into his embrace. Galahad held her and whispered to her, taking his time, oblivious to the people all around him. When he loosed her he smiled shyly at her and offered her his hand. She took it and helped him rise.

Tristan felt the blue eyes meet his as an arrow strikes a tree. "My lord king," he breathed. His legs buckled, and he found himself kneeling in the dust. "Sir Galahad."

A strong, browned hand reached out and raised him. "Tristan of Lyonesse. I bless the day you came to Lanascol. You rescued my daughter, who is more precious to me than any living soul, and you saved my kingdom. I thank you from my heart. What is mine is yours."

"Hardly that, my lord," Tristan responded weakly. "Your kingdom was in no danger with such a queen as your noble wife in command."

Galahad smiled, the seamed brown skin creasing along familiar lines in a handsome, fine-boned face. "She is worth three of me any day, as any one of my men will tell you." He extended his arm toward the doorway of the king's house, where Dandrane and Kaherdyn waited in ill-concealed impatience. "Come, lend me your shoulder, if you would. I believe Dane has a feast prepared. Although in truth, I have not much stomach for it, having got so used to foreign food." With one arm wrapped about Tristan and one hand on his staff, Galahad made his slow way up the wide steps and back into his home.

True to his word, he ate little enough at dinner, and no animal flesh of any kind. But he looked pleased when others ate and drank, and Iseulte, who sat beside him, could not take her eyes off him. He talked little about his travels; mostly he wanted to know what had happened in Lanascol in his absence. He questioned Tristan and Kaherdyn about the defeat of Ryol, their travels about the kingdom, the building of the army, the state of relations with the Franks and Alemans, and any news of his youngest brother, Gallinore, King of Brittany. Mention of Iseulte's ordeal was carefully avoided. Eventually, as the candles dimmed and the wine went round, talk inevitably turned to his pilgrimage. He sighed heavily and his eyes grew distant.

"It is another lifetime," he said slowly, half to himself. "It is another world. I left my youth there, Dane, in the white hills around the City of David."

"Is that where you were wounded? How did that happen? Were there bandits?"

He smiled wistfully. "Oh, no. Not there. We fought a pitched battle there. This wound in my thigh was from a Persian arrow."

The queen gasped. "You led an army against Persians? Dear God!"

"No, my dear, not I. A Hebrew king, clever as a fox. I'll give you the details another time, if you like, but I'm growing tired of talk." He smiled a quick, apologetic smile. "I've had so little of it, you see."

Queen Dandrane signaled the torchbearers nearer. "You'll let me send for the physician, surely. We must find a way to heal your wound."

He laughed. "Do you imagine they have no physicians in the East? I assure you, my wound has been examined by a dozen skilled physicians, true men of learning, not charlatans armed only with leeches and spells. I was half a year in a desert hospital working the poison out. It has knit as well as it ever will. Men can do no more. Let it be. It is the Lord's reminder to me that a humble spirit is a great gift and pride a curse." He lifted Dandrane's hand to his lips and gazed into her worried eyes. "What was it but pride that made me think that I, like Christ Himself, could carry the world's sins on my shoulders? What was it that made me go all the way to Jerusalem to discover what I had left at home? Pride and vainglory, nothing more. You see again how thickheaded I was born. I learned on David's hilltop what you have known all these years: that I am no more and no less than an ordinary man. My own misdeeds are more than I can handle. I need take on no others." He glanced gently at Iseulte, whose head was bowed.

Dandrane blinked back tears. "You are first among men, my lord, who would be last. That is wisdom as old as Solomon."

Kaherdyn rode at Tristan's side in the warm November sun. Most of the hardwoods stood gray and naked along the forest road, readying themselves for the coming winter snows, but along the edges of the lake the pines grew green right down to the water's edge.

"How's your father today?" Tristan asked.

"About the same." Kaherdyn pointed across the lake to an island in the middle. "My father used to spend a lot of time on that island when he was a boy. So did my grandfather, Lancelot, in his youth. It's pretty, isn't it? But somehow it's never called to me." He smiled quickly at Tristan. "In fact, it gives me the shivers sometimes. The locals think it's haunted."

"Indeed? By whom?"

Kaherdyn shrugged. "Who knows? I don't believe in phantoms."

Tristan smiled. "Clear-eyed Kaherdyn. Of course you don't. Your path is straight."

"No," Kaherdyn said solemnly. "It's not."

"What? Trouble with lovely Lionors? I thought you had her father's blessing."

"I do." He looked quickly away and shut his mouth on what he had been about to say. Tristan glanced at him and smiled. Kaherdyn was nearly eighteen, no longer a boy, with broad shoulders, strong arms, and thick chestnut hair that women loved to touch. Surely whatever problems he thought he had were easily surmounted.

"Well, then, marry the lass next spring. Your father won't object. Queen Dandrane practically raised her, she has been so long in her service."

"But my father *does* object," Kaherdyn blurted, reddening.

Tristan pulled up his horse and stared. "In heaven's name, why?"

Kaherdyn looked at him, shame, despair, humiliation, and then hope passing in successive waves across his face. "I promised I wouldn't tell you," he said at last. "I ought not to have said so much. I promised Father. He sent me to find you and ask you to go see him. I don't know what he wants, Tristan, but I think it may be partly about that."

Tristan scratched his head in bewilderment. "What do I have to do with your marrying Lionors? Well, if your father's waiting, let's not delay. Race you back?"

Kaherdyn grinned, his good humor restored. "Oh, there's no hurry. He had just sent for a hot bath when I left. He'll be hours yet. It takes him forever to get up and down, his joints are so stiff."

Tristan frowned and started his stallion forward again. "He was not so afflicted a month ago."

"Mother says it was because the weather was warmer then."

"I wonder how he will survive the winter. Perhaps it is a consequence of so much time spent in the sun."

"Do you know what Sir Bellas told me, Tristan? My father killed seventeen hill bandits by his own hand as his traveling party passed through southern Gaul. And saved thirty children from a massacre by some barbarous Massalian lord. And rescued a Hebrew maiden from stoning outside the holy city—I tell you, Tristan, the more we learn about what went on in those four years, the more amazed I am. Is Bellas telling me lies, do you think?"

"I shouldn't think so. Why would he? And he was there."

"But if Father did all those things, why won't he talk about them? He's as silent as Iseulte about his exploits."

"A good deed done in darkness," Tristan said slowly, "is a better deed than one done in light for all to see. Who needs to know about it but the ones concerned?"

"But he deserves praise for such deeds!"

"Of course. But perhaps he has already had all he wants. He's not a man who feeds on praise." Tristan frowned. "And he literally eats almost nothing. Have you noticed, Kaherdyn, how thin he's getting?"

"I know his leg is worse. He can hardly walk without his staff." Kaherdyn hesitated and then asked in a halting voice, "Do you think he's come home to die?"

Tristan shrugged, and moved to put heels to his horse. "It had crossed my mind."

He found Galahad in his chamber sitting straight in a tall-backed chair. The windows were shuttered against the evening chill and the room was warm with two glowing braziers, yet Galahad wore a heavy cloak over his white robe and a blanket over his knees.

"My lord Galahad."

"Arise, Tristan. Loosen your tunic and roll up your sleeves or you'll be sweating soon. I know it's overwarm in here. But my bones are cold." He waved his chamberlain out of the room and told the sentry on the door to let no one in. "Please be seated."

The brilliant eyes lifted to Tristan's and once again pinned his will to the wall. Tristan met that gaze with the qualm a soldier feels in meeting his new commander's eye. "Tristan of Lyonesse, I am honored to have you in my household. In the months since my return I have come to know you, and I find only honor in you. I knew your father and admired him. I know of the brave deeds you have done in Britain, both on behalf of your uncle and on behalf of the kingdom itself. I am honored to offer you a home here."

"My lord, the honor is all mine."

"I speak of a permanent home."

A light frown flicked across Tristan's brow. "Thank you, my lord. You are graciousness itself."

Amusement pulled at the corners of Galahad's mouth, but when he spoke, his voice was grave and gentle. "I am asking you to marry my daughter."

Tristan blanched. The room reeled, and he grasped the arms of his chair.

"Dane and I have worried about Iseulte for years," Galahad continued. "No suitor ever stepped forward for her. I used to fear it was my reputation that frightened them away, but in truth I think the explanation is simpler. Since Hoel of Brittany died and left the running of his kingdom to Lancelot's heirs, the noble families of Less Britain are all my kin. My brothers' sons are younger than Kaherdyn. And everyone in Britain persists in believing that I am dead. There is no one eligible for Elen." The blue eyes flickered. "And there is only one man I have met who is worthy."

"My lord." Tristan found himself on his feet. "My lord, it is impossible."

"Kaherdyn wishes to marry," Galahad continued, looking idly down at his hands. "Young Lionors, a distant kinswoman. I have only one objection to the match. Iseulte is one and twenty and unwed. When he marries and brings his bride into the house, supplanting Iseulte's place, he makes a spinster of his sister." A tender note crept into the even voice. "Surely, after all she has borne, she deserves better." He looked up at Tristan. "Is that not so?"

"Yes," Tristan breathed, gulping for air. "She's a noble-hearted woman. And brave. And beautiful. But my lord—"

"You do like her, Tristan? Dane gave me to believe you two had become the best of friends."

"Friends, yes, my lord. Without a doubt. I can tell her anything, and she me, but—"

"The love of a friend is often the truest of all. And you are more than a friend to Iseulte. You are the only one she speaks to. You are her healer, Tristan. With scars such as hers, she may have need of you her whole life."

Tristan paused, breathing rapidly. "My lord, I can't. It's impossible. Have you asked her? No, I see you haven't. She would not accept me. She knows my heart. She knows that I am promised to another. Surely she deserves a more devoted husband than a man who will always regard her as second best."

Tristan braced himself for a stinging rebuke, but when Galahad spoke, his voice was low and gentle.

"You are promised to a woman who is the wife of another man."

Tristan nodded miserably. "Yes, my lord."

"Well," Galahad said softly, "my father once faced just such a dilemma."

Tristan gaped. He sank slowly down into his chair, his heart roaring in his ears, and listened.

"In the end, we put our feelings aside and do what honor demands. To do else, we demean ourselves and debase the love we hold so dear. If she were free, you would wed her. Unimaginable joy would be yours forever." The blue eyes narrowed in a sad smile. "But she is not free. More than that, she is married to your sovereign lord, a man to whom you owe service and allegiance."

Tristan's head hung lower. He nodded dumbly.

"Then you know that your promise is a vain one, made in the heat of passion, and impossible to keep." Galahad's voice grew even gentler. "She has not been able to keep her promise, either."

Tristan bowed his head. Here was the wound that had kept him awake so many nights, the enduring pain he had striven so hard to hide from everyone. And now a stranger, a man he had known two months, whom he had supposed knew nothing at all about it, had struck his sorest spot with unerring accuracy.

Galahad lifted the wineskin from the flame, filled a silver cup, and handed it to Tristan.

Obediently, Tristan drank. "A promise is a promise," he whispered.

"Yes."

"I must leave, then."

"I will not prevent you, but there is no need. You are welcome in Lanascol for as long as you like to stay. You are welcome to make Benoic your home. We, all of us, love you as though you were already family."

Tristan looked up at him with drowned eyes. "But if I stay after Kaherdyn marries, there will be talk. About why I stay so close and do not marry her. It's not fair to Elen."

"No," Galahad said quietly. "It's not fair. But it's not new."

Tristan's throat closed. "What do you mean? Has there been talk already? Is that what you are telling me? Have I shamed your daughter?"

Galahad shook his head firmly. "No. Without you, she would be dead. You are the joy in her life, son. Very nearly her only joy. It never does any good to listen to kitchen gossip. Ignore it. Iseulte would want you to stay at any cost."

Tristan leaped to his feet and strode around the room, muttering under his breath. "If I stay, I am the cruelest man alive; if I go, I am an unfeeling, ungrateful wretch. If I break my promise, I am cursed; if I keep it, I am no more than a miserable sinner, already damned. O God! I cannot see the honorable path. There is no honor for me anywhere."

"Yes," Galahad said evenly, "there is. Sit down, Tristan, and calm yourself a moment." Galahad watched him with compassion. "You chastise yourself because your life is full of mistakes, errant judgments, wrong choices, even sins. But which of ours is not? You are not damned if you can put those hurtful acts behind you and go forward a better man. God forgives us all. We can begin anew." Galahad grasped his staff and slowly rose to his full height. Tristan slid off the chair to his knees. "I will not tell you what honor is, for this you know as well as anyone. I tell you only, do not despair. Seek a new path, find the straight road. Hope is always with us. That is God's great gift."

He made the sign of the cross over Tristan's head and slowly and stiffly moved toward the door, leaving Tristan bent double on his knees.

33 ✝ ISEULTE OF THE WHITE HANDS

On a clear day in December Tristan stood in the marble Roman chapel on a hillside in Benoic, surrounded by the white blaze of candles, while a priest spoke the solemn words that bound him for life to Elen of Lanascol.

After the wedding the small procession wound up the hill to the king's house, Dandrane following Galahad's litter, Kaherdyn and Lionors walking hand in hand behind the bride and groom. Last night's snow had carpeted the world in crystalline brilliance, a blinding blanket of light marred only by their footsteps. It was fitting, Tristan thought numbly, that he should embark on a new life on such a day. The whole world was clean, cold, unmarked, and dead.

The feast began as night drew down. All the young men in the army cheered Tristan, toasting to his happiness over and over again amid their dancing, jesting, and singing. Neat Gaulish wine flowed like water and the wedding guests grew wild as the night wore on. At the climax of the evening, Dandrane revealed the surprise she had been hinting at all week. Old Rhys, the master bard of Wales, stepped into their midst and bowed low.

"My lord Tristan," he growled in his rough speaking voice. "How glad I am to see you still alive. God bless you, sir." He beckoned to his apprentice to bring in his harp. He gave them all the old sweet tales of Britain: "The Song of Maximus," "The Lay of Arthur," "The Parting of Lancelot and Guinevere," "The Defeat of Cerdic," and one or two tales of his own devising about events more recent. His singing voice was clear and true, carrying to every corner of the hall with a melancholy sweetness that brought tears to many eyes. At the finish, Tristan pulled the gold brooch from his shoulder and pressed it into the old bard's hand.

"Bless you, Master. You speak to all our hearts. Would our lives were all like your heroes' tales, with noble endings."

The bard peered down at the brooch. "The Eagle of Lyonesse?"

"Take it, Master. I have no more need of it. And you have done me a service tonight. You have taken me back to Britain, which my eyes shall never see again."

Rhys bowed low. "The future is what we make of it," he murmured, as the queen signaled her women to lead the bride out. Pale Iseulte, her black hair braided with garnets and river pearls and a laurel garland around her brow, raised her eyes briefly to Tristan and then lowered them demurely as she turned to go. A cheer rose from the wedding guests, and Rhys raised an eyebrow.

"Congratulations, my lord. She's a beauty."

"Oh, God," Tristan breathed. "Is it time already? Sing me another song, good Rhys, a long one, that lasts until the dawning."

The old bard looked at him knowingly. "My lord is an unwilling bridegroom?"

Tristan smiled bitterly. "Alas, no. Let it not be said I did this with my eyes closed. It was by my will I chose it. Yet . . . yet I would put it off a little longer. Sing for me, I pray you."

"Very well, my lord." He bowed again to the king and queen. "I give you the tale of Tristan of Lyonesse and the giant Marhalt."

The room was dark when Tristan opened the door. An applewood fire burned low in the grate, shedding the only light. He glanced furtively toward the big bed but saw only an unmoving bulge in the bed furs. After a moment's hesitation, he took his own garland from his head and let it fall to the floor. He stirred the fire to life, added another log, lifted the wineskin from its stand, and poured himself another cup of wine. He drank it standing. Finally he put down the cup, squared his shoulders, and walked to the bed.

"Elen. Are you awake?"

"Yes."

He sat down beside her. "Sit up and talk to me."

Still the furs did not move. "I am afraid."

"Of me? It's only Tristan. I won't harm you. Come on, sit up. We haven't said two words to one another in one long, dreadful month. I need to speak to you."

She pushed herself up slowly. They had dressed her in an ivory gown trimmed in white fur, and they had removed the lacings from the bodice so that the fabric parted as she moved, revealing the sweet curve of her breasts. Tristan took a slender white hand in both of his. For the first time in years he felt the stirrings of desire. Rosy firelight played across her face, highlighting her cheekbones and throwing her magnificent eyes into shadow.

"How beautiful you are," he whispered. "You deserve a better husband than I can make you."

She smiled in quick relief. "Oh, Tristan, I do not worry about that. Just be who you are; it is enough. But I fear I will not be able to be a wife to you. It is you who deserve a better wife than me."

"What does any man want in a wife but a good companion?" he asked, bringing her hand to his lips and watching her face. "We two are already companions of long standing. And you are beautiful besides, sweet-tempered and brave."

"Not so brave," she quavered. "And that is not all most men want. They want a willing breeder of sons." She gulped audibly and stiffened as he lifted the palm of her hand against his new-shaved cheek. "I don't think—I'm not sure I can—lie with you."

Tristan pressed his lips into her palm. Her raised arm parted the fabric of her gown even further and his voice caught in his throat. "I understand your fear. Nothing need happen between us, Elen. Nothing at all. No one will ever know but us."

Her eyes widened and caught the light, blazing blue. "And God."

"Is that so important? You are even braver than I thought."

She bit her lip and pulled her hand away. "It is not a marriage without. Why did you accept me if you did not want me?"

"Not *want* you?" He laughed hoarsely. "Oh, God! How little you know about desire." He ran a finger along her jaw and down her neck to the open bodice of her gown. "There is no fire in all the world like this fire," he breathed, drawing her closer and touching his lips to hers. She bore it stiffly at first, but after a moment, her lips relented and returned his gentle pressure. When he pulled away, her face was flushed with color and a dawning excitement danced in her eyes. "Lovely Elen, I accepted you because I mean to spend my life in Lanascol, and I want you as my companion always." She nodded shyly, her breath coming fast and a little shallow. "And why, if you are so frightened of a man's touch, did you accept me?"

After a struggle, the blue eyes lifted to his. "Because I love you."

He looked away without meaning to. "A gift, a great gift. But I am not worthy of such a treasure."

"Because you still love Essylte? I know that, Tristan. You needn't try to hide it. She is in your heart, and she always will be. I don't mind. I love her, too, because she is part of you."

"You're a generous woman. Indeed, you shame me." He took her hand again and held it. "You have borne with courage the worst men have to offer. Be patient with me tonight, and I will offer you the best. It need not be a sacrifice." He leaned forward. "Lovely Elen," he breathed into her ear, "let me lead you to the wellspring of desire." She trembled violently as his arm slid around her shoulders and pulled her closer. "Come, hold on to me. That's right. You're safe in my arms, and I in yours. We are here together. Don't be afraid to touch me; I'm only an ordinary man."

He kissed her softly, moving his lips over her face, her mouth, her jaw, while his hand slid slowly through the parting of her gown. His own heart raced against his will. He spoke to her gently, keeping his voice calm, keeping his touch gentle as he moved his hands over her body, easing her slowly to relaxation and then gradually to pleasure, conquering her fear. Her breathing quickened, her face flushed lightly, and her eyes looked up at his in growing surprise as her body responded to his touch of its own will.

"Tristan," she whispered, "I feel—like a waterfall."

He laughed lightly. "There are many currents in the river of bliss. Heaven waits at the end, I promise you."

Betrayal! The thought flashed across his mind with the speed of a sword stroke and stayed his hand. Essylte—had he not promised Essylte fidelity unto death? He stared down at Galahad's daughter, breathing hard. Essylte had been compelled to break her vow, but he was not—this he did of his own will. He knew it by the fire in his loins.

"Tristan," she whispered. There was an ache in her voice, an ache he recognized. Her arms reached out to him.

He hesitated half a moment, knowing that despite her apparent willingness he must continue at a snail's pace. But his body, fully reawakened after so long a sleep, cried out in exasperation. Before he knew it he had taken her in his arms, parted her thighs, and moved to cover her. Then the night exploded.

She screamed. Wild, frantic, in abject terror, she pounded on his shoulders with her fists, thrashing, kicking beneath him, forcing him up. She knocked over the candle stand at the bedside, she pulled at his hair, she sobbed aloud for the angel of death.

"Elen! My God, Elen!" He rose to his knees and pulled her up, hugging her tight against his body, holding her immobile while she screeched and sobbed.

"Leave me alone! Animal! Swine! I hate you! How could you? Oh, God, I am dirty, how dirty! I will never be clean!"

"Elen, sweet Elen, it's Tristan! Don't you know me?"

But she sobbed mindlessly and ferociously fought to escape his grip. He waited, it seemed like hours, while she clawed at him and howled, until the sobbing died to whimpers and, her strength spent, she sagged listlessly in his arms. Carefully, he lowered her to the bed, covered her with furs and then sank down beside her. For a long time he lay absolutely still while the pounding in his head slowed and the fire that consumed him subsided to ash. When her breathing fell at last into the slow rhythm of sleep he closed his eyes. *Saved from betrayal by a woman's fear,* he thought, his face hot with shame. *What have I done to the woman I would die for? Dear God, let her never learn of it!* He shuddered and turned on his side away from Iseulte.

When he awoke the gray light of morning streamed in through the open window and with it a chill wind. Iseulte stood at the window, staring out, wrapped in a heavy gown and cloak with her hood pulled tight around her face.

Tristan pushed himself up on his elbows and frowned. "Elen? Where are you going so early?"

She started at his voice and looked quickly down. "Away. Just away." There were still tear tracks on her face, and her voice was harsh with weeping.

Tristan pulled on his bedgown. "What do you mean, away? Away where?" Shivering, he went to the window and pulled the shutter closed. Iseulte slid to her knees, her beautiful hands upraised and clasped together.

"Forgive me, my lord," she said hoarsely. "Please. I beg you. I *must* have your forgiveness."

"Your hands are ice." He stooped and lifted her bodily, carrying her back to the bed. A shudder went through her as he put her down. "Just sit there a moment. I'm not going to touch you, I'm going to stoke the fire."

It did not take long to get a good blaze going, but the room was still so cold he could see his breath in the air. He hurried back to the bed and huddled into the furs beside her, teeth chattering. "If you are trying to kill me with cold, you may well succeed."

He regretted the jest the instant he made it. Her pale face flamed and tears filled her eyes.

"Put me away, Tristan," she whispered. "Put me away and be done with me, if you can't forgive me. I can never be your wife."

"Forgive you for what? Don't be ridiculous, Elen, I will never put you away. I meant what I told you last night. We can be whatever we want to each other. It doesn't matter to anyone but us." She was shaking horribly, and he put an arm around her shoulder. Her body was as rigid as a board. He hugged her gently. "We are what we are. Friends. It's enough for me."

"It isn't a marriage."

"Who says? It is to us. And I believe it is to God as well."

"But—we haven't—"

"Consummation is unimportant unless sons are needed. You and I can do without children. Let Lionors bear sons for Lanascol; as Kaherdyn's wife, it is her duty."

Iseulte shook her head slowly. "You are so generous. I would not shame you for the world. Last night I—I did not mean to deny you. But I couldn't help it."

"I know that."

"You were so sweet to me, so gentle and so kind." Her eyes flicked quickly to his and then dropped. "I did—I did like it, you know. At the start."

He smiled. "I know."

"I don't know what happened. Something came over me. I—I remember a dark shadow above me, swooping down." She shuddered. "It had talons. It was coming for me." Tristan squeezed her closer. She looked steadily away. "I don't remember anything after that. When I awoke at dawn, you were lying beside me with bites all over your chest and bloody scratches on your back. For an instant I thought the monster had—had attacked you, too." Her voice quavered close to tears. "But then I realized there was no monster but the one living in my head. I did that to you."

Tristan lifted her chin and gazed into her brilliant eyes. "There is no monster in your head. You are not yet healed from your ordeal, that is all. It was too soon. As for the scratches, they are only skin deep. A long way from my heart."

For the first time he saw a glimmer of a smile. "Thank you," she whispered.

He kissed her gently and pulled her down onto the bed, gown, cloak and all, and held her in his arms until, together, sleep overtook them.

On the day of the vernal equinox a courier arrived from Britain. Galahad lay on a pallet in the garden, carried there to benefit from the strengthening sun. Dandrane attended him, reading to him in her melodic voice sacred verses from the Holy Book. Lionors and her women were in the weaving room, frantically stitching and weaving against her upcoming wedding day. Kaherdyn and Tristan sat together in the king's workroom, reading dispatches, dictating to the scribe, planning a summer campaign against the Franks should diplomacy fail to settle the border dispute between them. Iseulte, in a comfortable old gray gown and patched blue girdle, curled on the floor at the end of the room, playing with the newest litter of puppies.

The courier was a young man who stared nervously at everything about him. When the page announced him he bowed low and went down on one knee before Tristan.

Tristan looked up from his work and smiled, pointing to Kaherdyn. "There is the Prince of Lanascol, lad. Address yourself to him."

"Yes, my lord," the young man quavered. "But the message I carry is for you, if you are Tristan of Lyonesse. I come from Tintagel."

Color drained from Tristan's face. He rose unsteadily. Iseulte came immediately to his side and drew Kaherdyn away.

Kaherdyn shrugged. "Call me when you want me, Tristan. I'm going to run this battle plan by Father."

When he had gone Tristan came around the worktable and stood before the courier. "Arise, man, and give me the news. Do you come from the Queen?"

"Aye, my lord."

"How does she?"

"I am instructed to give you no news of her, my lord."

Tristan drew a long breath. "Give me the message, then."

The courier reached into his pouch and placed something small and cold in Tristan's hand. Tristan stared down at his own golden ring with the eagle of Lyonesse carved into blue enamel. It was the ring he had given Essylte on her wedding night. His own voice resounded from the past: *You have my heart, Essylte, and no one else. And if it comes to damnation, we shall walk through the gates of Hell together, arm in arm. . . . This is a token of our promise. . . . Remember, when you see it, that you are Queen of Lyonesse, and my wife.*

His fist closed on the ring and he cleared his throat. "Did she—did she send no message with it?"

"Only two words, my lord," the courier gulped. " 'Never return.' "

Tristan froze.

Iseulte stepped forward and raised the courier, taking his arm and leading him to the door. She reached into her pouch for a gold coin and pressed it into his hand.

"Tell me quickly, lady, yes or no," he whispered furtively. "Did Sir Tristan really marry?"

She nodded slowly, her glance flicking to the stone-faced sentry beside the door.

The courier's shoulders sagged. "We had a bard with us at Tintagel three weeks after the thaw. Old Rhys of Wales. He told us he had sung at Sir Tristan's wedding feast. He caused much grief in Cornwall, I can tell you. We thought my lady would die from weeping."

Iseulte laid a hand on his sleeve and gazed pleadingly into his face, mouthing words.

"What is it, lady?" He glanced anxiously up at the guard. "What does she say?"

"My lady has been dumb for years," the guard replied with a quick bow toward Iseulte. "No fault of her own, but there it is. She can be understood if you watch her lips."

Iseulte mouthed the words again, but the courier shook his head. "Might as well be Greek for all I can make of it."

"She said," the guard told him gently, " 'Tell your lady Sir Tristan loves her still.' "

Iseulte made the guard a reverence and turned away. As the door closed the courier caught a glimpse of Tristan on his knees, bent double, hands covering his face.

"I'll be damned," the courier whispered. "And just how would she know that?"

"If anyone knows it, she does," the guard replied stiffly. "That was Iseulte, the king's daughter. Sir Tristan's wife."

The garden was crowded with servants and courtiers. Queen Dandrane and the physician bent over the king's pallet while onlookers muttered prayers under their breaths.

"He lives," the physician pronounced uncertainly. "But only just."

Kaherdyn, the battle plans rolled in his hand, pushed through the throng to look down at his father's wasted body. A lump rose in his throat. The left side of Galahad's face sagged as though some sculptor had tired of his clay and made a halfhearted attempt to erase his work.

"What happened?" he asked hoarsely.

Dandrane wiped her eyes and drew a trembling breath. "I was reading to him. And then he started talking to me, reliving old times, all the adventures we had been through together when we were young. The light was back in his face. He even laughed. He hadn't talked so much in so long, I begged him to take care and preserve himself, but he just smiled and told me God would take care of him. He—he told me about a dream he's been having lately, about returning to Britain, to a—a place in Wales, that he would like to see it once again, that he wanted to take us all to Britain when the weather warmed. But then—" She gulped hastily and clutched Kaherdyn for support. "His lips stopped moving, his eyes rolled skyward and then closed, and he sort of—crumpled." She shuddered. "After that I couldn't wake him."

"Hot water and blankets," the physician mumbled. "Rest, complete rest. Don't move him once you get him inside."

Dandrane looked at the man as if seeing him for the first time. "Will he live?" she asked. "What are his chances? For how long?"

The physician hemmed and hawed, but in the end he answered her. "My lady, it is not likely. If he lives through tomorrow, he may last a week or a month, but his God has laid His finger on him, and claimed him. You can see the Maker's mark."

Dandrane straightened. "If he lives through tomorrow, we will take ship to Britain." The crowd buzzed, the physician remonstrated, but Queen Dandrane was firm. "If he wants to go to Britain, we will take him. If God sent him the dream, surely God will preserve him long enough to enable him to fulfill it."

34 ⛨ CAER MYRDDIN

Tristan leaned over the ship's rail and peered at the cold green waters sliding past the hull. Behind him sailors tugged at the great sail as the oars came out, for they were leaving the Severn estuary and entering the wide, tidal mouth of the River Tywy on the southern coast of Wales. Somewhere far across the estuary ran the northern coast of Dumnonia, where, above a rocky cliff, Guvranyl's house overlooked the same sea. The sailors chanted as they rowed upstream toward the old Roman town of Maridunum, and Tristan watched as the banks of the tidal river, steep on the west, flatter on the east, grew slowly closer. Here, myriad fishing coracles lined a pebbled beach; there, a local trader wallowed at a wharf with her decks piled high with wool; and farther upstream, near the Roman bridge that spanned the Tywy, a sleek, painted merchantman from more distant waters rode serenely at anchor, casks of pressed oil or wine still strapped to her decks.

He stared hard at the foreign vessel and tried to guess from which sun-drenched city she had come, trying to keep his mind busy, fighting off the memory of his last glimpse of the Severn—that midnight race from the tempest in beating rain, the long climb up the cliff to Guvranyl's villa with Essylte warm and fragile in his arms. He grimaced and turned sharply away.

Coming up on deck, Iseulte saw the movement. "What is it, Tristan? Are you ill?"

He forced a smile. "A little queasy. It will pass. How is your father?"

She shook her head. "It's Britain, isn't it? It's not the sea. It's your homeland and all that it holds." She took his hand and held it firmly. "But I am so glad you came. It would have been so much harder for me without you. And I believe it will do you good as well."

This time he smiled more easily. "Not if you keep calling me by my name."

She colored. "Dear God, did I forget? And this is Wales!" She shivered and glanced swiftly behind her at the busy sailors.

"Never mind. No one noticed. How is your father?"

Her face lightened. "Better, Marcus, I'm glad to say. Not awake, but breathing quietly. Mother is with him. Kaherdyn's still seasick." She paused. "The closer we get, the better Father does. Strange, isn't it?"

"Perhaps. Perhaps not. Nothing about your father is ordinary."

Together they stood and gazed out at the approaching shore. On the rising land of the western bank, drab wattle buildings huddled against the wharves, seaward shutters opened to the April sun like newborn eyes squinting at an uncertain world. A thin curl of smoke marked the roof of an inn, where something was already warming over a peat fire, although it was a mild afternoon. Beyond the town rose a cluster of low green hills dotted with sheep and an occasional farmhouse, squat, round, with a conical roof of thatch. In the distance the rising land hinted at mountains, and the land breeze still smelled of snow.

Iseulte pointed ahead to the arched Roman bridge. "That's where we'll be going. Mother says we must cross that bridge."

"Easy enough. It looks unguarded. Look at the stone. Built to survive the Saxon raids, and it's been kept in good repair. I wonder who the commander is."

But Iseulte was staring hard at the thinly inhabited eastern shore across the bridge from the town. "The river road must be up there. The Christian monastery should be around that bend. Somewhere up yonder there's a mill, if it's still standing."

"A mill? Is that where we are bound?"

"We're going to Caer Myrddin and the mill is on the way."

"What's at Caer Myrddin?"

"I've no idea. I'm just repeating what Mother told Kaherdyn."

"Well, it can't be hard to find. Maridunum's not a big place. There are only two roads in the whole town, from the look of things—the shore road to Caerleon and the river road." He leaned his back against the railing and looked down at her curiously. "Why all the secrecy, do you suppose?"

Iseulte looked up at him. It flashed through Tristan's mind that she herself presented the greatest danger to him, with those brilliant eyes that seemed to cast a staring spell on everyone they met. Like her father, she stood out in any crowd, she drew the eye of every man. Few could meet her gaze and turn away. He knew Iseulte herself was unaware of this. He often wondered if it might have been her startling eyes, so clear, so direct, so powerful, that had aroused Ryol's raging need to conquer her. Those eyes might determine his future as well, for merely by accompanying her he risked recognition.

Iseulte dodged his question. "Mother begs you will find us a room at an inn, if there is one." She slipped a small leather bag of coins into his hand. "And would you see to the harbormaster, too? I hope that's enough, but I confess I know nothing about harbor dues."

Tristan looked amused. "It depends on whether Vortipor's still King of Dyfed, the old skinflint, and whether or not he's planning a summer campaign. Don't worry, I'll see that we're not cheated. Tell the queen I'm certain there's an inn. When does she wish to go ashore?"

"At dusk. So no one notices him."

"In a place this small nothing goes unnoticed. But old and frail as he is, he's unlikely to be recognized. If anyone asks, we'll tell them we're taking him to the monastery to be healed at Ninian's spring."

Her great blue eyes lifted to him, blinking back tears. "Oh, Tristan, perhaps we should! Is it really a healing spring?"

He leaned down and pressed his cheek to hers. "No, my dear, it's just a tale of mine. Hold on, now. We're nearly there."

She nodded, and together they turned to watch the shore approach. On a hill above the bridge, two low stone buildings formed a courtyard. "Look at those barracks," Tristan murmured. "Neat. Orderly. Right on the road. Someone knows his business. I wonder who the commander is."

"Why? Does it matter?"

Tristan shrugged. "It does if he knows me."

Her hand trembled on his sleeve. "Be careful, then, I beg you. For my sake, if not your own. I can't do without you, Tristan."

He smiled and bent down to kiss her lips. "Marcus, if you love me."

The inn turned out to be little more than a one-room hut with outbuildings clustered behind it, but the walls gleamed under a recent limestone wash and the roof was newly thatched. A dozen scrawny geese and chickens pecked discontentedly along the verge of the road, but the door stood open to all comers and the landlord, a cheerful, heavy man with a ring of grizzled hair around his balding pate, stood on the threshold and welcomed Tristan in.

"You're a stranger, sir," he ventured, placing a tankard of mead on an ancient oak table that ran the length of the room. Too thick to burn, Tristan guessed, and too heavy to steal, it must have survived a century of Saxon raids. A handful of villagers sat at the far benches, near the peat fire. They rose as he entered and resettled themselves closer to the door, leaving him the best seat and a degree of privacy.

He bowed politely in return. "My thanks, friends." He drew off his cloak and was aware of five pairs of eyes staring at his sword.

"We don't get many strangers here," the landlord suggested, hovering at his elbow. "Sailors off the ships, mostly, and them thieving foreign devils. Rarely a warrior."

"Foreign devils? Oh, you mean the merchantman. What's she got aboard her? Wine?"

The landlord nodded. "Oh, aye, wine aplenty in her belly, wine from southern Gaul, all headed for King Vortipor's cellars. But oil on her decks, my lord, and some of it coming here."

Tristan flashed a grin. "In time for supper?"

He was rewarded by the landlord's delighted smile. "Indeed, my lord, most happy to oblige. Just let me know your pleasure. A fat fowl, perhaps? Or a leg of mutton?"

Tristan glanced hastily out the window at the chickens and wondered if the landlord's sheep had stood the long winter any better. "Er, no. Fish is preferable. Hot fish stew. Something light. There are ladies coming ashore later."

The landlord rubbed his hands together and winked knowingly. "Aye, the sea do make them ill, don't it? Not travelers, women. Will my lord and his company be wanting a place to sleep?"

Tristan looked doubtfully at the shabby curtain that separated the common room from the kitchens. "If there's room for us all. We are five, and one an invalid."

"Oh, aye, don't worry, my lord. There's room and to spare. A good bed out back, and two stuffed pallets. And a loft with plenty of straw." He paused, scratching his chin. "Will there be horses?"

The landlord knew perfectly well he had come off the ship, alone; he was asking, as politely as he could, for news. The villagers, too, listened intently, although their faces were buried in their mead. Tristan knew it was time to weave the man his tale.

"Oh, no, no horses, although I'd be obliged to know the name of a trader hereabouts. I came off that Breton ship that sailed in this afternoon.

Name's Marcus Cunomorus. I serve young Kaherdyn, the Breton prince. He hopes to heal his father at Ninian's well."

"Spring," the landlord corrected eagerly. "It's up the river road at the house of the Christian sisters. My name's Rufus, my lord, at your service." The round eyes flickered. "Yours is a Roman name, my lord, but surely that's a Cornish accent."

Heads rose at the far end of the table, and Tristan found himself faced with five pairs of hostile Welsh eyes. *So much for Percival's unity*, he thought bitterly, *if here in Dyfed the old hatreds still burned so bright.*

"I was born in Cornwall," he admitted easily. "But when I was a lad King Markion cheated my father out of his land, so we went to Brittany, where more honorable men prevail." He paused for a swallow of mead and let the statement sink in.

The Welshmen glanced surreptitiously at one another, and the landlord's smile grew nervous. "Aye," he said softly, "I can't deny I've heard such tales before."

"Best be careful of your tongue, stranger," one of the villagers mumbled in an accent so thick Tristan could barely comprehend it.

Rufus nodded. "Speak no ill of the High King Markion," he said loudly. "We're all loyal Britons in these parts. We honor the King."

But Tristan noted the grim faces and the small beads of sweat along the landlord's brow. "Do you? Well, you can have him, then, and welcome to him. You'll never convince me he's not an arrogant, greedy bastard."

Sharp, meaning looks flew between the men. One of the villagers nodded solemnly at Rufus, and the landlord sighed heavily in relief.

"Yes, indeed," he breathed. "We've heard that, too. King Markion's no friend to us. Not us Welsh."

Tristan raised an eyebrow. "But I thought he took a Welsh princess to wife. The next High King will be a son of Wales."

Once again the landlord and the villagers exchanged meaningful looks. The landlord cleared his throat. "I see you've heard the official tale, the one the kings of Wales and Cornwall like to put about." He leaned closer until Tristan could smell his last meal on his breath. "But there's another story, one many of us think may be closer to the truth."

A small thrill slid up Tristan's spine. "Oh? What tale is that?"

But Rufus backed away, smiling nervously. Tristan placed a silver coin on the table and looked up slowly into the landlord's eyes. "Another tankard of mead, if you'd be so good."

The silver coin swiftly disappeared into the fastness of the landlord's tunic, and a villager rose without a word and closed the door. When Rufus had refilled everyone's cup he sat down himself at the table.

"Well," he began in a conspiratorial whisper, "have you ever heard of Tristan of Lyonesse?"

Tristan paled. When he found his voice, he was annoyed to hear it quaver. "He was Meliodas's son, was he not, whom Markion banished? He died at sea, I heard."

"That's as may be, my lord. No one knows his fate. But it's known all over Britain that he loved our Essylte with a passion undeniable and true. And she him. But the maid was already promised to the old goat of Cornwall, may Percival of Gwynedd roast long in Hell!"

He spoke emphatically and the villagers thumped their cups on the table in assent. "Old Markion shut her up in Tintagel to keep her away from Tristan. Indeed, he's spent so much time keeping young Tristan off he's let the Saxon terror creep halfway across Britain!" Rufus nodded knowingly. "But you can't gainsay a true love, my lord. It can't be done. There's those of us in Wales think those boys of hers are Sir Tristan's and not Markion's. And if what I hear is true, there's those in Camelot that think so, too."

Tristan stared at him, struggling to keep his panic from his face. "Surely you exaggerate. Markion's no fool, whatever his other faults. He wouldn't raise the bastards of an adulterous wife as his own heirs."

"Indeed," Rufus whispered, "he would not, and he is not."

"What!"

Rufus looked gratified at Tristan's shock. "This is news to my lord Marcus, eh? He's tried twice to take the boys from her, but each time she hid them from his envoys, and the men had not the nerve to beat the truth from her. So a month ago Markion sent the Queen word that as soon as the Saxons give him leave, he will go to Tintagel and take the boys away himself. I wouldn't give a fig for their chances then."

"Dear God!"

One of the villagers raised his head and nodded. "He'll kill 'em," he said with relish.

"Aye," agreed his neighbor. "They're in his way."

"But why?" Tristan gasped. "Has the Queen borne him no other sons since Tristan's exile?"

They all shook their heads.

"No," supplied Rufus, "although it's said she's miscarried twice."

"On purpose."

"Drank a potion."

"Witch's brew."

Tristan stared at them all in horror. "Percival wouldn't stand for it! They're his grandsons."

"He's got troubles of his own."

"Gaels on his coast."

"By the time he hears of it, the deed'll be done."

"The King of Cornwall don't care two straws for us Welsh and never did. That's a fact."

"And he don't care to raise a pair of Welsh boys as his heirs, God curse him," the landlord finished triumphantly.

Tristan was breathing fast. "This can't be true. These are rumors, the kind that run rampant and feed on their own wind. Who told you these things?"

Rufus straightened. "I got it from young Cadoc," he said defensively, "at the equinox, when he was home to bury his father. He's stationed at Caerleon under Sir Bruenor, another Cornish dog." Rufus hawked, turned his head, and spat.

Bruenor at Caerleon! Tristan's head reeled. "And where is King Markion now?"

"Fighting Saxons. *West* of Vindocladia, if you can believe it."

"So close? How is it possible? What is Britain coming to?"

The men nodded in agreement. "Dog days," a villager asserted.

Rufus drained his tankard and rose. "They say Markion's a madman. They say he kills whatever's in his path and asks questions later. And they try to blame his vile temper on our Essylte. They say she refuses to do her duty by him, out of love for Sir Tristan. They say she bloodies him well when he forces her and makes him pay for his pleasure. It has put him out of temper with everyone. She'll not bear him sons, and he'll not have the ones she bore. A pretty kettle of fish, that's what Britain's in." Rufus strode to the door and opened it wide to the golden light of the westering sun. "What we need, what all Britain needs," he finished devoutly, "is another Arthur."

The villagers drained their tankards and thumped them on the table. Rufus pointed north toward the gold-green hills. "Up there, that's where the old folk be sending their prayers, tonight and every night. The old folk who remember Arthur."

Tristan rose unsteadily. "To the monastery?"

"No, no. The good sisters are holy women and generous with alms, but they have no power. No, Sir Marcus, here in Wales we pray to the source of Britain's strength. To that hill they call the heart of Britain, where Merlin lies imprisoned in the rock until Arthur comes again and calls him out of his long sleep."

Tristan sighed in relief. He recognized both words and cadence; it was the end of "The Lay of Arthur," long a favorite among the Welsh. But the landlord's next words left him speechless.

"Caer Myrddin. It lies up yonder beyond the mill."

✳ ✳ ✳ ✳

Tristan stood on guard outside the wattle shed where Galahad lay abed. Queen Dandrane rested in a chair by her husband's side, and Iseulte and Kaherdyn curled on pallets on the floor. The furnishings were mean by any standards, but at least the bedsheets were clean and the place well swept. There had been a moment of awkwardness when Kaherdyn offered to take the night watch, on the grounds that, as a married woman, Iseulte's rights took precedence over his. Tristan smiled wryly to himself. With his upcoming nuptials postponed until his return, Kaherdyn could think of little else but weddings and beddings. On shipboard he had been overly careful to allow Tristan privacy with his sister, and every time she so much as hiccoughed he wondered aloud if she was with child. Tristan assured him, as politely as he could manage, that he preferred to stand guard over the royal family than make love to Iseulte at the foot of her dying father's bed. Kaherdyn finally took the point.

But the young man's concern annoyed him. He hoped fervently that once he was married to Lionors, Kaherdyn's persistent interest in his sister's marriage would die a peaceful death.

The door behind him opened and Dandrane reached out. Her eyes were huge. "He's awake!" She clutched his arm. "He wants to go. Now."

"Now? But it's past midnight. The escort is asleep on the ship—"

"We need no escort. You and Kaherdyn can carry the litter. Can you fetch us a torch or a lantern, do you think, to light our way?"

"But my lady, it's dangerous. To be abroad at night in a country we don't know—"

Her shadowed smile stopped him. "But we *do* know it, Galahad and I. We know it well. I will guide you. Iseulte will light the way. Go now. Hurry. There may not be much time."

When he returned with the lantern he found Galahad already on the litter, swaddled in blankets against the cold spring night. Two bright blue eyes glittered in his haggard face.

Iseulte held the lantern and led the procession while Kaherdyn carried the head of the litter and Tristan the foot. Dandrane walked beside her husband, holding his thin hand, out onto the shore road, across the stone bridge and onto the dirt track that wound uphill beside the river. It was a moonless night and very dark, with patchy clouds across the stars, and so cold that the ground crunched underfoot. No one spoke, except the queen to direct her daughter, and they met no one on the road. They passed by the sleeping monastery at a bend in the river, and a burned-out farmhouse, long abandoned. Once a dog barked in the distance, and Tristan fancied he heard the echo of sheep bells from the hills, but nothing moved in the solemn night but the gentle bobbing of the lantern.

Suddenly Dandrane spoke. "Halt there."

Iseulte raised the lantern high, and out of the gloom rose the spectral shape of a dilapidated building, the roofing gone, the walls showing gaps where wood and stone had been burned or torn away. Iseulte moved closer, and by torchlight they all saw the great wheel of a millstone tilted drunkenly against a pile of rubble.

Dandrane pointed to a sheep track that wound uphill past the mill. "Up there."

The path twisted through sheep meadows, hardwood copses, and rough brambles, winding around the hill as it climbed, up and up, narrowing with each turn. Iseulte stopped when the path forked at her feet, the larger trail to the right descending gently into a meadow, the animal track to her left twisting uphill between blackthorn nettles into a dark wood.

"Let me guess," Kaherdyn grumbled. "We go left."

"Yes," Dandrane whispered. "Yes. Like your father, you know the way without knowing how you know it."

Kaherdyn shot Tristan a doubtful look over his shoulder but trudged on in his sister's wake.

Iseulte went twenty paces and stopped again. She raised her lantern and pointed ahead. In a natural shelter under the budding trees they saw a lean-to, and within, a pile of fresh hay and a tub of water.

"A stable!" Kaherdyn exclaimed. "Then someone lives here."

Dandrane looked unsurprised. "A stable it is, but no one lives here."

"But the hay is fresh, and the water, too."

"The locals keep it so. They dream that Myrddin, like Arthur, will return to them someday, and they want to be ready for him. Come, give me the lantern, Iseulte. I will light you the rest of the way."

They struggled up a narrow track beyond the trees, through a cleft of rock and at last came out on a grassy ledge before a low, rounded cave mouth. Without hesitation Dandrane walked inside. Sweat beaded Tristan's brow as they followed with the litter. Anything at all could be in that cave—wolves, bears, boars, mountain cats, even bandits—yet the woman took possession of it as if it were her home.

"There," Dandrane said, pointing to a level stretch of flooring along the wall. "Put him down there." Tristan and Kaherdyn lowered the litter gently and gingerly flexed their arms. Dandrane knelt down next to Galahad.

"We are here," she said breathlessly. "See? This is Caer Myrddin. The villagers have left meal cakes and a skin of wine."

Startled, Tristan saw by the lantern light that this was true. On a cairn built just inside the cave was a clay platter piled high with homely offerings.

The cave itself was small, six strides by three, but high enough for a tall man to stand upright. The hard dirt floor had been recently swept, and the old brazier, half rusted, had been heaped with fresh coals. Someone tended this place, that was certain.

"Cover the lantern."

He jumped. Everyone stared at the pallet, recognizing the voice. Galahad watched them, his face immobile but his eyes alive. Iseulte obeyed and dropped the cover over the lantern. Darkness sprang at them. They stood blind and powerless, hardly daring to breathe, until gradually their eyes adjusted and their night sight could discriminate between shapes and shadows.

"Take me inside," the voice commanded.

"Inside *where?*" Kaherdyn wondered. "We *are* inside."

"There's another cave behind this one, deep in the hill," Dandrane said in a low voice. "Take the lantern, Iseulte, and follow me." Kaherdyn and Tristan lifted the litter and followed her into a dark fissure at the back of the cave. Iseulte clung to Tristan's tunic, holding back as far as she dared, shaking so hard the lantern rattled in her hand.

The procession halted almost at once. "It's gone!" Dandrane's panicked whisper echoed off the damp stone that enclosed them. "Galahad, it's gone! I can't find the entrance! Iseulte, the lantern."

"No," came the reedy voice from the litter. "No lantern. You will find it only in the dark."

Silence descended. The effort of speech had taken its toll; harsh, shallow breathing came from the litter. It was the only sound. No one dared move. Their fear was a palpable presence among them.

Dandrane's whisper hovered on the edge of sound. "Then how—?"

"Elen," the voice breathed. "Elen can."

Iseulte's fingers clutched Tristan's arm. She shook her head wildly.

"Elen," the voice repeated, "found it before."

Tristan stared down at the shadow of her face. "You have been here before?" Again she shook her head wildly.

"Yes, she has," Dandrane said quietly. "She was three years old. She found the inner cave all by herself. Come up here with me, Iseulte. I'll take the lantern. Now stand where I am standing."

Trembling, Iseulte obeyed. It was so dark she could not tell whether her eyes were open or closed. Quaking, hardly able to stand, she put her hands out for support and felt the cold, moist stone under her fingers. It beckoned to her.

Elen. She heard Tristan's whisper through the whirling blackness of her terror. *A calm soul.*

She drew a long breath and emptied her mind of thought. Her hands slid over the rock with a will of their own, exploring every hollow, every crevice, every cleft—there! A chasm, a hole, just big enough to hold her body. As she inched forward, holding her breath, she had the sudden, uneasy sensation that the rock itself was parting to let her through. The absurdity of the notion made her stumble. She lost her grip on the stone and fell forward, not into rock, but into nothingness.

"Father!" she cried out, and her voice rebounded, ringing and hollow, from the depths of the hill.

"Iseulte." They were there beside her, they had followed her through. She could hear their steps on the ringing stone and their shallow breaths echoing about her ears. She pushed herself up from the rock floor and stared blankly into the engulfing blackness. Even with night sight, she could not see a single thing.

"Now." Galahad's voice came out of the dark, the voice of a king. "Light."

Dandrane drew off the lantern cover, and they all cried out together in amazement. Before them yawned a great cavern, pillared in stone and shimmering with light. From cave floor to vaulting roof, slender columns of pale stone rose, glistening with damp, hundreds of them, marching as far into the shadows as the eye could see. A pool of still water encircled the columns, throwing back the lantern light in a thousand, iridescent colors, flashing brilliant as the facets of a crystal, filling the very air with light.

Tristan blinked, half blinded by the dazzle. "The Hall of the Otherworld," he breathed, and made the sign against enchantment. His words echoed around the cavern, resounding like a dreadful pronouncement.

"Or the Gate of Heaven." Tristan looked down to see Galahad's eyes narrowed in amusement.

"Sir," he breathed, "Christian or pagan or godless heathen, this is a sacred place."

They stood a long time in silence, taking in the wonder of it. From beyond the reach of the light the sound of dripping water reached them, and from somewhere far above them, from some hidden fissure in the hill itself, blew a draft of sweet air, light as a cat's-paw touch upon the cheek.

Galahad's lips worked stiffly in his wasted face. "Take me to the ledge."

It was only then that Tristan saw a limestone ledge protruding from the water, half hidden by the gleaming pillars. Dandrane's hand began to shake, and the quivering light danced and flashed off something sitting atop the ledge, but at that distance Tristan could not see what it was. He nodded to Kaherdyn, who gulped audibly. "Let's go."

The water was only ankle deep but so cold it was instantly numbing. The ripples they made shattered their reflections into a thousand splinters of light. Tristan caught his breath as he got near enough to see the objects on the ledge. He recognized them: a wide krater of beaten silver set with gems, and a long spear with a tip of forged steel honed deadly bright. These were the Grail and Spear that Galahad had searched for all over Britain, the fabled treasures of an ancient king that had the power, the sages said, to keep Britain whole forever. No wonder the locals called Merlin's Hill the heart of Britain!

In awed silence, they set the litter down on the ledge beside the treasures. Tristan saw the whites of Kaherdyn's eyes as he crossed himself with a badly shaking hand. Dandrane had gone perfectly still. Tristan reached for Iseulte and held her close. Her lips were blue with cold, and she was so numb with emotion that she barely breathed.

"Elen." Galahad's voice was clear and resonant. "Elen. Daughter. Come here and touch the Grail."

Iseulte shrank back into Tristan's arms, but Tristan led her forward against her will. To the astonishment of all, Galahad's hand lifted and reached for hers. "Don't be afraid, Elen. Nothing can hurt you here. God is with us, can you not feel it?" She nodded slowly. "You are a brave child. But since your abduction you have lived every day with fear in your heart." She nodded again. "Marriage to Tristan has brought you peace of a sort, but it has not healed you of your fear. It is a companionship of friends, not a union of lovers." Iseulte lowered her eyes and nodded again.

Kaherdyn shot a swift look at Tristan. "I knew it!" he breathed.

"When you were a child," Galahad continued gently, "you took this krater in your hands and brought it to me. It did you no harm. It will not harm you now. Lift it and look at the writing etched around the rim."

Iseulte hesitated, then slowly reached out to the gleaming Grail and lifted it between her hands. Hundreds of tiny amethysts set in delicate gold chasing glittered in the light. Around the rim ran antique, formal Latin lettering. *"Whoso thirsts, drink ye and be restored. Whoso wanders, hold me and find rest."* She jumped at the sound of her own voice, so calm and steady, and stared unbelieving at her father.

Dandrane wept to hear her daughter speak. She set the lantern down and pressed Galahad's hand to her wet cheek. "Bless you."

"Kaherdyn," Galahad commanded, "take the spear."

Forcing himself forward against his fear, Kaherdyn reached out and raised the spear, hefting it in his hand, amazed at the perfect balance of the ancient weapon. Here, too, ancient Latin etchings ran along the length of the polished shaft. *"Whoso trembles, take this and fear not. Whoso is lost, by my strength shall be preserved."*

A smile touched Galahad's lips. "This is my legacy to you both. You have seen the heart of Britain. Live long, and preserve the land of your forefathers."

Iseulte placed the Grail between Galahad's hands. "Father, can you not be healed as well?"

"My pretty child, do not fear for me. I go to join all those I have lost: Lancelot, Arthur, Gareth of Orkney, and many others." He smiled with the right side of his mouth. "Your place is with Tristan now. Stay beside him, whatever comes. Be one with him, in flesh and in spirit, in joy and in sorrow. He will serve Britain, and his sons after him." His hand touched her brow in blessing. "Go now, and let me have a word with Kaherdyn. Come back for me at dawn."

In the outer cave it was cold as well as dark. Tristan went to the rusting brazier and felt around in the dark for the flint and tinder he thought he remembered seeing nearby. At length he found them and after a struggle struck a spark into the tinder, which he blew into a flame and set beneath the coals. He tended the nascent fire anxiously, letting it absorb all his attention so that he need not speak to Iseulte. Her presence seemed to surround him like a shadow, insubstantial but menacing nonetheless, and the desire to steadfastly ignore her, like a naughty boy attempting to ward off the punishment he knew was coming, was too strong to deny. But as soon as the coals caught fire and lit the little cave with a dim glow, he grew ashamed of his cowardice and turned to her.

She stood at the cave mouth, looking up at the wheeling stars, her back to him. His childish subterfuge had been unnecessary, had gone unnoticed.

"Elen." His voice sounded strange, even to him. "Come sit by the fire."

When she turned around the firelight lit her solemn face, ethereal in its grief. He saw her suddenly as a stranger might, a breathtakingly beautiful woman with an otherworldly air of innocence and wisdom. He realized, as her shadowed eyes met his, that she was a mystery to him. He did not know her at all.

"The stars are out. The king star is still there, in the north. I thought— I thought it fell in a hail of light whenever—whenever a great king dies."

He walked to her side, and as he approached she drew her cloak more tightly about her body. It was a small movement, a gesture only, but it spoke worlds. He let his hands fall to his sides. "You've heard too many bards' tales."

She nodded, avoiding him adroitly as she moved toward the fire. She spread out her hands above the flames, those beautiful, long-fingered hands that had earned her the name she was known by, and shivered. An ache struck Tristan's chest. He wanted desperately to please her, but he knew the choice before him.

"He is dying." She said it flatly.

"Yes. He has been dying since before he came home."

Another shudder. "I know." She settled herself before the fire and kept her eyes on the flames. "I know why he came here. But why did you?"

"To be with—" he stopped. He had said it so often to himself he almost believed it. But after that interlude in the cave, the time for pretending was past.

"No," she said quietly, "not to be with me. To be in Britain. Ever since we landed you have been on fire to leave Maridunum. All I ask is that you allow me to go with you."

"How can you know?" he breathed. "Am I made of glass?"

She shook her head sadly and spoke to the fire. "I look at you with eyes of love, Tristan. I know your heart. Ever since she returned your ring you have wanted to come back and settle things between you. I know you will go down into Cornwall. I will not try to stop you. But I want to go with you."

Tristan moved awkwardly toward her. His heart pounded and his breath stuck in his throat. "Markion is going to kill my sons!" At last she looked up and met his eyes. He steadied. "They told me in the tavern—they heard it from a soldier at Caerleon. I don't know how old the news is; it could be months. It might already be too late. He has tried twice before and she's kept him off, but this time he's coming himself. I *must* rescue them if they still live. You see that, don't you?"

"Of course," she said calmly, "But you will need an army the size of Markion's. We don't have enough men in all of Lanascol."

"I have no time to raise an army. I will go myself."

She did not reply. They stared at one another in silence. At length she turned and looked down at the fire. The wavering light lit tear tracks on her cheeks. "I see. And where will you take them, to be safe?"

Tristan shut his eyes. "I don't know. I don't know. Into the forest, perhaps. To Less Britain. Anywhere he can't find them."

She stifled a gasp. "You would take Queen Essylte to Lanascol? To my home?"

"I'm not talking about the Queen—"

"Of course you are."

She said it calmly, and all his protestations died on his lips. He stood silently over her while Iseulte wiped the tears from her cheeks and stared into the fire. "If you take them to Less Britain, you will start a war. They are Markion's declared heirs, after all. And I'm not sure—I'm not sure Kaherdyn will give her sanctuary."

Tristan fell on his knees at her side. "Then I will do something else. I don't know what. I will think of it when I get there. But I must go." He raised his hands in supplication. "Please, Elen. Let me go."

She went very still and avoided his eyes. "Why is it," she whispered, "that everyone, *everyone* else calls me Iseulte and you do not?"

"I—I—I prefer Elen," Tristan said, floundering.

She shrugged. "Never mind. I know the answer. You simply cannot bring yourself to call me by her name."

"Iseulte!" He grabbed her hands and held them hard against his breast. "Forgive me for it. Don't let it matter. Don't destroy what is between us. Go home with Kaherdyn and your mother—"

"What *is* between us, Tristan? Look into your heart and ask yourself."

"I already have," he whispered.

"Is it worth preserving?"

"Yes."

He felt her soften. She drew a trembling breath but no longer tried to pull her hands away.

"Then let me come with you. You need me for camouflage. No one knows me here. I can protect you, at least as far as Tintagel."

"It's too dangerous. You will be safer with Kaherdyn."

"But I choose the danger. Don't protect me against my will. I would rather be with you than anywhere, and I will not leave if you are not with me."

Tristan pressed his lips into her hand. "I do not deserve you."

"And I did not deserve Ryol," she answered softly. "Deserts don't matter in the least. Remember my father's admonition to me: I will stay beside you, whatever happens."

"And remember his other admonition," said a voice from the back of the cave. "Be one with him in flesh as well as spirit." Kaherdyn strode angrily out of the shadows and frowned down upon them both. "Where are you going, Tristan, that you want to leave my sister behind?"

"Hush, Kaherdyn!" Iseulte spoke sharply. "This does not concern you."

"But it does. Father has just now bound me with an oath to look after you. It's an oath he ought to have made Tristan swear, and I wondered why he didn't. Now perhaps I will find out." He turned to Tristan, who rose and faced him. "Where are you going?"

"Into Cornwall."

"Cornwall! Whatever for?"

"To save my sons from the High King's wrath."

"Sons!" Kaherdyn stared at them both. "What sons? Whose?"

Iseulte rose and took his arm. "Listen, Kaherdyn, oath or not, this is none of your concern. When the time comes to leave, you will take Mother home. I will go into Cornwall with Tristan and we will take ship from there."

"I forbid it!" Kaherdyn cried.

"Prince Kaherdyn." Tristan bowed gravely. "I owe you an explanation, both as your sister's husband and as your ally. I pray you will hear me out."

"That's better," Kaherdyn grumbled, calming. "I will hear you, Tristan. Let us go outside."

"Kaherdyn!" Iseulte glared at her brother. "Try to remember you are not yet king. This man is my husband. He saved me from a fate you yourself could not have borne. Whatever he tells you, remember this: He has already earned our mercy."

Outside on the cold hill the two men sat wrapped in cloaks under the dimming stars. Tristan told Kaherdyn about his long love for Essylte of Gwynedd. He spared the boy nothing; he admitted his wrongdoing at every turn. When he had finished, Kaherdyn sat silent a long while.

"You only left her to save her life."

"Yes."

"Why did you marry my sister?"

"Because I intended to spend my life in Lanascol, and as your father pointed out, I could not live in such close proximity to her without taking her to wife unless I wished to make her the butt of gossip. And also because she wanted the match and I had no right to deny her."

"But you did not desire her?"

"On the contrary," Tristan said softly, "I desired her to the point of anguish."

"Then why have you not lain with her? Do not deny it—my father saw it straightaway."

"No, I don't deny it. But it is not from lack of desire either on her part or on mine. Kaherdyn, try to understand the fear a woman feels when she has been used the way Ryol used her."

"I don't want to talk about that!" Kaherdyn said sharply. "I am talking about you."

"But you *must* talk about it if you are to understand. To be so helpless against one's fate! Many women suffer from ill use and degradation at men's hands and are powerless to prevent it. They have no champions to fight for them against their husbands or their kings. Have you never imagined what it must be like? We who wield swords and can ride anywhere we wish unquestioned, we would stifle in an hour if we lived the lives they live. We can fight openly against our enemies. They cannot. We can seek our own vengeance. They cannot. We can control the ebb and flow of events. They cannot, unless they can manipulate a powerful man. Your sister has suffered because she is a woman, and so has Esmerée, and Branwen, and even Essylte the Queen. That's why your father spoke to her about fear. It is her fear, which she cannot help, which keeps me from her bed."

"In truth?" Kaherdyn said unhappily.

"Ask her yourself."

"She'll snap my head off," he said ruefully. "I dare not."

Overhead a falling star tore across the lightening heavens from horizon to horizon. Tristan crossed himself sadly and Kaherdyn shot him a curious look. In the east the first hint of gold struck the distant hills. Kaherdyn rose. Below them they heard women's voices in the cave.

"Well, Tristan, you are honor bound to go to Cornwall, and Iseulte is honor bound to follow. I have sworn to protect her, so it looks like Mother will be going home alone."

"You are wise beyond your years, Kaherdyn. Such understanding surprises me. But then, you are the son of the Grail Prince, may he rest in peace."

Kaherdyn frowned. "It's dawn. We should go back and get him."

"Too late."

As Tristan spoke, the ground beneath them shuddered and moved. Tristan grabbed Kaherdyn and pulled him to the earth. Together they rolled down the shifting sides of the hill, while earth and sky roared around them. They landed in a ditch filled with nettles. Boulders crashed through the underbrush, missing them by inches, and rocks and pebbles showered down upon them. At last, when the earth was still, Tristan struggled to his feet, bleeding from nettle scratches and bruised from the battering landslide. He coughed as a huge cloud of dust settled over the quiet countryside.

"The hill is gone! Iseulte! Iseulte! Dandrane!"

"Mother!" Kaherdyn cried, clutching his shoulder as he scrambled up. "Tristan, they were in the cave!"

Together they fought their way up and over the debris, climbing to the place where the cave had been. The grassy apron before the cave mouth was still there, just recognizable beneath piles of dirt and stone, but the hill itself had slid into a low mound. The cave was gone, and all that had been inside it.

"Elen!" Tristan wailed.

An answering cry came from below them. They scrambled down the sheep track and found Iseulte and Dandrane crouched low in the natural stable under the trees.

"Thank God!" Tristan took Iseulte and enfolded her within his arms.

Kaherdyn ran to his mother. "He is gone," she wept, stroking her son's hair. "He is gone forever. He died in my arms, and God Himself has buried him in the hill."

"Well." Rufus stood in the tavern doorway and scratched idly. "I wonder who those people really were. Stuff and nonsense, that tale about Breton princes. Witches and magicians is closer to the truth."

Behind him the villagers nodded in sage agreement.

"No strange doings up yonder on Caer Myrddin until they came."

"First a light all night, and then the magic storm. Struck Caer Myrddin and nowhere else. Witches for certain."

"No prince would send his mother home alone. On a ship. Across the sea. No prince worthy of the name."

"They bought Rhydderch's best horses. That Marcus knows his horseflesh."

"His name's not Marcus. I heard that young beauty call him Drustan. Or Tristan. A man with a false name can't be trusted."

"Tristan!" Rufus breathed, watching the fading dust cloud on the Caerleon road. "I wonder. . . . Wouldn't that be a tale to tell my children! Do you suppose it could have been? . . ." He scratched again and yawned, feeling in his pouch for the heavy coin purse. "Well, God bless them all, I say, whoever they were. They paid well."

35 ⚔ THE NIGHT WIND

Dinadan and Guvranyl sat alone at the long table throwing dice. Behind them unshuttered windows gazed out on a tranquil sea, and the evening breeze, warm and laden with all the scents of spring, poured softly in around them. Dinadan rose abruptly.

"Go on!" he scoffed. "No one throws dragon's eyes thrice in a row. You've weighted them, Guv. This time you have."

Guvranyl belched. "I've killed men for lesser insults."

Dinadan shrugged. "Kill me, then, and avenge your honor. I'd give anything to wield my sword with a purpose once again. Another year of this forced inaction and I'll throw myself into the sea."

Guvranyl rose. "As punishments go, it could have been much worse, and you know it well. Thank God your father spoke up on our behalf, or we'd be pushing up daisies like Regis, Dynas, and Filas." He shook his head sadly. "We bet wrong on that roll of the dice, lad. We must take what comes. Be thankful it's only guard duty at Tintagel and not labor in the quarries. I'm too old for that." He walked stiffly to the hearth and lifted the wineskin from its stand above a low flame.

Dinadan watched him, scowling. "You drink too much, Guv. Don't try to tell me you don't hate this imprisonment as much as I do."

Guvranyl drained the wineskin and stared at Dinadan with rheumy eyes. "I won't deny I'd rather be home in Dumnonia. As you'd rather be with your young wife in Dorria. But—"

"*And* my daughter of eighteen months, whom I've never seen!"

"Aye, that's cruel of Mark. But if I can't be home, I'd rather be here than serving in his army."

"Seriously, you old soldier? Why?"

"Because he's not a leader of men and he's no tactician. Every time he took us into battle I'd be thinking how very much better Tristan would have done it."

"Damn you, old man! You swore me an oath you wouldn't speak his name."

Guvranyl grinned unevenly. "I was drunk when I swore that. So were you."

"Yes. Well, I drink too much, too. Any news from the scouts?"

"Not yet."

"I suppose the old goat really means to come himself?"

"Oh, yes. Last time she nearly had his eye out. I thought perhaps he'd leave well enough alone after that, but his message was clear enough. He's coming himself."

"To take the boys." Dinadan's lips twisted in a wry smile. "It will be the end of me when he finds them gone. But he made me Queen's Protector, and thus I am bound to serve the Queen."

"Where are they going this time?"

"I don't know. I'm not hiding them myself. I've sent for Pernam at the Queen's request. He's the only one we can think of who has both the courage and the power to deny Markion. He should be here any day now. I just pray he gets here, and gets away, before the King arrives. After that"—he grimaced and reached for the wineskin—"they can fight it out between themselves." He squeezed the last drop of wine into his mouth, then dropped heavily into the King's carved chair.

"Five to one she sends him packing," Guvranyl offered.

Dinadan raised an eyebrow. "You know, I might take that bet this time. She's not well."

"No? Looked fine at breakfast. But still nursing her winter cough."

"It's more than that. It's a weariness of spirit. Since the turn of the year, she's just given up."

"She's young still. Plenty of life left. Mark my words, she'll kill Markion before she'll let him take her sons away."

"Yes," Dinadan said absently, staring into the distance. "She might."

A tap came at the door and the captain of the house guard entered and saluted.

"Oh, good," Dinadan breathed. "Pernam at last!"

The guard bowed to the space between them. "Travelers upon the road, my lords, seeking shelter for the night. A Prince Kaherdyn from Less Britain and his sister, Lady Elen, and Sir Marcus Cunomorus, who travels with them."

"Shelter?" Dinadan wondered aloud. "Shelter from what? It's a mild night in May."

"I've not heard those names before, Morven," Guvranyl replied. "Does the knight wear a badge?"

"A hawk, my lord."

"Brittany's badge is a silver boar."

"His is a small subkingdom, my lord. He says you'll not have heard of it."

"Are there only three of them? Harmless enough, I wager. Eh, Dinadan?"

Dinadan shrugged. "Where can they be going on the shore road, I wonder? Well, do as you like, Guv. You're master of Tintagel."

Guvranyl returned to the guard. "What are they like?"

"I didn't get a good look at the knight, my lord. He was busy with the horses. But the prince is seventeen or so, and his sister is a beauty."

"God preserve us from beautiful women!" Dinadan groaned, but Guvranyl smiled at the sudden warmth in the guard's voice.

"Very well. I'll receive them. Alert Merron to see to the rooms. Oh, and Morven, send for more wine."

"Yes, my lord."

When the door had closed, Dinadan scowled and adjusted his sword on his hip. "I wonder what on earth is keeping Prince Pernam? Ask these travelers if they've seen anyone on the road."

"Aren't you staying to greet them?"

Dinadan yawned. "Not me. I'm off to bed. Too much dicing and drinking. Too much boredom to be endured."

"Don't forget to check on the Queen before you go."

Dinadan smiled bitterly. "Oh, aye, I obey all his orders. Be sure and tell him so. I'll make damn sure there's no one in her bed. Why he treats her as if she entertains the army in his absence, I'll never know. Sheer orneriness. He only ever had one man to fear."

With that, Dinadan closed the door and trudged away through the dimly lit halls toward the Queen's stairs. The two sentries he passed were asleep at their posts. He shrugged and let them sleep. But as he turned the last corner he stopped abruptly, every sense alerted. The stairs were in darkness. The lamp had gone out, and the air was heavy with the pungent scent of a wick recently snuffed. His sword leaped into his hand.

"Who's there, in the Queen's name?"

He heard a soft noise from above him, the slip of steel against leather as another sword left its scabbard.

"Who goes there? Announce yourself!"

"Shhh." The whisper sounded in his ear. He whirled, and a firm hand came down on his wrist. "Don't wake the guard, Dinadan, my old friend. I need his sleep."

Dinadan gasped aloud. *"Tristan?"*

An arm slid around his shoulders and hugged him tight. "Ah, God, you are the last man I expected to find *here*! Is this your punishment, then, for standing by me? Guard duty?"

"Tristan!" Tears sprang to Dinadan's eyes as he hugged his friend. "You are alive! Thank God! We never knew for certain."

"You didn't believe the bard, then? *She* did."

Dinadan sobered instantly. "Aye. She did indeed. But all bards are liars at heart, begging your pardon, Tris. I wanted proof." As his eyes adjusted to the dark he made out the dim outline of Tristan's head against the wall. "How did you know about the bard? How did you get here? Where have you been? It's as much as your life is worth to set foot in Britain—did you bring an army?"

"No," Tristan replied softly. "No army. I came with Prince Kaherdyn and his sister."

"You're Marcus Cunomorus!"

"Yes."

"By God! You have some nerve, using Mark's very name! And where did you find that Breton prince? Have you been all this time in Brittany?"

"In Lanascol. Prince Kaherdyn is my kinsman now. Lady Elen is my wife."

Dinadan gasped. "Jesu! Then it's true?"

"Yes and no." Tristan gripped his arm. "I must see her, Din. I must see her now. Tonight. You have to cover for me."

"Good God, Tris, you brought the woman *here*? Are you completely mad? You can't expect to—"

"I must see her."

"You can't! Markion's coming."

"I know."

"I won't let him take the boys. Don't worry. I've sent for Pernam."

"You're a good friend, Dinadan. Better than I deserve."

"But you can't see her. I can't let you. I have standing orders from the Queen herself."

Tristan paused, breathing audibly. "When did she give those orders? After the bard's visit? Those orders came from the depth of the wound I gave her. Give me a chance to set things straight between us. She will thank you for it after."

"Let it go, Tristan. It's over. Let the poor woman heal. It will only make things worse to rake it all up again."

"*I must see her.*"

Dinadan shook him by the shoulders. "Have all my sacrifices been in vain? Filas, Dynas, Regis, Branwen, Grayell, Guvranyl, and a hundred others who paid the price for backing you—was it for nothing? Tristan, I have a daughter I have never seen because of you."

Tristan embraced him and pressed his lips to Dinadan's cheek. Dinadan sighed wearily. "You'd kill me, if you had to, to get to her. I know you would. All right, I yield. If she doesn't have my head for this, Markion will. Either way, I am a dead man."

"Come with us, then. Come with us to Brittany. Bring Diarca and the child. We will all escape together."

"On foot? We won't get far."

"Our ship lies off the coast of Lyonesse. It will wait a fortnight for us; that's plenty of time to get to Dorria and back. Come with us."

"You think Essylte will travel with your wife and her brother? Have you lost your senses?"

"She will when I tell her the truth of how things stand. But you've got to give me the chance. Stand here and guard the stair."

Dinadan laughed lightly. "Oh, no, you can't get in without me. I've the key to her chamber door."

Tristan drew a sharp breath. "He locks her *in?*"

"That's not the half of it. She's his prize bitch, and nothing more. He whips her if she doesn't mind."

Tristan bit off a cry. "I'll kill him the same day he sets foot in Tintagel! I swear by God I will!"

"Shut up." Dinadan grabbed him and dragged him up the stairs. "If you value your worthless life, shut up and follow me."

Together they crept up the stairs to the landing. No sentry stood there now, for a heavy lock and chain secured the door. "She's abed," Dinadan mumbled under his breath. "My orders are to check on her every night and see that she's abed and alone."

"Filthy sonofabitch's whelp. I'll give him the slow death he deserves."

"He loves you, too. Remember that. Ah. Here we go."

Dinadan pulled the chain from the door and pushed it open.

Iseulte stood at the window and gazed out at the western sea. "What a beautiful place Cornwall is. Every cliff looks out at the ends of the earth. In Lanascol we have nothing so dramatic. We look out upon a sea of trees."

Guvranyl gestured to the servant to refill her winecup. "I'm sure it must be a very lovely place, my lady." He turned to the russet-haired young prince who brooded by the unlit fire. "How does Less Britain? We've had no news for ages."

"Everything's quiet enough," Kaherdyn grumbled.

"Are you on your way home, then?" Guvranyl prodded.

Kaherdyn flashed his sister a meaningful look. "Eventually, Sir Guvranyl. My sister had a hankering to see Cornwall first."

Guvranyl frowned in evident disbelief.

"We came to Britain to bury my father," Iseulte explained, turning her brilliant eyes upon him and rooting him where he stood. "He wished to die in Wales. Afterward, I made Kaherdyn bring me overland through Britain. I had never seen it—the Summer Country, Dumnonia, Cornwall, Lyonesse . . ."

"Um, er . . ." Guvranyl coughed discreetly. "It's odd I had no warning of your approach. You must have passed through Caerleon. The commander there is a Cornishman. Sir Bruenor would have sent me notice."

"We took a ferry across the Severn," Kaherdyn said quickly, "and so missed the fortress. Our guide said he knew of a shorter way."

"Ah, then Sir Marcus has been to Britain before? Where is he? I should like to meet him and know whom he's fought for."

"Indeed," Iseulte said absently, turning away, "I believe he is a Briton born. He will join us here directly. I beg your patience on his behalf."

Guvranyl bowed low, enchanted by her beauty, her grace, her remarkable eyes. "Granted." He turned back to Kaherdyn. "If you traveled through the Summer Country, you must have stopped at Camelot."

"Er, no. We heard rumors of fighting thereabouts, and I did not wish to endanger my sister."

"You were misinformed, my young lord. King Markion is away at the wars, but they are east, much farther east. It's a pity you didn't see the place. You have missed one of the greatest sights in Britain."

"Well." Kaherdyn squirmed. "Another time, perhaps."

Guvranyl looked at him curiously. They made a strange pair, the brilliant woman who looked at everything with an intense interest he could feel across the room, and the sulking young man who refused to look at anything, who clearly wished to be anywhere else on earth than where he was. What could have brought them to Tintagel, if they had missed such unavoidable crossroads as Caerleon and Camelot?

"Sir Guvranyl!" The door swung open to admit a guard, breathless with excitement. "Prince Pernam!"

Pernam swept into the room close behind him, his hood thrown back, his gray eyes flashing. "Guvranyl! Alert the Queen! Markion is upon the moor!"

Iseulte gasped aloud. Pernam turned, startled, and saw her and Kaherdyn. He inclined his head. "My apologies, lady, for the sudden intrusion. I did not know Sir Guvranyl had guests."

Iseulte could hardly breathe. "Markion, did you say? The High King himself? Is coming here?"

"Yes. Not swiftly—there's a long procession of torches coming across the moor. He'll make a ceremonial entrance." He turned to Guvranyl. "That gives us time. Esmerée is even now waking the boys. Where's Dinadan?"

"Abed, my lord. Shall I send for him and wake the Queen?"

"No!" The words burst from Iseulte's lips. Everyone stared at her. She lifted a pale face to Pernam. "I beg you, sir, I beg you not to disturb the Queen."

"But the High King will want to see her," Pernam said gently.

Iseulte gulped. "Even so, let it wait until the last moment. Please. I have no right to ask it, but—please."

Pernam lifted a hand to her chin and gazed into her eyes. "What concerns you so? You have honest eyes, but you are hiding something. Give me truth, lady. Who are you?"

"My name," Iseulte breathed, "is Elen of Lanascol. But I am known as—Iseulte of the White Hands."

Pernam looked blankly at her, but Guvranyl drew breath sharply. "Oh, my God. *Oh, my God!*" He looked around wildly. "Marcus Cunomorus! Where is he?"

Pernam frowned. "Have you lost your wits? I've just told you. He's upon the moor."

"No, no! Not Markion. The knight who rode in with these gentle folk. He's down at the stables somewhere."

"No, he's not." They all turned to the door.

"Dinadan!" Pernam cried in relief. "Awaken the Queen. Markion will be here within the hour."

But Dinadan gazed in open wonder at Iseulte and walked toward her like a man in sleep, heedless of the excitement around him. He lifted her hand to his lips and bowed low. "Lady Elen. Wife of—Marcus."

"You must be Sir Dinadan. He has told me much about you."

"He has told me absolutely nothing about *you*," Dinadan responded gravely. "He should never have brought you to Tintagel."

Iseulte smiled quickly. "I know why he is here, my lord. Do not fear for me. My eyes are open."

"No one can be that generous."

"That's what *I* told her," Kaherdyn added sullenly from his corner.

"Some things cannot be prevented." Iseulte glanced at Pernam, whose eyes widened with apprehension. "If there is any hope that we may someday have a life together, I had to bring him here. There wasn't any choice."

"I take it," Pernam said evenly, "that Marcus Cunomorus is my nephew's idea of a disguise?"

Iseulte looked bewildered. "Prince Pernam is Markion's brother," Dinadan supplied. "Tristan's uncle."

Iseulte made a reverence to Pernam. "Then we are kin, my lord. Tristan is my husband."

"Dear Lord." Guvranyl's legs buckled, and he landed heavily on a bench. "Dear Lord, preserve us all. Do you mean to tell me Tristan is *here*? In Tintagel? *Where*, for God's sweet sake?"

"Where do you think?" Dinadan's lips lifted in a bitter smile. "I found him on her stairs when I left this chamber nigh on an hour ago."

"And you let him in." Guvranyl made it a statement. He shook his head slowly. "No good will come of it. We are dead men all. If you value our lives, get back there and warn them of Markion's approach. He'll kill them both if he finds them and he'll be here any minute."

"Markion? *Here?*" Dinadan jumped like a man coming to his senses. But as he reached the door he froze, then whirled around, white-faced. "Too late."

"The King!" a guard cried, and Markion himself strode into the room, followed by his torchbearers, his warrior-companions, and a train of servants.

"Too late for what, Dinadan? Ah! What's this? A feast? A celebration? With guests?" He nodded to Iseulte and Kaherdyn, who made him reverences, and frowned at Pernam. "What are you doing here, brother? Come to rescue my wife's bastards? Too late, indeed!"

Guvranyl rose shakily to his feet. "My lord King. Welcome to Tintagel. This is Prince Kaherdyn of Lanascol, and his sister, Lady Elen. They have stopped the night with us on their way to—on their way to . . ." His voice trailed off uncertainly.

"On our way home to Less Britain," Kaherdyn said firmly. "We had no idea you and your company were expected, my lord, and we have no wish to be in the way. If you will give us leave, we will take ourselves off to bed and leave you to your homecoming."

Markion's eye ran over Iseulte with appreciation. "Must you go so soon, Prince Kaherdyn? We don't get many visitors at Tintagel. I would be honored if you and your handsome sister would grace us with your company a while longer. I must see to my wife; afterward I would be glad to sit and talk with you both over a skin of wine."

Kaherdyn had opened his mouth to decline when Iseulte smiled at

Markion and curtsied low. "The honor is all ours, my lord King. Must you see to your wife so soon? Surely you are entitled to rest from your journey first."

Markion's smile broadened. "Well, well. Perhaps it can wait a little." Kaherdyn gaped.

"I will see that their chambers have been prepared," Dinadan said nervously, backing toward the door.

Markion eyed him sharply. "You stay here. That's a job for the seneschal. Hasn't it been done?" He turned on Guvranyl. "Eh, Guvranyl? What's this I hear? Neglecting your duties? Spending too much time with the wineskin again? Have their beds and horses been seen to?"

Guvranyl blinked in confusion. "Beds, certainly, my lord. Horses, I don't recall—yes, Marcus Cunomorus saw to the horses." Guvranyl gulped suddenly as Markion reddened.

"*Who?* Is this a jest?"

"No, brother," Pernam said calmly. "Marcus is the man who traveled south with Prince Kaherdyn and his sister as their escort. There is no jest."

"Well, then, where is he?" Markion snapped.

No one moved. Markion stared at them all, first in anger, then in astonishment, then in consternation. He walked slowly to Kaherdyn, to Iseulte, to shaking Guvranyl, to close-lipped Pernam, to white-faced Dinadan. None of them could meet his eye. "You're afraid," he announced, watching their faces. "You're *all* afraid. Why? Of what? Of me?" He smiled, but no one smiled with him. "No one who deals honestly with me need fear me. Ask Dinadan, here. I'm only cruel to traitors and—" he stopped as Dinadan flinched. Markion's face hardened. "Marcus Cunomorus." He whipped around and glared at Kaherdyn. "Less Britain!" His lips lifted in a snarl. "*He's here!* Isn't he? That fornicating bastard son of a pagan whore! Where is he? Speak!"

No one spoke. Markion whirled and pointed to his men. "You, you, and you. Draw your swords and stand by the doors. No one leaves. *No one.* Kill the first one who tries."

"My lord!" Iseulte fell to her knees and raised her hands to him. "He is my husband. I beg you, do not harm him!"

"Your husband!" Markion sneered. "Then you should have kept him at home in your bed, lady. His life is forfeit here."

"I beg you, my lord! Show him mercy. He came—he only came to say farewell."

Markion was already at the door. He turned back once more. "That's what he told you, is it? Then you haven't known him long." Iseulte's eyes filled with tears and Markion grunted. "If he's anywhere else in Tintagel but in her chamber, I'll let him live until morning. But if he's with her—so help me God—if he's with her, he'll die a slow death tonight!" Then he turned on his heel and was gone.

The double-flamed lamp cast a soft glow across the Queen's bed, across her red-gold curls sprawled over the pillow, aglow in the lamplight, across her face, pale and shuttered in sleep, half turned away. Tristan crept noiselessly to her side, slipped off his cloak, unbuckled his swordbelt, dropped them softly on a chair, and knelt down at her side. He hardly dared breathe. Every long-dead fiber of his body reawakened at her nearness, every forgotten impulse rekindled, every long-vanquished hope was reborn within his breast. He lifted a hand and touched her hair, a harper's touch, a sigh across the strings. "Sweet Essylte."

She stirred dreamily and settled deeper into the pillows. Her lips moved in a whisper. "I saw him again. In my dreams. He came back to me."

He bent his head closer to her lips, her scent filling his head. "Who has come, love?" His lips brushed hers, a gossamer caress. "What lucky lover meets you in your golden dreams?"

Her eyes flew open. "Dinadan!"

He frowned. "Dinadan?"

In a flash she rolled away from him and pushed herself up, breathing hard. She stared at him wildly, unbelieving, her hair in a riotous jumble, the breast of her gown rising and falling in a quick, unsteady rhythm as she fought for breath.

"Essylte . . ."

Her jaw tightened. Her eyes welled with tears. Before he had time to draw another breath she drew back her arm and struck him hard across his face.

"I took you for a better man!" she spat. "I thought you were Dinadan!"

Tristan hardly flinched. He could not believe he had ever left her willingly. He could not believe he had endured three long years without her. She filled the room with her righteous fury, her glorious rage. She lit the night.

"He has always been worth two of me."

"How dare you! How dare you come here!"

"My heart, how could I not?"

"Get out! Get out!" Her voice rose in a dangerous crescendo. "Oath breaker! Adulterer! Liar! Thief! I'll call the guard!"

Tristan leaped onto the bed and grabbed her, covering her mouth with his hand. "Be still! If they find me here, they'll kill me before your eyes."

"Let them!" she gasped, fighting him off. "Let them! Die for me the way Branny died for you!"

He pushed her flat on the bed and forced his mouth on hers. She scratched and clawed him like a caged beast. She bit his lips and kicked against his weight, but the enormity of desire so long denied, of suffering and separation, of wild tears, spent dreams, and bitter loneliness, overwhelmed her rage and left her defenseless against his tenderness. She wept as she held him to her breast, wept as she kissed him and drew him close, wept even as she yielded, aflame with the heat of his desire, to the undeniable power of his need. A sense of hopelessness possessed her, a bittersweet certainty that he was her fate, her doom, her death, her life, her only love, and that it was all come upon her at this hour.

"Tristan . . . Tristan . . . I am undone!"

"Essylte," he whispered, holding her as if to press her into his own flesh, to make their union solid, indivisible, eternal. "You are mine, now and forever. In life and beyond. We are one, joined in spirit, in soul, in flesh." He spoke in sighs, his lips against her neck, as his breathing slowed. "No one will ever come between us again. I swear it."

Tears slid down her cheeks even as she cradled him against her body. "Not my husband? Not your wife?"

He fumbled on the bed for his discarded tunic and drew forth the blue enamel ring. He slipped it onto her finger. "*You* are my wife, Essylte."

"You married that Breton girl. After all your promises to me."

"A marriage of words, like yours to Markion. But I never lay with her."

She gazed up at him and pushed his hair from his eyes. "No? Then you shamed her, and her family, too."

"I did as she bid me, Essylte."

"Indeed?" She shut her eyes tightly. "But Mark did not do my bidding, Tristan. Ours has been a marriage of more than words since the night that Branny died."

Tristan bowed his head. "I know, my sweet."

"That makes this adultery."

"No. No. Do not speak of it. The love we share—"

"Not speak of it?" She pushed him away, eyes blazing, and straightened her nightdress. "I *must* speak of it. Yes—it is only fair. We deserve one another, you and I. But let our eyes be opened. You must know every last indignity of my suffering, every last humiliation, every wrenching diminution of my soul. Whether it is God's punishment for our sin or the retribution that comes of its own will from men's actions, I do not know, but you must hear it. Listen, Tristan, while I tell you what the brute has done to me."

Tristan sat beside her in the bed, holding hard to her hand.

"That very night—after you leaped from the window and Branny drank the poison—that very night he came to my bed, heavy as I was with Ysaie, and lay with me. It pained me fierce, which was what he wanted, and I could not keep from crying out. No—say nothing. Be still, I command you. It is your punishment to hear it, as it was mine to endure it. It was the last time he came into my chamber. After we left Lyonesse he never came to my bed. But he—he took me in other places."

Tristan gasped. She shot him a sharp look. "For a warrior, Tristan, you don't show much control. I have learned to hide behind a wooden face while my heart is screaming. Attempt it, for my sake. Or I shall not get through this."

"All right. All right. I will."

"My confinement with Ysaie was a long one. He was big, and was three days being born. I thought I should die, then. I know I prayed for it. I bled and bled until there was nothing left of me. He had to be put to the wet nurse, for I had no milk, no strength; I could not lift my head from the pillow for a fortnight. And through it all, I had no one to talk to, for my dearest Branny lay deep in the soil of Lyonesse. My only solace was that Mark kept away. Far away. He never even sent to learn of the baby's birth or if I had survived it. He was gone to Logris, thank God, fighting Saxons.

"Then, when Ysaie was three months old and I had regained my feet and something of my color, he returned. He began a campaign of insults designed to humiliate me before his men, before his courtiers, before even my own servants. At dinner he would slide his hand under the table and up my skirt. He allowed no protest—he struck me when I objected. He would open my bodice and expose me to his men and his dinner companions. He would take my breast in his hand and ask them all if they had ever seen a finer."

"Christ!" Tristan's face flushed dusky red. But Essylte went on, heedless of the interruption.

"When I tried to leave he would not let me. He told me it was his right. A few of the men had the grace to be embarrassed and turn away, but most of them enjoyed it. Little by little they began to egg him on. I was no more than his prize cow that he showed to everyone." She shut her eyes so she would not see Tristan's tears and continued evenly, "I often went up on the northern battlement to be alone, to weep for you and Branny and all that I had lost. One day he followed me, and when he found me in tears, he grew enraged. He accused me of pining for you, but I would not admit it. He told me I would bear him a real heir or I would die. And then he forced me."

"He broke his oath to me that day!"

"Once in Gwynedd a man tried to rape me," she whispered, tears seeping from beneath her lids. "He would have done it but for Branny. It was—awful. I used to have nightmares about it. But Markion was—a thousand times worse." She shuddered. "He enjoyed my pain. He bent me back over the parapet, until I was nearly upside down. To struggle meant instant death." She bit her lip. "That was the last time he took me in private. After that, he raped me as a matter of routine. He did not much care where it happened, so long as it was public. He took me in hallways, in front of the guards; in the kitchen garden, with all the cooks looking on; in the stables, for the amusement of the grooms; outside in the castle courtyard, on the cobbles, and once—the last time—in the middle of the hall at dinner."

"Oh, God! No more—no more, I pray you! The black-hearted fiend!"

"His men would lay bets on his staying power. All the women hid behind doors, for his men learned to enjoy the sport as much as he. The ones who disapproved were posted elsewhere." Tristan thought of Sir Bruenor at Caerleon and regretted that he had not stopped to see the man on his way to Cornwall. Perhaps he could have come to Tintagel with reinforcements.

"If he caught me going up the stairs, he would grab me and lift my skirt. If he caught me coming down, the same. The only place he would not touch me was here, in my chamber, and in the nursery garden, the two places you had been. If I protested, he beat me. And I—I always fought. I could not help it. I could not bear it!"

"He shall die for this."

"I grew to hate him with a passion so virulent, so wild, I plotted long how I could kill him. I had Branny's herbs, and her book of charms, and what little I remembered of my mother's spells. I made a concoction for him. I have it in the chest, all ready for him, but he never came to me. Twice I conceived the heir he wanted. . . . Oh, Tristan, I can hardly speak this—I sealed my damnation on the day I drank the broth that rid me of the child." She looked at him dry-eyed. "I killed my baby. I killed them both. He never knew. He thought I had miscarried. The second time, last winter, I nearly died of it. I know it was wicked, I know I am damned, but I would do it again if I had to. Oh, Tristan! My loathing has taken me so far from God!"

"I was a fool to leave you. I should have known I couldn't trust him— better we died together in Lyonesse than you should suffer thus."

"I believe I did die in Lyonesse," she said slowly. "I am not the person I used to be, and neither are you."

"My love. My sweet, enduring love." He bent over her and kissed her. "Why didn't you send to Percival for help?"

"I did. But what had Markion done but assert his rights as a husband? My father told me I must bear it as best I could. It was not his right to interfere."

Tristan shut his eyes. Long ago, Pernam had said the same to him when he wished to save Esmerée from Segward. "You didn't tell him everything you just told me—he'd have come with every warrior in Wales."

"No," Essylte admitted. "I've never told the whole truth to anyone but you." She clung to him a moment, then pulled away. "Our love," she breathed. "Is it a blessing or a curse? Between us, we have killed Branny, and two babies, and many others who did not deserve to die. We have placed our sons in jeopardy. Mark is on his way here to kill them."

"I heard the tale in Maridunum—that's why I'm here. To take you and the boys away with me. A ship lies waiting off the coast of Lyonesse. I've brought help—this very night we shall escape from Tintagel and fly away south."

She smiled then, the indulgent smile of a mother to her wayward boy. "Of course. We shall escape and live forever in a land of golden dreams. You have always been a dreamer, Tristan."

"But my dear—"

"Don't you yet see? The size of your army does not matter. How could it ever be? There is so much more between us now than love."

Tristan pulled her closer as if his physical touch could soothe her agony. "What suffering you have borne! Let me take you away from this stifling prison and into the sweet air outside. Your scars will fade with time and distance, and your heart will heal."

She said nothing but turned her face away and slid out of bed. She walked across the room to a great carved trunk and fumbled with the catch. Tristan quickly pulled on his leggings and his boots. But when she turned around she carried not her traveling clothes, but his old horn lap harp with horsehair strings. Merlin's harp.

"Play for me, Tristan, would you? I should like to hear your music again . . . in the time that we have left." Her voice sank to a whisper as she spoke and he missed the last words.

He took the old harp from her hands. "I never dreamed you had this. I thought it was lost forever."

"I brought it home from Lyonesse. Next to our sons, it is all I have that is yours."

He curled on the bed and tuned it lovingly. "I shall sing you a traveling song, sweet Essylte. Get you dressed and ready for the road."

She smiled sadly. "Never mind that. Just play for me."

"Within the hour we'll be gone!" he urged.

She nodded wearily and reached obediently for her comb.

Essylte stood at the shuttered window with the night wind breathing through the cracks, listening to the roar of breakers far below. Tristan's voice rose and fell with the liquid cascade of the harp in a song of love, bittersweet and enchanting. The years dissolved as she stood and listened. Once again she was back in her father's castle, kneeling with Branwen at the bedside of a handsome stranger while he beguiled them both with his beauty and his song. Her heart lifted. The night wind whispered in her ear. Was it possible she might rediscover hope if she could get beyond the confines of her prison? She had despaired so long that hopelessness had become a habit. But here was Tristan, sitting cross-legged on her bed as if he had never left. His voice, his strength, his beauty, his passion—all were undiminished. If she should let him have his way, if she could rely on his promises, if only she could get beyond this devastating fear, beyond Mark's reach—

"Tristan!"

He looked up, startled at her cry. "Love?"

"Swear to me now you won't leave me again."

"I swear it."

"Promise me we will be together always."

"Until death, sweet." He placed his hand over his heart and extended it toward her. "It is a vow."

The door burst open and Markion strode into the room.

The two men stared at each other. No one moved. No one breathed. In the same instant both men lunged for the sword that still lay in its scabbard on the chair. Tristan, encumbered by the harp, was a trifle slower. Markion got there first.

Breathing heavily, Markion faced them, a drawn sword in each hand. "By God, I've got you now! Caught you red-handed, you fornicating villain! Death is too good for you. No!" he barked at Essylte, "don't bother to plead for him. Say farewell, if you like. He's mine now."

Essylte shrieked. "Tristan!"

Tristan dove under the bed as the sword came down, rolling out of sight. Markion bent and stabbed viciously at the crawl space. A hand shot out, grabbed his wrist, and wrenched it sideways. Markion half fell, catching himself on the bed, but the sword skittered across the floor. Tristan swarmed after it. He leaped to his feet, sword in hand, to see Markion grab Essylte by the arm and pull her in front of him, placing the blade of his sword against her neck. He smiled contemptuously.

"I'll not battle for the right to kill you," he snapped. "Drop the sword or watch her die."

Tristan lowered the sword. "Coward. Let her go. This is between you and me."

Markion laughed. "To the victor go the spoils? Oh, no. She's my best weapon against you. Yield, Tristan. This is your deathday."

Tristan tossed the sword onto the bed, halfway between him and Markion. Essylte whimpered as Markion jerked her aside.

"Put your hands behind your back," Markion commanded. Tristan obeyed. Mark walked up to him until the two men stood face-to-face. "You bitch's spawn." He spat into Tristan's face. Tristan twitched, but before he could move, the point of Markion's blade pressed cold against his ribs. "You've ruined Cornwall, you traitorous dog. You've ruined Britain. My father's dreams, *your* father's dreams, *her* father's dreams—all come to nothing. *Over a woman!*"

Over Markion's shoulder Tristan saw Essylte bend over the chest and lift something from it.

"You would never understand it, Mark, if I had time enough to tell you the tale from its beginning. Leave it that we must be enemies."

Markion smiled. "So long as we both live, we must. But I intend to live long without you. You've done making a fool of me. Good riddance to you, harper."

Markion thrust his knee into Tristan's groin and, as he doubled, slipped the blade in between his ribs. Tristan gasped once and slowly crumpled to the floor. Essylte screamed. She flew to his side and bent over him, trying to staunch the flow of blood with her bedgown.

"Tristan! Oh, Tristan, don't leave me! I am ready, love, I am ready to follow wherever you lead—to the golden land, to the Paradise of your dream . . ." She bent her head in a long, keening cry, the ends of her hair afloat in the dark pool of Tristan's blood.

Markion raised the dripping blade again and squinted at it in the flickering light. "Killed with his own sword. How fitting." He tossed the sword away, and it clattered across the floor. "I've another blade for *you* if you want to join him." He reached for the sword on the bed.

Essylte looked up at him with drowned eyes. "Go ahead. I beg you."

Markion grunted and sheathed his sword instead. "I won't give you the satisfaction. Better you should live to service me." He clapped a hand to his groin and grinned. "Now that his shadow no longer lies across your bed, I think I'll visit you here. Make ready, for I'll be back tonight."

He spun on his heel and went out the way he had come, slamming the door behind him.

Essylte cradled Tristan's head in her lap and stroked his hair. Her body shook with unvoiced sobs as tears splashed down on her hands, on his hair, on his livid face. His dark eyes looked up at her, struggling to keep her in focus.

"Don't be afraid," he breathed. "There *is* a land of golden dreams. I am going to it now."

A spasm crossed his face. A thin stream of blood dribbled from his lips, and the light in his eyes began to fail.

"Don't go, Tristan! My dear heart, don't go without me."

Love. His lips formed the word but no sound came out. His breath had stopped.

Essylte pressed her cheek to his, closed his eyes, and slowly rose. Her bedgown was smeared with blood, her face ragged with grief. Only her eyes were calm. She went to the winestand and poured wine into a silver cup.

From the painted wooden box she had taken from the chest she withdrew a black linen bag. Outside the door she heard Markion's shouted orders to the guards. Beyond the window came the sea sounds on the night wind, breathing a gentle summons like a soul in passing.

She pushed open the shutter and with a small smile emptied the bag into the winecup, stirred it carefully, and knelt beside Tristan's body. Already the guards were thundering up the stairs.

"Husband," she whispered, lying beside him and taking him in her arms. "My beloved, wait for me."

As the door burst open she downed the wine.

EPILOGUE
✝ THE HAZEL AND THE IVY

Iseulte stood in the apple orchard wrapped in a thick cloak. Overhead gray skies lowered, muffling the sound of the sea and drizzling a light, cold rain. At her feet stretched two long scars of naked earth, ugly against the new green of the orchard grass. No headstones marked the site. No carved cross, no crown, no mark of honor due a prince's grave. Only a shoot of ivy to mark his resting place, and a hazel sapling to mark hers.

Iseulte looked up as a tall robed man came toward her from the nursery door. She attempted a smile and made him a reverence. It was thanks to Prince Pernam that they at least had ground to rest in. Markion had wanted them thrown into the sea, food for fish.

"Prince Pernam."

He bowed. "Lady Iseulte. We are ready to depart. Kaherdyn is with the horses in the courtyard, and Esmerée has the children ready. You may travel how you will, riding with your brother or with us in the wagon. But time is short. Mark may always change his mind."

"I must tell you again, my lord, how grateful I am for all your efforts on our behalf. You have made the past week bearable, I don't know how."

Pernam's arm slid around her shoulders and held her tight. "It is a dark time indeed. But there are better days ahead. When you are back in Lanascol, those boys will light your life. In five years you will hardly remember the woman you are today."

Iseulte wiped a tear away. "I shall not forget Tristan so soon."

"You will have his image ever before you in his sons. Remember, too, that you are welcome to visit us, to leave the boys with us for any space of time. Esme loves them for his sake as much as you do."

Iseulte smiled sadly. "He sowed love wherever he went. He was a rare man, both brave and tender, both warrior and bard. He let everything touch him. He turned no one away. I feel so for Sir Dinadan. I have never seen such grief in a grown man. How did you ever persuade the King to send him to Lyonesse? I thought Markion would kill him, too."

Pernam sighed. "My brother's temper is quickly aroused, but quickly cooled once the cause is settled. In a calm moment, I made him see sense.

He has no time to divide Cornwall by seeking vengeance against men who were Tristan's friends. He has Britain to think of, or what is left of it. He has Saxons to fight. And unless he wants to face an invading army led by Tristan the Younger in twenty years, he had better acknowledge the boy's claim to Lyonesse and let someone trustworthy keep his kingdom for him. Mark agreed to it readily enough once I laid it out thus. After all, it costs him nothing and gains him much. Old Guvranyl will go with Dinadan, I think, unless he retires to Dumnonia."

"Bless you, Prince Pernam," Iseulte whispered. "No one else will die, and Tristan's sons will have a future."

"Perhaps." Pernam frowned. "It depends on what happens to Britain. In twenty years Lyonesse may be Saxon land if it hasn't sunk into the sea."

"God forbid."

"Raise those boys to be leaders. For when Markion dies, they are his heirs."

Iseulte looked startled at the thought. "Not just Lyonesse, but Cornwall?"

"Not only Cornwall," he returned gruffly, "but Britain."

She caught her breath and looked down at the twin graves. "What a gift you have bequeathed me, my love," she whispered. "I am to be the mother of kings." She crossed herself slowly. *Good-bye, dear Tristan. I shall never see you more, but in my dreams.* She straightened and took Pernam's arm. "See how the ivy you planted over his grave has grown and entwined itself around the hazel over hers. In just three days. It is a miracle, my lord. A sign that they are still one, even in death. And that God has forgiven them."

Pernam shook his head as he led her away. "I shall never understand your God, who first damns men and then forgives them for their sins. The Great Goddess is perfectly clear about transgressions: Either a thing is wrong or it is not."

Iseulte smiled gently. "That is because our God became a man and sinned Himself. Our God knows the value of forgiveness. Our God is love."

Pernam raised her hand to his lips and kissed it. "As far as I'm concerned, that's His most redeeming feature. I shall miss you when we part, my lady queen."

She frowned up at him. "Not queen, my lord, but—" She stopped as his kind smile broadened.

"You forget who he was, the man you married. He was King of Lyonesse."

Iseulte bowed her head as they stepped out into the cold rain of the courtyard. "But I thought of him," she said in a low voice, "as a musician whose music healed my soul."

Pernam handed her into the covered warmth of the wagon. "He was always torn between the two sides of his nature. It was his fate. He was born between the stars."

When Markion returned to Tintagel eight months later, bloodied from the Saxon wars, he cut down the hazel sapling over Essylte's grave and ripped up the ivy over Tristan's. Nevertheless, they grew again within a fortnight. Twice more Mark cut them down; twice more they grew. Ill health and bitter wounds sapped his will at last, and with a disgusted wave of the hand he let them be. The ivy entwined about the hazel until they grew to be one plant, indistinguishable from one another except in their foundations, and climbed together toward the sun.

⚜ THE HOUSE OF CORNWALL

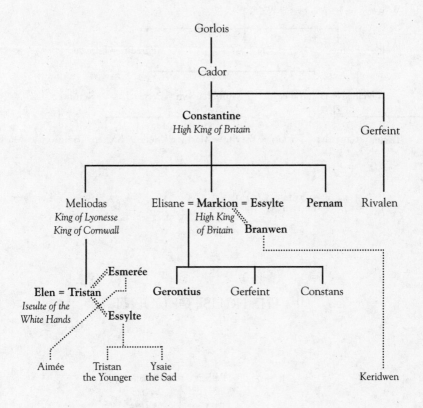

KEY:

=	Marriage
∷∷∷∷∷∷∷∷∷∷	Sexual relationship outside of marriage
─────	Denotes legitimate relationship
··············	Denotes illegitimate relationship
Boldface	Characters who appear in this book

✠ THE HOUSE OF GWYNEDD

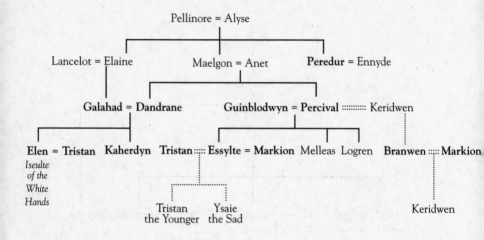

Pellinore = Alyse

Lancelot = Elaine   Maelgon = Anet   **Peredur** = Ennyde

Galahad = **Dandrane**   **Guinblodwyn** = **Percival** ⦙⦙⦙⦙⦙⦙ Keridwen

Elen = **Tristan**   **Kaherdyn**   Tristan ⦙⦙⦙ **Essylte** = **Markion**   Melleas   Logren   **Branwen** ⦙⦙⦙ **Markion**
Iseulte
of the
White
Hands

Tristan   Ysaie
the Younger   the Sad

Keridwen

✠ THE HOUSE OF GUENT

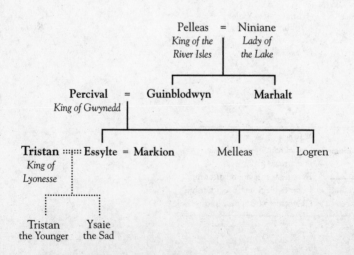

Pelleas   =   Niniane
King of the   *Lady of*
River Isles   *the Lake*

Percival   =   **Guinblodwyn**   **Marhalt**
King of Gwynedd

Tristan ⦙⦙⦙⦙ **Essylte** = **Markion**   Melleas   Logren
King of
Lyonesse

Tristan   Ysaie
the Younger   the Sad